32,359

Harris, Marilyn.
    Eden rising.

DATE DUE		
SEP 8 1982	APR 6 1985	JUN 10 '88
SEP 3 1 1982	APR 2 2 1985	DEC 16 '89
OCT 1 1982	MAY 2 0 1985	JUL 1 7
OCT 3 0 1982	APR 1 1986	FEB 1 0 1990
NOV 1 5 1982	MAY 1 9 1986	MAR 1 3 1990
DEC 1 0 1982	DEC 2 9 1986	DEC 2 7 1990
DEC 3 0 1982	JAN 2 9 1987	JUL 2 9 1991
JAN 1 7 1983	MAY 1 3 1987	OCT 3 1991
FEB 1 2 1983	AUG 4 1987	FEB 2 1993
MAR 6 1984	OCT 7 1987	MAY 8 1993
JUL 2 1984	JAN 2 0 '88	
NOV 2 4 1984	FEB 1 5 '88	

EDEN
RISING

Also by Marilyn Harris

EDEN RISING

MARILYN HARRIS

G. P. Putnam's Sons
New York

Copyright © 1982 by Marilyn Harris
All rights reserved. This book or parts thereof
may not be reproduced in any form without
permission. Published simultaneously in Canada
by General Publishing Co. Limited, Toronto.

Library of Congress Cataloging in Publication Data

Harris, Marilyn.
    Eden rising.

    I. Title.
PS3558.A648E3   1982   813'.54   81-19893
ISBN 0-399-12687-2   AACR2

PRINTED IN THE UNITED STATES OF AMERICA

Second Impression

For Judge
who makes everything possible

In those distant days, as in all other times and places where the mental atmosphere is changing, and men are inhaling the stimulus of new ideas, folly often mistook itself for wisdom, ignorance gave itself airs of knowledge, and selfishness, turning its eyes upward, called itself religion. . . .

—George Eliot

Religious ideas have the fate of melodies which, once set afloat in the world, are taken up by all sorts of instruments, some of them woefully coarse, feeble, and out of tune, until people are in danger of crying out that the melody itself is detestable. . . .

—George Eliot

The blessed work of helping the world forward happily does not wait to be done by perfect men. . . .

—George Eliot

Mortemouth,
North Devon Coast,
England
June 4, 1874
Midnight

She had been dreaming of men screaming and dying with open, untended wounds when the pounding sounded at the door and awakened her and she realized she was cold.

"Who is it?" she gasped, fighting through the cobwebs of nightmare sleep. She sat quickly up and clutched the blanket to her, lost momentarily in the darkness of the small room which had been attached, like an afterthought, to the back side of the Mortemouth Methodist Church.

An urgent male voice came faintly through the thick oak door. "Susan? Are you awake? You must come. Something terrible—up at Eden . . ."

She recognized the voice, Reverend Christopher, and recognized the message as well. Too often something terrible. Here. Down in the village. Up at Eden. Made no difference. In this world or in the shadowy realm of sleep, far too often something terrible . . .

"Just a . . ." she called out incompletely, and swung her legs out from beneath the blanket and felt an objecting ache in her back from the hard lumpy mattress and thought with fleeting regret that when she'd been a girl it had made no difference where she'd slept. Now, at thirty-four—

"Susan?" Reverend Christopher's voice came again, more urgent. "Are you there? We need you. Please . . ."

"Yes," she called back.

In the unseasonable cold of early June she shivered and grasped the neck of the heavy muslin nightgown. As she hurried toward the door on feet which felt as though they were encased in ice, she tried to clear the last of the nightmare from her mind. The dream had been so real, as real as the war almost fifteen years ago, the senseless Crimean conflict, thousands of men screaming for the blessed mercy of death. Fifteen years ago? Had it been so long? Would it never fade and give her peace?

"Susan? Please, can you . . . ?"

Again the male voice cut through her thoughts and, as her hands reached out for the heavy crosslatch, she wondered what precisely was the nature of this emergency. Was it Caroline Butler's baby in need of delivering? Or Sam Watkins losing his battle with the killing fever? Even in a village as small as Mortemouth, there was an abundance of human need. How presumptuous of Susan to think that she, a single woman, could do anything to help. Yet since the Crimea and Scutari and the profound influence of Miss Nightingale, the only course of action that had made sense to Susan Mantle had been a life dedicated to at least the illusion of service.

In the dark she found the latch and with renewed purpose slid it noisily back. With both hands she pushed open the heavy door and found on the other side what she knew she'd find, the portly, rosy-cheeked Father Christmas visage of Reverend George Christopher, shepherd to the little Mortemouth Methodist Church, who now, upon seeing Susan clad only in her nightdress, stepped back, mild shock on his cherubic face.

"What is it?" she asked quickly in an attempt to ease the shock and remind him that he had, most successfully, conveyed urgency.

"It's . . . that is to say . . ."

"I need light. May I borrow . . . ?"

"Of course," he said, and blushed crimson as he extended the flickering lantern to her. The cold wind coming off the quay caused the flame to dance and in turn cast dancing shadows over his face and black coat. "I'm sorry to disturb—"

"It's all right," she broke in, and tried to ease his embarrassment and hers as well. "What is it? Has there been an accident? Someone . . . ?"

"It's John Murrey Eden. Something . . . terrible . . ."

Armed with light and with renewed conviction that there was divine work to be done in this life, she halted in the very act of closing the door.

"Eden?" she repeated, peering through the dark. What could she possibly do for John Murrey Eden? For that matter, what could anyone do?

She knew who he was, as did everyone in the West Country, knew as well what had happened to him in the last few years. In fact, she'd seen him first in that very hospital in Scutari that had been the scene of her recent nightmare.

"Susan?" The urgent male voice turned suddenly considerate. "Are you all right?"

"Yes," she whispered, and heard the breathless quality of her own voice and wished the nightmare would leave her alone. Well, now it was time for her to turn her attention to Mad Box John, for that's what the children called John Murrey Eden, who lived at the top of the cliff walk in what was once the grandest castle in all of the West Country—in all of England, according to some.

"Give me a minute to dress," she said, and tried to convey to Reverend

Christopher that she was back on track. "I'll do it quickly and leave the door open a crack so that you can tell me . . ."

"No . . ."

". . . what happened. You said it was urgent," she reminded him, and didn't give him a chance to protest further, and drew the door to within a foot of the latch and moved hurriedly back to the bed, taking the lantern with her. She spied the chair over which she'd placed her simple brown nurse's dress. Plain it was, but good fabric cost money, and she'd never had an excess of that.

"Are you still there, Reverend Christopher?" she called out, and drew forward her thick petticoat and pulled it on beneath the nightdress.

"Y-yes, but . . ."

"What's happened? To Mr. Eden, I mean," she repeated.

"He . . ."

At the same time, she heard other voices, male, approaching from the left corner of the church, hurrying down the cobble walk toward her room, where Reverend Christopher waited.

One called out in clarion tones, "Is she . . . ?"

"Dressing. She'll . . ."

"He's gone up now. There's quite a crowd gathering . . ."

"It looks like he's got something . . ."

"Terrible!"

"There are children watching . . ."

"Get the children away!" she heard Reverend Christopher call out angrily over the puzzling and incoherent exchange. "Have their parents lost their minds? Tell them to take the children . . ."

"Can't control them, Reverend," someone called back. "They want to be there. They don't like him—you know that—feel he's responsible for . . ."

As other voices swirled around the speaker, Susan drew down the brown dress over her head and welcomed its warmth and pondered briefly the mixed blessings of her profession as traveling nurse and midwife on the West Country circuit. The only aspect of life that seemed to visit the village with any degree of regularity was tragedy and its equally black twin, disaster, like the mysterious disappearance of herring last year. For a community dependent upon the small fish, which once ran in schools of thousands, it seemed whimsical of God to one day and without reason cause them to disappear. And where the people might have turned to the soil to supply them with what the ocean now denied them, Fate then sent them three devastating winters and three equally wet summers where nothing had grown, but only molded and rotted in the ground.

Though only a young man in the Crimea, in his early twenties, John Murrey Eden had looked fifty. Miss Nightingale, as Susan recalled, had taken a special interest in him, having known his father, Edward Eden, in one of the Ragged Schools of London.

"*Perceive the links in the chain,*" Miss Nightingale had said. "*His father shaped my soul. Now I'm responsible for his son. . . .*"

"Susan, are you ready?"

"Coming," she called, stooping to retrieve the lantern.

"Susan, are you ready? We must hurry."

Without answering she drew up the hood of her cloak over her long, still-mussed hair and hurried through the partially open door and looked out over the shadowy narrow courtyard to see a large gathering of twenty-five, perhaps thirty, men, all looking back at her. A few carried torches which lay flat under the duress of the cold north wind and sent hordes of ghosts dancing over the plain brown brick walls of the church.

"Ah, good," Reverend Christopher said vaguely, and started to reach for the lantern, but Susan shifted it to the other hand, knowing that she, not he, would set the pace up the steep and treacherous cliff walk which led to Eden Castle.

Without a word she hurried down the four narrow steps past Reverend Christopher, who looked relieved that at last someone else had taken the lead, and saw as well the men part for her, and hurried through them down the narrow passage which led to the cobblestones, which in turn led the length of Mortemouth to the foot of Eden Point and the narrow goat trail which spiraled upward to the imposing castle that had cast its shadow, for better or worse, over the citizens of Mortemouth since the twelfth century. As she walked, a sizable tail of excited men and boys gathered behind her.

When had it happened? When had Susan Mantle, daughter of an Exeter farmer, become someone to follow?

Suddenly she shivered. On more than one occasion God had, contrary to rumor, sent her more than she could shoulder. It was a lovely myth that He was incapable of misjudging one's capacity to endure and prevail. Her ordination had been long and haphazard and, occasionally filled with defeat.

"Clear the way!" she heard a man shout close beside her as they turned into the cliff walk and encountered a chattering group of young people. A girl, whom she recognized as Milly Slade, appeared to be weeping softly in a young man's arms.

"What is it, Milly?" she asked, and was not given a chance to finish.

"Oh, it's turrible, Miss Mantle!" Milly sobbed. "He's goin' to drop her, or worse, jump with her. I know he is. He's daft, you know, turrible daft, has been for years."

Susan tried to make sense of the gibberish. Her? What her? She had understood that John Murrey Eden inhabited Eden Castle alone, with the exception of an occasional brave visitor from London.

Now, drawing a long breath, Susan forced herself to move past the attraction of young people and braced her body for the first steep incline of the cliff walk.

With conscious effort she slowed her step and felt the "tail" of nervously chattering men adjust their pace as well, and looked ahead to see two old women, one lantern between them, clinging to the cliff side of the walk, their sunken eyes glittering feverishly in the excitement of the night.

"It's too cold for you," Susan called out kindly, feeling the unseasonable chill in her own bones, knowing they must be dangerously cold. Why were they out and about at this hour? They had no business . . .

As Susan drew near, she suggested over the shrill wind, "Go on home with you both, please, to a toasty fire and a cuppa—"

"I served him, you know, I did," announced one old crone over the wind. "I was in the banqueting hall the very day Lady Harriet looked upon him for the last time." Suddenly the old woman crossed herself and shivered anew in a way that had nothing to do with the wind and clung more fiercely to her companion.

"He tweren't a bad young man," she added, smacking her lips over toothless gums. "There's more of his father in him than anyone wants to know. It's her he's got now. It's her . . ."

The crowd behind pressed against Susan, having caught up. In the faint light she saw their excited expressions, drawn-down lips, glittering eyes. The old woman who claimed to have served John Murrey Eden stepped closer. In the spill from the lantern Susan detected a bluish tint to her lips.

"I know what's goin' on up there, I do," she vowed. " 'Tis a wrestling match atwixt God and Satan. They both want his soul, don't you know."

At that moment a blood-chilling wail struck her ear, a male cry, or so it seemed.

Out of the corner of her eye she saw the two old women cross themselves again with bony fingers upon skeletal and sunken breasts. "I'd stay away if I were you, pet," one advised earnestly. "Satan is winning." She tapped the side of her nose. "But then, he always wins, now, don't he?"

Hurry, a small voice of reason advised quietly inside her head. The old woman was right on one count. The persistence of evil in the world was awe-inspiring. And where evil did not triumph, all too often passivity did.

Her thoughts were interrupted by a close knot of climbers up ahead. She'd seen them earlier but never dreamed she'd overtake them. There were four men in all, all weaving slightly with that telltale lack of balance which marks inebriation. Obviously they'd stopped at the Green Man before deciding to go where the true excitement was. Now in their staggering she observed from several yards back that they were occupying the entire path, arms locked. If they were aware of her fast approach, they gave no indication of it.

She broke speed and felt trapped, caught between the arm-locked men up ahead and the pushing, scrambling crowd behind.

"Coming through, please . . ."

. . . and saw the man on the extreme left turn slowly as though he wasn't quite certain whether the voice was real or merely part of the wind. Then the second turned, then the third, and at last the fourth, though there was a painful collision with the jagged cliff wall as the path suddenly narrowed, and all four jockeyed for their share of the limited space.

As the fourth rubbed his shoulder, the other three staggered about in a limited circle, all squinting at her, their faces ruddy and weathered from constant exposure to the wind. She recognized them as fishermen from Mortemouth.

"Who . . . ?" one slurred, and leaned heavily upon his mates.

"It's only me. Miss Mantle," she called out, smiling, pushing back the hood of her cloak so that they might see her clearly and recognize her. Everyone did, from the Bristol Channel to Clovelly. Now she lifted her face to the sliver of a moon in the hope that her familiar features would be illuminated, the drunken men would recognize her and let her pass with a minimum of difficulty."

"I said, who . . . ?" one of the men slurred again, and squinted into the darkness and, in his eagerness to see, lost his balance and would have toppled over the edge of the cliff walk if it hadn't been for the quick action of his mates.

Susan marched forward, thinking to thread her way through them while they were still struggling to identify her. Up close she recognized one of them, Tom Babcock, a local herring fisherman. His infant son had suffered lung fever last year. The child had survived, but Susan feared that his hearing was now impaired.

" 'Evening, Tom," she called out, drawing even with the men, who seemed to be exerting massive effort simply to stand erect.

Suddenly from out of the shadows she felt a hand descend upon her left shoulder. Massive and strong, it spun her about. She dropped the lantern and for a moment the entire world was converted into a whirlwind blur of black ocean and dancing whitecaps and distant eyes of light. In an effort to remain upright, she reached out toward the center of the men for any available support and found it on a broad chest and in two rough arms that within the instant ensnared her and drew her close to a bewhiskered mouth from which emanated the smells of all the breweries of the world.

"Ha! Caught you, plain Miss Sparrow," the man laughed, and though she was struggling inside his enforced embrace, she looked up into the massive face and realized that she had never seen him before. Not of Mortemouth, she was certain.

"Please . . . let me . . . pass," she suggested with an admirable degree of calmness, for there was no cause for alarm. It was just the ale—too much of it—that had made them aggressive, and perhaps the fact that John Murrey Eden, whom they loathed, was suffering again, and that, of course, was worthy of celebration.

"Pass, pass," the giant teased good-naturedly, though he did nothing to release her. In fact, she felt his arms become a vise about her shoulders, a gesture that was in contradiction to his teasing. Then she felt one enormous hand work its way up her waist, closing about her breast, drawing her yet closer, the grizzled face bending over her, making it necessary that she look sharply to the left in an attempt to avoid intimate contact.

The sudden struggle attracted the attention of all those men near enough to see. She was aware of them halting on the path behind her as though they too had encountered an insurmountable barrier.

"Please . . ." she gasped, pushing with her one free hand against the massive barrel chest. "I'm needed up at—"

"You're needed here," the man hissed in her ear, and inevitably the arms tightened even more and she felt that one straying hand explore further, venturing back and forth across her breasts, the fingertips finding the softness, then plunging into it.

After a moment of panic she reminded herself to stay calm. She'd been in similar situations before, many times, worse than this.

But as the hand pressed further and the mouth came closer, she saw the

14

gathering crowd, a few struggling to catch their breaths after the climb up, Reverend Christopher wearing a shocked and outraged expression but all of them holding their ground, as though they were frightened of the giant.

"Please . . ." Susan gasped, and continued to struggle against the massive barrel chest and tried equally hard to avoid the grizzled stubbly whiskers that continued to bend close over her face.

"Please let me go," she repeated, trying to keep her voice as normal as possible.

"Let you go," parroted the giant, grinning. "Come back with us to the Green Man and show us what you got in your nurse's bag. Eh, Tom? Wouldn't you like to see . . . ?"

As all the men laughed, Susan suddenly—and to her surprise—pulled free. She wrenched left as the giant threw back his head to the right and invited the others to join in his sport.

Freed, she backed hurriedly up the path, all the while keeping a vigilant eye on the stumbling, giggling men.

"Leave her alone, Simon!" It was a weak voice compared to the giant's, and then she heard it again, as though the voice knew it was inferior and needed to repeat itself. "I said leave her be!"

As no hands had as yet made insistent contact, she dared to look back from her position near the cliff wall and saw that Tom Babcock had come to her defense, though the pleasure was mixed because on his face she saw the completion of the chain, the practical application of *Do Unto Others*, and she *had* sat with his infant son for three nights. But she saw as well that he was clearly outmatched both in physical size and in weight of authority. The top of Tom's head barely reached the giant's shoulder.

Still he came, leaning into the path's incline, his face placid as though he were confronting merely a bothersome neighbor or tradesman in need of gentle correction.

"Leave her be, Simon, is what I say."

At the same time, she saw Tom step upward to a position directly behind Simon and only lightly touch his arm. Simon whirled on the light touch as though it held real threat, and the last Susan saw was that enormous hand draw back in what seemed an eternity of gathering strength and finally shoot forward pistonlike and deliver an awesome blow to the side of Tom's jaw.

Sickened by the crack of bone on bone and the sight of poor Tom literally airborne in his backward-tumbling descent down the path, it was Susan's turn to feel splintering intentions. If she stayed to lend her assistance, Simon would merely relaunch his conquest, and undoubtedly some other knight-errant would start up the hill to offer her rescue. Carried to its logical conclusion, she foresaw herself never reaching the top of the cliff walk and saw as well the path behind littered with the groaning bodies of would-be rescuers and saw no point to either projection.

So . . . she ran. She gathered up her skirt and bowed her head into the incline—at its steepest here at mid-point—and heard an uproar of laughing men coming from behind as most cheered her on her way. She looked ahead and tried to draw deep breath for her bursting lungs and—to her surprise—saw a gnarled hand reach down in assistance and saw ahead of her on the path only a black-hooded figure, faceless, and heard a voice of no clear sex say hoarsely, "Hurry! You're needed, though you may wish old Simon had got you first."

In the momentum of her speed she couldn't break pace, and took the outstretched hand, grateful for the assistance, and was well past it when it occurred to her to look back for clearer identification, and when she did, she saw at the side of the path where the specter had stood—nothing, merely the silky heads of high rush weeds bending under the duress of the harsh channel wind.

Where . . . ? she thought, momentarily alarmed, then belatedly realized the path had followed the contours of the cliff and had curved, and the figure, whoever it was, had disappeared behind the cliff wall.

Hurry! You're needed, though you may wish old Simon had got you first.

She still felt the chill dampness of a hand covering hers and vowed when the crisis was over to inquire about the black-hooded figure. Hurrying on toward the fortress towering above her, she looked up as though the jagged crenellation had called to her. She hadn't realized how close she was to the top, for she saw more than crenellation now, saw the castle itself, enormous, imposing, a constant and steady landmark from her youth, along with Exeter Cathedral and the wild loneliness of Exmoor.

Still struggling for breath, she thought of all the stories of Eden Castle she'd heard as a child, and had believed. Slowly she resumed speed as though the weight of her thoughts had steepened the incline in the last few yards. She remembered her father's perennial and classic rage at "them Edens," the ancient question which always confronted mankind, confronting him with new immediacy and frustration, "why some slept warm and dry and others didn't, why some hurt all the time and others appeared never to hurt . . ."

At least Susan knew more than her father had known, knew the vast importance of that one benign word: "*appeared* to hurt . . ."

All men hurt. And women. It was that simple and that sorrowful. Nearing the top, she heard voices beyond her thoughts, heard a female voice shout, "Who's comin'?" over the wind, and looked up to see a sizable greeting committee, forty or more men and women, a few children, shifting as restlessly as rush reeds under the pressure of the wind.

"It's only—" she called back, ready to identify herself, when a strong male voice cut in. "It's her. It's the nurse. Let her pass. She can . . ."

She never heard the nature of his vote of confidence, for at the announcement of her identity, the group moved back to permit her to climb to the very top of the path, where a woman greeted her by shouting, "He's up there, he is," and she pointed a finger toward the sprawling castle, where still Susan had seen nothing human or threatening save the outline of the castle itself.

She pushed back the hood of her cloak and felt the hair close to her scalp wet with perspiration despite the cool wind, and looked closely at every jagged edge of crenellation, thinking she'd missed something and was, in fact, still missing it.

"I don't . . ." she began to the woman, and was quickly offered an explanation.

16

"Oh, not there, dearie, but on the channel side, right down that path there, near the Eden graves, don't you see, or right above them."

As the woman spoke, Susan followed the direction of her hand and saw little but that strange brooding terrain which was characteristic of all the moors, grassy yet virtually devoid of all else, with gaunt ribs of rock, heather, and wind-tortured clumps of gorse and bracken. No reassuring trees or hedgerows, fields or meadows, just the bleak repetition of emptiness and desolation.

She drew one final lung-filling breath and glanced briefly behind her, expecting to see the sharp descent, and saw nothing and remembered that the woman had led her away from the treacherous edge and had now abandoned her for whispered gossip among her friends, having pointed the way to where something was going on that required Susan's attention.

With no offers from anyone to guide her farther or assist her in any way, she shrugged the hood of her cloak farther back onto her shoulders and felt the good clean coldness of ocean wind and tried, as she started off alone down the path, to resurrect from memory an image of John Murrey Eden as she'd last seen him in the army hospital at Scutari, his right shoulder wounded from the massacre at Station Number Seven on the Brassey Railway. She'd heard it all, every grim detail, not from Mr. Eden, who had been strangely silent during the days of his recuperation, but from other survivors of the same tragedy. Not that there had been that many. She tried now to remember the final count of the dead. There was something safe and objective in a number, far better than the memory of men's screams which had awakened her earlier on this bizarre evening. Over five hundred, she recalled; and as always, the dead had been the fortunate ones. For days, weeks, the less fortunate had hobbled or been carried off the ships at Scutari Landing, many amputees who had endured the first surgery under rough battlefield conditions, some clearly insane from the weight of the pain.

Suddenly Susan looked up to discover that she'd wandered off the path, moving toward the cliff's edge, away from the castle, as though her instincts, if nothing else, were trying to warn her . . .

Then she heard it again, that deep plaintive wail that seemed to start low, then climbed the length of the scale, though it was not a human scale, for she'd never heard a human voice make that piercing cry.

Before she stepped back up onto the path, she looked again in the direction of the sound. Straight ahead, wasn't it? It seemed to be, and she saw through the shadowy night yet another group of Mortemouth's citizens several hundred yards up ahead, lantern flares dancing at macabre angles under the pressure of the wind. From where she stood, a distance removed, they seemed to be simultaneously looking up at something and yet backing away.

"Hurry!" someone shouted, and she quickened her step.

As she approached the large gathering, she saw their faces, their eyes recording something at the top of the castle. A few, incredibly, were grinning. But most bore stiff frozen expressions, varying degrees of horror, several of the women pressing the hems of aprons to their mouths, the men standing deceptively casually, hands shoved into well-worn trousers, the tension manifested in the manner in which teeth chewed at the corner of a lip.

Suddenly a communal and sharp intake of breath issued from the closely watching crowd and at last the stragglers from the cliff walk drew near and caught her in their flow and pushed against her as though at last forcing her to turn and face whatever spectacle was taking place at the top of Eden Castle.

She could see a dark shape, the figure of a man, though the head seemed to blend with the shoulders, the shoulders with the torso, until, reaching midsection, it appeared to elongate as though he were carrying in his arms another . . .

"Who is . . . ?" she began of anyone who cared to answer, and never finished, for suddenly the specter stepped closer to the edge of the escarpment, bearing the silent figure with him, a figure detailed now, as Susan observed, by the fullness of the thick skirts.

A woman.

"Who was in the castle with him?" she asked, and wished that someone had the knowledge to answer.

But apparently all were lacking, for in the split second before the wind died, no one answered, either through lack of knowledge or the greater fascination that the figure was less than a single step from the edge of the roof, only the shortest of movements separating him and his mysterious cargo from the edge and the sheer descent down to gravel four stories below.

"Who is with him?" she demanded, and for a moment thought irrationally that she must find a quick way up and relieve him of his burden before they plunged over the edge, either singly or together. But there was no quick way up, none that she knew of. Before her, skirting the walls of the castle, she saw the gravel path which led back around the northern expanse of castle, on around to the western front to the gatehouse, through the gatehouse and inside the inner courtyard, up the steps of the Keep, where the trail disappeared into the vastness of the castle itself.

Again the man moved closer to the edge, his cries rising with the wind, the same cries she'd heard for the last fifteen minutes, a depth of mourning that could not and should not be maintained.

"Are there servants?" she asked, beginning to address those directly on either side of her. She needed specific answers.

Suddenly, from behind, she heard a puffing though familiar male voice. Reverend Christopher's.

"Thank heavens," she exclaimed, pleased to see someone moving toward her who might have information and the courage to share it.

As she waited for him to push his way through the crowd, she glanced over her shoulder, to see the tableau at the top of the castle unchanged, the bearded figure with face and features obscured still tottering on the brink, the woman in his arms unmoved as far as Susan could tell, apparently not protesting her fate in any way, though occasionally the persistent wind lifted a skirt and altered the silhouette and gave the appearance of life and movement.

Standing next to her now, Susan saw the same old woman she had encountered earlier on the path, the only font of willing information on the scene, apparently. "It's his retribution, don't you see?" the old woman announced over the wind, smacking her lips in a curious manner, as though the words tasted good.

18

"For what?" Susan inquired.

"Who are you?" the old woman demanded, squinting over the limited distance that separated them. "Oh, it's the little nurse." She grinned, answering her own question. She stepped closer, and Susan smelled a garlic plaster. "You got your work cut out for you up there, now, ain't you, dearie? If I was you, I'd just turn . . ."

Behind her she heard the familiar puffing and looked back to see Reverend Christopher, more red-faced than usual, draw even with her. "I was afraid of this. How many times I have tried to reach him with the promise of God's forgiveness, but he really didn't want . . . forgiveness." The bewilderment in his voice reflected the greater bewilderment of his soul. Who in their right mind would turn down God's blessed forgiveness?

"He's not seen things clearly for ever so long," Reverend Christopher went on, whispering.

How long the tortured man and his cargo would be content merely to howl at the moon, she had no idea.

"Who is with him?" she interrupted.

Reverend Christopher looked up toward the crenellation as though somehow the distance and shadows had altered and now he could see. "Well, I'm . . . not certain," he murmured, his eyes becoming two slits as he peered upward.

"Who was in the castle with him?" Susan asked urgently.

"No one," he said flatly. "No one was in the castle with him."

Surprised, Susan was certain that this was misinformation. How could that be? The Eden family was large, like most of the great families of England, half-brothers and -sisters and countless London associates. As frequently as three years ago the only carriages she ever encountered crossing the moors were elegant London coaches, all bound for Eden. No, she was certain that Reverend Christopher was mistaken when he said that John Murrey Eden lived in the castle alone.

"Then who is in his arms?" she asked.

But before he could answer, a voice, steady, unperturbed, male, came from behind. "It's the Lady Harriet," this voice announced calmly. "Mr. Eden's aunt, or mother, or lover, or mistress, depending upon which tattler you choose to believe."

Even as the voice spoke, Susan turned, hearing the weight of authority she needed. There was no speculation or guesswork in those clarion and slightly arrogant tones. Someone *knew*. She saw in the dim night a pencil-thin, yet erect male figure, dressed in a black coat. His face was old, with a solemn expression in his eyes and thin drawn-down lips. His hair was wispy and white and seemed to lift under the force of the wind as though it had a will and energy of its own. She couldn't remember having ever seen him before in her life.

Still he spoke on in a deep, well-modulated voice, a touch of sorrow audible in his tone, a deeper sorrow in his eyes. "It's the Lady Harriet, yes, I'd bet on it." He nodded, looking effortlessly up, as though something had provided him with a clearer vision.

"And you are . . . ?" Susan began, feeling the need to identify the strange old man who might, with luck, lend her a particle of understanding concerning the grim and apparently fixed tableau at the top of Eden Castle.

Yet at the very moment when she'd invited the old man to speak, he fell silent and looked as though he were on the verge of moving away.

Reverend Christopher lightly touched his arm and drew him back and tendered the introduction. "This is Mr. Bates, Susan," he said, stepping closer between them and looking simultaneously up at the top of the castle. "He served as butler to the Edens for . . . oh, how many years was it, Mr. Bates?"

Butler! Here was a stroke of fortune, her first.

"For the better part of my productive life," Bates said solemnly, head still lifted. The deep hollows of his gaunt cheeks caught and held pools of shadows from the surrounding torchlights.

"I was brought up from Chatsworth, from the noble Duke of Devonshire, by that man himself," and with a moving degree of reflection he nodded toward the distant man.

"He paid me a king's ransom, he did," Mr. Bates went on, a new and discomforting bitterness creeping into his recall. "In those days his money could buy anything, though I was warned it was tainted. But you see, I was young and had no conception of the darkness into which I was stepping . . ."

He seemed in turn loath to speak and then eager to do so, and Susan felt the conflict of the moment, and didn't want to add to it but felt such an urgent need for information. "*Is* there anyone in the castle with him, Mr. Bates? Please, if you know . . ."

But now Bates was looking down on her as though seeing her for the first time.

"My name is Susan Mantle, Mr. Bates," she said, doing nothing to disguise or soften the impatience in her voice. "I'm a traveling nurse out of Exeter and was in Mortemouth when Reverend Christopher summoned me here tonight. I assume we all want the same thing, to try to bring them both down alive and intact—"

"Too late for that," Bates said bluntly. "One is already dead."

"One . . ." she tried to repeat, and couldn't, for suddenly it seemed to her that the wind as well as the surrounding voices had fallen silent, listening.

Bates nodded, a grim, economical confirmation. "Her," he said. "Lady Harriet. I suspected it last . . ."

Abruptly he broke off as though aware he'd said too much. In his lean, enclosed face she saw the code of all successful butlers who always were hired not for their knowledgeable ways in managing a great house but rather for their inhuman ability to see everything and reveal nothing.

"Please, Mr. Bates," she urged, trying to draw both men a distance away from the crowd, which continued to grow in numbers. "Please tell me what you know. It might help to—"

"They both are beyond help," he interrupted, his voice topping hers. "Don't you see? One is dead, and one wants to be dead. Leave them to heaven, or in the case of Mr. Eden, to the hottest fires in the lowest hell."

She looked away at this harsh sentence and wished that she could anchor the old man in the present, as opposed to slipping in and out of what apparently was an awesome and destructive past.

"Do you still reside at Eden, Mr. Bates?" she asked politely, though with new directness and greater urgency, for she'd heard an angry swell from the audience, had heard one drunken male voice shout, "Why don't you jump, you bastard?"

Quickly she prayed that the voice had not carried to the top of the crenellation. "Do you, Mr. Bates, still live within the castle?"

"Miss," he said archly, "do I look capable of inhabiting a pigsty? No, I left the castle years ago, as did all men of reason and civility."

"Who cared for . . . ?"

"He cared for himself."

"And the Lady Harriet?"

"The same, though it was harder on her in her blindness."

Blind. Only then did Susan remember the stories that had circulated around Lady Harriet Eden, how she'd tried to mutilate herself and had succeeded in blinding herself. Susan hadn't believed them. "How do you know this, Bates, if you no longer reside in the castle?"

"I have access, miss, and certain orders from a London firm."

"What London firm?"

"Mr. Eden's. Who else?"

"Who in the London firm directs you?" she asked, remembering that this man was more accustomed to interrogation than polite inquiry.

"Alex Aldwell."

"Mr. Bates, will you come with me and show me the fastest way up there? Please . . . ?" she asked, already starting off, confident that he couldn't refuse so sensible and humane a request.

"For what purpose?" he demanded imperiously, and even before Susan could reply, Reverend Christopher sputtered indignantly.

"For . . . what . . . purpose? Look for yourself and discern the purpose. This circus must be brought to an end, and soon."

"It will be, sir, I assure you, so long as no one interferes. I was told by London to watch but not to interfere."

"Whoever told you that was a barbarian and a fool," Reverend Christopher snapped. "I cannot stand by with a clear Christian conscience and watch . . ."

Susan had heard enough, and now heard more in the wailing wind, heard a lamentable sob, the fearful sound coming from the top of the castle. Whatever the nature of Mr. Eden's offenses against man or God, no punishment in heaven or on earth should be capable of producing such a wretched sound.

So while the two men engaged in useless argument, she stepped out of the triangle and hurried toward the castle's north wall, hoping to find a path which would lead her around to the gatehouse, across the grille into the inner courtyard and ultimately into the castle itself.

"Miss, I must firmly request that you not interfere," Bates called out after her.

"Take it up with me, Bates," the Reverend Christopher sputtered. "I'm the one who fetched Miss Mantle. She has a way with the hurt."

Bates laughed, a dry, bone-rattling sound. "She'll need more than that to deal with Mr. Eden," he said acidly. "He has destroyed everyone else. Let him destroy himself."

Bates continued protesting as though Eden Castle was his private domain.

"You'll only be doing more harm than good, I swear it," and she heard his old voice crack under the duress of speed and emotion.

"How so?" challenged Reverend Christopher. "I was a frequent visitor at Eden—"

"When? Not recently."

"No, I concede, not recently . . ."

"No, of course not. No one has visited Eden since . . ."

She broke speed, listening, curious for a date. It might be helpful for her to know how long the disintegration had been taking place.

"Since when, Mr. Bates?" she called over her shoulder, hoping the man did not resent her so much that he ceased talking to her altogether.

When, after several moments, she heard no response, she increased her speed and left the two men stumbling after her.

"If it wouldn't be asking too much," she heard a breathless Reverend Christopher entreat, "the man might speak if we would only break our pace . . ."

"Can't," she replied bluntly. "No time. Fall back if you must, but . . ."

"You'd best be falling back yourself," she heard Bates warn. Even his pious old voice was beginning to suffer under the duress of speed. "The gatehouse is locked and barred. No one has passed in or out since I left several . . ."

Abruptly she stopped. "Why didn't you tell me?" she demanded. Apparently he'd known from the beginning that there would be no access in this direction.

"You didn't ask, miss," he replied tersely, "or give me a chance to inform you. You simply took off into the night and . . ."

"Then where?" she demanded. At that moment she heard the distant voices of the crowd. Something had happened to excite them further.

"Where?" she demanded again. "Surely there is an access route inside the castle somewhere."

In the dark she couldn't see the old man's face, and for that she was grateful. "There *is* a way in," he replied with a maddeningly calm voice.

"Where? Hurry! Will you show me?"

"I must ask first . . ."

"What?"

"What is your intention once in?"

"To find a way up," she said, doing nothing to hide the incredulity in her voice. "To find a way to avert that tragedy that is now being witnessed by most of Mortemouth."

"Impossible."

"Why?" she demanded, her incredulity growing rapidly to outrage.

"Because Mr. Eden wants nothing more in this world than to die, and in all matters, Mr. Eden accomplishes what he wants, what he sets out to accomplish."

"Then he will have to say that to me before—"

Bates laughed. "Mr. Eden does nothing but what pleases him. What fails to please him or gets in his way gets snuffed out like a burned-down candle."

She was aware of Reverend Christopher leaning heavily against the castle wall, still drawing tortured breaths.

"Then why did you come for me?" she asked him, remembering the rude pounding on the door, her harsh awakening.

In an attempt to answer her question, Reverend Christopher tapped on his chest with one fist as though to aid the passage of air through his lungs. "I came for you because you are needed," he said simply, "and because I strongly disagree with this . . . gentleman and because life is sacred and must be maintained and preserved at all cost."

As he launched into a small tedious sermon, she thought bleakly that she could have argued the point with him, about life, that is, though perhaps not effectively, for she was undecided in her own mind.

Then it was up to her to find an alternative route. If the gatehouse was bolted, surely there was a passage or a gate left carelessly open on the east wall, the place where a low scattering of outbuildings huddled against the fortress of the castle, the place where horses once were shod and sheep sheared, farm implements stored, though she knew for a fact that the farm equipment had not been used for several years, the rich fertile land on Eden Rising going to weed and ruin.

"Miss! I must ask again, where do you think you're going?" demanded Bates.

"To find for myself what you apparently refuse to show me."

"I assure you that you will find nothing that way except a full meadow of Eden dead and a crumbling path that leads the length of the headland to . . . nothing."

A full meadow of Eden dead. A curious phrase; and then she realized. The Eden graveyard. What else? Was he telling the truth? Was the castle impenetrable? Perhaps so, but for the sake of her own conscience she had to find out for herself, and on this conviction she'd just started off again when she heard his voice, more practical, certainly more resigned, as though in her persistent determination she'd proved something to him.

"Very well," he said, a weariness of resignation in his voice. "Come with me," and now saw him push aside his long black coat and reach into an inner pocket, fish blindly for a moment, head raised, body angled away from the search. And at last apparently he found what he was looking for, tucked it inside the palm of his left hand, restored his coat, and walked on.

By way of showing her gratitude, she kept silent and purposefully fell a step or two behind the thin old man and felt very much in her "woman's place" and recognized his resentment. She encountered it daily, even from those who benefited most from her nursing skills.

Of course she was almost beyond caring now, and stumbled along the mud-soft border, feeling her shoes grow heavy with caked mud, feeling the weight of male superiority, hearing a new and ominous silence in the night, no more shouts or jeers coming from the distant crowd. Something had stunned or shocked or frightened them into a new and disturbing silence.

Hurry! the voice dictated again from inside her head.

He's not a man, but the Devil.

That judgment would have to be left to God.

Coming from behind, she heard Reverend Christopher fretting out loud, voicing her fears. "Why are they suddenly so quiet?" he asked of anyone who cared to answer.

Bates had a ready answer. "Not many of them have ever seen the Devil in the flesh. It must be an impressive sight for them."

As long as words were once again the order of the day, Susan spent a few for herself. "Did you always view Mr. Eden as such?" she asked. "One wonders why you spent your entire lifetime in his employ."

"Always," came the terse reply. "Always!" came an even more emphatic repetition. "The first time I ever saw him at Chatsworth, I knew I would weaken before him."

Despite the darkness, she heard the bitterness of regret, yet was puzzled that he would blame Mr. Eden for his own succumbing to material temptation.

"How, precisely," she asked, "did he corrupt you? Mr. Eden, I mean. Surely you were capable of resisting—"

"No, I was not," he snapped, "nor would any man, when faced with that Lucifer."

"Then he offered you money?"

"More money than I'd ever seen before, or dreamed of."

"Still, you could have resisted—"

"No!"

Well, she could understand that, too. Existence and the conditions of existence were not always compatible to the "theory" of goodness. Parts of her own past were bleak testaments to that.

She looked ahead to see the vast expanse of the north fortress wall coming to an end. In the dark it resembled a mammoth extension of the cliff wall itself.

"Mr. Bates, where . . . ?"

"Straight ahead," he commanded, lowering his head into the powerful convergence of sea and channel wind. "Beyond the gatehouse there's a small door in the south wall." He paused and held up his left clenched fist. "I have the key."

There was such self-satisfaction in this claim that for a moment his voice lightened and she wouldn't have been too surprised to see a grin upon his bony features.

"Miss," Bates demanded suddenly, breaking his speed, the force of the converging winds lessening as well, "what is your precise interest in all this, besides good works and a clear Christian conscience?"

The direct question caught her off guard, preoccupied as she was with the castle itself. She faltered, then managed, "As I said, Reverend Christopher—"

"I did, indeed," Reverend Christopher blustered as though he too were annoyed by the impudent question. "Miss Mantle has a miraculously soft touch with the ill and wounded, and I thought—"

"Mr. Eden is neither ill nor wounded," Bates cut in, increasing his pace and simultaneously throwing back his voice.

"I would argue that, and suggest that he is both," Susan contradicted.

"Then he's been thus all his life, for the theatrical which you have just witnessed from the headlands has been his sign and signature for as long as I can remember. He 'performs' everything. Everything in his life is a lie." Bates shook his head. "He missed his natural calling, don't you see? He should have gone on the stage."

She listened, though she found what she was hearing hard to believe.

24

No one could artificially produce that sound of human distress and misery which at intervals punctured the already restless night.

But before she could argue the point, she heard him call out, "Over here," and followed the imperious wave of his hand to a spot near the crumbling gatehouse. One grille, she observed, had fallen altogether and now rested at a sideward angle. The other was only half-raised, giving the impression of a large open mouth on the verge of devouring anyone foolish enough to pass beneath it.

But apparently Mr. Bates had no intention of entering the gatehouse, for she saw him march straight past it, taking care to step over and around the accumulated debris which had blown against the grille, both from inside and out, under the force of the perennial wind. Inside the gate, pressed against it in various positions of crucifixion, she saw weeds, straggly bits of bracken and newsprint clinging to the bars like prisoners wanting out.

"Over here!" she heard Bates shout, and looked up, and in the dark at first couldn't see him and then saw the elongated shadow moving across the high stone wall, a short distance from the substance of the man who was bent over a small arched door which appeared to have been constructed in the wall itself of weathered wood and remnants of wood carving in both the upper and lower panels. It had been a very handsome and very secret door at one time. For what purpose, she had no idea, but it was her estimate that they would come out on the other side near the central staircase, having walked the length of the courtyard on the outside.

"Please hurry," she urged softly as Bates bent over the low lock and fumbled for the key. Behind, she heard Reverend Christopher, just catching up, whispering a humorous but heartfelt entreaty for God to "lighten the weight, Lord, just for a moment."

"Light would help," Bates complained in a terse voice, and belatedly it occurred to Susan they should have brought a torch. But surely, once inside the castle, they would find all the torches and lamps they required.

In an attempt to soothe, she voiced this conviction. "Inside, I'm sure we can find sufficient illumination for—"

"You are consistent, Miss, only in your erring judgment," Bates pronounced. "There has been no real illumination inside that tomb for months, years. Does a burial ground have need of light? On the express orders of the monster himself, all wall torches, all fixed standards, were removed and disposed of in a bonfire truly worthy of Lucifer himself."

Caught between this bizarre announcement and the projection of a darker passage up to the top of the castle, Susan foundered. "W-why? I . . . don't understand . . ."

"Of course you don't," Bates snapped.

Angered at the delay, she reached forward and felt the heavy brass key still in the lock. She stepped closer, grasped the stubborn key and gave it one vigorous turn, and to her surprise felt no resistance, in fact felt the door give and creak slowly open on hinges as rusty and neglected as the lock itself.

Susan was convinced that all along he'd been capable of opening the door but had feigned difficulty. She saw a new acquiescence on Bates's face, a new truce as it were.

25

"Follow me," he commanded. "I am the only person in the world, save one, who does not need illumination in order to navigate through the twists and turns of Eden."

As though to demonstrate the validity of his claim, he set a brisk pace, so brisk that she hurriedly ducked her head to pass through the small opening and was forced to step quickly to keep up, and there was no time to check on the progress of Reverend Christopher.

Once inside the inner courtyard, she discovered that it was as she'd suspected. The main thrust of the castle loomed straight ahead, next to the gigantic Keep and Close. As she hurried across the cobblestones, she kept a vigilant eye on the high thick-walled charnel house and tried not to dwell on the humanity that had suffered and died inside.

Then, just as she was about to make it safely past those thick doors, she saw to the left another gruesome relic from the past, the thick, tar-coated whipping oak, once an enormous tree felled and transported from the woods beyond Exeter, the broad trunk stripped of all softening foliage which identified God's purpose for it and left it for man's.

Reverend Christopher now appeared directly behind her, having successfully squeezed his girth through the narrow door in the castle wall. In fact, coming alongside her, he took her arm as though to assist her beyond the gruesome past, a touching and considerate gesture of chivalry.

"Are *you* all right?" she whispered as he came alongside her. "The narrow door, I mean . . ."

"Oh, yes, quite." He nodded. "My own fault, you know—or rather the ladies with their scones and cream."

"What was it for? The door in the wall."

Bates shrugged. "I haven't the faintest. Part of the original castle, I'm sure. There are three in all, I believe, one in each wall, proof that the first Eden was a forward-thinking chap who knew that there would always be a need in such a grand place for ready and secret escape routes."

She smiled, finding the hushed chat a pleasant diversion from the urgency of the evening. It took her mind off what might be awaiting them up on the parapet.

"You've never been here before?" Reverend Christopher asked, darkness masking the surprise on his face but not in his voice.

"No," she admitted, and wondered what possible cause could have, in the past, brought her here. "Why?" she asked further. "Am I unique in that respect?"

"Well, yes, rather," he hedged. "At one time, shortly after all the fancy renovations, those gates were thrown open two, sometimes three times a year, at least on every festival day. All of Mortemouth would come, and most of Ilfracombe as well, and anyone else who happened to be passing by and was in need of a roll and a roast chicken, or simply the clasp of a friendly hand."

They paused, having reached the bottom of the Great-Hall stairs, and gaped up. "In his good days," Reverend Christopher concluded quietly, "there was never a more generous and gracious gentleman than John Murrey Eden."

She started up the stairs, seeing that Bates had already reached the top and was now fussing with the massive oak Great-Hall door.

As she gained access to the door, she found herself confronting total blackness, not a spill or trace of light coming from any source, and she sensed an immense and oversized hall used in better times for massive public receptions.

Using her hands like a blind man, moving them as perceptively as possible through the empty black space before her, she proceeded straight ahead for a few steps and at last realized the foolishness of her predicament.

"I take it you have been a guest at Eden before?" The arch voice came from behind and needed no identification.

"No," she said quietly, stopping where she was, as the surrounding darkness was a literal blockade.

"Then I assume you haven't the foggiest notion where you are going?" Bates inquired further.

"No," she confessed. "My only wish is that we might move faster."

"Oh, my," Bates sneered. "We are being chastised by the woman."

Then training won out over breeding and a moment later she heard rigid footsteps pass very close to where she stood, heard as well the ominous command, "Follow me, if you can. I believe the only lamp left in the castle is in the library. We must have light. There is little chance of making it up to the roof without it."

Reasonable, though one or two questions did lodge in her mind as she tried to fall into step behind the sound of his footsteps. Why was there only one lamp in the entire castle, and why was it in the library? And second, what was that hideous odor which seemed to increase as they made their way across the Great Hall, a terrible combination of soiled linen and rotting or rotted food and something else, the smell of the dead or dying.

She'd thought to ask all these questions, but at that moment something skittered between her feet, something solid, of substance, that caught briefly on the hem of her dress and caused her to jump nervously to one side, her hands clawing frantically at her skirts for fear the scurrying thing had attached itself, and all the while her eyes searched blindly in the blackness for a clue.

"No need to be alarmed," Bates called back, having heard her frightened movements and rightly interpreting them. "Undoubtedly it was just a member of the large and ever-growing rat population of Eden Castle."

She stood trembling, her hands still clutching her skirts, and thought how peculiarly uncomforting the truth was, almost always, without exception.

"I say, are you all right?" came Reverend Christopher's concerned voice in the dark. "I mean, it didn't nip you or anything?"

"N-no," she stammered, afraid to move in any direction.

"Yes, it's rats," confirmed Mr. Bates. "Contrary to popular myth, they didn't move into this ship in great numbers until it started to sink, some two or three years ago."

In the dark she heard a skeletal laugh, like dry bones. Moving again, she tried to relax, and at the same time she placed one hand over her nose in an attempt to diminish the awful smell. "I still don't understand," she confessed bluntly, feeling that words would help both the odor and her fear. "Why do you hate him so?"

For a moment there was no response, only the slow steady clack of footsteps resumed.

"Because," she heard him say, to her amazement, "he possesses that mixture of folly and evil which often makes what is good an offense and what is offensive appear to be good."

Suddenly all three stopped, as though their respective muscles were being controlled by one mind.

"And because," the disembodied voice went on in the dark, "he has ruined every life he has ever touched. He is a soul-murderer." This voice seemed not to belong to Bates. This voice was echoing and measured and spoke with that finality of absolute experience.

Having had the last word in this manner, Bates proceeded on across the Great Hall, and now to her amazement Susan discovered that she could see him, only vaguely and in outline, but it was enough and helped to keep Bates in her sights. She decided there must be a light coming from someplace and was grateful for it.

He possesses that mixture of folly and evil which often makes what is good seem offensive and what is offensive seem good.

"This way," she heard Bates call out, and saw him even more clearly, as though they were approaching the invisible light source. Also at this point she noticed the Great Hall narrow into a single corridor and observed to her left a great black shading which might be a staircase.

"Wait here," she heard Bates command, and observed before them a large cavity. Door frame? Door opened, she saw a deeper darkness on the other side. The library, she speculated, clasping her hand more firmly over her nose in weak defense against the noxious odor which seemed to be yet increasing.

As they had been ordered to wait, both she and Reverend Christopher did so, though under the enforced idleness he paced nervously back and forth in the narrow corridor and, just as she was about to speak in an attempt to ease the tension, she heard coming from deep within the darkened room a sudden crash followed immediately by a long curse which ultimately dissolved into angry sputtering. Obviously Bates had collided with something.

"Are you . . . all right?" Reverend Christopher called shyly in. "You will let us know if you need—?"

"Nothing," came the offended voice on a gasp.

Suddenly she saw the first flicker of light out of the corner of her eyes, like a timid flash of lightning. Yet when she turned on it, it was gone, the black of the library merely black again.

Reverend Christopher obviously had seen it as well. "Bates, I say, I take it you found—"

"A lamp, yes," came the toneless reply.

"Do you need . . . ?"

"Help, no. Oil, yes. It's empty."

Disappointed, Susan leaned heavily against the door frame and tried not to think about what was happening on the parapet. She feared that it had resolved itself one way or the other. And yet they were gaining ground. If only . . .

Then she saw the light again and held her breath as the spark grew.

"Bravo!" called out Reverend Christopher. "Bates, well done!"

Susan added her thanks mixed with new urgency. "Now we can move with greater speed, can't we, Mr. Bates? We really must . . . ."

The old man did not respond in any way and stood at the far end of the room and fiddled endlessly with the wick and windguard, adjusting everything with maddening thoroughness. He moved at a snail's pace through what in the dim light appeared to be a clutter of furniture, some shrouded by dull gray canvases, others stripped and pushed awry, the foul odor which she'd detected out in the corridor even stronger here.

Again she covered her nose and saw that Bates was moving toward them, bringing the lamp with him as well as a bizarre invitation. "Would either of you care to see the inner graveyard of Eden Castle?" he asked with suspect ease.

The macabre words seemed to approach very slowly in the semidarkness.

"Down here," came Bates's voice again.

She saw Reverend Christopher with a massive questioning look on his face. As for herself, she stepped all the way into the musty room, the better to see precisely what was going on at the far end, and saw a strange sight, the lamp burning well now, a stable pool of light in a dark sea, while a black silhouette lit what appeared to be two massive candlelabra spaced an equal distance apart.

"Mr. Bates?"

"The inner graveyard is what I said," the old man repeated, and his voice sounded breathless, as though under the duress of exertion. "Step forward, both of you," he commanded, and simultaneously the candles flared and joined the limited illumination of the lamp, and at last the far end of the library was illuminated. She saw a mussed sheet-enshrouded chaise, a low table cluttered with what appeared to be mugs, dishes, cutlery, an overturned chair draped unceremoniously with shirtwaists, a crude area which recently had served as living quarters for someone.

But most mysterious of all was what appeared to be an enormous painting, the focal point of the flanking candles as well as of the entire room.

Susan found herself turning first in one direction, then the other, trying to take it all in, trying hard to understand the man who had inhabited such chaos for the last several years. She drew near to the bright circle of light enhanced by candles and observed how the mussed couch had been dragged into perfect alignment with the large painting, which was not hung but merely rested precariously on a large standard.

To one side of the painting stood Bates, a pointer in hand which he'd found somewhere during his search for oil. "Can you see?" he called out as she came to a halt directly before the painting.

She nodded and was aware of Reverend Christopher coming to a halt just behind her. But a moment later she was aware of nothing except the painting itself and its subject matter, which she saw clearly as Bates lifted the lamp and held it close, a mobile sun which illuminated a most dazzling array of rainbow colors in the shapes of four gossamer gowns, the four women themselves arranged precariously on the edge of a high marble parapet, four very different yet seductive beauties gazing out over a blue sea, their attention focused on a spot just beyond the frame of the painting, one a pale fair beauty more girl than woman, and next to her a more aggressive yet physically smaller and older woman, and next to her a dark exotic woman, Indian-appearing, or so it seemed in the flickering light, and last, the most beautiful of all, a young classic face with streaming fair hair, frankly sexual, portrayed with that dewy silkiness of a pampered woman's flesh.

Who they were, she had no idea, but together they formed a spectacular harem, so diverse and yet so united in their focus as though, despite their differences, they were waiting for someone under a communal tension.

"Who are they?" she asked quietly, somewhat intimidated by such collective beauty. She'd been cursed all her life with what Miss Nightingale had, with Christian generosity, dubbed "a good English face" and "vast hidden qualities." Natural beauty impressed her.

"Oh, I knew them all," she heard Reverend Christopher boast. "Knew most of them firsthand. That there is Miss Elizabeth, truly a good soul, almost despite herself . . ."

As Susan searched the four for the reluctant Christian named Elizabeth, she saw Bates nod.

"Elizabeth Eden," he confirmed, and stood back and, with the tip of his pointer, indicated the older woman. "The nearest thing to a mother that Mr. Eden ever possessed. In fact, many thought she was his mother, as she had been the constant and devoted companion of his father, Edward Eden. But I have it on good authority that she was not his blood mother, though she raised him and loved him and forgave him more than anyone else."

"Where is she now?" Susan asked, quickly praying that this proud beauty was not the lifeless cargo in Mr. Eden's arms up on the parapet.

"Dead," came Bates's flat reply, followed by a halfhearted resurrection, "probably. . . ."

"No!" Reverend Christopher protested with something less than complete conviction.

"I said 'probably,' " Bates snapped. "She was the last to leave some years ago and was on her way to Paris to join her good friends in the revolution of the Female Communes."

"Why did she leave?" Susan asked, her imagination performing cruel feats, seeing the lovely Elizabeth bloodied in the distant conflict across the channel.

"Why else?" Bates smiled, enjoying his role as authority at least where the women of Eden were concerned. *He* told her to leave, Mr. Eden did, told her to get out. He didn't want her here, and blamed her for everything."

Again Susan heard a shocked protest coming from Reverend Christopher, who moved a step ahead of her. "Not true," he grieved. "Surely not true. She was . . . so good, so loving. I can't believe . . ."

"No," Susan agreed quickly, "and I'm sure that Bates doesn't know for certain either. Perhaps she is . . ." Suddenly she glanced behind her into the deeper darkness of the room, thinking she had heard something. "Mr. Bates, I feel that we must—"

"Only a moment, miss," he scolded, "and I beg you to use your head. This painting is the map to the man. The only way to gain knowledge of John Murrey Eden is through these dead beauties."

"Dead," she tried to repeat, shocked. "Surely not all . . ."

"As good as." Bates nodded and stepped back to the painting. Wielding the pointer, he started at the left edge of the canvas and tapped his way across a sad roll call.

"Young Lady Lila Harrington, unfortunate enough to have served as Mrs. John Murrey Eden for a short duration, though long enough to conceive and deliver two sons and die."

Susan had heard the rumor once that there were Eden sons. But she'd never believed it, for where was the wife? Dead, apparently.

"And this lovely creature," Bates went on, "was Mr. Eden's Indian mistress, Dhari, brought back from the ashes of Delhi by Mr. Eden as one might bring back a wild boar after a successful hunt."

"Dead, too?" Susan asked weakly.

Bates shrugged. "Who knows? She had no tongue, you know. She lost it when she betrayed her own people. Mr. Eden used to say she was the ideal woman, cooperative and silent."

The old man laughed, and Susan heard a rattling in his lungs and knew what it meant. Still, she resented the laugh, especially following such a grim announcement.

She had no tongue, you know.

Suddenly, coming from someplace above her, she heard that great and intolerable wail. Reflexively she moved rapidly back through the clutter of furnishings, past the striking and tragic women of Eden. Whatever the nature of their grief, it would have to wait for the greater grief which still pursued her, that single animal howl of such duration and substance that she felt literally as though it were running her to ground.

"Miss, wait! You don't know the way," Bates shouted over the ungodly sound.

"Then show me, and quickly," she shouted back, stumbling once in the darkened end of the library, trying to find the door in the dim spill of light from Bates's single lamp.

"You must wait," Bates called out, and she looked back over her shoulder to see the two men in faltering pursuit. Directly ahead she saw a darkened cavity which she trusted was the door, and without pausing, she hurried through it and found herself in a new darkness, the cry overhead still raining down upon her, and she thought: nothing human could sustain it this long.

"To the right," she heard a begrudging voice instruct from behind. "Back into the Great Hall, then keep sharply to the left . . ."

To the right first, he had said, then sharply left around the Great-Hall arcade. Using the wall for support as well as guidance, she found herself feeling the way and felt the dampness of stone and shivered.

She lived long enough to conceive and deliver two sons and die.

Where were they now, those hapless children, while their father . . .

"Keep sharply left," Bates barked, "or else you'll end up two floors below in the kitchen court."

Still using the arcade wall for guidance, she pondered on his last instruction and sensed an intersection coming up and saw first in the dim light from Bates's bobbling lamp the massive outline of what appeared to be an equally massive staircase, flanked on either side by lesser arteries, smaller ascents, the one on the left cutting sharply away from the larger one, the one on the right appearing to lead straight into the heart of the castle.

Keep sharply left or else you'll end up two floors below in the kitchen court, and again she was grateful for the instruction which was directly opposed to her instincts, which told her to go straight up the large staircase. Surely so prominent an artery led to the top of . . .

Lost in thought, her feet obscured by the darkness, she miscalculated the first rising and stumbled and went heavily down on one knee and protested softly with one startled gasp, yet knew no damage had been done and righted herself quickly.

In the brief interim she heard heavy padding footsteps and saw both men evolve out of the darkness, the one in the lead lifting his limited light high, the one behind inquiring, "Are you all right, Susan? Still in one piece?"

"Yes." She nodded. "Which way now, Mr. Bates?"

"To the left, I said," the old man snapped. "If you'd only waited and . . ."

". . . let me take the lead" was the rest of the implied scolding, and now he did take the lead and Susan had only one request and made it as tactfully as she could. "Just hurry, please," she murmured, and stepped to one side as the glare of light rushed past, the lean old man heading toward the smaller staircase, which seemed to cut away from the heart of the castle and lead to yet another darkness.

The unearthly wail which had accompanied every step since they left the library suddenly ceased, a ghostly cessation which proved as unsettling as the wail itself.

For a moment all three froze on the narrow staircase, and as her hand was on Reverend Christopher's arm, she held it there, needing the feel of something human, though at the same time she felt a trembling and wasn't sure if it was coming from her or him.

She looked ahead and saw Bates angling the lamp upward as though all that the mystery required for a satisfactory solution was a dim and unreliable light.

"Please, let's hurry," she begged again, pushing past Reverend Christopher, feeling like a harried mother herding two recalcitrant schoolboys.

"What point?" old Bates demanded with maddening deliberation. "I suspect now that it's all over."

"We don't know . . ."

"Do you hear anything?"

"No, but . . ."

"Then why do you insist . . . ?"

"Because we must see what has happened." She looked back beseechingly at Reverend Christopher.

"She's right, Bates. Lead on, and quickly. It's been my experience that silence is worse than wailing, is not the abode of peace we mistake it for."

Bates opened his mouth as if in protest, but then, probably curious himself, continued his upward climb.

Hurrying after, she kept her eyes downward in search of hazardous footing that might cause her to stumble again, and in the process she lost the light and looked up to see the glow disappear around the distant corner and was tempted to call out "Wait!" then changed her mind and broke into a run in an attempt to catch up and listened briefly for sounds coming from behind and heard none and determined that they'd left Reverend Christopher far behind, and increased her speed and suffered the optical illusion that she would never reach the end of this corridor in time to catch the light . . .

But a few moments later she saw the corridor end abruptly in a blank stone wall, saw two narrow twisting staircases lead off to the right and left, and paused in an attempt to catch her breath and tried to determine the direction of Bates's lamp, and saw to the right a pale orange glow and instantly decided, "To the right," and took the narrow staircase running.

After three turns she encountered him as he pushed his way through a low door, which she observed led to a corridor identical to the one they'd just left.

"From now on, keep up," he scolded. "Don't lag behind. It can be dangerous."

She had no intention of lagging behind, even if she had to maintain a run to keep up, for while this corridor appeared to be identical in size, it was altogether different in other ways. No elegant portraiture lined these cold barren walls, no tapestry, no runner underfoot to soften the stone floor. This corridor clearly had been used only for passage. As she was thinking, with relief, that no one had inhabited this melancholy place, she saw a partially opened door, the heavy oak still a barrier, but she saw a pale glow coming from deep inside the chamber, as though someone had lit a lamp or left a small fire burning.

She hesitated. If Mr. Eden had taken up residence in the library downstairs—and there was every evidence that he had—then obviously he had not been in the castle alone. Someone else had shared his isolation. But who?

Unwilling to lose sight of Bates's lamp, she broke into a run and called out, "Wait, please," and didn't know if he'd heard her or not until she reached the end of the corridor and looked up to the left and saw him, leaning against the stone wall, his face in shadow a map of exhaustion and rigid gloom.

"I . . . suppose we . . . are too late," he gasped. Then, in a curious non sequitur, he added, "No decent woman would . . ."

"Who occupies that chamber, the one we just passed?"

"No one. There's no one in the castle except—"

"There was a light, or fire—"

"Not possible."

"You passed by it as well."

"One more staircase. Are you prepared?" He didn't wait for her answer.

Fatigue or something caused him to break his vindictive pace, and now she had little trouble keeping up, even as she surveyed this passage, the smallest yet. Two people would have difficulty passing each other. By reaching out on either side, she touched both walls, which seemed to be growing colder and damper, as was the air itself. She smelled sea breeze and knew they were nearing the top of the castle and, despite the torturous journey up, she was grateful to the old man for showing her the way, for she would never have found it by herself.

"Here . . . is the last," said Bates, tight-lipped.

"But . . . the door is closed," came the breathless voice from above her. As she climbed up the staircase, she saw him beyond the last turn, the lamp on the step below where he stood, pushing upward against what appeared to be a trapdoor in the ceiling.

"Here, let me," she offered, and sidestepped the lamp and counted hastily, "One . . . two . . . three!" On the count of three, both pushed, and she heard a scraping, felt the heavy door lift, felt Bates, the taller of the two, take the brunt of the weight on his shoulders and ease it carefully to one side.

At that moment a strong downdraft from the exposed opening swept over them and extinguished the lamp.

In the sudden darkness she closed her eyes, weary of obstacles. "Did you bring a lucifer?" she asked, lifting the dead, though still smoking, lamp in an attempt to show it to Bates, who now appeared decapitated, his head invisible through the opening of the trapdoor.

If he replied, she didn't hear, and foolishly she continued to hold up the dead lamp as though it were capable of giving off light. When Bates continued to stand in the opening, apparently disinclined to move through it or step out of it, she called out, "Can you see . . . ?"

"Nothing."

"Let me . . ."

"I said I could see nothing."

Amazed at this final obstacle after a night filled with obstacles, she was on the verge of pulling on his trouser leg when she heard a scuffle of steps coming from the opposite direction and turned on the sound.

"Who . . . ?" she gasped, terror mounting. The long passage through the castle had taken a toll. Nothing could evolve from out of those shadows . . .

Still they came, struggling footsteps which Bates apparently had yet to hear.

"Please . . ." she begged the inhabited darkness, "speak and identify . . ."

"Susan?" came a gasping raspish voice. "Who do you think it is? No one in their right mind . . ."

She felt a small collapse of relief at the voice and in her imagination sketched the body around it, Reverend Christopher, who obviously had navigated the treacherous castle corridors on his own and had at last found them.

"I say, why the bottleneck?" he inquired on the step below her.

"Mr. Bates," she said wearily, confident that that would suffice as explanation.

"I can see that," Reverend Christopher replied, a bit snappish. "Here, let me . . ."

All at once Bates withdrew his head and collided on his way down with Reverend Christopher, who was just starting up. For a moment both threatened to dislodge the other, and all three would have tumbled down to the first landing had there been room for such a tumble. But for once the narrow confines kept them intact, save for awkward balance, until at last Susan edged past both and moved to the recently vacated position directly beneath the trapdoor.

"No need," Bates called out.

34

"I don't . . ."

"It's empty," he announced, "as I thought it would be. No one in sight, no one at—"

"I can't believe that," Susan protested.

"I tell you, you won't find Mr. Eden there. . . ."

"Then where will we find him?"

"In hell, where he belongs."

Again she heard the disturbing hate and wondered why he felt thus for his tempter when he had been the one who had given in to temptation.

In the dark she was aware of Reverend Christopher trying to comfort the bitter old man, while at the same time trying to relight the lamp.

At that precise moment a small flame flared in the lamp and she found a rough stone shelf, like the stirrup on a saddle, obviously designed for a foot up, and without hesitation she took it and reached through the opening for something of leverage and grasped at handfuls of air. Yet with surprising ease she gained the roof and for her efforts received a wintry blast of channel wind directly in the face with such force that her eyes stung. Quickly she averted her face and looked down through the trapdoor to see a pool of light and at the center the grinning Reverend Christopher extending the lamp up and commending her. "Good girl! Now, be quick. What do you see?"

Again she shivered, painfully aware how ill-equipped she was for this task. The rescuing of lost souls was Reverend Christopher's domain. If she possessed any ability to serve, it was only in a secondary way, after the physical pain had been eased if not obliterated.

"Go on, Susan. You can do it," urged Reverend Christopher, who appeared only from the head up in the opening of the trapdoor. Clever man to sense her doubt.

"You're the only one."

Doubly clever to remind her that there was no one else. Now with a sense of mission she secured the hood of her cloak and turned once in a tentative circle, her eyes searching for a glimpse of the specter she'd seen from the headlands below.

Nothing—but as yet she hadn't turned full circle, and she required a few moments to get her bearings, facing south now, the force of the wind blowing at her from behind, pushing against her as though urging her back down into the safety of the trapdoor. She looked carefully at all the angles and aspects of the place, and saw nothing except the occasionally deceptive outlines of chimneys, endless configurations of red brick to accommodate the countless fireplaces below. Silhouetted against the night, some resembled broad, squat, square men.

If he wasn't here . . . But she canceled the thought.

"Susan?" Anything . . . ?" Reverend Christopher was still by the trapdoor.

"No. I can't find . . ."

"Look over the edge. Go on . . ."

The command was delivered sternly, as though he knew she had been postponing it. In a curious self-comforting litany she repeated two words, "Please God," beneath her breath as she approached the edge and stopped short by about five feet, a vantage point which revealed nothing but a breathtaking view of the channel, like a broad black ribbon stretching endlessly in either direction, and the large brooding dark landmass which was Wales.

Move closer. There was nothing in the distance that required her as witness. Distances generally accommodated themselves. Only the close at hand . . .

Closer . . .

To the edge. So close now she could lift her foot to it, and with it she suffered a moment's lightheadedness. The abyss came quickly. Nothing now for her eyes to inspect save the gray yawning emptiness.

She leaned farther out and saw . . . Nothing. The place where the villagers had stood in excited company was empty. Obviously there had been a conclusion of some kind. She stepped yet closer and searched the headlands in either direction.

"Susan, please tell us . . ."

Slowly she backed away from the edge, and out of consideration made her way to the trapdoor. "Nothing, I'm afraid, Reverend Christopher," she said, keeping her voice down despite the blowing wind.

From someplace lower down the narrow staircase she saw a scuffed pair of black boots. They seemed to give off a feel of sullen impatience.

"That's not possible," Reverend Christopher protested. "He was there. You saw him with your own eyes. Look again, Susan."

A useless suggestion, she thought, as the place where she was standing was limited, as was the place below. Still, she humored the old man and exactly retraced her steps, moving first to the edge of the parapet.Though she was looking out over the channel, she was seeing more clearly the massive portrait of the women of Eden. Suddenly she sensed movement. She glanced toward the trapdoor, thinking that Reverend Christopher had called to her again. But the trapdoor was empty. Only the glow of the lamp was visible, like an opening into a limited hell.

Slowly she started back away from the edge of the parapet, the feeling growing stronger. She was not alone. There was unquestionably company somewhere, hidden from view, in the shadows, close by.

As the feeling grew, she increased her step, astonished that she only felt it now, the presence of another, the absolute conviction that there was someone else.

Yet where? She moved quickly to the far side of the roof, that distant crenellation that she had never inspected, focusing on the side where she'd first seen him. But perhaps, sensing rescue, he had taken refuge in one of those distant shadows.

As she passed close to the open trapdoor, she looked down, hoping to see Reverend Christopher to inform him that she would be beyond his line of vision for a few minutes and that he was not to worry. But he was no place in sight. Even Bates's scuffed boots had disappeared.

For a moment she stared down into the vacuum and felt a profound sense of abandonment. Where had they gone? She might have need of them at any moment. And this was their domain, not hers. She was just . . .

She caught herself in time. No need to assign blame. She retrieved the lamp, hoisted it upward, and made a conscious attempt to hoist her courage with it, and took a few tentative steps away from the safety of the trapdoor to the all-encompassing darkness of the roof.

Please hold, she prayed, and cupped her free hand around the windguard, lending the lamp double protection. In the exact center of the castle was a large protrusion which appeared to comprise the core of the castle itself. What it contained, she had no idea. Perhaps storage, perhaps the children's nursery. Whatever, it protruded like a squat, square fortress which had to be circumvented. Beyond this large obstruction, the roof was jagged with other, smaller protrusions, some chimneys, the purpose of others unknown.

Now she made her way carefully around these smaller obstructions, stopping about every three steps to listen to the wind, hoping a human voice would evolve out of it, something to signal a location.

She halted her step again. Now she thought she heard breathing, a heavy labored sound which at first seemed to arise from the wind and pulsate rhythmically with it. But in the next moment the wind rushed by and she continued to hear a faint rasping, like a slowed pulse.

"Is anyone . . . ?" she began, feeling a sudden and urgent need for the sound of a human voice. At the same time, she moved all the way to the crenellation, still searching the shadowy horizon for an outline more flexible than stones and mortar, something malleable of flesh and blood. But still she saw nothing save the rigid sawtooth design repeating itself in endless duplication.

The wind was behind her now, a discernible pressure which seemed to be pushing her closer and closer to the edge. Suddenly weary of fighting the wind, she turned on it, and in the process her eyes fell on what appeared to be a shapeless lump collapsed against the south wall of the large rectangular protrusion.

For a moment she gaped at it. Quickly she looked away, then looked back, only to see it constant, a gray-black something which was neither brick nor mortar and did not accommodate a chimney or a nursery.

Her eyes felt sealed to the mysterious shape which, if it was human, lacked a recognizable head and shoulders. What it most resembled was a fisherman's discarded tarpaulin, which, worn with overuse, had been pitched against a brick wall to rot.

See it clearly, a voice urged from within her. *Move away*, came a countering voice. Though the latter was the wiser of the two voices, she obeyed the first and lifted the lamp. Steadily her steps guided her closer, until at last the limited light caught too much and she saw first the cradled cargo, a frail woman's frame held in a most loving embrace, her face completely obscured by a black covering of some sort and even the covering doubly obscured by the angle at which she was being held, and from both came no movement. Even the persistent wind seemed loath to ruffle their garments, which, while thick, spoke strangely of deep chills.

The immediate relief that she had found them alive was instantly replaced by the question: *Were* they alive? When she was about ten feet from them, she stopped and sent the lamplight in a limited arc. It did well to reach the mottled hem of what appeared to be a very worn and soiled black gown. The folds, caught up in the embracing arms, revealed highlights of a light substance, like chalk or dust.

She shifted the lamp, covered it, and found the most revealing clue to date, a small, slender, naked white hand resting limp in the black dusty folds, one small piece of human flesh, clearly a woman's, thus providing an accurate map to the rest of her.

Slowly Susan lowered the lamp, and in its descent she saw for the first time the sprawled tips of a man's boots, the laces undone, the edges curled loosely back. No one could walk in such footwear. The best that could be accomplished would be a kind of shuffle. As she knew that the frail hand was feminine, she knew also that the disreputable boots were masculine. It was a man buried inside the abandoned tarpaulin, which she saw now was a heavy and well-worn dark gray cape, voluminous, either designed initially for a larger man or worn now by a diminished one.

By lowering the lamp again and drawing a few steps closer, she saw a bare expanse of ankle inside the undone boots, pitifully thin and diminished, like a child's.

This wasn't Mr. Eden. Though grievously wounded and spiritually weakened by the horrors of the war which had overtaken him in the Crimea, nonetheless that Mr. Eden had managed to impart a bewildering strength at the height of his illness. Lying on the simple cot at Scutari, his right shoulder swathed in bandages, his eyes riveted to the ceiling, he had resembled a fallen giant only momentarily disabled, perhaps merely catching his breath before he would rise again.

Not so this man, whose head and face she had yet to see clearly. The ravages of something were too clearly visible in his extremities, in the undone boots, the thin white ankles, the sprawled legs, the manner in which he clasped the woman to him, as though she were his only source of life.

"Mr. Eden?" she murmured, and raised the lamp in search of shoulders, head, face, that strikingly handsome countenance which had converted the normally stern nurses of Scutari into giggling schoolgirls.

Nothing.

She stepped closer and extended the lamp in search of the top half of the man and found a new specific. The cloak here was hooded. Someone had found the late-night wind and the confrontation with God a chilly business and, though perhaps death had been the object of the evening, the chill of living had prompted him to lift the hood and secure it and, in this tortoise-like position with the woman clasped in his arms, sleep rather than death had overtaken him and, with the protective barrier of the brick wall blocking them from the wind, they both had relaxed in their warm cocoon, not bothering to inform anyone that their passage into the next world had been temporarily postponed.

"Mr. Eden?" she called out again, thinking to rouse him and get them both moving toward the trapdoor and the protection of the castle. "Mr. Eden, please. You must . . ."

Before she could deliver herself of the imperative, she saw the gray cape stir, or rather saw something within it stir, not precisely an awakening, for she doubted if the stupor into which he had fallen could accurately be called sleep.

She stepped back and held the lantern steady and watched his head lifting heavily from the chest, as though invisible weights were attached to the chin. Nothing else moved save that slowly lifting head, the cloak falling farther back, the configuration of snarled and matted hair blending with the frayed edges of the cape and hood and, on one side, made even more complex by the obscured face of the silent woman.

Susan held her position and her breath and thought of Lazarus and wondered if this was a resurrection or merely prelude to a true death.

Then all at once the lifted eyes surfaced from their black pools. The lips, chafed and dried from crying out to heaven, met and painfully parted; the lower cracked, and a small thin stream of red ran slowly down into the beard. The lips moved again as though the speaker thought he had spoken and was amazed that there was no reassuring sound vibrating in his ear.

She considered speaking to him but wasn't certain that he saw her clearly or at all. "Mr. Eden?" she murmured again, bending closer. "Can you . . . ?"

But she never finished, for all at once his arms, lost in the gray and voluminous cape, strengthened, tightened, grasped the female form more closely to him, and at the same time his eyes made direct contact with Susan's, proving that he did see her and was capable of communication.

"Help . . . her," was what he whispered, and in the slant and angle of his features Susan saw nothing which reminded her even vaguely of the John Murrey Eden of Scutari.

Before he made the tortured plea again, Susan placed the lamp close by and started to honor his request. But suddenly it occurred to her that whatever help she might be capable of giving would be useless as long as Mr. Eden maintained his death grip on the woman.

"Please, let . . ." she requested, aware of the incomplete nature of her request.

For a moment he looked up at her with a bewildered expression as though in that moment too many veils of living had lifted.

It wasn't that Susan hadn't seen the expression before. She had, frequently on the faces of dying men in the last moments of consciousness.

Alarmed, she met his eyes and started to make inquiry concerning *his* needs, and realized he probably was beyond articulation, and saw his lips move again, "Please . . . ," and realized that it couldn't be postponed any longer, her examination of that lifeless figure in his arms.

"May I . . . ?" she asked, slipping her arm around the woman's neck, and felt the lifelessness, the skin already turning cold.

Although she was supporting the woman's weight, he refused to remove his arm and merely went with her as she eased the woman back out of his embrace and gently placed her prone on the roof floor.

Slowly Susan sat back on her heels, her hands moving aimlessly above the woman's head and face, which were still obscured by some sort of head covering, a thick black veil which fell almost to her waist and appeared to be attached to the top of her hair. The style, though certainly not the color, reminded Susan of the happiness of brides.

But this was not a bride before her. She saw now beneath the woman's garments an outline of a leg pitifully thin, a child's waist, no visible sign of a female's anatomy, no breasts, no curve separating waist and hips. Someone either had forgotten to eat or had lacked sufficient interest, and now the only flesh remaining on the body was just enough to hold the skeletal structure together, and in some places even that was stretched dangerously thin.

Look upon the face, she urged herself, that barometer of human endurance and suffering, and accordingly she reached for the hem of the mysterious black veil, her every movement gentleness itself, when suddenly coming from him she felt a restraining hand, and looked up as he clasped her wrist with a grip from which she could have easily broken free, but she didn't, fascinated by both the fact of restraint and the hand itself, as skeletal in its way as the female form, yet filled with surprising strength and soiled.

"I must see," Susan said soothingly to the restraining hand, "if I am to—"

"N-no," came the faltering protest.

"Mr. Eden, if she can be helped, let me . . ."

She was going to say "try," but then there was no need. There was only a moment's indecision; then slowly his hand slipped from her wrist, fell the short distance to the roof floor, where it lay unmoving at a disjointed angle, like a marionette with loosened strings.

She waited to see if he would speak further, either in protest or instruction. It was while she was searching his face, waiting for verbal communication, that she saw tears, not many, and he made no attempt to wipe them away, as though he didn't even know they were there, or didn't care.

Seeing him thus, she experienced a sudden wrenching sensation. "Mr. Eden, please," she comforted, reaching out for the hand that continued to lie lifeless upon the roof floor.

She started to say more, then changed her mind and moved back in order to lift the veil. All about her now was that musty smell, as though someone had dressed hastily in garments which had been stored in old trunks with never a thought of wearing them again. The odor seemed to emanate from both. She looked at the spent, thin female figure. Was this thin shell the remains of one of the dazzling beauties she'd seen downstairs in the massive painting of the women of Eden?

As her hand laid the veil back over the woman's head, Susan's first instinct was to look away. But it would serve no purpose to look away, for what she saw before her surely was a distortion of light and shadow, and on this false hope she reached for the lamp and brought it closer and held it near the woman's face, and that proved to be the most foolhardy gesture she'd made all evening.

Nothing, no human sin or series of sins, would warrant such hideous mutilation, and at last she forced herself into a brief examination of what once had been a woman's face. The eyes were gone, the sockets empty save for two deep pools of loose and useless flesh. Then, as though the act of blinding had not been enough, there were deep ridges of scar tissue which cut in peaks and valleys down both sides of her face, a curiously symmetrical damage, as though the weapon had known about symmetry and respected it.

Without warning her horror began to diminish and was replaced by an even more painful emotion, pity. But neither was negotiable on this cold roof. So confirm the woman's life or death and let her rest in one world or the other.

Quickly she slipped her arm beneath the woman's head and lifted her clear of the mussed garments and black veil. In the process the veil fell completely away and for the first time Susan saw close-cropped stubbly gray hair, no effort made at style or grooming, the edges jagged, as though the blinded eyes had perhaps tried to direct the shears.

As she drew the face closer, cradling the head and neck as Mr. Eden had recently done, she looked up to see his reaction to the pitiable sight which she suspected he knew by heart.

Then she gently placed her cheek against the still lips and held it there and sheltered them both from the wind, which seemed to be subsiding, while she searched for the sensation of a more meaningful wind, a gentler one coming from the woman herself, signifying life.

But there was nothing, and with the tips of her fingers she felt along the narrow tendon which ran the length of the woman's neck. Sometimes the pulse of life would mysteriously register there when it would register no place else.

But nothing.

The woman was dead, though she'd not been dead for long; Susan was certain of that. There still was a degree of warmth in her extremities, the curled tips of her fingers, the frail hands themselves, which now lay pooled and lifeless in her lap.

Glancing at John Murrey Eden, she saw that his head had fallen heavily forward onto his chest, as though he were worn out. At first she was afraid that he had passed to unconsciousness. Then she saw his head lifting, gathering strength, until at last he was sitting upright, his face lost in the mussed and ragged beard.

With some difficulty he found Susan's eyes, and to her despair, his lips moved again, a sad repetition of his initial request. "Help . . . her . . . "

"I'm . . . sorry," she murmured, delivering herself of a partial message. "There is nothing or no one who can help her. . . ."

She started to say more by way of softening the message, somehow making it more palatable. But there was neither chance nor need, for he had understood from the first, possibly even before he had made his request, and slowly he was moving again, his arms reaching out for the lifeless woman and at last effortlessly taking her from Susan, though immediately he fell back against the brick barrier and took the dead woman with him, his left hand pressed against the small of her back, his right stroking alternately her thin arm and then the stiff, butchered gray hair, his voice lost in the unorthodox union.

All she heard clearly was, "My love . . ." mourned over and over again, and slowly she sat back on her heels again, forced to watch the unchanging tableau.

She glanced toward the small square opening which led through the trapdoor to the heart of the castle. She couldn't do alone what had to be done up here. Her first task was perhaps the most difficult, and that was somehow to remove the dead woman from his grasp as peaceably as possible.

She looked again toward the trapdoor and saw, like an answered prayer, a round head fully covered with bright red curly hair, and a pair of sturdy shoulders, which daily had grown stronger by hauling filled herring nets to boatside.

Tom Babcock? She made a first faltering identification because he had emerged facing away from her. But then, grasping the edge of the trapdoor opening, he slowly turned, searching every shadow as closely as she was searching him. And when she saw it *was* him, she marveled at God's occasional readiness to oblige.

"Tom, over here," she called, and was aware that the wind had

41

increased and was forced to call a second time, and this time he saw her and pulled himself quickly through the trapdoor and hesitated, once up, as though impressed with the height, the night, the fact of his presence on the roof of Eden Castle.

"Over here," she called again, and stood, the better for Tom to see her.

She waited until he was less than three feet away to speak, not wanting just yet to draw Mr. Eden back to this world with the presence of a stranger.

"Miss Mantle," Tom gasped. "I thought you might be needing help," he said, ducking his head in that curious way that most men addressed her, as though she were a cross between their mother and their schoolmistress.

She nodded an affirmative yes and could have said more by way of explanation, but at that moment his eye fell on the two at her feet.

"What . . . ?" Tom began, and suddenly began to back steadily away.

"Please," Susan entreated, and reached out for his arm.

"Is . . . it . . . ?" he asked, still looking down.

She nodded and tried to turn him away. "Will you help me, Tom?" she asked.

Though he nodded vigorously, he repeated his half-formed question as though not believing her. "Is it . . . ?"

"Yes, it's Mr. Eden," she confirmed. "Now, if you would help . . ."

"And the other? Who is . . . ?"

"I don't know," she said. "Where's Reverend Christopher?"

"Downstairs," he said.

"And Mr. Bates?"

"Oh, he's right over . . ." He seemed to jerk his head in the direction of the trapdoor. She glanced in that direction and saw that he was right, saw the scarecrow head just emerging through the opening, where he too swiveled about and at last found them and, apparently impervious to time or circumstance, called out at top voice, "What is it? You must come down, now. We can't have the place filled with . . ."

Choosing to ignore him, she drew near to Tom and asked, "If I can get him to release her, can you carry her . . . ?" She halted in mid-sentence. Where did they take corpses in Eden Castle? ". . . to the kitchen court?" she concluded weakly.

· " 'Course," Tom said with new and reassuring eagerness, and at last seemed to relax a bit. "And him," he asked, "what about Mr. Eden?"

She had no ready answer. They would deal with him later. For now, the first order of the day was—

"I say, miss, did you find him or has the peacock long since flown the coop?"

"Please!" she shushed as she drew close to Bates, who appeared to draw back until he was pinned against the opposite side of the opening, as though she were a contamination. She bent down the better to speak without being overheard. "He's here," she whispered, trying to see beyond Bates's gaunt shoulders down into the narrow stairwell itself, still searching for Reverend Christopher. He would know what to do with the fact of death. But he was no place in sight, and Susan took the only course open to her. "He's here," she repeated, "but he's not alone."

"Of course he's not alone!" snapped the old man, as though he could just barely tolerate her presence. "Anyone could see that clearly from below. The question is, who?"

Susan overlooked the sarcasm in his voice. "It's a woman," she described quietly, "frail and older than Mr. Eden—or at least she appears . . ." She paused before going on. "And her face is . . ."

"Oh! My heavens! That would be Lady Harriet!"

"Who is she?"

Bates seemed to soften. "His aunt," he said patly, too patly. "Perhaps his aunt," he said again, emphasizing the "perhaps." "At least that was the general opinion. His father's brother's wife." He peered up at Susan, confirming her suspicion that he was relishing this opportunity to reveal something. "Though some claim they were lovers."

Shocked, Susan stared at him. Had the old man lost his mind, to speak so casually of such matters? "I *am* sorry, miss." He grinned. "You did ask a question. I was only trying to oblige."

"She . . . must be removed," Susan added, trying to clear her mind of all matters but the most essential.

"Removed where?" Bates demanded. "They got up here. I say let them get down."

Then suddenly he was saying nothing, all his energy concentrated on pulling himself up through the trapdoor. As he labored, she asked if he had any information on the curiously missing Reverend Christopher.

"Where do you think he is?" Bates retorted, still brushing the dust from his trousers, the wind whipping his white hair into a froth. "To fetch help—though I entreated him no. We mustn't have the castle overrun, you know."

"The woman is dead," Susan said bluntly, her voice low but sure. Anything to end the old man's senseless rambling.

"I . . . beg your pardon?"

"I said the woman is dead. I'm certain, Mr. Bates." And then, before the man could challenge her, she asked, "What happened to her face?"

He spoke only two words, though they were so incredible that Susan was certain she'd heard incorrectly.

"Self-imposed," was what he had said.

"I . . . don't . . ."

"She inflicted the damage on herself. But what matter now," he added with admirable largesse, "if the woman is dead."

At that moment Reverend Christopher's face appeared, red-cheeked and puffing. "Susan, what . . . ?" he gasped.

"Over there," she said.

Bates swiveled his head. "Is he . . . ?"

"Not dead," she said, and heard movement coming from beyond the trapdoor and looked over to see three men emerging onto the roof.

"We was sent, Miss Mantle," said the first man to reach her, "to help fetch Mr. Eden back down. If you'll just tell us . . ."

How did he know her name? Then she saw his face clearly in the uncertain light, recognized him, Sam Oden from Mortemouth, a fisherman with too many children and a worn-out wife and generally not enough to eat.

"Is that him?" Sam asked, and drew her attention back to the two slumped against the brick wall.

She nodded.

"And who would that be?" Sam asked further, approaching the lifeless two as though they were merely a problem to be solved.

"I'm . . . not sure." Susan faltered, mildly intimidated by his aggressive behavior. Suddenly it was as though he had taken charge.

"It's his mum, would be my guess," Sam announced full voice to anyone who cared to hear. What was most curious was that no one seemed shocked by it. Clearly the village had known everything for a very long time. Whether they knew the extent of the intimacy which had existed between mother and son, she didn't know and had no time to find out, for suddenly Sam stooped down near Mr. Eden and commenced speaking calmly, coolly, as one would to an ill child.

"Mr. Eden? Can you hear me? 'Course you can. Ain't nothin' wrong with your ears, now, is there? You probably don't remember me, but I worked for you, years ago when you was bringing this old place back from the dead . . ."

Susan listened, fascinated by this one-sided conversation. Maybe after all, this rough fisherman could penetrate.

"Are you cold, Mr. Eden?" she heard Sam ask. "I'm sure your . . ." He paused. Obviously there were secrets to be maintained even under these grim circumstances. "I'm sure your old auntie is," Sam went on after a brief pause. "Why don't you let us give you a hand up?"

She saw him start to reach for the frail figure in Mr. Eden's arms and saw at the same time a protective tightening.

Sam looked up at her, the lamplight catching on his strong and now puzzled features. It wasn't a call for help, not yet.

"Lookee, Mr. Eden," he tried again, settling back on his heels like an enormous grasshopper ready to jump, "it ain't a matter of you not being able to trust us. So what do you say, Mr. Eden? Let me take . . ." At that moment Sam reached down for the small hand which lay like a fallen leaf among the grays and browns of heavy garments.

There was only an instant contact, but apparently that was enough. Suddenly the grasshopper was hopping, his long legs propelling him up and back, a single word escaping his lips in frightened repetition. "Gawd! oh, my Gawd! Gawd!"

Quickly Susan stepped forward, gathering Tom Babcock as she moved, to whom she delivered a single clear instruction, "Take the woman from him." For a second she was afraid he either hadn't understood or wouldn't obey. But by the time she'd pushed her way through the gaping men, Tom had taken over the lead and the woman was lifted clean, when suddenly Mr. Eden came roaring up out of his grief, an awesome sight, features and limbs evolving out of the amorphous primordial lump. Reaching out with one massive swoop, he recaptured the hem of her layered garments, and for several macabre moments there was a grotesque tug of war.

Susan stepped closer and tried to place a gentle though restraining hand on his arm.

"Mr. Eden, please don't . . ."

As poor Sam tried words again, Mr. Eden took advantage of the distraction and pulled completely free and once again grasped the dead woman to him like a thief, his eyes filled with a mad glittering light that spoke of other realities, and for a moment he backed slowly, defiantly away from them, nothing to impede his backward retreat from culminating in the sheer drop of four stories onto the gravel of the graveyard below.

Suddenly a new fear surfaced in Susan's mind. In his present state of mind he could accomplish the leap unwittingly, for he wasn't looking behind him. What he most desired was in his arms, and what he most loathed was directly before him in the form of the slowly approaching, carefully tracking men.

Then something turned in her mind, a fragment of a recent memory, the large canvas downstairs in the library, *The Women of Eden*, one in particular. Elizabeth Eden.

The nearest thing to a mother that Mr. Eden ever possessed.

"Mr. Eden," she said suddenly, and stepped through the low-crouching men who continued to track him to his destruction.

"Elizabeth," she said flatly, though loud enough for all to hear, particularly the one who still backed toward the edge of the roof, now less than five feet away.

"Elizabeth," she said again calmly, merely speaking the name but hoping that if once there had been anything between them, then perhaps the name alone would remind him of other faces, other realities.

"Mr. Eden," she said, "think of Elizabeth. Think how much it would hurt her if you were . . ."

But the man continued to back away, clutching his burden.

"Mr. Eden, please," she entreated. "Elizabeth," she repeated. "Consider Elizabeth and how much she loves you."

Suddenly, when she least expected it, the struggle stopped. The head had been thrown back when something had penetrated and apparently distracted, if not soothed.

Tom Babcock moved away holding the dead woman, and Sam Oden put a restraining hand on the man's shoulder. As though realizing he had lost his burden, Mr. Eden suddenly roared upward, as if to pursue Tom, and it was several moments before Sam and the others wrestled Eden to the floor, when the great head finally ceased its thrashing and appeared to stare straight up at her.

Suddenly Sam Oden's mates, aided by a most unlikely ally, Mr. Bates, appeared before her, carrying a long thick piece of rope which trailed behind Bates like a fitting tail, and even as she watched, helpless, the four of them, working in efficient unison, the long rope tail shrinking as it was wound around and around the fallen man, pinned his arms, on down to his upper legs, until Eden resembled nothing quite so much as the prize kill in a big-game hunt.

At that moment, the struggle erupted again, all the more awesome for its futility, and she watched as long as she could as he tried to pull free of the rope and, unable to do so, commenced to propel himself like a malformed crab, using the back of his head and the heels of his boots for leverage, the strain of incredible effort upon his face.

As the torturous effort of locomotion earned him a few useless inches, Mr. Bates stepped forward and lifted one boot and placed it directly in the middle of the man's abdomen. As he held it there and watched the slow-dawning awareness on Mr. Eden's face, this grin broadened.

"I don't think that your royal Highness is going anywhere without the permission of these . . . gentlemen."

45

"Please . . . let him go," Susan begged, and saw the four of them still bent over, growing brave. Sam Oden halted the outraged thrashing by merely stepping forward and standing on the long outflung hair.

"Don't!" she cried, at last finding her voice and the will to use it, confronting the senseless brutality with the weak weapon of entreaty. "Mr. Bates, I beg you. Please release him. There's no need—"

"No need?" Bates parroted, encircling the fallen man to a position where he could confront her over the body. "The man is a suitable candidate for Bedlam. Look at him. With little effort and no concern for us he could take his final step over the edge and take us with him, one or all." At this excessive claim he pointed a melodramatic finger toward the edge of the roof. "Now, surely, miss, you don't want all of our deaths on your conscience."

By way of support, Sam Oden contributed, "He's strong as an ox, miss. He really is. I mean, he looks . . . shriveled like winter apples, but there's granite in there someplace."

Sickened by the spectacle, Susan noticed that all had fallen silent now, staring down at their accomplishment. Bates seemed to relish the moment more than the others, who continued to exhibit a certain hesitancy, as though, despite their unschooled intelligences, they, more than Bates, knew that sometime, somehow the bondage would have to be removed and the man would come storming up out of rage, his targets clear—the three who rendered him thus.

Then it was her time to move. "Please, Sam," she said quietly, her voice hovering below the roar of the wind, "lift him up and carry him downstairs to the library. I think he's been—"

"No!" The strong objection came from Bates, who stepped forward, clearly challenging her.

"Why not, Mr. Bates?" she asked, still hoping to see Sam Oden and the others following her order.

But she didn't see anything, and only at the last moment heard Bates: ". . . so I think, while it is certainly desirable to transfer him, he must be taken immediately to the proper authorities."

It was only on the last words that Susan came back to herself and to the precise voice speaking madness. "Authori . . ." she tried to repeat and couldn't and there was no need, for Bates was more than happy to repeat it for her.

"Of course authorities. She was dead," Bates explained, as though to slow children. "Wasn't she, miss? Oh, you tried to whisk her away, but Bates knows the feel and look of a corpse, and if she was dead, which I assure you she was, then someone must be responsible for that death, and we all know who that someone was, and now Mr. Eden can add murder to the long list of offenses which God will confront him with in the next world. But in the meantime, we humble folk are compelled to live by the same laws, whether he likes it or not."

As he spoke, his voice rose from sarcasm and wheedling to outrage and fury. The degree of hate which Susan felt spilling out of the thin man was awesome.

But what did he want? What, in the throes of this ancient outrage, was he failing to articulate? "Yes, she was dead," Susan said quietly. "But I don't believe Mr. Eden was responsible, as you suggest, Mr. Bates."

"Oh? And how can you be so sure? Are you a constable or an inspector or an examining physician?"

"No," she agreed readily, "and I can't be sure. But I have had experience, and in my judgment the woman starved to—"

"Starved!" Bates mimicked. "Miss," he said archly at the end of the laugh, "Sam Oden's people might starve, or mine, or, as they do every year, any number of Mortemouth folk, but I assure you, as one who knows that anyone blessed to inhabit this castle does not, will not, cannot starve to death . . ."

He had his audience—Sam Oden and his two mates, who undoubtedly all their lives had heard about the Eden wealth and Eden plenty.

". . . so I propose, miss, that we haul the garbage out, right enough, but instead of giving him escort down to his grand library, that we haul him direct to the constable in Exeter."

"He is helpless!" Susan countered angrily. Yet what could she do? Reverend Christopher, who had been an ally, had disappeared, bearing the body of Lady Harriet, along with Tom Babcock. With their disappearance had gone the last vestiges of reason. All she was left with was pious anger and illiterate curiosity.

"All right, men," she heard Bates command, and looked back to see the three of them closing in on Mr. Eden, all more than willing to take their orders from Bates, who seemed to know precisely when the reins of leadership had shifted and who held them now.

As the three of them lifted him bodily, his head fell back disjointedly and for a moment she thought that he had blessedly lost consciousness. But then she caught a brief glimpse of his eyes, open, staring at nothing.

"No objection, miss?" Bates inquired with suspect thoughtfulness.

"Yes, Mr. Bates, many objections, but none that can be discussed here, at this moment, in front of Mr. Eden."

"All right, men, then haul the rubbish out in any way you see fit."

In spite of the strain of effort, all three men nodded to the command, which simply gave them permission to make the passage as rough as possible.

Then they were moving, and she caught up with them at the trapdoor. As Sam Oden stooped to slip through the narrow opening, she bent over the helpless man who had been lowered to the floor with unnecessary roughness.

"I'm sorry," she murmured.

Then Mr. Eden was hoisted aloft again and angled awkwardly down through the narrow trapdoor.

Bates called out instructions in one direction. "Proceed directly through the castle the way we came up, and down into Mortemouth, where we'll fetch a wagon, and stop for no cause or no man," and all the time he spoke, he slowly disappeared after the others.

Gone! Then she'd better rouse herself and follow closely after.

He had tried to tell her to go away. Who the woman was, he had no idea. But it mattered little. She had looked kindly at him, and that he couldn't bear.

47

Suddenly he felt himself slipping from their grasp on the sharp downward angle through the trapdoor. Four hands made a grab for him, but too late, and seconds before his head struck the stone floor, carrying the full weight of his bound body behind it, he could see what was going to happen and welcomed it, and at the same time lowered his head and let his shoulders take the brunt of the fall.

He shut his eyes and bowed his head in an attempt to absorb the pain, and wondered how long it would take them to kill him. No matter. He'd been too cowardly to accomplish the task himself. Let them do it for him.

Harriet . . .

At the thought of her he bowed his head, and though he didn't will it, a single moan slipped out.

"Easy, men," someone sneered close above him. "His royal highness isn't used to such rough passage. Kid gloves, that's what he's accustomed to."

With his head bowed, John thought he recognized the voice. Slowly he looked up and felt something cool and wet rolling down from his left temple, and was only then aware he must have scraped his forehead.

Bates!

He'd thought so. He'd endured that arrogant bastard every day for too many years.

As the ancient fury built, he struggled against the ropes that held him, and ceased only when he realized he had no more energy and that he was providing his tormentors with a source of amusement.

"Ever seen anything like it?" one asked, standing back, a note of clear delight in his voice.

"Did oncet," came the flat reply. "Went up to London town to visit me brother, and he took me to the circus at Bedlam."

"Come on, lift him high and let's carry him out."

Bates . . .

The best head butler in all of England, or so the Duke of Devonshire had claimed, and John, of course, hadn't rested until he'd lured him away from the duke, paying a king's ransom in the process. He'd known that first year that the rigid man had been miserable. Eden wasn't Chatsworth, was rougher, more isolated, cut off, and worst of all, tainted with the scandal of John's own life.

Still, instead of releasing him, John had merely appealed to his greed, to the natural greed of all men, and Bates had reluctantly remained in service at Eden and, in the process, had become a modestly rich man. He might have become a wealthy man if he'd had wit and cunning. But lacking both, modest riches had been all he could manage.

All at once John heard the voice again, encouraging, "That's it, men. Now you've got the hang of it. Like a dead animal, that's the best way to carry him. Don't you agree?"

As pain compounded pain, John felt his body weight hang suspended. He gave himself over to the harsh rocking motion and tried not to dwell on his dead hands, numb from lack of circulation, and wondered what had intervened, what had come between him and the goal he most urgently desired.

48

Something . . . A voice had spoken a name, and that name had meant too much to him—Eliz . . .

He felt only distracted chaos in all parts of his mind. No more false shadows of hope, no more specters of fear, real or imagined. If he'd lacked the courage to end this futility on the parapet of his empty castle, then he had every reason to believe that the men carrying him now, and certainly the one following after, would be more than happy to end it for him, perhaps before the dawn of a new day.

He was sorry for that. As he'd directed his life, he would have liked to direct his death, with Harriet in his arms where she belonged, where she had always belonged, already passed on, waiting for him on the other side, where together they would revel in their unique love which this world had denied them.

This world? Why was it so difficult to comprehend? How had he known to go to her apartments last night? He'd gone there before only in the beginning, when his sickness hadn't as yet done its worst, when he'd first been aware that they were the only ones in this vast castle, Peggy gone, then Bates. He'd needed her then, had envisioned them together. But night after night he'd knocked on her door and called out to her, but had always found the heavy bolt thrown, and ultimately he'd lost his temper and pounded on the door until his hands had bled; then he had turned his back on her barricaded door and had barricaded himself in the library.

And in this isolation he'd lost time, and days and weeks and months had turned into years and he had lived only in the presence of the Alma-Tadema painting of *The Women of Eden*, and in his remembrance of the past, which ultimately had done the greater damage, for he carefully avoided thinking on happy times. They hurt too much. Rather he dwelt on the betrayal and deception, for those suited him better.

"Lift him up," came the command from behind. "We want to deliver more than a corpse to the constable—"

Abruptly the voice broke off, and John, eyes closed, listened for the cause. "Put him down," he heard Bates whisper fiercely, and sensed that someone was coming from the opposite direction, up from the lower floor, which would mean that it wasn't the woman. They'd left her above on her knees, praying. *She'd* been the one who had spoken the name that had—

"I say, what in the . . . ?"

This voice *was* coming from the opposite direction, was male and puffing and sounded more baffled than anything else. "I say, Bates, have you lost your mind? What in the . . . ?"

Then he felt himself being dropped from a distance of several feet onto the stone floor, his back receiving the full weight of the fall, the impact penetrating through to his chest, where he felt his lungs deflate.

For a moment he was aware of nothing except his need to breathe and his total inability to do so. He tried to turn first right, then left, but the trusslike rope prohibited significant or effective movement. He tried to draw his knees up, hoping to ease the strictures about his chest and force air into the useless lungs. But even that was denied him by the rigid bondage encasing his legs and ankles, and in a final effort to draw breath, he lifted his head and purposefully struck it against the stone floor.

"Turn him over!"

49

He heard the cry from a great distance and at first wondered what a child was doing wandering about Eden Castle.

Then he heard it again, louder.

"I said turn him over—quickly?" and with the second command the blackness spread over all his vision and he thought it was just as well and realized that the cry had not been that of a child, but of a woman.

Then he heard it a third time, that half-angry, half-frightened female voice raised in a strident command. "Are all of you deaf? I said turn him over! He can't breathe. Can't you . . . ?"

The circle altered; two broke rank and moved quickly back.

Then she was upon him, the same "she" that he'd seen up on the roof.

"Easy," came her voice, and, on his side now, he felt hands on his back working their way through the layers of garments, hurried yet strangely calm, filled with authority.

"We . . . ain't done nothin' to him," came a pouting voice from the circle of men looking down.

"Help me," he heard the woman say, and felt a tugging at the rope which was tightly laced the length of his body. "Remove this bondage, now," came the female voice again.

"And I say no!" came Bates's equally determined counterreply.

"I say," came Reverend Christopher's puffing voice, "why is . . . the gentleman being treated like . . . I say, Susan, what in the . . . ?"

Then John heard the woman's voice. "Mr. Bates here claims that Mr. Eden is responsible for the woman's death," and heard nothing else, though there were voices all about, but for himself his head was filled with the echoing possibilities of that single sentence.

Responsible for . . .

Of course he was responsible for Harriet's death. He *was* responsible for all their deaths, literal and figurative, large and small, all driven away by him, his will and compulsion: Dhari, Mary, Elizabeth . . .

Eliz . . .

The single name halted his thoughts as up on the roof it had halted his final step into oblivion.

Elizabeth. The closest person to him, the nearest to a mother. He stared blankly out at a world gone mad and wondered what had become of her. Dead too?

Before he could provide himself with an answer, one of the voices above him grew belligerent.

"I have witnesses, Reverend Christopher," it threatened. "Three men who saw the evidence of a body in his arms and one—Tom Babcock there—who helped to carry her down. Now, surely Tom knows the feel of a dead woman."

For a moment the silence suggested that Tom Babcock did not know the feel of a dead woman. "It was dark," he muttered.

"You don't need light," Bates bellowed, "to feel the lifebeat . . ." Now he began a deadly pursuit of the young man. "Well, come on, Babcock. Tell us the truth, as you'll have to tell it on the stand in Exeter. How did the lady feel to the touch?"

"Cold, sir. She was cold, but then, so was I, and I ain't—"

"Did she so much as stir once on the passage down to the kitchen court?"

"No, sir, I don't believe she did, least not that I seen, if you know what I mean."

"Didn't that suggest something to you?" Bates demanded angrily.

Then John heard a voice that echoed his prayer. "Please, all of you. Hold your arguments for the proper forum, and in the name of decency, please release this man and let him walk upright through his own castle, perhaps to the chapel, where he can confront and question his God in private."

Confront and question his God!

How quaint. In the past he had carried his own god around inside him, like a willing and docile transient. No power for good or evil had ever emanated from this free rider. The true power source was John himself, and it had always been thus and would always be thus.

"Please release him." There she was again, and Reverend Christopher, still suffering a degree of confusion that apparently knew no bounds, joined. "Yes, please do, Mr. Bates. If you truly believe in your ridiculous accusations, then there will be a time and place—"

"They are not ridiculous, and I do firmly believe in them," Bates pronounced imperiously, "and I, for one, am tired of seeing him and his kind get away with everything, while the rest of us pay for their errors. . . ."

Had they paid for his errors? Errors there had been, but he was not aware of anyone paying for them but himself. First off, there were so many of them. Who would know even where to start?

"No, I won't release him," Bates now exclaimed, as though he'd just reached a hard decision. "He's going to stay just the way he is, because if you don't know how slippery the Devil is, the rest of us do."

John heard the woman again, close by and still angry. "Look what you are doing! You'll be delivering a corpse if you're not . . ." She drew closer, so close he could see the tip of her shoe beneath her skirts. "Loosen his collar. You're pulling it tight, like a noose."

Almost immediately he felt the stricture loosened, his shirtwaist ripped above the neck.

Then all around he noticed a strange silence, no one speaking or protesting, as though all were focused on a communal fascination. He was still suspended between the various hands that held ankles and shoulders secure, his head free-floating, though gravity was taking its toll. What in the hell was the delay now? Why had all voices, all life, ground to a halt?

Then he felt a twisting pain which seemed to start in the area of his left rib cage and cut a burning path up the side of his neck and on up in a scorching path directly into the center of his skull.

In the last moments of consciousness, and though he was actively opposed to it, he sensed a surrender. The numbness was spreading, invading his head now, to the very center of that cap of pain. As soon as it reached the threshold behind which thought resided, he would not have to think or perceive or feel ever again.

Then it did, and a savage blackness covered everything, and somewhere he sensed ages of humiliation, a select status, and a simplicity worthy of hell. . . .

Eden Castle
June 21, 1874

Alex Aldwell sat uncomfortably in the back of the rocking, jolting carriage and tried to brace himself against the potholes and ruts, and worse, against the realization that he'd broken his vow to himself and was now in fact returning to Eden Point and John Murrey Eden.

"Gawd!" The self-disgust combined with a particularly deep rut in the road, and as the high thin carriage wheels struggled for mastery over the rough terrain, Alex did the same and braced himself with one stiffened arm against the opposite side, while with his right hand he felt inside his pocket for the last message, three in as many weeks, from—what in the hell was her name?—Susan something, and co-signed by the old Methodist preacher Reverend Christopher from Mortemouth. They had been calm, neatly penned messages, though each had grown more urgent, informing "Mr. Aldwell" as a close personal friend and business associate of Mr. Eden's "indisposition."

Indisposition? What in the hell did that mean? As far as Alex was concerned, John had been "indisposed" for the last four years, locked in the grand library with only the painted images of *The Women of Eden* to keep him company, shunning all visitors, including Alex himself that first year and, on occasion, Aslam, until at last both had grown weary of making the long trek from London to North Devon and Aslam had said it best: "We'll guard his empire and leave him to God."

On occasion Alex had severely doubted if even God wanted anything to do with him.

Lost in grim thought, Alex braced himself on either side of the narrow carriage and stared blankly out at the passing moors. Not far now, though the road had deteriorated along with everything else. Alex could remember the time, four, five years ago, when under the surveillance of John's constant maintenance a lady could traverse the road from Exeter to Eden and never so much as ruffle a feather in her bonnet. Now? Alex's insides felt as though they had been beaten on a washboard, and his head as well.

As the sense of devastation and waste swept over him with new and powerful impetus, like a late-breaking wave, he braced his boots against the carriage floor and closed his eyes and tried to resurrect an image of John Murrey Eden as he'd first known him.

Surprisingly, the image sat very close to the surface of his consciousness and stirred him deeply, that fair, brash, and arrogant young god who had pumped him dry for information concerning the fortunes to be made or stolen in India. They had been ward mates at the army hospital in Scutari, Alex an erstwhile soldier of fortune just returned from a vagabond's life in India and suffering an embarrassing case of dysentery. They had parted, Alex for England, never dreaming that the brash young man was indeed on his way to India. It was a wonder and a testament to his cunning that he survived in that treacherous land.

Then Fate, clever Fate, had brought them together again in the form of an advert in a London paper for a foreman for the building corporation of John Murrey. And Alex had been a foreman—and a damned good one— and had then been in need of employment, and how was he to know that the John Murrey Company was the same as the young John Eden he'd befriended at Scutari?

Suddenly the carriage took a rude jolt to the left and Alex opened his eyes to see the bleak brown-and-green landscape whirring past in a blur. What in the hell was the driver's hurry? He grabbed for the window and jerked it down. "Pull on the reins, up there! No hurry back here, though it would be nice to arrive in one piece. . . ."

All he could see from his angle was the square shoulder of a gray cape and a firmly anchored flat-brimmed hat. At first he wondered if the man had even heard him. But a few moments later he felt the carriage breaking speed.

Daring to relax under this more sensible speed, Alex leaned heavily back into the cushions and wished to hell he could remember the female name that had been affixed to all three notes. Susan something, but he wouldn't swear to it. He might take a look, for the third and last message was tucked inside his pocket, but even that simple gesture required too much effort, and he was bone-weary. In the old days he and John had been capable of making the trip and stopping at every pub between Eden and London, and still arrived fresh as a spring morn and almost always on time.

Gawd! How time had managed to change everything. Both here and back in London. A struggle it had been there as well as here, the boy Aslam thrown headlong at the green age of twenty-one into the treacherous waters of London's financial world, taking the reins of the John Murrey firm, regardless of whether they had been formally proffered. And that first year it had been touch and go, mostly "go," as many employees, ranging from solicitors to engineers, had decided that they couldn't work for a "dark-skinned nigger," no matter who he was. And, of course, who he was was damned impressive: John's adopted son and the true great-grandson of old Bahadur Shah Zafar, the last descendent of the mogul emperors, the last mogul king himself.

Still there had been a damaging exodus, and for about fifteen months Alex had looked about the once gigantic and profitable firm and had seen only shipwreck and impending disaster.

But it had been Aslam who, with cold objectivity, went quickly about the task of shoring up the most dangerous ruptures, convincing the most valuable employees that it would be mutually profitable if they remained. And it had been. Of course, what few knew was that they were working for one and the same, for Aslam had become what John was, more English than Indian, Cambridge-educated, probably a bit quicker than John and—most important—more in control of himself.

Even when Alex and John had been working at peak capacity, there had been something childlike about John: *Come on, Alex, let's run away for a few days and tell no one.*

Hard-earned moments of self-indulgence, true, but self-indulgence all the same. In the four years that Aslam had held the reins of the firm, Alex had never seen similar behavior. In fact, the young man seemed ill-at-ease with leisure, seemed most comfortable and at home seated behind John's enormous desk in the mansion in Grosvenor Square, all rooms closed off and shrouded save John's top-floor apartments, all the staff dismantled except for one, an ancient crone named Maudie Canfield, who trudged the four flights of stairs without a grumble whenever she heard Aslam's bell.

Once, years ago, Alex had been foolish enough to believe that John's love for Aslam would draw him out of his grief and back into the bustle of financial London. But thus far it hadn't, and now, realistically, Alex knew it never would.

Without warning he felt a hot stinging behind his eyes. How close they had been once: Alex Aldwell, the country bumpkin turned soldier of fortune, an ox of a man with only enough of a brain inside his head to keep the world from taking advantage of him; and John Murrey Eden, a man young enough to be Alex's son, yet smarter, quicker, cleverer—with a face and a form which confirmed the biblical promise that we had been made "in His image." Well, not all of us, but a few—John Murrey Eden, for one.

Under the weight of unexpected feeling, Alex bowed his head. What the hell? There was no one about to see him but the seagulls gliding in the bracing sea wind.

Alex breathed deeply. It had always been thus, that magic essence of ocean and heather. In the past he'd seen John shed the worries and cares of ten men with the first whiff of that elixir.

Eden . . .

Whispered or shouted, it had made no difference. John Murrey Eden could ponder the word as though his mind were collecting all the good memories to him—memories of Lila, the once lovely and now dead wife, the two perfect sons, Stephen and Frederick, in Ireland now with their maternal grandfather . . .

"Oh, John!" Alex mourned aloud, his memories painfully converging. Outside the window he saw a blurred vision of the coastline, the carriage veering to the right, the gates of Eden less than ten minutes away. It was here at this exact turn that the guards on horseback would always intercept the entourage, confirming identities, one's right to pass, and John would be hanging halfway out of the window, more boy than man, inquiring of the guards a report of recent weather, the growing season, an ill child, or how the herring were running.

And sometimes John's two sons would be waiting for him—Stephen, about three before all the tragedies descended, and Frederick, two—small, compact, cherubic miniatures of their father, particularly Stephen.

Gawd! Where were they now, those two lads? And would John ever see them again, and would he recognize them if he were to see them? Not a fit way for a father and his sons to live, whisked off by their grandfather Lord Harrington and the madman Charles Parnell, and all this happening four years ago while most of the family still inhabited the castle. How old would they be now? Stephen at least seven, going on eight, and Frederick always condemned to tag a year behind.

The scene outside the winow blurred under the duress of memory, and for a moment he saw the twin cherubs. "My most precious possessions," John had once called them. And nothing had given Alex greater pleasure than to see John down on his hands and knees with both boys giggling atop his back, the most gifted and powerful man in England a helpless slave to the whims of two young dictators whose combined weights did not exceed fifty pounds.

"Eden Gate ahead!"

The cry jarred him back to the present and painfully reminded him that perhaps he'd made a mistake in returning, despite the urgent messages. Aslam had warned him. There was nothing he or anyone could do, short of planning John's funeral, and since none of the urgent messages had mentioned the kindness of death, then he assumed that no death had occurred.

Then what? What calamity after four years had taken place in Eden Castle, forcing some stranger's hand to summon help?

Suddenly the carriage stopped abruptly. The premature halt threw Alex forward. As he reached out quickly to brace himself on the opposite cushions, he bent down and looked out of the window on his left.

"What in the hell . . . ?"

They weren't even through the gatehouse yet. He lowered the window and gaped ahead. There it was, a good seventy-five yards straight . . .

He blinked and tried to clear the distortion of fatigue and emotion from his eyes. He thought he had seen . . .

"What do we do now, sir?" the driver asked with admirable calm, considering that at that moment he was looking straight into the barrels of at least a dozen breech-loading shotguns, not very new-appearing—but then, neither were the men who shouldered them, a mismatched troop if Alex had ever seen one, men he suspected would be more at home in a herring boat swilling the nets.

In the lead was a strange duck, arrow-thin, garbed in tight-fitting black frock coat which, like everything else in this grim tableau, had seen better days.

Now this comic band was standing not so comically in an almost straight line, as though guarding the gatehouse from trespassers, though for the first time Alex's attention was drawn away from the makeshift homeguard to the gatehouse itself, a narrow sheltered passage which was wholly blocked by one of the grilles which had apparently slipped its track and come crashing down, leaving a confused tangle of heavy chains dangling uselessly from the overhead pulleys.

All right, Alex advised himself, opening the carriage door. Go out and reason wtih them. Try as gently as possible to point out that there really was no need to guard a gatehouse that was completely impassable to start with.

"Hold your position," he warned the driver beneath his breath, "and keep the horses still."

"They're hungry."

"Who isn't?" He started forward at a casual pace, hands shoved lightly into his pockets.

Suddenly he stopped, listening. He *was* in a bad way. He was hearing things now, what sounded for all the world like a . . . . pianoforte?

He came to a halt about twenty yards from the home guard. Had the wind of Eden grown so rare that now it was capable of forming melody patterns? For that's what he heard, a sad though lilting tune expertly played on an old pianoforte, the upper registers tinkling across the quiet morning like small harbingers of beauty and order.

He lifted his head to the delightful sound, amazed as much by its presence as anything. In this vast landscape of misspent and wasted lives, such a heavenly sound seemed to be in direct contradiction.

He listened to it a moment longer. Then with the most conciliatory voice he could muster, he smoothed back his mussed hair and went forward, calling out, "Hallo . . ."

With luck and grace, God might, on Judgement Day, forgive her a few of her minor and thoughtless sins. But Herr Spindler? Never. For the manner in which she was now butchering Chopin's "Fantasy Impromptu" he would see her punished in that unique hell reserved for the heathen who did not view a pianoforte as a celestial instrument.

Of course, in all fairness, the offense was not totally her fault. Part of it lay with the very handsome though wretchedly cared-for pianoforte itself, dated and labeled in rosewood inlays "Pleyel, Paris 1836."

That was years before her birth, an antique really, a lavish gift from one Eden to another on some far-distant and happy occasion.

Suddenly she heard a soft groan coming from the library. Within the instant her fingers were again on the keyboard, something simpler this time, Chopin at Majorca.

Between rests in the melancholy piece she turned her ear in the direction of the library. He was, as she suspected, quiet now. Not asleep. She knew better than that. But somehow soothed by the music, even music badly played.

As her fingers formed certain chords, she marveled again that he was still alive. On that dreadful night three weeks ago when they had bound him like a wild animal and half-carried, half-dragged him down from the castle roof, she had been afraid for him, for the duress that he, as well as they, was inflicting on his body. When the seizure had come—and it had

56

been awful, blood seeping from his mouth and nostrils—she knew instantly what had happened, a stroke as Miss Nightingale had called it. Death was the best remedy, she had said further, with the sympathetic but objective judgment which had made her the greatest professional in all of England. Such patients never got any better, and some—for too long—never got any worse, like Mr. Eden.

Every morning she awakened from her cramped position in the big wing chair she'd shoved into position beside his couch in the library, certain that she'd find him dead. But what she had found every morning for the last three weeks had been a pulse, faint at first but persistent. And as the first days had evolved into a week when she'd sat with him through fevers, she prayed that God would be merciful enough to take this servant, for the worst punishment He could send this once-strong man would be a life of impairment.

That had been her prayer in those first days. But at some point when it had been clear to her that either God was not going to answer her specific prayer or that John Murrey Eden was fighting with every ounce of limited strength he could muster, then she had ceased offering up that prayer and remembered, "Thy will be done, not mine," and devoted herself completely to his case.

As she brought the nocturne to a close, she thought she heard a human voice raised in "Hallo" a distance away. No, only her imagination, the natural result of too much isolation and too little sleep. Once a day—sometimes in the evening—if he wasn't too busy Reverend Christopher would trudge up the cliff walk and bring her a basket of muffins, a round of cheese, and always an encouraging word. But beyond that she was alone in this immense tomb with only a half-dead man and a handful of zealous home guards for company.

Bates . . .

A fearful man, she'd decided a long time ago, who now had marshaled a vigilante group of fishermen who stood guard night and day outside the castle gates, awaiting the day when Mr. Eden's health permitted him to face the justice that they were forced to face every day of their lives.

Somberly Susan stared down at the keyboard, recalling the words she'd exchanged with the old man—sometimes angry, always futile. The dead woman— "Mr. Eden's victim"—had been buried, without ceremony, in the Eden graveyard three weeks ago.

Still overwhelmed by the madness, Susan shook her head and glanced back toward the library door and wondered if Mr. Eden even knew what had happened to him. She removed her hands from the keyboard, where they had rested for several minutes without striking a note, and abruptly stood. How much longer could it go on? And how much longer could she abandon her other patients on the circuit? She was long overdue now . . .

Yet what to do? She'd sent three different messages to the John Murrey firm in London. Reverend Christopher had given her a name—a Mr. Alex Aldwell, who, according to Reverend Christopher, was Mr. Eden's close friend and business associate. In each message she'd tried very hard to be precise and yet brief, not clearly defining Mr. Eden's seizure, for she hadn't been certain just precisely what had befallen the man. But what had it gained her? Exactly nothing. No response. Either Reverend

Christopher was wrong about the depth of the relationship which existed between Mr. Eden and this Mr. Aldwell, or else that relationship had soured, like everything else in this dreadful place.

Suddenly an idea occurred. What if she were to move Mr. Eden outside into the dazzling sun which shone brilliantly through the open door of the Great Hall. She sat up on the piano bench. Yes, it had always made a difference with the patients in London. Then she would do it. But could she? Even a reduced Mr. Eden was still a large man . . .

She bowed her head, then caught herself and looked up into the same empty rectangle of sunlight which only a few moments earlier had provided her with hope. She blinked.

It wasn't the same empty rectangle. Something was filling it now, the silhouette of a man, massive, in shades of dark and light, merely standing there, one arm braced against the right door frame as though he were tired and in need of support.

Her first thought was that it was one of the home guard come to ask a favor or to inquire the condition of Mr. Eden's health. They reminded her of vultures waiting perversely, not for the body to die, but for it to live, so they could pounce on it and carry it away.

But in spite of her surprised shock, she looked again across the Great Hall and decided, no, it wasn't a member of the home guard although for a moment or two she was unable to say how she could be so certain.

Would he never speak? Surely he had seen her, though now she noticed that his eyes were caught on a specific room deterioration. Near the top of the high ceiling there were large cathedral windows; three were broken. "It's seen better days," came the deep, weary male voice from the door. The words seemed to sail effortlessly over the distance that separated them. She thought in a second that it sounded like a voice accustomed to addressing men.

"I'm sure it has," she replied, and thought how weak and womanly her voice sounded in contrast.

"Would you . . . ?"

She'd thought to ask him his name, nothing more, but apparently he had mistaken the half-formed sentence for an invitation to come all the way into the Great Hall, which in the next minute was precisely what he was doing, at the last minute remembering his short black narrow-brimmed hat, and scooping it off schoolboy fashion, holding it awkwardly before him.

"I'm sorry," he apologized, and she was amazed to discover how ill-at-ease he was. With the distance of the great hall separating them, he seemed confident.

"You are . . . ?" she began.

Suddenly a look of remorse warmed his face. "Oh, Gawd, I'm sorry," he apologized. "You must have thought . . ." The grin faded as he shook his head in self-abnegation.

"Aldwell," he pronounced with renewed conviction. "Alex Aldwell, down from London . . ."

Although she'd only recently been thinking on him, it took her a moment or two to connect the reality of this man to the name she'd addressed on three different occasions. Then she did.

"Yes," she said, smiling back at him. "Yes, of course. Mr. Aldwell. I wrote to you . . ."

"Several times . . ."

"I'm sorry. I had no way of knowing if my earlier efforts . . ."

"They did."

"Then I *am* sorry . . ."

"No need. I tried to get here sooner, but . . ."

"It wouldn't have made any difference."

"Are you alone here?"

"Except, of course, for Mr. Eden and . . ."

"Them?" With that he jerked his head back toward the sun-filled door to the Great Hall. Since there was no one there, she assumed he meant Bates's comic-opera soldiers beyond.

"Yes," she replied, and wished again they all would go back to their herring boats. Yet at certain moments, particularly late at night, she was glad they were out there.

During the interim, Mr. Aldwell stepped closer and appeared to be staring beyond her, as though looking for someone.

"Mr. Eden is bedridden, Mr. Aldwell," she said.

Quickly he nodded, as though he'd known that all along, though he added a curious postscript. "Then he's . . . still alive?"

"Yes," she replied, "he's still alive, but you won't recognize him. He's not the same man . . ."

"What happened?"

"A seizure," she said simply.

"How long had he been ill?" Mr. Aldwell asked now, suddenly lowering his voice as though fearful of being overheard.

"To the best of my knowledge, he hadn't been ill at all," Susan replied. She was speaking, of course, of physical illness. After having watched Mr. Eden each day and large parts of each night for the last three weeks as he'd cried out, first calling one name, then the other, she suspected that he was suffering from a deep spiritual illness, the outlines of which she could only guess at.

Mr. Aldwell seemed surprised at this information, as though certain that such a serious condition as existed now had to be preceded by earlier and equally serious illness.

As he continued to stare, she tried to explain and gave him a brief accounting of how Reverend Christopher had summoned her to Eden Castle, hoping that perhaps she could alter the impending tragedy which was about to take place on top of the high crenellation.

He listened attentively and quietly until she spoke of the dead woman in Mr. Eden's arms. Then his attention vaulted. He started toward her.

"Who . . . ?"

"Reverend Christopher identified her as Lady Harriet—Mr. Eden's aunt, I believe he said."

Mr. Aldwell seemed to be suffering for Mr. Eden now. "God help him . . ." Then he asked, "How . . . did she die?"

"My professional judgment—and Reverend Christopher agrees with me—was that she died of starvation."

"My God!" The pain broke on his face and seemed literally to turn him about and leave him facing the Great-Hall door, where for a few moments she could chart easily the agony as it moved down his neck into his shoulders, everything about the large man visibly collapsing.

Then suddenly she heard his angry voice demanding, "Where were the servants?"

She looked up to see Mr. Aldwell confronting her as though she were responsible for the sad state of affairs at Eden.

"Gone," she said, taken off guard by the accusatory tone of his voice.

"All of them?" he demanded further, his sense of incredulity growing.

"When I arrived, yes."

"How did they live?" he asked frantically, and only at the last minute did he seem to realize that his question had been answered in the very fact of the disintegration of Eden. Their eyes met and held, she trying to offer comfort without words, he rejecting it.

"My God!" he repeated, and again his despair turned him about and propelled him forward almost half the distance back to the Great-Hall door.

"You know, I told Aslam," he called back to her. "Yes, I did. Several times. I said we can't just . . ." Abruptly his voice broke.

"Mr. Aldwell, don't blame yourself, please," she begged.

He was silent for a moment and then angrily pointed outside. "What in the hell are they doing there?" he demanded.

"They're waiting for Mr. Eden's recovery." She came up alongside of him on the top step and joined him in gazing out at the unofficial sentries.

"What is their interest in John?" Aldwell asked.

She stepped back and lifted her face to the sun, which was warm, and rubbed her arms. "They believe there are charges to be brought against him," she said bluntly.

"What . . . charges?" Mr. Aldwell asked, altering his line of vision, shifting it to her.

"Serious ones, Mr. Aldwell, though ridiculous on the face of it."

"What charges?"

"They feel that somehow Mr. Eden was responsible for the woman's death."

"John? Responsi . . . ?"

Still he appeared more bewildered than anything else. She was on the verge of repeating herself when abruptly he turned away.

"My God!" she heard him whisper, and while she knew it wasn't a prayer, she knew it wasn't a curse either. He went on, his back to her, and the strong channel breeze seemed to blow a few of the words away. "Don't they know . . . ?" He began angrily and never finished, and glanced out at the distant men.

"Why?" he demanded again. "What has John ever done to them but hired and fed and clothed a great many of them?"

"That's not the point, Mr. Aldwell," she said gently. "Most of the villagers have lived their entire lives in the shadow of Eden. If they have worked inside the castle, the case would be even stronger against the Eden family—"

"Why?" he demanded, his indignation growing.

60

"Mortemouth is a poor village," she said, feeling as though she were commenting on the obvious. "Children starve to death every year down there. Did you know that? Look at the close physical proximity of the two worlds. Questions of equality and justice are bound to occur to the simplest minds . . ."

His anger appeared to be receding. "Still, John earned . . ." He broke off mid-sentence and glanced back toward the home guard. "Dear God, how he worked, and how much the firm needs his steadying hand now."

"I'm sure it does."

"Is he . . . ?"

"Come, I'll take you to him."

"No, wait!"

Although she had already turned back toward the Great-Hall door, dreading the impending meeting and wanting only to get it over, she was surprised to find a restraining hand on her arm. Apparently he was dreading the meeting as much as she.

"There's nothing to be afraid of, Mr. Aldwell. He's—"

"I'm not . . ."

"He's very ill, that's all. But he's still alive and fairly young . . ."

He turned away and she saw him fumbling in his waistcoat pocket, and a moment later he withdrew a mussed linen handkerchief and made two awkward swipes at his eyes and blew his nose. She waited with him and saw his line of vision again, aimed straight toward the home guard beyond the gatehouse, and saw, along with him, something new, Bates staring back at them, his rigid thin form like a single black slash on the blue horizon.

"Bastard!" Mr. Aldwell muttered beneath his breath. "I daresay he's waited all his life for this moment."

"Do you think he can bring charges against . . . ?"

"He can if he wants to. It won't make any difference. I'm taking John with me back to London." He looked sharply over his shoulder at her. "If he can travel, that is. Do you think . . . ?"

Whereas before she'd been fairly certain that Mr. Eden was capable of surviving such a journey, now she felt fully her responsibility. She knew that Mr. Aldwell would abide by her decision.

"Perhaps . . . probably. We'll see," she murmured, safely equivocating. How peculiar! Only a few moments earlier she'd wanted nothing so much as to be freed from this curious duty. Now . . .

"How soon?" Mr. Aldwell pressed further.

The direct question brought her back to her present dilemma. "I'm . . . not certain. Care will have to be taken. . ."

"Of course."

"The journey will have to be done in stages . . ."

While he nodded cooperatively to everythiing, suddenly it occurred to her to consider Mr. Eden's wishes. What if, even in his diminished state, he had no desire to leave Eden? To force a change of environment upon him could be fatal.

"What is it?" Mr. Aldwell asked, seeing the indecision on her face.

"I . . . was just thinking . . ." She broke off.

"What were you just thinking?" Aldwell persisted. "Were you worried about them?" He jerked his head in the direction of Bates and his guards.

She grabbed at the false excuse. "Yes," she lied. "Bates was fully prepared to transport Mr. Eden to the constable in Exeter three weeks ago, immediately following his seizure. It was only Reverend Christopher's persuasion that saved him."

The indignation on Mr. Aldwell's face escalated to anger. "Well, the bastard has me to deal with now," he exploded, and swiveled back around, dividing his fury equally between her and the man for whom it was originally intended. "I just wish he would try to stop me," he said, his voice falling ominously low.

"Come, Mr. Aldwell," she said with sudden dispatch, weary of postponing this difficult moment. "Maybe it will be your face, your presence, that will penetrate through Mr. Eden's silence."

He nodded soberly, as though he too were ready to get it over with. "He's . . . in a bad way, then?" he asked with gruff ingenuousness, and followed anxiously after her back into the Great Hall.

"Yes."

"Where is he?" Mr. Aldwell asked, coming up on first one side, then the other.

"In the library," she replied without looking back.

For a few moments she sensed him falling behind, sensed as well his incredulity. "That's . . . where I left him."

Interested, she glanced back but never altered her step. "Why did you leave him? And when?"

"About four years ago," he said, at last drawing even with her, though up close she could see the reluctance on his face.

"And why?" she persisted.

Mr. Aldwell shook his head. "He was . . ." He hesitated. "Oh, hell, I don't know what he was," he concluded, annoyance joining his sorrow. "I tried for days, weeks, to reach him. Miss Elizabeth too, before she went to Paris with her friends."

There was that name again. Elizabeth. The one that Susan herself had recently invoked. "Would you know where she is now?" she asked, thinking that news of the missing woman might mean something to Mr. Eden.

But "Gone" was all the man said, and he said that rather patly, as though he'd been quizzed before on the matter and had simply concocted the most economical answer he could think of. Now he repeated it with ominous variation. "Gone. Along with all the rest of them. And though it pains me to say it, John brought it on himself . . . yes, he did."

She considered pursuing the harsh indictment, then changed her mind.

"Come, Mr. Aldwell," she invited now, "your friend is waiting. He needs you now as he's never needed you before."

At the direct and urgent invitation, Mr. Aldwell looked almost pleadingly at her. "Is . . . he . . . ?"

"Come and see for yourself," she repeated. "I sense a deep bond of affection between you."

"Aye," he agreed readily.

"Then come. I assure you that now he is completely abandoned and we must overlook his offenses of the past, whatever their nature. Let God judge him, as He will judge all of us. For now, our responsibility is not his soul, but rather his body, and that has suffered a grievous blow. Come. You may be the very one who makes the difference."

She tried to make her voice a soothing instrument. But for several awkward moments she wondered if he intended to heed her or not. Had he traveled all the distance from London to turn his back on Mr. Eden?

"Mr. Aldwell, please . . ." she entreated. "I must go to him. Feel free to follow or to stay. . . ."

Then, with a sense of dispatch, of getting it over with, he turned sharply on his heels and set a fast pace toward the corridor that led to the library, his head bowed, shoulders elevated and hunched, his entire massive body struggling at a forward-leaning angle, as though he were approaching one of the mightiest storms of his life.

He had not expected it to be so difficult. Nor had he expected to remember so much. The approach to the castle had been nothing compared to the castle itself. There all the years that he'd spent with John and the others had come crashing down upon him, as though he'd just lived them.

The tragic irony of the moment was not lost on him. The remarkable man who had brought them all together and welded them into a family was the same man who had driven them apart, each vowing never to return to Eden so long as John drew breath.

"In here, Mr. Aldwell."

At the specific direction, he looked up to find himself before the library door, the woman beckoning him forward.

"Mr. Aldwell, are you feeling well?"

Apparently the dread had registered on his face, or else she was skillful at reading men's minds.

"No, I . . ." he began, and apparently she sensed the nature of his hesitation and moved to offer comfort.

"He's your friend and he needs you. It's that simple," she said, indicating, if nothing else, her ignorance regarding the past and John Murrey Eden. Nothing that man ever did, had done, or would do could be defined as simple. He was a master of convolution, at pitting one individual against another and always asserting his will above all else.

Strangely enough, this brief excursion into hate and resentment seemed to fortify him, like a glass of good port on a January day, and just as the woman was retracing her steps, ready to comfort further, he found the courage to march past her and into the library.

From where he stood just inside the door he saw the vast shelves stripped, the thousands of rich morocco-leather-bound books gone. Where? To his left, like deserted carriages in a storm, stood a row of the mahogany stepladders used for reaching the higher shelves. The arrangements of tables and chairs and reading desks had been pushed into the extreme northwest corner and the various Oriental carpets had been rolled up and shoved beneath the tables, their fringed ends protruding like snuffed-out cigars.

63

The room resembled nothing now, its original purpose lost. He stood a moment longer, consciously avoiding the extreme depths of the room to his right.

"This way, Mr. Aldwell . . ."

It was the woman again, forcing him in the least desirable direction, though in the moment of turning he spied another safe harbor, the massive Alma-Tadema painting *The Women of Eden*.

Even with the distance of the library stretching between him and the painting, he still could see it clearly. The scale was enormous, each individual woman twice as large as life.

Now those women held him enthralled, all of them as evocative on canvas as they once had been in real life, filling the cold corridors of this ancient castle with their light and laughter and beauty and love.

His favorite was Miss Elizabeth, that proud woman to the left of center. He understood Miss Elizabeth better than the others. No aristocratic blueblood there, except of the spirit, and then she was the bluest of all. Started her days, she'd once told Alex, as a prostitute on the lanes of St. James's and, at fourteen, had ended up in the common cell of Newgate, where she'd had the good fortune to meet Edward Eden, John's father.

"Were they truly that beautiful?" The question came from his left, from the little nurse named Susan.

"Oh, more so." He nodded. "Though each was unique. Dhari there was a beauty. Aslam's mother, you know," he explained, "but the rarest jewel and John's favorite was his cousin, young Mary, there at the very edge. Mary was irresistible, alive, vital, laughing, as stubborn as John, loving and now . . . wounded. And gone. Married an American, she did, without John's blessings, in fact with only his curses. Gone to America, which was as good as being dead."

"She's lovely," came the comment from his left. "And of course the other one is John's wife. Lila? Was that her name?"

Alex nodded, suddenly weary, not of the painting but of all the tragedy embedded in the paint. It was over. All of it. Those lives, those women. He hadn't received word from any of them for literally years. Gone—as though they had never existed. And all that remained was this canvas. *How could that be?*

Now, of his own volition and without any urging or assistance from the nurse, he started forward with a determined step, heading toward the high-backed couch, where he suspected the true tragedy rested.

Behind him he was aware of the woman keeping pace. "Mr. Aldwell, I think you should know . . ."

This voice bore no resemblance to the soft one that had made inquiry about the beauties in the painting. This one was tense and trying to warn him of something.

Too late. His determined step had carried him too rapidly to the high-backed couch, where, with nothing further to obstruct his vision, he glanced down . . .

"Oh, my dear God!"

. . . and was unable for the moment to mask his shock. Instead, he stepped closer until he was standing directly over the high-backed couch, his attention caught and held by the blank fixed stare in those eyes which

64

appeared to be lost in two black hollows. Then he realized that John wasn't seeing anything, not of this world at any rate.

He watched a moment longer and tried to determine the cause for such a bleak fixed gaze. Then a terrifying thought occurred. "Is he . . . blind?" he whispered, fearful that John could hear what they were saying.

Quickly the nurse shook her head. "No—at least, I don't think so."

"Then . . . what . . . ?"

"It's like a twilight sleep," she said. "It was Miss Nightingale's belief that they generally are more aware than we give them credit for."

"They?"

"I've worked with other patients who have suffered seizures."

He nodded, not absolutely certain that she'd answered his question.

"I'm . . . sorry, Mr. Aldwell. Perhaps I was remiss in not more adequately preparing you."

"Not necessary," he murmured, and waved his hand in dismissal and felt there were a few words that were necessary, a few questions to which he would like to have direct answers.

"Miss . . ." he began, and stopped.

"Susan," she said, and simultaneously stepped forward and without hesitation placed a hand on John's forehead. She held it there for several moments, and as far as Alex could tell, if John was aware of her close proximity or Alex's, he gave no indication of it. The eyes never wavered from their fixed spot on the ceiling, the brows slightly knit, as though someplace in the vicinity of the ceiling was an imponderable mystery.

"Still too warm," the nurse said quietly. "I can't understand . . ."

"Fever?"

She nodded. "Slight, but it does persist."

"How . . . long has he been thus?" he asked now, though curiously he turned his back on the couch and took refuge in the painted beauty of *The Women of Eden*.

"From the beginning," came the reply, which seemed to carry with it a note of astonishment.

He looked back.

"From the beginning," she repeated. "From when Bates and his men bound him and carried him—no, dragged him—down here. That's when he suffered the seizure."

"And there has been no alteration?"

"No, none. Except . . ."

"What?" Hopeful, Alex drew nearer, but not wanting to get so close he could see the face again.

"He used to weep, almost constantly. Now . . ."

Alex didn't wait for the full explication. "Does . . . he speak?"

"Not intelligibly," came the reply. "He speaks most eloquently with his eyes. And"—her smile grew as though they were merely talking about a misbehaving child—"he swings a most effective right hand."

Alex looked puzzled. How the weak man lying on the couch could swing his arm, Alex didn't know, and was in no mood to find out.

Suddenly the remaining question in his head seemed massively unimportant. Would he improve? Obviously not. Would the torturous trip to

65

London and skilled physicians make any real difference? Probably not. Was he even capable of being transferred back along the bone-jarring and neglected route without doing greater and more pronounced damage to himself? Most certainly not. And how far removed was death? Not far. Surely not far. The man resembled a corpse now.

Then it was settled. Alex would remain here for a polite length of time, an hour, perhaps two. Then he and the sullen London driver would make for Exeter, a friendly inn, a prolonged rest for the horses, a good charred beefsteak and an endless bottle of bloodred port in which he could obliterate at least the memory of the man lying there. As for the richness of the man himself, that would be with Alex always.

To that end he stood up straight and tried to form the first words of what he hoped would be a graceful exit.

"Well, I thank you for writing to me and informing me . . ."

"I think we can construct a comfortable litter on which to . . ."

She was suggesting that he take John back to London!

Now he felt a desperate need to refute such a suggestion.

"He can't possibly travel. Can he?" he asked tentatively, not really caring how she answered. In his own mind he was resolved.

"Oh, I think he can," she said with exasperating calm.

"You can't be serious."

"Why not? The damage was done with the first seizure. I have no reason to believe that there will be others."

"But he looks . . ."

"His appearance is deceptive. He's lost flesh, true, but he eats little. In London, surrounded by family and friends . . ."

"He has no friends and no family."

She stared at him for a moment as though trying to determine if he was telling the truth. "I . . . can't believe that."

"Believe it. The family—what's left of it—is scattered literally all over the globe, most of them having vowed not to return so long as John . . ."

Abruptly he caught himself and looked quickly down on the skeletal face, staring eyes. "Are you certain he doesn't hear and understand?" he asked, his voice low.

Immediately she shook her head. "No, I'm not certain of anything. There's no way of measuring the damage until the patient can speak for himself, can take the initiative in describing his own feeling."

"And John has not . . . ?"

"No. All he's done, as I've said, is weep. Oh, on occasion, in moments of frustration when he tries to make the body work as it once did, he seems to speak a name, but never clearly. For most of the time he seems placid, content to do as he's doing now, study that one spot on the ceiling."

John himself had taught Alex long ago that any difference of opinion could be resolved with the proper purse. Then first he had to establish what pay she generally received as a circuit nurse—not much, he was certain. Then all he had to do was double it, triple it perhaps, at least until he could make other arrangements from London. Of course, the only family member available for consultation in the matter was Aslam, and Alex already knew what his judgment would be—practical, and probably right. In London John would be nothing but an albatross.

66

All right. Then at best Alex was asking for two, possibly three more weeks of the nurse's time. Surely she could afford him that, particularly in view of what he was about to offer her.

"Miss," he began, and would have continued except at that moment John lifted his eyes for the first time, disengaging them from the ceiling. For a moment they seemed to roll backward into his skull, a hideous image which appeared to leave him sightless. But then they reappeared, and for one terrible moment he seemed to look directly at Alex, the eyes, which only moments before had been fixed on the ceiling, now closely studying Alex's face as though, despite the obscuring veils, something like recognition was stirring.

She saw it as well, and bent down until she was close to his ear, her right hand still caressing his forehead, her eyes trying to chart everything at once.

"Do you know who this is, Mr. Eden?" she asked, smoothing back the matted and tangled hair. "He's a good friend, an old friend. Take a closer look . . ."

At this suggestion Alex saw the pale brow knit again, the eyes definitely engaged, though as yet nothing registered on his face and certainly no words had been spoken.

Then, to Alex's consternation, the woman was motioning for *him* to step closer. "Come, Mr. Aldwell, the light is dim here, and his eyes . . ."

She never finished her statement about John's eyes, for at that moment they closed, as though a state of complete exhaustion had overtaken him. His head rolled to one side on the hollowed pillow and, to all appearances, he had fallen instantly asleep.

At least that was Alex's grateful judgment. Under the weight of that brief but penetrating gaze, he'd felt his soul falter. How many times he'd seen that same intense gaze on John's face.

But the nurse was unwilling to give up.

"Mr. Eden, please," she begged, "look again at Mr. Aldwell. He's come so far to see you, and is so worried. Please . . . try . . ."

"I don't think, miss, that he's—"

"You have to try," she repeated, and her voice cracked, and this time the admonition was addressed not to John but to Alex. "You see, Mr. Aldwell, he doesn't know what he can do at this point in his recuperation, and I suspect that Lady Harriet's death has taken a toll of his spirit. So you see, he must be urged to try, or else . . ."

"Or else what?" Alex asked, curious to know the complete prognosis.

She told him without hesitation. ". . . or else he will die. Unused muscles atrophy. Neither can the loss of flesh persist, though he seems fortunate to possess hidden reserves, both literal and figurative, and I think London will make a difference as well. I understand that London is more his home than Eden, so I'm certain there must still be friends there who are capable of making a difference in his recovery."

What *was* she talking about? And by the time Alex had refocused his attention away from his quick exit, he heard what sounded dangerously like a plan of action.

"So I think, with Tom Babcock's help, we can construct a makeshift litter that will fit snugly into the carriage, where Mr. Eden will be able to ride with a minimum of discomfort."

"I . . . don't . . ."

But the list of negatives was so monumental that Alex faltered as he attempted to list them, and into the vacuum came the soft though determined female voice.

"I know he'll rapidly improve in London, Mr. Aldwell. He's so cut off here, has been for too long. It would be of great help also if some of the family could be notified and summoned home. In his sleep he sometimes calls out certain names . . ."

"Who?"

"Harriet, of course, and as often Elizabeth . . ."

Fortunately there was no need to comment one way or the other on her last request. Harriet was dead, as she knew all too well, and Elizabeth had disappeared across the channel in Paris with her revolutionary friends. Four years ago Aslam had received instructions from her to sell her London house at number Seven Saint George Street, once her greatest pride. Aslam was to place it in the hands of an estate agent and not to sell until he could fetch the highest price. Then the proceeds were to be sent immediately to Elizabeth in Paris.

Recalling all this, his mind grew glazed again. He assumed that Aslam or one of the clerks would still have that address, but what guarantee that she would still be there? Reports coming out of Paris the last few years had been grim. Female incendiaries. Women taking an active part in the revolution.

"And, best of all, you will be able to avail yourself of Miss Nightingale's experience in these matters of seizures. You'll find her almost every morning at St. Thomas . . ."

He nodded, though paradoxically he still was rejecting everything she was saying. Just as soon as she gave him a chance, he would come forward with a series of rebuttals as impressive as her proposals.

"Now, all that remains," she added, "is to decide what day to aim for. I think Tom can—"

"Just a minute, please."

At least he'd managed one interjection, though if she'd heard it, she gave no indication of it.

"And beyond the construction of the litter, nothing remains to do except to close the castle and, of course, one way or the other to disband the home militia outside the gate, but that shouldn't be too difficult. Old Bates is clearly the ringleader. I think that if he—"

"Just a minute, I beg you . . ."

"—and I'm sure you can hire some capable woman from Mortemouth who will carefully pack away everything left of value."

"I must insist," Alex now said, mustering a degree of force, raising his voice in an attempt to top hers.

For the first time, she looked directly at him—and said nothing.

Then it was his turn, and he stepped close to the high-backed couch, which had become for them a kind of barricade, Susan on one side, Alex on the other. Unfortunately, from this close proximity he caught another glimpse of John's face, and, to his shock and horror, he saw the eyes open again, this line of focus aimed at Alex himself.

"What . . . ?" he muttered, and stepped back, as though driven back by the eyes.

"It's all right, Mr. Aldwell. He can't really see you. Sometimes he passes the entire night with his eyes open. I suspect the small optical nerves have been damaged in some way."

"Then he *is* blind?" Alex asked, his shock growing.

"No," she replied, "because occasionally his eyes will follow me. I suspect he's seeing light and color, at least. Oh, don't you see, Mr. Aldwell, these are the very reasons why you must take him back with you to London now. He needs modern treatment, up-to-date equipment. There is absolutely nothing I can do for him here, except—"

"Out of the question," Alex snapped, still not recovered from those possibly sightless eyes staring up at him. "What I mean to say," he began, moving to a safe position at the head of the couch, where he did not have to look down on those eyes, "is that I think it would be foolhardy to transfer John to London at least now, at this time."

He'd expected objection coming from her. Instead, she stood quietly on her side of the couch, hands folded neatly before her, her face strangely calm, as though she'd expected this.

"Go on, Mr. Aldwell," she invited.

"I disagree entirely," he said. "There's no one in London to care for him," he explained bluntly. "I'm afraid he would end up in hospital, in a ward, served by disinterested women who lack your skill, there to languish until death blessedly intervened."

She spoke one name. "Elizabeth . . ."

He replied with one word. "Gone."

"She can't be reached?"

He shrugged. "I don't know."

"The rest of the family?"

"Gone."

"And yourself?" she asked with disarming directness.

The rapid repartee had provided him with the illusion that he was winning. Now she had destroyed that illusion with two words.

Still he had ammunition and didn't hesitate to use it. "I am not a nursemaid. Even with training I would make a poor one. My job is in the field, with men. Besides, I love John too much to watch him die. I really couldn't bear that."

"I don't think he's going to die," she said with cool optimism that shamed him.

"Well, I think we both have to concede that that is God's decision."

"Conceded," she said briskly. Then, to Alex's amazement, she too moved away from the couch and disappeared behind a small wooden screen which he'd just noticed at the far left-hand corner of the library behind the painting of *The Women of Eden.*

From this distance her voice sounded slightly strained. "Then what *are* your plans, Mr. Aldwell?"

"I had thought," Alex commenced, "to hire someone here to stay with him. You're wrong about his fondnesss for London," Alex went on, lying. "He loathed London, he really did, the poisonous air, the crowds and noise . . ."

He paused, thinking some response might be forthcoming from behind the screen.

When none came, he went on, moving as directly as he dared to the

69

heart of the matter. "Someone who . . . knew how to deal with this. Someone who . . . and I'd pay handsomely, I would, certainly make it worth someone's while, yes, I would, and further, I'd see that the castle was at least partially staffed in order to give that someone a hand, if you know what I mean."

He broke off. At that moment she appeared in front of the wooden screen, a dark blue cloak tied over her shoulders, a small, well-worn portmanteau in hand, a look of civil determination on her face.

"Then I wish you well." She smiled, not unpleasantly, and adjusted the tie at her throat. "He requires almost constant attention, Mr. Eden does, but you must always urge him to try—"

"Where are you going?" he demanded.

She smiled and checked the clasp on the portmanteau. "On my way, Mr. Aldwell," she said simply, not looking at him but proceeding on past the painting, then the couch with the man silently staring.

"You see, I'm three weeks late on my rounds as it is. There are others waiting who expected me some time ago. I told Reverend Christopher I would remain at Eden only until family arrived. Then—"

"But family hasn't arrived yet," he interrupted, grasping at straws.

For the first time she looked up. "I understood you to say there wasn't any."

"I never said that," he denied, following after her to mid-room. If only he could keep her talking, perhaps he could persuade her or, better still, let her set the size of the purse and watch him meet it.

"Then what *did* you say?"

"I said simply that they were scattered, some as far as America."

"Oh, my. Well, I certainly couldn't wait for that arrival."

"And I'm not asking you to."

"Good. Well, then, I wish you both all the best—"

"Please wait," he called after her, desperation growing, "and hear me out, I beg you."

Something—either the entreaty or his tone of voice or both—caused her to halt her step when she was less than ten feet from the library door. For a moment she stood facing away from him, as though she didn't want to look back.

"I'm afraid I haven't made my position very clear," he began on what he thought was a conciliatory tone.

"I didn't realize that you had made the long journey from London to discuss *your* position," she said, and he heard a distinct edge to her voice and knew that he had begun badly.

"What I'm trying to say," he began again, "is that there is no one in London capable of giving John the kind of care that he—"

"You've said that," she interrupted again, "though I must confess I find it as hard to believe now as I did the first time I heard it. I have been at Eden for only three weeks, and of course I realize I'm seeing an altered and disrupted Eden, but I know, because of what I see and what Reverend Christopher has told me, that Mr. Eden's herculean efforts in restoring the castle four years ago were for one purpose and one purpose only, and that was to provide a family seat for Eden family and friends. This family was of vast importance to him, or so Reverend Christopher has said. Now," she said in the manner of a conclusion, "I find it difficult to believe that the family who gained so much in so many ways from John Murrey

Eden find it inconvenient to come to him in his time of greatest need."

As she spoke, her voice became harder and more condemning, and at the first break Alex said simply, because it was the truth, "You . . . don't understand."

"Mr. Aldwell, please don't say that again. It sounds ominously like a convenient carpet under which we can sweep all the droppings of our soul's decay."

"But you don't—"

"I understand enough, that the man whom you profess to love is lying over there in desperate need of familiar hands, a familiar voice—"

"You do very well."

"I tend to the needs of his body."

"What more could he . . . ?"

He had asked the incomplete question, sincerely wanting to know. But when he saw the shocked expression on her face, he realized again that he'd made a dreadful mistake. And, since she seemed not only willing but eager to leave again, he threw diplomacy to the wind and moved straight into the heart of the matter.

"May I make a proposition?" he demanded with a strength of conviction he did not feel. "I will return to London immediately, this very afternoon, and send dispatches by the fastest couriers to all members of the family, relating in full the recent turn of events here and imploring them to regather immediately for the purpose of . . ."

He faltered. The request sounded ludicrous even in thought. Lord Richard, John's half-brother, had vowed never to return to Eden until John's death.

". . . for the purpose of looking to the well-being of John himself," he went on, despite the battle raging in his mind. "I'll do this," he concluded, "if only you will remain at Eden and provide him with the care he needs until the first arrival."

"No," she said simply, and started toward the library door.

"Forgive me, but I am prepared to offer you more than adequate compensation."

"No, thank you, Mr. Aldwell," she called back, at the door now.

"It shouldn't be but a matter of weeks," he lied, pursuing her.

"I have other duties," she said, marching down the corridor which led to the Great Hall.

"I said you would be generously compensated," he repeated, "and I'll hire a partial staff so your only duties will be the care of Mr. Eden."

He expected another rejection, but this time she said nothing, though she continued her march across the Great Hall.

"Did you hear?" he called after her.

This time he raised his voice and shouted and heard a thin edge to his tone as well. She couldn't leave. He couldn't care for John. And to live constantly with those dead and staring eyes was too much to ask of him.

"Please?" he called again, desperation increasing.

She was drawing ahead of him by several yards, marching toward the arched door of the Great Hall and the rectangle of sun beyond.

"Miss, please. Just a minute more of your time, then I shall plague you no longer."

No, he was convinced of it. She wouldn't stop again. Stubborn bitch.

71

There was nothing in her pace to indicate that she'd even heard him. *What in the name of God was he going to do now?*

Suddenly she stepped up to the threshold of the arched doors and the sun fell in cascades around her, and as though the weight of the sun had proved too heavy, at last she stopped and stood staring straight ahead.

Encouraged, Alex ran to catch up with her, and stopped short when he felt his voice was within easy range.

"Then, tell me, please," he begged. "I need help," he said simply. "Instructions, at least. Surely it won't delay you to . . ."

Ah, good. At last she was turning toward him. Perhaps if he could keep her talking, she might change her mind. How would it hurt her to take up temporary residence in this grand old castle?

"Just a few instructions, please," he said, smiling, his manner as conciliatory as possible. "For example, are there medicines, and if so, what and how are they administered and when?"

He looked up, startled by a sudden noise, and saw that she had dropped her portmanteau, a terrible expression of shock on her face as she appeared to be looking directly at him.

Well, what in the hell had he gone and done now? Made a simple inquiry about John's care, that was all. Not for himself, mind you. It was his intention to go down into Mortemouth and hire the first willing and fairly able-bodied female he could find . . .

But now, what *was* the matter with her, and why that awful expression on her face, her eyes fixed with frightening intensity on something—not Alex, for now he had determined that she was looking beyond him to some sight at the far end of the Great Hall.

Just as Alex was on the verge of turning to see for himself, he saw her cheeks go pale, both hands lifted in distant assistance of something or someone, and she started slowly approaching him with that same startled and shocked expression, mouth opened, and, as she drew even with him and passed him by, he heard her breathe in prayer . . .

"Dear God . . ."

. . . and as she passed, he followed her with his eyes and saw . . .

Gawd!

At the far end of the great hall, leaning heavily against the wall, using both hands for support, crouched a ghostly specter, two painfully thin legs protruding out from beneath what appeared to be a voluminous nightshirt, his face from that distance lost in the tangled mat that was his hair and beard.

John . . .

With his attention splintered between the man clinging weakly to the far wall and the woman trying to reach him, it occurred to Alex that perhaps his diagnosis of John had been false and premature. He found very little relationship between the man whom he'd seen earlier lying senseless on the couch and this man trying incredibly to stand upright without the assistance of the wall.

At the sound of her rapid approach, Alex saw him look up from the effort of standing. For a moment the rapid change in focus threatened to topple him altogether, but he reached out again with both hands and appeared to chart her approach with great interest.

As Alex was only a few feet behind, he could hear what was said.

72

"You shouldn't be up, Mr. Eden," she murmured as she halted abruptly, one hand out, reaching in assistance, then quickly withdrawing, as though John were a hot stove.

For a moment the three of them merely stood, each suffering his own incapacity. John, the true focus of attention, seemed most lost of all, as though, having gained the corridor, he now suffered complete disorientation.

She apparently saw his bewilderment and moved to ease it. "Would you like to return to bed now, Mr. Eden? I think you've done very well for one day, but now I . . ."

But at the moment her hand moved out in assistance, John shook his head once, and still using the wall for support, eluded her hand by easing down several feet. The movement, the gesture, carried with it a curious demented quality. Alex thought: How old he looks, how worn, how truly ill.

"Would you help us, Mr. Aldwell? He must return to bed now."

Of course he was prepared to help in any way he could, though as he started toward John with the intention of lifting him up, John suddenly came violently to life. His head lifted and he scrambled farther down the wall, his head commencing to shake in a slow, measured refutation.

"Come on, John," Alex soothed.

"No violence, please."

Her strange request caused Alex to halt in his approach to John. Half in anger, half in bewilderment, he looked back at her. What did she think he was?

"You said to assist him. That was my only intention."

Then he heard a new sound. It vaguely resembled a human voice. Susan was already at John's side, supporting him on the left, her face as moved and astonished as it had been in the Great Hall when she first spotted him.

"What did you say, Mr. Eden?" she inquired casually, almost as though she were trying to make light of it.

From this close proximity Alex saw new effort forming on John's face. The mouth was open, and occasionally the teeth were bared, like a primordial reaction against the failure of his body to perform as he expected it. Then he heard that sound again, accompanied now by several short expulsions of air.

"What is it?" she coaxed gently, still supporting him in one arm, her head down, as though she knew how embarrassed he was by his appearance and therefore was trying to spare him.

When the inarticulate sound came again, she mentioned to Alex to come closer. "I think he wants to say something to you."

Suddenly the weak man objected strenuously. He tried to wrench away from her assistance. In the process he lost his balance and fell to his knees, where he seemed to hold himself erect for a moment. Then the collapse was complete, facedown, his left arm curved at an inhuman angle beneath him.

"Lift him," she commanded sharply, and Alex had already done so—or was in the process, reaching for John's shoulders. As he turned the dead-weight in his arms he saw John's face up close, no color, not a trace of color except for the bluish tinge around his lips.

"Is he . . . ?" Alex began, and never finished, for John stirred in his arms. The eyes fluttered open once, then closed. Alex had thought that he was either asleep or passed out. Now he appeared to be neither, for he looked directly at Alex, not necessarily in recognition, for there was nothing of recognition in the look.

Still half-kneeling with John supported in his arms, Alex felt stunned by the look. "He doesn't know me," he muttered.

"I think he does," she contradicted quietly. "I think he wants to speak, and I think further that he has overheard and understood everything that we've said."

Alex doubted that. But it didn't make any real difference, did it? If the seizure had rendered him speechless, then it really didn't make any difference what he had heard or perceived.

Newly aware of time passing, of the hazards of this place, this man, Alex vowed once again to be gone as soon as possible.

"Listen!" The admonition came from the nurse and seemed foolish, as Alex wasn't making any noise.

"Listen!" she whispered again, and the two of them now stared down into John's face, where, under the strain of effort, his eyes tightly closed, his lips moved, one word formed with painful effort.

"Stay," was what the pronunciation sounded like. "You . . . stay," he repeated, this time opening his eyes and looking directly at the woman. "Go," he added, to Alex this time.

Though the message was halting and fragmented, nonetheless the meaning was clear.

Though it was precisely what Alex had wanted, for a moment he suffered a sense of severe hurt. "You . . . heard?" he asked of the woman, who sat back on her heels, hands resting in her lap, her gaze still focused on John, as though she expected him at any moment to open his eyes and explain the command.

"It was clear," Alex said further, "and his desire, not mine, this time."

He spoke softly, still supporting John in his arms, ready to lift and carry him back to the couch in the library as soon as he could determine her state of mind.

"Will you?" he prodded to her bowed head. "Stay, I mean."

She appeared to be listening closely, watching John's face. "I . . . had no idea . . ." she murmured.

"What? I don't—"

"He can walk," she said, a tone of marvel in her voice.

"And speak," Alex contributed.

"Yes." And for the first time she smiled up at him. "Do you know what that means, Mr. Aldwell?" she asked further, and the smile broadened. "It means that his recovery is almost a certainty, depending on . . ."

"What?"

She shrugged and with one hand gently smoothed back a strand of John's hair that had fallen across his forehead.

"It depends on what?" Alex asked again, pleased, though still skeptical, that total recovery was within the grasp of this terribly ill man in his arms.

"His will," she said simply, "his determination, his spirit."

Now, and for the last time, he urged again, "Will you? Stay, I mean. At least a fortnight."

"I . . . shouldn't . . ."

"You must. He obviously trusts you. Believe me when I say there is no one in London . . ."

For the first time in several minutes she looked up. "You will write to Elizabeth?"

He nodded broadly and dared to hope. "Consider it done."

"And the others?"

"Yes, I give you my word."

"I'll need help."

"Hire as many as you like."

He thought she might say more, but instead she stood with slight effort from her kneeling position and, without a word, started off across the Great Hall, heading toward the arched doors.

Surprised, he watched her for a few moments, thinking foolishly that she was merely confused, that she'd lost her sense of direction, that the library was back in the other . . .

"Where are you going?" he called after her, still bewildered by her rapid move in the wrong direction.

She was just this side of the Great-Hall door approaching her portmanteau when . . . Of course. She'd simply retraced her steps to retrieve her luggage.

Now, without turning about, he heard her issue a spate of commands. "Please carry Mr. Eden back to his couch in the library, Mr. Aldwell, and be so good as to sit with him until I return. I must make a brief trip down into Mortemouth . . ."

She stopped talking and appeared to look down at the luggage in her hands as though not absolutely certain how it got there.

"And . . . this," she said. "Would you be so good as to return this to—"

"Certainly," he interrupted, working hard to conceal a smile of relief. He came up quickly before her and took the luggage, as though he viewed it as collateral. This would assure her return. In an attempt to further conceal his pleasure at this turn of events, he asked quietly, "You really have hope for John, then?"

"Of course," she said, straightening her cape and reknotting the tie at her throat. As she started off once again toward the Great-Hall door, she called back another instruction. "There is limited food down in the kitchen court, Mr. Aldwell. Help yourself and see that Mr. Eden gets as much as he wants. I'll return as soon as I can."

Alex postponed John's transfer back to bed and hurried toward the door through which she had recently disappeared. A few seconds later he lifted his hand to his eyes and squinted toward the gatehouse. The home guard was no longer marching in that ragtag fashion. Now they stood closely grouped around someone who occupied the core. Also in rapt attention was the stick figure, Mr. Bates.

Suddenly Alex looked back at John. Maybe, just maybe, he should take him back to London. For everyone's sake. He now recalled Aslam's one fear where John was concerned, that in a diminished and uncaring state he would be a likely victim for kidnappers, who could hold the John Murrey firm to ransom. And of course the scandal sheets would poison public opinion and the firm would be forced to pay the outrageous sum.

Then, staring outward again, Alex saw an interesting development, old Bates and the woman walking slowly and very privately away from the others, both heads down, as though deep in plans or conversation.

A very real threat there as well, one which the magistrate in Exeter might find rather fascinating, to say nothing of a bored and restless populace. John Murrey Eden arrested for the murder of Lady Harriet Eden. It could prove the grandest theatrical of all the recent Eden dramas.

Gawd! What to do?

For a moment longer he stood indecisively, caught between the mysterious and prolonged conversation going on beyond the gatehouse and the vulnerable silence coming from the far end of the Great Hall. That once-powerful man could be used for anyone's purposes now, and Alex found that realization unbearably sad.

By midnight that same night Susan looked around her surroundings, impressed anew with the power of money. Though she had pleaded for assistance from old Bates for over an hour on her way down into the village, it had been Mr. Aldwell who had accomplished the feat of pressing the old man and his home guard into service. And how had he done it? By the simple waving of a sizable purse and the promise of several gold pieces if they got all accomplished in the course of this night.

Susan had never seen such industry. Immediately following her return from the village, Mr. Aldwell had shown her this pleasant apartment tucked away at the top of the grand staircase on the second floor, only a deceptively small and unobtrusive door marking it. She had seen it before and had assumed that it was a storage closet of some sort.

Thus her surprise when Mr. Aldwell had unlocked the door to reveal a cozy three-room flat, self-contained in the heart of the castle, with a small, doll-sized kitchen and a cozy sitting room furnished more simply than the other chambers she'd seen in the castle. To one side of the sitting room was a bedchamber into which the men had moved one of the four-posters from the third floor, and to the left a second, smaller bedchamber into which they had moved her few belongings. By leaving the door open, she could hear Mr. Eden at all times, and these smaller rooms were so much easier to tend and to heat than the cavernous library.

Now, as Susan sat on the settee, feet propped up before a crackling fire, she realized that for the first time since she had been pressed into service at Eden, she was almost warm.

Outside in the corridor she heard Mr. Aldwell settling up with the home guard. A clever man, Mr. Aldwell. He'd promised the men regular wages if for the next few weeks they continued their watchful vigil outside the gatehouse, not for the purpose of absconding with Mr. Eden, but rather of keeping him safe.

The male voices outside in the corridor continued to hum. More exchanges? More bargains? More money? Mr. Aldwell seemed to have an endless supply of it. But she was grateful to him for having found this comfortable little corner. According to Mr. Aldwell, it had been constructed and furnished to accommodate the tutor for Lady Harriet's children, Lord Richard and Lady Mary, when they had been young, a mean-spirited Yorkshire gentleman named Caleb Cranford and his equally mean-spirited sister Sophia, both of whom had run the household with a harsh and unloving hand.

Well, no matter. It was Susan's intent to make the narrow confines of these rooms a safe harbor. Just then she heard footsteps passing by the door of the apartment and rose to see who was there.

"Mr. Aldwell, what is it?" she inquired, hurrying down the steps, then stopping short of the one where he sat,

Then an idea occurred. Perhaps Bates had proven too contrary, had refused to agree to Mr. Aldwell's requests, preferring to pursue his pointless game of revenge.

"Don't worry, Mr. Aldwell," she soothed. "I suspect that in reality Mr. Bates is a great deal more bark than bite. At least that's what Reverend Christopher tells me, and he's known him for—"

Abruptly he shook his head, though still he didn't look up at her. "Bates gave me his word that he would bring no charges until John was well enough to know what he was being charged with."

She was pleased but surprised by the generous concession.

"Furthermore," Mr. Aldwell went on, "he and his men *will* stand guard on the castle until my return, for the sole purpose of protecting you and Mr. Eden."

"I'm grateful, though I don't think that was necess—"

"It *was* necessary," he said bluntly, swiveling around and glaring at her for the first time. "Of course, they all will be handsomely paid, a fact which should ensure both their loyalty and their zeal. Besides," he muttered, voice falling as he contemplated the step on which his feet were resting, "I don't think you realize how many enemies a man like John has collected over the years."

"Surely if enemies do exist," she said, "they exist in London and not here."

"They are everywhere," he said patly, "and they are highly mobile—or can be—and may have waited for years for the first breach in the wall. Now they fully intend to close in, as old Bates did, with a pocketful of ancient grievances."

"If you felt there was real danger, Mr. Aldwell, why didn't you take him back to London?"

"No!" The reply was lightning-fast and final.

She started to pursue it further, than changed her mind. "Then will you be more specific?" she asked in a businesslike manner. "If I alone am to be responsible for Mr. Eden until the arrival of the family, I must know more about these threats. How will they come? Who will they be? Is there protection—?"

Suddenly he stood up. "I wish I could tell you more. There is considerable dissension within this family. His half-brother Lord Richard Eden was, at last word, living in a house in Kent. John had arranged a union between Richard and a young woman named Lady Eleanor Forbes, good family but impoverished. But first there was a stumbling block that had to be removed, a man named Herbert Nichols, a colleague of Lord Eden's at Cambridge. Rumor had it that the two men were sodomites. John met with Professor Nichols in private and threatened to reveal all to the authorities unless the man immigrated to Australia and vowed never to set

77

foot in England again. Lord Richard found him in his attic room some hours later, dead, hanging by the neck."

She closed her eyes. "Then it is Lord Richard who has threatened . . . ?"

"Not in so many words."

Mr. Aldwell began to range in a limited area back and forth on the broad step, hands shoved into his pockets, his shoulders lifted high in protection, either against the chill in the air or the chilling nature of his words.

"Aslam saw Lord Richard last year," he went on. "They were very close once, Aslam and Richard, and Richard told him then that he wanted very much to come forward and reclaim both his inheritance and his castle, but would not, could not, as long as John inhabited it."

"And you believe his own brother would harm him?"

"Half-brother. And blood makes no difference where vast amounts of money and property are concerned."

"And what else?" she asked. "I had thought that my only responsibility would be to nurture him in his illness. I had no idea that there were others, besides God, who had designs on his life."

He looked sharply up, interrupting his pacing as though she'd said something that had interested him. For a moment she thought he would reply, but he didn't, and at last spoke when he was the farthest distance from her, with his back turned, his words muffled.

Surely she had misunderstood. She could have sworn he had said, "John's sons . . ."

"I . . . beg your pardon?"

"I said his sons," he repeated, looking directly at her.

Sweet Lord. He was being overtheatrical. "His . . . sons? Surely you can't mean that. They are mere babes—"

"—traveling in the custody of their maternal grandfather, Lord Harrington of Wiltshire, who is convinced beyond a shadow of a doubt that it was John's selfishness that killed Lila, Lord Harrington's only child, John's wife."

"Still, two young boys and an old man," she murmured, finding no real threat there, only tragedy.

"Yes, merely two young boys and an old man, living in the house at Avondale of one Charles Stewart Parnell . . ."

She blinked up at the name. "The Irish revolutionary?"

He nodded, apparently pleased with the look of shock on her face. She was beginning to understand.

She started to inquire about the bizarre nature of that relationship. How had two young aristocratic English boys fallen into the suspect hands of a lunatic who wanted to put the torch to the whole world?

"And then," Mr. Aldwell continued, "we should mention a few competitors who have been driven out of business by—"

She held up a staying hand. "No, please," she murmured, and walked a few steps up toward the top of the staircase. "I will simply trust no one who appears at the gate, and I hope you gave no one orders to repair the fallen grille. While it's unsightly, it does provide us with a margin of safety. The inner courtyard can be approached only by foot, thus diminishing—"

He nodded. "In fact, I have expressly ordered Bates to leave the grille as it is."

"Good." She reached the top of the stairs and looked back on the man who stood at mid-step. "Anything else, Mr. Aldwell?"

He hesitated. "I have left sizable purses with both Bates and Reverend Christopher. Anything that you request is to be delivered to you as soon as possible."

She looked down on him. How quaint. She was capable of taking full responsibility for Mr. Eden's life, but she was not capable of spending a few English pounds. She started to protest and changed her mind. She lacked the energy to articulate her feelings.

"One more thing," she asked. "Please give me a tentative length of time before the family arrives." Good Lord, if they came, would they come to cure or kill him?

He faltered. "I will write to Elizabeth first, in Paris . . ."

"Does she have cause to want to harm him?"

Slowly he shook his head. "No. She loved Mary and Richard and John's two sons and Lila. They were *her* family as well as his. His offenses against them hurt her—"

"And you think she'll come?"

"Oh, yes. If she's able."

That was an ominous "if," and Susan realized for the first time how much she dreaded this confinement that hadn't even begun. "Please write to them all, Mr. Aldwell, as soon as possible, and inform them of the serious nature of Mr. Eden's illness, remind them of Christ's forgiveness and, unless they consider themselves greater than Christ, urge them to return to Eden as soon as possible."

"I'll do it." He nodded and added encouragingly, "By this time tomorrow, messages will be going in four different directions. In the meantime . . ."

"I'll do my best. Please go now, Mr. Aldwell. I'm counting on you as heavily as you are counting on me. In a way, we are the only two in Mr. Eden's world who are still capable of helping him."

He rubbed his hands together and withdrew a pair of well-worn leather gloves from his coat pocket. "I was . . . thinking. Should I tell him good-bye?"

"He's asleep now," she said.

He nodded too quickly, thus confirming her suspicion that duty and obligation, more than desire, had prompted the need for a good-bye scene.

Alex bowed from the waist; withdrew the shapeless hat from a back pocket, stuffed it into his left hand along with the worn gloves, touched his free right hand to his forehead in salute, then with almost military precision he turned about and walked smartly down the grand staircase and did not once look back.

She stood on the top step and watched him go with painfully mixed emotions. His words had disturbed her, his initial unwillingness to take any responsibility for "his good and beloved friend" had disturbed her. Yet, on the other hand, perhaps this was for the best. Where Mr. Eden was concerned, she was a clean slate, thus enabling her to be as objective as a good nurse ought to be.

She stood a moment longer and felt her heart accelerate. It was so vast, this castle. What human being or scores of human beings required this much space?

Still she stood, hearing the curious illusion of a voice talking quietly to himself—or so it seemed.

There! She heard it again.

She glanced over her shoulder toward the apartment door, which she'd left ajar for the express purpose of overhearing.

"Mr. Eden?"

Through the door she felt the first warming of the small but effective fire. Then she saw the door leading to Mr. Eden's bedchamber open, the soft glow of a lamp coming from within. Quickly she gained the door, pushed it silently open, her eyes falling on Mr. Eden, his head resting awkwardly on the pillow at the distorted position of either sleep or unconsciousness, his mouth reflexively open, hands lying at his side, his entire body beneath the coverlet bespeaking lack of consciousness.

Then who had been speaking?

Just as she was in the process of turning away from the bed, she felt her heart accelerate, and looked back, startled.

Then, with relief, she saw that she had been mistaken, for in the shadowy half-light of one burned-down lamp, she thought—no, she could have sworn—that she had seen Mr. Eden's eyes open. . . .

Close call, that.

What had happened was that his mind had wandered away from this disreputable bed in the Cranfords' musty old apartment and had taken flight back to his father's Ragged School on Oxford Street, the two of them sharing a second-floor bedchamber—like father, like son—playing endless games of possum beneath the covers of their communal bed while Elizabeth shouted like a fishmonger from the bottom of the stairs for John to come and attend to his studies.

And how his father had held him, in the closeness of a playful embrace at first, then something altering between the two of them, something transforming both, the child—for John couldn't have been more than three or four—and the father clinging to each other beneath the coverlet as though good, simple Elizabeth represented all the threats and hazards in the world.

That's where his mind had slipped, and he had been talking with his father, and so vivid had been the memory, and so moving, that he'd forgotten the woman in the room and had carelessly opened his eyes, thinking her gone.

But there she was, staring intently down on him, as for one split second he had stared with equal intensity up at her.

He thought he heard a voice now coming from the sitting room. Where in the hell was the bastard Aldwell? Gone, he hoped—and forever.

John had seen the revulsion in Alex's face as he'd lifted him back onto the couch in the library, then later up here. Good friend, hell!

For now it suited him to be ill. He held perfectly still, thinking the woman outside would hear him and come running again. But she didn't, and he tried to stretch his legs beneath the covers, and experienced that peculiar sensation which had plagued him off and on during the last few weeks, the sensation that he possessed only one leg, his right.

But he had no intention of discussing such a complicated physical ailment with a circuit nurse.

Suddenly a sharp, uncomfortable twinge spread across his skull, a curious though blessedly short-lived numbness spreading down over his neck and shoulders. Perhaps his judgment of her was too harsh. There was something pleasant in her attendance. At least she was constant, her touch gentle.

Harriet dead. . . . Over. That brief though perfect love. She had been so frail. . . .

Carefully he opened his eyes and looked slowly around. A mean room, small, limited. On the ceiling directly above the small lamp table on the left was a blackened circle where the flame had burned too high. No wall decorations, no softening tapestries. My God, he had paid a fortune for Brussels tapestries. Where were they now?

Suddenly the chaos and the ruin that now were his life broke all around him. No tears. Too late for tears. Was it too late for everything? Would he be given another chance?

Papa, do you love me?

He closed his eyes and in the self-imposed blindness he felt, after all these years, his father's arms about him.

His father . . .

Regarding the Eden wealth, my lord, I now surrender all claim to it . . .

Madness, John muttered, and recalled how he had run from the magistrate's chambers that hot July morning. But something more. It had not been merely the act of a madman that had done such devastating damage to their relationship after that.

Suddenly a terrifying thought occurred. He would die here, in Caleb Cranford's old bed, in this small mean-spirited apartment, attended by a stranger, abandoned by all. And by the time his family was notified and came drifting slowly back—not to see him decently buried, but to claim, like scavengers, whatever part of Eden wealth they could make off with— by the time all that happened, he would be lying liquidly in his grave, the worms already at work.

No!

Someone had to come, someone who once had loved him and would be willing to at least try to forgive him.

Elizabeth.

She was the closest, in Paris. She would respond to Aldwell's letter, he was certain of it. Dear good Elizabeth, more his mother than . . .

Elizabeth.

The name kept reappearing in his mind like a beacon on a dark night. How much he loved her and would welcome her back into his good graces. Then, with Elizabeth established at Eden, it wouldn't be long before the others followed, for they had always looked to Elizabeth to set the pace and the tone.

In his new state of ease, brought on by the projection of a new and dazzling future for Eden, he smiled.

Elizabeth.

The mere thought of her, the sound of her name, brought him peace. He loved her so, always had, always would. She would come to his aid.

He was certain of it.

La Rochelle
House of Detention,
Paris, France
July 3, 1874

Despite the limited comfort of their privileged cell on the ground floor, Elizabeth sensed hazards in the night and looked up from her small lamp which illuminated her sewing box and her sharp shears, and allowed her embroidery to fall limp in her lap.

She stared at the darkness beyond the bars toward the end of the corridor, hearing footsteps where no footsteps should be.

"Did you hear anything?" she asked Eugenie, who had been dozing off and on all evening. Normally Elizabeth would have been content to let her sleep, but with a start she realized she was suffering an emotion she hadn't truly felt for years. She was afraid.

There! She heard it again, someone in the darkness meeting someone else, then both standing stock-still. Though she had no clock to state the time, she needed none. After four years in prison she was expert at judging the tortoiselike passage of the leaden nightime hours.

After midnight now, she was certain. No one ever moved around after midnight, certainly not in this part of La Rochelle. In the common wards, those unspeakable pits of filth and degradation, there was movement all night long. Thank God the general had discovered her talent with the needle and, needing a female companion for the young Countess Eugenie Retiffe, whose father did not think she'd been punished enough after four long years in this unique circle of hell, moved both women to this small barred cell, which had appeared like heaven after the horrors of the common wards.

And here they would remain, Elizabeth until her four-year sentence had passed on December 10, 1874, and poor Eugenie until her father felt that she had been cured of her "dangerous revolutionary inclinations."

Dangerous? Eugenie? Elizabeth smiled. The girl had been a pitiful creature back in 1871 on the barricades, endured by the others only because of Louise Michel's initial kindness to her.

We need assistance from all quarters, even aristocratic ones. Let her serve with us. We will be sending back to her father an enemy.

Well, Louise hadn't had many lapses in judgment, but there certainly sat one. Still, it wasn't a fair assessment. The girl had performed to the best of her ability, and during the last four years everyone had suffered and had stood shoulder to shoulder against the inhuman nightmare that was La Rochelle.

Slowly Elizabeth became aware that her own eyes were as fixed and as staring as poor Eugenie's were.

Nightmare . . .

That was a proper assessment, all right, and she dared to relax from her needlework for a few moments, though she knew she'd have to finish Eugenie's work as well as her own by dawn, or the general would be angry. His only daughter was marrying within the week, and for the last four weeks Elizabeth and Eugenie had stitched monograms on lace handkerchiefs, lace bodices, lace petticoats, and other intimate pieces of apparel where Elizabeth had never dreamed monograms could or should be stitched.

But what right had she to complain, when nobler women like Louise Michel were now serving unspeakable sentences at hard labor in remote places—"where their screams could not be heard"—like New Caledonia. And many other whom she'd grown to love and respect during the revolution now lay in unmarked graves scattered throughout the various cemeteries of Paris, some of the bodies of those executed reclaimed by their families, but most abandoned to a pauper's grave.

The grim remembrances of the past came unexpectedly. Silently she said a brief prayer for her dear friend Louise Michel—*pray God she was still alive*—and said another prayer for all those who had been executed.

Punishment . . .

The word resounded incongruously through Elizabeth's mind as she retrieved her needlework and commenced to stitch a pale pink rose in the corner of a petit-point handkerchief.

Why punishment?

What had any of them done that had not sorely needed to be done? In fact, the miracle was that it had not occurred sooner, women for the first time in history manning the barricades, loading guns, fighting oppression and injustice with the same zeal and dedication as men, and equally as ready to pay the price.

Suddenly she leaned sharply over, unmindful of the needlework, which was becoming crushed in the process.

She *was* afraid. *But why?* For Elizabeth, freedom was less than a year away. During her confinement she hadn't quite learned to live with the guilt brought on by her easy sentence. Four years at La Rochelle House of Detention, while Louise Michel . . .

Louise dead?

That was a possibility she couldn't deal with, not yet. Once she was freed from this place, it was her intention to return to London and sell the rest of her belongings, enough to purchase passage to New Caledonia, where she would try to barter for the release of as many women as she could.

That thought, filled with purpose and movement and hope, gave her courage to lift her head and glance at the sleeping Eugenie and even to face the darkness beyond the bars again, listening.

There *was* something . . .

"Eugenie, please wake up," she whispered, poking the young girl's knee, hoping to rouse her to wakefulness.

Listen!

"Who is it?" she called out softly through the bars, confident now that someone was out there in that black passageway. "Is there . . . ?"

Quiet now. Surely it had been only her imagination. Elizabeth took up her sewing again.

Captain Jouenne . . .

Why had she thought on him now? Captain Jouenne, the prosecutor in most of the trials of the women incendiaries, a short, squat, dark, arrogant Frenchman, nothing distinguished about him. You could see his double a thousand times on any given day on any Paris street. Pencil-thin mustache, dark uneasy Gallic eyes, a paragon of mediocrity on whom Fate had played the cruelest trick of all, had somehow given him the airs and illusions of superiority.

She could see him still so clearly, strutting between the bench and the prisoners' dock, could still hear that offensive voice. ". . . these women are moral monstrosities, more dangerous than the most dangerous man," Captain Jouenne had raved, playing broadly to the all-male tribunal and the all-male bench, as well as the all-male gallery. "The emancipation of women has been preached by scholars, and look where we are led by all these dangerous Utopias. Have they not held out to all these wretched creatures bright prospects, incredible chimeras: women judges, women as members of the bar! Yes, women lawyers, deputies perhaps, and for all we know, generals of the army! Certainly, faced with these miserable aberrations, we must believe we are dreaming. . . ."

Then she could remember no more and stood abruptly and knew now what she had known then, what was clear to all with half an inclination to see, that what Captain Jouenne was putting on trial was the idea of education for women. Again, unaware that her needlework had now joined Eugenie's on the dirty floor and, under the duress of her recent recall, she strode as far as the limited cell would permit—about eight feet—until her feverish forehead was pressed against the cool bricks.

It seemed so long ago, yet the fury was still so fresh.

Beware the danger of a revolution which is not permitted to happen.

She still remembered the words of Louise Michel. Resting her forehead against the wall, she caught a sudden glimpse of the patchwork quilt that had been her life. She'd started in the common cell of Newgate Prison in London. Would it end as it had begun, in a cell in a French prison?

Abruptly she scolded herself for her morose thoughts. What nonsense to consider her life ending! She was in her prime and, most important, alive with purpose. Hadn't Louise Michel told her to wait in London? Word would come to her there about the movement. She would be one of the few on the "outside," free, as it were, to continue the cause while awaiting Louise's release.

She turned away from the wall as though she'd found the courage in that one thought to face the next hour. How good it would be to see certain people! Lovable old Alex Aldwell, and even Aslam, though he bore the characteristic and dangerous drive of John, and in a curious way she now was tired of driven people.

This last thought caused her to pause. She looked intently down on the table and small circle of light, seeing neither table nor light nor sewing box nor shears, seeing instead one face that once she had loved more dearly than any other in the world. John.

Would she find the time and energy, she wondered, to journey to Eden Point? She was certain he was still there, flourishing no doubt. John had a singular talent for flourishing.

She began effortlessly to wrap a single pink thread around and around her finger, seeing neither thread nor finger, seeing nothing that belonged to this foreign and brutal French world, seeing instead a clear and moving progression of the extraordinary events that had bound her life inextricably with that of John Murrey Eden.

Suddenly on the opposite side of the cell Eugenie gave a loud snore that sounded like the neighing of a horse.

Early morning now. It had the feel of early morning, a dead heaviness in the air, like a universal fatigue.

John. . . . The young man she'd helped to raise.

She thought the name so slyly, as though she were trying to fool herself. Years ago she'd made a melodramatic exit from Eden Castle, vowing, along with Richard and the others, never to return.

John Murrey Eden. . . . Like a son.

Abruptly she stood, enjoying a curious flow of energy at the mere thought of the name. He *was* remarkable, not in the same ways his father had been, but in different ways.

Noise again. Where was it coming from? Nothing mysterious about it now, boots moving heavily without fear of discovery or need for concealment.

"Eugenie, wake up," Elizabeth whispered, nudging the silly sleeping girl harder than ever. "Eugenie, please . . ."

They were coming closer, the sound of those boots, more than a single pair she was certain, at least two, maybe . . .

"Eugenie . . ."

She spoke the name aloud, and the sound of her own voice jarred her back to a degree of good sense. Why was she afraid? The cell door was locked, the key tucked safely inside the mug on the small table. She reached for the mug and knocked it rolling on the floor.

"Eugenie!"

She heard the hysteria in her voice. There was nothing she could do in such a state. *Be calm.* It could just be guards moving from one area of the prison to . . .

Where was the key?

Hurriedly she lifted her skirts and pressed her feet into the search, swinging them in wide arcs across the floor, hoping to hear the telltale rattle of a piece of metal. It was here; she knew it. It had always been here, concealed safely either by herself or by Eugenie. All that she had to do was . . .

"Eugenie, please wake up."

Fear and confusion mounting, she went down on one knee and reached under the table into the darkest corner, her fingers tearing at the emptiness, moving out in all directions.

"Eugenie, please help . . ."

As she looked up in entreaty, she saw the dull-eyed girl looking directly down on her, eyes wide open, her expression noncommittal, though Elizabeth could not see one trace of sleep.

"Eugenie, the key," Elizabeth begged, still bewildered by the girl's placidity. Couldn't she hear the approaching threat?

"The key, Eugenie, Do you have . . . ?"

The question incomplete, she saw the girl staring at the empty darkness beyond the bars, which were no longer empty.

Evolving out of that darkness were two duplications of every communer's nightmare, the dark blue, red-splotched uniform of the soldiers. Fédérés, these two like all the others, curiously faceless beneath the square-brimmed and perching little blue hats—monkey-grinder hats, Louise Michel had called them.

Still on one knee searching for the key, Elizabeth looked up again at Eugenie's curious behavior. Generally given to groundless hysteria, the girl now seemed to be a model of quiet courage.

"Eugenie . . ."

Too late. Elizabeth saw something matching between the unnatural calm on Eugenie's face and the same calm on the two soldiers, who simply stood on the other side of the bars, two fixed images staring blandly in, while Elizabeth, the only pocket of movement in the cell, continued to search for the key, even though she knew now that she would never find it.

"Madame?"

The male voice cut through the silent confusion and was followed by a question which Elizabeth didn't understand and which was all the more terrifying because she understood all too well the meaning and the message, and looked slowly up and saw one soldier holding up the key for her inspection, holding it gingerly, as though it were hot or wet or soiled.

Betrayal? Why? What had she ever done to Eugenie Retiffe except befriend her when no one else would? She might have found the courage to ask this question if there had been time. But now she heard the key grating in the lock and saw Eugenie gathering up her cloak beneath which was her valise, packed and bulging. Obviously in exchange for the key, a bargain had been struck.

As the cell door swung open, Elizabeth tried once more to find the breath and courage to address the silly young girl. Didn't she know these men were not to be trusted?

"Eugenie, be careful," she called out as the girl slipped easily past the two soldiers, who allowed her to pass without offering the least resistance.

For just a second the girl looked back at her, and Elizabeth thought she saw a faint look of apology on her face.

Well, then, what business did she have with these two, who now stood inside the cell, the door closed and locked behind them, grinning down on her with an expression she'd seen before on male faces.

"What . . . do you want?" she asked, growing strangely calm when

86

confronted with this ancient threat. "Surely there are younger, fresher Frenchwomen in La Rochelle." She smiled, trying reason, knowing it would fail. She stood beside the low table, using it for support against the tidal waves of revulsion which were beginning to sweep over her.

No!

Beware the danger of a revolution which is not permitted to happen.

She'd been through this too often before. The two soldiers resembled the strutting peacock Captain Jouenne, as one was loosening the tight gold collar around his neck. Jouenne used to do that near the end of a day of lengthy testimony.

"Please," she whispered, seeing the expressions on their faces alter to something more threatening. The one on her left began to move quietly into position behind her, thus shattering her focus. She couldn't keep her eyes on both of them.

"What did you promise Eugenie in exchange for the key?" ske asked quickly, moving back from both men, the three of them now forming a triangle. If she could get them talking, she might stand a chance.

But either they didn't understand her any more than she understood them or their time here was limited. She sensed the one behind moving down on her, and then she felt something coarse and knotted pulled back between her teeth, distorting her mouth, causing her to gag briefly, and for a few moments longer she struggled, although she knew it was useless, as all similar struggles had been useless. She had never won this battle, nor had any woman.

So, although she knew the battle was lost, had been lost before it had ever commenced, nonetheless she struggled mightily, feeling herself being drawn backward and down, her arms pulled over her head, a rapid and excited exchange taking place between the two soliders, one giving instructions, the other following, while she found herself flattened on the cool floor, knowing what was ahead for her, knowing there was nothing she could do to alter it in any way, hoping only that it would not be accompanied by brutality and torture as so often it was. Morley Johnson had beaten her senseless first. And the first time it happened, at fourteen, the fat old magistrate had been amused by her fear as he'd held a poker hot from the fire close to her breasts.

Then suddenly the struggle was over. She moved away from the remembered horrors of the past to the new horrors of the present and felt twin pains running the length of her arms and was aware that the soldier behind her was standing on her arms, his boots pinching, while he leaned over her, upside down and smiling. Gathering the two sides of her bodice, one in each hand, with one effort he ripped it open well beyond her waist, where, laughing, the second soldier grabbed for the two ends and tore it the rest of the way. The same was done to her petticoat, until she lay bared before them and saw their sporting ardor change to something else, something more intense, as for several moments they stared down at her, their hands moving over their own garments independent of their eyes, fingers nervously fumbling with buttons and belt buckles, an occasional low comment greeted with a nod, while she closed her eyes and thought of the women, many her friends, who had been massacred on the barricades by men in uniforms identical to these, summary executions without benefit of trial or magistrate.

As knees roughly forced her legs apart, she looked above and saw the second soldier grinning down on her.

Then the assault was launched, body violated, soul plundered, pain accompanying the rough penetration, hands uninvited moving over all aspects of her body, while she, with head pressed back, tried to endure and remain intact, for there would be work to be done after it was over.

As the rhythm of the attack increased, the soldier standing on her arms urged his compatriot on by putting new pressure on her wrists. The hobnail boots were cutting into her flesh, which in a way was a blessed distraction.

Only once did she cry out, and it was her cry that seemed to satisfy him, and he shuddered heavily and slowly withdrew and wordlessly the two changed places and the second attack was under way with no word spoken, merely a satisfied weariness on the part of the first and an eager enthusiasm on the part of the second, and for the second time Elizabeth felt the coolness of air rush across her body, until it was covered by the soldier.

Only six months, and she'd be home.

John . . .

The pain was increasing. Dear God, help . . .

Then, when she didn't think she could endure, she felt the soldier go limp atop her and heard a curious sound above her, applause, and a delighted male laugh, and looked up to see the first soldier applauding the performance of the second. She felt the incredible weight leave her body, felt the despicable sticky moisture between her legs, felt the sensation of hands and teeth still upon her, and, most welcome of all, felt the pressure leave her arms as both men exchanged comments, grinning, though neither looked down on her once, not in condemnation, not in pleasure. She had simply served as an inanimate receptacle, something used and now discarded.

They moved leisurely about her, stepping over her as though someone had carelessly left a piece of refuse in their path.

They stood with their backs to her now, only the low table separating them, restoring their garments, talking quietly between themselves, their conversation, whatever its nature, frequently punctuated with a low guttural laugh.

After it was over, there would be work to be done.

Could she stand? She had to. Only those capable of standing could man the barricades; Louise Michel had said so. The dark blue uniforms were coming again . . .

Stand up!

Slowly she drew herself forward and onto her knees.

Hurry!

Time was always of the essence. *The enemy must not be allowed to anticipate your next move.*

She stumbled once on her torn dress, and was certain the two would turn and see her. But neither did, so engrossed were they in their low conversation, the restoration of endless gold buttons on their tunics.

Leaning heavily on the wall for support, she raised herself all the way up, impervious to the torn dress. Before her she saw the wicker sewing box which the general had given to her for the purpose of embroidering his daughter's trousseau. And there, next to the basket, the sharp long shears.

She did not discriminate. She was well beyond the ability to pick one and reject the other. She simply followed Louise Michel's instructions. She held her weapon steady, upraised in her right hand, for her left had been injured in some way by the hobnail boots, and she saw two blue-coated backs before her and she simply moved on the nearest and added strength to her weapon by stumbling on the hem of the torn dress as she brought the shears down, and felt the good resistance of a penetration, the sharp blades going the length of the back with her fall, cutting a swath through fabric and flesh, and before she fell to one side she heard the joyous music of a man's scream of agony, and saw a wake of glistening red spread out over the torn back and, as she fell, she saw him fall in the opposite direction, the shears still protruding from his back.

She struck her head on the stone floor as she went down, but unfortunately the blow wasn't enough to render her unconscious, and though stunned, she was fully aware of the shocked and angry face now glaring down on her, and she knew in that moment that it was over for Elizabeth Eden.

She tried for a few sorrowful moments to return the stare of the man standing over her. But then he spit on her, and as she tried to wipe the slime from her face, she felt a displacement of air as he drew his boot back and brought it forward with all his strength against the side of her head, the force of the blow causing her neck to crack, her ears to ring, and leaving her in a semi-black world, aware only that she would never see John again, or Mary, or Richard, or Eden.

Beware the dangers of a revolution which is not permitted to happen.

For her the battle was over. Shortly she would be free to go and find Edward Eden, and that was a moment she joyously anticipated. The only time this world had made any sense to her had been in those golden days when she had lived with Edward.

Then, though unschooled and untutored, she had understood everything. . . .

Eden Castle
July 28, 1874

Indulging in the classic petulance which he felt was an invalid's right, John slumped beneath the lap robe in the chair on the headland and tried not to listen to the woman's voice, though it was pleasing enough. It was her choice of reading matter which had plagued him for the past two weeks, since she'd first decided that both his soul and his body needed a warming light.

What in the hell that was supposed to mean, he had no idea. She'd said it often enough, though not once had she ever stopped to explain it. And not that he'd ever asked . . .

" 'Why, O Lord, do You stand far off?' "

Her voice drew him back with the curious question. Had she read it or spoken it aloud from her heart? He glanced slyly to his left and saw her sitting primly on one of the stone benches which his grandfather had arranged on the length of the headland.

This woman had bathed, combed, changed, and fed him for a lost number of days. Suddenly the realization gave him pause. How intimately those small hands supporting that dog-eared Bible had moved over him. The second realization was even more astonishing than the first. No other woman in his entire life had ever done for him what this woman had done.

As she continued to read from the small black leather Bible, he abandoned his train of thought and let his mind drift.

Harriet dead . . .

Suddenly the droning voice fell silent. "Are you in discomfort, Mr. Eden?" she asked gently.

He shook his head, embarrassed. When would the realization cease to hurt? Harriet dead . . .

Either she didn't see the slight shake of his head or else she was determined to force him into speech. "I beg your pardon?" she inquired politely, and from the downward angle of his vision he could only see the brilliant green grass and the dusty hem of her dark blue dress.

Again he shook his head, feeling embarrassed and childlike before her. She was damned self-possessed for a woman, he'd give her that much. He'd seen her with old Bates and his motley crew. She kept most of them on a short string, without them even knowing it.

"It would help, Mr. Eden," came the soft voice on his left, "if you used speech more often. Your impairment will never get better until you try."

Angered by the accusation of impairment, he almost responded but caught himself in time, knowing that his anger had been her goal, and now he refused to give her that satisfaction.

Instead he stared straight ahead out over the channel, which was an almost unbelievable shade of blue on this mild July afternoon. Abruptly he closed his eyes. Her voice resumed its reading.

" 'Why, O Lord, do you stand far off? Why do You hide Yourself in time of trouble?' "

Elizabeth?

When would Elizabeth come home? He needed someone who understood him. Not a stranger. Aldwell had been here . . . when? Surely there had been time to get a message to Paris by now.

Aldwell . . . Bastard. John had seen clearly the way Aldwell had looked down on him. Finished. That's what his expression had said. John Murrey Eden finished.

Not that he would have wanted to return to London. He wasn't ready for London yet, though he was beginning to experience an increasing sense of urgency. Alex Aldwell, though a disappointment, wasn't his main concern. Aslam held that unique position.

" 'He boasts of the cravings of his heart, He blesses the greedy and reviles the Lord . . .' "

Oh God, would she never cease? Would he be forced to speak in an attempt to quiet her?

"When . . . Aldwell return?"

The sound of his voice, impaired and halting, intersecting her fluid one, seemed to startle them both. She looked up and blinked, as did he.

"Mr. Aldwell?" she repeated, trying to make the transition. "I'm afraid he didn't say. If you wish, I can send a messenger—"

Quickly he shook his head. He didn't want Aldwell to think he needed him. But a man in attendance would be a pleasant change.

"I know how difficult it is, Mr. Eden. This waiting, I mean," she said quietly, and out of the corner of his eye he saw her stretch in a becoming way, both hands planted on her hips near the small of her back, neck extended, the gesture lifting her breasts. She wasn't beautiful—not by conventional definition. But she *was* fascinating to watch, her self-assurance, her confidence.

Without warning, she looked up, as though embarrassed by his gaze. "I'm . . . s-sorry," she murmured, and glanced down and saw the Bible in her hand and held it up, as though it were a splendid idea. "Shall I read?"

91

"No."

Confronted with his blunt rejection, she foundered, then slowly lowered the Bible back to her lap and sat like a child chastised.

"Would you like to exercise?" she asked a moment later, her face once again flushed with the excitement of a new idea.

To that hideous suggestion he said a second resounding, "No."

If given his choice between the Psalms and exercise, he'd choose the former.

"It would be good for you," she said, obviously unaware of the depth of his loathing. "I could call Bates and Sam Oden . . ."

He was certain she could. The whole ridiculous home guard lounged less than fifty feet away in a patch of sweet fragrant clover—that is to say that everyone lounged except the madman himself, Bates, who stood at a semistiff angle, his gaunt face taut with condemnation of everything he saw, the two of them primarily, but also such gross offenders as the green grass, the brilliant sun, and the lace of whitecaps on the channel.

In a very definite way John knew precisely what was making old Bates so antagonistic: John himself—for allowing the willful destruction of the world of Eden, the rarefied world of company and festivals and comings and goings, of master and servant. When John failed to keep his world intact, he simultaneously destroyed old Bates's world, for the latter could not exist without the former.

Ostensibly now—at least according to Bates himself—they had agreed to Mr. Aldwell's terms because they didn't want to let the "prisoner" out of their sight.

"What's he paying them?" he asked suddenly.

"Paying them?" Susan parroted, bewildered, obviously having difficulty following the turns of his mind.

He looked toward the small knot of men lounging on sweet clover. Apparently—though she now understood the question—she still was at a loss to provide him with an answer. "I . . . don't know, Mr. Eden," she confessed, seated straighter on the bench. "I believe money did change hands, but how much, I . . ."

Plenty, he was certain of that—for two reasons. One: Alex was always good at putting men on the payroll. It had been a bone of contention with them in the past. Then, two: there was the matter of Bates himself. John, if no one else, knew him for what he was, a rigid and unbending but honorable man who had agreed to sell him a portion of his soul. Nothing new there. Men sold their souls, either in part or whole, every day, then conveniently forgot about the transaction. But something in Bates would not let him forget, and John found himself now gazing at the old man with a degree of admiration. A man *should* be angry when he parts with his soul.

"Shall I call Mr. Bates for you, Mr. Eden?" she offered now. "Perhaps he can—"

"No."

Tired of turning his head first in one direction, then the other, he slumped deeper beneath the lap robe and brooded out over the channel. In a way, and in spite of everything, the moment was peaceful, just her silent presence and the good fragrant day and the high warm sun and a curious though delightful sense of no past, no present, no future.

"Bates, stay close," John muttered as they approached the gatehouse and the rocking motion of his chair began to take a toll. His back ached, his head ached, his dead left leg had chosen this moment to come briefly, painfully to life, and now a hot shooting pain was running the length of his body, commencing at a point in his calf and shooting all the way up to the base of his skull.

Also he was aware of the stunned expression on the old pencil of a man walking close beside him. "I . . . beg . . . your pardon, sir?" came the chilly inquiry. What gave John hope was the almost reflexive "sir" that appeared on the end of the taut query and seemed to soften it all.

"I said, 'Stay close, please.' " John repeated.

"Stay . . . close?" he heard Bates repeat, the bafflement on his face extending to his voice. "Why, sir?"

There it was again, that reassuring "sir," and John knew precisely what it meant and how to exploit it. "Because she's driving me crazy, that female is," John lied, knowing that it was probably the only explanation to which Bates would relate.

Right on target. John heard the old man snicker, a good male sound of derision, and a moment later he was joined by Sam Oden and Tom Babcock, the only two within hearing distance. The others had run ahead to throw open the narrow gatehouse doors.

"It's rumored in the village," Sam Oden said conspiratorially, "that Susan Mantle will heal your body and take your soul for payment. If you're not careful, that is."

"Stay . . . close, Bates," John repeated, cursing his sluggish tongue for forcing him to speak with all the fluidity of a village idiot. "I want . . . you . . . tend me," he added, pleased to see that while his tongue might be sluggish, his mind was not.

He had no use for Bates as an enemy. But he had a hundred uses for him as an ally. And he suspected that down deep, Bates felt the same.

"I must ask you to repeat what you last said, sir," Bates demanded, sniffing at the air with a frown, as though in some way he found it lacking.

Despite the circumstances of the moment, John loved that arrogance and imperiousness. In fact, if the truth were known, it was for those twin characteristics that he'd paid a king's ransom for Bates in the first place.

"All right," John sighed with an air of strained patience. "I . . . want you to tend me," he repeated, and abruptly ducked his head, embarrassed by his sluggish tongue and lips.

"Tend you?" Bates repeated. "I . . . don't understand . . ."

"How much clearer need I . . . ?" Drawn to anger in a very short time, John sat back in the chair and tried to control his impatience.

Apparently the request at last registered, though Bates's face still was a mask of bewilderment. "I am not a man's man," he said archly, and drew himself up. "I am a butler."

"I know that," John snapped. "I'll see to it that Aldwell provides you with a purse for your . . . effort."

There! Thank God. One complete sentence. He could do it; he just needed practice.

His impatience softened by a brief sense of accomplishment, he looked up, wondering what in the hell more needed to be said. They understood each other better than this. Bates had already sold him a portion of his soul. What matter another small piece?

"Come on, Bates," he urged now. "What do you say?"

For a moment nothing moved on the thin old face. His eyes seemed to become completely fixed and lifeless. Then, through pursed lips held so rigid that it was a miracle words could escape at all, the old man spoke.

"I say to you, Mr. Eden, that you are an insane man, the devil incarnate, and a half-dead man as well. Tend you? I would sooner tend a basketful of vipers. It would be far the safer undertaking, and if I were the last man left standing on this earth and you were to approach starving, naked, and dying of thirst, I would not so much as lift this little finger to ease your pain."

John blinked up. It was going to be a bit more difficult than he had imagined.

"What am I asking, Bates, that is so . . . demanding? I thought my health was of paramount importance to you."

The release of hate seemed to provide the old man with a degree of relief. In fact, now he even deigned to smile. "Your health is of paramount importance to me," he confirmed, inserting one hand in his pocket, an unprecedented gesture for that normally ramrod-straight man, "but I'm not certain that you fully understand your position here, sir."

"Explain it to me," John demanded, still reassured by the ever-occurring "sir."

"Gladly," Bates replied, and waited until the two men who had been carrying John's chair settled in the tall grass, clearly as fascinated as John by the explanation to come.

When all was quiet, save for the soft whistling wind and a single cartwheeling gull, Bates stepped back and commenced to speak. "Though your manner and attitude seem to deny it, sir, a woman is dead, was found dead in your arms in a singularly grim tableau which would have brought the full weight of the law crashing down on our poor lesser heads—"

"She did not die there," John muttered, head down, cursing the old bastard for inflicting such pain of memory.

"I beg your pardon, sir?"

"I said, 'She did not die there,' " John shouted. "She was dead when I found her."

"Where was that, sir?"

"In her chambers."

"How did she die?"

"I don't know."

"But she was dead when you found her?"

"I said so, didn't I?"

Precisely what had triggered the weakness, he had no idea. The thought of Harriet dead, all the remembered sorrow, combined with the gaping men who now had been joined by the woman coming softly up behind his chair—curious at first, then stunned into silence, as were the men, by the spectacle with which John was providing them.

"What . . . happened?" he heard a gentle female voice inquire from behind.

"He asked me to . . . tend him," Bates repeated, and John thought his voice sounded less imperious now.

"Tend him?"

"I don't know, ma'am. He never explained . . ."

There was another moment's silence, during which John enjoyed the unique sensation of standing outside himself, looking down on the ill man along with everyone else. Surely, surrounded by all these good Christian hearts, one at least could find it within himself to forgive him.

Then one did, though it was a most surprising "one" and John wasn't absolutely certain that forgiveness was the motive.

"I'll tend him, miss," old Bates volunteered now. "He needs a man. But I want it clearly understood by all, that as soon as his health improves, I am personally escorting him to Exeter. Would you ask him if he understands that?"

"Why don't you ask him yourself, Bates?"

Oh, she was a cool one, that one was, who healed bodies in exchange for souls.

"I said I'd tend you, Mr. Eden, sir, if you wish. But you must understand my intentions. As soon as you are able, we will go to Exeter; is that clear?"

Yes, John understood all too well. Further, he understood that such a journey would never take place.

"Did you hear me, Mr. Eden?"

Then it was John's turn. Slowly he lifted his head. "Thank you," he murmured, then added brokenly, ". . . forever in your debt . . ."

Even the wind seemed to fall silent out of respect and pity and attention.

Without looking up, he said to the nurse, "Would it be possible, Miss Mantle, to accommodate all these good men inside the castle? It would be very convenient for them, closer than Mortemouth. Plenty of rooms, and I hate to think of them chilled and hungry."

For a moment he wasn't certain if anyone had heard or understood. On either side out of the corner of his eyes he saw Sam Oden and the other giant rising slowly to their feet, their gaze fixed on John with a distinct air of disbelief.

Bates, as always, was chief spokesman for their confusion. "We . . . don't understand, sir," he stammered, though John suspected that he understood all too well.

"Move into . . . castle," John repeated, still not looking directly at any of them. He didn't have to. He knew very well the thoughts spiraling through old Sam Oden's head, and those very same thoughts would be duplicated by the other men from Mortemouth. Never in their wildest dreams had they ever entertained the notion that one day they would inhabit Eden Castle. Eden Castle was, at best, the place where—if one was very lucky—one went into service.

"Of course," John murmured weakly, as though on the verge of denying his own idea, "if it's asking too much, please . . ."

"You mean you want the men to move in, sir?" Bates prodded further, apparently not understanding at all.

John nodded. "More . . . convenient . . . for them . . . more comfortable . . ."

Then all understood and were stunned into silence. John's muscles were beginning to grow stiff. He needed to move, stand, walk, if he was to function again at all, but he did not relish using a frail woman as a crutch. No, the presence of men in the castle would be a help to John, if no one else.

"It would mean extra work," the nurse contributed with typical practicality.

"Hire . . . help," John stammered.

"Oh, not necessary, sir," Bates soothed. "These are good men, accustomed to doing their share. They'll pitch in."

Incredible! Was this the same man who only a few minutes earlier had condemned John and dismissed him as being the devil?

"Then it's settled?" John smiled wanly and for the first time looked up at them all, an attentive audience.

"Settled, sir." Bates nodded.

As Sam and Tom Babcock moved into position beside the chair, Bates held up a restraining hand. "No," he ordered and, shocked, John looked up.

"Mr. Eden will walk back into his castle," Bates pronounced. "Come." He gestured to the two men who had carried the chair thus far. "Lift him to his feet."

"Wait a minute," John protested vigorously, not particularly enjoying this turn of events. He was incapable of walking anyplace. Didn't they all know that?

"All right, heave!" Bates ordered, and before John knew what had happened, even before he could protest, he felt himself leave the confinement of the chair, felt himself dangle for a moment between the twin towers of Sam Oden and Tom Babcock, felt their generous strength supporting both his arms, and looked down, and to his mortification saw the bathrobe fallen open, revealing his bare knees.

"Perhaps we should postpone the first walking lesson until Mr. Eden is more appropriately garbed," Miss Mantle interjected. "Also, I think that one of Eden's endless corridors would be a more reliable setting than this bumpy terrain."

Bless her, John thought, and felt the men cover him carefully and ease him back down into the chair.

He needed clothes. Bates could find them someplace in the castle. He needed to move and exercise the phantom leg. Bates would help him along one of Eden's "endless corridors," as the woman had put it.

In short, he needed to become whole again. There were tasks yet ahead of him, and the thought of surrender was intolerable.

"Select any chamber you wish," he called out to the men who moved beside him. "And we'll open the Grand Dining Hall," he exclaimed to Miss Mantle, who was walking beside him. "It will be good to see it in use again. And hire all the kitchen help you need. I don't want you spending all your time in that miserable kitchen."

The more he talked, the better he felt. It was over, then, this long night. Anything would be better than the half-death of the past, and until his real family came to their senses and returned to his sheltering wing, then this one would serve.

"What are you staring at?" he asked of Miss Mantle, who gazed down on him with a curious expression.

"There's color in your cheeks," she said in a marveling tone.

La Rochelle
House of Detention,
Paris, France
September 26, 1874

Still in a state of stunned shock, Elizabeth glanced up at the single burned-down candle and signed what she knew would be her last letter to John, and allowed her signature to dry without benefit of sand, staring at the name as though it belonged to someone else, as though someone else were seated in this cold narrow cell in the bowels of La Rochelle House of Detention under sentence of death for the stabbing murder of Lieutenant Jean Dauguet.

"My Father Who art . . ." she murmured quickly, and fought against the rising fear and wished she weren't alone. Even Eugenie Retiffe would be welcome company on this cold September night in this wretched place.

And it wasn't as if it would all be shortly ended. The French magistrate had ordered that her sentence of death by firing squad be preceded by two months' confinement in the dungeons of La Rochelle. To those women of the communes who had faced the firing squad before her—they had said what a blessing death was after the dungeons.

Now, at the conclusion of the letter that had left her drained, she was aware for the first time that her fingers were numb. There was no feeling whatsoever halfway up the palms of her hands. Quickly she tucked them beneath her arms in search of body heat and at the same time looked down on her evening's work.

Letters. Last letters—although she suspected that she would write "last letters" again, as she'd written them twice before. She was always thinking of something else she wanted to say, first to Mary and Burke in far-off America. To Richard in Kent she had written long paragraphs on this peculiar matter of forgiveness. Neither John nor Richard would know any true peace on this earth until one or both found it in their hearts to forgive.

97

Abruptly she stood from the low table. Why was she doing this? Then slowly she sat back down again and clung to the edge. Two months to think about it, to envision it. No more! And it wasn't as though she was without hope. Only last night she'd found a crudely penned note pushed beneath her cell dooor. "Louise Michel does not despair," it had said simply. Most of the night she had lain awake trying to understand it, thinking that another message might be delivered.

But nothing more had come, and in this enclosed, low-ceilinged cell she never saw her guards. There was a small door cut into the bottom of the larger one, and through this opening each night was shoved the sustenance of the day. At first she hadn't been able to eat it. In the semi-dark of one candle she could scarcely see it, which had been a blessing, but still there was the odor.

Don't think about it, she warned herself sternly, and gathered up the letters she'd written this night, another to Mary and Burke in America—she'd promised them to come for the birth of their firstborn—another promise she'd have to break, and a letter to Richard addressed to Forbes Hall in Kent, although God alone knew if he was still there. And last, the letter to John which she had just completed, entreating him to mend the chasms which had sprung up between all members of this family.

Now she stared at the candle burning steadily toward its end and wished she were just starting the day again, her allotment of one fresh candle just passed through the small door. Since there were no windows, no light source at all, the empty designations of night and day held no meaning. Therefore she was tempted to burn the candle continuously, and in the beginning had done so, until she'd realized that, burning steadily, the candle had limited life. After a few days of experimenting, she'd discovered that it was far preferable to be in blackness for shorter, though more frequent, intervals than to watch the candle burn consistently and know the length of the darkness that was yet ahead of her.

It was her guess now that she had about two minutes of light left. No matter. She was through writing for the evening. And she was tired—of everything, of thinking, of dreading, of missing, of being cold and hungry, and so terribly tired of being alone.

Louise Michel does not despair.

Then neither would she, though she knew that to be only a false show of bravado. Never in her life had she been so afraid.

At that moment the candle burned out. Left in total darkness, she clasped her hands before her and bowed her head and closed her eyes. And prayed.

Eden Point
October 15, 1874

Amazed at the miracle that had taken place in just three short months, Alex lifted his glass of port to John in belated but heartfelt tribute. He hoped the others about the table forgave him this moment's intimacy.

"To you, John," he said to the top of the head of the brooding man at the end of the table. "To Eden's very own phoenix."

Susan Mantle smiled and murmured, "Yes," directly across from him, and in her eyes Alex saw fatigue and a good sense of accomplishment. The remarkable woman *had* worked a miracle, though earlier she'd denied all credit, all responsibility, crediting only John and his will.

"What's a phoenix?" Tom Babcock asked, seated next to Miss Mantle.

All at once the brooding man at the end of the table lifted his head and looked directly at Tom. He'd been toying with his fork with his right hand—Alex had observed that he seldom used his left—and now he tossed that fork with a clatter onto his plate. "A phoenix, Tom," he began, his voice low, the speech slightly slowed, as though he were trying very hard not to make a mistake, "is a half-witted bird who doesn't know when to stop rising from his own great pile of ashes."

The cynicism settled heavily over everyone at table, and in the quiet interim Alex once again looked with astonishment upon this motley collection of humanity, all of whom apparently had been invited by someone in authority to sit and eat at the Eden table.

Directly across from him was the little nurse with the will which almost matched John's. Alex wondered if John would ever know the size of his debt to her. He doubted it.

And farther down he saw—by God, no one in London would believe this—Bates seated *at table* in the Grand Dining Hall, eating with the

99

company as though all vestiges of butler had been eradicated, the divisions of a lifetime removed in a few short months.

But the greatest change of all, he was certain, was John himself. Incredible! Alex thought, leaning back in his chair, watching John still speaking with Tom. As he watched, Alex tried to find a trace of the terribly ill man he'd left here—for dead—less than three months ago.

Leaner, this John was, a bit bony about the neck. The shirt collar hung too loose and the line of the jaw was a bit too sharp. The hair was longer, the beard untended and flecked with gray, and there was the matter of the left arm, which remained in hiding beneath the table. And of course the most obvious difference of all between the old John and this new facsimile was the silver-topped black ebony walking stick that rested against the back of his chair and was pressed into use whenever John moved, supplying the impaired left leg with support.

Still, in spite of all this, the recovery had been miraculous, and now it would be a privilege to escort this "phoenix" back to London, if for no other reason than to see the expressions on certain faces who had hoped that death at least would be a worthy adversary for John Murrey Eden.

Also Alex was relieved to find a relatively hale and hearty John for another and sadder reason. It was only a matter of time before Alex would have to reveal the true nature of this return visit, that letters had gone out to Elizabeth in Paris, to Mary in America, to Richard in Kent, over three months ago, and follow-up letters had gone out six weeks ago, and thus far no one had deigned to reply to the news of John's serious illness, and certainly no one had come rushing home.

It was Alex's opinion—and Aslam had agreed—that the first family function which might conceivably draw them back would be John's funeral. Of course, he had no intention of putting it in those harsh terms. It would serve no purpose. But if John was still anticipating a warm and all-forgiving family reunion, then he'd better disavow himself of the foolish dream, because it wasn't going to happen.

Abruptly Alex looked up from his thoughts to see Mrs. O'Donnell, the newly hired cook, offering him the decanter of port. "No, please. I've had plenty, and thank you," he murmured, sensing his moment approaching. John knew—if no one else at table knew—that Alex had not journeyed all this way for a glass of port.

"I do wish to extend my compliments to the cook, however," Alex went on, hoping to postpone the set of urgent questions he saw forming on John's face. "How long has Mortemouth been concealing a gem such as yourself?" Alex smiled, not necessarily trying to extend the conversation but curious about the woman's origins. Her cooking did not exhibit the simplicity of a country woman. She knew what all the spices were and used them with the hand of an artist.

"Oh, I'm not from Mortemouth, sir," Mrs. O'Donnell answered, clearly nervous that the focus of attention had unhappily fallen on her. "Oh, not that it ain't a pretty little village," she added hurriedly to the men from Mortemouth seated around her, "it's just that . . ." Her embarrassment vaulted; her voice drifted.

John sat up, taking notice. "Tell us where you *are* from, Mrs. O'Donnell," he demanded, a tone in his voice which seemed to say that as long as the subject had been launched, let's see it through.

For a moment the focus slid down the table and landed heavily on the woman. Alex was sorry for that. He'd simply intended to pay her a well-earned compliment.

Then: "Ireland," she said, and the silence around the table grew heavy.

Ireland. John's two sons had been spirited off to Ireland four years ago.

"Where in Ireland?" John demanded, and sat up at table and reached behind for his walking stick as though he must make ready to move.

For a moment Mrs. O'Donnell hesitated. She appeared to glance nervously about the table. "Dublin, sir," she said at last, and bowed her head at the end of the confession and began to fold and refold her napkin, the second glass of port forgotten.

Again Miss Mantle came to the rescue. "And I can assure you she is a gift from God." The woman smiled, trying to send comfort to the far end of the table, where it was sorely needed.

Grateful, Alex felt the tension was ready to ease in all quarters save one, and that was the man still brooding down the table in the direction of Rose O'Donnell.

"If you are from Dublin, Mrs. O'Donnell, what are you doing on the North Devon coast?" John asked, stroking the silver head of his walking stick.

"Me . . . husband," Rose O'Donnell stammered, ". . . died. I couldn't pay the landlord and couldn't find me no job. So I thought I'd go to London, where I'd heard all things were possible. But the Lord led me here and that kind lady took me in and I'm not sure where I am, sir, or how long me good fortune will last, but I get down on me knees every night and thank God for it, and for you."

If the tension about the table had been heavy before, now it was merely paralyzing. The man who had forced the unpleasant confession seemed to be suffering the most.

"I'm . . . sorry," John muttered, grasping the walking stick, though he was still seated. "I quite honestly don't remember your arrival."

"I know sir. It's as Miss Mantle says, you have your own cross—"

"Well, welcome to Eden," he said gruffly, cutting off her expression of gratitude and sympathy and looking nervously around as though he expected someone to get him out of this awkward predicament.

And they did. Or rather she did, Miss Mantle, who stood abruptly and began to gather up the scattered cutlery. "To work," she announced broadly, as though extending the advice to everyone. And accordingly the men stood up with such speed that their chairs scraped noisily on the floor. They conferred briefly with Mr. Bates for a moment, then started off at a brisk pace toward the door.

"Sorry we have no cigars, Mr. Aldwell," Miss Mantle apologized, "but I wouldn't let you smoke them in the company of Mr. Eden . . ."

Alex smiled and nodded. "Never touch them," he lied.

Then she was gone, hoisting the heavy tray of dishes with only slight visible effort, following after Rose O'Donnell, who had just left the Grand Dining Hall.

As the woman's heels sent back an efficient click, Alex saw John grasp the walking stick with even more strength, that ominous preoccupied

101

brooding expression very much in evidence on his face. As soon as she eased the door closed behind her, John gave in to a relatively quiet explosion.

"Women!" he muttered, as though he knew she was still outside and thus within earshot. "If it hadn't been for that noble gentleman there," he said, indicating the scarecrow Bates, who now sat conspicuously alone at the far end of the table, "she would have driven me into my grave by now."

Alex disagreed. "I would say that she has done an admirable job of keeping you out of your grave."

To this comment John said nothing. "Amuse yourself for a moment, Aldwell," he snapped, and started away from the table with a pronounced limp, leaning heavily on the walking stick.

For a moment Alex felt a stirring of pity. He was still watching closely as John drew near to Bates. He saw him glance back the length of the table toward Alex. Was that an accusatory look on his face? What the hell? Why were they whispering? Since when had John kept secrets from him? And in his recuperation had he forgotten how untrustworthy old Bates was? Three short months ago he'd wanted John's hide.

Then the conversation at the door was concluded. He saw Bates hover over John as though to make certain all was well. As always, John dismissed the concern with a wave of his hand and watched the man through the door, waited until he closed it behind him, then at last turned to face Alex with the entire length of the room stretching between them.

For a moment Alex wondered if he needed assistance and considered offering it, then changed his mind as he saw John renew his grasp on the walking stick and bow his head into the effort of walking.

"I see you helped yourself," John called out when he was at midpoint of the table.

Alex nodded and lifted his glass as though to confirm the evidence. "I hope that was all right."

"Of course. Don't be foolish. In fact, pour one for me while you're at it, and I'll try to arrive there before it evaporates."

At this small display of self-pity, Alex thought he detected a greater display of effort on John's part, as though the impairment had worsened in the last few minutes.

"Oh, Alex," John mourned, "I never thought I would come to this, a cripple."

"Well, I wouldn't call you a cripple, John," Alex replied. "Perhaps briefly . . . incapacitated. But if that nurse has her way . . ."

"Why didn't you want to take me back to London?"

Oh, Gawd! Alex turned quickly away on the pretense of warming his hands. In truth, he needed a moment. So! John had overheard everything. He remembered once suspecting as much but had been unable to bring himself to believe that the lifeless and unresponding man was capable of . . .

Enough time had passed. "I didn't think you were well enough to travel," Alex said, turning back to face the accusation.

"She said I was."

So he'd overheard that as well. "At that time she had her own schedule to pursue. I did not feel she was making that judgment in your best interests," Alex responded, struggling to maintain at least a degree of outer calm.

"I could have received excellent medical care in London," John muttered.

"You were receiving it here."

"Of questionable quality."

"I don't call the results questionable."

"I can't walk."

"Three months ago you couldn't sit up. It will take time—"

"What is your news? When will they arrive? I need a crew of men out here. Much to be done to get this place ready."

Stunned by the rapid transition, Alex felt the need for time and distance.

"Well?" John demanded, apparently abandoning his hurt over Alex's lack of loyalty.

For a moment all Alex could do was to shake his head in an idiotic fashion, all the while trying to deal with this man who was making plans for renovation for a family that would never arrive.

"John . . ."

"Elizabeth. What have you heard from Elizabeth?" John demanded. "Of course, she should have been here by now, but I'll forgive her for her tardiness. Is she still in London? Tell her I need her here. That should draw her away from her dressmakers and her salons quick enough."

"John, please . . ."

"Don't tell me. She's not still angry with me, is she? Surely not after all these years." At some point the demanding arrogance had disappeared and in its place was a small boy, hurt, abused, in need of gentle reassurance.

For a moment Alex found himself seriously considering a small harmless lie. How much easier to say, yes, that Elizabeth was still angry with him than to tell the truth. But he couldn't do that.

"John, I'm afraid that . . ."

"Did she speak of me at all?"

Alex turned away back to the fire. "No."

For a moment there was only silence and the faint crackling of the flames. Then: "Alex, are you . . . ?"

"Yes, I'm certain, John," Alex said forcefully, resenting both the man's ability to manipulate and his willingness to be manipulated. "She said absolutely nothing about you because she isn't at her dressmakers or in her salon in London. In fact, she isn't in London at all."

"Has she married?" John asked with sudden interest.

Unable to see either the point or the relevance of the question, Alex dismissed it. "I don't know. All I know is that the first messenger was unable to find her, and the second messenger *was*."

For the first time in several minutes, the frown left John's face and he smiled. "Thank God."

Then Alex could keep still no longer. "The second messenger located her, with great difficulty, in the La Rochelle House of Detention in Paris. He was unable to find out the nature of her offense or the length of her sentence. He said the French—"

Before he completed the message, John had angled the chair into posi-

103

tion and now sat heavily, his face upraised, brow furrowed, as though Alex was using a foreign tongue and the words were not registering.

"La . . . Rochelle, a house of . . ."

"A prison," Alex said flatly. "That's what the French call it."

"I . . . don't . . ."

"Neither did the messenger, though it was his opinion she'd got caught up in some of the women's antics a few years back, that march on Versailles, burning down half of Paris in the process . . ."

But if John remembered anything, it was impossible to tell. The mind had apparently caught on one word and could not move past it.

"I must go to her," came the insane pronouncement from the man slumped in the chair.

"John, that's—"

"—the only sensible course of action," John countered, on his feet now as though the forward movement were capable of propelling him across the channel. "You said yourself the French were hostile to—"

"I didn't. The messenger—"

"No matter," John said, and dismissed it with a wave of his hand. "She needs me. She . . . needs . . . *me*!" And all at once, quite incongruously, he laughed. "That is miraculous, isn't it, Alex? I sit out here concentrating on how much I need her, while all the time—"

"John, listen to me. It would serve no purpose—"

"Serve no purpose! My God, I'd do the same for you—"

"What? What precisely do you intend to do when you arrive in Paris?"

"Get her out, of course. What else?"

"How?"

John faltered. "Hire a solicitor. Get a new trial . . ."

"You have no jurisdiction and less power in France."

"Money is power, Alex. My God, I thought you would have learned that by now."

"In London, yes . . ."

"Also in Paris."

"What if she's guilty?"

"Of what?" Again John laughed, a hearty sound considering the nature of their conversation. "My God, Elizabeth couldn't commit a serious crime if she put her entire mind and soul to it, you know that. She used to scold Mary for stealing irises in Hyde Park."

Alex was forced to concede the truth of this claim, but the fact remained that the messenger had located her in a prison.

"I know what happened," John claimed flatly, and took another chair halfway down the table, as though he were growing tired and too stubborn to admit it. "While Elizabeth was never very good at committing crimes, she was always excellent—first rate, as a matter of fact—at choosing the wrong companions with which to associate."

True again. Alex could not refute this. "Still, John, I don't think that you—"

"I'll leave immediately," John pronounced. He was up to another favorite trick of his, a rare talent for hearing only what he wanted to hear. "The sea air might even be good for me," he went on, seeming to gain energy as the idea gained momentum. "I'll find her. Yes, I will," he pledged, "and I'll get her out and I'll bring her back to Eden and I promise I'll forgive her everything, and then the others will come . . ."

Abruptly he stopped, some minor key entering the major harmony of this greatest of all family reunions. "I take it you did . . . not hear from the others?" he asked, looking back over his shoulder, the expression on his face suggesting that he already knew the answer.

"No," Alex confirmed, and, not wanting to dwell on the absence of news, he took up the theme of his newest worry. "John, listen to me. You can't go running off to Paris. It's a very different Paris now than—"

"I don't give a damn about Paris," John exploded, his anger, Alex suspected, aimed at the silent and unresponding family. "I'll fetch Elizabeth and not linger, I can promise you that. You know very well my feeling toward the French," he muttered. "Yes, we'll leave immediately. See to the arrangements, Alex. I'll go and tell the others. Of course, they are welcome to stay here until our return. I don't want to appear ungrateful . . ."

Stunned by this new turn of events, Alex tried to choose the right moment in which to jump in with his objections. and when none seemed forthcoming, he jumped in anyway. "John, I—"

"And I don't want to go by way of London," John said, talking quite volubly now and keeping pace with his words—or at least as much as the left leg would permit. Without warning, he looked up as though a stunning thought had just crossed his mind. "The f-firm . . ." he stammered, and briefly all color seemed to have left his face, and for one incredulous moment Alex suspected that this was the first time the firm had crossed his mind.

". . . is doing well." Alex smiled, pleased at last to find some good news to relate.

"Aslam?" John asked.

"You'd be proud of him." Alex nodded. "Four years ago I wouldn't have wagered one pound on the lad. Now I'd stake my life's fortunes on him."

"He is . . . in charge?"

"Absolutely," Alex said, still amazed that for years John had exhibited no interest in the major effort of his lifetime, the largest, most profitable construction firm in the British Empire. He was prepared and even eager to give him figures, the impressive statistics of growth and good management. "We have a workshop in Scotland now, John. Aberdeen."

But if the news of expansion penetrated at all, John gave no indication of it. Instead he turned away from the news and walked in the opposite direction, head down.

"John, regarding this . . . trip to Paris . . ."

"Yes, as I said, we'll leave immediately."

"I can't go to Paris with you, and you shouldn't go."

For several moments John looked back as though bewildered by the blunt announcement, and Alex braced himself for the anger which would surely explode any minute now.

Instead, with complete calm John turned about and looked benignly down on the table. "I didn't ask you to go, Alex," he said, a raw chill to his voice. "Nor did I ask your opinion concerning my plans."

"But you can't go alone. Your health—"

105

"I have no intention of going alone."

Suddenly there was a light rap on the door. "Mr. Eden?" The voice, filled with hauteur, was familiar. Bates.

"Come in, Bates." John called out, and Alex thought he detected a new cordiality in his tone.

The next moment the door was pushed open and the man stood, ramrod-straight, exhibiting an almost militaristic bearing.

"Bates, what would you say to a brief ocean voyage, across the channel and deep into snail-eaters' territory?"

Despite the hauteur, a look of bafflement crossed the old man's face. "Where, sir?"

"France, man," John exploded, in remarkably good spirits considering the variety of bad news that Alex had shared with him this day. "I need a man to accompany me on a very important rescue mission. Are you game?"

For the first time Alex saw Bates glance down the length of the table to where Alex stood, as though asking without words why *he* wasn't going.

"Responsibilities . . . in London," Alex said, and hoped that it would suffice.

Apparently it did. Either that or John didn't give him a chance for further inquiry. "We'll need a roadworthy carriage and passage from Dover . . ."

As John listed his various needs, Alex returned to the fire, suffering a peculiar splintering of emotions. No longer was he John Murrey Eden's "running man." Obviously someone else had been selected for that role. And he had willingly surrendered the job. Then why was he so resentful of the new association which was being formed at the end of the table, Bates at some point drawing forth a small black leather notepad, still writing after John had ceased itemizing, stopping only with John's gentle humor: "You must escort me, Bates. No choice, for after all, I'm your prisoner."

Bates looked up from the notepad. His lined face seemed to freeze with thought for a moment. Then a subtle smile rearranged the lines, and though he didn't respond, he did nod.

"Well, then," John added, "be about it."

Bates slapped the notebook closed, tucked it safely inside his vest pocket, and asked one simple question. "The time of departure, sir?"

Without hesitation John replied, "Tomorrow morning."

"Impossible, sir."

"Why?"

How many times in the past Alex had been confronted with that questioning look! Now, thank God, it was someone else.

Bates met the challenge admirably. "Simple, sir. There are eight carriages in the carriage house and none have been road-tested in over four years. There are wheels to mend, axles to check, interiors to be—"

Never a man to abide detail, John bellowed, "Then when?"

Again Bates seemed to be flourishing under the weight of his new responsibility. "One week."

"Five days."

Bates nodded. "I can do it."

John beamed and looked upon the man as though he were a national treasure.

"One thing more, Mr. Eden," Bates said, moving toward the door.

"Yes?"

"We'll need funds."

All at once John laughed. "Funds?" he repeated, and glanced up toward Alex at the fireplace.

"Your name is credit enough in England, John," Alex explained. "But it will mean nothing once you reach Calais."

Bates nodded, a strained but genuine understanding springing up between the two men, a sense of a banner passed.

Apparently John saw it as well. And disliked it. "Well, give him a letter of credit, for God's sake, Aldwell."

"The French couldn't give a damn about your letter of credit, either, John," Alex said, grateful now that it was Bates and not he on the threshold of this mad journey.

Stymied, John exploded. "Well, what in the hell do you suggest?"

But it was Bates and not Aldwell who solved the problem with admirable dispatch. "May I make a suggestion, sir?" he inquired with impeccable politeness.

"Please do."

"If it isn't too much trouble for Mr. Aldwell, he could have a courier—guarded, of course—ready and waiting for us at . . . say, the Haunch of Venison in Salisbury, an easy ride from London and not too far removed from the turnpike that will take us around the city and down to Dover . . ."

Alex listened closely, knowing what was coming. It was a sensible idea.

". . . a portfolio with funds, part in English pounds, part in French francs."

Then John understood as well, and the gloom of unsolved problems vanished. "Excellent idea."

Bates beamed.

"Well, what do you say, Aldwell?" John demanded.

Alex agreed. "A workable idea, John, and instead of an armed courier, I'll bring the portfolio myself."

He had hoped that the offer might elicit some sort of response. But it didn't. Without a word John went immediately to where Bates stood, and propelled him toward the Great-Hall door, his voice low, issuing a spate of commands. Both men kept their voices down, thus adding to Alex's sense of having been shut out.

No matter. In a very real way he was ready to be "shut out" of this part of John's life.

He looked up out of his thoughts and saw Bates just leaving. John appeared to watch him as well, a mixed expression on his face which Alex found impossible to read from that distance. Then there was no need, for John had turned about and was just starting back into the room, head down.

Alex waited in silence, thinking he should be on the road tonight. Aslam would have to be informed of the impending journey and the need for a sizable amount of funds.

"John, you must be careful on this journey. I wish I could talk you out of—"

"You can't, so save your energy."

"It could be very dangerous for you."

"How? I don't plan to break any laws, French or otherwise."

"The French don't need the excuse of a broken law."

"Oh, for God's sake, Alex, what am I supposed to do? Leave her in prison? Don't you think she'd try to help me if the situation were reversed?"

"Her sentence is nearing its end. At least that's what the messenger—"

"No," John announced with renewed conviction. "I regret every day now that she has spent there. I must go to her, ask her forgiveness for all of my offenses against her in the past and then seek her help in bringing the rest of the family back to Eden." He shook his head and looked up bleakly. "Oh, Alex, I've made such a botch of everything, haven't I?"

The honest question stopped Alex altogether. He'd never heard the old John reveal such a perception.

"In many ways, yes," Alex agreed, in truth thinking how mild a word "botch" was for the ruined lives which John Murrey Eden had left in his wake.

Then, almost childlike, John looked up out of his fatigue. "Do you think it's too late?"

"For what?"

"You know. To ask them . . . to tell them . . . oh, you know. I'm sorry. I *am* sorry, that sort of thing."

As a blueprint for a future apology, it left a lot to be desired. Still, considering its source, it was a remarkable start.

"Well, I think I'll make preparations for my own departure, John," Alex announced with sudden dispatch.

At the same moment, a soft rap came at the door, accompanied by a well-familiar and equally soft voice. "Mr. Eden, I've been appointed your walking partner for the day. Mr. Bates appears quite busy . . ."

Alex saw John look up at the sound of the voice. For less than a second he saw something which resembled pleasure on his face, but either Alex was mistaken or else John quickly canceled it.

"Come," he called out gruffly, and even before the door was pushed open by the nurse, John muttered beneath his breath, but loud enough for Alex to hear: "Women!"

Eden Point
October 22, 1874

Susan didn't mind the added chore of walking every afternoon with Mr. Eden. In fact, she looked forward to it, though on occasion it was chancy, what with the mid-autumn rains just beginning to set in. At first she was afraid of the dampness, for Mr. Eden's sake, but in the last week, with the positive action of the journey ahead of him, he seemed to have grown stronger, indomitable almost.

If the sight of Mr. Eden walking unassisted brought her pleasure, this sight she now viewed seemed to cast her inexplicably into a strangely sobered mood: the grand carriage which Bates had had eight men working on for the last few days now stood waiting and ready outside the castle.

Gilt and purple, it caught every reflecting ray of the sun and hurled them in colorful profusion about the inner courtyard. To the left, just coming up the steep brick stairs which led down into the kitchen court, was Sam Oden supervising a caravan of young boys from Mortemouth who—for a very handsome day's wage—were now bringing up the trunks belonging to Mr. Bates and Mr. Eden.

Mortemouth's only tailor, old Mr. Robbins, had worked night and day for the past week in an attempt to make Mr. Eden's old wardrobe fit his new lean frame, though how long it would stay lean, Susan wasn't prepared to say. Under the skillful artistry of the little Irishwoman Rose O'Donnell, the bill of fare coming out of the kitchen was playing havoc with all their waistlines.

No matter. It was all coming to an end tomorrow morning, as a matter of fact, with the dawn departure of Mr. Bates and Mr. Eden—for Salisbury first, then Dover, then Calais, and finally Paris.

Despite the fact that Susan was standing in a bright spill of sun, she shivered. Paris. It sounded so far away and so foreign. Down below, she

109

saw Bates in a long dark blue butcher's apron, sleeve rings on his upper arms, directing the confusion with remarkable skill, while to one side stood Mr. Eden . . .

There her inspecting eyes stopped. *Thank You*, she prayed quickly under her breath, and said no more, for she knew that God knew she was thanking Him for that miracle, that man who, a few short weeks ago, had lain paralyzed and partially speechless upon a mussed couch. Now she saw the man standing erect, the lines of illness slowly disappearing, under the patina of late-fall sun, his new lean frame growing taut and supple with the daily exercise, his spirit recovering as well under the anticipation of the journey.

And how well now he and Bates understood each other and seemed to get on, each responding to the other's needs scarcely before those needs had been voiced.

John Murrey Eden . . . She thought the name quietly and to herself, thinking curiously that despite the intimacy of her caring for him, she still didn't know him.

Suddenly she shivered again and prayed—as she had prayed repeatedly before—for their successful journey. Then she looked up in an effort to see if Mr. Eden was ready to commence their walk. They had emerged from the Great Hall about a quarter of an hour ago and he'd politely begged her patience while he inspected the coach.

Behind her, coming from the Great Hall itself, she could hear the women who, like their sons, had been hired on the basis of a day, reshrouding all the furnishings and all working under the strict orders of Mr. Bates, who had blossomed into the "grand Organizer"—at least that's what Mr. Eden called him to his face, and it seemed to please both.

Closed. With sadness Mr. Eden had informed her only yesterday that to the best of his knowledge this would be the first time in the history of Eden that the castle would be completely closed, no one in residence, no staff, no game warden or ground warden, no farm crews, nothing.

She remembered his face in that moment, a new desolation worse than any she'd seen during the height of his illness. Gently she reminded him that, with God's help, it would only be temporary, that he'd return soon bringing Elizabeth, who in turn would coax the others back.

John . . .

The thought of the name drew her attention down to the man, who now was being taken on a brief inspection tour of the carriage by Mr. Bates, who was at the same time instructing the parade of boys where to place the trunks for easy loading.

Bates was doing the talking. The other was staring up at her with a directness that caused a blush to erupt on both cheeks.

Why was he looking at her in that manner, as though he too were having trouble understanding the nature of partings and good-byes?

Why he felt a compulsion to look up at just that moment, he had no idea. He hadn't even been aware that she was standing there until he'd seen movement out of the corner of his eye and had glanced up, and now he saw her just starting down the steep Great-Hall steps.

". . . and I'm sure you'll agree, Mr. Eden?"

The question came from his left, the efficient voice of old Bates, who,

110

like Miss Mantle, had worked long and hard on his behalf and for the success of the journey. For one curious moment the realization that others served and sacrificed on his behalf moved him.

"Mr. Eden, did you hear? Are you feeling well?" It was Bates again, apparently having seen the drifting look in John's eyes and assumed that it was related to his health.

"Very well, thank you." John smiled apologetically, and was aware of Miss Mantle approaching him from behind and keenly aware of Bates awaiting an answer before him.

"I'm . . . sorry, Bates," he apologized again. "I'm afraid I was wool-gathering."

Bates smiled as though he understood. "I was just pointing out the arrangement of the trunks," Bates explained.

"I'm sure that under your efficient hands they will be arranged brilliantly," John said, and meant it.

Aware of Miss Mantle waiting a few steps away, doubly aware that this would be their last walk together, he stepped forward and brought his meeting with Bates to a close. "You've done a splendid job," he said, hoping to inject the tone of a conclusion in his voice. "We'll leave at dawn as scheduled." He lowered his voice. "On that other matter . . ."

"Arranged, sir. She's agreed to the morning, though she's quite apprehensive."

"Tell her there is no reason. It's her services I seek, nothing more. . . . "Well, then," John exclaimed, stepping back from the coach and joining Susan at the bottom of the stairs. "And what is your opinion, Miss Mantle? Of the coach, I mean. Do you think it will safely transport me to Dover?"

"I do, sir. It's a grand carriage, and Mr. Bates here has indeed gilded the lily."

John saw the humor in her face and saw as well the line of her vision to the rather overgrand gilt coat of arms on both sides of the carriage.

"Well, it will serve its purpose," he said, swallowing a minor hurt. He'd rather liked that gilded coat of arms. "You'd be surprised how country inns respond to that gewgaw."

She nodded and looked to be on the verge of saying more. Instead: "Shall we go?" she invited.

He nodded and started off toward the gatehouse, setting an easy pace, smiling at the workmen, some of whom he knew personally from the past, others he did not. As they passed by the Keep, he realized that she was walking a step or two behind and wished she'd catch up. Without thinking, he reached back with his hand and made contact with hers and drew her forward.

Though he thought he detected a brief look of shock on her face, she covered it quickly. "If you're feeling weak, Mr. Eden . . ."

"Not weak," he countered, "just alone. You don't mind walking *with* me, do you?"

"No, of course not."

"Good. Then what will be our direction today?"

"The headlands?"

"No, not the headlands," he said, feeling more exuberant with every step.

"Then where?" she asked, guiding him in a careful path toward the gatehouse. "Surely you're not going to attempt the cliff walk down into Mortemouth?"

He laughed at the suggestion. "No, not today. Besides," he added, glancing about at the bustling courtyard, "it's my guess that most of Mortemouth is up here today."

She smiled and nodded and seemed to settle into an acceptance of his hand about hers. He saw a faint though becoming blush color her cheeks. Then he looked ahead and saw the workmen standing back in polite deference.

"Watch your step," she cautioned, pointing out the rise which led through the gatehouse.

"You're lookin' well, sir, Mr. Eden. Long life to ye!" one of the workmen dared to call out.

John stopped, amazed and moved that the man—any man—would care how he looked or felt. "Who said that?" he asked.

Then he heard Miss Mantle's voice. "It was you, wasn't it, Charley Spade?" she asked with a kindness that seemed to soften the tension and cause a giant of a young man to duck his head, as though in an attempt to cover the brick-red blush which covered his face.

"Wasn't it you, Charley?" she asked again, and reassured him further. "I'm certain that Mr. Eden wants only to thank you for your kind interest. That's all, isn't it, Mr. Eden?"

John nodded. "Of course. I was just . . . curious . . ."

"Come forward, Charley," Miss Mantle urged, extending her hand to the still-clustered workmen, a few of whom were parting in an attempt to make room for the young giant named Charley Spade.

John gaped, amazed, as the man moved forward, clutching a worn tricorn hat of ancient vintage between well-blackened hands. He appeared to be well over seven feet tall, with the square broad shoulders of a young Hercules, close-cropped flaming red hair topping a square and massive forehead, small deep-set blue eyes giving an assurance of shrewdness to a face massed into firmness by a compressed mouth and strong chin.

As Miss Mantle led the man forward, John thought how helpful it would be to have such a man on a journey, and started to initiate a line of questioning, but Miss Mantle launched forth into a most interesting introduction, which briefly proved distracting.

"Charley Spade, you know Mr. Eden, of course . . ."

"I do, miss, yes."

"But, Mr. Eden, do you know Charley Spade? You should, you know. According to Reverend Christopher, his grandfather provided a rather unsavory service for your grandfather."

"I . . . don't understand," John murmured, still fascinated by the man's size.

Without a word Charley grinned and lifted his right hand, finger pointing at the blackened and immense whipping oak which sat to the left of the Keep.

"Me grandfather was the premier whipman of the West Country and practiced his profession exclusively for your grandfather Lord Thomas Eden."

Whipman? The fact that such an unsavory job would be labeled a profession shocked John.

"Me grandfather lived on the estate until he died almost twenty year ago," Charley went on, "and me dad knew yours"—abruptly the massive face softened—"but the Prince of Eden never had no use for such as whips and things."

John smiled, affectionately remembering the gentleness of his father. No, his father would never have recognized the intrinsic value of a good whip.

"Well, so much for the past," John said gruffly. "You, Charley Spade, what are you up to now?" he asked, finding the massive frame and ham-like hands incredibly suited to his needs and purposes.

"Working for Eden"—Charley grinned—"just like me dad before me and his dad before him."

"What is your employment at the end of this day?"

"Whatever I can get, sir. Running herring, most likely, but I don't like it. They smell awful, have you noticed?" The massive nose wrinkled, as did the square forehead, and his mates, all fishermen no doubt, jostled him good-naturedly.

"Do you have a family?" John asked.

At this Charley Spade laughed heartily, threw back his enormous head, and laughed straight up at heaven. "Now, what self-respecting woman would have me, sir?"

No family, no permanent trade or profession, able-bodied, apparently suffering some delusion of a bond with Eden. It looked promising.

"Do you drive a carriage?" John asked.

"If it has horses I can, sir." Charley grinned, beginning to enjoy center stage, surrounded by his mates, who from time to time would nudge each other in the ribs with their elbows.

"Can you repair carriages?" John asked further.

"I repaired that grand one there, didn't I?"

"Have you an appetite for travel, Charley?"

"Don't know, sir. Never been no place beyond Ilfracombe."

"Not even to London?"

"No, sir. Me parents caught the fever when we was young, and we all scattered and learned ourselves how to put bread in our mouths."

John gazed at the man, seeing in all aspects of him an answered prayer. "Who are you responsible to now, Charley Spade?" he asked.

"No man," Charley answered without hesitation.

John smiled. "Then would you have any objection to working for me?"

Apparently the big man failed to understand. "I just got done working for you, Mr. Eden."

"No, I mean on a full-time basis."

A murmur of impression arose from the others as all glanced curiously at Charley.

"I . . . don't . . ." Charley stammered, and though he didn't mean to, John lost a degree of patience.

"Work for me, man," he shouted, "in my permanent employ, like your grandfather worked for my grandfather."

The bewilderment on Charley's face turned to apprehension as he glanced nervously toward the whipping oak. "Oh, sir, I don't think . . . no whip, you see. Ain't got no . . . no, I don't think—"

"Not as a whipman," John bellowed, instantly regretful of having bellowed. "As my driver," he explained, trying to rouse all the patience he could muster. "Mr. Bates and I are leaving for France tomorrow. We need a good steady driver and a strong back in the bargain. Are you game?"

"F-France?" Charley stammered.

"I said so, didn't I?" John snapped. He wasn't any good at dealing with these people. He should have summoned Bates and let Bates do the hiring—

Then Miss Mantle stepped forward with an ease of manner and calmness of spirit. "May I, Mr. Eden?" she asked politely, as though sensing his need.

"Please," he muttered, and turned away from the gaping men and again looked with longing at the passing day. Behind him he heard her delicate voice, like a steady melody, followed by the only words he'd really wanted to hear, Charley's agreement, his voice newly sobered by his instantaneous elevation in the world.

Then it was settled, and with dispatch he turned back to shake hands on it—would Charley Spade even know what a gentleman's handshake meant?—but instead found himself confronting Miss Mantle, who now stood between him and his new employee, a questioning look on her face, as though she'd asked a question and he had not heard.

"I'm . . . sorry . . ." he murmured.

"Charley's wage, sir. What did you say you would pay him?"

Clever! John stepped back from the direct question to the waiting Charley, who looked eagerly at him, the grin on his face the size of a half-moon at harvesttime.

"I . . . didn't say," John muttered.

"Well, I think you should, don't you?" Miss Mantle went on undaunted. "After all, you are asking Charley to leave his home—"

"Don't mind none, miss," came a very sensible reply from behind.

John turned about, thinking that this repudiation would silence her. But it didn't. Instead she took Charley by the arm and led him out of the group until he was standing separate and apart, his grand qualifications clear now for all to see. John studied him in this angle and decided quite simply that there probably was nothing the man could not do that required physical prowess.

Still, almost plaintively, he argued with Miss Mantle. "I'll see to all his needs," he said. "That should be enough."

"Come, now, Mr. Eden," she chided gently. "Everyone here knows that a man must have more than his needs taken care of!"

Did they all know that? John didn't, and from the puzzled look on the faces of the men, particularly Charley Spade, they didn't know it either.

Damn! Hemmed in! Nothing to do but make a pittance of an offer for this ox. He would be of invaluable service, of that John was certain.

"Fifteen shillings," John offered, doing nothing to conceal the anger in his voice. What business was it of hers? "Per month," he added pointedly, delighted to see the initial look of approval fade from her face. As for Charley Spade, he looked stunned, as though someone had just delivered a blow to his midsection.

"Per week," she countered.

"Out of the question," John said.

"Then I must advise Mr. Spade to say no to your . . . offer, which in truth is not an offer at all but the very worst form of exploitation, as you so well know."

John stared down on her and wondered what Alex Aldwell had offered *her* as a wage for caring for a half-dead man.

"No," John said, unable to believe the words that were forming in his head. "I offer Mr. Spade fifteen shillings . . . per . . . week."

He had intended to say more, but the stunned gasps coming from the workmen precluded speech as they gathered about Charley Spade and slapped him on the back and dared to ruffle his close-cropped hair.

John waited out the men's excitement, all the while concentrating on her eyes, the color of the channel on a sunny day. *There* was his reward, that simple look of gratitude. As though the expression was not reward enough, she stepped closer, away from the chattering men. "Thank you, Mr. Eden," she said. "You won't miss the money and it will provide Charley with his first sense of self-respect. Besides," she went on, "he will defend you with his life now, and that will mean a great deal to those of us who . . . care for you."

Strange, that hesitancy in her words.

Then his new employee was coming forward.

"Mr. Eden," Charley began, and with those two words he appeared to have moved himself beyond his ability to speak.

"No need," John said gruffly, hoisting his walking stick into the air, a clear signal the interview was over. He increased his speed away from the still-gaping men and proceeded beneath the arch and out onto the headlands, thinking that Miss Mantle was directly behind him, only to look back from a distance of about forty feet to see her in close conference with Charley Spade, the large man nodding to whatever she was saying.

Ah, here she was, approaching slowly, head down, checking each step.

"Everything settled?" John called out, knowing that it was, seeing beyond Miss Mantle's slim shoulders to where Charley Spade stood, his great cow eyes watching both of them.

"Oh, yes." She smiled, stepping up alongside him, her arms crossed as though she were chilled. "I just wanted to be certain that he fully understood what had transpired and what would be expected of him."

"And did he?"

"Yes," she replied. "It was a good idea to hire Charley Spade. I shall feel . . ." Abruptly she stopped and glanced back to where he trailed a step or two behind.

"Miss Mantle, wait!" he called out.

"What is it?" she asked, looking back.

"You started to say something but checked yourself. What was it?"

"I don't remember."

"Of course you do."

"Yes," she agreed with a suddenness which suggested she knew as well

115

as he that they were playing a game. She walked slowly away again, head down. "You've been seriously ill, Mr. Eden," she began. "I'm not even certain that you should be undertaking such a difficult journey—"

"It will be—"

"But since you are, and since I'm quite certain there is nothing anyone can say to dissuade you, then I will feel better knowing you have competent assistance."

The way the wind was blowing the fringes of her hair was fascinating, lifting individual strands in a gentle pulling motion away from her face, which was suddenly so earnest. He found himself wondering what it was about her he found so appealing.

Be attentive! a voice inside his head sternly counseled.

"And you feel that Charley Spade and old Bates are . . . competent, as you put it?"

She smiled. "Competent? For a man in your condition? No. Better than nothing? Yes . . ."

"What precisely is my condition?" he asked, leading the way out across the headlands, but at a more prudent pace. Also the brief interim had given him a chance to plot a route for this afternoon's excursion, one which might be of interest to her, though the first leg of the trip took them over well-trod territory back across at least a part of the headlands.

"You can't be serious," she said, coming up alongside him.

"Oh, but I am," he said, and liked the way she walked beside him, her attention his.

My God, he really didn't want to leave her.

". . . and beyond that it is impossible to tell precisely what and how much damage has been done."

Damn! Why did his mind insist upon drifting?

"I'm sorry, Miss Mantle. My mind . . ."

She looked up at him. "I know," she said. "That too is the result of the seizure. I wish when you feel up to it that you would go to London and see Miss Nightingale. She has become the leading authority on—"

"No," he said, cutting in. "London has little appeal—"

"Are you warm enough, Mr. Eden?"

He responded to the soft inquiry with a scant nod and wondered why he felt so self-conscious around this woman. He couldn't remember when in his life he'd wanted so terribly to say the right words, to make the right responses.

"Tell me about yourself, Miss Mantle."

"No need to worry about—"

Unfortunately their voices came simultaneously, one blurring the other.

"I'm sorry—"

"No, I—"

"It's damn chilly. Are *you* warm enough?" As he tried to hide his embarrassment, he took refuge in the weak subject of her thin shawl.

"I'm fine," she said, though both seemed to have increased their pace against the chill and accelerating wind.

"You know, it might help," she said, her voice raised in competition with the giant breakers which were beginning to crash on the rocks far below the cliff, "if we turned inland."

116

He nodded and struggled to maintain the pace which he had set. The numb leg did not work well under pressure and seemed to him at times to belong to someone else.

"We'll cut in up ahead," he said, and realized with a start that he was shouting, that the wind within minutes had risen to gale force. "Not through the woods, though," he added, smiling. "We've seen the woods. Today I want to show you something else."

Now he looked ahead, hoping he'd remembered correctly at which point the castle wall gave way to the hidden door and access to the overgrown terrain beyond the family graveyard.

"Will you be off tomorrow as well?" he asked abruptly.

She nodded. "Oh, yes. I have several long weeks of work to catch up with—"

"There it is," he cried out now, spying the rusted black hinges where he remembered them and reaching out for her arm in order to redirect her.

"Where are we?"

"You'll see," he said, and drew her close and smelled that lovely scent of soap and lavender which it had been his privilege to waken to every morning for the past several months.

He sensed her interest as they drew near to the door, and was pleased to see her launch forth into a removal of clinging ivy that obscured the latch.

"There's one just like it in the south wall." She smiled. "How long have you known about this one?"

"All my life," he said, pleased that the wind seemed to have subsided.

She looked up, surprised. "Then you were born here?"

"No."

"London?"

"No."

"Where?"

"Shropshire," he said. "I'm a Shropshire man."

The news seemed to puzzle more than illuminate. "How did Elizabeth happen to be in Shropshire during her confinement?"

For a moment he looked down on her as she stooped to remove the last of the ivy. Was she seeking? So many others had in the past.

"Elizabeth is not my mother," he said, recalling unhappy times against his will.

"She raised you. At least, that's what Reverend Christopher—"

"She is not my mother," John repeated, and heard the edge in his voice and decided to do nothing to soften it, and reached out and pushed against the rusty door with all his limited strength and was pleased to hear it give with first effort.

Briefly they stood a distance apart, each assessing this gray and gloomy place where jagged stumps raised distorted faces out of moss and leaf-scattered earth, where full-grown dead trees had fallen and over the years had been allowed to remain fallen in fixed positions, their limbs rotting into macabre angles, like men undergoing torture.

He saw her shiver. "Of course, you know what it is," he said, leading the way through the least obstructed part, heading toward the clearing beyond the graveyard and the cobblestone path which led to their ultimate destination.

"No. I'm sorry, I don't know . . ." she stammered.

"Over there," he said. "That will be cleared and smoothed for all those Edens not yet born." He walked ahead, aware that straight up was that implacable fortress, four stories high, the exact point in the crenellation where he had stood with Harriet in his arms entreating Heaven to take them both.

"Mr. Eden, why don't you sit for a moment? Here, here's a dry . . ."

Apparently she had seen him stumble and, in a flurry of half-sentences, had caught up with him and had established a firm grip on his arm and was leading him now with surprising strength toward a smooth fallen tree trunk which seemed to have formed a natural bench. He did not resist.

"Come," she urged, gently continuing to lead him over the uncertain footing, and once changing her mind. "Perhaps we should return to the castle. This dampness . . ."

"No, just . . . sit . . . minute . . ."

"But you have a long journey ahead of you tomorrow . . ."

"Hours of . . . confinement. Let me . . . move . . ."

His tongue had grown sluggish again. Damn! What was the matter with him? What in the hell was the nature of his illness, one minute well and functioning, and the next weak and helpless?

"Here," she urged, angling him about as though he were a cripple and guiding him down onto the fallen log.

He did as he was told, for he had no choice. His knees were trembling as though palsied, as were his hands.

"We really should go back, Mr. Eden," she said, kneeling before him on the damp earth, her face slanted into angles of concern. Suddenly he felt an irresistible compulsion to touch—merely to touch—that good strong face, and so he did, very gently, his right hand cupped in sincere gratitude about the firm jaw, his fingers extending over her cheek in one direction and down her slender neck in the other.

"You know that I will never be able to repay you," he said, his voice husky under the duress of the moment.

"I require . . . no pay," she answered, obviously startled by the small intimacy but doing nothing to move away from it.

"What *do* you require?" he asked, thinking surely there would be something he could do to ease her life, as she had eased his.

"Nothing. I swear it." She smiled, blushing slightly. "Your good health is reward enough. I pray for it nightly."

Again he felt a shuddering weakness which seemed to commence at the top of his head and move slowly but steadily the full length of his body, like a devastating wave, that left him weak and sweating. "I'm . . . not certain," he murmured, "that your God is paying the closest of attention—"

"Don't say that," she interrupted sternly. "He is always here, with you as well as with me."

At that precise moment John felt the first drop of telltale moisture, the gray and swollen clouds about to release a cold rain. To run back to the castle was out of the question. To remain here in this future burial ground for the yet unborn was equally out of the question.

At that moment she felt those first drops as well, and the worried look on her face suggested a distinct though temporary loss of faith.

"Come, there's shelter not far." He thought she was going to protest as he led her in a direction away from the castle. But as the rain had increased in those few short moments, she ducked her head, took a firm grip on his arm, and followed after him through the overgrown jungle.

At the extreme south edge of the graveyard he found the beginning of the crumbling path which led, as nearly as he could remember, back into the far eastern edge of the castle grounds proper, past the large sheds and outbuildings where, when he'd first arrived at Eden, he'd served time as an odd boy while everyone tried to determine the authenticity of his parentage. Beyond the scattering of outbuildings, beyond what once had been the monstrous and mountainous compost heap, beyond the livestock pens—empty now and likely to remain so—on the very edge of the green woods was Eden Rising, the place where the fields and meadows and pastures of Eden commenced.

And there it was, precisely as he'd remembered it, the comfortable cottage which in the past had served as shelter for various wardens important to the functioning of Eden Castle.

"Up ahead." He pointed, gazing through solid sheets of rain at the questionable shelter which nestled into autumn-brilliant trees at the end of the heavily rutted road.

She looked up. "Thank heavens!" She shivered. "I hope there's firewood."

John hoped there was more than that—a reliable roof, for starters, or better still, a reliable floor. To the best of his knowledge, the cottage hadn't been occupied since his youth.

"Almost there," she called out as though to encourage new strength within him.

Then a few minutes later there it was before them, looking terribly small and plain and ugly when compared with the enormous castle in the distance.

"Watch your step," he called out, seeing the bottom plank rotted.

She gave him a grateful look and moved to the extreme edge and clung to the banister, which looked none too steady itself. Still, it held, and with her in the lead they made their way up the four precarious steps to the questionable shelter of the overhang through which gushed numerous small waterfalls, an ominous omen of what they might find inside.

"Do you have a key?" she asked, trying to brush the wet hair out of her eyes.

"No, but I don't think we'll need one," he pointed out, indicating the door, which, from the top of the steps, he could see was attached by one hinge only.

She saw it as well and stepped gingerly around the main cascade coming through the overhang and pushed open the door. Even above the music of the rain he heard the single hinge squeal in objection to sudden use.

"Come, please," she called to him from just inside the door, where she'd gone ahead on an inspection tour and apparently found the interior, if not better, at least no worse than the exterior. "Mr. Eden, please," she called again with fresh urgency. "The last thing you need is a damp chill. Hurry . . ."

There it was again, that remarkable tone of concern in her voice. He started forward, leaning heavily on the walking stick in an attempt to avoid slippery places, and at last reached for her extended hand, when she took him the rest of the way into the semidarkness of the old cottage. Once they were through the door, she closed it quickly behind them. Though it possessed only the one hinge, it seemed to hang better closed than opened.

"That might keep some of the chill out," she murmured, "though I doubt it," and brushed past him in her usual efficient manner. From the continuously changing angles of her head, he knew she was taking it all in, every cobweb-filled corner and every inch of the debris-littered floor.

For a moment neither spoke as she walked slowly about the large room, still shivering now and then, for he could see the clear contours of her back through her rain-soaked dress. Of greatest interest to her was the large fieldstone fireplace, which looked as though it had been dead and cold and empty forever. Quickly she bent over, apparently to study the flue. "If we had wood . . ."

"We have wood," he said, pointing out two wooden chairs and a decrepit table.

She looked surprised at the suggestion. "We couldn't burn . . . furniture."

"It's not furniture," he said, feeling remarkably good, all things considered.

"What is it?"

"Rubbish."

"It seems wasteful . . ."

He moved into the center of the room, took one of the crumbling chairs, placed his good right leg against the back legs, and with only slight pressure leaned against it once and it collapsed. A short time later, with the added bonus of a tin of dry lucifers they found behind a brick in the fireplace, a fairly decent fire was crackling in the fire well, the warmth banishing the chill—at least in one small corner of the room, which was really parlor, lounge, and kitchen together.

The chairs destroyed for firewood, she found a bench against the kitchen wall and laboriously dragged it into place, twice commanding him not to help, and finally they settled somewhat stiffly on opposite ends of the bench, while the fire blazed and warmed the center section.

"It could be quite comfortable," she said, still looking about, her hands smoothing the rain from her face.

Outside, the storm had increased. Through the smudged front window it resembled night instead of afternoon. "We may be here awhile," he said, not really objecting to the idea and hoping she didn't either.

She looked up as though she was about to say something, then changed her mind. "Bates will be worried." A smile crossed her face as she braced herself with both hands on the bench and began gently to swing her feet. "I don't think I've ever seen a man change so much."

Alert, he looked up from his own persistent woolgathering. Where had

120

he gone this time? No particular destination, just a soft velvet drifting, the mind charting its own course independent of the will. "Yes," he agreed, not certain what it was he was agreeing to but seeing an expression on her face which seemed to require a yes.

"Bates," she chided gently. "I said I'd never seen a man change so much. You've won him over, completely. A few weeks ago he wanted only to transport you to Exeter and prison—"

"I know," John interrupted, back on track, fascinated with the reddish play of the fire on her face. "I don't think that anything has really changed," he added, looking away. "By accompanying me on this journey, he can still keep me in sight."

"Oh, I don't think that's why he's going," she objected.

It really didn't matter to him why Bates was going, or what, if any, were his ulterior motives. There *was* something that did matter to him.

"You," he began awkwardly, wishing he could talk to her without looking at her. There were soft curls of hair still plastered against her forehead and cheek. "Where will you go? Tomorrow, I mean, when the castle is closed."

"On my rounds," she said without hesitation, still swinging her feet, the faint rocking motion apparently soothing her. "I'm so late as it is, I scarcely know where to start."

"Where do you generally start?"

"Exeter. That's home base, a good place to refurbish medical supplies, bandages, you know."

"And then?"

"Usually down the coast, starting with Mortemouth or concluding there."

"How far?"

"A little beyond Clovelly, though not far. Depends on how busy I've been, if there is a fever or—"

"Who pays you?"

"No one pays me."

"How do you live?"

She smiled at the question. "I must confess, I wonder that myself sometimes. But in all the years I've been a circuit nurse, God has provided."

"God?" he asked, doing nothing to mask a certain archness in his voice.

"Yes, through His instruments of men. I have never lacked for a warm bed or a dry room or a bowl of hot soup." Suddenly she lifted her head upward toward the rain-leaking roof. "Except now," she laughed, and moved a short distance down the bench toward the center.

"Charity, then," he said, curious about this woman who apparently made it a practice to give herself away, expecting nothing in return.

"Charity, Mr. Eden? No, I don't think so. I try to the limits of my ability and training to give the very best service I know how to give. When I'm on the circuit I go where God directs me and where people need me—as God brought me to Eden when your needs were so apparent and desperate."

Abruptly he looked away. He disliked hearing about his needs for some reason, particularly from a circuit nurse who lived mainly on the gener-

121

osity of others. Since she was still gazing at him and causing him to feel uncomfortable, he stood, and felt a sharp pain run the length of his spine. He wavered for a moment and leaned heavily on the walking stick.

Instead of rushing to his side as he'd expected her to do, she held her position and quietly advised, "You might want to sit a moment longer."

"No, I don't," he said, more to cross her than anything else. "Where do you stay in Mortemouth?" he asked, making his way slowly across the puddle which had already formed on the floor.

"Reverend Christopher lets me stay in the small room behind the church."

"And how do you eat?"

She laughed at his persistent line of questioning. "I told you, Mr. Eden. God always provides. Look how He's provided of late. I don't know when I've eaten so well. Rose O'Donnell is a jewel, and she claims she taught herself."

Newly interested, John hobbled back to the bench, crossed in front of where she sat, and paused before the fire to warm his hands. "What do you know of her, this O'Donnell woman?"

"Nothing, as I've told you, except that she presented herself at the gates when you were so ill, and the men brought her to me, and I asked if she could cook and she said it was what she did best, and that was that." There was a pause. Then softly: "Why? Has she offended . . . ?"

"Oh, no, I was just curious. She doesn't strike me as an itinerant."

"I don't believe she is."

He looked back at her. "She claims to be."

"I know, but still I see . . ."

"What?"

She shrugged. "Sorrow, loss, a need for a new life . . ."

"Not a transient?"

She paused for a moment before answering. "She's transient now, obviously. No home . . ."

Then it was her turn for drifting. He heard it clearly and looked back at her. But her head was bowed, face obscured, and he saw nothing of the expression which had accompanied such a mournful phrase as "No home . . ."

In the silent interim he looked about at the ruin which surrounded him. Dear God, how could anyone ever live in such a place? No room, no scope, no space, everything crude and narrow and limited.

"It's charming, isn't it?" came a soft voice close to his elbow, and, surprised, he looked up to see her on her feet passing this odd judgment on the same surroundings which recently he'd dismissed as dismal.

He looked with surprised good humor at her. "Hardly."

"I don't mean as it is," she explained, "but as it could be."

He'd heard that before, too. "Elizabeth used to proclaim and preach optimism as well. '*We can fix it, a little scrubbing, a little paint . . .*'" Even as he quoted her, he could hear her voice, that same voice that had called to him all through his boyhood. Now, for the first time, he felt the pain of memory eased by the realization that they would be reunited soon.

"You love her very much, don't you?" Miss Mantle commented quietly, leading him back to the fire as though she didn't approve of him standing chilled and apart.

"She raised me." He nodded, settling back onto the bench.

"When you find her, you'll bring her back to Eden, of course."

At the image of an Elizabeth so easily manipulated, he had to laugh. "One does not transport Elizabeth anywhere without her express permission, but, yes, I hope to . . . persuade her that I need her." His voice drifted again, but this time with purpose. He really didn't feel capable of sharing the tragic past with anyone.

In an abrupt change of subject, he looked up. "Do you really like this place?" he asked, amazed.

She nodded. "I think it's a lovely cottage that has just been neglected and needs only care and patience to restore it."

He looked away first. A thought had just formed, persistent, clear, with a feeling of rightness about it. "Would you accept it—this cottage, I mean—as payment for services rendered during the last difficult weeks?"

He did not look at her, but waited patiently for her response, which he felt certain would be in the affirmative. People who relied on the generosity of God rarely turned down any gift. Then, too, he had ulterior motives. By making her a gift of this crumbling dust-filled cottage, he was guaranteeing in a way that he would see her again, and somehow that was important to him.

She bowed her head and looked intently at the floor, studiously aligning her feet with the cracks. "We really should—"

"Go back," was what he was afraid she was going to say, but at that moment several volleys of thunder cut through the steady rain. The rain seemed to increase, and the thought of leaving even this questionable shelter was absurd.

"Will you?" he asked.

"Will I what?"

"Accept the cottage as payment . . ."

"I couldn't do that, Mr. Eden."

He started forward. Had she understood? Suddenly angry that he wasn't being taken seriously, he leaned forward and demanded, "Why in the devil won't you take it? It certainly would make it easier on you. Instead of staying in churches, here you would have your own home, let your patients come to you—and they would, from all over the West Country."

"*You* wouldn't have come," she reminded him.

"Yes, I would have. Not in the beginning, perhaps, but later."

There was another feature about her that he didn't care for, her damnable insistence that she knew precisely what he was thinking and feeling.

"How could you have?" she demanded. "You were unconscious for several days, lacking in the ability to make certain judgments."

"I've improved," he grumbled.

"Of course you have," she agreed, smiling, "and will continue to do so—but not unless we get you back where it's warm and dry and . . ." As she talked, she moved past the two front windows, leaning over to check on the gray, boiling clouds. Nothing had changed, and though he was cold to the bone, he was momentarily grateful for the enforced confinement.

"Please," he said quietly, now altering his approach. Anger seemed to be wasted on her. She simply didn't respond to it. Too bad. His anger used to bring Mary to tears in less than ten minutes. It was a harmless tyranny and frequently very useful. But not here, not with this woman.

"Come, Miss Mantle," he invited, a different voice and attitude catching her attention, and drew her back to the fire. He smiled. "If I'm cold, you must be . . ."

"I am," she confessed, "but I'm not just recovering from—"

"Please accept it," he interrupted as she returned to the fire and settled on the edge of the bench. "It's doing no one any good as it is," he went on. "Consider it your home. Do what you will with it—"

"Mr. Eden, please," she protested, her voice low, as though embarrassed. "I cannot accept a gift as grand—"

"Grand?" he repeated, laughing. He looked around at the ruined interior, small waterfalls cascading in from the failing roof. From where he sat—and even if he looked in all directions—he could see nothing which, under any circumstances, could ever be called grand. Confronted with such diverse visions, he feigned retreat. "Well, I had wanted to give you something . . ."

"No need . . ."

"I obviously felt that there was a need," he said, peeved, and caught himself in time. "Consider for a moment if our positions were reversed, if I had been largely instrumental in rescuing you. Wouldn't you feel a debt of gratitude that begged to be repaid?"

She appeared to be seriously considering the question, perched on the end of the bench so far away. "I would have been most grateful, of course," she said, staring into the fire as though her response was coming from the flames. "Still, I don't think I would have thought in terms of a gift. Instead I would have to assume that God, using you as His servant, had rescued me for a purpose, and that the best way I could repay you would be to find out what that purpose was as soon as possible and try to meet it."

He found himself watching her, his mind drifting.

"Are you listening, Mr. Eden?"

No, of course he hadn't been listening. He looked away from her into the fire. "Well, while I respect your wishes, I must repeat my own as well. I shall give Alex Aldwell all the particulars he needs, and he, in turn, shall instruct Aslam to see to it that a new deed of property is drawn up for this game warden's cottage that is located behind Eden Castle on the lands known as Eden Rising—"

"Please, no," she protested.

Suddenly a terrible thought occurred to him. "You're not a married woman, are you?"

She shook her head and looked genuinely distressed. "No, but—"

"Good," he said with renewed energy. "As a wife I'm afraid you couldn't own property. As a spinster—"

"It will be a waste of time."

"So be it. It's yours and it will always be here."

"I did not seek it, and I don't want it."

"I know."

"And I do not now accept it."

"But it accepts you." He smiled, wishing she wouldn't get so agitated. As a gift it was nothing, would perhaps be considered worthless and an insult in certain circles.

Abruptly she stood and walked toward the door, pushed it open, and peered out. From where he sat he could see that the rain had subsided.

"I think we can make it," she said without looking at him. "I must get back."

"I didn't mean to offend you."

"You didn't," she said, still looking out at the chill gray day.

"I'm afraid I did." He wanted another refutation. Instead he got only silence. "Miss Mantle, please come back for just a moment."

At last she looked at him. He *had* offended her. "Tell me what I should do," he asked, pretending a weakness, both spiritual and physical, that he did not feel. "All my life my generosity has gotten me into trouble. I try to give to those I care for what I think will please them, and always I drive them farther away." Near the end the pose broke, as did his voice. When had he started speaking the truth? He bowed his head and felt a chill the fire could not dissipate. In the silence of the room, with only the diminished rhythm of the rain, he closed his eyes and felt a soul-deep loneliness. "I . . . don't understand," he muttered.

At first there was no response. Then, just when he'd given up waiting for a response, he heard an inquiry. "What is it that you don't understand?"

He looked up and wondered where to start. "I created an empire and have no one to share it with. I nurtured and treasured and adored those fragments of my life and tried to bring them together as my family, and I only drove them from me, possibly forever. After India and Scutari I wanted only peace—there had been so much death—and yet it followed me here to England and inhabits me and all those I love."

No pose, this. It was the confessional of his heart, and the mystery.

Then: "Mr. Eden, the death you speak of is a natural part of all life."

"No, not this—"

"It visits all, every day in some form or another."

"No—"

"Yes. What you have reference to is something else."

"Death—"

"—but not natural death. Not the blessed conclusion of life, but death of the spirit and—the worst of all—death of love."

He started to protest again but changed his mind. *Death of love.* That was precisely what had happened. He had killed the love of all those who had mattered most to him.

"You employ your will like a weapon, Mr. Eden. Did you know that? It's an incredible will."

Now he looked up, stunned by her criticism.

She saw the expression on his face. "Would you prefer that I didn't speak?" she asked.

Of course he would prefer it, particularly if she was going to criticize.

"Tell me if you don't wish me to speak, and I will refrain from doing so."

Why couldn't he tell her? The desire was certainly there, the words formed.

"Very well, then." He heard the soft rustle of movement as obviously she took up her position at the end of the bench.

"I've watched you for several months now," she began, her voice still so musical, masking the unpleasant nature of what she was doing, "and I must confess that on that night we . . . brought you down from the parapet, I prayed for your soul, for I felt certain you would not live to see dawn."

There! Wrong! Dying had been the farthest thing from his mind that night. Since then there had been moments when to close one's eyes and never have to open them again would have been highly desirable. But not that night. His rage had been so great that Death would not have dared to approach.

"Then your illness," the voice went on, seeming to retreat as though she'd expected resistance and longed for it. "I felt again as though at any time you could withdraw that incredible will and go effortlessly."

Will had had nothing to do with it. Didn't she know that?

"Then, in all ways and every day, I watched not you but your will at work. In those first tentative efforts to speak, then to stand, then to walk. It was almost as if you were defying your body not to cooperate."

He heard a curious sound, as though she'd started to laugh, then changed her mind. "The will, used in that manner and for that purpose, is right, and, in your case, awesome."

Safe behind the blinders of his hands, he considered looking up, then changed his mind. He suspected she wasn't finished.

"But, Mr. Eden . . ."

Aha! There was that tone of transition he'd been waiting for, the all-encompassing "but."

". . . you can't—not successfully, at any rate—use that will for the purpose of manipulating other lives. You can suggest, point out, and in many cases warn, but beyond that, more harm is done than good. And of course in the end what generally happens is precisely what did happen. You only succeed in destroying the very relationships you are trying to secure."

She was silent. Had she run dry so soon? He'd expected several more minutes of clichés and homilies.

Now . . . nothing. The chill damp air inside the cottage hung heavily about him. He reached down for his walking stick where he'd let it drop to the floor. He retrieved it and stood immediately, struggling for balance, determined not to let her see any single aspect of his weakness.

He said nothing until he had reached the door and stepped through it, pleased to see the rain over—scarcely a mist now, but icy cold. "I think I'll return now, Miss Mantle," he said, allowing his voice to fall with all its natural imperiousness.

"Stay here, if you wish," he added with an indifferent wave of his hand. "Accept it, if you wish. Do anything you bloody well wish, but please never again give me the insight of your . . . superior wisdom."

Good Lord, he'd not expected it to sound so harsh and condemning. He looked back into the room, although he'd vowed not to. She sat unmoving on her end of the bench, head down, resembling a chastised child. The sight of her hurt cut with unexpected sharpness.

"I'm . . ." He started to say "sorry," but at the last minute he grew hard and sensible. He really wasn't sorry. At least he'd relieved her of that damnable air of superiority. ". . . going back now, Miss Mantle," he called out, weary of the sight of her.

Once down the stairs, he had to sidestep a large puddle, and in the process, listened closely in an attempt to pick up any sound at all that might be coming from inside the cottage. Then he heard the telltale scraping of the one-hinged door; someone, restored enough to close it gently and follow after him.

"Mr. Eden?"

Damn! Hadn't she said everything there was to be said? Apparently not!

"I'm sorry for any offense I might have caused you—"

"No need," he interrupted airily, marching straight ahead and setting a fast pace that he hoped she couldn't match.

She had to hurry to keep up, which she did without objection, as though she knew he couldn't maintain it for long either.

"And I do wish you the very best," she went on, pulling the dirtiest trick of all on him. Elizabeth used to do this to him as well, return his harsh remarks, which were designed only to hurt, with kindness. It was one of the deadliest of female tricks.

"I hope that your journey to Paris is uneventful and totally successful and that you find Elizabeth and ask her to return with you to Eden. I know how important it is to you," she went on with uncanny accuracy. "Sometimes I think it's easier not to have a family, like me, than to have a large and loving one and lose them."

True, he thought, pleased that she'd returned to her senses.

For the rest of the way, nothing was said. By either. She seemed to walk with increasing energy, while he suffered a persistent and painful shortness of breath and a growing chill that on occasion caused his teeth to chatter. If she was at all aware of his discomfort, she gave no indication of it. She continued to walk ahead of him, lifting her face now and then to the still-boiling clouds, a new energy in every step, as though he'd said nothing at all to her that was hurtful.

Eden Castle
October 23, 1874

For all the rain and gloom of the day before, the morning of the departure dawned rosy and gold, as mild as an April morn, as though nature knew it would be difficult enough without adding the extra burden of unpleasant weather.

Susan stood at the top of the Great-Hall steps, waiting for Mr. Eden's carriage to depart. As soon as they had left, it was her intention to go directly down into Mortemouth, fetch her landau, and put as much distance as possible between herself and Eden by nightfall.

A rattling confusion coming from the direction of the stables caused her to look up. The six enormous horses were being led into place. At the same time, she saw a sudden movement emerge from the dark shadowy stairwell leading up from the kitchen court. She looked more closely at the shape shrouded in a black hooded cape.

Rose O'Donnell.

Susan started to call to her, wanting to say both good-bye and thank you, but at that moment the approaching horses intersected her line of vision, and when the animals had been led past the kitchen-court stairs, Rose O'Donnell was gone.

Susan blinked at the mysterious disappearance. Where could she have gone? Back down the steps was the only possible answer. Good, then Susan would have an opportunity to say good-bye after Mr. Eden's departure.

She looked again at the vacuum at the top of the kitchen steps. The area was still cast in changing morning shadow. Perhaps she'd imagined Rose O'Donnell. It wouldn't be too difficult. She was exhausted this morning, having stayed up late last night gathering together her belongings, hoping that the meeting in the library between Bates and Mr. Eden and Charley

Spade would end early so that she might have a chance to speak with him once again in private.

But the meeting had not broken up early and she had spent most of the evening packing and listening for sounds that had never come.

What had gone wrong yesterday? she now wondered.

At that precise moment Bates appeared, looking very dapper and smart in checked waistcoat, black trousers, and black snug-fitting coat, all of which made him resemble an exclamation point.

"Good morning, Miss Mantle," he called out cheerily, balancing a hatbox in one hand and a black leather case in the other. "It's going to be a beautiful day, I believe," he exclaimed, stopping at the top of the stairs and surveying the morning sky in the manner of a proprietor. "Good for a journey."

"I'd say so, yes, Mr. Bates." She smiled and drew her shawl more closely about her shoulders. "Is Mr. Eden . . . ?"

"Shortly," he said, hurrying past her down the steps, handing the black leather case as well as the hatbox to one of the young men harnessing the horses, where, with a wave of his hand, he signaled that they were to be stored inside the carriage.

At that moment, just emerging from the long staircase which led up from the kitchen court, she saw Charley Spade. If old Bates looked dapper, Charley Spade looked incredible. Now she grinned, along with Charley Spade and all his mates, who clustered about in clear admiration. A few even dared to touch the elegant though ill-fitting suit, and all were envious of the shiny gold buttons and black leather boots which fit Charley's bulging calves like second skin. In one hand he carried quite awkwardly a pair of heavy leather gloves—obviously Eden carriage drivers always wore gloves—while in the other he dragged a well-battered valise which from this distance appeared to be bulging as much as Charley himself.

Good, she thought, eyeing the valise. Soon, she predicted, he could shed the pretentious finery and slip comfortably into his own clothes. And if John Murrey Eden were truly wise, he'd say not a word.

As they stood waiting, she heard a tap-tap-tap on the landing above them. She looked back up at the top of the stairs and was stunned.

It was the young lion she'd first seen in the army hospital in Scutari. Not precisely the same, of course. The hair was streaked with gray near the temples, and the face itself bore new lines and hollows of illness. But for the rest of it, in almost all respects, from the proud attitude of his stance, to the cut of his new garments which clung to his new lean frame in a most becoming manner, to the almost blinding brilliance of his highly polished boots, this *was* Miss Nightingale's "young lion," *Punch*'s "most remarkable man," the *London Times*'s "genius," and, sadly, his own worst enemy.

For some reason known only to God, Susan suffered an embarrassing burning which felt ominously like tears. While he posed a moment longer, she took advantage of this last second's privacy to withdraw her handkerchief from the sleeve of her dress and wipe at her eyes.

"I trust you didn't catch cold yesterday, Miss Mantle."

As she heard the familiar voice approaching, she breathed a quick prayer for control. For both their sakes. "No." She smiled, looking up at

129

the man who now stood even with her on the step, though separated by about ten feet.

"I hope not," he said. "How ungrateful I would be to allow you to cure me, then fall ill yourself."

"I'm not ill, Mr. Eden, and neither did I cure you. You did that, with God's help."

She saw a familiar weariness on his face, as though he found few things more tedious than talk of God. She was sorry for that.

"Well," he said expansively, and looked about mid-step as though he'd dropped something, "a good day for travel, wouldn't you say?"

"I would indeed," she agreed, wondering which man she preferred, the weak and angry and uncertain one which she'd glimpsed in the cottage yesterday, or this arrogant, self-confident, and strutting peacock. It wasn't too difficult to discern which one *he* preferred.

"And you're leaving, as well?" he inquired now, carefully, meticulously drawing on gray kid gloves, while below in the courtyard over thirty-five men waited as each finger was being carefully angled into each opening.

"Yes," she said with abrupt sharpness.

"Where?" he asked, drawing a step nearer, shortening the distance between them.

"Clovelly first," she replied. "Reverend Christopher tells me there is fever—"

"A disgusting place"—he frowned—"built for mountain goats rather than human beings."

She saw effortlessly in her mind's eye the perpendicular little fishing village that did indeed cling to the side of a steep cliff and where the most beautiful climbing geraniums in all of England grew.

"Is that wise?" he went on, stepping closer.

"I . . . don't understand," she said, not having the vaguest idea what he had reference to.

"Going where there is fever."

"There are precautions one can take," she said, trying to reassure him. "I promise I will take them."

"The best precaution would be not to go at all," he said, scolding.

"It is my work," she said, equally stern.

For a moment the impasse held. She thought she saw additional questions forming on his face, and waited patiently to see if they would be forthcoming.

He too seemed to be waiting, his eyes fixed on some aspect of her face. "About the cottage . . ." he began.

"No."

"Will you—?"

"I said—"

"Then will you take care?"

"And you, too. . . ."

In the almost rapid-fire exchange she tried to memorize all aspects of his face and at the same time tried to be coherent, and, she suspected, failed at both. "You'd better hurry," she scolded lightly, turning away to hide her various weaknesses. "Salisbury by night . . ."

"Easy."

"On good roads . . ."

"Charley will get us there."

"I'm sure he will."

"Fifteen shillings per week," he grumbled, though with a smile.

"You'll sleep better." She smiled back.

He started to say something else—she was certain of it—even drew nearer. Then all of a sudden he changed his mind and started down the stairs, and in his eagerness to depart, he failed to rely upon the support of the walking stick and, as his left leg buckled beneath him, he went heavily and painfully down on his knees, striking his shins in the process, his right hand clawing for something to cling to in an attempt to prevent a more serious fall all the way to the bottom of the steep stairs.

Instinctively she reached out. And missed. And reached again, and felt his hand grasp at hers with a death grip.

"Mr. Eden!"

An excited parade, led by Bates, with a shocked and concerned Charley Spade following behind, hurried up the steps. Bates cast a suspicious glance at her, as though she were responsible for this embarrassment before going down with an offer of assistance to Mr. Eden, who continued to cling to her hand as though certain if he let go he would surely fall the rest of the way.

"Mr. Eden, may I . . . please let me . . ."

As Bates hovered, Susan gently but firmly withdrew her hand, thus making it available for Bates, who took it readily.

Leaning heavily on Bates and resembling a man twice his age, Mr. Eden made it down the stairs and into the carriage, where within the instant he settled back into the far corner and released the small purple velvet curtains, and the interior of the carriage and its unhappy cargo were sealed from view.

Again she'd wanted it to be so much more, but like the ill-fated walk of the day before, something had happened. Yesterday it had been the rain and her own foolishness. And today? She had no idea.

Without warning, she suffered a severe sense of deprivation.

"God go with him, please, and keep him safe," she prayed quickly, and realized it was perhaps the most urgent prayer she'd ever uttered in her life.

Exmoor Road
October 23, 1874

Rose O'Donnell stood beside the road about two miles from Eden Castle and watched the lingering, shapeless ground fog brush against her skirts and stared down the long rutted road and wondered how long the scarecrow man expected her to stand here catching her death, when she had pressing errands to be about.

Though dawn had broken, there still was a chill, and carefully she rested her portmanteau against her legs. With both hands she tightened the collar of her cloak and heard the wind whistling over Exmoor and looked in all directions and saw only fog and space and emptiness and desolation.

Like the devil Englishman hisself, she thought vindictively, and the sense of sin brought her comfort, God forgive her, and warmed her bones against the early-morning chill.

As she tucked her gloveless hands inside her cloak, she shivered, unseeing, and thought back on her early-morning escape. Not escape, really. Her job in that chilly grave was well over, and she had an earful for Lord Harrington—for which she'd get paid handsome, and every pence and pound of it would go into the tobacco tin which she kept buried under the large rubbish barrel in the back. And one day soon she'd have enough to purchase passage aboard one of them grand ships sailing for America, where she would be reunited with the most gorgeous man God ever created, her very own Denis Bourke O'Donnell, deported from Ireland along with nine others as a result of their revolutionary activities. Four years she'd existed without Denis' comfort. Oh, she told everyone she was a widow. It was easier and saved her the embarrassment of questions. But the day that Denis Bourke O'Donnell died would be the day that Rose O'Donnell contrived to crawl into her grave as well, God forbid.

She shivered again. The chill was penetrating. Winter coming. She hoped this was her first and last trip for Lord Harrington. She didn't like coming down to the devil's country. Of course, she guessed she wouldn't mind if the price were right, but she preferred to do his spying for him on home territory, as it were, and there were plenty of English bastards swarming over Dublin to keep her busy for a long time—at least long enough to get her that one-way passage to America, to New York City.

Abruptly she heard a distant rattling sound that disrupted the silence of the moors. She looked fearfully down the road to the end of the world, or so it seemed, and saw it, that grand carriage made small by distance—which was all right, for she'd like to prissy herself up a bit so she'd look her best and perhaps beguile the devil into thinking she was harmless company and he'd tell her more than she already knew.

Inside her voluminous cloak she felt for and found the silver mug bearing the Eden coat of arms she'd stolen from the Grand Dining Hall so that Lord Harrington would know she'd penetrated the enemy fortress. Of course, the more hard-and-fast information she had, the better, at least for the tobacco tin buried in the back, though she couldn't for the life of her understand why Lord Harrington gave a damn, God forgive her, about the madhouse that was Eden Castle. Of course, she believed children needed both a mother and a father, but Lord Harrington was doing a good job with the boys—with *her* help, of course. Frederic, the little one, seemed to grow more shy and uncertain every day, but Stephen bore an astonishing resemblance to the devil hisself. Anyway, both were getting along very well, thank you, without a father, and would continue to do so. Then what in the name of God had Lord Harrington sent her down here for—under cover, as it were—to "see what she could see and hear what she could hear"?

The noise from the rattling carriage was growing louder, though it was still a distance away. Oh, she wished it would hurry and get here and she could learn why the scarecrow named Bates had given her strict instructions to be waiting on this road at this time, "because Mr. Eden himself wants a word with you."

Gawd! Suddenly a terrifying thought occurred. What if he'd found her out, discovered that she was in the employ of Lord Harrington, and asked her to wait so one of his minions could do her in?

Fearfully she eyed the approaching carriage and crossed herself, started to flee, and was smart enough to realize that if she could see the carriage, the carriage could see her. No, she must hold her ground like a good soldier, like Denis Bourke O'Donnell would want her to, and meet the enemy face to face for the cause of Ireland and all those glorious men unjustly deported.

The rattling grew louder, a thunderous approach, a sound which could come only from hell. She reached quickly down and grabbed her portmanteau and flattened her hand atop her black bonnet, for accompanying the devil there was always a wind, and, as she saw the six enormous animals draw nearer, she was prepared to swear she saw fire coming from their nostrils.

Apparently the devil had spoken, for suddenly the horses broke speed, yet passed her by and came to a halt thirty feet on the other side. For several minutes no one moved in or around the grand carriage, and the only sound was the breathless and impatient snorting of the horses, which pawed at the ground and shook their huge heads as though angered by the sudden halting.

Slowly the carriage door started to open. One white-gloved hand was the only thing visible, and she kept it in her sights as though it alone was the symbol of all evil. Out of the corner of her eye she saw the giant on the high seat adjust the collar of his too-tight jacket, draw it up around his throat as though he too were feeling the chill, and she thought it strange that a minion from hell should carry such a chill within him.

The white glove expanded into a black-clad arm and shoulder, and suddenly the old scarecrow was staring out at her like she was a lesser thing.

"You!" he called out in his horrible British voice.

She drew herself up to her full five feet, two inches. "Me name is not You. Me name is Rose O'Donnell."

"I know your name," the old man shouted back, stooping on his way out of the carriage; then, while she was still trying to peer inside, he closed the door behind him and stepped gingerly down to the soggy tundra of moorland, doing a funny little jig in the process, searching for a patch of dry moss.

Rose did nothing to hide her smile. The old man looked like a stiff black grasshopper.

Apparently he saw the smile and snapped angrily, "Leave that!" and pointed at the portmanteau. "Step inside. Mr. Eden desires a word with you."

Before he had finished speaking, she was already shaking her head. "No, sir, I ain't gonna do that."

"I . . . don't . . . What do you mean?" the old man stammered, balancing precariously on one small square patch which he'd thought dry. Unfortunately he couldn't see the moisture creeping up on both sides of his once highly polished black boots.

"I mean what I says," she repeated. "I won't leave me portmanteau."

"I'll watch it for you," he snapped, and gestured toward the carriage door.

She started to argue some more, then changed her mind. Get it over with. Shyly she went forward, plunging her hands into the inner pockets of her cloak in an attempt to warm them, and as she did, she felt of her rosary with her left hand.

Before the carriage door, she briefly faltered. If he was the devil . . .

"Madam, do you require assistance?" It was the old scarecrow again.

"No, just getting me footing," she replied breezily.

Her first impression was one of night. How dark the interior of the carriage was after the bright sun of morning.

"Mr. Eden?" she called out tentatively, still clutching the crucifix. As she crouched inside the door, her second impression was how cramped a place it was, this gentleman's carriage. She wouldn't care to take a prolonged journey in it. Not half as big or as grand as Mr. Charles Parnell's carriage, the one in which he had transported her from Dublin to Lord Harrington's estate north of Dublin. Now, *that* had been a carriage, as grand as the man who owned it. But this one . . .

134

"Have a seat, madam," came a voice from the dark recess, and as her vision began to adjust to the shadows, she saw a shape slumped against the far window, all swathed in a dark cloak. Well, she knew who it was, and eased carefully down into the far seat opposite him. Didn't need a road map, not Rose O'Donnell.

"Your name, please," this weary voice now requested. And it *had* been a request, very softly spoken, a slight nervousness audible in certain words.

"Rose O'Donnell," she said, and sat up straight to look again around the cramped interior. "I looked for you, I did, the last few days." She smiled, turning on the charm which Denis Bourke O'Donnell said she had considerable.

The shape nodded, and she sensed a smile. "I wanted to thank you for giving me employ, taking me in, as it were."

"May I ask your destination?" came the voice opposite her, apparently not given to niceties.

"My destination, sir, is Dub . . ."

Oh, Christ, Holy Mother . . . She almost spoiled the pudding then, she did! She'd told the little nurse back at Eden that she was on her way to London in search of honest employment. She'd better remember her own deceptions or she'd get herself into plenty of hot water.

"My destination, sir, is London," she said, smiling at the shape, confident he didn't catch the near-mistake.

"And where is your home, Mrs. O'Donnell?" he asked.

"Dublin, sir. Born and raised there, married and widowed there, sir."

"Why are you leaving it?"

She glanced down at her lap and feigned grief. Or at least she hoped it looked like grief. "I need . . . a fresh world, yes, I do, sir, altogether fresh from first to last. You see, me husband, God rest his soul, passed on last year."

"Would you object to returning to Dublin, Mrs. O'Donnell?"

Shocked at first, she cocked her head toward the faltering voice. "I thought you asked me if I wanted to return to Dublin." She grinned.

"I did," came the quiet confirmation. "Of course, there will be more than fair payment for your troubles."

"I . . . don't understand . . ."

"Mrs. O'Donnell," the shape began, and straightened.

For the first time she saw his face close at hand. In the past she'd seen it only blurred and at a distance—across the Great Hall or making his tortuous way across the courtyard with the scarecrow Bates at his side.

Now he sat fully erect and pushed back the voluminous cape that had so successfully encased him, at the same time slightly dislodging one of the heavy drawn drapes at his elbow. A beam of bright morning sun instantly illuminated the interior of the carriage and revealed fine appointments— which she vowed to inspect more closely later.

Then she heard his voice again and discovered the voice matched the face, belonged with it, as it were. Soft, gently entreating. And false.

"I need your help, Mrs. O'Donnell," he was saying, his clasped hands folded tightly before him, his eyes down, as though he was praying.

"Me, sir?" Rose gasped, still stunned by that face. "I'm sure I don't know how—"

"Oh, you can be of immense service"—he smiled—"but what I have to ask of you is an enormous task. I don't know what prompts me to ask it of you, a stranger, except I sense a trust. I sense a good heart and, most important, I sense a past of deep grief and pain. Is that true, Mrs. O'Donnell?"

She nodded and bowed her head. Perhaps, just perhaps, there was a remote possibility, just a possibility, this wasn't altogether the devil hisself.

"Correct, sir, Mr. Eden." She nodded and fished through her pockets for the handkerchief she knew she didn't have. "I'm . . . so . . ." she began, and never finished, for suddenly an elegant linen handkerchief appeared within her downward line of vision.

"Please take it, Mrs. O'Donnell," the quiet voice urged.

"I . . . don't know when I can return it, sir," she murmured, eyeing the lovely linen square complete with inlaid lace monogram of three letters—JME.

"I'm not asking that you return it, Mrs. O'Donnell. In fact, please keep it."

There was a pause while she took the lovely hyacinth-scented linen-and-lace square and lightly dabbed at her eyes. "Now, sir, please tell me how I can serve you."

"How well do you know Dublin?" he asked.

"Dublin, sir?" She grinned. "I know it just about as well as I know the back of me hand. No, better! You see I was born there, I was, and raised there."

The news seemed to please him enormously. "Good." He smiled. "There is, close by . . ." he began, and suddenly faltered. "At least I've been told there is close by to Dublin an estate known as Avondale. Are you familiar with it?"

Suddenly she wished he'd draw the drapes again before her blush gave her away. Did she know it? She'd been in service there right after Denis Bourke O'Donnell had been deported, taken in along with the nine other "widows" who had nothing to do and no place to go, by that grandest of all gentlemen Mr. Charles Parnell.

"Avondale?" she repeated. "No, sir, can't say as I've heard of it. But if it's near to Dublin, I can promise you I can—"

"What I would like for you to do, Mrs. O'Donnell, is this." With sudden urgency and matching secrecy he leaned forward. "I would like for you— for a very handsome fee, of course—to return immediately to Dublin . . ."

Not bad, that, since it was her direction anyway.

". . . and once there, I want you to launch a very quiet search for Avondale. It shouldn't be too difficult," he went on, his voice exhibiting duress, "for it belongs to a criminal named Charles Parnell."

For just a moment her Irish heart turned with righteous indignation. "May I ask, sir, what I'm looking for in this place . . . What was the name, sir? Avon—"

"Avondale," he said, quick to supply her with the right name. And he was equally quick with the rest of his reply. "Because I have reason to believe that an archfiend named Lord Harrington is in residence there."

Well, now. An interesting turn of events. Lord Harrington and Mr.

Parnell had sent her in search of "the English devil," who in turn was sending her back in search of "the criminal" and the "archfiend."

"I . . . don't understand, sir," she puzzled, understanding perfectly well.

"Please," he begged, "hear me out and say yes, for you are my only hope . . ."

Oh, she liked that part!

". . . to regain my two sons, who were stolen from me over four years ago by Lord Harrington and his cohort."

Holy Mother, it was like hearing the same script from two actors who were merely inserting different names.

Now she repeated the name. "Lord . . . Harrington, you say?"

He nodded and sat up even straighter. The very one," he confirmed, "who four years ago, while I was in London and unable to stand guard, returned to the castle, where I had left my two sons in the safekeeping of a nursemaid, and after having talked his way past the guards, he took my sons, mere infants, their mother recently deceased, and spirited them out of the castle and out of England, and I've not seen them since."

Gawd! She'd not heard that. According to Lord Harrington the two tykes had been abandoned by their mother, who had died, and by their father, whose sole purpose in life now seemed to be to drink himself into oblivion. No, Lord Harrington had never said anything about stealing children.

"Two . . . lads, you say?" she asked quietly.

"Mere babes they were," he murmured. "One is named Stephen. The last time I saw him, he was four. The other is Frederick."

Frederick, oh yes, she could give him a more complete physical description than he could give her, having washed and scrubbed them, dressed and fed them, comforted and cuddled them, and, on occasion, even instructed them. For one incredible moment she felt a strong urge to tell him that the lads were doing well, though they were no longer babes. But she held her tongue and concentrated instead on this new dilemma.

". . . and this would be merely first payment," Mr. Eden was saying.

She looked up out of her confusion to see a large parchment envelope being extended toward her. A rather plump envelope, she observed, and as the gentleman was still talking, she merely eyed the envelope and listened carefully.

". . . and if you agree to what I've asked of you, Mrs. O'Donnell," he went on, "then we will take you as far as Exeter, where you can catch the train to the Midlands and depart on the St. George's ferry for Dublin. As soon as you arrive, I want you to take decent rooms, purchase a decent wardrobe, and hire a carriage and a competent coachman. Then from this secure and comfortable base you are to launch your search. When you are in need of additional funds, contact this man." He handed her a small card neatly engraved, bearing the name of one Alex Aldwell.

Yes, she remembered the gentleman from his brief stay at Eden. He'd seemed pleasant enough . . .

". . . and Mr. Aldwell will see to it that a bank draft is placed in your name in a Dublin bank. Do you understand?"

Oh, Gawd, yes, she understood! Everything. A plot, a plan made in heaven, where for an unlimited period of time and with little effort and less risk she could play both sides against the middle and in the process reap a harvest far richer than anything she might ever have dreamed of.

"Mrs. O'Donnell, are you well?"

The thoughtful inquiry came from that grand gentleman across from her—not the devil, surely not the devil—and besides, who was a child-stealer to be calling another man "the devil"?

"Aye, Mr. Eden." She smiled meekly, taking the large parchment envelope and estimating fairly accurately the number of notes inside. All that remained to be seen was the amount of each. A bit of quick multiplication and . . .

But she couldn't quite bring herself to do that yet. In fact, it would best serve her purpose to appear hesitant and doubtful. "Aye, of course I understand, Mr. Eden, and me heart breaks for them wee babes who was spirited away from you . . . but still I hesitates to serve you, because . . ." She broke off at the timely moment and saw the dark clouds of disappointment already gathering on his fine brow and tried to estimate the value of those dark clouds of disappointment.

"Why?" he asked urgently. "I am capable of making your life very comfortable. All I ask in return is your assistance and your loyalty."

"Oh, you have my loyalty, sir," she said quickly, "as you've always had it. No, my only hesitation is . . . fear of letting you down."

"I'm not bargaining for results," he said reassuringly. "I'm only bargaining that you will try to help me find my sons. If you do, you will be amply rewarded. If not"—he shrugged—"you are free to keep what you will have already earned."

Pleased that no results would be expected of her, she lifted the large envelope again to peel the edge only high enough to slip the business card into it, though in the process she caught sight of a number . . .

Ten!

Not possible. This lovely envelope could not possibly be filled with ten-pound notes. The thickness indicated . . .

"There are one hundred pounds there, Mrs. O'Donnell," he said thoughtfully, confirming what she did not think possible.

Easy, Rose, close your mouth. Keep your wits on a short leash.

". . . and there's more," Mr. Eden said, apparently unmindful of the miracle he'd placed in her hands. "All I want is news of my sons." Suddenly he pushed even farther back into the cushions, his face livid with anger. "My God," he exclaimed, "why should I have to bargain for my sons? *My* sons, Mrs. O'Donnell . . ."

And in his fervor she found herself agreeing with him. A man's sons were his most sacred possession. They were, in effect, his tomorrow.

"Please, Mrs. O'Donnell, say you'll help me. I promise you will never regret it."

"And where, Mr. Eden, do I contact you when I have . . . news?"

Suddenly the face brooding opposite her broke into a smile. "Thank you, Mrs. O'Donnell . . ."

He pushed open the carriage door and issued a soft command. "Bates, load the lady's luggage and direct Charley Spade to stop at the Coach Inn in Exeter. It will delay us, but no matter. Mrs. O'Donnell will accompany us to that point."

Without waiting to see his command had been followed, he settled back in the seat and gave her a most grateful smile. "We have about two hours to talk and chart a plan, Mrs. O'Donnell. So make yourself comfortable . . ."

She grinned and nodded. Gawd! Who'd have thought it? Rose O'Donnell riding in this fancy carriage with the devil himself.

Haunch of Venison
Public House,
Salisbury, England
October 24, 1874

Whenever possible, the young man preferred to sit in shadows. Alex had observed it too often not to take notice of it now and wonder at it and fear for it.

Alex pushed close to the crowded bar in the Haunch of Venison and glanced over his shoulder at the shadowed man who now ran the John Murrey firm with a most efficient and profitable hand. The way the fixed wall lamp cast its illumination, it looked as though someone had painted a line diagonally across his chest, casting the lower portion in clear concise light and the upper into the muddled darkness of night.

"Same, mate?" The barkeep grinned.

Alex nodded.

As the barkeep slid the filled mug across the bar, Alex caught it, sipped, and vowed to make it the last. After a long and satisfying swallow, he wiped the excess from around his mouth with the back of his hand and felt again a pronounced anxiety over this unscheduled meeting. Why Aslam had insisted upon coming at the last minute, Alex had not been able to discern. He and John would have to say what they wanted to say to each other quickly and transfer the large portfolio of funds; then Alex and Aslam had to be on their way back to London—a night's journey that would leave both of them exhausted for the stockholders' meeting tomorrow.

Why had Aslam insisted on this unscheduled meeting with John?

He looked up at the young man at the far corner table, his dark head bowed over a thick sheaf of papers.

What was it? Alex tried to guess and couldn't—which of course was why Aslam was head of the John Murrey firm and Alex considerably lower. Still, he had done battle for Aslam, had stood by him, had defended

140

him in those first tentative days when John had abandoned the reins of leadership and all of financial London had waited gleefully to see the John Murrey empire topple.

But of course it hadn't toppled at all, had it? Lord, no, it was stronger than ever, and all due to the brilliant foresight of that young man who preferred shadows, who with apparent ease had taken a good hard look at his adopted country four years ago and had determined—long before anyone else—that the fortunes of England would be changing in this decade. From 1815 until now, England had still measured her wealth largely in land and its products, and except in years of bad harvests, her food had been grown at home.

But, as Aslam had determined, the population by 1870 had more than doubled, and to feed these new millions, more and more food would have to be purchased abroad. Exports to pay for these purchases and for the purchase of raw materials would become the lifeblood of the nation.

Happily for the John Murrey firm, Aslam had figured right. He had taken the millions of pounds in profits from the company and created a monstrous import/export corporation with vast offices in St. Katherine's Dock and a fleet of twenty-eight seaworthy vessels, all of which flew the Union Jack but which, interestingly enough, bore the name the Star of India.

Across the aisle, a noisy dart game grew more so, everyone talking and laughing, shouting at full pitch. Someone shouted, "Shut the bloody door!"

Feeling the chill himself, Alex looked up from his brooding. Framed in the doorway was old Bates, bracing the door with the full length of his back, clearly holding it open for someone who had yet to appear. As the old man looked disdainfully out over the crowded pub, the voices around Alex fell. How well they must suit each other, Bates and John, Alex brooded, wishing he could remain invisible for the rest of the evening.

Now John stood framed in the open doorway, ignoring an ox of a young man who hovered nervously about. Clearly he had been told to "help" Mr. Eden, but Mr. Eden seemed to require no help, though Alex determined he looked tired, the flesh stretched tight over bone, and he seemed to lean heavily on the walking stick.

Amazed he still suffered a degree of love for the man, Alex considered going to him at once, then changed his mind.

"John," he called out, and surprised even himself with the force of his voice.

At once John looked in his direction, then turned immediately with a quick whispered command to Bates, who, within the instant, relayed it to the large man who still hovered, red-cheeked, behind John.

"John, good to see you." Alex smiled.

Almost shyly John returned the smile, shifted the walking stick to his left hand, and accepted warmly the outstretched hand. "The world is a wondrous place, Alex," he said quietly, glancing about at the pub, where, en masse, the patrons continued to stare back at him. "I've been estranged from it for several years, so perhaps custom has changed." He leaned closer. "Could you tell me? Am I doing something wrong?"

Alex laughed heartily. How becoming was this new uncertainty, and how promising. "No, I assure you," Alex said warmly. "You are doing

141

nothing wrong." He lowered his voice and clasped an affectionate hand on the shoulder, which felt so thin through the thickness of cloak. "You fascinate them, John, as you have always fascinated people."

John seemed to dismiss this as so much nonsense, and glanced back over his shoulder, as though checking on his two men.

"However," Alex said, "may I suggest we close the door, and they might not stare quite so hard."

John obliged with a suddenness that indicated he'd had no idea he'd been causing them discomfort. "I *am* sorry," he murmured, closing the door behind him.

During this brief moment, Alex glanced toward the table by the far partition. Aslam was in solid shadow again, the convenient shadow of the fixed wall lamp, though his papers still lay scattered over the table before him. Alex turned back to Eden.

"What can I get for you, John?" He watched the man settle with obvious weariness into a chair, his left leg extended stiffly. Alex was certain that Aslam's black eyes were seeing and recording everything.

"Nothing, thank you," John said.

"But you must be starved," Alex protested lighty. "It's late and the night is chill . . ."

"Nothing now," John repeated, at last looking up. "The warmth feels good. That's sufficient."

"Will your men share a room?" Alex asked, referring to Bates and the strapping lad who still hovered close to John.

All at once a smile cut through the weariness of John's face. "Bates? And Charley Spade? No, I'm afraid not."

Alex nodded and started up. "I'll tell the publican—"

"Not yet," John objected. "Please sit for a moment. I must talk with you."

Alex obliged, looking again at the table in the far corner. No sign of movement from the young man. What in the hell was he doing? It had been his idea to come and see John. Then why didn't he?

"I'm sorry we're late," John said, at last loosening the tie of the cloak about his neck. "We were detained at Exeter—"

"Nothing serious, I hope?"

"No, business. And I must talk to you about it."

Business? In Exeter? Alex drew his chair closer and motioned away one of the little rosy-cheeked barmaids who had been inching closer and closer ever since John had seated himself at the table. "All right, this business," Alex began, settling in the chair at an angle so his back was toward the far corner. Perhaps what he couldn't see wouldn't bother him.

"Yes." John nodded and shrugged the cloak all the way off, laid the walking stick crossways on his lap, and stared at it. "Do you recall from your last visit to Eden the woman named Rose O'Donnell?"

Alex blinked, struggling with the name, never his strong suit. "That wasn't the little nurse, was it?"

"No," John said, shaking his head. "This woman cooked for us for a few weeks," he added, trying to refresh Alex's memory.

"Yes," he recalled. "Some mystery to her, wasn't there?"

"Not really. She was newly widowed, unable to find decent employment in Dublin and on her way to London when she ran out of funds and stopped at Eden to replenish the coffers."

142

Suddenly Alex knew precisely what John was going to tell him. His sons! They were involved. The giant had indeed stirred—Aslam's phrase, not his—and now he wanted his sons back. It had always been inevitable; then why was Alex so surprised as John talked steadily, telling him of this new conspiracy between himself and Rose O'Donnell?

". . . and as soon as I return from Paris with Elizabeth," John went on, "I shall be returning to Eden. The woman knows to contact me there. But I have no idea how long this silly French business will take, and I have given her your card and London address. You are to reimburse her for every piece of information she sends you, no matter how small and inconsequential."

Alex nodded, grateful that Aslam was not present. Handing out banknotes to an unknown Irishwoman in Dublin for information that could not be verified would offend his good judgment. But Alex would oblige—for a period of time—out of his own purse for John's sake. Or, better still, perhaps the female sleuth would not uncover any clue until John and Elizabeth returned from France. Then John could deal with her exclusively.

"Will you do it for me, Alex?" John asked, a new urgency to his voice.

"Of course I'll do it. Haven't I always honored your requests in the past?"

Relieved, John sat back in the chair. "I want my sons back," he said. "Is it asking too much? Of course not," he answered his own question. "I had no idea that it would stretch on this long. Lord Harrington has no right. No right at all . . ."

"We'll find the lads, John. I swear it," Alex vowed, though he quickly suggested, "It may take time . . ."

"Thank you." John smiled.

"Where will she start, this Irishwoman . . . what's her name?"

"Rose O'Donnell, and she will start in Dublin or just outside it at Avondale, Mr. Parnell's home. If you recall, Harriet said that's where . . ." He slowed, then stopped altogether, as though a blockage of some sort had occurred. A few seconds later he picked up the fragmented sentence. ". . . that's where Lord Harrington was taking the boys."

"But that was four years ago, John. Surely he has established his own residence by now."

"I would think so." John nodded. "But Mrs. O'Donnell will be a skillful detective. She appears to be naturally curious and endlessly talkative. I've given her an initial payment which enables her to take decent lodgings and hire a carriage, buy some reputable garments and stay moderately well-fed. Thus armed, I doubt there is anything Rose O'Donnell couldn't accomplish."

For the first time a hint of a smile altered the skeletal face, and Alex recalled how much in the past John had adored intrigue.

"I wonder how they've changed, Alex," he murmured now. "They were so young . . ."

"I'm sure they've changed, John, and I'd be willing to wager they're not so small any longer."

Abruptly John changed the subject. He sat up and looked as though he was ready to stand. "Where do you suppose they had to go to find a decent stable?" he asked.

"Down the street," Alex replied, equally distracted, though his concern was not the location of a good stable but rather the still-shadowed man who continued to sit at the table by the far partition. *What in the hell was he doing?*

Alex leaned forward. "John, I did not come alone tonight."

"And who accompanied you?" John asked, smiling. "A lovely lady, I hope for your sake."

"No, I'm afraid not," he said with only a twinge of regret. "Someone much more important—to both of us."

At last he had John's interest. "Who?" he demanded, and Alex detected a new defensiveness in his voice.

"Aslam," Alex said simply, and without looking in that direction, pointed over his shoulder toward the corner.

For a moment it seemed all light and movement had departed from John's face. Considering the skull-like nature of the face, he resembled a poorly done death mask. "Where?" he asked quietly, as though he didn't want anybody else to know.

Wordlessly Alex glanced toward the far partition, surprised now to see the young man on his feet, as though he'd known at the precise moment when Alex had informed John he had not come alone.

"A-Aslam?" John stuttered, squinting his eyes into the interior of the pub.

Alex nodded foolishly, and stood immediately back. John followed slowly, forgetting at first the walking stick he'd positioned across his knees, having to grab for it at the last minute.

"Aslam, is it you?" John asked, projecting his voice slightly, a new warmth beginning to break through. But he continued to clutch at the walking stick with his right hand while he clung with his left to the edge of the small table, his shoulders stooped, his face slightly flushed.

As for Aslam, he seemed to be suffering a similar paralysis, though he stood ramrod-straight, as though with military bearing. The shadow cast by the fixed wall standard now covered the top half of his body.

Still they stood, until Alex sensed something besides nonrecognition stretching between them, something less palatable, which felt uncomfortably like . . . embarrassment.

Then Alex understood. It was coming from John, who obviously felt the full weight of his various impairments after his seclusion and illness. He must be aware too of the physical changes which had taken place. After all, he was the one who had to confront the looking glass every morning. Now . . .

"It *is* the lad, John, all grown up. Why don't you go and greet him?" Alex urged again.

Quickly John nodded, and, as though to hide at least a portion of his disability, he tried to take the first few steps without the aid of the walking stick. Fortunately both Alex and the table were close enough to prevent a serious fall. And, clearly sobered by that prospect, John waited a moment until he regained his center of balance, then pressed the stick into use. He was steady on his feet now, indicated as much to Alex, and this time started forward in full control, with a smile.

"Aslam," he called out again, and stood, his arms wide, a familiar gesture between them. Alex had seen him greet the boy thus for years. Now

144

Alex hoped the boy remembered this ritual greeting as well, for from the expression on John's face, he wanted very much to embrace the boy.

But still Aslam stood unmoving, his hands motionless at his sides. Not until John, with mounting confusion and embarrassment, lowered his arms and looked bewilderedly back at Alex did the young man deign to move. Even then it was with insolent deliberation. Two steps, and he was beyond the protection of shadows, though curiously Alex found himself wishing the young man was obscured again, for his dark face and patrician features revealed a chill objectivity amounting almost to indifference.

What in the hell was the matter with him?

"Aslam," John said, "it's good to see you."

In reply the young man simply gave a stiff nod of his head and instantly withdrew his hand, as though physical contact with John was loathsome. "And you," he said rigidly in that clipped way of his which Alex heard every day, but only now did he realize how wintry it sounded. "I understand from Mr. Aldwell," Aslam went on, "that you have been indisposed."

"Yes." John nodded, still not fully recovered from the rebuff. "But I'm quite restored now, thanks to a remarkable woman who simply refused to let me do anything but get better."

"How fortunate for you," came the voice of winter. "But then, you always were gifted when it came to finding women who would serve your purposes."

Sharply Alex looked up. What in the hell?

John apparently wondered the same, as briefly a look of bewilderment covered his features. "I . . . don't . . . understand," he stammered.

"Would you prefer to sit?" Aslam asked, his voice broadening along with his gesture, which took in two chairs at a near table.

"N-no," John stammered. "That is, unless you . . ."

"No, I stand whenever possible," the young man pronounced, and seemed to stare for a moment at John's left hand, which had begun to tremble visibly. "I understand from Mr. Aldwell," Aslam went on, beginning to pace back and forth in the limited area between chairs, "that you have undertaken a rescue mission to Paris on behalf of Elizabeth."

"Y-yes." John nodded, and leaned heavily on the table, an unfortunate position which caused him to slump before the ramrod-straight Aslam.

"Then I wish you well, for Elizabeth is worth saving."

This curious and insensitive statement seemed to create an even greater confusion. "Yes." John nodded. "She is being detained on some charge at the La Rochelle House of—"

"I know where she is, John. It was one of my men who located her for you. According to his report, her sentence is concluded in a few months. You might be wise to leave her in prison until the end of her sentence, help to drive the lesson home, you know."

With every word the young man uttered, the look of confusion on John's face grew.

Alex decided it was time to intervene. He drew forth a chair with a command that left no room for debate. "Please sit, John," and he was not too surprised to see the man obey. Under the strain of the mystery that was Aslam, John's weakness was increasing.

145

All he could say was, "No. I must go and fetch her. You see, she needs—"

From where Alex stood, he saw a cold light of amusement on Aslam's face. "Of course, if she needs you . . ." he repeated, looked back, and blurted out, "I see Richard, you know, quite often."

Helpless, John glanced up at Alex for direction. Unhappily, Alex had none to give.

"And . . . how is he?" John asked, his voice falling quite low, as though this mere boy was getting the best of him.

"Richard is fine," Aslam replied, ". . . most of the time. Of course, he misses his home Eden, as you know."

"He's welcome anytime."

"I think not."

John nodded slowly, though he did not look up at Aslam but concentrated on the silver head of his walking stick. "Where is . . . Richard residing now?" he asked.

"Forbes Hall. Kent. With his wife, Lady Eleanor."

At this John looked up, surprised pleasure cutting through the defeat. "Wife?" he repeated.

Aslam nodded, though the skin on his forehead tightened as though nothing displeased him more than John's pleasure. "Two years now. It couldn't be avoided, as you so well know. It was the pact you had made with her parents. Though both are dead now, Eleanor held Richard to his promise." There was a pause. "Both are miserable."

To this account John gaped wordlessly. Once he shook his head as though to deny something, but Aslam didn't give him a chance.

"Richard is honorable. He has at last impregnated her. She's carrying the firstborn. If it is a son, he has told me he will never touch her again."

Alex listened with shocked indignation. He'd not heard this before. For a moment no one spoke.

Just then the door flew open and Bates appeared, his keen eyes searching immediately for his master, finding him, and clearly not liking what he saw. Behind him trailed the young giant, who juggled effortlessly two large trunks, one on each shoulder. Hurriedly Bates whispered something to him and pointed toward the publican behind the bar.

"Are you well, sir?" Bates asked in a concerned tone.

When there was no response, Bates drew closer, on the verge of repeating the question, when suddenly there was movement coming from the far corner—Aslam gathering up his scattered papers, returning them all to a large portmanteau, and reaching for something inside the portmanteau, withdrawing a large flat black leather folder.

Everything restored to order and to his satisfaction, he walked slowly to the table at which John sat. "Funds," he said simply, "for your journey. If you require more . . ."

But John quickly shook his head.

"I trust you will find Elizabeth well and intact."

John nodded and still did not speak or look up.

"As soon as . . . you are fully recovered," Aslam went on, a new strain beginning to show on his dark face, "and, of course, if you are interested, I would like to apprise you of the progress of the John Murrey firm."

At last John looked slowly up, as though the familiarity of the name had attracted his attention. "I . . . would like that," he said.

"Well, then," Aslam said, stepped back from the table, and lifted his head as though in need of air. "I must return to London tonight. I wanted to see . . ." He broke off as though embarrassed by the unspoken sentence. For a moment it looked as though he would say something else, but at the last minute he changed his mind and walked rapidly around the table, past Bates, past Alex, and was almost to the door when John stopped him with a single word.

"Wait!"

Aslam obeyed instinctively. The voice that had spoken that word, though weakened now, once had carried with it all the authority in Aslam's world. So he waited, just at the door, his hand on the doorknob, his head down. "What do you want?"

Interesting, Alex thought. Both men were positioned with their backs to each other.

For several seconds it was as though John had forgotten why he'd called out. Then slowly he lifted his head. "Mary. Have you heard from Mary?"

Alex might have known. Mary. His favorite, his beloved cousin, Harriet's daughter.

"No, I have not," Aslam replied crisply.

Slowly John nodded. Alex couldn't be certain, but he thought he detected a sense of relief coming from John. Not knowing, on occasion, was far better.

"Thank you for coming," John said to the empty space beyond the table.

Aslam's head lifted, and Alex thought he might speak. But he didn't. He simply waved a backward hand in Alex's direction, drew open the door, and went out into the night, leaving the door open, as though confident someone lesser than he would close it.

For several moments no one moved. If there was any sound at all in the crowded pub, it had been drowned out by that deafening silence.

"Nigger!" came the hissed voice of old Bates. "Never did like the nigger. Treacherous, all of them."

Alex could have been mistaken, but he thought he saw John smile. At the same time, he lifted his head, found Alex, and asked a peculiar question. "Where's his carriage? I didn't see his carriage when we arrived. How are you traveling?"

Alex started forward slowly. There was so much John didn't understand, needed to know, and must know soon if he was to wrest any degree of power from Aslam's hands. "It's out there." he nodded. "A rented brougham, two horses. Aslam owns no carriage. Considers it a needless luxury. In London he walks about. Where he can't walk, he rents a . . . conveyance."

All the time he spoke, John's face was splintering again into new angles of bewilderment.

When the confusion appeared to render him speechless, Alex took the

147

lead. Aslam would give Alex three, perhaps four minutes; then the hired driver would be instructed to guide the rented brougham back to London—with or without him.

"John, please," Alex said quietly. "Complete this journey as quickly as possible. Rescue Elizabeth and come back to London, where you belong and where you are needed."

"Is it true, Alex, what he said about Richard?"

"I don't know. I see Lord and Lady Eden infrequently They don't journey about much and seem content in rural Kent."

"And Mary. Have you heard . . . ?"

"Nothing. But then, America . . ."

As Alex's voice lightened, so did his expression, anything to offset the gloom on John's face and the distance they had effortlessly strayed from the single most important point he had tried to make. If John wanted to retain any degree of power with his famous London firm, he'd better return and do so as soon as possible. At the door now, aware of Aslam's growing impatience, Alex stopped and looked back. It was his guess that John was finished. Perhaps the trip to Paris would kill him. In a way, it would be a blessing.

Then Alex had seen enough, and stepped through the door and closed it behind him, realizing sadly as he hurried across the cobblestones that the winds of change were upon them all, a torch-passing time, the "nigger pariah" of yesterday well on his way to becoming the richest man in the British Empire.

"Climb aboard," came the clipped voice from the darkness. "There is work waiting for us in London."

"Yes, sir." Alex nodded, reached one hand up for support, and only briefly looked longingly back toward the mullioned windows of the well-lit pub behind which sat the remains of the most remarkable man he had ever known.

What ceases to exist when someone dies?

Why were we wrong for so long about the sun going around the earth?

As long as John could keep his mind busy, he would not feel so acutely the pain caused by the confrontation with Aslam.

Damn him!

Suddenly he gripped the table with both hands, fearful of falling. The chair on which he was seated seemed to be tipping.

"Easy, sir," Bates soothed. "You need food and drink. I'll fetch—"

"No, nothing," John muttered, waving away both the man and his offer. He continued to hold on to the table until the world grew steady again.

"Come, sir. Charley's here. He'll help you upstairs. A good night's rest and we'll head for the channel and Miss Elizabeth. After all, that's what we came for, wasn't it? Forget the nigger."

For some reason John enjoyed hearing Bates call Aslam a nigger, though years ago when the boy had been growing up under John's protection, John had had men horsewhipped for the same offense.

Well, as soon as he fetched Elizabeth, he'd safely ensconce her at Eden and put her in charge of readying the old castle for all the various homecomings. His sons—surely Rose O'Donnell would locate them—and Elizabeth would write to Mary and tell her of John's illness, and surely Mary would come. And Richard . . . Yes, he could persuade even Richard to forgive him for past transgressions.

"Are you ready, sir?" Bates prodded again, clearly disliking the crowd that was now pushing around them.

And John disliked them as well. "Yes, Bates, shall we . . . ?"

"Here, lean on Mr. Spade, sir. He will assist you up to your chambers."

"Come, sir, don't stumble," Charley whispered, and turned him about, and he obeyed, as placid and helpless as a child.

"Elizabeth," he muttered as the name appeared without sequence on his consciousness.

"Yes, sir." Bates smiled, leading the way through the cluttered pub to the narrow wooden steps which led up to the chambers above. "Tomorrow bright and early we will go in search of Miss Elizabeth. But now you require food and rest. I promised Susan Mantle."

There was that name again, so solid-sounding against the indefinite pain of a vague past. John found in memory the face that went with the name, and both provided him with enough courage to make it through all those staring eyes—and worse, the realization of what he had become.

149

Exmoor
November 5, 1874

For four days and three nights Lord Richard Eden, fifteenth baron and seventh earl of Eden, had traveled from his present home at Forbes Hall in Kent to his ancestral home, Eden Castle, in North Devon, buoyed and kept moving by the beloved and well-read parchment which he now held in his hand.

In a blaze of autumn sun and weary of the endlessly rocking carriage, he looked to the parchment for relief, as it had provided him with the same every day since he'd received it over a fortnight ago.

Now, despite his burning eyes and the subtle and clever sense of guilt which had accompanied him with every mile since he'd left Forbes Hall and his burgeoning wife, Eleanor, Richard carefully spread the parchment upon his knees and cursed his failing eyesight, a memento from his scholar's days at Cambridge. He brought the fine, spidery script into focus, though it wasn't necessary, for he knew every precious word of it by heart and viewed it now as he'd first received it, as a literal lifeline, at least temporarily rescuing him from that horrible pit of cloying domesticity which now served as his life at Forbes Hall.

"My Dearest R" was the salutation, and with the mere reading of those words, the scent of the one who had penned them was upon him, filling the carriage with such clarity that it obliterated the miles of heather which stretched across Exmoor on either side.

For a moment Richard closed his eyes, literally unable to go on. Why did it hurt so, man's capacity to love? Yet it had always been thus—with Richard, at least—and not the pleasurable pain often described by poets. For Richard it had always been more pain than pleasure.

Now he looked beyond the salutation and heard the voice speaking behind the words:

My Dearest R,

The monster has left his lair for a few weeks. May I suggest an alternative to our customary rendezvous, a journey of longer duration but promising greater rewards? I long to see you in your natural setting, your rightful one, the one which I swear will be yours one day.

Come to Eden on the sixth of November, for one day, two, three—for as many as your other wife will permit.

Come to me, my dearest, and let us make that wretched castle live up to its name, at least for a while.

Your beloved,
A

Although Richard had long since finished reading what he knew by heart, he continued to stare at the elegant script.

Your other wife . . .

Poor swollen Eleanor. She didn't even suspect, so engrossed was she in her own world of infants.

Come to me, my dearest, and let us make that wretched castle live up to its name . . .

He smiled. They had their work cut out for them, to make of that place a true Eden. But dear Lord, he was willing to try. With his beloved near, he sometimes felt stronger than he'd ever felt in his life, able to accomplish anything. As for the muddle of his own life, so long as Eleanor wasn't too demanding, he would pretend to be a good husband to her. But if the child she was now carrying was a son, there would be no more physical contact between them. She was perfectly welcome to take a lover, as many as she required, but Richard would not enter her again.

"Where are we now?" he called out to his driver, feeling a desperate need to alter the course of his thoughts.

"Not far, sir—at least, I don't think so. Ain't never been in these parts. I'm a Kentish man—"

"Keep your eyes open for the turrets. You can't miss them," Richard shouted back over the whistling wind, holding on now with both hands as the rapidly turning wheels fought for traction in the heavily rutted road.

"Up ahead, sir, I see something. Would that be Eden?"

Excited, Richard drew himself close to the window on the right side of the carriage and looked through the spiraling mists and fog which had not as yet burned off in the brightness of the November sun. Then he saw it. "Eden," he murmured.

"Yes, that's it," he shouted to his driver. It was impossible at that moment to chart the antics of his emotions at that ancient sight, the square-towered crenellations protruding up out of the fog.

"Dear God," he whispered, gripping the window with both hands, feeling his face grow numb under the chill November wind. What a surprise that that cold tomb which contained the reality of every nightmare he'd ever suffered still was capable of moving him.

"Welcome home, sir," the driver called back to him.

Richard nodded. It was all he could manage.

A few minutes later the driver took the gatehouse at a clattering speed, and Richard leaned forward as the carriage slowed in its turn before the Great-Hall steps. On the first glance up those steps he saw the author of the parchment that had rescued him from Forbes Hall and his swollen wife. Merely standing there he was, hands on slim hips, smiling down as though the sight of Richard had brought him reciprocal pleasure.

Richard pushed open the carriage door even before the driver had brought it to a firm stop and started slowly up the stairs, his hand already extended to the one who was coming down the steps toward him.

Their two hands met first and joined them in a warm embrace. Richard closed his eyes. There it was again, that scent of spice and rose. Grateful for the scent and the one who wore it, he smoothed the straight black hair with his right hand and allowed that hand to fall gently in a caress the length of the back.

Confident they were alone and no one was watching save for the screeching seagulls overhead, Richard drew him closer and whispered his beloved's name.

"Aslam . . ."

Eden Point
November 5, 1874

Alone in the chill, musty interior of the cottage on Eden Rising, Susan sat on the bench which just a few weeks earlier she'd arranged for another. The fire was dead as well, a dead season. Even her heart felt strangely stilled, as though something else within her was providing the impetus for blood and oxygen.

Suddenly she felt a deeper chill and sat on her hands in an attempt to warm them, and wondered what had possessed her to stop off here when Reverend Christopher was waiting for her at this moment down in Mortemouth with a lovely pot of hot tea. Why wasn't she down in Mortemouth instead of up here in this cold and lonely place filled with nothing but bewilderment and the echo of his voice?

Softly she bowed her head. Why had she chosen that last afternoon for a "clear look at his character faults"? Dear God, what had possessed her? He had been ill, terribly ill. Whatever was lacking in his character, couldn't it have waited until he had recovered his health?

Sharply she lifted her head, as though she'd forgotten to breathe. It was a peculiar hurt she was suffering, not of the body, not like fever or a broken limb. This hurt was deep inside and therefore beyond healing.

Thirteen days, that's how long he'd been gone. She'd counted every moment, every hour. Surely he would be in Paris by now. Perhaps he'd already found Elizabeth, and both now were on their way home.

The thought, however illusory, comforted her, and she pushed up from the cold bench and smoothed the band about her waist and, still distracted, took two steps toward the dead fire, turned away, and stood as though warming her back where no fire existed. For the next few minutes she studied the ruined interior of the cottage. Every place she looked, she saw neglect, the entire structure in need of reinforcement from the inside as well as out. Still, it was sturdy-appearing and wouldn't take a great deal to . . .

No! She had no intention of settling in the shadow of Eden—neither the man nor the castle. Besides, she was needed in too many other places to settle comfortably in one. No, it had been a generous gift, and typical of him, but she would look her fill now and never return.

She got up, then paused, hearing something. It sounded like a carriage, distant yet coming steadily toward . . .

Him? Back already? It was possible. To Paris and back in almost a fortnight? Oh, quite possible.

To the gatehouse now, or so it sounded. Dear God, let it be he. Let her see him just once more, see that he was well and happy and reunited with Elizabeth, who undoubtedly would take excellent and loving care of him. Then Susan would leave his life forever and never again step foot on Eden Point. She couldn't. It would be too painful.

Out of breath, she nonetheless pushed herself harder and faster, making a broad arc around the farmyard, where puddles from yesterday's rain still stood. Proceeding at top speed, aware of her hair tumbling down her back, she hesitated as she approached the sharp corner of the castle itself.

See who it is first, instinct said. And if it is him, restore yourself to a degree of order.

Yes . . . and besides, her lungs were bursting for lack of air. Thus she came to an abrupt halt just steps away from the corner which gave a complete and uncluttered view of the inner courtyard. For a moment, as the sound of the carriage grew louder, she closed her eyes and lifted her face to the warmth of the sun and tried hard to still the agitation she felt.

Him . . .

As she heard the carriage slowing for the turn, she drew one last breath, then forced both hands into action straightening her hair, which had tumbled loose down her back. Hair tucked up. Shirtwaist straightened. Dear Lord, she must have resembled a wild banshee, tearing up the road like that.

The carriage had come to a halt. At least she could hear nothing—which she thought strange. Old Bates was fond of shouting orders willy-nilly. Then she remembered. Of course. The castle was empty. No one here to greet them. Then all the more reason to make her presence known. She could be of assistance to them—at least until Elizabeth could form her own staff.

She smiled at her own foolishness and took one step out, her line of vision fixed on the Great-Hall steps, the place where all carriages came to a stop.

But one step was enough, for it had provided her with a quick glance at a carriage she'd never seen before. This one was black and somber and very dusty from the road, as though someone had traveled a long distance without respite.

Who?

Postponing her disappointment, she pressed back against the castle wall and peered out again, just enough to see a man alight from the carriage. Not Mr. Eden. She knew his gait, manner, and profile as well as she knew her own. So, not Mr. Eden, but it was a gentleman she'd never seen before, tall, thin, slightly stooped, dark thinning hair. He stood for a moment, bowed in the carriage door, both hands gripping the sides, his line of vision fixed at an upward angle, as though he were viewing someone who had just emerged from the empty castle.

Not him . . .

Then came the first waves of disappointment, an actual pain at the base of her throat. She turned away and fought the weakness as best she could with reason. Of course it wasn't him. He'd not had time to go and come.

Suddenly she covered her mouth with both hands in an attempt to cancel the grief forming in her heart.

What was the matter with her?

Confused and frightened by feelings she'd never experienced before, Susan took one last look at the strange gentleman who had just climbed down from the carriage and who was now staring up at the top of the stairs, where no one . . .

With a start she leaned farther out. There *was* someone there, just emerging from the Great-Hall door, a man in a white shirt, coatless, tieless, as though he were in residence in the castle. Yet she knew they had left the castle closed and empty.

He was just standing at the top of the stairs now, though she could feel an incredible bond stretching between the two, both slim, though the gentleman starting up the stairs struck her as the older, for he climbed the stairs with effort, leaning into the ascent with each step—as Mr. Eden used to do.

Why did the thought hurt so? And why was the image that accompanied the thought almost unbearable?

Still in hiding, she watched the strange meeting, the man climbing steadily toward the younger, who, despite the distance, she discerned as being a foreigner, dark-skinned, long straight black hair. She continued to watch the two, mesmerized by their silence. Words usually were exchanged upon greeting, but not these two. Not that they weren't speaking. Volumes were exchanged in that silence.

Then . . . Contact, an aching meeting of hands first, then the embrace, coming as she knew it would, despite their maleness, for she had recognized in the pair the new pain which had taken up subtle residence within her own soul.

Need. Human need which failed to recognize gender.

Then the kiss, the younger man literally drawing the older man up the stairs and into his arms.

For several minutes Susan watched, aware that she shouldn't. *Who were they? And did Mr. Eden know they were here?*

No time for answers, as now Susan objected to her own spying and ran, retracing her steps back through the farmyard, around the empty barns and stables, running at breakneck speed, as though something were pursuing her.

She'd ask Reverend Christopher. He might know who they were.

No . . . She changed her mind. That could simply alert the entire village to the fact Eden Castle was once again occupied. She'd leave them be and try to bring her own splintered and cartwheeling emotions under control. Otherwise she would be of no good to anyone, least of all herself.

It was so easy to say, so difficult to accomplish.

Paris
November 8, 1874

Rain again.

Shivering despite the heavy lap robe, John pressed back into the far corner of the hired carriage and glanced at old Bates, who leaned nervously forward, checking the scenery outside.

Rain.

It pelted the windows, turning the scene outside into a cold blur. Was there ever a more wretched country? As John posed the question to himself and simultaneously answered it, he suffered a sudden bolt of memory, something connected with rain—though of a different sort, not an aggressive and incapacitating one like this, but soft, gentle.

Sit here, Mr. Eden, by the fire. It will warm . . .

The nurse. Why did she cling so to his consciousness?

"I think we may be getting close, sir," Bates said, clinging to the back of the seat with one hand.

"I doubt it," John grumbled, as he'd grumbled every day since they'd first set foot on foreign soil—an unhappy moment, as the French authorities had confiscated John's comfortable carriage at Calais. The horses had been stalled at a local inn—for a king's ransom—and the same corrupt French authorities had forced this wretched conveyance upon them, along with two swaybacked nags, and for this miserable package they'd had the unmitigated gall to charge the exorbitant price of four hundred louis.

On this occasion, as on many others, John had been so grateful that he did not speak their wretched language, which sounded less like a language and more like a nation of head colds. At least it spared his direct contact, and Bates didn't seem to mind. Apparently years ago as a young man Bates had received basic instruction in the French language so he could translate the menus of Chatworth's French chefs to its English guests.

In the rocking motion of the carriage John saw for a moment three of Bates, intense triplicates who all clung to the seat, their heads wet with rain from previous excursions, bobbing about like broken puppets.

Then suddenly: "Up ahead, sir. I think we've found it!"

"My God," John whispered, his eyes moving steadily down the long rows of high barred windows. On the third floor above he saw two pale hands wrapped around the window bars. Suddenly the realization that delicate and graceful Elizabeth was incarcerated someplace behind that miserable red-brick wall was more than he could bear.

"No, wait, Bates," he called after the man, who was just stiffly alighting from the cramped carriage. "I'll come with you. We must get her out today. Tonight at the very latest we'll be on our way back home."

He lifted his voice with the last pledge to include Charley Spade, who sat, drenched, upon the high seat, struggling to control the French nags who, like their two-legged counterparts, tended toward pointless hysteria.

"Hold them steady," John called up again, angling the walking stick into place. "By this time tomorrow I promise I'll buy you the largest piece of English beefsteak you can handle."

"You're on, Mr. Eden." Charley grinned. "And I'll be right here waiting for you when you come out."

John nodded, strangely moved by the loyalty of these two mismatched bookends. Well, he'd figure out a way to make it up to them later. For now the purpose of this entire miserable trip lay straight ahead through those high arched doors, covered by what appeared to be an impenetrable black iron grillwork. In front of the gate he saw at least half a dozen soldiers, their red-and-blue uniforms particularly bright and garish in the gloom of the rainy day.

Then the soldiers spied them, old Bates leading the way in his black frock coat, looking more like a member of the clergy than a butler. At the same time, the gibberish exploded, all six Frenchmen talking at once, gesturing wildly, while Bates with perfect and unswerving aplomb continued to walk straight at them.

"Bates," John called out. "Tell them that I want to see their commanding officer regarding an English prisoner. That's all they need to know." He came to a stop directly before Bates.

Of course, he should have known . . .

He reached into his pocket and counted out six large bills and handed them to Bates. "Their commanding officer," John repeated forcefully. "Now!"

Bates translated the few words and filled them with emphasis as he distributed the money. Several of the soldiers studied the notes before pocketing them. Most pocketed them directly, and a moment after, one was gesturing roughly toward John, indicating he was to follow after.

There! You see? It was as he had suspected. "Come, Bates," he commanded, sweeping through the knot of sullen French, who stood back, expressions of bewilderment on their faces, as though they knew they had been defeated but still weren't quite sure how.

Before the high black grilled gates they paused a moment. From inside, two soldiers shouted something in anger at the soldiers on John's side. One spit something back, a forceful declaration accompanied by a strong gesture. John held his purse at the ready and wondered if he would have to pay his way in at every turn.

Then he heard the cranking of the gate and thought briefly of Eden and wondered if the cottage was still cold and empty, and heard suddenly a fierce ringing in his ears. He closed his eyes until the dizziness passed, and opened them when he felt Bates at his elbow whispering, "You should have remained in the carriage, sir. I could handle the bastards."

John smiled and decided he could grow quite fond of the old man if he permitted himself. He accepted the support of his arm and whispered a reassurance. "I'm fine, Bates, as long as you are with me."

The sentiment seemed momentarily to undo the man, and it was John who led the way inside the grilled gate, which had no door other than the grilles themselves, which meant the temperature inside the prison corridor varied little from the temperature outside.

But cold was not John's primary complaint. Once they were through the grilled gate, an odor so poisonous and foul that he covered his nose with his hand greeted them and now permeated, despite his protective hand. Bates apparently had detected it as well, and withdrew his handkerchief, carefully folded it into a rectangle just large enough to cover his nose, and held it in place.

"What is it?" John muttered. Then he saw a soldier urinating against the wall, the hot piss causing small vapors of steam to arise in the cold air. He also observed what appeared to be human feces scattered up and down one side of the wall.

He reached into his pocket for another note for the officer whose jurisdiction apparently was the piss-filled corridor. "Give it to him," he instructed Bates, "and repeat our wish to see the commanding—"

But the stubborn sergeant had already seen the note and now grinned at John. "*Très bien, monsieur.*" He took the note before Bates had a chance to offer it and led the way down the chilly corridor. As the wretched odor increased, John wished he had followed Bates's suggestion and waited in the carriage. But he doubted the old man could have gotten this far, and he had the sinking feeling they had a lot farther to go before they reached Elizabeth. Again, at the thought of her confined in this place, his mind turned in dread. He stepped through the squabbling soldiers and led the way down the corridor in the only direction that was open to them.

The soldier ran after him, talking endlessly, apparently requiring nothing in the way of a response, because even Bates made no reply and pressed his folded handkerchief tighter against his nose.

During the last exchange inside the gate, John had heard one name with great and reverent repetition. General Montaud. Now he assumed that was their destination, though it looked merely as though they were going deeper and deeper into the prison, past a series of doors which led into larger halls—one clearly a dining hall, the repulsive odor of boiled cabbage joining the odor of human waste—and other, smaller chambers. Offices, John assumed, a scattering of prison personnel lounging about inside, women, their heads covered with white kerchiefs, wearing shapeless gray smocks, working in what obviously was the kitchen court. As they passed by, only one or two glanced fearfully up, their eyes wide and staring, a few red-rimmed, all gaunt and pale, ill-looking. For the second time, John suffered an almost paralyzing fear.

Then the soldier was speaking again, directing them away from the long corridor lined with closed doors, into a small arcade which appeared to skirt an impossibly large courtyard. The red bricks of La Rochelle formed three sides of the enclosed courtyard, while the fourth was a large gray army barracks. Despite the rain, which fell in solid sheets, he could see groups of soldiers trying to maintain formations in the steady downpour.

"*Allons!* " the soldier ordered, apparently not liking the fact John was studying the vast courtyard. They continued at a brisk pace until the man stopped before a door of heavy oak which suggested the corridor and chambers beyond this door might be of a warmer temperature. The French soldier let them through and firmly closed the door.

Aha! There was an important someone in this corridor who did not care for the chill day any more than John did. He noticed other changes as well. No foul odor here, no urine-covered walls. Here a lovely rich Oriental carpet ran the length of the narrow corridor, and every few feet there was a fixed pewter lamp.

For the first time since they'd entered this miserable place, John lowered his hand from his nostrils. The French soldier came to a halt before heavy double doors, where two additional guards stood flanking the rich mahogany panels. After a brief exchange, the soldier motioned them forward. "This way, monsieur."

John felt Bates's hand on his arm guiding him forward, and willingly he accepted the support. He looked up to see one of the French soldiers motioning them into a comfortable waiting room, a small fire crackling in a corner grate, a tall, slim dark-skinned young man in a dark suit working behind a desk, who scarcely looked up as they entered. Turkish, was John's guess. Perhaps years ago the general had brought back a souvenir from the Crimea.

"This way, sir. General Montaud will see you now."

At the moment the inner doors were pushed open, revealing a cozy cave of rose velvet and rich Oriental carpets, enormous bouquets of fresh roses everywhere. A large glistening crystal chandelier hung overhead and cast a soft light over every fabric and texture, a room more typical of a salon than a commanding officer in a prison, and more typical of a woman than a man.

"This way, monsieur," the French guard instructed. "May I present General Jules Montaud . . . ?"

Quickly John ceased his ogling—not because he'd seen everything. He hadn't. In fact, at that moment his eye fell on an enormous brass birdcage, more a house than a cage, and inside were three vividly feathered parrots, all perched on different levels, eyeing him steadily.

Then there was no more time for gaping, and he found himself standing before a delicate little Queen Anne desk confronting the most bizarre creature he'd ever seen, small, almost birdlike, partially balding on the upper forehead, with rows of collar-length black ringlets falling from the back of his skull. The general now looked up at John and smiled, coquettishly. An ancient face, or so it seemed, yet small, childlike in size but heavily lined, and covering one eye was a gold brocade eyepatch.

For the rest of him, he was meticulously dessed in the dazzling uniform of general, complete with gold epaulets and several decorations upon his chest.

It was John's intention to state his case immediately, using both Bates

159

and the French guard for translators in the event one faltered. But suddenly the general gave the guard a command and the man disappeared through the door, leaving them alone, except for Bates, who retreated back to the door, as though not absolutely certain whether he too should stay or depart.

"Stay!" John ordered, annoyed the old man couldn't see he was needed now more than ever.

"Why, sir?" Bates asked, apparently bewildered.

"To translate!" John shouted, and caught himself in time. He looked back at the strange man behind the desk and saw a smile which broadened, revealing three gold teeth.

"No need, I assure you, Mr. Eden. I speak, if not perfect English, certainly passable."

Surprised though relieved, John saw the man stand. On his feet he resembled a very old child. Most bizarre.

"May my aide serve you something? Brandy? Coffee?"

Why not? He was chilled to the bone. "Brandy, please," he said at last.

"And your . . . manservant?" General Montaud asked, glancing slyly around John to the open door, where the young desk clerk stood at attention next to Bates.

"He is not my manservant," John said tersely, disliking the cunning manner of the little general. "And he can speak for himself."

Apparently the general heard the terseness and seemed even more amused by it and glanced coyly toward Bates. "And what is your pleasure, sir? I mean, concerning a refresher."

My God! John looked back toward the mincing voice and saw clearly the sodomite behind it.

Apparently Bates had given him an answer, for now the man waved the aide away with a delicate white lace handkerchief he'd retrieved from somewhere, and as the door closed, he sat behind the desk and pressed the handkerchief against his nostrils, little finger arched.

John found himself caught in a kind of repellent fascination at the man's monstrous affectations, the manner in which his finger moved in serpentine fashion in and out of his mouth, the manner in which one hand smoothed back the semibalding hair, a delicate feminine self-caressing gesture.

"Please sit," General Montaud invited now, indicating one of the comfortable rose velvet chairs which flanked the white marble fire well.

Wary, John glanced in that direction, looking for visible reasons why he should not accept the invitation. He hadn't come to sit by a warming fire with a prim sodomite while Elizabeth languished God knew where. Still, it might be wise in the long run not to anger the man. John suspected he was in the presence of the absolute power of La Rochelle. The ease with which John might remove Elizabeth from its awful environs resided with the diminutive general, who was now coming around from behind his desk in mincing steps, smiling at old Bates. With one drop of his wrist he indicated Bates was to occupy the straight-backed chair to the left of the door.

To John's amazement, Bates obeyed. Now, as the general settled opposite John in the matching rose velvet chair, John caught sight of the man's footwear—rose velvet slippers with smaller roses embroidered on each toe.

Apparently the general saw his line of vision. "I adore roses, you know," he said. "When I attended your Cambridge years ago, I learned that roses are God's most perfect creations. They really are."

John groaned inwardly. Apparently the English had had a hand in the creation of this monstrosity.

"We French," the general said sadly, "we do many many things well—perfectly, even. Unfortunately, growing roses is not one of them. That, I must confess, you English do best."

Embarrassed for everyone and unable to think of a suitable response, John sat up straight, and with the air of a man losing patience, stated his case. "We have come, General Montaud, to secure the release of an Englishwoman whom we have reason to believe is being held unjustly prisoner here."

He was about to say more by way of explanation, but all the while he was talking, General Montaud had allowed his head to fall back against the rose velvet chair, eye closed, as though he'd put himself into some sort of trance. Then softly he spoke.

"No, sir, you are mistaken. We have no English prisoners here. Only French."

"No, *you* are mistaken," John contradicted, certain Alex Aldwell had not given him false information. "I received the information on good authority that she was being held at La Rochelle House of Detention. This is La Rochelle, isn't it?"

Slowly General Montaud opened his one good eye. "It is."

"Then she's here. And I would appreciate it if one of your guards would fetch her. If fines are due, I'll be happy to pay them. If any other form of restitution is owed—"

"What . . . was her offense?" General Montaud asked, and sat up straight—an unfortunate gesture, as his rose-velvet-slippered feet failed to touch the floor and he began to swing them.

"Her offense?" John repeated, and felt a need to stand, lest he reflect the idiocy of the man seated opposite him. "I don't know her offense," he replied honestly, and angled the walking stick into position.

"No, don't do that, sir." General Montaud sighed.

"Do . . . what?" John asked, bewildered.

"Rise in my presence. When I sit, everyone remains seated. Is that clear?"

In response to this mindless edict, John sat numbly. The point was to remain calm. At least that seemed to be the message which Bates was wisely, though wordlessly, conveying. Now, as though fearful John would be either unable or unwilling to carry it out, Bates started to rise from his chair several feet away, then seemed to change his mind, sat again, and projected his voice in a slow, mellifluent manner.

"General Montaud, if I may speak . . . ?"

"Of course you may speak. This is a democracy. Yet, there are too many deaths for it to be a good democracy. Terrible deaths, so many a few years ago, no roses, no flowers at all in Paris. Can you imagine Paris without flowers?"

At that the door opened and the slim dark young man in a tight-fitting black suit entered bearing a silver tray, a decanter of brandy, and three snifters.

"Ah, there you are, André." The general smiled, clearly distracted from his recall. "This is my very best friend. His name is André," he said, and the introduction extended both to John and to Bates.

The young man looked up embarrassed from the small table where he was pouring the brandy. He said nothing, but merely glanced at John with dark brooding eyes—which John had seen before, in the Crimea. Turkish eyes, shifting eyes, always looking for advantage and advancement, self-serving eyes.

As he stooped to hand John a snifter of brandy, André whispered, "Tell me the name of your prisoner and I'll try to find her for you."

Before John could respond, he'd moved on with the tray to where Bates sat by the door. Stunned by the whispered command coming from such an unlikely source, John watched carefully, thinking the young man would return for the information.

But he didn't. He lifted the tray and with only the briefest of backward glances left the room, and left John and Bates alone with the madman, who sipped at his brandy, lifted a single rose from a near vase and peeled off all the petals, dipped them into the brandy, and chewed and swallowed them contentedly.

Thirty minutes later John placed his empty snifter on the table and started to push out of the chair. He'd stared for so long at the macabre face opposite him that he felt if he didn't flee soon he would become as mad. But at the same time, the door was pushed open again and André reappeared, still bearing the silver tray, and something else, what appeared to be a gray folder tucked beneath his arm.

"Ah, André," mourned General Montaud. "Why did you go off and leave me alone with these . . . English? They are so boring, both of them."

As the man appeared to be literally on the verge of tears, André came close to hover over him and whispered something into his ear, a prolonged message which stretched on and on, the general appearing to listen closely.

"The name of your prisoner?" the general demanded suddenly, all boredom gone from his face.

"Elizabeth Eden," John replied, daring to hope it would be over soon.

General Montaud continued to study the gray folder; then a grin covered his face. "Correct!" he pronounced.

"She journeyed to Paris about—"

"—four years ago," the general read, lifting the folder until it obscured his face—but his voice was audible.

John sat up on the edge of the chair and noticed Bates in the same rigid position, as though both knew the importance of the folder.

"Ah, naughty girl," the general said, still reading, still obscured. "It says here, 'revolutionary activities . . .'"

Damn her, John cursed privately. He would have to talk with her. "If you would tell her that we are here," he went on, and though no one stopped him, he stopped himself, seeing the general look slowly over the folder, a shocked expression on his face.

"Sir?" John inquired, bewildered. In this new silence of shocked mysteries, John felt a sudden twinge of terror.

"Elizabeth Eden," General Montaud pronounced in a low monotone, not looking directly at John.

"She is here, then?" John inquired, thinking if he could just establish that, then the mysterious terror would dissipate, for he was certain he could get her out. After all, she was a gentlewoman, and English. Surely the French had no quarrel with . . .

"She has been sentenced . . . twice," the general said.

"Twice? I don't under—"

"Once for revolutionary activities. That sentence is almost served . . ."

"Good . . ."

"The second sentence has not been carried out."

"Second? What . . . ?"

"For murder, sir. It appears she murdered a French soldier. She is under sentence of death. The date of her execution is November 15. By firing squad."

The terror vaulted and exploded in his head. Then, incredibly, he felt an odd compulsion to laugh. They were joking. The French madman was joking, that was all.

For murder, sir. She is under sentence of death . . . date of execution is November 15 . . . firing squad.

There was the terror again. John pushed hurriedly up from the chair. "I don't believe it," he said flatly, and reached back for his walking stick. "General Montaud, I demand to see the prisoner. Immediately."

Suddenly the little general came to life and jumped to the floor with a screeching sound like a wounded bird. He picked up the gray folder and shoved it at John, the French tongue moving rapidly, a spray of spittle preceding him. Even while the diatribe was still going on, Bates drew closer.

"He says," Bates began, meeting John's eye for the first time and revealing a matching depth of terror, "that you are welcome to read it there"—with one hand he pointed toward the thick gray file—"though it is in French, so I doubt—"

"I don't want to read anything," John exploded, angling the walking stick into position.

Bates merely exhibited a stunned though persistent determination to translate everything the general was saying. Apparently he had been ordered to do so.

"The name of the murdered man was Lieutenant Jean Dauguet, a good officer, a good soldier," Bates said, a halting quality giving the flow of words an unreal quality. There was a longer-than-usual pause. Bates looked sharply at the old general, who fairly screeched in English now, "Repeat it as I say it!"

That, John understood; and he understood more—that the inexplicable terror he felt was perhaps justified.

"Did you hear?" the general screamed again at Bates. "Say it!"

John glanced toward Bates and saw a battle being waged on his face. With painful effort and eyes closed, Bates finally repeated it exactly as the general had said it.

"The . . . Eden whore . . . was given special privileges, special comforts due to the fact she was foreign and the government had no real quarrel with her, and in return for these special privileges she repaid us by willfully and with no regret plunging a pair of shears into Lieutenant Dauguet, then watching the lifeblood slip from his body." Stunned, Bates looked up.

John ignored the expression on Bates's face and turned immediately on the general, who now appeared to be brooding in hurt silence before the fireplace.

"Sir, I demand to see Elizabeth Eden," he repeated. "And I demand to see her now. I don't know how much clearer I can make it. And if you don't oblige, I shall be forced to contact my government and inform them of the treatment of a citizen of the British Empire—"

"She is a murdering slut!" the man screamed, so outraged John saw blood veins protruding from beneath the parchmentlike skin.

Bates again tried to intervene. "Sir. It's true, I'm afraid. Please, we must—"

"We must do only one thing," John countered. "We must find Elizabeth and take her out of this . . . ."

Suddenly a new terror pressed against him. What brutalities had been visited upon her? Was she able to travel, or would she first require the services of a physician? As the thought of Elizabeth ill or brutalized dawned on him, his rage increased. "I demand to see her," he said again, striding toward the door as though to say if he was not shown the way immediately he would find her on his own.

He had expected a new outburst from the general. Instead there was a moment's pause while he turned back to the fire. And when he glanced toward John again, everything was restored and in order.

"Of course, Mr. Eden," the general said with suspect kindness. "How propitious your arrival today. The prisoner has seven days left on this earth, more than enough time to—"

Then it was Bates who rushed forward with an insane interruption. "Don't, Mr. Eden, I beg you. Do not see her. Let her go. It's for the best—"

"Your manservant is wise." The man grinned. "Much wiser than you."

"I do not seek your definition of wisdom."

"You should, for you will regret what you are about to do for the rest of your life."

I demand to see her."

"And see her you shall."

Then Bates was at his side again. "Please. Don't!" he whispered fiercely. "You have your own health to—"

"Damn my health!" John exploded. "I have no need for health without Elizabeth." Where had the terror come from again? He thought he'd banished it. "Besides, I'm not as gullible as you, Bates. I don't believe a word—"

"Then I'll come with you," Bates offered at last with an air of resignation.

John and General Montaud—allied on at least one point—said "No" in tandem, General Montaud filling the chill air outside the waiting room

164

with countless official rules. John, in order not to hear what the general was saying, spoke as loudly and as rapidly, giving Bates his own reasons. "If I am to free her, I must talk with her, and she might be inhibited by your presence."

Despite the look of sadness on Bates's face, there was also a look of relief, as though the offer to accompany John had been obligatory at best.

While the general summoned someone with an imperious clap of his hands, John drew up the collar of his cloak in meager protection against the chill and gave Bates last-minute instructions. "Go and wait in the carriage with Charley Spade. Stay dry, both of you, inside, and tell Charley he may be asked to ride back to the channel."

"I . . . don't understand, sir."

Neither did John. If there was no truth in the old general's tale, then what was preventing Elizabeth from walking out now with John? On the other hand, if there had been a murder and a mock trial, then the decision must be overturned—and that would require help from high places.

"Sir?" It was General Montaud, again gleeful as a small contingent of French soldiers appeared in marching formation, their boots muffled on the carpet runner. "These men will accompany you to the place where the condemned prisoners are held until . . ."

Without another word to Bates or the general, though he felt their eyes upon him, he took his place at the rear of the soldiers, four in all. Why so many to escort him to the cell of a female prisoner, he had no idea.

As the parade started down the narrow corridor leading toward the cold arcade and the vastness of the prison beyond, John grasped his walking stick and fell into the rhythm of the march, trying to clear his mind for the reunion and trying not to think on what had transpired in the general's office.

Ahead he saw the door which led to the open-air arcade, saw the rain increase, coming in solid gray sheets, obscuring the vast courtyard with its mysterious posts and black iron spectators' box.

Such was the stuff that nightmares were made of.

She had long since learned the one important lesson of isolation and confinement: Do not think on the past. It was a form of torture more effective than anything her jailers could inflict on her. Neither was it wise to consider the future. The future was as dead as the past.

Therefore, that left only the present, but there was no need to view it as limiting or limited. There was, for example, this arrangement of wax flowers on which she was working. The wax was left over from burned-down candles, and she could mold and shape it by warming it in the palms of her hands, then forming individual petals and leaves, a graceful and accurate arrangement of roses and lilies.

Her warden, Madame Charvin, permitted her this activity, even though she knew it brought her pleasure, because upon Elizabeth's death she had promised the arrangement to Madame Charvin. In fact, of late Madame had commenced bringing her colored wax so she could work her artistry into the accurate floral colors.

Elizabeth enjoyed the work. It was in her memories she suffered most. "Edward," she whispered aloud, enjoying the sound of the name on the silent chill air. Slowly she lifted her fingers to the small candle flame in an attempt to warm them.

Dear God, she still was so frightened, still was not ready to die.

Suddenly she bent over and covered her face with her hands. Both were so cold—but it didn't matter. Neither were as cold as the thought of death, the cessation of life.

And no one even knew where she was. That was, in a way, both the hardest part and the easiest. Most of the time she was grateful she was going through this crucible alone. Yet sometimes she ached with longing for just a word from someone at Eden, though for what purpose? No one, not even John, could alter this. She *had* killed a man, with great and perfect premeditation. There had been a trial, hasty and unintelligible, but a form of a trial nonetheless, and the magistrate had passed sentence on her—death by firing squad.

Well, then, that was it, wasn't it? Nothing anyone could do, not even John.

With her hands extended over the small flickering candle, she concentrated on the tiny dancing orange-red flame—and saw John.

Suddenly the flame dipped low and almost went out.

Oh, dear God, enough! she scolded herself, belatedly realizing she had broken her own rule and was at this moment inhabiting the past. Of course, the unhappy past was not the one capable of doing any lasting damage. It was the blissful past that cut deepest, and those memories were all of one man—Edward Eden. Predictably, the self-inflicted torture took a toll, and slowly she bent over against the pain of ancient happiness. In the process she crushed the wax petal in her hand and, in surprise, looked down on the small misshapen lump. It would have to be done again—but no matter.

Listen! What was that? Someone coming? She could hear the scrape of boots on the stone floor. It wasn't time for anything. Not food, nor . . .

It wasn't November 15, was it? Not yet! She still had seven days in which she planned to pass a lifetime. Then what? And who?

Fearfully she turned about on the low stool to look through the bars of her cell.

Please, God, she prayed softly, give me strength. . . .

It was a descent into hell. As the guards rounded still another clammy gray stone corridor and started down to yet another level, John wished for a chance to catch his breath.

The four soldiers were chattering among themselves now. Blessedly they broke pace slightly to accommodate their conversation and John was able to do the same and concentrate less on maintaining his balance and more on studying his grim surroundings.

"How much farther?" he called out, received no answer, and knew he wouldn't, for these four didn't understand him any more than he understood them.

The corridor now was so narrow it permitted the passage of only one person. As they arranged themselves into single file, he looked over their bobbing heads and shoulders. At the far end he saw the pale yellow flickering of a light—a candle, most likely—the cell itself set apart and isolated from the others.

Then he saw that the soldier in the lead had come to a halt before the small cell, all of them joking and laughing now, continuously obscuring his vision, one producing keys. Why couldn't they stand still for just a moment so he could see exactly who . . .

Then he could. And did. And felt the weight of terror press down upon him, threaten to annihilate him, and simultaneously he prayed that it would—and prayed with equal zeal the image before him would fade from his vision and never reappear again, not even in memory. Despite the shapeless gray of the prison dress and the smudged filth on her face, he knew he had found Elizabeth.

Then he was aware of the four soldiers standing back, the cell door unlocked, nothing obscuring his path to this pitiful woman whose stylishness and grace and enchantment and warmth once had captivated the most powerful men in London, who now had fixed John with the same haunted vision he fixed on her, her mind clearly refuting what her eyes saw. Only then did it occur to him there had been changes in himself as well.

Still, he knew precisely the moment when her heart had convinced her head of his identity, for he saw her struggling upward from the low stool, either too weak or too ill to accomplish it easily. John, unable to watch the struggle any longer, hurried to her, reached out for her and drew her forcibly to him, and was shocked at how thin she was, more bone than flesh. Yet he enclosed her in his arms, letting the walking stick drop to the stone floor.

He wept with her and they clung to each other under the staring eyes of the soldiers, who ultimately sensed something rare in the moment and moved down the corridor out of earshot, as though they understood the need for privacy and respected it.

At various times during her four months of solitary confinement Elizabeth had suffered hallucinations. Therefore, when she had turned at the sound of approaching footsteps and had seen beyond the soldiers to that facsimile of John, at first she'd been certain she was being visited by a vision. On closer examination she'd seen something solid in his face that specters are usually spared—the heaviness of this earth. Still, she hadn't been certain until he stepped to the door of the cell and the candle had shed its limited light on his eyes—Edward's eyes. Though she still couldn't understand the new gauntness, the gray-flecked hair, or the lame left leg, she had known who it was and had tried to stand, had felt her customary weakness compounded by the shock of recognition. And that was when the "hallucination" had taken her into its arms.

Now she was the one who rallied first. "John?" she whispered, trying to ease out of his embrace in an attempt to see his face close at hand. "Is it . . . truly you?" She knew, but wanted *his* confirmation, wanted to hear his voice, his reassurance.

For a moment he refused to look at her, and still holding her, turned his face away as though embarrassed by his incapacity.

"John, come," she beckoned, reaching back for his hand, now spying the fallen walking stick. Slowly she bent to retrieve it, caught sight of her own gray prison garb, and again suffered a sense of misplaced pride. "Here . . ." She smiled, handing him the stick, attempting to smooth back her tangled hair at the same time. Occasionally Madame Charvin brought her a brush.

"Come," she urged again, saddened to see him so changed.

Under her gentle insistence he took the stick and angled it down. She thought she saw pain across his face as he moved awkwardly forward, and she grieved for the whole and perfect little boy who had darted ahead of her on walks through Hyde Park.

Near the low stool where she'd been working on her wax flowers she withdrew the bench. "Come, sit," she urged. Relieved, she saw him start down and sensed an unstable center of balance, and at the last minute reached out a hand in assistance.

"I *am* sorry." She smiled, sitting effortlessly upon the straw before him. She'd grown accustomed to the floor during her years of imprisonment and now found it far more satisfactory than the confinement of any chair.

"Are you . . . ?" He looked up with mild shock to see her on the floor.

"I'm fine," she said quickly.

He nodded once and looked briefly about the small cell, his eyes taking it all in, the dank red-brick walls, low ceiling, one cot, one table on which rested one candle. "My God!" he whispered in reaction to the cell.

She nodded and tucked the soiled gray prison shirt about her legs and drew her knees up. "I know." She smiled. "It isn't Saint George's Street, and certainly not Eden."

He looked down sharply on her for a moment, as though he didn't appreciate her poor attempt at humor.

"How . . . long," he began, "have you . . . been here?"

"Here?" she asked, not certain if he meant this prison or this particular cell. "Here about four months, since the trial. Before that I had a lovely cell upstairs with a high window, even. You could see the sky . . ." Recalling such luxury, she smiled nostalgically. Unfortunately his face bore quite another expression.

"How . . . long have you . . . ?" he began, and could not finish and let a weak gesture which encompassed the small cell complete the question for him.

"Been in prison?" she asked. And smiled. "Too long, I'm afraid," she said, evading the question.

"Elizabeth, look at me," he commanded. "How long?"

In a curious way, she felt reassured. So long as everything in the world did not change all at once, she would find it easier to deal with her last days here. To see John subdued and ill was bad enough. To have found his mind and spirit as changed would have been too much.

"I worked for the movement three months after I arrived from London . . ."

"And then?"

She shrugged, still unable to believe he was here, that they were chatting so casually of such matters. "A group of us were arrested, some deported. Louise Michel was sent to New Caledonia. You remember Louise . . ."

She couldn't tell if he did or not. There was on his face still a splintered expression of stunned disbelief. "What . . . year?" he stammered, apparently trying to put a time sequence together. For what reason, she had no idea.

Time meant so little to the prisoners of La Rochelle. It never behaved as properly in confinement as it did in freedom. Here, she'd observed, it either went too slowly, never moving forward at all, or moving far too rapidly, like November 15. Once—only yesterday—she'd had four months left. Now she had seven days.

"The year was 1870, John," she said quickly in answer to his question. "The same year that . . ." She broke off, aware too late of what she was about to say. See? There was a hazard in isolation. One tended to forget how to conduct oneself socially. She was about to say, "the same year you drove everyone away from Eden." "The same year Mary and Burke sailed for America," she substituted, hungry for news of everyone, but of these two in particular.

"Come along," he commanded absurdly, as though he'd seen enough of everything and now it was time to move on.

As he struggled to his feet, she gaped upward, still eager for news from the outside. "John, please tell me about—"

"I'll tell you about anything you want to hear," he said gruffly, breathing heavily from the exertion of standing, "but not here. Let's get the hell out of here."

As he made his way to the open cell door, she still found she was incapable of doing anything but gaping. Did he really think they were going to just walk out of here? Oh, dear Lord, how often she had dreamed it. But didn't he know . . . ?

"Come, Elizabeth," he scolded again, more sternly this time, as though she were a stubborn child.

"John, I don't . . ."

Then he was standing over her, awesome from this angle, extending his hand downward, indicating without words she was to take it.

"John, please, I can't—"

"Get up!" he whispered fiercely, high color rising on his face.

Stunned by his ingenuousness, his apparently sincere outrage, she took his hand and felt herself almost airborne as he pulled her upward. Still grasping her wrist in a viselike grip, he started back toward the open cell door, moving at high speed now, both hands fully occupied, one grasping her wrist, the other the walking stick.

But John managed only one boot over the line that separated her from her nightmare. All at once the four soldiers who had been softly chattering a distance away suddenly sprang to life, all shouting at once, all moving at once—ironically, not toward John, who had initiated the bid for freedom, but toward her, who had only followed.

As they descended simultaneously, they pushed John to one side, as though he didn't exist. As she felt the full weight of their hands on her shoulders pushing her down into the straw, she was sorry John would have to see her manacled. It would have been easier for him if he had not. She closed her eyes as she felt the prison skirt lifted, felt the cold iron band clamped shut on one ankle, the black iron chain pulled taut as the second iron was shut over her other ankle. All the time, the French soldiers were chattering, half in anger, more in annoyance, as though she were simply a child who had disappointed them. One held up wrist manacles . . .

Dear God, no.

But the others shook their heads and pointed toward Madame Charvin's arrangement of wax flowers.

Thus given the freedom of her arms and hands, she closed her eyes and heard them in retreat, still muttering in anger, and wondered where John was and what he was thinking—and was he strong enough to endure?

For several moments she refused to open her eyes, unable to face the answers to those questions. Then she did, and instantly regretted it and saw him flattened against the bars of the cell, his face even more bloodless as he stared down on her manacled legs.

She must speak to him. She was accustomed to the irons. She'd worn them day and night the first two months of her imprisonment after sentence had been passed. They could be dealt with.

"John, you mustn't—"

"I . . . am so . . . sorry . . .." But he couldn't finish and apparently felt instead a need to touch her, for all at once he was at her side, his arms about her.

She lost track of how long he held her. It didn't matter. The guards had closed and locked the cell door after them to prohibit any future escape attempts. And John, having seen their quick action where she was concerned, seemed to have momentarily surrendered in this battle of wills.

Gradually the tension seemed to ease in him, and thus in her. It had always been so. John had always set the emotional pace for all the family.

But for now nothing mattered except they were together, after she had thought she never would see him again in this life. While she wondered precisely how long they had, even that didn't matter.

"Is it true, then?" he asked.

"Is what true?" she asked, nestling closer into his arms against the day when he would be gone from her.

"They told me you were under sentence of . . . death."

She closed her eyes, appalled at how it sounded when spoken aloud. "Yes."

Did she want a blindfold, or did she want one last look at the miracle of blue sky?

"Would you tell me about it?" he asked, his voice as kind as she'd ever heard it. If only he'd discovered that becoming and soothing tone sooner, his empire and family might still be intact and she would not be . . .

She commenced speaking of the night months ago when she'd been sewing late with Eugenie Retiffe, when she'd heard the footsteps at a time of night and in a place where there should be no footsteps. It wasn't as difficult to tell as she'd imagined. Even the humiliation and degradation that had followed were bearable. It was almost over. Even memory then would be obliterated. She concluded with the magistrate's pronouncing the death sentence by firing squad, and then realized she had nothing else to say.

Just when she thought how good he was being in not interrupting, she heard him groan.

"Don't, John, please." She held him now, her arms tightly enclosed against the horror she'd lived with every moment of every day for the last four months. It could be accommodated, the sure and certain knowledge of one's imminent death. But the most stoic will could be undone with one brief expression of pity.

"It can be endured, John," she whispered, pressing his head close to her breast. "I assure you it can. I saw so much bravery during the revolution, women who—"

"Damn the revolution!" he exploded, and pushed away from her comfort.

And she knew *that* expression and regretted what it meant—more will, more inhuman effort expended in a futile cause. How much better it would have been to spend the last moments talking quietly about their rich past.

"The fifteenth, the bastard said," John announced.

She nodded and sat up straight, tried to stand and remembered the manacles were back in place, and instead curled her legs to one side and smoothed the prison skirt over them. Strange, but in his presence they were more of an embarrassment than usual.

"I . . . don't . . ." she began, watching the process she knew so well, having witnessed it off and on throughout his life since he was a little boy, the dynamo that controlled his spiritual center beginning to build a head of steam. On his feet, he retrieved the walking stick and commenced pacing the small cell. Four steps in one direction, three in the other . . .

"John, please," she begged, watching him, wishing he would hold her again and say nothing.

"No," he said sternly, shaking his head, still pacing, studying the floor as though the clue to the future was there, had been there all along and all he had to do was find it.

"Tell me of Eden," she begged, still trying to cut through the monumental energy building within him. "John, please tell me of Eden. There isn't much time. . . ."

"You're right," he snapped, and for the first time looked down on her. She saw the new strength, the new resolution falter, as though each time he looked at her, he suffered a new shock.

"Seven days," he said, speaking rapidly, "but we can do it."

"Do . . . what?" she asked, almost fearful he would tell her.

And he did. "I'm not alone, you know."

"Who . . . ?" she asked eagerly, hoping it was a member of the family. Of course they wouldn't have let him come alone. "Who, John? Richard? Is it Richard?"

"Of course not," he scolded. "I haven't seen Richard. It's Bates. You remember Bates . . ."

Bates? Yes. Pencil-thin, arrogant, and proper. She'd always suspected Bates didn't quite approve of her as a member of the Eden family. "Where . . . ?"

John shrugged and smiled, the first she'd seen on his face since he'd arrived in the dimly lit cell. "He was in Mortemouth and appeared when I needed him most. He's upstairs at this very moment with General Mon-

171

taud . . ." He broke off and stopped directly in front of her. "Do you know the general?" he asked, his voice weighted with innuendo.

She did. Madame Charvin had brought him down once not too long ago to show him her wax flowers.

"He's a bastard," John pronounced solemnly, "and a madman."

She smiled at the innocent assessment. "They are all mad, my dearest," she said. "The world has gone mad. I was able to judge that at the end of my first day on the barricades."

Slowly, almost wearily, he backed away until he found the security of a wall and leaned against it. "What . . . possessed you?" he asked, almost childlike.

For a moment she had no idea what he meant. "What . . . possessed? I don't under—"

"To leave England, me, Eden, and come . . . here."

She'd known all along she'd have to address herself to this sort of accounting, though for a moment she resented it. "I did not think of it as leaving England or you or Eden," she said, and realized she was lying—at least in part. Had life at Eden been different, she might have stayed. But there had been so much death and destruction and tragedy, the very air had seemed heavy with grief and she'd felt a strong need for fresh air, different horizons.

"It was Louise, primarily," she went on, not looking at him, easing the heavy iron ring around her left ankle where the flesh was being pinched. "You remember Louise Michel," she went on. "She spoke in London on several occasions. I held a salon for her once. She was a most eloquent woman, like no one I'd ever met."

She closed her eyes and enjoyed a precise image of Louise Michel, the close-cropped brown hair, a soul burning in dark eyes the chill of prison could never extinguish. Recovering quickly, she opened her eyes from the torture of memory and saw her arrangement of wax flowers awaiting finishing touches. For one instant she deeply resented John's presence and wished—God forgive her—he had not come, had left her alone to face what had to be faced.

"Did I . . . ?" he began, and broke off. Did I . . . ?" he began again. "Was I responsible for . . . driving you away?" he managed at last.

Again she was shocked by the ingenuousness of the question. Of course he was. "No," she lied. "I would have gone anyway. I had to. I believed so intensely in what Louise was preaching, the right of every woman to select her own destiny, to spend or waste her life."

"Did you have it so bad?" he asked, that small-boy quality to his voice again, clearly indicating he didn't understand her or the movement any more now than he had on that last terrible day in the Eden library years ago when, like a deranged man, he had shouted, "What did any of you want that I was not able and willing to give you?"

"Freedom," she'd answered then, and started to repeat the word, and decided: No. She was through explaining herself.

"Come, John," she invited, extending a hand to him with the thought of guiding him back down on the straw. It would be easier for both of them to sit than to stand. And she was weary of postmortems and what-might-have-beens.

"In addition to Bates," he said, ignoring her gesture, "there is a young man from Mortemouth who is serving as my coachman." He looked down on her with a curious expression, part smile, part astonishment. "He said he wanted to serve me." The soft astonishment grew, as though he were so accustomed to being hated that a desire on the part of anyone to serve him came as a shock.

"I don't doubt it," Elizabeth said, still amazed at how important it was for this complex man to know he was loved. "I imagine everyone in Mortemouth rejoiced at seeing you well and—"

She started to say more, but suddenly he interrupted. "Prepare yourself," he said with almost amusing melodrama.

She tried to match the new soberness in his face, and looked up. "Prepare myself . . . for what?"

"I'm leaving now to dispatch Charley Spade back to England on the fastest horse I can purchase in this godforsaken place. I will send with him a personal letter for William Gladstone—"

"No—"

"Hear me out. As prime minister he can intercede on your behalf—"

"No, John, I beg you . . ." She was on her knees, suffering fresh agony, the duress of this latest threat. Not Willie. He owed her nothing, and she was fearful a bid for help would be interpreted as payment due on an ancient debt. No! John had no right . . .

"John, please," she begged, still struggling up against the confinement of her manacles. Halfway up, in haste she lost her balance and fell back to the straw.

Just then the guards appeared, key in hand, and unlocked the door. John passed through it immediately. "If Charley Spade moves quickly," he called back through the bars, "I'll have you released well within the limit of time—four days, no more. And Gladstone will intervene, I'm certain of it. In the past he has quarreled with me, but not with you."

"John, no, I beg . . ."

Either he couldn't or wouldn't hear her protest and backed away from the bars, as though relieved to be outside the cell. She started to call to him again, but saw the single-mindedness on his face that she'd first observed when he'd been a boy of three.

With characteristic imperiousness he waved the soldiers forward as though they took orders from him. To her astonishment, they fell into precise formation and led the way down the dark, narrow corridor. Without another look in her direction, John followed. She sat frozen, listening to the cadence of their step, and found herself counting it off under her breath, and realized she passed a large part of her day in silent counting. Counting the bars which fronted her cell. Counting the number of candles on the low bench which must be transformed into flowers by next Tuesday.

Tuesday.

The word stopped her.

November 15.

All the way back up the long staircase, he purposefully kept his mind busy. Yes, they would go immediately to the stables he'd spotted not too far from their wretched boardinghouse in Rue Saint Jacob. While Charley Spade and Bates were selecting the best animal, John would pen a hurried though careful letter to William Gladstone, England's prime minister, informing him in clear terms of the barbaric indignities being heaped upon a British citizen who had been unfortunate enough to get herself caught in this latest example of French instability and hysteria.

The French soldiers led him upward at a fast pace. Twice they had to slow down as, with one backward look, they could see that he had trouble keeping up. He made himself hurry. Yes, he would write to Gladstone. What had she against that? John was certain the old man owed her a great deal, for the number of times she'd permitted him to . . .

The thought was like poison in his system, threatening both his breath and his balance.

The three soldiers in the lead drew farther and farther ahead, isolating John with the one man who continued to hover solicitously, supporting his arm, a gesture of kindness that baffled John but which he accepted gratefully nonetheless.

When they were less than fifty feet from the top, when he could see the first faint patch of gray day and smell the first whiff of fresh air, the soldier trailing behind reached out a hand—not in support, but in restraint.

Surprised, John looked back. The other three already had reached the summit and were now talking easily among themselves, apparently unconcerned about the two lagging behind.

"Monsieur . . ." the soldier began, something conspiratorial in his manner.

Annoyed by the attempt at fraternization, John gathered new strength from somewhere and pulled ahead by a step or two, and called back brusquely, "I'm sorry. I don't speak—"

"But I do," the soldier said with surprising facility.

John looked back again, his mind turning. If the man could understand English, he must have overheard everything that had been said down in Elizabeth's cell.

"No fear, monsieur," the soldier said, his manner, as always, surprisingly mild and reassuring. "I hear all," he said, "but say nothing. I swear it."

"I don't know what you mean."

"You must hear me," the soldier went on, drawing yet closer. Too close for John's ease.

"I have—"

"You have nothing," the soldier countered. "Nothing that matters here, in this place," he added, his voice suddenly growing harsh.

Shocked by this new tone and curious as to why the other three were purposefully leaving them alone, John turned to confront the man once and for all so that he could complete his climb out of this miserable pit and move on to the most important tasks ahead.

"Sir, hear me out," the soldier said now, so close to John he was required to do little more than whisper. "Your female friend," he went on, pointing back down the steps, "is doomed. There is nothing you can do to bring her back, for she is already dead."

"No."

"Yes!" This was accompanied by a strong hand on John's arm, one of

174

both restraint and support, as though the Frenchman was trying hard to convince him of something. "Now, if you truly care for her," the man went on, his voice still low, "there is one course of action which you must take."

"W-what?" John stammered, hearing the stammer, feeling the terror behind it. Who was this man? Then a thought occurred. He was offering John an escape plan. For money, of course. Why not? Here obviously was a wealthy Englishman who wanted to change the course of fate.

"I must ask you to say a word of this to no one," the Frenchman whispered, glancing up the steps at his three comrades, who were still chattering and laughing among themselves.

"Of course," John snapped. "What is—?"

"These are painful matters to discuss."

"Please, what . . . ?"

"Her execution, as you know, is set for Tuesday."

Execution . . .

John gaped at the word, still wholly unable to comprehend or accept the reality behind it.

"How you say, sir? Will you . . . witness execution?"

"There will be no—"

Quickly the man lifted both hands, as though in an attempt to stay John's anger. "In the event that there is," he went on, clearly choosing his words carefully and now backing a step away, "you must know how it is done. Our instructions on the first round are to aim only for the extremities. The arms, hands, feet, legs, if you comprehend. On the first round," the man went on, quietly talking madness, "death seldom occurs. The prisoner is not relieved of his agony until the second and sometimes even the third round, when our commander instructs us to aim for the heart."

For a moment John felt the steep dark stairs swirl about him. He glanced down and saw them liquid, as though underwater. In the other direction he saw the three soldiers had disappeared altogether.

"Do . . . you comprehend, sir?" the soldier asked.

No, John didn't comprehend, and said as much. "Why are you telling me this? As I said, there will be no—"

Suddenly, with new aggression, the soldier stepped back down to John's level and with one hand pushed him roughly against the cold wall. "You do not hear well, sir," he whispered fiercely, all earlier traces of sympathy and compassion gone.

John started to protest the rough treatment, but was not given a chance.

"You think you can strut in here and make your claims regardless of French law. You English . . ."

As the sentence dissolved into a sneer, John held his position a moment, then said abruptly, "If you'll excuse me . . ." He purposefully brushed past the man, in the process conveying he was no longer interested in what he had to say, when in truth he was more interested then ever.

The odds on Charley Spade reaching Calais, crossing the channel, making his way to London, locating Mr. Gladstone, obtaining from him an official letter of protest, then returning here—all within seven days—was unlikely to the point of being impossible. But a simple escape plotted by someone who knew the inside workings of the prison as well as the outside—that might work.

The soldier allowed him to climb laboriously upward for three steps before he stopped him—as John knew he would.

"My price is one hundred louis," he demanded, with just a touch of belligerence in his voice.

John stopped his climb and looked back. "For what?" he asked. "You've not stated the nature of your service."

Quickly the man shook his head. "I *have* stated it," he said. "On the first round we are instructed only to aim for the—"

"Enough!" John shook his head, not wanting to hear it again.

The man shrugged. "For one hundred louis I will personally give you my word my first bullet will go directly into her heart."

Stunned and sickened, John tried to speak and could not.

"I tell you, sir," the Frenchman said, stepping close at the very time he should have put a safe distance between them, "people think the firing squad is superior, kinder than the guillotine." Calmly he shook his head. "Not true. The blade kills cleanly, instantly. But bullets . . ." Again he shook his head, a look of mock sadness on his face. "I have seen men scream for the coup de grace, their flesh ripped open, standing in pools of their own blood."

John closed his eyes.

"Did you hear this time, sir?" the soldier prodded foolishly. "One hundred louis will buy you one clean bullet directly through the center of her breast."

There was nothing else for John to do but to stop the obscene mouth from speaking further obscenities. The only way to accomplish that was to destroy the man behind the mouth, and since he had a weapon, the heavy silver-headed walking stick, he lifted it quickly before the mouth could start talking again. The element of surprise combined with his sense of outrage, and he delivered one stunning blow to the side of the man's head, dislodging the grin as well as the man's footing.

The soldier buckled briefly, went down on his knees, a convenient position for John, who with extraordinary calmness stepped forward to deliver blow after blow to the man's upper body, sometimes striking his head, then his shoulders, now his arms, which had been raised in meager defense, multiple blows which caused rivers of blood. John wondered, even as he pursued the man down another step, why he didn't cry out for help.

Then he did, a raucous shriek accompanied by a continuous stream of outraged French. Still John lifted the walking stick and let it fall where it would, feeling genuine relief each time it struck bone, delighting in seeing the man cower on the step below him.

Did you hear, sir? One hundred louis will buy you one clean bullet directly through her heart.

So engrossed was he that he failed to hear the rush of boots coming down the stairs behind him. The twin grips on his shoulders were of such strength they literally seemed to lift him until he was airborne, in fear of falling down the steps over the very man he had beaten senseless. But the

176

same hands that lifted him also supported him and roughly turned him about and half-pushed, half-shoved him to the top of the stairs.

They were all talking at once, and he couldn't understand a word. No matter. What he could understand and what brought him the greatest pleasure of this miserable day was the quick backward look which he stole from the top of the steps at the man who had so offended him.

Now the soldier sat, hunched and bowed, on the step where he had fallen, blood pouring from his nose, the corner of his mouth, his forehead, the tops of both hands—a steady stream.

I've seen them standing in pools of their own blood.

So have I, John thought with pleasure, and even managed a smile for the three soldiers who now pushed him roughly ahead.

At that moment one of their rifles made a stabbing gesture in his ribs, the message clear, requiring no translation. Suddenly the exertion of the beating, the sense of terror he'd struggled against since his arrival in this place, the remembered sight of Elizabeth helpless, frightened, joined forces and conspired against him. The strength in his legs failed him and he went quickly down on his knees.

As the French chatter increased around him, he felt the rifle barrels prodding his ribs, back, and neck. Though he could not lift his head, he knew what was going to happen seconds before it occurred: the rifle butt lifted with a curse high in the air over John, who struggled up to his knees. With another curse it was brought down full force against the side of his head.

His skull felt as though it had been split open by the single blow. A seductive blackness was coming closer to the center where thought and consciousness resided. Perhaps for a few moments it might be best . . .

Welcome the blackness, a voice of wisdom urged.

He did.

For two hours Bates had maintained a constant vigil beside the bed in the low-ceilinged second-floor chamber of Monsieur DuCamp's questionable lodging house in Rue Saint Jacob, praying Mr. Eden would wake up, then praying he wouldn't, for then Bates would have to give him the bad news.

Now he kept a close eye on the large purple swelling on Mr. Eden's left temple and wished Charley Spade would hurry and get back with a physician, but he didn't hold out much hope. There were no private physicians left in Paris, according to Monsieur DuCamp, only "citizens' physicians." Bates shook his head, trying to understand. All of Paris now seemed to be suffering from a very messy and inefficient egalitarianism.

God, how Bates hated it, all of it—from this dark, cramped chamber which smelled of ancient cabbage, to the fulsome sense of democracy itself. No two men were sent into this world by their Creator the same.

He shuddered as the cold rain pelted the filthy window glass, and he saw again in memory that most fearful spectacle which had been inflicted on him a mere three hours ago as he'd sat awaiting Mr. Eden's return from his first visit with Miss Elizabeth in her cell at La Rochelle Prison.

177

Bates had known it would go hard for Mr. Eden, but he'd had no idea how hard until he'd heard a scuffle just coming in the door of that unspeakably filthy front corridor at La Rochelle. He had looked up in apprehension and had seen Mr. Eden suspended, lifeless, between two French guards, blood flowing in a steady stream from a wound on his forehead, his feet dragging.

But the bloodiest specter of all had been trailing behind, another soldier who continuously fought off the support of his mates, half-walking, half-stumbling but always pushing forward in demented outrage, ready to inflict more harm on Mr. Eden. And he would have, too, had not the overall ruckus brought the mincy-stepping little General Montaud scurrying from his comfy quarters, his chalk-pale cheeks ruddy as a Welshman's with anger over the turmoil at that moment taking place in his prison.

Bates, of course, had gone instantly to Mr. Eden's side and relieved one of the soldiers of his support. As the other had stepped away as well, and as Bates was not equal to Mr. Eden's deadweight, he'd had no choice but to let him slip, as easy as possible, to the floor.

As he'd struck ground, Mr. Eden had given a reassuring groan, confirming life if not dignity—it was the combination of the two that was so difficult to achieve.

Bates had run to the front doors, had cried out for Charley Spade, who still sat patiently beneath a mountain of lap robes in the cold steady drizzle of the day.

True disgrace when a man of quality, one of the most powerful men in England, was treated so barbarically by foreigners, and then at the end of the day could not find even a decent and comfortable lodging. Never had Bates seen this most unique phenomenon close at hand, an entire society straining with all its energy and with all its might to become common.

At that moment he heard a slight noise at the door and looked up, hoping to see Charley Spade's broad welcome face and, trailing behind, a competent physician. But the longer he kept his eye fixed on the oak door, the more convinced he became he'd imagined the noise. Either that or a curious chambermaid had been sent to spy on the "English" by Monsieur DuCamp.

"Mr. Eden," Bates called softly, daring to shake the rain-damp shoulder. "Mr. Eden, can you hear me?" Bates tried again and, receiving no response, stood stiffly and walked to the single narrow window. On the opaque glass it appeared to be raining coal dust.

The scene on the street below was a frantic, blurred chaos of grays, browns, and blacks, people hurrying every which way to avoid the rain, which had increased with nightfall. The intersection directly to his left was a clogged, hopeless bottleneck. Several soldiers were trying to bring order to the glut of rain-slick carriages and wagons, but without success thus far.

Confusion everywhere he looked, rampant confusion. Again he sniffed disaster in the moment, the day, the times, and thought the best action he could take on behalf of them all would be to load the still-senseless Mr. Eden aboard the hired mourning carriage and give Charley Spade instructions to head for the channel at the fastest speed. After General Montaud's parting order today, there was absolutely nothing more to stay for. Perhaps if he could remove Mr. Eden before consciousness returned, it might be easier . . .

He froze, still listening, and it came again, a soft moan from the bed, signaling . . .

"Mr. Eden, please. Can you hear me?" he called out, and was rewarded with the pale face upon the pillow turning once, then back in the opposite direction. Then at last a good healthy groan accompanied by a healthier curse, "Goddammit!" as one hand went gingerly up to the swollen goose egg on his left temple.

Mr. Eden winced at first touch, as did Bates sympathetically. Finally Bates guided his hand away from the injured area. "I wouldn't, sir," he said gently. "It was quite a blow."

"Eliz . . ." Mr. Eden tried to say, and something—either the effort or the thought—robbed him of sufficient breath and he closed his eyes, then made a logical request. "Brandy, Bates, please. Just one."

Bates moved immediately toward his trunk, where he had packed a bottle of brandy for medicinal purposes. Quickly he found it, poured a portion into a mug from the washstand, and extended it to Mr. Eden. When he didn't take it immediately, Bates carefully slipped his arm beneath Mr. Eden's head and elevated it enough for the man to sip.

And sip he did, drained the mug and made a face at it, shook his head once at the burning liquid, and though gasping for breath, found the energy and will to remain elevated.

"Are you—?" Bates began.

But Mr. Eden merely lifted a restraining hand as though to say he couldn't answer questions and move at the same time. Still seated mid-bed, his legs spread askew before him, he raised his head laboriously and appeared to be looking in all corners of the narrow room.

"Charley . . ."

". . . has gone to fetch a physician for you," Bates replied.

In response to the announcement concerning Charley Spade's destination, Mr. Eden looked displeased and swung his legs over the side of the bed.

"I . . . found her, Bates," came the mourning voice out of the bleak expression. "She was . . ." As he tried to describe what precisely he had found in the dungeon cell at La Rochelle, his voice broke.

"Don't think on it, Mr. Eden," Bates advised kindly, still dividing his attention between the man sitting on the side of the bed and the liquid flow of humanity on the street below the window.

"I can't get it out of my mind, Bates," Mr. Eden confessed quietly. "She bears no resemblance to . . ."

Again Bates nodded, pleased he was talking but wishing he'd talk on some other matter. "Come on, sir," he interrupted. "Let's make ourselves ready. There is nothing more for us in this godforsaken place. . . ."

At that Mr. Eden looked squarely at him, shock registering on top of pain. "What are you talking about, Bates? As soon as Charley arrives I have the most important errand of his life awaiting him, because if he is successful, I shall personally see to it that he never wants for anything again in this lifetime."

At this extravagant promise, Bates stopped, having run into a self-made

179

barrier of envy and resentment. Why should Charley Spade get such a rare opportunity? "I . . . don't understand, sir," he said honestly, and tried to read Mr. Eden's face, but it was difficult.

The man again had fallen into a close scrutiny of the floor, his mind apparently fully engaged in planning. "Bates," he called out, still not looking up, "what is your opinion of Charley Spade's capabilities?"

A curious question. "I . . . don't . . ."

"Is he capable?"

"Of what, sir?"

Anger surfaced for a moment and did apparent damage to his head. "Of . . . functioning," he said at last, gently holding his head as though trying to hold it together.

"Yes, of course. In a limited way," Bates responded, still baffled.

"Can he read?"

"Yes."

"Write?"

"Yes."

"He'll serve." Mr. Eden nodded, concluding the bewildering exchange. Then on the next breath with a wave of his hand he asked Bates to fetch his writing pad and clear the bureau, as he had "a most important letter to write."

"Sir, I think you should know—"

"I know damn well what I should know and what I must do!" he exploded.

Bates had seen it too often before to be shocked by it. "No, sir," he began rigorously, and might have been allowed to finish, except at that moment there was a knock at the door, the door was pushed open, and a very wet, very miserable Charley Spade stood there with a foolish announcement.

"I was told that no French physician would come out on such a night for an Englishman," he grumbled.

Standing, though unsteady, John gaped at him a moment, then with a quick wave motioned him into the room with a brusque announcement. "I have no need of a physician, Charley, particularly a French one. What I do have need of is your effort and your services on behalf of the woman we have come to rescue. Are you willing?"

Again Bates retreated to the window, curious as to the nature of Mr. Eden's "needs," doubly curious why Charley Spade had been chosen over himself.

As Mr. Eden guided Charley to the fire, the large man pledged his loyalty and his service in any way Mr. Eden saw fit to use them.

"A journey, then," Mr. Eden pronounced, settling slowly back into the horsehair chair.

"A journey. Very well." Charley nodded, looking up from the small fire and warming his backside. "Where?"

"Back to London."

At the calm announcement, Bates started forward. "An excellent suggestion, sir," he agreed. "Might I suggest that we all retrace our steps just as soon as—"

"No. Just Charley," Mr. Eden said flatly. "I want you to purchase the fastest horses, change them as often as you need, but do not stop and do not rest until you are standing before the private desk and are in the private company of Mr. William Gladstone."

"I . . . don't . . . I'll do it, but I . . . don't . . ." Out of this incoherency Charley shook his head soundly. "I . . . ain't equipped, sir, to converse with the prime—"

"I'm not asking you to converse with him," Mr. Eden said. "All I want is for you to hand him a letter, place it directly into his hands and wait while he reads it, and do not leave until he supplies you with an answer. Then you are to leave London immediately bearing that response and return here. Is that clear?"

From where Bates stood at the window, it was clear. Mr. Eden was making a final desperate bid for clemency for the woman. But according to the confusion and bewilderment he saw on Charley's face, nothing was clear.

"I . . . don't . . . London, sir? Now? I'm not . . . sure . . ."

As Mr. Eden moved closer with surprising patience to explain it again, Bates closed his eyes and wondered if now was the time to inform Mr. Eden of General Montaud's last command. He would have to know sooner or later, and it might relieve him of a torturous second explanation to Charley Spade.

"Sir, if I may interrupt—"

"In a minute, Bates," Mr. Eden said brusquely. Then back to Charley. "Now, you must look at me, Charley," he began patiently, "and listen carefully. . . ."

There was one last pledge of devotion and vows of success, a firm handshake, and then apparently it was time to turn to more practical matters.

"Bates," Mr. Eden called, recognizing him at last, "buy clothes, the fastest horse in Paris, the quickest route to the channel, a knapsack of cheese and rolls so he won't have to stop, and ample funds for more horses, should he require them along the way." He stopped for a moment, thinking. "Can you do it," he asked, "within the hour?"

"I can easily, sir, but—"

"Good, good," Mr. Eden repeated, and looked vaguely about the small room as though momentarily he'd lost his train of thought. "Then be off with you both. Give me the hour in which to pen the letter—possibly the most important letter I've ever written in my life."

"Mr. Eden," Bates tried again, "I must tell you something."

"Can't it wait?" was the weary response.

Bates stepped back to make way for him as he moved heavily toward the small writing bureau. "No, I'm afraid it won't keep, sir," Bates persisted.

With a slap Mr. Eden opened his writing portfolio, then sat back in the chair as if to say his attention was Bates's, at least for a few minutes.

"General Montaud . . ." Bates began, testing the name on the air.

"Bastard!" John muttered beneath his breath.

Bates ignored the curse and went on. "He was quite . . . upset with what happened at La Rochelle to—"

"As well he should be!" John snapped, voice rising along with his temper. "I've never seen such conditions, unspeakable, not fit for animals, let alone humans. And Elizabeth . . ." Suddenly he closed his eyes.

181

"Sir," Bates said with renewed conviction and resolution, "you must not return to the prison tonight . . . or ever, for your own safety." In the absence of a response, Bates glanced toward Charley Spade, who now seemed to share Bates's concern. "Did you hear me, sir?" Bates asked. "General Montaud said—"

"Who gives a damn?" Mr. Eden asked sullenly.

"You should," Bates went on undaunted. "Give a damn, I mean, for the general said if you ever returned to La Rochelle he would imprison you."

Slowly Mr. Eden looked up from the blank piece of stationery, a look of stunned disbelief on his face. "On . . . what . . . charge?"

Bates drew a deep breath. At last he had the man's attention. "Oh, one of many." He counted off the fingers of his left hand as he tried to recall the incoherent dancing little man who'd almost set the soldiers on all of them.

"Attempting to lead a prisoner to escape; attempting to bribe an officer; attempting to plant seeds of revolution in a prisoner's head; attempting to murder an officer of the . . ."

Now paradoxically there appeared a smile on Mr. Eden's face. "Is that all the little weasel could come up with?" he asked, as though vastly amused by the whole affair.

"No, sir, there are others, but I can't remember—"

"Nor should you clutter your mind with such . . ." All at once he looked over his shoulder and saw Charley Spade still warming his backside at the fire. "You still here, Charley?" he asked, peeved. "You'd better be about it."

"*Sir!* " With all the force Bates could muster, he stepped between Mr. Eden and Charley Spade and made an impressive pledge of his own. "If you return to La Rochelle, you will do so alone, and if you walk through those wretched gates, it is my judgment neither you nor Miss Elizabeth will ever walk out of them alive."

For a moment it was impossible to tell what was moving behind Eden's taut forehead.

"I . . . m-must see her again," he stammered. I can't—"

"General Montaud said you would be permitted in the prison one-quarter of an hour preceding her execu . . ." Bates broke off, unable to say the word.

Mr. Eden seemed to be aware of the thoughtful omission and appeared grateful. Then he turned abruptly about in his chair, reaching for the penpoint, while at the same time issuing a command. "Then move, both of you. It's more important than ever that Charley Spade reach England and sanity. Gladstone will respond. I know he will. He was very fond of Elizabeth. Then let's see what our little French bastard does with an official protest from the prime minister of England."

Disbelieving the new and easy acquiescence, Bates stood stock-still.

"Move! Both of you!" Mr. Eden bellowed. "Must I do everything?"

Something in the tone sent Charley Spade and Bates hopping for the door. Eden bowed his head until his forehead was resting on the table.

He resembled for all the world a man who suffers an invisible boot pressing against the back of his neck.

* * *

It was approaching ten P.M. when John stood on the rain-slick pavement outside DuCamp's lodgings and handed over to Charley Spade the letter addressed to William Gladstone, which he tucked for safekeeping inside a waterproof pouch.

"Guard it with your life," John said simply. "You have until Sunday evening. Then you must be on the road back to Dover. Do not wait for schedules. Whatever you require, purchase it outright. You have my signature and letter of credit. It will obtain anything you need in London." He was aware of Bates listening closely, a step behind. Sick with the odds against success, John added, "And remember Alex Aldwell. If you encounter problems, contact Mr. Aldwell immediately and he will . . ." He disliked having to involve Alex because he was no longer absolutely certain of his loyalty. Still . . .

"Not to worry, sir." Charley Spade grinned down from the horse with an encouraging confidence. "It is my plan to reach London no later than Saturday morning bright and early. It is my plan to be speaking with the prime minister before he takes luncheon that same day. It is my plan to be on the road to Dover by Saturday evening, and it is my plan to arrive here at this very spot no later than Sunday evening or Monday morning, when—if you will wait for me to wash the dust off me face—I'll drive you personal to La Rochelle, where together we can present to the French slime Mr. William Gladstone's angry words."

The grin was infectious and the confidence more so. "God go with you, Charley." John smiled and stepped back with a salute.

Then with a yell Charley turned the racer about, guided her skillfully through the traffic of Rue Saint Jacob, into the large boulevard which led to the Seine, and opened her up immediately to a canter, then a gallop. The last image John had was of a large man bowed skillfully over a flying horse, both man and beast working in perfect concert, speed the goal of both.

Talbot House,
Dublin, Ireland
November 11, 1874

"If you're fully restored, Mrs. O'Donnell, I want to hear everything."

As Lord Harrington settled behind his writing bureau, he wished he were closer to the blazing fire. He looked up at the mullioned windows covered with solid sheets of cold November rain and recalled September, when those same windows had been thrown open so he could hear the boys playing on the green.

Boys . . . Stephen, please . . . Dear God, help him . . .

Quickly he crossed himself and reached for his rosary, placed it atop the bureau, and then turned his attention back to Rose O'Donnell, who had only just arrived from her hazardous mission to the North Devon coast.

"Please, Mrs. O'Donnell, tell me everything you learned as briefly as possible. Then you must go and see Stephen. He is so ill and has been—"

"How long has the lad been ill, Lord Harrington?" she asked.

"Too long," he replied. "The doctor came once and said . . ."

Directly overhead Lord Harrington heard footsteps. The nursemaid, no doubt, moving to comfort Stephen. Worried, Lord Harrington looked up at the beamed ceiling as though he were capable of seeing through it.

As Rose O'Donnell launched forth into a self-pitying account of the hardships imposed upon one while traveling—particularly "an attractive widow lady"—Lord Harrington put off listening to her and concentrated on the soft tread of footsteps overhead, moving twice back and forth between the bed and the water basin.

How had the lad fallen so sick so quickly? Just last week he and Frederick had made a steeplechase of the staircase and lower corridor. Old

184

Crosset Fletcher had threatened to leave unless Lord Harrington intervened immediately "on behalf of sanity."

". . . and you should have seen me, my lord, when I arrived after that ordeal. . . ."

Lord Harrington nodded, not having one idea which ordeal she was referring to. "Please reach the point, Mrs. O'Donnell," he urged with an unprecedented display of patience. "I want very much for you to look in on Stephen."

"Who's that up there with him now?" she asked, apparently having heard the footsteps as well.

"Deasy Morgan," he replied, wearily knowing she would object and the account of what she'd found at Eden would be postponed again.

While the feisty woman launched a vicious attack on little Deasy, Lord Harrington eased back in his chair and mourned the lack of sweet and gentle femininity in his life. All that seemed to have died with Lila, his beautiful daughter Lila, whom John Murrey Eden had assiduously wooed, courted, wed, and killed.

Deep inside he felt ancient grief, yet surely he'd spent it all. He had wept for days, nothing and no one capable of comforting him save Elizabeth. Dear Elizabeth, the only decent person he'd found when he moved into that cold tomb known as Eden Castle. Eden. . . . He scoffed privately, only vaguely aware that Mrs. O'Donnell was still crucifying Deasy Morgan.

"Mrs. O'Donnell," Lord Harrington interrupted, "I must beg of you, please get on with your report. If Deasy Morgan is indeed inept, then she will need your guiding hand even more upstairs, as will Stephen."

Though anger had been her first reaction, as he continued to speak soothingly the flash of anger disappeared, replaced by a benign look of self-righteousness. He knew the look well, had even worn it himself on occasion, the look of all good Catholics who believed they alone held all the truly important keys to divine communication and understanding.

Irritated, he asked sharply, "Did you find him, Mrs. O'Donnell?" He knew full well she had.

"Well, of course I found him, I did," Rose O'Donnell began with admirable directness. "But when I first heard of employment at Eden, they were saying that Mr. Eden was being measured for his coffin." Abruptly she leaned back and shook her head. "But what I found when I arrived at them crumbling gates was far from a corpse. It was the woman who had died. The Lady Harriet."

Lord Harrington bowed his head. The name was beloved, as was the lady who wore it. Harriet dead? Lonely, secluded Harriet, who always wore a veil to cover her blindness.

"Starved to death, or so they said."

To this gruesome announcement Lord Harrington looked up. "Starved to . . ." he tried to repeat, and couldn't.

". . . and I can't remember her name," he heard Rose O'Donnell muse now.

He looked up from his mourning for Lady Harriet to see Rose O'Donnell studying the ceiling. "Who?" Lord Harrington asked, vowing to keep his mind on the matters at hand.

Above, he heard footsteps again. *Dear God, let the fever break.*

"The other one I was told about at Eden," Mrs. O'Donnell said snappishly. "Not dead yet, but had got herself into a fair pickle. Oh, yes, Elizabeth. That was it, Elizabeth."

Still not fully recovered from the shock of Harriet's death, Lord Harrington was unable for the second time to believe what he was hearing. "Not d-dead?" he stammered, denying death even before she had confirmed it.

"Oh, no, sir, not dead. Just went and got herself locked up in a French prison for . . ." She broke off and looked about as though fearful someone would overhear her. ". . . for revolutionary activities," Mrs. O'Donnell said with impressive melodrama, her arched eyes narrowing to two slits. "Mr. Eden shouldn't have gone, according to his nurse, Miss Mantle, but there was no stopping him, and when he got the ox Charley Spade to go as his coachman and old Bates to run interference for him, she said her mind was easier and that it really didn't make any difference anyway, because Mr. Eden had to go and fetch Miss Elizabeth because he didn't stand a chance of luring the rest of the family back to Eden without the assistance of Miss Elizabeth."

"Mrs. O'Donnell," Lord Harrington said. "Tell me of Mr. Eden. Had he . . . was he ill?" he asked.

"Yes," she went on without inflection. "Yes, Mr. Eden has been ill, seriously ill. And Miss Mantle says—"

"Who is this Miss Mantle you speak of?" Lord Harrington interrupted.

"The nurse," Mrs. O'Donnell replied, "the little circuit nurse, that's who."

"Do you think I should take the boys away, Mrs. O'Donnell?" he asked abruptly. He'd always needed someone to give him direction.

"Take them away where?" Mrs. O'Donnell asked with admirable strength.

"I don't know," he confessed. "Away from here. It wouldn't be too difficult for a skilled investigator to locate us."

A curious smile covered her face, which she quickly canceled. "Well, no need to run and hide yet, Lord Harrington. First, let's get Stephen well and out of bed," she began.

Suddenly he felt a surge of gratitude to the gossipy common woman. "Yes," he agreed, smiling.

"Then—say, about a month from now—I'll make a return trip, just to check on things, if you know what I mean. No employment this time, just a brief look-see on me friends—and I made me one or two while I was cooking there—then I'll be able to tell you if Mr. Eden is back and, if so, what precisely is going on. And on the basis of that journey, then you can make your decision concerning where you want to take the lads—maybe even America."

Now Lord Harrington listened with total absorption. America! No, he hadn't even thought of that, and felt certain it wasn't a wise destination and wished he didn't have to take them anyplace. Still . . . "A good idea, Mrs. O'Donnell," he said, giving the devil her due. "But I do hate to keep asking you to make that treacherous journey into enemy territory, as it were. Perhaps next time I'll ask Deasy Morgan to accompany you. She could—"

186

"Don't need no one to accompany me, Lord Harrington," she said with sudden anger. Least of all Deasy Morgan," she added with a sneer. Either I go alone or I don't go."

He glanced at her for a moment, still not quite able to fathom the woman. No matter. The journey had accomplished its purpose. The monster had awakened, but he was in far-off France now.

Mrs. O'Donnell had risen to go to Stephen. "Wait! I'll accompany you . . ."

"No need. I know the way."

Harriet dead . . . Elizabeth imprisoned . . .

As the two thoughts took root in his mind, he stood up rapidly as though to abandon them along with his chair.

"Mrs. O'Donnell, please wait," he called after the woman, who was already halfway up the broad staircase.

Stephen Eden, age eight, had been asleep and dreaming of a place with long gray corridors. Though he was hot and the corridors were cool, still he was frightened because he was lost and certain he could never find his way back to Talbot House. So he made himself open his eyes.

The first thing he saw was Grandpapa, who looked like he was lost in a nightmare as well. Stephen was glad to see him, and he lifted his arms, wanting to be held, then realized he was acting like a baby—or worse, like Frederick, who whined all the time for someone to hold and rock him.

But apparently Grandpapa didn't care and hurried to the bed. Despite Deasy Morgan's protest—she'd just put a camphor pack on his chest—Stephen snuggled into his arms and was glad the gray corridors were gone, yet wondered if he would ever see them again.

"Grandpapa," he murmured, nestling closer and wondering why he was shivering and burning up at the same time.

Suddenly, over Grandpapa's shoulder, he saw the witch herself, Rose O'Donnell, materializing out of the gloom of the corridor. When had she returned, and why didn't she just go away and stay away, and he wouldn't want to tell Frederick, who surely would cry . . .

"Good day, Stephen," the witch said. "I hear you've been a bad boy and gone and gotten sick."

He felt Grandpapa ease his hold to look sternly up at Rose O'Donnell, but with one hand she waved Grandpapa away from the bed. Stephen was disappointed to see how docilely he went. In fact, everyone in the household, including Frederick and Deasy Morgan and even old Crosset Fletcher, moved when commanded to do so by Rose O'Donnell.

"Let's have a look," she commanded. Again with a wave of her hand she motioned for him to draw down the blanket and draw up his nightshirt, which he did without hesitation, because he knew from hard experience Rose O'Donnell's was the voice to be obeyed.

Her hands were cold, and as Stephen pinched his eyes shut, he heard Deasy's voice as light as music but, as always, making no sense at all.

As Deasy chattered aimlessly to the air, Rose O'Donnell moved her icy fingers down Stephen's chest like she was counting his ribs. "Are his bowels moving?" she asked anyone who cared to answer.

Deasy stepped closer to the bed and stared mournfully down. "Like doorknobs," she beamed in response to Rose O'Donnell's question.

As Rose O'Donnell's examination continued, Stephen looked over her shoulder to see Grandpapa standing before the rain-splattered window, hands clasped behind his back, staring sadly out at the day. That was one thing Stephen didn't like about Grandpapa. He seemed happiest when he was sad.

"Bleeding," Rose O'Donnell announced, raising up from bending over with her ear pressed against his chest. "That's what he needs, a good bleeding."

"No!" This strong protest came from Grandpapa, who didn't look so sad any more as angry.

"Congestion and infection," Mrs. O'Donnell pronounced, and folded both hands together before her and looked like she was challenging Grandpapa.

"He's too little and too weak," Grandpapa argued, coming closer to the bed, fixing Stephen with a frightened eye. "It isn't necessary—"

"And how long has he been like this?" the witch inquired, circling the bed, playing with a big ring on her finger, twisting it then looking at it.

Grandpapa looked helpless.

Deasy followed Rose O'Donnell around the room, looking at the ring with her. "That's gorgeous, ma'am. Where did you pick up that pretty?"

"How long?" Mrs. O'Donnell repeated sternly, and pointed back toward Stephen.

Deasy answered accurately for a change. "Last week."

"Bleeding!" came the pronouncement again, and this time Stephen saw Grandpapa weaken.

"A week is too long for this fever," Mrs. O'Donnell said, and shook her head down at Stephen as though it were his fault.

Still hesitant, Grandpapa drew out his rosary beads, which generally he kept hidden in his pocket. "Perhaps I should fetch the doctor again from Dublin," he said.

Stephen watched his fingers move quickly down the small black beads.

"And pay a king's ransom in the process," Mrs. O'Donnell said. "I guarantee it—and for the same prescription."

Grandpapa seemed to be listening closely. The money was what made the difference. Mr. Parnell always told Grandpapa the English had robbed him of everything, and money was always a problem, what with high prices and bad crops.

"Is it . . . truly necessary?" Grandpapa asked. He looked like he was the one who was sick, and not Stephen.

"Would I have suggested it if it weren't?" Rose O'Donnell said, her tone angry.

Deasy moved close, a light smile on her face. "I was bled once, Lord Harrington, sir," she confessed, curling the corner of her apron around one finger and looking sideways at the floor. "Didn't hurt a bit, no sir, it didn't, and the next day, just like the doctor said, I was good as rain."

The witch looked up as though surprised by the support from this unexpected quarter. For a moment she didn't appear to know what to do with it. In the end she decided to do nothing and commanded Deasy to go to the kitchen and fetch one of Crosset Fletcher's sharpest knives.

At that Stephen decided it was time to pay closer attention. He had no idea what "bleeding" meant, but if it involved sharp knives, he wanted no part of it.

". . . Papa," he whispered and heard how strange it had sounded. He'd meant to say "Grandpapa," but it had taken too much energy, and now he looked up, surprised, to see Rose O'Donnell staring angrily down on him from one side of the bed. Grandpapa was on the other, though he didn't appear angry, just puzzled.

"You . . . haven't been talking to him about you-know-who, have you?" Rose O'Donnell now demanded angrily.

"No, of course not."

"Then why . . . ?" Abruptly Rose O'Donnell broke off, though she continued to stare down on Stephen as though she were trying to put a curse on him.

"It appears I got here just in time," he heard the witch say.

"I knew he was getting worse, but I didn't know——"

"I don't think we want Mr. Eden aware of the unhappy fact his son is——"

"Don't!" The stern voice was Grandpapa's, who sometimes didn't like to hear people say certain things.

"Then let me care for him. I know what is best for him."

"All right," Grandpapa replied, as though impatient or annoyed or both. "I'll be downstairs in the library. Tell me when it's over."

"Of course, Lord Harrington."

There was something in the tone of both that alarmed Stephen, his Grandpapa's easy surrender and the witch's tone of triumph. The wrong person had won, as always, and something was going to happen to Stephen that he would be powerless to alter, and it was going to hurt and, instead of making him better, it was going to make him worse and unable to find his way out.

". . . Papa," he murmured, and wondered again why he was calling out "Papa" instead of "Grandpapa."

"He said it again," the witch said, furious. "Are you *sure* you haven't been talking to him about his father?"

Father.

"No, dammit, I told you. I'd be an idiot to do that, now, wouldn't I?"

Still relatively safe behind his closed eyes, Stephen listened to the voices swirling about him, male and female blending.

Father . . .

. . . rather than Papa or Grandpapa. Suddenly he had the clearest of visions behind his closed eyes of a tall man—not Grandpapa—strong, with fair hair and a darker beard that tickled Stephen's face, a man that looked like one of the Norse gods in his mythology books, and this god came into the room where Stephen was playing with building blocks. Where the room was, Stephen had no idea. But there the man was, a giant, who at first frowned down on Stephen as though he'd displeased him in some way. But that couldn't be, because the next thing Stephen knew, hands reached down and lifted him and he was in the air, his feet sailing out behind him, looking down at the god's face—and it was no longer displeased, but grinning wildly up at him, whirling around with him until the large room and everything in it blurred.

"Ah, here we are. Good girl." Rose O'Donnell brought him back from his memory and deposited him in Talbot House, where he saw Deasy standing wide-eyed in the door, her broad white apron filled with mysterious items.

"Well, come, come," Rose O'Donnell said sharply, waved the girl forward, and commenced to arrange the items on the bedside table.

Stephen tried to look in all directions at once, at the ominous things being placed on the table, at the starched and rigid expression on Rose O'Donnell's face, and—worst of all—at the fearful one on Deasy's face.

"Isn't old Crosset coming?" Rose O'Donnell demanded, looking back through the door as though the second woman were lurking outside waiting for an invitation.

"No, ma'am," Deasy murmured, newly respectful of the witch. "She says to tell you to use this to close him up, leastwise he'll bleed to . . ." Abruptly she broke off. "Oh, ma'am, do you need me? I'd like to—"

"Of course I need you," Mrs. O'Donnell snapped. "Holy Mother, I can't do everything by myself. Now, go and prop the lad up on his pillow."

"Come on, Master Stephen," Deasy urged halfheartedly.

For a moment he thought she was going to cry. He would have liked to oblige her, but he had no more strength for "coming on." Where precisely it had gone, he had no idea, but even the thought of lifting his head from the sweat-dampened pillow was more than he could manage.

"Deasy . . . what . . . ?" He tried to ask a question, but she never gave him a chance and shushed him up, at the same time raising him to a half-sitting position, where his head wobbled bonelessly about for a moment and at last fell back into the familiar hollow of the pillow.

From this vantage point he saw Rose O'Donnell coming at him with a piece of heavy twine—the sort old Crosset Fletcher used to tie the legs of chickens together before she put them in the oven—and she was bringing closer that heavy crockery pot which old Crosset used to fill with chips of ice from the icehouse for Stephen and Frederick to munch on during hot summer days.

But there was no ice in it now, and no reason for it to be in Stephen's room, because it wasn't hot summer. Rose O'Donnell placed the big bowl on the side of his bed and apparently saw the expression on Stephen's face.

"Oh, come, now. You're a big boy, a man almost. When my Denis Bourke O'Donnell was a man of nine, he was the sole support of his blessed mum and nine brothers and sisters. He went down into the mines and came up with the best of them, and earned a full day's pay every day of his life until the bloody English—"

"Mrs. O'Donnell . . ."

The timid voice was Deasy's, and for once Mrs. O'Donnell listened to her and nodded in apology. "I'm sorry," she muttered to Stephen. "It's just that you and Frederick have had it too easy, far too easy, and if you're ever going to grow up and be decent men . . ."

He listened closely, feeling his lack and sorry for it, and tried to withdraw his arm as she reached for it. But she was stronger and bigger and sat on the edge of his bed and boldly pushed up his nightshirt sleeve and commenced to tie a heavy piece of twine about his upper arm, not so tight it hurt—he did want to be a man—but tight enough to be uncomfortable. He had to close his eyes and deal with the sudden rush of tears which were flooding in from behind his eyes.

It was while his eyes were closed that he felt strong hands grasp his right arm, lift it, hold it steady. Then he felt the pressure of a cutting edge, felt it cut deeply, stinging into the flesh of his arm, heard a very small voice inside his head prudently advise, *Don't look.*

But foolishly he ignored the voice. He opened one eye and saw a nightmare sight. Blood, more blood than he'd ever seen before, streaming freely, unabated, from the cut on his upper arm! Running down over his wrists, breaking up into smaller channels over his fingers, and ultimately streaming down into the big crockery bowl!

"Papa!" he screamed, terrified, uttering the first word that came to mind, an unfortunate selection, for Rose O'Donnell renewed her grip on his arm and looked down on him.

"Who are you talking about when you say that word?" she demanded, squeezing his arm, causing the rivers of blood to increase and crest, his entire arm red now.

"No . . . one," he lied, and again tried to twist away from the terrifying ordeal.

But now it was Deasy who held his shoulders securely, and he closed his eyes against the fearful sight of his wet red arm and thought on the Norse god who had carried him through endless gray corridors, scaring him sometimes, tickling him at others, a mix of feelings Stephen couldn't understand—like now, except just thinking on him made him not quite so afraid.

"Stephen! Answer me! Who do you mean when you speak of Papa?"

But the low ugly voice could threaten all she wanted, for he was no longer alone. Behind his closed eyes, Papa had appeared, so clear in all aspects, and was now approaching Stephen across a wide place—where it was, Stephen had no idea, but it was wide and green and the sun was shining. As Papa came closer and closer, Stephen thought: Yes, it's him, the same one who used to pick me up and whirl me around and tickle my cheek with his beard.

Despite the threats of the old witch and the sight of his blood-coated arm and the throb of the cut through which every beat of his heart seemed to be amplified, he looked up behind his closed eyes and smiled and ran to meet him, calling out with every step, "Papa!"

London
November 12, 1874

A lesser man than Charley Spade would have turned back at New London Bridge and the worst traffic jam in the history of the world. But if Charley Spade resembled an ox, he had the tenacity of a bull terrier, and besides, he knew how much Mr. Eden was counting on him and he couldn't let the man down.

So it was he arrived in London town on Saturday, Market Day, the day the creatures were brought in from the surrounding farms to Smithfield's for sale and ultimate consumption, the day Covent Garden spread wide its stalls and filled them with fruits, vegetables, and homemade sauces and jams and jellies, the day when London decided to "go to the stalls" all at once.

"You can't make it that way, guv," Charley shouted at a fast-moving brougham which cut through the line of wagons and climbed up onto the bridge to add to the clogged congestion.

But the driver never even acknowledged the warning, brought the whip down over his horses, and eased through between a large milk wagon and a straw wagon, then turned sharply, unexpectedly to the right and disappeared down a narrowing cobblestone alley that appeared to lead nowhere except back to the Thames.

Curious, Charley—more mobile than most with just a horse to manage—eased up with no difficulty between the congestion of wagons and looked down the steep, narrow alleyway and saw the brougham moving along a narrow ledge of embankment that ran parallel to the river.

So, with only a fleeting thought to the moot question was it the wrong or right thing to do, he brought the whip down lightly over the horse's back and guided him carefully between the wagons down the embankment, not having one idea where it was leading him but hoping it was away from this awful place of screaming, shouting voices.

"Gawd!" Charley muttered only a few moments later, and wondered what he'd gone and gotten himself into now, for suddenly he looked up to discover he was the only rider in sight. Everyone else was walking, trying to keep dry in the slow drizzle which had just commenced. For a moment he tried to steady his horse, which was growing nervous with so many people passing at such close quarters. And still they came, all the people of London town—or so it seemed.

"Hey, don't!" he shouted as he felt hands pull on his stirrups. "What do you—?"

But he never had a chance to complete the question, for suddenly something was brought down across the back of his head. At the moment of impact he thought of walnuts, of when he was a child how his father would go up the coast near to Bristol and gather baskets of walnuts, and all year long they would crack and eat them.

The last sensation was of falling from the height of his horse, the horse itself spinning and rearing, as scared as Charley.

Gawd! North Devon seemed like paradise after this hell. As a fierce ringing erupted in both ears, he vowed if he ever made it back to his little fishing village, he would never again leave that blessed paradise of clean wind and sun-swept beaches, where politeness still mattered, where you greeted your neighbor with a smile, and where men did not go about knocking other men in the head.

Never at his best when aroused from a deep sleep, Alex Aldwell swayed, bleary-eyed, in the door of his house near Hanover Square and wondered what in the hell Jason was doing on his stoop at this hour of the night.

"All right, Jason. Try again," Alex invited, trying to clear his head of sleep, for Jason had come from Aslam, and that was a source to be taken seriously.

"It's as I said, Mr. Aldwell," Jason began again, looking mildly heavy-eyed himself, as though Alex wasn't the only one whose sleep had been interrupted that night. "Lord Eden took the man in, then suggested I come right away over here and fetch you because of the letter which was all the man had on—"

"Wait!" Alex commanded, holding up one hand as though to stay the confusion before it overtook both of them again.

"No time, sir," the tall man interrupted. "It was bad enough finding a naked man left on the stoop, but then Mr. Eden opened the letter, and—"

Alex started forward. "Mr. . . . Eden?" he asked, bewildered.

"The young one. Master Aslam," Jason explained, a look on his face which suggested he understood Alex's confusion. For years there had been only one Mr. Eden—John Murrey Eden.

"What . . . naked man?" Alex asked tentatively,

"Can't remember his name," Jason said apologetically, "but he come from North Devon and went to Paris with Mr. Eden—the other one."

"You say he's from Devon?" Alex asked.

Jason nodded. "Naked he was, like the day he was born. And he was left by a man and a woman, and he was wearing the woman's cape in an attempt to hide—"

"All right, wait," Alex commanded wearily again. "Come inside. I'll get my clothes on and we'll—"

"No!" Jason interrupted, then apologized. "I'm sorry, sir. Of course get your clothes on, but Mr. Eden—the other one—asked me to ask you to call at this address, if you would be so good, and deliver this letter. Most important, he said it was."

Bewilderment mounting, Alex took the letter. It felt thick, and the seal had been broken. Apparently Aslam had read the contents. But most significant of all was the name of the addressee written in bold strokes by a hand as familiar to Alex as his own.

John Murrey Eden. John had written this letter. Again Alex gaped down, stunned at the addressee. . . . *Mr. William Gladstone?*

Carefully he took the letter out of the heavy parchment envelope and stood with his back to the fire and read the familiar handwriting.

"My Dear Mr. Gladstone," the salutation read, and Alex smiled, recalling the past stormy history that had existed between John and "the people's Willie," a mutual loathing if there ever was one. Then Alex felt his pulse quicken and his eyes read faster and faster, unable to believe what he was reading.

". . . *her execution by firing squad is scheduled for the morning of November 15.*"

Her . . . execution?

He looked up quickly at Jason, who seemed to know the nature of the message.

"Did anyone read this beside Aslam?"

"Lord Richard Eden," said Jason.

Alex looked up sharply again. "Richard's in London? When?"

"Last evening, sir."

"Why? I thought that Lady Eleanor was . . ."

Oh, Lord, would Alex never learn? There were some questions, some subjects, one did not discuss with servants. And this was certainly one of them.

"No, he said nothing to me, sir," Jason replied with admirable diplomacy. "All that was requested of me was that I deliver this to you and that you in turn deliver it to Mr. Gladstone at the earliest possible convenience."

"Of course," Alex murmured, reading on to the end, John asking—no, John demanding—intervention on behalf of the English government for the blatant mistreatment of a British citizen by a foreign government.

"All right," Alex said with dispatch. "Did you bring a carriage?"

"No, sir. Just a mount. I figured I could—"

"Quite right. Is he winded?"

"Blaze? Go on. He's tethered out front."

With only the briefest of stops in his bedchamber to slip on jodhpurs and boots, Alex rushed out the door and saw before him on the darkened pavement Jason's magnificent Blaze. A horse and a half, Alex thought as he strained upward for the stirrup of the enormous chestnut stallion. Once he was up, the horse turned skittish, as though aware a stranger was aboard.

"E-easy," Alex soothed, leaned forward to pat the massive neck, and urged the animal forward.

Execution by firing squad . . .

Dear God . . .

Suddenly Alex brought his heels down and the horse shot forward, speed increasing until the shop windows were a blur on either side, the echo of the horseshoes on cobbles like the reports of rapidly firing guns.

Grosvenor Square,
London
November 12, 1874

"Will he be all right?" Lord Richard asked Dr. Jacobs as he raised up from examining Charley Spade, whose bruised body was a mute map of the poor man's fall from his horse and subsequent assaults.

Dr. Jacobs, sleepy-eyed and sullen from his early-morning arousal, nodded and slowly lifted the gauze and oil with which he'd treated the worst lacerations. "Oh, I'm sure he'll be fine," the old man said, and Lord Richard observed the cuffs of a nightshirt protruding from beneath the black coat.

Richard was relieved and looked down on the young man who had been delivered to the doorstoop of the Grosvenor Square mansion without fanfare or explication, simply dumped, as it were, without a stitch on, bereft of everything save for the lady's cape and the leather pouch about his neck, which apparently the assailants had been in the process of removing as well, for half the strap had been cut away.

From the shadows near the door came a clipped and familiar voice. "Thank you for coming, doctor. My clerk will be around in the morning to compensate you for your lost sleep."

Aslam. As always, safe in shadow. And at the mention of compensation, Dr. Jacobs nodded, walked to the door, then advised, "Have one of your female servants look to his head bandage in the morning and, if draining, replace it with clean linen."

After he left, there was no sound in the room. Richard returned to the couch where young Charley Spade had been placed. On the opposite wall in the deep fire well a fire crackled. Only then did Richard realize how strange it might have appeared to Dr. Jacobs, both he and Aslam in their dressing gowns.

No! Not strange. Richard was a house guest in the residence now occupied by the firm hand which so ably was conducting the family business in the absence of its founder.

Would he never move away from that door?

Richard continued to wait, ready to take his cue from Aslam, but there was no predicting what the man was doing or thinking or what his mood would be when he deigned to speak.

"Are you feeling well, Richard?" Aslam asked at last. "Perhaps Dr. Jacobs should have—"

"I'm well." Richard smiled, renewed by the young man's appearance. Forbes House in Kent and all the various albatrosses contained therein were momentarily forgotten in the slow, elegant approach of this most English of all Englishmen.

"What do you make of him?" Aslam asked, slowly encircling the couch on which lay the still-senseless Charley Spade.

"What's to make of him?" Richard shrugged. "Clearly he's one of John's men, bearing tragic news, one more accounting for John as he banks the fires of hell."

A little amazed at the degree of bitterness which had surfaced in his voice, Richard moved quickly away from the couch in a direct line to the sideboard, where he poured two clarets and carefully carried them back to where Aslam was standing, hands in pockets, staring down on Charley Spade.

"Will he sleep forever?" he asked as he took one of the clarets. "There are questions I must ask."

"You'll have your chance, but probably not before this evening."

"He's in no condition to ride—"

"Ride where?" Richard asked, momentarily forgetting the entire purpose for Charley Spade's presence in London. Then he remembered. "God, no. But someone must. Gladstone's response . . ."

"I don't think he will," Aslam said quietly, moving away from the couch and taking the glass of claret with him to the fire.

Surprised, Richard looked up. "Why not?"

From the fire Aslam smiled. "Because he's not in London."

Richard started forward. Perhaps Aslam had simply heard a rumor. "Where is he?" he asked.

"In Wales. On a walking tour," came the soft reply. "My clerk had occasion to confer with one of his clerks last week. He was told then Gladstone's office would be closed until early December. He's quite fond of walking, you know."

Distracted, Richard nodded, though his thoughts had already crossed the channel to a single cell somewhere in that unhappy city that now was Paris. "Elizabeth . . ." he murmured, still unable to believe the letter, wishing, along with Aslam, that Charley Spade would awaken so he could respond to direct questions. "Then why," he asked suddenly, "did you have Jason take the letter to Aldwell if you knew . . . ?"

"Because I want Aldwell to learn it for himself, so he can truthfully report to John that every possible effort was made. I want my word to count for nothing. In fact, I would much prefer not even—"

Suddenly a low groan came from the couch. The giant was stirring. "Oh, Gawd!" he groaned again.

Richard moved closer, wanting to question the man. "God *was* with you," he said gently, bending low over the head which thrashed upon the pillow, then grew still out of respect for the pain which obviously was shattering his skull.

"What . . . hap . . . ?" Charley tried to say, and at last opened his eyes and took one look around, and apparently decided he hadn't an idea in hell where he was.

Richard saw the confusion blend with pain and fear and moved closer in an attempt to alleviate at least two of the man's discomforts. "You're in London, Charley, in the house that belongs to Mr. John Murrey Eden. You were brought here by a man and a woman who failed to identify themselves . . ." As he talked, Richard carefully charted the changes in the young man's face. But of changes there were few until Richard spoke the words ". . . thieves and cutthroats . . ."

Then Charley moaned again as though briefly reliving the most terrible moments of his attack.

"Charley, would you like a brandy?" Richard offered kindly.

With the offer the remembrance of the attack was dissipated. "That . . . would be helpful," Charley murmured.

"Very well." Richard nodded. As he went to the sideboard, he exchanged a smile with Aslam, who continued to stand before the fire, apparently content to let Richard conduct the interrogation.

"Better?" Richard asked after Charley had sniffed and swallowed and coughed and swallowed again.

The man nodded, and the brandy did seem to have cleared his head, for now he looked about the room with new alertness, clutching at the hem of the blanket with both hands, as though he had just become aware of his nakedness.

"Me . . . clothes . . . ?" he gasped, and looked up searchingly at Richard.

"Gone, I'm afraid," Richard said sympathetically. "The same ruffians who knocked you from your mount and took . . . everything. But you are safe here, and I will personally see to a complete new wardrobe and horse and anything else you might require when the time comes."

This seemed to soothe the man, though he continued to look nervously about the room until his eyes at last landed on Aslam. Suddenly, fresh terror surfaced from somewhere and Charley Spade struggled up from the couch, his eyes fixed on Aslam. "Him! It was him who robbed me. I swear it!" he gasped. Then he repeated the accusation louder. "I swear he was the one. What's he doing here? Come to finish the job?" he demanded, half raised on his elbows.

But Richard stepped forward, soothing. "You must lie still and rest. We need to ask you some very important questions concerning Mr. Eden and Elizabeth. So would you . . . ?"

But the man wouldn't, so ready and excited he was to identify one of the culprits.

Again Richard tried to soothe and explain. "Clearly what has happened," he began, "is a case of mistaken identity. Someone who resembled Aslam was one of your assailants." He waited, trying to read the perplexed expression on Charley's face. "Do you understand?" he asked.

He gestured toward the young man near the fire, who had yet to respond to the false charge in any way. "This is Mr. Eden's adopted son, Charley, the man who is conducting Mr. Eden's business affairs in Mr. Eden's absence. Now do you understand?"

Slowly the man nodded, but not before first scrutinizing Aslam with a last thorough look. "May have been someone else," he muttered. "Looked just like him."

"Of course," Richard agreed. "Now, do you mind if I ask you a few questions about what you found in Paris?"

Charley Spade sank slowly back into the comfort of the pillow and shook his head. "What we found, sir, can be summed up in one word: Hell! That's what we found."

"And how is John? Mr. Eden, I mean."

"Oh, not good, sir, not good at all. Sometimes he looks . . ."

"He looks what, Mr. Spade?" Richard prodded, curious.

Charley shrugged. "You know, lost, like he's lost his compass, if you know what I mean."

Suddenly there was a direct question coming from near the fireplace. "What is the nature of Mr. Eden's illness, sir?" Aslam asked with clipped politeness.

"Seizure, sir, least that's what Miss Mantle calls it."

"Who is Miss Mantle?"

"A nurse." Charley grinned. "A circuit nurse, sir, who does more good in a day than most folk do in a lifetime. I don't know what the West Country would do without—"

"Are they serious? These seizures."

A quick look of indignation crossed Charley's face. "Right serious, sir, and the next one—according to Miss Mantle—could kill him if he's not . . ." Abruptly Charley stopped talking, as though a new fear had just occurred to him. "It was me who carried him out of that wretched place where he found Miss Elizabeth. Bleeding, he was, and four French soldiers following after him, ready to pounce again and finish him off, and he just hanging there between them, looking half-dead."

Something about the crude description caused Richard to feel weak. "Elizabeth?" he asked quietly.

Charley hesitated. "Well, now, sir, I never saw her for myself, nor did old Bates. The bastard general who runs that foul pit only let Mr. Eden go down. But he was gone ever so long, and when he come up, it's like I said, he had had him an altercation with someone—"

"Elizabeth," Richard repeated, trying to keep the man on track.

"Quite bad, sir, or so I understood Mr. Eden to tell old Bates. She'd lost flesh, he said, and turned total white on the head and . . . Oh, yes, he said they had manacled her ankles so she couldn't escape."

Suddenly, to Richard's complete shock, the large man started to bawl noisily, easily as a child does, without shame or apology. "Oh, sir, it grieves me to talk about it."

If Charley Spade was having trouble accepting the impending tragedy, Richard wasn't faring so well himself. He too turned away.

"What are the charges brought against her?" If there was any significant emotion in Aslam's voice, Richard could not detect it.

"Murder, sir," Charley replied promptly, sniffling noisily and wiping at his eyes with the back of his hand.

"Whom?" Aslam quizzed further.

Charley shrugged. "Some frog. You can be sure he deserved it," he added, bristling with hostility.

"Was it a jury trial?" Aslam asked further, but apparently Charley had no knowledge of the nature of the trial.

"Oh, I'm sure I don't know, sir," he moaned. "All I know is I must be on the road no later than midnight tonight, and in me pocket I must have a letter from Mr. William Gladstone, 'cause I promised Mr. Eden. Can I make it, sir?" Charley asked, now half-raised on his elbows. "Can I be on the road by—?"

"Do you feel up to another ride?"

"Oh, yes, sir."

"Then I see no reason . . ."

Aslam stepped forward with a suggestion. "Perhaps Jason should go with you, in case . . ."

Charley Spade looked from the shadows where the voice had originated to Richard, who sat close to the couch. "Who's . . . Jason?"

"Jason was Mr. Eden's London coachman, a good man and a strapping one."

Charley blinked rapidly, as though someone had just challenged him. "Don't need no one else," he muttered.

"You could have used assistance last evening," came the voice from the shadows.

"Can he ride?" Charley asked with new belligerence. " 'Cause I don't plan to slow for no man."

Richard tried to calm the man. "If you don't wish—"

The voice from the shadows became more insistent. "But I do."

Puzzled, Richard looked in that direction. "I . . . don't understand."

Without a pause, Aslam explained. "If anything goes wrong, I don't want John to think anyone here contributed to the inevitable tragedy." He paused. "Mr. Spade, Jason can ride, I assure you. Furthermore, he can proceed if you . . . in any way falter again. Do you understand?"

From the expression on Charley's face, Richard wasn't absolutely certain he did. But at least he wasn't protesting anymore. And now Richard fully understood. It could end only one way, with a volley of bullets, and when John surfaced from his grief long enough to search for a culprit, as was always John's custom, then Aslam wanted to give him no cause to look to London.

"Then it's settled," Aslam said, finally crossing to the couch. "There is a trunk of garments on the floor below. Please help yourself to whatever you wish. There are boots there as well. As soon as Jason returns . . ."

As Aslam laid plans with dispatch, Richard saw new confusion cutting across Charley Spade's face. "Wait a minute, sir," he protested. "I got to get Mr. Gladstone's response."

"Of course," Aslam said, and moved back into the shadows. "Mr. Aldwell is at this minute seeing the prime minister. In the meantime, it won't hurt, will it, for you to prepare yourself, so that when word does arrive, you are immediately ready to ride?"

For a moment it looked as though Charley was trying very hard to find something in the quiet voice to argue with. But apparently he could find nothing, and at last stood. "Where did you say this here trunk was?" he muttered, still clutching the blanket.

"On the floor below," Aslam repeated. "Go along with you, and, as I said, take what you want. As soon as Aldwell returns—"

"With the response from Gladstone," Charley announced defiantly.

There was a pause. "Perhaps," Aslam replied, and this seemed to satisfy Charley, who at last pushed up from the couch, wobbled a bit, and left the room.

Richard held his position by the couch and stared down with unwarranted interest at the mussed linen and coverlet, seeing neither. "She will . . . die, won't she?" he asked.

At first there was no response. Then: "Perhaps my clerk was mistaken. Perhaps Gladstone changed his plans and is at home and at this moment writing . . ."

Did he believe his own words? Or had they been spoken solely for Richard's comfort?

"Not necessary," Richard said. "You know how I feel about false hope."

"As we all do. But at this point we can't be certain if it's false, can we?"

La Rochelle
House of Detention,
Paris
November 13, 1874

"Are you frightened?"

Elizabeth looked up at the question and shifted upon the straw and massaged her ankles, grateful to Madame Charvin for having the manacles removed.

"Yes," she replied honestly, "though sometimes I feel as though I've used up all my fear and what I feel now is a kind of numbness. And sadness, that too." She spoke carefully, trying to be as articulate as possible, not necessarily for Madame Charvin's benefit, but for her own. She still couldn't quite understand why her life was ending here in this place, in this fashion.

Madame Charvin, as though aware of the importance of her own question, did not push for further explication and contented herself with admiring the lovely wax flowers which Elizabeth had just presented to her.

They had turned out well, quite to the astonishment of Elizabeth herself. Now she curled her legs sideways and tucked her bare and filthy feet beneath the hem of her equally filthy dress, and thought how strange that almost on the eve of her death she'd discovered a talent. It had never occurred to her she might be good with her hands.

Suddenly it came again, that sharp realization of limited time, of the ordeal ahead of her and—worst of all—her lack of faith in her own ability to meet it. She'd heard screams for the last several months, men mostly, a few women, the soft dronings of a priest drowned out in that last moment of terror when one must face the fact you are seeing everything for the last time.

For the last time. . . .

"Elizabeth?"

She looked up to see Madame Charvin looking down on her with what appeared to be grief as deep as her own.

Elizabeth managed a brief smile of reassurance, and thought how fortunate she at least had Madame Charvin. The warden had never shown her anything but courtesy and kindness, had from the beginning brought her small comforts that had made the solitary cell at least momentarily bearable.

"I hope you like them," Elizabeth said now, looking up at the wax flowers, lilies mostly, because Madame Charvin had said they were her favorites. Elizabeth had hoped to break the mood of mourning on Madame's face. But instead of breaking it, she seemed only to have compounded it, and now, to her complete consternation, she saw Madame remove a handkerchief from the pocket of her dress and dab at the corners of her eyes.

No! No tears. That was the one thing Elizabeth would not endure, would not permit. "Madame, I beg of you . . ."

Quickly Madame nodded, as though she understood, and almost in anger she shook her head. "I am sorry," she apologized, her English very good for a Frenchwoman. "I won't stay," Madame Charvin said. "I fear I'm intruding . . ."

"No, please. Just . . . no tears."

Again the woman nodded and slipped the handkerchief back into the pocket of her dress. Suddenly, to Elizabeth's complete surprise, Madame Charvin declared, "I hate this job. I really do."

Elizabeth smiled. What normal woman in her right mind wouldn't hate it? "Then why do you . . . ?"

"I must." The woman shrugged, and primly restored a strand of hair to the knot at the back of her neck. "My husband was the male warden until his death twelve years ago . . ." Quickly she crossed herself.

"Before General Montaud?" Elizabeth asked.

". . . took Monsieur Charvin's place," Madame sniffed. "Half a man—in every way," she added.

"And you stayed on?"

"Where would I go? A widow with two children . . ."

Fascinated, though shocked, Elizabeth asked, "Your children grew up here?"

"Of course," Madame Charvin replied, and she too seemed to be enjoying the chat. She came around the low table and sat on the edge of the bench, leaning forward, her arms resting on her lap.

From Elizabeth's position, seated on the straw, she thought she saw the remnants of what once had been a beautiful woman. It was hard to determine her age, but Elizabeth guessed late fifties.

"Where are they now? Your children," Elizabeth asked.

"Dead," came the flat reply. For a moment the single word seemed to echo endlessly about the small cell.

Stunned, Elizabeth looked more closely at Madame's face. Nothing for the children either? But if there was any degree of grief or mourning within the woman, it was so deeply buried as to be invisible.

"Wh-when? How?" Elizabeth asked.

"Auguste died when he was just a baby . . . five. There was nothing anyone could do." Her voice was flat and without inflection, as though she were speaking of the weather or a new ruling. She didn't look at Elizabeth as she spoke, but rather laced her fingers together, then drew them apart, then laced them again.

"And Marie," she went on, and abruptly stopped, as did her interlacing hands, the tension increasing, "was found dead in the courtyard on April 14, Thursday, at six-twenty in the morning, in the year 1868, by the morning guard as the shifts were changing."

"How . . . did she die?" Elizabeth asked, without bothering to open her eyes and look up.

"Oh, she was murdered, of course." Madame Charvin declared almost breezily, as though it was something Elizabeth should have known. "And she'd been raped—or so the doctor said."

"I'm so . . . sorry . . ."

"Oh, it was a long time ago. It all belongs to another life. Sometimes one's progression through this world seems made up of separate lives, doesn't it?"

Elizabeth nodded, grateful for the woman's control. "Did they ever discover who . . . ?"

Madame nodded quickly. "Prisoners, of course," she said. "At least, that's what General Montaud claimed. The fact that all prisoners are locked up at night and Marie was discovered in the courtyard, a place where only staff and soldiers go, seemed not to make a great deal of difference."

"Was there a trial?"

"No, there was a circus," Madame Charvin muttered. "General Montaud used the case for his own advancement. Four miserable wretches were unjustly accused and shot, and the guilty went free . . . until . . ." All at once she looked down at Elizabeth, the blaze of a smile on her face. ". . . until you punished him," she added.

"I . . . ?"

"I have proof—eyewitnesses—that Marie was assaulted and murdered by Lieutenant Jean Dauguet."

Elizabeth looked up. Lieutenant Dauguet, the same officer for whose murder she would shortly die.

"Are you . . . certain?" Elizabeth whispered.

Madame Charvin nodded broadly. "Eyewitnesses, as I said."

"Why didn't they come forward during the trial?"

"Would you? It was not in their best interests to do so."

Shocked, Elizabeth said, "But your daughter. I should think that the true solution to such a—"

"She was dead. What could we do that would bring her back? I knew who had done it, and at the time, that was enough. And further, somehow deep inside I knew he would be punished. I didn't know how or when, but . . ." Still smiling, she gestured down on Elizabeth, and briefly the smile faded. "I just wish . . ."

"No," Elizabeth said quickly, and stood, holding on to the wall for support until she found her center of balance.

"Please," Madame Charvin whispered, following after her. "Let me do something, anything, to ease these last few hours. I have access to opium. It will render you senseless. Let me . . ."

But Elizabeth merely shook her head and moved away to the far side of the cell and wished the woman would speak of something else.

"They are letting the press in, you know. It will be a carnival."

"Please . . ."

Suddenly Madame Charvin grabbed her elbow, thus halting her flight around the narrow cell. "Elizabeth, you must listen to me. I have tried every avenue that is available to me, and a few that are not, to alter the sentence, to have it reduced, to postpone it, in an attempt to give your English friends a chance to intercede."

"I didn't ask——"

"I know you didn't ask. But I did it anyway, to the point I made a pest of myself at the Ministry of Justice and . . ."

Elizabeth dared to look back, briefly hopeful.

"It will go on as scheduled, and because you are a foreign woman, the press will be allowed to . . ."

It made no difference—it really didn't—and Elizabeth turned slowly away and moved toward the dark corner of the cell.

Edward . . .

That was the only name that made the moment bearable.

Edward.

"Please, Elizabeth, let me do something." It was Madame Charvin again, burdened with her weight of gratitude and not quite knowing what to do with it.

How ironic! As Elizabeth had plunged the shears into Lieutenant Dauguet, she had simultaneously ended his life and hers and had given Madame Charvin's new meaning.

"What can I do?" Madame again. All right, ease her burden.

Elizabeth smiled at the persistence of female vanity. "A bath," she said without hesitation. "A long, luxurious hot one, with fragrance, please."

Madame Charvin nodded. "Of course. In my own apartments. You shall have it——"

"Wait! I'm not finished," Elizabeth interrupted playfully.

"Good! Ask away!"

"A dress. A new one. Blue. Very elegant," Elizabeth added, coming all the way out into the light of the candle. A blue dress? Where had that request come from? She'd been wearing a blue dress on the night in Bermondsey when Jack Wilmott had brought Edward's body home. "Yes, a blue dress," she repeated softly, "if it isn't too much——"

"You shall have it," Madame Charvin declared. "The prettiest in Paris. I shall go now and return for you tomorrow eve." Abruptly she broke off, a look of pleasant conspiracy on her face. "Oh, what fun we will have. I promise. . . ." Now she walked to the door of the cell and signaled to the guards to let her out.

As the key grated in the lock, Elizabeth concentrated on the narrow opening that led to freedom for some but would lead to death for her.

What was death?

Was one's concept of oneself constant, or was that too of this world and abandoned along with hopes and fears and dreams and loves?

If so, then there was just cause for premature mourning, for, in the case of known death, one mourned for oneself, that self that had accompanied, stood by, pleased, disappointed, amused, gratified one all life long. Would that self die?

As the cell door closed and locked behind her, Elizabeth thought she would not look. But she did, and she was glad, for she saw the once-beautiful Madame Charvin, who had lost a husband and two children in this circle of hell, and she decided she probably couldn't find anyone more appropriate to spend her last night with than Madame Charvin.

Now Madame gave her a warm wave, and by way of response, Elizabeth smiled and watched the woman march off down the corridor, and counted, with increasing intensity, the number of times Madame Charvin's sharp heels struck the stone corridor floor. She continued to listen until she could hear them no more.

When all was silent again and the two guards had gone back to their pipes and cards out of sight beyond the corridor, there was no sound in the cell, in the corridor, in the prison, in the world, save the accelerated beating of her heart. Elizabeth fell to her knees in the straw and thought of one name, one man.

Edward.

Would she see him? If only she could be certain, then not only would she not fear the moment of her death, she would welcome it.

Monsieur DuCamp's Lodging House, Paris
November 14, 1874

Never skillful at waiting, the last few days had served as a new kind of hell for John.

There were certain rituals to be observed morning, noon, and night, and these had kept him on the tentative balance he now maintained as he sat in Monsieur DuCamp's cramped and smelly reception room before a small and smoking fire, forced to listen to French chatter, glaring at what had to be the ugliest wallpaper in the civilized world—an arrangement of bile-green fern interspersed with broad-leafed orange flowers.

"Café, monsieur?"

Stirred out of his loathing for the surrounding world, John glanced up at the little waitress, one of Monsieur DuCamp's numerous offspring. "Yes," he replied, full-voiced. "But that is not café in your pot there. That is caramel-flavored acid. So to that I will say, 'No, thank you.' "

At the sound of his voice, the conversations going on about him died. Good. Silence was better, though he saw the old watchdog Bates start forward, a familiar red blush on each cheek, as he was again called upon to smooth feathers John had ruffled. John watched for as long as he could bear to watch as the old man explained something to the young girl, who fortunately did not understand a word of English.

While this obnoxious exchange was going on, John checked his watch—going on four P.M.—and dared to think the unthinkable: *What if Charley Spade did not . . . ?*

"Shall I fetch you a brandy, sir, in lieu of coffee?" It was Bates again.

Though John would have welcomed the comforting numbness of a half-dozen brandies, he felt on this night he must be alert. Everything was packed and loaded on the carriage. They had signed out of their rooms—

hence the necessity for waiting here in this disgusting public room filled with belching women and farting men.

But as soon as Charley arrived with Gladstone's letter of clemency, it was their intention to deliver it promptly to General Montaud, fetch Elizabeth, and leave immediately for the coast, where John had planned to hire a packet; and with luck, dawn would find them in English waters.

Execution . . . by firing squad.

He leaned forward sharply in his chair, as though someone had delivered an invisible blow to the back of his neck. Peculiar, how those four words seemed to be permanently lodged in his head, and no matter what he did, they continuously presented themselves for his scrutiny.

Damn! Where was Charley Spade? He promised . . .

Suddenly John stood up, a movement so startling that all eyes in the room turned to him. For a moment he didn't know what to do. Confined by the rain and by General Montaud's last angry edict, he had no choice but to wait here, though it was killing him to do so.

"Sir, may I suggest . . . ?"

Bates's voice, filled with advice, only seemed to enrage him further, and without a backward look he strode angrily to the door and hurled it open, as though it offended him, took the vestibule and the corridor with equal outrage, and proceeded on beneath the arched front door, out onto the rain-wet pavement, where halos cast from the gas lamps caught and reflected every light source in the puddles that had collected between the cobbles.

He lifted his face to the night sky and breathed deeply of the cold, wet, smoke-scented air. It was still raining, though it was just a drizzle now. The wind had died and the Rue Saint Jacob was alive with people scurrying about after the confinement of a downpour.

In an attempt to check his anger, he turned up the collar of his coat, positioned his walking stick, and started slowly down the stairs, not really wanting to join the rabble on the street but preferring it to the plain, bovine, middle-class faces which now occupied Monsieur DuCamp's reception rooms. He wouldn't go far. Just a stretch for his legs. Perhaps when he returned, Charley Spade would be waiting for him.

As he fell into the pedestrian traffic, he discovered first that everyone else was moving too slowly—plodding, shuffling creatures going no place, with no sense of direction or purpose.

But at the end of the street where the intersection angled off toward the Seine in one direction and Saint Germain in the other, he suddenly discovered the foot traffic was moving so fast he couldn't keep up.

He tried to move off the pavement and onto the side of the road, but fast-moving carriages prevented that. Now, as the foot traffic increased even more, he found a relatively safe harbor in a large courtyard which fronted a church—Gothic in style, with gas lamps flanking the large doors and casting upward shadows on the square bell tower.

Strange he'd never noticed the church before. They must have passed it several times going to La Rochelle. He must have been occupied with thoughts of Elizabeth . . .

Elizabeth . . .

He'd tried every hour of every day to cleanse his mind of that last image of her, seated on straw, her ankles manacled.

The thought still was unbearable. Hungry for diversion, he saw a large gathering near the church doors, a curious circle of some sort with something at the center holding the audience's attention, a single plaintive instrument filling the night air with a simple melody.

Upon closer examination, he saw the ghostly white faces of a troupe of mimes, their eyebrows arched, garbed wholly in black except for their white faces. About six in all, he observed.

The audience seemed hushed now, their attention focused rigidly on the drama taking place in the arena before the church doors.

Suddenly the single piping instrument grew even more plaintive, and he saw now that the church itself was apparently part of the mime, for a priest stood in the high arched doors. Not a real priest, he felt certain, for the figure was part Satan—my God, how clever!—the priest mime wearing two disguises. On one side were the black robes and cassock of a priest holding the church standard in his hand, a two-faced mask drawn tightly down over his head with fixed and staring eyes, while on the other side, as the actor rapidly turned, John saw the Satan figure, one half of the black robe bright glistening red satin, a predominant horn, the standard pitchfork, the same benign and passive face of the priest. All the mime had to do was turn in one direction to be a priest, then in the other to become Satan.

A few moments later the figure lifted his arms, beckoning, and the mimes ran through the doors of the church, the audience following, proceeding up the broad steps in an orderly, hushed fashion.

Before John realized what had happened, he found himself alone on the wet pavement where only moments before the crowds had jostled him and each other in comforting closeness. Suddenly self-conscious, he looked about. For just a moment he suffered an impulse to follow, to see what drama would transpire under the skillful hands of the painted actors.

Then he heard a human wail coming from the church. He stood still for a moment, listening, and it came again, still louder this time, more frightening, like a cry from Hades.

As John felt the hair on his arms rise, he backed away from the closed doors of the church. He wanted nothing to do with what was going on inside.

This world was hell enough without adding God's heaven to it.

Paris
November 14, 1874

Charley Spade knew they were late, regretted it, and at the same time wished that something, anything, would happen to delay them further.

But with the exception of the rain squall which had slowed them down crossing the channel, the journey had been speedy and uneventful, the West Indian more than keeping up the pace. Now as with difficulty they tried to maneuver their way through Paris traffic, Charley looked anxiously around in an attempt to get his bearings.

"The river!" he shouted to Jason, who sat erect on his horse. "If we could find the river, I think . . ."

Jason nodded, as though he'd understood. Damned clever for a nigger, and Charley was the first to admit it. He also now was prepared to admit he hadn't wanted to travel with Jason at all, hadn't thought it necessary.

But the worst, the very worst, was the fact of the empty pouch inside his rain-soaked coat pocket, the leather pouch that was supposed to have contained the letter of clemency from Mr. William Gladstone on behalf of Miss Elizabeth.

Walking? In Wales? What man in his right mind went to Wales to do anything? And why couldn't Mr. Gladstone walk about in London if he was of a mind to do some walking? And what would Mr. Eden do now? And how could any of them just stand by and let Miss Elizabeth . . . ?

He couldn't even think about it, and as he drew his exhausted horse up to a busy intersection, he looked to the left and saw the twin spires of Notre Dame and knew instantly where he was, and knew he didn't have much time before he would have to confront Mr. Eden with the news the

210

mission had failed, and unless God Himself decided to intervene, one of the noblest, rarest, kindest creatures who ever lived would be . . .

"Jason!" Without looking up, he called for the man to catch up.

Without a word, Jason drew even beside him, his dark face glistening from the steady rain which had been falling since they entered the city.

For a moment Charley stared at him, wondering why he'd summoned him, when for the most of the journey he'd tried to separate himself from this traveling companion. Finally he said, "I . . . can't . . ."

"Can't what?" said Jason, steadying his horse. "Are you ill?" he asked, peering more closely at Charley, as though trying to find a clue there.

In some exasperation and not wanting to confess openly to cowardice—certainly not before this man—Charley delivered one sharp jab to his horse and shot across the muddy street and realized instantly he should have turned toward the church, not away from it. But in that moment he had found the perfect solution to all his problems.

Lost! With little effort he could contrive to get lost, and since Jason was even more of a stranger to the city than Charley, and since neither of them spoke the language and as they had been unable to find anyone who spoke the King's English, well . . .

For the first time on that wet and miserable journey since he'd left Mr. Eden, Charley smiled. Of course, it wasn't a permanent solution, but it was a good postponement—at least until Charley could think up a report that would make sense and not make him look so bad, one that might even evoke a little pity in the bargain. On that note of faint optimism, Charley bent low over his horse, like a man intent on reaching his destination.

By the next intersection the traffic had cleared and they were the lone riders on a quiet lane lined with small darkened shops.

"Is it far?" Jason called from a few paces behind, his voice hushed, reflecting the new surroundings.

"Not far," Charley called out, and begged God to forgive him and turned his horse down yet another narrow lane, going farther and farther away from the church, deeper and deeper into foreign territory.

Would God forgive him?

He had to forgive him, didn't He? For it was God Himself who had made Charley Spade a weak man, thus a cowardly one.

Eden Castle
November 14, 1874

It was lovely in the autumn sunset and Susan allowed herself one moment's indulgence because it would be the last.

With perfect deliberation, like a man drinking a treasured wine after a long period of self-imposed abstinence, she stood on the elevated spot of ground called Eden Rising and saw only beauty magnified. On the western horizon was a solid line of fire, the licking flames of the dying sun performing with great virtuosity in the last moments before darkness.

Before the fiery backdrop of orange and crimson, claret and purple, every lesser thing was silhouetted in black. Even the great square castle itself sat inert and unmoving, its emptiness somehow manifested in its glazed windows and the tattered banners which hung lifeless from high standards.

A dying time.

The words struck against her mind with ecclesiastical accuracy. Quickly she drew her cape about her shoulders and faced in the opposite direction toward the southeast, toward Exeter and London, and the channel and Paris.

John.

She closed her eyes, still quite bewildered concerning the nature and most specifically the cure for this new illness which had stricken her and which now threatened to undo everything she'd worked so hard and long to achieve in her life.

They should have been back by now, Bates and Charley Spade and the woman Elizabeth and . . .

John.

The pain was as precise as though someone had driven something sharp

212

directly into the center of her chest, and so specific she gasped for breath and moved quickly away from the road, thinking to head back to the small gate through which Bates and Reverend Christopher had led her that first night and outside of which she'd left her landau while she said good-bye to the castle, to the cottage, and to the memory of the man who had, without warning, occupied, in the manner of a marauding army, her mind and her heart.

Now there was one further view she would like to look upon again for the last time, for she intended never to pass this way again. London was her destination now, as soon as she was finished with this sentimental stop, London with its oceans of human need, enough to neutralize and annihilate the most persistent and painful memories.

Through Reverend Christopher, who had sensed her despair, she'd heard of a man and his wife in London, William and Catherine Booth. Mr. Booth was establishing himself as a dissenting minister concerned with the outcasts and the poor of society.

The mission appealed to Susan, the localized cry for help, the need to submerge herself in a cause greater than any she'd ever been associated with before. Mr. Booth and his wife were in desperate need of help, according to Reverend Christopher. A simple tent in Whitechapel in the East End of London served as their "Church for the Christian Mission to the Heathen of Our Country." Concerned for the poor and their lack of faith, Booth was in the process of demonstrating a true Christian ministry to the world.

"You cannot reform a man morally by his intellect," Reverend Christopher had quoted Booth as saying. "You must reform man by his soul."

Susan liked that. She suspected William Booth had taken a careful look at the organized church and had found little evidence of it being God's earthly residence. With dismay and a degree of disillusionment, she too had witnessed the bishops' huge salaries, the endless debate on vestments, incense, processions, and ceremonies, rather than its ministry to the poverty-stricken, the hungry, the despairing. The clergy offered the poor only benevolent smiles and occasionally a handshake. Its main concern was to defend its beliefs and uphold Christian orthodoxy against the secular thoughts and intellectual challenges of the day. Help for the poor sat somewhere very near the bottom of the church's list of priorities; income to restore buildings and sustain church personnel, very near to the top.

Lost in thought, yet excited by a sense of this new mission, Susan looked up from the ruts in the road toward the cottage on Eden Rising, pleased to feel nothing but the excitement of the challenge and the journey ahead.

Reverend Christopher had assured her she would be welcomed in London with open and very grateful arms, particularly with her medical training. She would be invaluable to the mission. In return for her services, she would be paid nothing, would be provided with a single cot and what food was left over from the common kitchen.

A chill wind gusted behind her, a harbinger of winter.

Then accept it, she scolded herself harshly. Accept the fact God intended her to serve Him alone—for every attempt at companionship she'd ever tried to cultivate in her life had always failed.

Besides, how silly she had become in her solitary treks up and down the

West Country. At this very moment—no matter where he was or what doing—John Murrey Eden probably didn't even remember the name of the nurse who had cared for him after . . .

Though she'd been walking with admirable purpose and determination down the road, abruptly she stopped. Ahead twenty yards was the cottage.

Dear God, how she missed him, that man who probably did not even remember her name, that strange and complex man who once had lightly touched her hand as though testing, allowed it to rest atop hers for a moment before quickly removing it, the same man who stood accused of ruining every life he'd ever touched.

"I wish you well," she whispered to the late-evening air, and vowed with simple sincerity *never* again, under any circumstances, to allow her heart and soul to be invaded as this one man had invaded and conquered hers.

Love was an illness to be perennially avoided—as she tried to avoid pox and fever and all infections which undermined the system and against which there was no protection.

Resolution made! Good-bye!

She turned and ran back down the road, her feet slipping in the ruts, her vision blurred, the natural strain of self-discipline . . . and loneliness.

La Rochelle
House of Detention,
Paris
November 14, 1874

Single-handedly, Madame Charvin had taken the simple bureaucratic activity of pulling strings and had elevated it to a fine art. She was proud to be able to accomplish almost anything within the walls of the prison, anything except a prisoner's escape, and she'd never dared to arrange for that, because, quite simply, if it didn't work, her own head would roll, and she was still quite fond of her own head.

So when the prisoner Elizabeth Eden had requested a fragrant hot bath and a new blue gown as her last wishes before facing the firing squad, Madame Charvin at the last moment had effortlessly arranged for both.

As she surveyed the clock on her mantel—shortly before midnight—she wiped her hands on her apron and turned to confirm the readiness of Elizabeth Eden's last wishes. In the center of her comfortable parlor stood an enormous copper tub, large enough for the prisoner to stretch out if she so desired. Halos of steam still rose from the jasmine-scented water, bathing the entire room in a fragrant fog. If everything went on schedule, the guards, friendly ones, bribed ones, would return with Elizabeth Eden in ten minutes. By that time the water would have cooled just enough for comfortable submersion. Then it was Madame's intention to gently wield the scrub brush herself. She could have brought in one of the female prisoners for this menial task—there were plenty of ladies' maids among the still-imprisoned female incendiaries who had attempted to put the torch to Paris four years ago—but Madame Charvin wanted this chore for herself, because in truth it was no chore. She felt such a debt to this remarkable Englishwoman who would be dead by this time tomorrow.

Abruptly she turned away from her fixed gaze on the shimmering copper tub. Something pinched, hurt.

Dead.

215

She lifted her head, and in an attempt to ease the temporary discomfort, she walked quickly into her bedchamber for a final check on the lovely blue gown which had been delivered to the service entrance of the prison and carried up to her apartment in a wicker case safely concealed beneath a layer of fresh linen.

It *was* beautiful, Madame Lemel's finest—or at least so Madame Charvin had been assured that afternoon when she'd called personally on Madame Lemel's salon and made her request complete with size and had been shown three blue gowns. She had selected this one with Elizabeth Eden in mind. Silk it was, the color of the sky over Mont Saint Michel on the afternoon of an early-June rain, an azure blue with white watermarks which fell in cascades of elegant silk from the small nipped waist to the floor, not a decoration anyplace on the skirt, for none was needed.

Again Madame Charvin tried to draw a deep breath and couldn't. She turned away from the blue silk gown and glared at the door. Where was that blasted maid? She'd sent her on this last errand hours ago. The prisoner would be here soon, and Madame Charvin wanted everything in readiness, did not want them to be disturbed until . . .

My God, what was the matter with her? Sharply she shook her head in an attempt to clear it of the grim images which continuously presented themselves for her inspection. A cup of coffee might help, or a brandy. Yes, the latter. So what if they both got a little tipsy? It was her intention to sit up with Elizabeth for the rest of the night until the soldiers came for her at six in the morning. She would be allowed a last few minutes with one individual of her choosing; then she would be led out to the courtyard, placed against the firing post, her hands bound behind her, and she would be given the choice of a blindfold or none.

Take it!

A sudden knock at the door caused Madame Charvin to jump. She clasped a trembling hand to her throat. "Come," she called out, and was forced to say it again, louder. "Come in!"

A moment later the apartment door was drawn open and one of the prison maids pushed in a small cart on which rested a yellow teapot, two cups, a large covered platter, and a tiered plate containing a lovely arrangement of delicate cakes and cookies.

"Very good," Madame beamed, glad for the prompt delivery and doubly glad for the distraction. From where she stood she saw clearly the terror in the young girl's eyes. She knew very well what the meal was and whom it was for.

"Run along now and tell no one," Madame ordered the girl. "What you saw here is no one's business, is that clear?" She was on the verge of telling her good night and to close the door when she heard the telltale shuffling of a manacled prisoner.

Why manacled? Dear God, she wasn't going anywhere.

"You, girl, run along . . ."

But too late. Standing half in, half out of the door, the girl stiffened, her attention fixed on the shuffling feet, joined now by the smart click of heeled boots. The escort, no doubt.

God be with us and make us strong.

Madame Charvin prayed quickly and crossed herself and took a final appraisal of everything in order, steam still rising from the copper tub, the smell of jasmine everywhere—like Versailles in early May—a stack of clean white linen, a simple soft white dressing gown, and in the bedchamber, just the corner of the bed visible, the elegant gown itself.

The footsteps came to a halt outside the door.

"Madame Charvin?" The male voice seemed strangely out-of-place. Still, she must respond.

"Come." For the last time she adjusted her twisted bodice, straightened the French knot which sat at the back of her neck, and turned to greet her good friend Elizabeth Eden from London.

But as the guards appeared, flanking and supporting between them what appeared to be a very frail and ill woman, all of Madame Charvin's resolutions faltered. When the two guards and the maid departed the room, Madame Charvin half-walked, half-carried Elizabeth to the nearest chair. The blankness in the woman's face alarmed and frightened her. It happened sometimes—Madame Charvin had seen it before—the subtle diminution of a prisoner's senses as the moment of death appeared, the mind's way of defending itself against what was coming.

"Elizabeth?" Madame Charvin smiled kindly. "It's me. Remember? The wax flowers you made . . ."

"Of course I remember, madame," came a soft voice, and Madame Charvin knew instantly there was nothing wrong with this remarkable woman's wits. In fact, for the moment the sentence of death seemed to be pressing down on Madame Charvin rather than Elizabeth Eden.

"Come," Madame Charvin said, cutting off the thought before it became too destructive, "let me help." She stepped back and pointed toward the copper tub filled with hot fragrant water. "We'll bathe first," she suggested, "then I . . ."

Elizabeth nodded, and with Madame Charvin's help made her way slowly toward the tub, where her hands commenced to move slowly down the long row of buttons.

"Here, I'll do it," Madame Charvin offered, and Elizabeth did not protest, trailing her fingers through the water, a smile on her face, eyes closed as though the sensation was pleasurable beyond description.

Buttons undone, Madame Charvin slipped the awful dress down, watching as it fell the rest of the way to reveal a small, almost childlike body, the shoulder bones and ribs visible, the slender legs, shapely save for the two bleeding and chafed bands about the ankles where the manacles had cut deep. If Elizabeth felt any immodesty, she gave no indication of it, instead concentrating on the water, the fragrance.

"Jasmine," she murmured. "Thank you. I had no idea you could really do it."

A bit offended, as though her reputation had been questioned, Madame Charvin answered in mock indignation. "As I told you, you might have requested anything except . . ." She had started to say "escape" but changed her mind. Why flirt with false hope? "Anything," she repeated, "and it would have been yours. I would have seen to it personally. It is the right, you know, of every condemned . . ."

She broke off. Not that she'd seen anything on Elizabeth's face that had informed her she'd said too much. In fact, she couldn't see Elizabeth's face at all, for she'd turned back to the tub, leaning heavily against the edge. Across her shoulders and back Madame Charvin saw gooseflesh.

"I'm . . . sorry, Elizabeth," she apologized.

"No," the woman said without looking up. "We can't avoid it, can we? So we mustn't be afraid of it."

Madame Charvin shook her head.

"Heaven!" she heard Elizabeth gasp, and looked back to see her just stepping into the hot water. There was a slight wince as the lacerations on her ankles came into contact with the water. But the discomfort was short-lived. With help she eased all the way down into the water, her eyes closed, face lifted.

"Oh, madame, it *is* heaven."

Madame Charvin, not trusting herself to speak, hovered for a moment to make certain all was well; then she stepped back. "I'll leave you for a while," she offered, thinking perhaps Elizabeth would want a brief interval to herself.

"Oh, no, please, madame," Elizabeth protested sharply, sitting up. "Please . . . stay," she begged. "I've been alone . . . too long, and will be . . ." As she faltered, she bowed her head over the water.

To Madame's consternation, she thought the woman was weeping, and realized afresh this would not do at all. She retreated to the sideboard, poured two snifters of brandy, and carried them back to the center of the room. "Here," she commanded, extending one snifter over the water.

But there were no tears on Elizabeth's face. She took the snifter with a quick smile.

"Heaven!" she murmured, eyes closed.

Monsieur DuCamp's Lodging House, Paris November 15, 1874 Three A.M.

For the first few hours of the long evening, Bates had tried to keep pace with Mr. Eden, his aimless wanderings, the repetitious movement around Monsieur DuCamp's small parlor, then out onto the cold rainy pavement, where for several moments he'd search each passing carriage.

Now, weary at three A.M., Bates slumped on the settee. *Where was Charley Spade?* Bates made a little sound of contempt and suffered a major regret that he had not gone himself. He'd offered, twice, and twice had been rejected on the grounds of his age.

"What time is it, Bates?" The taut, exhausted voice came from the fire, where Mr. Eden had been pacing in small circles for several minutes.

"A quarter past three, sir," Bates replied, glancing at the large mantel clock directly in front of Mr. Eden. "Sir, may I suggest . . . ?"

All he was going to suggest was a short interval of rest. But he never had a chance to complete the suggestion, for, without warning, Mr. Eden pushed open the double doors of Monsieur DuCamp's lodging house and stepped out onto the portico.

In growing despair, Bates sat up straight and peered through the lace panels of the wavy glass windows. From this angle he could see the street was deserted except for the play of lamplight on moist canals, the light beams cutting strange, irregular patterns every which way. There was not a conveyance in sight, nor a pedestrian. He took a final look through the lace curtains at Mr. Eden standing alone on the edge of the pavement, the collar of his cape turned up, his head swiveling in one direction, then the other, alert to every sound.

Bates stood as rapidly as age would permit and hobbled to the door, thinking to close it, but at the sound of his boots, Mr. Eden whirled about, looking directly at him. Bates knew if he lived to be one hundred and fifty he would never cleanse his memory of that expression, a tortured combination of hope and despair.

"My God!" Bates breathed heavily, and quickly closed the door on such a face, wishing he'd stayed in North Devon, hating his past, resenting his present, and dreading his future.

Somehow he had felt so safe then.

La Rochelle
House of Detention,
Paris
November 15, 1874
Predawn

Madame Charvin had faced many difficult ordeals in her life, by the very nature of her profession. But possibly the most difficult one of all was watching Elizabeth Eden arranging her hair as though for a ball, when in truth in less than two hours the woman would be dead.

Briefly Madame closed her eyes to rest them from the torturous sight, and enjoying a moment of self-imposed blindness, she wondered bleakly if she would have the same courage as the little Englishwoman if their roles were reversed.

How deftly the woman wielded the hairbrush, bending her slim lovely neck at a becoming angle in order to catch the tiny curling neck hairs. Each time she straightened, Madame Charvin caught a clear look at the woman's face and was newly astonished. Never had she seen such concentration, though there was just a hint of a smile at the corners of Elizabeth's mouth which seemed to say, "I know better than anyone how frivolous and vain this is, but still it must be approached seriously."

"Madame!" As Madame Charvin spoke, the single word seemed to echo about the small apartment. It was the first word spoken in over an hour and served to startle both women.

Elizabeth glanced up expectantly into the looking glass. "You spoke, madame?" she asked.

"Yes. I wondered . . ."

What had she been wondering? How they would survive the next hour, the last before the guards came? Against the onslaught of that thought, Madame Charvin bowed her head. It was then the thought occurred, so devastating that for the next few moments she could not look up. No, dismiss it. Now, before it took root and grew and spread and flowered.

221

"Madame Charvin?" It was Elizabeth again, concerned. "You mustn't. Remember, we promised. No fear."

No fear? Madame Charvin had never in her life known the degree of fear she was now experiencing. And yet, what was the alternative? That they sit here, both of them, passively, like canaries awaiting the arrival of the cat? How stupid.

"Madame Charvin, is something wrong?"

"I'm well," Madame Charvin muttered, and stood immediately to pace to the far corner of the chamber, requiring a few minutes alone before she shared her madness. She was fully aware as Elizabeth tracked her with her eyes, still trying to determine the exact cause of the change which had come over her in the last few minutes. When Elizabeth saw Madame staring back, she quickly averted her eyes by ducking her head in order to secure the clip tightly at the back of her neck.

All right, keep busy for just a few more minutes, Madame Charvin brooded, thinking on the first step—which, if she agreed to this lunacy, should take place almost immediately. Elizabeth Eden, fully dressed—in the blue gown, if she insisted—but the gown as well as her new coiffure would have to be well covered in one of Madame's prison-issue cloaks, drab dark gray heavy wool and smelling of old urine, like everything else in La Rochelle.

Then, with her identity obscured, including her fair hair and English features, Madame Charvin would lead her to the long passageway which led to the small service entrance, which in turn emptied out into one of the busiest thoroughfares of Paris, a narrow artery which tried to accommodate the goings and comings of all prison personnel, plus the three hundred workers from the sprawling match factory opposite. There were times—early in the morning, like now—when the soldiers were forced to halt all conveyances at the end of the street and the passengers spilled out onto the pavement and proceeded to their various destinations on foot. With her identity obscured beneath the dark cloak, who would stop and question one more woman who appeared to be moving with dispatch toward a private destination?

Madame Charvin closed her eyes, momentarily overcome by the hope that it might work, it could work, it should work. Energy was being generated deep within her, in the place where every rebellion, major and minor, had gone into hiding after being annihilated by practicality and good sense for the last forty years. Now it seemed as if all those other lost opportunities, quiet agreements, docile obedience, joined forces with this newest and most deadly revolution to give impetus to a plan, hastily conceived, and Madame Charvin could not now think of one reason why it could not work.

How often she had run the gamut daily, adjusting her cloak, hood raised—for she did not like to be seen and identified on the street, nor did most prison personnel. There was always the possibility a recent parolee bearing a painful grudge would be waiting.

So anonymity was—and always had been—the order of the day passing from inside to outside, and Elizabeth would be anonymously garbed. Once out on the street, Madame Charvin would be of no further assistance, except to give her instructions on how to reach other equally clogged thoroughfares. From where Madame Charvin stood, it seemed Elizabeth's safety lay in taking refuge in very public places, at least for a few days.

Then, after the search—and there would be a search, for General Montaud did not take kindly to any escaped prisoner, let alone those who eluded his crack firing squad—Elizabeth should be able to leave the country undetected with her kinsman.

What was his name, the man who was here and who had behaved so badly? And what relation was he to her, and could he be trusted? He had failed so miserably the day the guard had half-dragged him up from the dungeon cell.

Abruptly Madame Charvin turned back to face Elizabeth. "What is your relationship with the gentleman who was here recently, the one who . . . ?"

She stopped speaking, stunned by Elizabeth's expression. Madame Charvin had no idea that such a simple question would produce such a painful vacancy on that face which earlier had been amused by her own vanity.

"I . . . raised him," Elizabeth said to her hands.

"Then he's your son?"

"No," Elizabeth replied with matching quickness. She looked up, and again Madame Charvin was so moved by the depth of emotion she saw in that pale face that she regretted bringing up the subject.

As though Elizabeth had been following the progression of her thoughts, she asked, "Why do you inquire? Is he . . . ?"

Madame Charvin shook her head and tried to speak as reassuringly as possible. "Nothing, I promise you. I'm certain he will return today and—"

"*No!* Please, he mustn't," Elizabeth protested, starting out of the chair. "Please, madame, I beg you, see to it that he is not allowed in during . . ."

"I have no control," Madame Charvin replied as calmly as possible in an attempt to calm Elizabeth at the same time. "I do not make that policy, have no authority to enforce—"

"Oh, no, please!" the woman went on, speaking as though Madame Charvin had not spoken at all. "He must not be permitted to witness . . ." Suddenly she stopped. One hand covered her mouth as though to prevent an outcry.

In that moment, and with no further debate concerning the rightness or wrongness of her action, Madame Charvin reached a decision which—regardless of its success or failure—would drastically transform one of their lives, perhaps both.

"Elizabeth, you must listen to me as carefully as you have ever listened before. If you follow every instruction to the letter, I think I can help you out of here."

She started to say more, realizing time was short, that ideally such an insane scheme should have been planned weeks ago, every guard movement noted, money obtained along with identification papers—oh, so many things that would simply have to be left undone. But perhaps the element of surprise would ultimately benefit them. No one knew at this point but Madame herself, thus no chance for leaks of secrets or revelations of any sort.

"Elizabeth, did you hear what . . . ?"

At last she saw a faint alteration in the dead eyes. "Help . . . me . . ."

"I will," Madame vowed. "I'll help you out of here." Furiously she dragged a chair close. "There will be tremendous risks, of course, but you have nothing to lose."

Where before there had been no words, now they spilled out in an incoherent stream of hope. "Madame, please tell me. I'll take the risks. Just tell me your scheme, what I must do to help make it work." In her growing excitement, she angled her chair around, and now the two women were seated knee to knee.

"All right," Madame Charvin declared, and felt the warmth of hope and found it a singular miracle. "All right," she repeated. "My scheme is this—and though it sounds simple, it is filled with danger and you must understand that if caught, nothing will be altered for you."

"Go on . . ." Elizabeth faltered and lowered her head.

Madame Charvin grasped both of Elizabeth's hands. "Now, this is what we are going to do. . . ."

Monsieur DuCamp's Lodging House, Paris November 15, 1874 Dawn

Dawn.

Whether John was even aware of the small fingers of light splintering the safe darkness, Bates could not tell. The night had diminished him in some way. Bates watched the tortured image as long as he could, then slowly pushed himself off the uncomfortable settee which had been his bed. He wanted to remind the man opposite him of what remained to be done on this morning before they could shake the dust of this despicable city from their boots and head for the channel. "Sir, time is passing," Bates said, and heard the idiocy of his own remark. In an attempt to cover his embarrassment, he withdrew his pocket watch and angled the face toward the dying lamp at the end of the settee.

Five-forty-five.

For Mr. Eden's last meeting with Elizabeth Eden they were to be at La Rochelle at six-fifteen. It was a fifteen-minute carriage ride, longer if traffic was fierce, and with Charley Spade still among the missing, Bates would have to take the reins this morning. Repeatedly yesterday he had tried to dissuade Mr. Eden from this senseless form of self-punishment. He'd not come right out and said so, but as much as it grieved him to even think it, he knew: Elizabeth Eden was a dead woman. He'd been amazed Mr. Eden had not realized Charley would not survive in London. But of course, Mr. Eden was not himself, had not been himself for some time.

The simple fact was that if Mr. Eden was forced, through some misplaced sense of duty and obligation, to witness this execution, there would be two corpses at La Rochelle on this day.

"Sir," Bates prodded, feeling he had to at least give the impression of performing as a loyal servant, just in case Mr. Eden was truly more aware than he appeared to be.

"Sir, the hour is . . ." He started to say "late," but at that moment Mr. Eden stirred.

"Must . . . wait," Mr. Eden slurred. "Charley Spade is due . . ."

Never, Bates concluded to himself. Charley Spade would not appear in Paris this morning. Unless Bates missed his guess, Charley Spade quite probably was still in London, either in some dockside pub passed out in the sawdust or else he'd met a bumpkin's end with a knife between his shoulder blades.

"Sir?" he tried again.

"Wait . . ." Mr. Eden murmured.

All right. So be it! They could wait all morning, for all Bates cared, certainly well past the hour of six-thirty, when the French soldiers would take their positions in a straight line, rifles at the ready, and . . .

Let her die alone and in peace.

"Very good," he said obediently, having been told they would wait. "Very well," he repeated, and slipped his watch back into his pocket, wondering only briefly what manner of God it was who presided over the debacle known as the human race.

226

La Rochelle
House of Detention,
Paris
November 15, 1874
Dawn

Their only disagreement had been a minor one, whether or not Elizabeth would wear the blue gown beneath the gray prison-issue cloak.

Madame Charvin had been opposed on the grounds Elizabeth was to pass for her, and never in her entire life had she ever worn so fancy a gown.

But Elizabeth had insisted, and now, buoyed by her imminent escape from this nightmare place, she stood back to survey the lovely blue silk in the full-length glass. She caught a glimpse of Madame Charvin's furrowed brow and instantly regretted causing the kind woman additional worry.

"Madame, please," she entreated, turning away from her reflected image to confront the woman directly, "there is no way I can repay your kindnesses to me. Indeed, I owe you my life—"

"It may not work," the stern woman grumbled, still worried.

"I think it will," Elizabeth countered, "and so do you, or you would never have suggested it. But please, let's not argue in our last moments together." She stepped closer and took Madame Charvin's hand. "I do know if God is with me and I make my way successfully to freedom, as long as I have a mind and a conscience I will remember you every day in my prayers . . ."

Madame Charvin turned away and shook her head brusquely, as though the expression of gratitude had embarrassed her—or worse, moved her.

But Elizabeth persisted. "No, let me finish, then I shall disguise myself beneath your cloak and bother you no longer."

"You should be off now," Madame Charvin snapped, seeming to grow

227

angrier as the moment of parting drew near. "It's none too soon, you know. The guards have already—"

"I know," Elizabeth soothed, "and I'm ready. Just let me say one more thing. If this day has a happy ending and I see dawn tomorrow, I'll make my way to England, and once there, to the West Country, to Devon and a place called Eden Castle. If you are ever in need of anything, you are to contact me there. Do you understand? And if France ever becomes . . . unsuitable, you are to come to me and I will see to it you have a home of comfort and security always. Do you understand?"

She had been so intent on getting it all said that she had failed to notice the look of pain on Madame Charvin's face. At first she was shocked, for she'd said nothing to cause pain. "Oh, madame, please don't," Elizabeth murmured, reflexively embracing her. At first Madame resisted the offer of closeness, but as Elizabeth stood her ground, Madame thawed and ultimately succumbed. For several moments the two women clung to each other as the most loving of friends.

"What . . . if it doesn't work?" faltered Madame Charvin.

"Then I'm no worse off than I was before," Elizabeth said with a calmness she did not feel. It would work. It had to work. She'd make it work.

"Do you have my purse?" Madame Charvin asked, stepping away from Elizabeth's arms and fishing blindly in her pocket for a handkerchief.

"I do." Elizabeth smiled. "Right . . . there." She glanced toward the dressing table and spied the well-worn black satchel belonging to Madame Charvin, the same one she'd carried in and out of the prison every day for the last fifteen years.

"The guards have sharp eyes," she had cautioned Elizabeth. *They will recognize the purse."*

As Madame Charvin returned the handkerchief to her pocket, Elizabeth went back to the dressing table and caught a glimpse of the gown as she passed by the looking glass. It *was* lovely. Once away from the prison, she planned to remove the coarse-woven cloak and blend with all the other Parisians who were making their way to the channel and a holiday. She'd thought once of trying to contact John. She was certain he was still in Paris. But it was too risky. On that point she and Madame Charvin had been in complete agreement.

"You must hurry," Madame Charvin urged, growing more nervous with each passing minute. She picked up her heavy gray cloak. "Here, it's chilly, and this will warm. Now, I want you to tell me once more, what will you do?"

As Elizabeth tied the cloak around her shoulders, she tried to remember the instructions which Madame had given her earlier. "I leave here," she began, keeping her voice down, "and I proceed to the end of this corridor, and I . . . wait . . ."

"For what?"

"Until the six-thirty guard is changed."

"And . . . ?"

Elizabeth closed her eyes. It had not seemed very complicated when Madame had first related it to her. Now, why did it seem so complex— and worse, unworkable?

"And . . . ?" Madame Charvin urged, a new tension in her voice.

". . . and when there is no one patrolling the passageway, I run for the stairs."

Madame Charvin closed her eyes in apparent relief. "Then what?" she demanded wearily.

Elizabeth wondered if she was not at the moment regretting her involvement in this business.

"Then what?" Madame snapped, all the while taking items out of her large satchel, putting other items in.

"Then I take the passageway down," Elizabeth stammered, "taking care always to keep the hood in place."

"And if you meet someone and they speak?"

"I keep my head down and I say . . . nothing."

"Good." Madame nodded sharply. "I never speak, especially early in the morning. The fewer words exchanged the better, I always say. Remember that. No one will suspect you if you remain quiet. But if you speak . . ."

"I won't," Elizabeth promised quickly. She was beginning to suffer a growing fear. Yet why? It was as Madame had said when she'd first presented the escape plan. Elizabeth had nothing to lose.

"Madame—" she began, thinking there was so much to say.

But instead Madame Charvin interrupted again. "At the stairs, what?"

At the stairs . . . What?

What was the matter with her? "At the stairs, wait until I see the kitchen entrance fully opened."

Madame Charvin nodded. "Yes, good. Why?"

"Because . . ." Did it really matter?

Madame Charvin heard the hesitancy. "Because the kitchen is brightly lit and the new shift coming on will have sharp eyes. This will be your most hazardous passage, unless . . ."

She broke off. Elizabeth saw her eyes momentarily glaze. "No matter," she contradicted. "As soon as you see the night staff gathering, move down. Usually I am the last one through the door, simply because I don't like their early-morning chatter and so I time it thus. I urge you to remember that, because I suspect in that manner we are very different . . ."

Oh, yes, Elizabeth thought. After the loneliness and isolation of four years in prison, she would chat with a post if she thought there was the least chance of getting a response.

". . . so I urge you maintain your silence always, keep the hood in place, and hold the satchel in this manner." She demonstrated, clasping the satchel under her left arm and holding it securely against her body. At the conclusion of the demonstration, she thrust the satchel toward Elizabeth and waited expectantly.

Elizabeth took the satchel and imitated Madame Charvin and apparently passed muster.

"Good, good," the stern-faced woman pronounced, glancing behind her at the clock on the mantel, which now said a quarter to six.

"Time," Elizabeth heard Madame whisper, and saw her look back, her face a mixed script of fear and hope. "Oh, my dear," she fretted nervously, "I'm certain I'm forgetting something."

229

"Nothing, and how can I ever thank—?"

"Of course. Once outside, then what?"

"Mix quickly with the crowds," Elizabeth said. "I believe you said there would be crowds . . ."

"And there will be. Move away immediately from the prison side. Returning guards will recognize me and try to speak. Move to the opposite side, as though you were coming from the match factory."

"Yes, to the opposite side."

"Then?"

"Then . . ." Elizabeth faltered again. Then what?

Madame reached for the satchel and drew it open. "In the envelope there are seventy-five louis. It's all I had on hand—"

"No, I can't—" Elizabeth protested.

"You . . . have . . . no . . . choice," Madame snapped, placing emphasis on each word. "Now, listen carefully. You are to go on foot to the second intersection directly north of the prison. There, on the right-hand corner, you will see the place where the hired chaises are waiting. Go to the first and say only one word. 'Calais.' He will understand and will take you to the place where the coaches depart for the channel. Do you understand?"

Seventy-five louis. How could she ever repay the woman? "Yes." Elizabeth nodded reluctantly.

"Now, you must go," Madame said, urging her toward the door.

Although it was what Elizabeth had wanted for four long years and despaired of ever accomplishing, now she hesitated.

"Hurry!" Madame Charvin commanded. "The guards change at six-thirty sharp. The execution is scheduled for immediately following. When they come for you, I'll stall as long as I can, saying you aren't fully prepared . . ."

Elizabeth realized clearly that they both were taking enormous gambles, but perhaps Madame Charvin's was the greater of the two. If caught, Elizabeth's life was over. If the escape was successful, La Rochelle and everything it stood for was behind her. But either way, Madame could lose. To what extent and how much, Elizabeth couldn't guess, and doubted seriously if Madame herself knew.

They were before the closed door now. As Madame's hand moved toward the bolt, Elizabeth reached up and caught it, pressing it lightly to her lips. The gesture caught Madame off guard, and at first she started to withdraw her hand, but then some strange tempering need intercepted.

"God go with you," Madame said softly and drew her close.

"And you," Elizabeth whispered, kissing the woman lightly on both cheeks.

"Go!" Madame urged, nothing mournful about that stern face now.

Elizabeth nodded, secured the tie on the hood beneath her chin, drew the folds of the prison cloak around the blue silk gown, clasped the satchel beneath her arm in precisely the fashion Madame Charvin had demonstrated, and without hesitation turned to confront the shadowy emptiness of the corridor outside the door.

Freedom was about twenty minutes away. Surely God would not be so cruel as to deny it to her now.

Paris
November 15, 1874

The Countess Eugenie Retiffe had spent the night in her family chapel in Notre Dame Cathedral, praying to the Holy Mother for forgiveness for her soul as well as for the soul of the Englishwoman Elizabeth Eden.

Now, as she slumped against the brocade velvet of her private carriage, she felt the same emptiness she'd suffered every day since her premature release from La Rochelle Prison.

"Turn here!" she called up to her driver, stirring herself long enough to take note of street signs, aware of what she was doing but powerless to stop herself.

As the carriage veered sharply to the left, heading into the congestion of the narrow artery that ran behind La Rochelle Prison, she closed her eyes to the glut of humanity and imagined instead Elizabeth Eden's sorrowing eyes after she had plunged the shears into Lieutenant Dauguet, the look of betrayal aimed at *her,* Eugenie, who had struck a bargain a few days earlier with Dauguet, who had craved for himself English flesh. All that had been required of Eugenie, in exchange for her release, had been that she contrive to leave the cell door unlocked. No problem, that. Elizabeth Eden had trusted her implicitly. And what harm, Eugenie had thought, if Dauguet had his way? The Englishwoman was certainly no virgin. It had been rumored she had served as mistress to several prominent English politicians. Then how would it hurt if . . . ?

"Stop here!" she cried out, seeing the congestion up ahead, as the prison shifts changed.

She felt her driver angle the carriage to one side of the pavement, and tried again—as she'd tried every hour of every day since it had happened—to finally and securely close the door on the past. It was over, did

231

not concern her. The fate of the Englishwoman was up to God. Eugenie Retiffe had not asked her to come to Paris and involve herself in stupid politics—for that's what they were. She could see that now, and looked back on her involvement with the communes as merely a difficult part of growing up. At least that's what Papa had said, and since her betrayal of the Englishwoman and early release, Papa had begun to love her again. And Mama, too. And it was nice, far nicer to be clean and perfumed and wearing pretty little frocks like this one than to be locked in a miserable cell, exposed to the illiterate guards.

Reflexively she shuddered. No, she was far happier now. For a moment she stared, unseeing, out of the carriage window. Far better off, far happier . . .

Then why was she crying? Why did she want more than anything in the world to stop that firing line?

Executed!

She still couldn't believe it, not even after Papa had shown her the announcement in the paper. She'd cried then, and both Mama and Papa had comforted her, promised her a holiday in the south, and reassured her that whatever fate befell the Englishwoman, it was not Eugenie's fault.

Quickly she crossed herself and thought: Tell Jean to take you home. Papa will be waiting. Morning coffee on the terrace, the smell of autumn . . .

But despite the cascade of pleasing images, she could not give the order to her driver. Every time she drew breath, she saw in her mind's eye a graphic, horrifying image of Elizabeth Eden bound to the large post in the inner courtyard, head lifted . . .

Eugenie's own head fell forward with a suddenness, as though a cord had been snapped.

She saw that her carriage resembled an island, while all about poured floods of humanity, the two shifts changing simultaneously, the prison's as well as the factory's. She could sense the agitation of her driver as he tried to ease the horses.

"It will be over soon," she called out, remembering it didn't take long for the street to clear.

A sudden movement to the left of the carriage drew her away from her thoughts to the place where she saw a contingent of soldiers pushing their way hurriedly through the crowds, rifles at the ready, their heads swiveling first in one direction, then in the other, as though they were searching for someone.

An escapee? she wondered with mixed feelings. Few ever successfully escaped from La Rochelle except those who were permitted to "escape," for the purpose of being shot down in the process.

A larger contingent of soldiers was fanning out through the crowds. Clearly someone *had* escaped. Eugenie watched the soldiers for several moments with a mixture of fear and pleasure. They were not searching for *her*. She, thank God, did not have to be dragged back into that red-brick nightmare. Whoever had managed freedom this far, she wished them well. As several soldiers passed close to her carriage, she closed her eyes as she'd done so often when she'd been imprisoned—the ostrich scheme, foolishly assuming if you couldn't see them, they couldn't see you.

She waited to give them a chance to pass. Then she opened her eyes and wondered what had prompted her to come here. Surely the execution was over by now and Elizabeth Eden was at peace.

Oh, dear God, enough, she groaned, weary of thinking, of feeling guilt, so much guilt.

Was the woman blessedly dead now? And when would it be possible for Eugenie to join her?

"Proceed!" she called out through the open window, noticing the crowds were diminishing. She certainly didn't want to be here when the hearse wagon came rattling through those low gates with a single coffin lashed to the back.

"Please move," she called out, wondering why the driver did not obey her.

I'm sorry, Elizabeth. Please forgive me.

Suddenly she covered her face with her hands. The battle was threatening to tear her apart. Quickly she lifted her head, as though the spiritual fury was taking a toll on her physical body. As she did so, she spied, just stepping out of the low prison door, a stark and familiar figure, the gray-hooded cloak and worn satchel of Madame Charvin, the female warden of La Rochelle and the most powerful woman in the prison. Eugenie watched her for a moment as she passed through the gates with scarcely a nod to the two guards. She seemed different somehow, her step not as . . .

Suddenly it occurred to Eugenie this woman could tell her everything. Had the execution taken place? Something about her step suggested it had.

"Wait here," she called up to her driver.

"Madame Charvin!" she called out, aware her voice had not carried over the noise of the crowd. "Madame Charvin, please wait."

Surely the woman had heard that. Then why didn't she stop?

"Madame Charvin, please, it's me. You remember . . ."

Eugenie was still pushing her way through the crowds that continued to come between her and the stubborn Madame. Of course. Madame Charvin had always been fond of the little Englishwoman, as had Eugenie. Then the bowed head, the obscured face, and the refusal to stop even for the courtesy of a question clearly meant only one thing, that the execution had taken place. It was blessedly over—for all except those who had loved her.

Still, she had to know, had to exchange a few words with the woman who had last seen her alive. She doubled her step, slowly gaining on the old woman, who had yet to turn and recognize her in any way, though Eugenie was certain she had heard her cries, for everyone else had.

"Madame Charvin, I command you to stop!" she called out, still gaining on the woman, who had to know someone was calling to her.

"Madame Charvin!" Eugenie called out a final time and, at last, reached out for the gray hood that obscured the woman's face and pulled.

All during the treacherous passage out of the prison, Elizabeth had kept her head down, had childishly counted off the square tiles of each passageway, had kept one face, one name, steadfast in her mind as the only certainty she had against the tremors of fear that had threatened on several occasions to bring her to her knees.

233

Edward.

For each time she thought his name, she saw his face, and that single image gave her courage.

Edward.

John's father, yet how different they were.

Had someone called? Through the low door, out of the gate. *Dear God, please, I don't want to die.*

Keep going, head down, don't look up. Through the gate. The guards said nothing save, "Good morning, Madame Charvin."

Someone *was* calling to her. Madame Charvin said not to reply. Then she wouldn't, though it was an insistent someone. She heard the call again, and the sound, rising feebly over all the other sounds, caused her heart to accelerate.

Keep walking; don't look up or speak.

"Madame Charvin, wait, it's me . . ."

No, please, she begged quietly, thinking *Edward* and trying to find the image of his miraculous face in her fear. But it was gone. She couldn't resurrect one feature.

"Madame Charvin!"

The voice was gaining on her; the crowds nearing the end of the street were diminishing, so there was no one behind whom she could take refuge. If the persistent voice caught up with her . . .

Suddenly she increased her speed, thinking to gain the end of the street before the voice caught up with her.

"Madame Charvin, I command you to stop!"

Would God be so cruel?

Then she felt it, at first only a slight tugging at the gray hood, as though Fate hadn't quite made up its mind whether or not to let her proceed to freedom or . . .

Then the hand tightened on the heavy fabric and the tugging increased.

"No!" Elizabeth cried aloud at the precise moment the insistent hand pulled the hood free. She turned and confronted the shocked and horrified eyes of her betrayer.

Twice betrayed, she thought, in the moment before she ran. *Eugenie Retiffe. Dear God, why?*

"Elizabeth!" the pale woman cried. At the moment she spoke the name, the random street noises, the rattle of near wagons, the shouts of soldiers and barking dogs, all the reasonable shields which might have obscured the single name, fell silent.

But in the new and unholy quiet, that one name seemed to hang forever in the still air, amplified and echoing, gaining attention as far back as the prison gate. The sound of the name, combined with the face, the head, the fair hair, all reflecting and confirming the image of the new escapee, all this registered with three soldiers who were hurrying toward the intersection and who now glanced once at the curious confrontation—Madame Charvin's garments, Madame Charvin's satchel, but not Madame Charvin.

"Wait!" one shouted as Elizabeth broke into a run.

"Wait!" the second shouted.

Still she ran, hoping in a way they would fire on her now and end it—for it was over.

But they didn't fire. Instead, it was a simple matter for the first two soldiers to overtake her, and with one violent shove they pushed her to the ground. As the cobbles rose up, she felt her forehead in painful collision with the stones. Stunned, she was only partially aware of others closing in around her, of the cloak being torn off, as though they needed full confirmation it was not Madame Charvin. As she looked up, she felt restraining boots pressed against both ankles and wrists, heard the peculiar music of the French language—now harsh and staccato—saw a large circle of angry male faces gaping down on her.

Grieving the plan had not worked, that God had been so displeased with her He had denied her this last attempt to gain her freedom, certain now it was over, no more hope, she looked beyond the soldiers' angry faces, beyond the crowd which had quickly gathered in curiosity on all sides, beyond even the deathly pale face of Eugenie, who had pushed close for one look, then turned away sobbing.

Elizabeth cast her vision beyond everything that was worn and ugly and betraying and found, directly overhead, a circle of high blue sky, reminiscent of the blue which favored Eden's skies.

"Edward," she whispered once more before she saw the butt of a rifle raised directly over her forehead and knew it would render her senseless.

In the last moment of consciousness she thanked God for this one blessing.

Monsieur DuCamp's Lodging House, Paris November 15, 1874 Nine A.M.

"Damn you!" Mr. Eden shouted.

Bates knew if the man attacked him he was a dead man, for fury and rage had given to Mr. Eden an awesome strength, and while the previous illness had taken a toll, there was not one sign of weakness visible now. Like an injured bull, he had come raging up out of his predawn stupor long enough to discover Charley Spade had not returned and the hour of the day was approaching nine o'clock, two and one-half hours beyond the time of Elizabeth Eden's execution.

Bates attempted a weak defense. "Sir, you said to wait—"

"God, no!" Mr. Eden whispered to no one in particular, and was out of the front door. He'd lost his walking stick someplace and was limping visibly, stumbling once halfway down the stairs in his haste and fear, grappling at the banister until he could right himself.

Bates moved right behind him, seeing his direction, the black rented carriage waiting at the edge of the pavement. "Wait, sir, and I'll . . ."

But Mr. Eden, despite his apparent fatigue, wasn't in a waiting mood. With difficulty he swung himself up onto the high seat and had already taken the reins when Bates joined him, breathless from the sprint but grateful Mr. Eden's fury had at least diminished to the point it was no longer aimed at Bates.

John slapped the reins down across the horses. The animals, startled by the sound and the sudden sting, bolted away from the pavement, and for a few moments the carriage ran out of control across the intersection, narrowly avoiding a collision with a large hay wagon.

"Sir, let me . . ."

But as Bates reached for the reins, Mr. Eden held them fast and with effort brought the carriage under control, though never at any point did he attempt to reduce their speed. Once beyond the intersection, Bates opened his eyes long enough to determine Mr. Eden was on the proper route which ultimately would lead them to La Rochelle.

As the brilliant colors of the autumn morning blurred on either side of the high carriage seat, Bates sent his heart in search of blessings and could find only one—and that was a poor one—the realization his ploy had worked, that no matter how painful this moment was, it was nothing compared to what Mr. Eden would have suffered if he had arrived at La Rochelle in time for the execution.

A quarter past nine, his pocket watch said. Long since over. Elizabeth Eden was with God and at peace. Now all that remained to be done was to find just a small portion of earthly peace for John Murrey Eden.

La Rochelle
House of Detention,
Paris
November 15, 1874
Nine-fifteen A.M.

She regained consciousness in a small cell off the courtyard and thought at first in her stunned state it was already over. She felt little or no pain, save for the dull throbbing on the left side of her forehead. Other than that, she felt a strange peace, a feeling of passage, of something having occurred that had somehow removed her from all earthly struggle.

Yet here she was, sprawled facedown in a most indecorous position on a meager bed of smelly straw, all similar to her cell downstairs. But there was one thing different about this that made it paradise compared to the cell in the dungeon.

Sun! There was a sun somewhere close by. Not shining directly on her, but close enough for her to see, despite her blurred vision, the miracle of blue shadows, the manner in which golden light met, then receded from certain objects.

"Ah, our pretty is awake!"

Still lying facedown on straw, she heard the male voice, knew who it was, and considered turning to confront him, but changed her mind. That too required energy she didn't have. She was a corpse whose heart inconveniently continued to half-beat. But not for long.

"Madame, I spoke to you. Your countrymen are renowned for their courtesy. Where is yours?"

She heard the heavy tread of additional boots in the cell now.

"Lift her!" came the stern voice who earlier had wanted her courtesy.

She heard the boots come closer, felt hands grasp her beneath her arms, and suddenly she was lifted.

Once standing, all support left her and for a second she wobbled unstea-

238

dily before them. She would have fallen altogether had it not been for another set of hands which took her by the arm and led her to a low three-legged stool, sat her down, and hovered long enough to see she could manage on her own.

"Now, madame, look at me," came the arrogant male command.

"Sir," she murmured, her eyes at last meeting the small watery eyes of General Jules Montaud. He was elegantly garbed this morning in full uniform, a pair of highly polished black boots replacing the bedroom slippers, his small chest laden with ribbons and medals, gold epaulets glittering in the morning sun. Something important was taking place in La Rochelle this morning, she thought, to warrant such official and pompous splendor. Then she remembered. *Her* execution. That's what was taking place.

For several moments the general seemed content merely to stare at her, his brow furrowed, his thin black curls in disarray below his bald pate.

"Madame, how difficult you make everything for yourself," he softly mourned.

She nodded once and reached one hand up in an attempt to contain the throbbing pain in her head. "I'm afraid I always have, sir," she admitted with a smile. "A friend once said of me—"

"You have no friends now," the voice cut in, suddenly angry.

How could she have angered him? She'd not been given a chance to speak. She looked up and saw the pacing had stopped, the general confronting her directly.

"I will admit you did have one," he said, his voice low and ominous, "but she will be dealt with, I can assure you, and when we're finished, let her see how kind the world is to an ugly old woman with no funds, no kinsmen, no place to go."

Madame Charvin? Was he speaking of Madame Charvin?

"Jules Montaud can abide many things," the general went on, leaning close over her, "but what he cannot abide is disloyalty."

"I don't know what you're talking about," Elizabeth said suddenly, knowing it was the wrong thing to say even as she formed the words, but saying it anyway.

"Yes, you do," General Montaud snapped, then reached out and grasped her face with fingers of steel and held her fast. "We have both Madame Charvin's cloak and her satchel—"

"She did not give them to me; I stole them."

"Liar!" screamed General Montaud, exploding with fury, still grasping her face with bruising strength.

She tried to pull away, but two of the young soldiers behind her, each grasping an arm, held her tight. As she groaned, she saw the rage on Montaud's face subdue into a smile.

Though her eyes were closed, she heard someone open the cell door. She didn't bother to look because she didn't care, though she did overhear a brittle exchange.

"Too late, Father. She's compounded her sins of murder and thievery with the sin of a lie."

"All her sins are redeemable in God's eyes."

"Then God is more generous than any of us ever dreamed."

Although she'd vowed not to look on the man again in this life, the soft, repentant, almost graceful voice drew her attention upward despite her avowed intention.

The first thing she saw was the black hem of a priest's garment, delicate lace at cuffs and collar, a rotund, globular man of average height who stood before General Montaud with soft and sympathetic eyes, an elegant Bible in hand, open, a black rosary dividing the pages.

She had asked for no priest, was not Catholic, and therefore was not entitled to their ritual of death. She was about to say all this when suddenly General Montaud dropped to his knees before the priest. His head fell forward on his chest and he appeared to be in great pain, spiritual if not physical, though it was difficult to tell, so consummate was his mournful posture.

"Father, forgive me," he begged in a voice which in no way resembled the imperious, arrogant voice of a few moments earlier.

Stunned by this rapid change, she watched and listened. And did not understand.

"Does God believe I enjoy my most difficult task?" General Montaud whined. He had found the priest's hand and was now kissing it over and over again, halting only long enough to press it to his forehead now and again.

"God understands everything," the priest interrupted in a high-pitched voice, which startled Elizabeth. Because of the man's girth, she had expected a larger voice.

"Does He, Father?" General Montaud asked, lifting his head for the first time, those soft white features arranged into angles of sad remorse. "But then, of course He must," he went on, answering his own question. "It is His unpleasant task to administer divine justice. It is mine to administer earthly justice."

The priest nodded vigorously. "True, my son. He knows . . ."

"Everything?" General Montaud prodded. "Does He know that public executions of prisoners makes me physically ill? That it requires a full week for me to recover from one?"

"I am certain He does."

"But He also knows that it must be done, doesn't He?"

"Of course. And He sends to you a particularly rich blessing because you are among the chosen. You are His intermediary here on earth to see His commandments are carried out."

The male voices droned on for several minutes. "God help me!" Elizabeth prayed, surprising even herself with her unexpected failure of nerve. Death *was* obliging her, was standing in her very presence, and now she didn't want it, wanted nothing to do with it, wanted to strike any bargain possible. Let her spend the remainder of her natural days here in this cell, with only that one ray of sun and those miraculous shadows, let her—

"Madame, it is time to repent," the priest said, moving away from the kneeling figure of General Montaud. "Your time on this earth and in this life is limited. God is preparing to receive you, and you, in turn, must prepare to receive God."

He was standing directly over her. From her downward vision she could see beneath the black hem the tops of gold slippers. Ornately embroidered on the toe of each, in gold-and-black thread, was the symbol of the cross. So fascinated was she by finding the cross in such an unlikely place, she missed the next few minutes, focusing on the tiny crosses which perched just to one side of the priest's big toes.

"Are you, my child?"

At the sound of the high-pitched and insistent voice, she tried to clear her mind and vision of toe crosses, tried to lift her head in search of the full question. "I'm . . . sorry. I didn't . . . hear . . ."

"Are you ready to receive God?" the priest repeated.

"I wasn't aware I had become separated from Him."

Outside the door and beyond in the courtyard she heard voices, many voices, a crowd gathering.

Edward.

"Are you frightened?" the priest asked with unexpected bluntness.

"Yes," she replied with matching honesty.

"That is because your soul is not at peace. You must confess all your sins. Then death will be effortless."

Slowly she glanced around at the semicircle of male faces, knew what they thought of her and what she was, and knew what they wanted to hear in a confessional.

"I . . . have nothing to confess," she murmured, and bowed her head, suddenly embarrassed. Men had approached her in the throes of love and desire all her life, and she'd never once been humiliated. But these men, each passing moral judgment on her, embarrassed her to the quick.

"God will never receive you with blasphemies such as that," the priest scolded sternly. "Kneel before me and confess your crimes, your sins, your . . ."

Suddenly she felt his hand on her shoulder. She tried to stand in an attempt to put the limited distance of the cell between them, but her knees were weak.

"One last chance, my child," the priest intoned, his voice calm, as though he hadn't been too surprised by her refusal of his dubious services. "Kneel and confess."

"No."

"Kneel and confess."

"I have nothing to confess."

"You murdered a man."

"In self-defense."

"In God's eyes that makes no difference."

"It should."

"Do you presume to instruct God?"

"When I think He warrants it."

"God forgive her, for she knows not . . ."

Suddenly the absurdity vaulted. How foolish, all of it, herself included, a lifetime of effort, the petty fears of trifling anxieties which at the time had loomed mountainous before her. And most absurd of all, the energy, the incredible energy required in order to wage the battle with life.

From her vantage point she saw too clearly. There had been less than half a dozen moments in her entire life that had been capable of transcending the smallness of inconsequential action. There had been fewer than three people—only one, really—who had enabled her to glimpse the shore of that extraordinary spiritual country that lay beyond the confines of this reality.

New movement, new noise drew her attention. She looked up to see the six young soldiers in formation, two by two. Her head turned in all directions. Was it time?

Too soon!

She tried to ignore the woman crying within her and concentrated on the folds of her blue silk gown, which, despite the dried bloodstains, was still lovely.

Poor Madame Charvin. . . .

Now the soldiers passed before her where she sat on the low stool, each managing to look her straight in the eye before he quickly crossed himself and moved on.

The fourth, an incredibly young-looking boy with bright red hair and brighter cheeks, stopped before her, crossed himself, and whispered, "Forgive me . . ."

"You've not offended me." She smiled, wanting to touch his hand, which was so close, but she dared not. She watched him as far as the cell door, wishing he'd look back so she might give him a last reassuring smile, but he never lifted his eyes from the floor.

"One last chance, my child . . ."

She looked up to see the two remaining in her cell: General Montaud, and of course, the priest, who had pocketed his rosary and was now thumbing through his elegant new Bible. Again she was struck by the realization nothing on this priest looked worn, not even the man himself, though he was clearly well past middle age. His brow was unlined, no telltale track marks of time around his eyes or mouth. Even the black cassock looked new, as did the delicate lace which Elizabeth was certain had never been laundered. Everything new, unused, untested.

"God gives one and all, from the mightiest king to the lowliest sinner, a second chance," he pronounced, not arrogantly or unkindly, merely a statement of fact to which he had dedicated his life.

"Did you hear, my child?"

Why did he persist in calling her that? She was not his child.

"Kneel and confess."

She tried to speak and couldn't, and managed only to shake her head.

"Leave her alone, Father. She's beyond redemption," snapped General Montaud. "Come . . ."

She looked up, not at the indictment but rather at the command. Did he mean for her to come? Was it to be now?

But he ushered the priest out of the door, then followed after him, closing the cell door with a sudden slamming. A second later she heard the bolt sliding, then silence.

Slowly she turned upon the stool, thinking someone had been left. But no one had. She was quite alone in the cell, hearing only the thunderous beat of her pulse, aware of her hands folded and trembling in her lap, her mouth dry with fear.

Hurry, Death.

Someplace, somewhere, she would find a future for herself. That's what she'd told John on that morning over four years ago when she'd turned her back on Eden as well as on . . .

John.

Thank God she would not have to see him again, though she loved him

242

with all her heart. If she were granted one last wish from that angry God who wanted only to hear her confession, it would be that somehow John could make amends to the family he so desperately needed and had so grievously offended.

A slow-moving ray of morning sun crept over the high coal-dust-stained window and somehow managed to filter down on her. There was so much she would miss, so many faces she would never see again, so many voices she would never hear.

She heard the cell door open but lacked the will, energy, and desire to look up. Of far greater comfort and fascination to her was the pattern of light and shadow warming her hand.

His only coherent thought as he stood in the low doorway of the small cell was that—miracle of miracles—he was enduring the unendurable. The palms of his hands still ached from the death grip he'd maintained on the reins during the high-speed trip to La Rochelle. He remembered praying twice—God forgive him—that old Bates's ploy had worked and that the execution had already taken place.

But upon their arrival at La Rochelle a short while ago they'd heard that the Englishwoman had attempted an escape and that the execution had been postponed until nine-thirty.

"Fifteen minutes," the guard barked as he drew open the heavy cell door, "not a second more. That one has thrown off the entire prison schedule," he muttered, bobbing his head toward the woman who sat slumped on the small stool, staring intently at the back of her hand. She didn't even look up as the cell door was closed behind him.

Courage, he begged himself. Remember, *she is the one in need of comfort, as she has comforted you since you were a child.*

"Elizabeth?"

As he spoke her name, all his good intentions fled, and as she looked up, frightened, and he saw the wound on her forehead, he found himself incapable of further speech. He took one step forward and opened his arms. She appeared to hesitate for a moment as though she wasn't certain if the offer of shelter could be trusted. Then she got up and reached out to him. He held her close and felt dull and senseless with grief he could not, for her sake, display.

For several minutes neither spoke. John was content with the silence and the closeness, until he remembered both were limited to fifteen minutes.

Once he had had a lifetime, now only minutes.

Though it was the least important matter on his mind, it seemed safe and therefore appropriate and he asked softly, "Where did you manage to obtain that gown? If you're not careful, all female prisoners will demand one as pretty."

"It . . . was pretty, once," she whispered, looking down at the dried bloodstains.

"And still is." He smiled and carried her to the low stool, where he eased her down, holding on to her for a few moments to see if she could manage for herself.

Now she looked up at him with an expression of intolerable sadness. "I . . . wish—"

"For what?" he interrupted, settling himself stiffly on the cold floor before her, holding on to her hand as he used to do when he was a child.

"I wish you hadn't come," she said.

"Why?" he demanded with mock sternness. "You would have come to me, wouldn't you?"

The simple logic of love seemed to penetrate. And soothe. She reached out her right hand and smoothed back his hair.

"Of course." She smiled, caressing his face. "Please help me to speak directly, John," she said quietly, but with new strength and conviction. "I was mistaken earlier when I said I wished you hadn't come," she went on. "We both know what will take place in a few minutes, but we mustn't think on it now. It will come soon enough."

Please, don't! a voice begged from deep inside him, and somewhere the child within him ran away from the nightmare and successfully blotted out everything.

"You must listen," she begged with greater intensity, as though she knew him well enough to know precisely what he was doing. "If you love me now or have ever loved me," she said, "then promise me one thing . . ."

He nodded.

"If I could share the rest of my life with you, I would work diligently for one cause, the restoration of your family, all those people who love and need you and whom you love and need, drawn back to you and to Eden. Do you understand?"

The damned tears could not be controlled, so he dared not look up, and again merely nodded.

"You need them, John, more than they need you, I suspect. Otherwise, you wouldn't have behaved as you did. Please understand, my dearest," she whispered. "I say this out of the endless reservoir of love I feel for you."

"I . . . drove *you* away as well," he muttered.

Incredibly, she smiled. It was reflected in her tone of voice. "Yes, but I always knew I would return. I always knew the man I raised and loved as my own son would see the pattern and direction of his life and find it as foreign and as lacking as did all those who loved him."

Slowly he looked up, weary of concealing his grief. If their last minutes were to be honest ones, then grief must certainly be given its due.

"I . . . d-don't understand," he stammered, uncaring if the tears were visible.

"You are your father's son," she said simply. "Oh, John, promise me further you will find your sons and bring them home where they belong."

He nodded.

"And Richard and his wife, they must be reinstated, both in your affection and at Eden, for only through them will the line continue."

Again he nodded.

Now for the first time she reached out for his hand and held on as though it were the only lifeline in a tumultuous sea. "And Mary needs you more than anyone else," she whispered.

Her voice broke and John saw Mary in memory after the police had brought her back to Elizabeth's house in Saint George's Street, her once lovely hair butchered close to her scalp, rope burns on her wrists, the grisly script of the assault writ clear upon her face—and *his* hand behind it all, his pact with the three ruffians whom he had hired to frighten her.

But the weight of memory could not be borne, and apparently she felt his pain. She slipped to her knees before him and gathered him to her with surprising strength. For a few moments he closed his eyes and was a child again back on Oxford Street.

"But first and most difficult of all," she murmured, caressing his hair, the back of his neck, "you must forgive yourself. If you can find it in your heart to do that, the rest will follow, I promise you."

He held on to her as she had held on to him earlier, and blindly nodded, wishing his life would end here, before they came for her, before . . .

"Remember me," she whispered.

John continued to cling to her, and told himself he did not hear the cell door opening.

"Time, madame," General Montaud said loudly, cutting through the murmurs of promises requested, promises given. "Well, I see she got on her knees for you," the general went on, "which is more than God can say."

John started up with a sense of nothing to lose, would have risen instantly to his feet had it not been for Elizabeth's restraining hand.

"Don't, please, John," she begged. "He can say nothing that will hurt us. Listen to the voice of your father. He's here, speaking to us both. Can you hear?"

From the radiance on her face he was certain she was hearing something not of this world. But as for himself, all he could hear was the crowds outside the cell; and the reality he was facing—the most awesome moment of his life—he was totally ill-equipped to meet.

With a wave of his hand, General Montaud summoned two soldiers into the small cell. "Visitors out!" the general commanded. "I kept my word; now, you keep yours."

John tried for one last time to memorize her features against the moment they would be taken from him. But every thought process seemed to balk at the effort, and all he was aware of were the two soldiers coming around behind her, reaching for her arms.

At the precise moment he started angrily forward, two more soldiers appeared in the room, though these two were led in by an unexpected ally—old Bates himself, who appeared to position himself between them and where John stood.

Bates looked awful—half-dead with fatigue . . . and something else. As soon as they had successfully rescued Elizabeth from this wretched place, John vowed to give Bates a holiday.

Now: "Get her things," he commanded of Bates, at last aware why the old man was here. He'd come to help with her luggage. "Where are your belongings, Elizabeth?" he demanded, outraged to find the soldiers already restraining her.

Her eyes seemed to be trying to warn him of something, but all he could see clearly were the dried bloodstains on the blue silk bodice.

"Release her!" he commanded with all the old authority and imperiousness he could muster.

245

"Sir, please, I beg you," came Bates's fatigued voice from behind.

"Get him out of here," came the second male voice, arrogant, insistent.

"No . . ."

He heard only old Bates's single protest before he felt his own arms wrenched behind him.

"Take her out of here, Bates. I command you. Did you hear? Make them release her and take her quickly to a place of safety where my father can . . . You must!" he begged, struggling against the combined strength of the two French soldiers, years younger and in their prime.

"Sir, please come . . ." said Bates, realizing for the first time that his master was no longer rational.

"Get him out of here," came General Montaud's command again, and now he felt himself being half-dragged, half-carried to the door, though he continued to struggle for one last look, one word . . .

As the cell door closed behind him, the two soldiers tightened their grip and continued to drag him toward the low arched entrance which led to the courtyard.

"Please, sir," Bates continued to plead, hobbling first to one side, then the other, "I beg you. Let me lead you out of—"

"No!" John struggled again, his arms wrenched backward at a painful angle, until it occurred to him if he were expelled from the prison a second time he would have absolutely no chance of helping Elizabeth to escape.

And escape was still very much a viable possibility—at least in one part of his mind. He looked ahead through the arched entrance into the courtyard to see a crowd of almost a hundred people—some from the prison community itself, trustees and staff, curiosity seekers, journalists, and a large contingent of officials.

"Sir, please, there is no point, nothing more that can be done . . ."

Bates again. But John did not respond.

A few steps beyond the arched door, the two guards halted. They said something in French, and he waited, head down, for Bates to translate.

"They asked if you were man enough to walk by yourself to the spectators' box," Bates murmured.

The second soldier spoke. Bates translated. "General Montaud has given them instructions to stay with you. One more outburst, and you will be expelled." Suddenly his voice fell silent and he stepped close to John, his right hand extended in desperate entreaty. "Oh, please, sir, let us depart now, before . . . It will serve no purpose . . ."

John watched the old man and saw, not fear for himself, for he suspected Bates to be almost fearless, but something else. And as he spoke, the voice of reason and sanity was urging him to listen and take heed.

Ultimately he was left with only silence. Yet he knew what he had to do, had known all along.

Slowly he straightened up, briefly rubbed his upper arms where the grip of the guards had impeded circulation. As he passed beneath the archway and started across the upper end of the courtyard, he was aware the crowds fell suddenly silent, as though with his appearance the main attraction was about to commence.

Papa, who is Elizabeth? Is she my mother?

246

No, but she loves you very much and you are always to love her.

"Sir, please, the general himself has advised against this." Old Bates was back, and from the echo of softly treading footsteps, not alone. The two guards were shadowing, but ready to pounce at the least provocation.

If anything happens to me, John, take Elizabeth to Eden and stay with her.

Yes, Papa.

"Sir, please . . ."

But he merely walked ahead, passing by Bates as though he were invisible. Other voices from other places were filling John's head now. His father was walking with him, as vivid, as real as when they had walked together when John was a child.

Do you love Elizabeth, Papa?

Oh, yes, John, very much.

Why?

Because her heart is filled with love.

The black wrought-iron enclosure had two entrances. John took the nearest and saw half a dozen people ease more closely together to make room. When he turned about, he saw Bates and the two guards standing a few feet away. But of greatest interest to him was the small pompous figure who stood in the far archway, Jules Montaud.

Promise me, John, that you will find your sons and bring them home.

Stephen? Frederick? Where were they?

Directly before him in the enclosure he saw a thick black iron bar which ran the width of the enclosure. He reached out with one hand and found it cool but steady, lifted the other, and held on. Bates had been right. He shouldn't be here, because now he doubted seriously his ability to survive. But what was so admirable about survival?

"Sir, please, there's still time to depart. It will serve no . . ."

No!

Across the courtyard he heard the sound of boots marching and looked slowly up, *knowing.* He saw a limited formation of six soldiers, rifles at their shoulders, march in under the command of General Montaud himself.

Then all was quiet in the vast courtyard, the soldiers' boots silenced as they aligned themselves perfectly on the firing line, rifles at ease at their sides, heads erect, eyes straight, facing the three tall posts a distance away.

Papa, help me.

John gripped the iron bar.

I love you, Elizabeth.

He held this thought steady in his mind and tried with all his might to use it as a shield against what was coming.

With his eyes focused on the opposite archway, he saw, perhaps even before anyone else, the hem of that blue silk gown, then the woman herself materializing, small between the two guards. Trailing behind, he saw a rotund black-frocked priest, Bible open and in hand, intoning something.

Elizabeth . . .

247

He spoke her name softly, under his breath.

The crowd now caught sight of her, and he heard a discernible gasp as her beauty registered. Only as they approached the large central post did he observe her faltering in any way, then only very subtly. The guards led her forward until she was facing the post. Then John saw her courage desert her, saw her head, once erect, fall heavily forward.

He closed his eyes and cursed the God who would permit this morning to happen.

He stepped forward until his forehead was pressed against the sharp edge of the black wrought-iron cage, tried to clear his eyes of persistent tears, and wished with childlike simplicity the nightmare would end, and realized with mounting waves of grief that, even as a child, the only person capable of soothing his nightmares had been . . .

"Elizabeth. . . ."

He merely whispered the name, but as he did, he felt something break within him, a major disruption in the feeling, knowing, perceiving part of him. He did not mourn its disruption, but rather welcomed it, clung to it, and prayed only that it would not now desert him.

Never before in Bates's entire sixty-seven years had the world seemed so completely without point or purpose as it did at this moment, for two people were being destroyed for no reason save the mentality of a nation that believed ". . . from time to time it is necessary and wise to kill a few in order to warn the many."

Struggling to control his outrageously offended sense of justice and humanity, Bates tried to maintain a grip on his own feelings, knowing full well Mr. Eden would be unable to, though at the moment, he seemed the picture of docility. Bates turned to the woman. The priest was making the sign of the cross on her forehead. He thought he saw her turn her head away, but he couldn't be certain. In the next moment both the guards and the priest moved away from the post, all walking slowly and in formation back to the area of safety behind the firing line.

Bates was struck by how quiet it was, no sound. The rifles were ready, all six soldiers in the firing position. All life in the prison courtyard was suspended, along with General Montaud's saber, which he held waist-high, his eyes hurriedly making a final check of everything, stopping to dwell the longest on Elizabeth Eden herself.

Enough! Drop it! a voice screamed in Bates's head.

Then it fell, with a sharply barked command, and the first reports came like the slamming of heavy doors in a wind, accompanied by one single inhuman cry of protest from Mr. Eden, who jerked reflexively forward, the cry of "*No!*" leaving his throat in a continuous torturous trail. The crowd turned and was spared the atrocity which had occurred at the opposite end of the courtyard, the first volley of fire slamming the woman against the post with such force her neck cracked. Now her head slumped disjointedly forward upon her chest, the red target torn away as the bullets ripped through her flesh, another red circle, wet and glistening, taking its place. Blood seeped from other wounds on the slim torso. The head lifted only once after the initial shots; then head, body, legs, all slumped against the bondage, and still blood poured forth, wetting the sandy ground, staining the blue silk.

Over and above it all there still persisted the animal cry of protest which echoed about the courtyard, reverberating off the arcades and ultimately shattering every ear, every heart, and every sensitivity within hearing distance.

Most others looked away at the second volley. Mr. Eden did not. As fresh explosions of blood and flesh ripped through the blue silk gown, the scream ceased at last.

Bates tried to see the remains of the two who had died here, the woman hanging grotesquely on the post by the backward angle of her bound hands, and the second corpse, who still stood upright. Mr. Eden's hands now tried to maintain their grip on the iron bar, but could not for their violent trembling. Bates turned his back on the carnage to face the empty arcade which led ultimately to the street, and bowed his head to do something he had not done since he was a boy of five.

He wept.

Talbot House, Dublin, Ireland November 15, 1874

For several days Lord Harrington had maintained a constant vigil at Stephen's bedside, had watched Rose O'Donnell come and go with her various tortures disguised as ministrations, and had found himself thinking more and more often of the gentleness and ease with which dear Elizabeth had been capable of getting the boys to do anything. After Lila's death and while John had buried himself in his work in London, Elizabeth had become a surrogate mother to the two children.

Now, in the early-morning hours, bleary-eyed from lack of sleep, Lord Harrington watched the pale drawn face of his elder grandson and found, curiously, he was unable to keep his thoughts away from Eden Castle and those marvelously happy days at the beginning.

He shifted uncomfortably in his chair—it had served as his bed the better part of the night. As he tried to stretch his cramped muscles, he thought how pleasant it would be to see Elizabeth again.

Suddenly he felt a strange suffocation in his throat, as though an air passage had been blocked. He tried to straighten his back, keeping a close eye on Stephen, who continued to sleep restlessly upon his pillow. Twice in the predawn hours the boy had called out, "Papa!" in his delirium. The sound of the small voice uttering that word had deeply moved Lord Harrington, caused him to think on his own lost child. Now, as the inner conflict mounted, he got up and made his way to the French doors which gave a perfect view of the east meadow, where the foals were kept in the spring and where the boys loved to play.

Now there was a chill fog covering the ground, a light chill rain beginning to pelt the glass panes. It was a winter mood, a winter scene, and somehow it suited him.

Behind him on the large feather bed he heard a sudden restlessness. Looking back, he was surprised to see Stephen awake, watching him.

"Grandpapa . . ."

The small voice carried and thrust a question into Lord Harrington's mind and soul. Why had God permitted two such innocent lambs to be brought into the world, then abandoned?

"I'm here." He smiled, hurrying to the bedside, where the normally robust and ruddy Stephen looked shrunken, diminished by his illness.

"What is it?" Lord Harrington inquired, concerned, leaning closer. "Can I get you something? Water?"

The boy shook his head and closed his eyes. He was weak and growing weaker; Lord Harrington knew that much. He'd exchanged harsh words last night with Rose O'Donnell over the boy's treatment, was prepared to have them again today if the senseless bleeding did not stop.

"Stephen, what is it?" he asked again, concerned with how pale and lifeless the boy was becoming.

"I . . . dreamed," Stephen began.

"Of what?" Lord Harrington prodded, curious to know the nature of the nightmares which caused the boy to cry out so often.

"I . . . don't know, Grandpapa," he whispered, "but it was as real as Talbot House."

"It was a house?"

The boy shook his head and swallowed hard. "Not a house," he said. "Big. Bigger than Talbot House, with long dark passages."

Lord Harrington listened carefully, fearful of the boy's dream even before he had identified it. "And what else?" he prompted.

"Frederick was there," Stephen said, staring up at the ceiling, "but he was real little, just a baby, and . . ."

"What happened?"

"I was in a room, a big room, and it was warm because there was sun coming from . . . someplace, and I had been asked by . . . someone . . ." As his memory faltered, he looked up at Lord Harrington as though help could be forthcoming.

". . . to sing," he concluded. A half-smile altered the paleness on Stephen's face. "I was . . . scared, I remember . . ."

"Of course you were, though without reason. Can you remember who asked you to sing?"

The boy nodded. "A lady. Her face and head were all covered in black. I couldn't see her face."

Lady Harriet. Stephen had seen Lady Harriet, and the long dark passageways were Eden Castle. Yet it had been at least five years ago, the boy a mere babe himself.

"What else?" Lord Harrington prompted, curiosity joining his concern. How odd! He too had been revisiting Eden via dream and memory.

"There were . . . some other ladies present," Stephen went on. "Several, and some I couldn't see very clearly. There was one . . . dark, like Indian dark . . ."

Dhari! John's mistress.

". . . and there was a nice woman." Stephen smiled, closing his eyes. "She hugged me as I passed her by, and she smelled so good."

Elizabeth, without a doubt, Lord Harrington thought. He'd once con-

251

templated marrying the woman after his wife had died, after he and Lila had moved to Eden. But she wouldn't have him. Lord Harrington suspected years ago she'd given her heart to John's father, Edward Eden.

"And Mama was there," Stephen said at last, his small thin voice filled with sorrow.

"How . . . do you know it was your mother?" Lord Harrington asked.

"I know." The boy shrugged with supreme self-confidence. "When I finished the song, she hugged me and kissed me and said she loved me more than anything in the world."

Lord Harrington turned quickly away from the boy's close scrutiny.

"Grandpapa?"

"Yes," he said kindly, back safely turned.

"This isn't . . . my home, is it?"

He looked back. "For now it is," he said.

"But it hasn't always been."

"No."

"Is my name Harrington or Eden?"

"You know the answer to that one."

"Then I'm an Eden?"

He hesitated. "Yes."

"Then where is my father?"

Lord Harrington gaped at the boy who had just voiced the question he'd dreaded having to answer for the last five years. "I . . . don't know," Lord Harrington said.

Just in the process of walking farther away, he looked back to see Rose O'Donnell in the doorway, bearing the various pieces of equipment she'd been using too long in an attempt to cure Stephen.

"Lord Harrington," she said brusquely with a sharp nod of her head, as though she sensed his antagonism. "You must let the boy rest."

He nodded quickly, hearing a plaintive sound from Stephen, as though the boy had perceived the new presence in the room and the pain which always accompanied her appearance.

With sudden resolve Lord Harrington vowed not to have it today. He would get rid of the woman first before he'd allow her to continue with the daily bleedings, which clearly were not healing. "Mrs. O'Donnell," he commanded with unexpected sharpness, then foundered without the least idea what he would say next.

She raised up from her position bent over Stephen. As yet she'd inflicted no damage, content merely to feel of his forehead. "Sir?" she asked. The backward angle caused her to resemble a large vulture with its prey.

"I . . . was thinking . . ." *What*? "I . . . would like for you to . . . return to Eden for me, if you will, that is."

At last the old woman raised all the way up from Stephen's bed, a new light on her face. Something had caught her attention.

"But, sir, I only just returned from—"

"And now I want you to go back."

"I . . . don't understand."

"You said Mr. Eden was returning from France with Elizabeth Eden."

"He went to fetch her, yes."

"I would like to know if they are safely returned."

She nodded once, though an expression of bewilderment still lingered on her harsh worn features.

"Of course you will be justly compensated," he reassured her.

"I . . . was thinking on . . . him," she whispered, nodding toward the boy.

"I think he's beyond danger now," Lord Harrington said without conviction, wondering how much the boy's mysterious dreams were contributing to his debilitating illness.

"I don't know." Rose O'Donnell hesitated. "It seems such a long trip for such a—"

"I said you'd be justly compensated," Lord Harrington snapped.

The woman seemed to hear the anger more clearly than anything else. She moved away from the bed, her "patient" momentarily abandoned for this new prospect. "And return here immediately?" she inquired, clearly trying to set the limits for her excursion.

Lord Harrington nodded vaguely. "If you wish, you may take additional time . . ."

Slowly she encircled the large double bed, looking down on Stephen but not seeing him. "And you're certain you can handle him?" she asked, coming up alongside the bed.

Lord Harrington nodded, again without conviction. His first wish was to get her away from Stephen.

"I'll not be able to make the same time in this weather," she warned.

He nodded. "I said to take your time. . . ."

"Anything else?" she demanded, abandoning the equipment on the side table by Stephen's bed. Lord Harrington saw from a distance the dreaded knife and white crockery bowl into which the blood was spilled, and saw as well the wide look of fear in Stephen's eyes.

In answer to her question, he thought for a moment and decided. "Yes. Find out, if you can, the disposition of the entire family, how Elizabeth Eden fared during her imprisonment in Paris, and the others as well. All of them."

"Including the grand cock himself?" Mrs. O'Donnell smiled coyly, knowing full well the degree of Lord Harrington's interest in John Murrey Eden.

He turned away from the offensive woman and the equally offensive question. "I'm sure that will be made known to you the instant you pass through the gates," he murmured, turning back to the window.

For several minutes he heard no sound, and as the silence stretched on, his curiosity prompted him to look over his shoulder. To his annoyance, he saw the old bitch praying over Stephen. He started to stop her, then changed his mind. He didn't want to give his true feelings away. He still needed Rose O'Donnell, who was, if nothing else, greedy enough to serve as a reliable go-between.

For a moment she looked sternly down on Stephen, then said, "Now, I want only good reports on you when I return, do you hear?"

Stephen appeared to listen carefully. "Are you going to see my father?"

Even Rose O'Donnell seemed to be taken off guard. She looked sharply up at Lord Harrington, then back down on Stephen. "Of course not. I don't even know who your papa is. So how could I see him? You are a silly thing . . ."

When the door was safely closed again, Stephen looked up. "She lied, didn't she, Grandpapa?"

For a moment Lord Harrington couldn't reply. If Stephen was capable of seeing through Rose O'Donnell, what would prevent him from seeing through Lord Harrington himself with equal facility?

"My father isn't dead, is he?" Stephen asked. "That's what everyone has told me, but I know now it isn't true."

Lord Harrington moved away from the questions, still unable to reply.

"I've dreamed of him every night. I've seen him so clearly. He's ill, Grandpapa, and sad—but not dead."

How long could he hold them here? How long before . . .

Lord Harrington found the thought insupportable. He went directly to the doors, pushed them open, and stepped quickly out to welcome the freezing rain, which cleared his head, if not his heart.

Paris
November 15, 1874
Evening

John Murrey Eden had spent the better part of the day trying to obtain Elizabeth's body—to no avail. Now, Bates thought, he resembles a dead man himself, as though at the exact moment the lifeblood had drained from Elizabeth Eden, it had drained out of him as well.

"Sir? We'll be ready shortly. Are you certain you are capable of traveling?"

As he bent close to Mr. Eden, who sat in Monsieur DuCamp's parlor, he saw the vacancy in the eyes and was stunned anew.

Yet, despite the seriousness of this new silence, Bates had not been overly concerned. There had been far more pressing matters at the time, such as how Bates was going to drive the large coach back to Calais, all the time attending to Mr. Eden.

But fate had even managed to provide a solution for that, because as they had made their way back to Monsieur DuCamp's, Bates had spied a familiar figure slumped across the rump of a horse, an equally familiar—though surprising—figure sitting with a bit more dignity in charge of the reins. The "prodigal" had returned, Charley Spade in the mysterious company of black Jason, both much the worse for wear. There was a slight wound on Charley's jaw, and both reeked of whiskey; an empty pouch lay beneath Charley's jacket containing . . . nothing.

Thank God! Bates had breathed with relief as he'd inspected the pouch. If that had come too late . . .

Bates had thought once the unexpected appearance of the man who had been Mr. Eden's most trusted driver, the West Indian named Jason, would make a difference, but it hadn't. Jason himself appeared to be in only slightly better shape than Charley Spade, though apparently it had

255

been Jason who finally with difficulty had led them safely back to Rue Saint Jacob.

Returning from the ordeal at La Rochelle to find these two disreputable men slumped on one horse, Bates had given them exactly three hours to make themselves ready for the return trip to London.

"Sir, I beg you," Bates whispered now, keeping his voice down, as the small room was beginning to fill with dinner guests for the first sitting. "We'll be ready to leave shortly. Would you like . . . ?"

But there was nothing. It was as Bates had predicted. Two had been murdered this day.

Beyond the arch he saw the West Indian making a last trip down the stairs with the final trunk. "Jason!"

At Bates's first call the man deposited the trunk in the hallway and presented himself.

"Would you please assist Mr. Eden to the carriage while I . . . ?"

There was no need to complete the command. Jason approached with sad reverence the chair where Mr. Eden sat. Without a word he reached down for the lifeless arms and guided him up, murmuring, "We must go home, sir. We must go home."

In the next moment, as Jason was attempting to turn him toward the front door, Mr. Eden's knees buckled. He would have collapsed altogether if it hadn't been for Jason's superior strength. Quickly he lifted Mr. Eden into his arms and carried him, childlike, through the gaping guests.

Bates hurried ahead to open the front door and encountered a very pale and bleary-eyed Charley Spade just hurrying in.

"There's a woman outside," he murmured to Bates, keeping his voice down. "Wants to see Mr. Eden, she does." That was all he said. He hoisted the trunk effortlessly onto his shoulder and marched on through the door, leaving the muddle to Bates, who peered out and saw an old woman dressed entirely in black slowly approaching him. A heavy dark cloak obscured the specifics of her features, and in her arms she clutched a flat rectangular wicker case—more than clutched it. Clung to it as though it were the only source of life itself.

Charley Spade, who stood to one side of the old woman, a hand on her elbow, was saying, "Mr. Bates, please. This lady would like very much to speak with Mr. Eden. With your permission, of course."

"On what matter?" Bates demanded sternly.

Charley Spade looked up at the question. "I . . . don't know," he faltered.

Bates drew a sharp breath. "Madame," he began as kindly as possible, "Mr. Eden has suffered a severe shock today and now requires privacy. If you would be so good as to state the nature of your business with him, I will be happy . . ."

All at once, for the first time, that coarsely woven black hood lifted, revealing a worn old French face which, to Bates's surprise, was streaming tears.

"Madame!" he repeated in concern. "Come," he murmured, giving in, and took her arm to guide her toward the carriage and the open door, thankful to let her see Mr. Eden.

To his surprise, the woman seemed to draw away hesitantly at first, as though in protection of the wicker case. Then he saw her look ahead into

256

the carriage, spy her goal, and, still clutching the container under one arm, pull herself into the carriage to settle stiffly in the seat opposite Mr. Eden.

Bates considered the civility of an introduction and only at the last moment realized he didn't know the old woman's name. "Madame, you must . . ." he began, and never finished.

Suddenly she pushed the black hood all the way off her head and in the process revealed the severe dark gray dress of La Rochelle Prison. She clutched the wicker case to her with even greater strength and murmured a splintered introduction of her own.

"Mr. Eden, I had to see you. I . . . spent the last night with Elizabeth Eden. My name is Madame Charvin."

Should she have come? That question continued to plague her even as she sat opposite the ghostlike man, aware that what she had to say and do would only contribute to the hell he'd already walked through.

Yet there was *her* purgatory to consider as well. She'd been dismissed by General Montaud, her funds confiscated, turned out on the street with only the clothes on her back. Of course this mattered, but not so much as the question which continued to haunt her. *Could she have stopped it*?

She looked at the man opposite her. Lord, but she felt as though she knew him. In the last week Elizabeth Eden had talked constantly, compulsively, of two men, John Murrey Eden and his father, Edward Eden. The father was dead, and now the son looked as though he would have given his kingdom to follow them both to the grave.

"Sir, hear me out. I'll be brief. I had to come," she went on, and thought surely to capture his attention this time. But still his gaze had not altered. In fact, the only movement discernible was a trembling in his left hand.

Now there was movement from the old man who hovered just outside the door. "Go ahead and state your business," he suggested with an air of helplessness. "We have no way of knowing if Mr. Eden . . ."

As his voice dwindled, Madame Charvin understood. Still clutching the wicker case with its precious cargo, she leaned up. "Did you hear me, sir?" she asked softly. "She talked of you with the greatest of love." She hoped to comfort, thinking to ease her own pain in the process.

"I have something I must give to you, but first give me your attention. . . ." Still there was nothing moving in the face opposite her. "Here," she said, thrusting the wicker case across the narrow aisle, weary of the encounter. "I heard you had requested her body," she said, hearing the absurdity of her own comment, "and I felt you should know why it was denied you."

For the first time she saw a barely discernible movement on Mr. Eden's face. It was only in the eyes, which seemed to lift as though the man were flinching from an anticipated blow.

"Since the communes four years ago," she spoke on, her hope buoyed by that one faint movement, "the prison has made it a policy to dispose of all executed prisoners for fear of martyrdom and the rebirth of the movement. . . .

"Here, sir," Madame Charvin said finally, and thrust the wicker case all the way across the aisle. "I was fortunate to get it. . . ."

At first she saw no alteration in his face.

257

"Take it," she urged again.

At last she discerned a shifting in the dead eyes opposite her. "What . . . ?" was the only word which escaped through the dried lips.

"It's her dress, sir, the last thing to touch her, and I can vouch for the fact it made her happy, and she looked so beautiful . . ."

At first she was shocked by the sound of strangulation. Only when she looked down was she aware all the time she'd been talking she had been unclasping the wicker case, had lifted the lid, and . . .

Dear God! Why hadn't she noticed it before in the cellar where the bodies of executed prisoners were taken before secret burial in a monastery graveyard outside Paris. She had a friend who tended these bodies, and he had said she could have the dress. There, in the darkness of the dungeon, she'd failed to see what she saw now: the bloodstained bodice, the blue silk fabric ripped where the bullets had torn through her.

"Madame, please!" Bates interrupted, indicating the atrocity which she had witlessly brought to Mr. Eden.

"Of course," she murmured, appalled at her own stupidity. Thinking to remove the painful object from Mr. Eden's sight, she reached across for the wicker case.

But Mr. Eden was grasping it with both hands.

Bates interceded. "Sir, let her remove it. You don't—"

Whatever it was Bates thought Mr. Eden didn't want or need was never stated. Suddenly, with surprising strength, Mr. Eden successfully ensnared the case and drew it to his side. His left arm wrapped around it in a protective gesture while the other slowly touched the stained fabric.

For a moment Madame Charvin looked between Bates and Mr. Eden, praying for direction, for an excuse to vacate this unhappy place. At last it came from Bates, who reached a hand up and gestured for her to come forward.

She did willingly, taking only a brief backward look at the man bent over the soiled, stained dress.

"I'm . . . so sorry," she muttered as Bates took her arm to turn her away, though as he did, a sudden cry came from the front of the carriage.

"Sir!" The alarmed voice belonged to Bates, who stepped forward. Madame Charvin saw the cause of their alarm—Mr. Eden himself, who had now stepped out through the opposite door of the carriage, still clutching the wicker case, directly into the early-evening traffic of the street.

"Sir!" Bates called again, panic rising in his voice as he hurried back to the pavement, prepared to step off into the same flow of carriages and wagons which now, with some difficulty, were trying to avoid the man as he stumbled toward the far curb.

"Wait, sir!" Charley Spade called down, looking at Bates this time. "I'll go." With that, Madame Charvin saw him jump down from his high seat.

The old man, Bates, called up something to the black man, instructing him to stay with the carriage, then he too started across, both men in pursuit of the man who had already disappeared into the pedestrian traffic across the way.

She turned once, without direction, on the cobbles. Where was he going? Where did he hope to find safety and comfort in this insane world? Where was *she* to go? How would an old woman survive, unprotected?

She stood for a moment, head cocked to one side as though awaiting an answer. But there was none, save for the bells of Saint Germain des Prés announcing evening matins. Of what earthly good were bells when the soul was deaf?

She bowed her head and started slowly down the street in search of a reason to be alive.

"After him! Quick!" Bates shouted, literally shoving Charley Spade ahead of him. My God, what would they do if . . . ?

"Hurry! Find him!" It was unthinkable what had happened. One moment Mr. Eden had been sitting docilely in the carriage awaiting departure for England, and the next . . .

Breathless from his sprint, Bates drew to one side in an attempt to catch his breath, at the same time craning his neck to see up ahead over the onslaught of people.

Where were they?

Surely Charley Spade could overtake him. Mr. Eden had not had more than a few minutes' head start.

As the pedestrian traffic around him increased, Bates clung to the red-brick wall for a moment longer, feeling curiously numb, as though a decision had been made.

Transitions! God, how he hated them, always had. And what in the name of God had possessed Mr. Eden to bolt? And what if Charley Spade could not find him and bring him back? And what would a half-dead man, who did not know the language nor care to know it, do in Paris? And who would understand the mysterious and grisly contents of that wicker case?

Bates continued to cling to the brick wall, and realized he was afraid. Not for himself. He could always hang on to some small piece of sanity for the simple reason he'd never had the courage to invest that much of himself in life.

Rather, he was afraid for John Murrey Eden, who had made it a habit of investing all he had in every aspect of life, who had started on a descent this night from which Bates feared no man could rise intact.

Grosvenor Square, London December 5, 1874

With the unhappy impatience of a man who was one place and knew he was needed elsewhere, Lord Richard read the hastily penned note from Bates for the third time and found it made no more sense than it had when Aslam had first thrust it at him earlier this evening.

Disappeared?

That was the most puzzling word of all. "Mr. Eden just . . . disappeared."

Lord Richard stood up from the narrow confinement of the writing bureau, feeling an uncomfortable mix of anger and apprehension begin to build inside him. Would he never be free of John Murrey Eden? Since they had first met as mutually unhappy boys that stormy night at Eden Castle so long ago, John had always managed to occupy one-half of Richard's consciousness, either in love or hate.

Now he paced restlessly before the dying fire, listening for the familiar sound of a boot on the stairs outside the door.

Aslam.

He should have been home by now. A late-night dinner meeting with the board of directors of the Great Northern Assurance firm had called him away. *They* were courting Aslam, hoping to woo a small percentage of the firm's massive profits for private investment.

Thinking on the young man, Richard glanced quickly toward the door, then looked back into the fire, suffering a twinge of guilt. He shouldn't be here at all, what with Eleanor's confinement due to end any day. He should be in Kent with her at Forbes Hall.

Eleanor. Her first child. It had been a difficult pregnancy and surely would be a difficult delivery. He did love her, he thought with curious sorrow. He desperately wanted the child to be a son, next in the long line of barons and earls that stretched unbroken back to the tenth century. In that roundabout way his tumbling thoughts brought him directly back to the tragic letter from old Bates which had just been delivered by special courier this afternoon.

If something had happened to John, Eden Castle was his again, and his son's.

"My Dear Sirs," Bates's letter began, penned in a neat though broad penmanship. The first paragraph tended toward fulsomeness and social amenities, the old man informing them of Parisian weather and Parisian temperament. Then, without warning, came the most incredible line in the letter: "Following Elizabeth Eden's execution by firing squad, Mr. John Murrey Eden disappeared into the congestion of evening traffic, and despite the concerted efforts of myself and Jason and a colleague from Eden Point, Mr. Charley Spade, we have been unable to trace him."

There was more, but each time Richard read the letter, he found it increasingly difficult to get past that paragraph unscathed. Every sentence, every word, carried with it a complete set of hazards.

Following Elizabeth Eden's execution by firing squad . . .

Suddenly Richard felt weak. "Dear God," he prayed. He bowed his head and thought of the date inscribed on the letter: November 20, five days after the execution. Was the message still true? Was John still missing?

Listen! There was a footstep. Aslam? He couldn't tell, looked in that direction and suffered a split-second image of Eleanor, swollen and uncomfortable with child, missing him—at least, that's what she'd wept out last week as he was preparing for this brief sojourn. Business, he had told her, comfortable with his lie, for it *had* turned out to be business, family business, though he hadn't known that when he'd left Kent. Still, there it was, a family decision pressing, which could . . .

He sat up straight and heard it again, hesitant footsteps coming up the stairs. Not Aslam, who frequently took them two at a time.

A knock at the door, followed by a crackling, very breathless old female voice. "Mr. Alex Aldwell, wanting to see you, Lord Richard. What words shall I use?"

Richard stared a moment longer at the letter, only then remembering he'd sent a message around to Aldwell's flat, asking him to come around to the Grosvenor Square house as soon as possible. With regret he remembered he'd told Aldwell nothing of the contents of the message, which meant there was Aldwell's grief and shock to be dealt with, and like everyone else who had known Elizabeth Eden, Aldwell's heart had been taken prisoner years ago.

"Send him up right away," he called through the closed door.

A few moments later he heard new movement on the stairs, heard a forceful knock on the door, and even as he was in the process of calling out "Come," the door opened and there was Alex.

"Well, where are they?" he demanded. "I came as fast as I could. I had a damned meeting over in Southwark, but I felt they'd understand, and Elizabeth particularly. I'm sure she remembers what it was like in those good early days of the John Murrey firm. No rest for the evil. And John, is he . . . ?" Aldwell looked around the room, confused.

"Alex," Richard began, thinking, after a brief warning of bad news, to let the man read the letter for himself.

"Well, where are they?" Aldwell demanded again, hands on hips, clearly ready for a reunion. "Come on, Richard, where are they hiding?" Aldwell grinned. "In the bedchamber?"

He took three steps toward the door, then slowly stopped. "Where are . . . ?" he tried to ask, obviously couldn't, and took one additional look about the large room. "You sent a . . . note," he said feebly.

Richard again decided not to interrupt, to say nothing until Alex indicated with his silence he was ready to be told.

Then it came, a sudden draining of all life, though his eyes seemed to have found the crumpled letter in Richard's hand. "I . . . trust your wife is well, Lord Richard," he said with strange formality, approaching the fireplace and gently taking the letter from Richard, though not looking at it immediately.

"As well as can be expected," Richard answered. "Delivery soon, we hope."

"So!" Alex exclaimed nervously, lifted the letter, and read.

When several minutes later no sound had broken the silence, Richard stirred himself from his close vigil on the fire and saw Aldwell slumped on the sofa, his head down, still clutching the letter.

"I'm . . . sorry," Richard began, moving toward the collapsed man. "I should have been more . . . specific."

Disjointedly Alex shook his head and turned away, as though speech were still beyond him.

"Did you read the letter in its entirety?" Richard asked, following after the man to the sideboard, where he was in the process of pouring himself a brandy. Good. It would help to clear both the head and the heart.

"I read it." Alex nodded, draining the glass with one swallow.

"And . . . ?"

"And what?"

"What is your opinion?"

Aldwell looked at his empty glass as though he were contemplating another. "I have no opinion," he said gruffly, moving away from the sideboard, as though away from temptation. "He killed her," he accused suddenly, seeking the safe warmth of the fireplace. "I heard him that morning," he confessed, "years ago. He was a madman, insane, he was," Aldwell went on. "He'd had a couch moved down to the library, you see, claiming that . . . Lila was up there, his dead wife, and she wanted him dead as well . . ."

The large man spoke slowly, each word individually pronounced. "And all he did all day long and all night was stare up at that goddamned painting and talk to it.

"If it hadn't been for Elizabeth . . ." Again his voice broke.

Richard returned to the sofa, mindless with grief.

"Well," Aldwell said at last, a degree of dispatch in his voice, as though he knew better than anyone the futility of what they were doing, "if you're asking me direct what I think should be done about . . . the disappearing man . . ." The emphasis on the word "disappearing" was weighted with sarcasm. "In my opinion . . ." He paused, as though assessing privately what he was about to state publicly.

Into this new silence Richard heard a steady, measured tread on the stairs and recognized it immediately. "Aslam," he murmured to Aldwell, who, looking up, had already heard it as well.

"Has he . . . seen . . . ? Does he know?" Aldwell asked as Richard started toward the door.

"Oh, yes. It was addressed to him."

At that moment the door was pushed open, and there he was, tall, slim, sober, those dark eyes immediately recording everything.

"The meeting," Richard began. "How was the board of directors?"

"Satisfactory," came the blunt reply as Aslam meticulously closed the door. "Good evening, Aldwell. I'm glad you're here. We'll need two recording clerks tomorrow morning at the general board meeting. I will make a major proposition concerning the disbursement of stock dividends."

Richard saw Aldwell nod. He saw both men carefully avoid eye contact with each other, neither speaking on any subject at all, as though the most logical one, John Murrey Eden, must be avoided at all costs.

Fascinated by this unexpected drama, Richard perched on the back of the sofa and wondered how he would manage going through it all again—for Eleanor would have to be told. After the birth of the baby, of course.

Abruptly his thoughts came to a halt. Aslam was adjusting the small gas lamp and opening a large brown envelope, looking for all the world like a man preparing to work.

Richard returned to the sofa and lifted Bates's letter into the air. "I think before we get settled into other activities, we have an important piece of unfinished business."

Both men looked up. Alex turned slowly, a weariness to his face, as though memory had assaulted him again and taken a toll. "Eden's ill-equipped to handle . . . things on his own," Aldwell muttered. "If he's truly taken off on his own, then he will be dead shortly, if not already."

Richard saw Aslam sit up straight, the writing portfolio totally forgotten. "Do you think that's possible? The fact of his death, I mean."

Alex nodded. "Of course. He was ill when he left here. Elizabeth's death . . ." Again something overtook him and all he could do was shake his head.

"Then I suggest we do nothing," came the clear, clipped voice of the man behind the desk, who had once again begun to thumb through the large file. Richard detected a new pleasure in Aslam's voice, as though the thought of John dead was extremely pleasing to him.

Still, to do nothing . . .

"I don't think we want to do that, Aslam. Some effort should be made . . ."

The young man looked serenely up at the challenge. "And why not?" Aslam replied lightly. "I have no intention of providing old Bates and his two cohorts with a French holiday while John does what he's done best all his life, which is to stage his own drama to the amusement of no one but himself." He paused and again looked searchingly, hopefully at Aldwell. "Do you really think he might be dead?"

Alex nodded. "If not now, soon. He's cut off, you see. No way to communicate, no funds, according to Bates." He shrugged. "Oh, God!" he breathed heavily, as though the thought were insupportable.

So grief lurked just beneath the death sentence as well as the condemnation.

"Can old Bates be trusted?" Aslam asked, his voice low.

Alex looked up, puzzled. "I don't under—"

"Can we believe what he says?"

"Well, I'm not certain we have any reason to doubt his word. Why would he make up something like . . . ?" Alex looked merely puzzled at the dark-skinned young man. "If he is alive—I can speak with a degree of certainty—he is suffering—"

"John adores suffering," Aslam broke in. "It is by far his favorite pastime."

"Aslam, please . . ." Alex requested.

"And his second favorite pastime," Aslam went on, "is to inflict suffering on others."

Richard exchanged a quick glance with Aldwell, as though the large man were seeking advice on how and what he should do.

"Do what you will." Aslam stood up and headed toward the bedchamber door. "You will anyway." At the door he stopped and turned back. "I doubt if either of you knows John Murrey Eden in precisely the same manner as I do. But I can assure you *he* will do as he wishes in all matters. If he wishes to disappear, as Bates's letter naively suggested, he will remain out of sight until he is ready to be found. If he's still alive, that is. And nothing you can do will aid the process in any way. Still, do what you will. I want no part in it . . ."

With that he closed the door behind him, leaving Aldwell and Richard staring at the closed door.

Richard was on the verge of apologizing for him when he looked around to see Aldwell rereading Bates's letter. Finally Alex drew his heavy black jacket more closely about him and started toward the outer door. "I will be leaving in the morning on the packet from Dover," he said softly to Richard. "Tell Aslam I will take my own funds for now but expect full compensation in the future. I will return as soon as I hire a competent investigator who will bring us proof of either his life or his death. Also, I will see to it Bates understands precisely what I want him to do."

Puzzled at this contradiction of intent, Richard asked, "Why must you go? We could hire a man from London, send a courier with funds, even instruct Bates to . . ."

But all the time he spoke, Aldwell was shaking his head. "No," he said as Richard fell silent. "I must go. But I'm not going for John. You must make that clear to Aslam. John Murrey Eden can rot in his own private hell—if he hasn't already—as far as I'm concerned." Without looking up, he concluded, "I'm doing it for Elizabeth. She never ceased to love him, and if she were here now . . ." His voice broke.

Richard had thought to say something else, but before he could organize his thoughts, Aldwell was on his way down the steps. Struggling to keep his mind away from dangerous images, Richard bolted the door, thinking as soon as he'd had one small fortifying brandy he'd join Aslam in the bedchamber. But as he turned, his eye fell on Bates's abandoned letter.

I'm not going for John Murrey Eden, who can rot in his own hell. I'm going for Elizabeth.

No matter what he did or what he thought, he could not rid his mind of the image of the woman as she once had been, as she'd entered his life, graced it, warmed it, and left it forever richer.

He looked about frantically and thought he shouldn't be here at all. He should be with Eleanor, enduring the last few days of her pregnancy. Yes, he would leave London in the morning, immediately following a shopping spree during which time he would select rubies for Eleanor, to show his gratitude to her for producing his son.

For a few moments it helped to plan, but ultimately he'd planned everything and there it still was, Bates's letter with that nightmare message: *This is to inform you that Elizabeth Eden was executed by firing squad on November 15. . . .*

London
December 15, 1874

Susan shivered at the back of the freezing tent in Whitechapel and tried to concentrate on the angry words of William Booth, who seemed more like a military man than a man of God. Yet his good works were undeniable, and nightly Susan gave thanks to God for directing her faltering footsteps to this man and his vision, his calling, his service.

Tall, black-bearded, lean; deep-set eyes which saw clearly every flaw, frailty, and injustice that ran rampant in this London world, William Booth did not speak when he could shout, did not walk when he could run, did not comfort when he could challenge and affront, like now.

"Look at you," he cried to the one hundred or so men and women huddled together inside the tent which served as meager protection against the biting December wind. "God demands of you unfaltering obedience under any circumstances, any conditions, and yet you shiver in a faint wind and lack the energy and will and discipline even to raise your voices in a song of thanksgiving. . . ."

As the nightly tirade continued, Susan pulled her heavy cloak more tightly about her, trying hard not to be aware of the creeping numbness in her feet and ankles. Reverend Booth was right. The warmth of God's love should suffice. But it didn't always.

"This is our Christian mission to the heathen of our country," Booth went on, his voice strong and loud, resonant in the cold night air, no sign of faltering, never a sign of weakness or hunger or despair or any of those bothersome hells that plagued ordinary mortal men. In most ways Catherine, his wife, was exactly like him. Susan had never seen such zealous dedication to the cause of unhappy, suffering humanity. In the two weeks since she'd joined their Christian mission on a voluntary basis, she'd witnessed acts of selflessness worthy of a saint.

266

Reverend Booth's primary enemy—besides the bone-racking poverty and disease which plagued London's dockside population—was the church itself, the organized prosperous church that had totally forgotten Jesus was a friend of publicans and sinners and outcasts, that perhaps before you gave them the sublime knowledge of the love of God you may have to give them food and a roof for the night.

In addition to the poor, the curious, the cold, and the hungry, the large tent gave shelter to Reverend Booth's entire volunteer task force of over fifty men and women, Susan among them. Most of them were young, but there were a few older, who had been searching all their lives for a cause greater than themselves to which they could give themselves. Like Susan, perhaps they had been running from a certain destructive force in their lives. Now all had come together, hungry as the lost flock for purpose, direction, and knowledge of that greatest of all lights, God's love.

Suddenly the powerful voice coming from the platform at the front of the tent fell silent. She looked up, to see Reverend Booth bend over the edge of the platform, his hands reaching down to someone, his face obscured by the sharp downward angle of his head. A new hush seemed to fall over the large tent as Reverend Booth helped a man climb up on the platform.

"Ladies and gentlemen," the reverend shouted out over the silent tent, "may I present a lost lamb, a man who in despair turned his back on everything life had to offer him, which was considerable."

Leaning from side to side in an effort to see over the tall man standing directly in front of her, Susan caught only fragmentary glimpses of the platform. Standing head down next to Catherine Booth, she saw a lean man, bearded, gray hair, his head bowed, eyes closed as though he was at prayer.

One phrase stuck in her mind as she struggled to see the "lost lamb" who . . . *turned his back on everything life had to offer him, which was considerable.*

Curious, but in the dock area of London one did not tend to think of lost lambs as having "considerable." She knew from recent and painful experience that the apparently blessed of this world frequently suffered the most, like . . .

John. John Murrey Eden.

She allowed the name to march very sedately through her mind, as though to test it. As a test, it failed. With the very first syllable the man himself was before her in perfect clarity, his eyes, the line of his jaw, the way the sun struck his forehead.

For a few moments she lost all contact with the cold tent, the once "lost lamb" standing between Catherine and William Booth. Silently she turned away from the platform, pushed gently through the crowds behind her, apologizing to the few who looked annoyed at the disturbance, but finally made her way to a deserted place near the rear of the tent, where the chill draft was converted into a cold, angry wind that whipped the hem of her long black skirts and sent shivers of cold over her.

She gripped the stiff canvas and clung to it, appalled she'd not progressed with this private Gethsemane as far as she once had thought. It had been her hope, in leaving, to leave all memory, all feeling behind as well. Instead, his face rose before her, and as she tried to concentrate on

267

the tent, she heard the "lost lamb" introduced as Lord Someone, who had found his silver spoon bitter-tasting and empty.

Susan listened, trying to discipline her mind to the testimony of service. Yet she continued to cling to her small hold on the frozen canvas tent, and still he was there before her, wholly resurrected, until at last his image and his memory were everywhere, in the howling wind, in the mixed voices coming from the platform, and—worst of all—in the pronounced and prolonged silences of the audience itself. Everyone now was listening intently to what was being said.

Still she tried not to see or hear him, suffered both sensory illusions and went weak with need. She closed her eyes and wept as she had not wept for two weeks since she'd arrived in London. She couldn't do it, exist without him, or at least without obsessive thoughts of him, for even in the pain of recall she found life more palatable than without his memory.

"Sister, are you well?"

The voice of concern came from behind. She brushed away her tears and looked over her shoulder and saw Cassie Helms, the large robust woman who had been the first to receive her two weeks ago at the Christian mission.

"Sister?" Cassie inquired again, leaning closer, as though a look at Susan's face would reveal all.

It didn't reveal all, but the sight of tears gave dear Cassie a boost in the wrong direction. "What a good heart you have, Sister Susan," she murmured, placing one ample arm around Susan's shoulders, "to be so moved by a mere tale of salvation. I will tell Reverend Booth. He will want to talk with you, I know, for he has often said the truest love springs from the fullest heart."

The memory of John was still so strong that Susan lacked the energy to offer a correction.

"Come," Cassie urged, apparently hearing Susan's mysterious grief increase, "you must meet Lord Simmons for yourself and allow Reverend Booth to see the visible manifestation of your loving heart."

Again she lacked the strength or the desire to correct the misinterpretation, adding cowardice to her spiritual weakness. What was the matter with her? She hadn't asked for this frailty, had done nothing to court it, prompt it, or encourage it. She wanted only to be free of it and of him— and of all the pain that was pressing down on her.

"Come, Susan, a word from Reverend Booth and your grief will abate. I swear it."

Don't swear, dear Cassie, she thought bleakly, and knew with a sinking heart she was not yet cured of this most awesome illness, and suspected that if a cure existed, it was to be found in long hours of back-breaking labor. To that course of action she pledged her life, and what was left of her heart.

Paris
December 25, 1874

Aldwell felt battered after four days of listening to old Bates describe in graphic detail the barbaric death of Elizabeth Eden and John Murrey Eden's subsequent disappearance. He had bolted without funds, without the slightest knowledge of the French language and, according to old Bates, without purpose or destination.

Aldwell glanced impatiently at his watch and tried not to hear this new description of "that saint's last moments upon this earth." Old Bates clearly enjoyed his role as eyewitness to the grisly tragedy, and for once Aldwell was grateful to the Yuletide revelers who drank noisily at the tables around them in the crowded Saint Sulpice Coach House.

He had been in Paris since December 21, and outside of vaguely accomplishing what he had come for, he'd been here exactly four days too long. And yet what he had accomplished had left him strangely dissatisfied, as though there were a major piece to the puzzling disappearance of John Murrey Eden which even old Bates had overlooked.

In the last few minutes before the coach arrived which would take him back to Calais and the night packet across the channel to England, Alex decided that he was incapable of hearing one more time how Elizabeth Eden had refused the blindfold and had looked her murderers straight in the eye.

"Bates," he said sternly. "We can do nothing for Elizabeth now." He felt awful just saying those words, but there was the truth of it, and the sooner he and everyone else faced it, the better.

Impatiently he turned to look out of the smudged mullioned windows, where a fine sleet was exploding against the casements.

"So you think this inspector will be able to locate John?" It was Bates

269

again, newly quieted, as though—at least for the time being—he had talked himself out.

For that Alex was grateful. For the question itself he was less grateful. It reminded him of the dandified little Frenchman who had applied to their advert. His portfolio had been impressive and he had claimed his specialty was the tracking down of famous and notable persons. Although his price had been exorbitant, Aldwell had paid it on the condition the man report daily to Bates, who was staying on at Monsieur DuCamp's lodging house in the event John came to his senses and returned. Charley Spade and Jason would remain with Bates, at least for a time.

"About Monsieur Clichy," Alex went on, finding it somehow very difficult to keep his thoughts moving in a given direction, "be certain to keep your appointments with him every evening, and if he manages to uncover anything, you let me know at once. By special courier."

Bates nodded, his face a mask which said this was old territory and no need to go over it again.

Alex lifted his mug and drained his mulled cider, wondering if he had time for another and hoping he didn't, even though the steaming liquid would be a good protection against the cold drive to the coast.

"Food, sir?" Bates invited considerately, pointing to the huge side of beef roasting noisily on the spit over the open fire. "It will be a long and cold—"

"No. No, thank you," Alex said, shaking his head. He turned again to the window and peered out. No sight of the coach, but he did see that awful mix of flesh and bone and ragged clothes and cadaverous bodies that always attended the comings and goings of every coach that left from any inn the world over.

Beggars, most of them were, footpads, thieves down on their luck, all hoping for a coin or two from the travelers, who—or so the beggars figured—must have coin to spare if they were paying someone actual money to take them from here to there.

Turning away, Alex saw the large coach pulled by eight horses just turning out of the lane at the end of the road.

"Well," he said, standing with dispatch, seeing absolutely no need to linger. They had said everything that had to be said at least twice.

"Safe trip, sir." Bates smiled, standing as well.

A bellowing voice shouted out the arrival of the coach, and it seemed to Alex half the crowded inn got up and made their way to the door. His heart sank. There was no way all these Frenchmen would be able to get on. But as it turned out, only eight were boarding the coach for Calais, including Alex. The others were apparently only well-wishers.

Bates maintained silence until it was Alex's turn to mount the coach. In one hand he held his small portmanteau, with the other he clamped his soft-brimmed hat, so it wouldn't be dislodged in the strong winter wind.

"God go with you," Bates shouted over the bustling of the crowd.

Alex nodded, thinking he'd never felt a colder wind, and knew the channel crossing would be miserable. As he settled stiffly into the window seat, a fat priest settled next to him, smelling of garlic. For several additional minutes the coach bobbed and sank lower under the weight of heavy trunks thrown atop and secured. Grateful he had brought just one small bag, Alex eased it under his seat.

At that moment the confusion threatened to turn into chaos as the fat priest withdrew from a large case an immense and smelly sausage. Outside the carriage Alex saw the innkeeper, clad in a brown-splotched apron and rolled-up shirtsleeves, wielding the stick end of a large broom, which he swung wildly at the band of beggars, who, tempted by the meat, were creeping ever closer to the carriage, threatening the friends who were seeing off the passengers.

Despite the ugliness of the moment, Alex's heart went out to the beggars. He'd been one of their brotherhood, had been down and alone without funds and terribly in need. Remembering his own grim days following his return from India years ago, he studied the frozen men, saw them all inadequately clothed against the biting wind. A few wore the old army-issue square cap which had been the uniform of the Crimea. Most, Alex realized, were the approximate age to have served in that senseless conflict—which for some reason made the scene even more intolerable.

But the innkeeper was having his way, still swinging the handle end of large broom, dispersing the beggars. Most of them backed away, a few ng their hands in angry and obscene gestures, but most merely ted, like that one, tall, gaunt, his head totally obscured by a rather -looking hooded cloak, which undoubtedly he'd stolen.

ewcomer to the ranks of beggary, was Alex's guess. The cloak, for ng, and for another, that curious wicker case he clutched to his n as he turned away from the muddied area around the coach. ded, finding it easier to concentrate on the retreating beggars Bates's upturned face.

lex heard the cry of the coachman and shifted closer to the in an attempt to put at least an inch of space between himself who had now devoured over half the long sausage, punc- low, deep, pleasurable burps.

ch started forward, Alex lifted his hand to his forehead nd wondered bleakly if the man might as well not be on ith him returning to London.

ain cut through the chaos of departure. *John staged his as he will stage his reappearance when he's ready.*

red and closed his eyes. John, he thought, and ver he was, and thought how much simpler life so.

London
December 25, 1874

Seated alone in the Grand Dining Hall of the mansion ir
Square, Aslam listened to the silence and waited for Maudie
appear with his dinner. The silence suited him, as did the s
alone—and the dinner most certainly would, for over the
had learned to the letter what he liked. Everyone w
learned that lesson early on or they did not serve him
perfectly aware of his imperiousness, and cultivated it a
his great-grandfather, who had been the last emperor
pire until the British had turned Delhi into a caldron o
treachery and corruption. Then, as though the bas
been unable to live with their own monstrous crea
day afternoon they had set the torch to the ent
Palace, his great-grandfather, and three t
wealth, and tradition to the ground, and, ir
out of his birthright to the Peacock Thron

The silence of the room held. A few
thoughts under control. It might have beer
stayed, but he'd remained too long as it wa

Seated at a table designed to serve fifty,
would never make it to Kent in time for Chr
nor chose to bring forth her child today, she w
that brought him the greatest degree of pleasu

Richard would return to him as soon as the wor
her awful cargo. Then he and Aslam had vowed to re
rest of their lives. No more female impregnations, reg
this birth. If the Eden line continued, well and good; a

and good. Besides, as Aslam had pointed out to the amusement of both, there were always John's offspring to corrupt the line further.

Impatiently he looked over his shoulder toward the service door that led down to the kitchen, wondering what the delay was. How long did it take to prepare one hard-boiled egg and a cup of buttered noodles? Not that he was hungry. But he might as well eat now and get it over with. It was simply a bodily necessity, the consumption of food an obscene waste of time.

Outside the windows he heard a distant tinkle of bells, several shouts of "Merry Christmas!" and a sudden sharp peal of a child laughing. He closed his eyes and envisioned a scene so removed, so distant and foreign to this London world, that for a moment he gazed upon it with complete objectivity. But the longer he kept his eyes shut, the clearer that foreign world became, more than clear, literally upon him, absorbing him, welcoming him. A hot, dusty red-dirt courtyard baking in a high-noon sun, old men sleeping around the shaded edges, like discarded bundles of old rags, and there a trellis with climbing red flowers as large as a man's hand. Beyond the high walls of the courtyard he heard a din of street noises, wagons, livestock, vendors hawking, but inside this courtyard it was safe and peaceful.

Until . . .

He groaned softly, bowed his head, and consciously tried to open his eyes but couldn't, as though the scene were holding him against his wishes, certainly against his better judgment.

"Dinner, sir. Sorry to be late. Couldn't get the . . ."

Where was he? Whose voice was that?

"Are you well, sir? Why don't you let Maudie—?"

"Get out!" he whispered, never raising his voice, confident this old woman would obey him—and she did.

The scene faded mercifully, to leave him leaning heavily on his elbows, his hands serving as blinders in a futile attempt not to see his home—or what was left of it after John Murrey Eden had finished exploiting it.

No, it was gone now, blessedly, but he was newly aware of the depth of his hate for John Murrey Eden. *He* had been the trespasser, the corrupter, the very embodiment of the English conqueror, who had marched into Aslam's quiet, sun-drenched country, had proceeded to take any and everything he wanted, from jewels to women to territory to privilege, with no thought or consideration for right or ownership or consequences.

Aslam rubbed his eyes, weary of reliving the past, the origin of his hate for John, and stared straight down into his plate filled with one boiled egg and a small mound of buttered noodles. His hands shook as he pushed up from the table and the bland, uneaten food. Later. Perhaps later. He walked to the high windows and stared down at the empty street. At the far end of the crescent he saw a black-clad figure, a curious black lace parasol hoisted aloft in weak protection against the persistent sleet. There was no special reason why this particular woman caught his eye, except for the fact she had the street and the pavement all to herself.

He paused a moment longer to watch her, thought of her sex and found a new reason to loathe her, a total stranger. As she drew nearer, he noticed wiry tufts of red hair visible beneath the prim broad-brimmed black hat, saw clearly the gewgaws about her neck, chains, pendants, drops, an imprisonment of cheap jewelry, all worn with a distinct air of pride, as though confident of her extreme beauty and good taste.

What in the . . . ?

In surprise, he leaned forward as he saw the woman pause before his Grosvenor Square mansion, her eyes squinting at the facade of the house. Then she started up the steps, lowering her parasol and shaking off the moisture which had accumulated.

Enough, he scolded, blotting her from view by returning to the table and his now cold meal, finding everything on the plate as repulsive as the woman, yet knowing he had to have sustenance of some sort, as it was his intention to pass the rest of this miserable day sorting through the countless blueprints which cluttered his desk. Sometimes it seemed to him a simple matter to make all of London part of his new empire, not just the limited John Murrey firm.

He heard the bell ring. The woman from the street. Then it occurred to him—she was a friend of Maudie Canfield's, who probably had invited her for Christmas dinner in the basement kitchen. At first Aslam was tempted to give in to anger, then changed his mind. Maudie Canfield had served him well and loyally for the last four years. She hated John Murrey Eden with admirable and vocal force, having suffered repeatedly from his displays of temper when he was in residence here. No, let old Maudie have her friend in for the day. He would require nothing more of either of them.

He drew the platter of cold food closer and speared the egg, drawing the sharp blade of a knife through it twice, feeling the slight resistance of the hard yolk. The quartered egg, chewed but once, then swallowed, slid thickly down his throat, followed by another quarter, then another, until all was devoured, simply because the body required it to function. He experienced neither taste nor pleasure. All he required to nurture and sustain him was his deep and abiding hate for John Murrey Eden. If he was truly at last dead—and Aslam firmly believed he was—his one hope now was it had been a prolonged and painful death.

What relief, what pleasure that thought brought him, his only true pleasure on this abysmal and pointless Christian holiday.

At sixty, Maudie Canfield puffed her way up the kitchen stairs, heading toward the front door of the Grosvenor Square mansion, where the bell had already rung twice and undoubtedly would do so a third time.

"I'm coming," she called ahead to the impatience on the other side of the door, wondering who it could be on this day. Standing before the front door, she fumbled with the latch, peering closer through the smoked glass to see only black shadows in the shape of a woman's full skirts, a cape and umbrella.

Female? What female would be out and about today? The latch slid and fell free and she drew open the door. "Yes?" she demanded harshly, peering through the slot, seeing the woman whole now and finding the reality even more bizarre than the shadows. It was a woman, all right, but she looked more like a traveling jeweler, one of those colorful peddlers who wear their wares.

"What is it?" Maudie demanded after she had stared all she wanted.

"I have come to see Mr. Eden. If you will . . ."

Now, that was a strange bit of news. Why would Master Aslam be meeting a woman like this?

"Is he . . . expecting you?" Maudie asked.

"Of course!" the woman snapped. "Just announce me. Tell him Rose O'Donnell is here—with news," she added pointedly.

Maudie decided that the woman was not to be trusted.

"Well?" Rose O'Donnell demanded. "Are you going to leave me freezing on your stoop, or do you know the amenities?"

"Come," Maudie muttered, a little less than hospitably. She stepped back from the open door, beginning to shiver herself. "You wait here," she ordered with new sternness, and closed the heavy door behind her.

At the dining-room door Maudie lifted her right hand and knocked once. No response.

She tried again, and waited, looking back over her shoulder at the woman, who was giving the black-and-white-marble reception hall a pretty thorough going-over. As Maudie knocked the third time, the aggressive woman glanced angrily in her direction, as though the lack of response was her fault, along with everything else.

"Let me," she said, and swept toward Maudie, dislodging her from her position at the door. To Maudie's horror, the woman knocked but once, then pushed open the door and swept into the dining hall without even having received permission to enter.

"No," Maudie gasped, but it was too late.

"Sir," Maudie began apologetically, and let the word carry her all the way across the threshold, heading toward the cold, rigid figure who was staring at the crude woman as though she were an apparition. The woman's face wore the same expression.

"Who is he?" she demanded with an arrogance that made Maudie flinch.

"Master Aslam, this woman says—"

"Where is Mr. Eden?" the woman interrupted, striding closer to the end of the table, where Aslam continued to sit in a state of stunned horror.

Quickly Maudie stepped into the breach. "This *is* Mr. Eden," Maudie said quizzically. "I thought you said—"

"That . . . is . . . not . . . Mr. Eden," Rose O'Donnell pronounced. "Where is Mr. Eden?" she demanded again, holding her ground, studying Aslam with a condemning eye.

"Get out!"

There was neither volume nor threat in his command. It simply came with all the deadly swift accuracy of a thrown knife.

Unfortunately, Mrs. O'Donnell went right on speaking. "I demand to see Mr. Eden," she announced, her voice taking on a screech-owl quality. "I have struck a bargain with the gentleman and I am here to deliver my part of the bargain. Now, if one of you will be so good as to—"

At that moment a voice cut through the babbling female voice. "I am Mr. Eden," was all it said, as though that were sufficient.

And to most rational people it might have been sufficient, but to Rose O'Donnell it wasn't.

"How amusing! What precisely is going on here? I know Mr. Eden personally, you see. Therefore, I cannot be duped. And further, I know you for what you are, despite your English clothes. You're a nigger, plain and simple, probably in the employ of Mr. Eden, who will be very displeased when I tell him what his servants are—"

Suddenly Aslam's hand moved like a lightning bolt toward the side of Rose O'Donnell's overrouged cheek to deliver itself of a single blow which echoed about the quiet dining hall like the report of a gun.

There were two gasps. One of shock coming from Maudie herself, for in all her sixty years she'd never seen a man strike a woman. The second gasp came from Rose O'Donnell, who had fallen to one side under the force of the blow and now clung weeping to the back of one of the chairs.

"Madam," he said, his tone quiet, his manner almost polite, "I repeat, I am Mr. Eden, and I have struck no bargain with you. If you are referring to Mr. John Murrey Eden, then I fear your bargain, whatever its nature, is as worthless as the man with whom you struck it. Mr. Eden is dead and therefore relieved of the temptation to be dishonorable again."

Maudie listened. Mr. Eden dead? She'd not heard that before. In fact she'd thought Mr. Aldwell had run off to Paris in an attempt to find Mr. Eden.

Aslam stepped through the door now and took three steps across the entrance hall before he turned back. His words were for Maudie. "Get her out of here," he said, his voice low, "and never open the front door to strangers again."

"Sir, she claimed she knew you."

"A false claim."

"I'm sorry—"

"Get her out of here. Is that clear?"

Oh, it was clear, all right, despite the sobs coming from the woman in the dining hall. Maudie glanced first at the man walking up the stairs, head erect, then back to the sound of complete ruin coming from behind her.

"Mrs. O'Donnell," Maudie began, with the intention of offering comfort before she ushered her out, but at the moment she spoke the name, the woman, whose face now bore the imprint of a single hand, rose hastily from the chair, her hands trying to cover her tear-streaked face.

"I'll tell the police, I will," she sobbed. "And how was I to know Mr. Eden was . . . ?" Apparently she couldn't bring herself to say the word, and rushed past Maudie in a straight path to the doors. With some difficulty she drew one open just wide enough to slip through it.

By the time Maudie reached the door, Rose O'Donnell was halfway down the stairs, her head bowed, still holding her injured face.

Forbes Hall,
Kent
December 25, 1874

In her extremity Lady Eleanor Forbes Eden looked up from the massive four-poster, no longer embarrassed by her bared, heaving belly. She grasped the ends of the twisted cloth which she held between her clenched teeth and saw a semicircle of strangers staring down on her naked body. Three women—two she'd never seen before—and the short, plump, elfin figure of old Dr. Brackish, who had prowled these Kentish woods for as long as Eleanor could remember, setting bones, stitching cuts, delivering babes.

Suddenly she felt an upheaval in the lower part of her stomach, a pain as sharp as she'd ever experienced in her life, and the awful sensation that the thrashing infant was trying to escape through the wall of her abdomen.

She gave in to one short moan, bit down harder on the twisted cloth, and felt the two strange women draw her legs farther apart and prop them up.

"Brandy, doctor?" Mrs. Eunice asked quietly, wiping at Eleanor's brow. Eleanor knew Mrs. Eunice and liked her, the most experienced midwife in Kent, who had spent the last few days talking to Eleanor, telling her what she could expect at the time of delivery.

In answer to her question, the doctor shook his head. "Not yet," he said, giving Eleanor an encouraging smile. "She's a brave girl, and it's a peer of the realm she's bringing forth. Now, she doesn't want to be half-senseless for this momentous occasion, now, does she?"

The old man's question was aimed directly down on Eleanor, who shook her head weakly and wondered how long before the next upheaval, how long would it go on before the "peer" arrived, and would it be male? *Oh, please, God, yes!* Where was Richard? Why couldn't he have seen fit to be here for the birth of his son?

At this last painful question, she groaned in a way that had nothing to do with her physical ordeal. She felt the old doctor's hand on her stomach again, fingers splayed as though by merely feeling the angry infant he could predict and prophesy.

"Not long, my dear," he comforted. Then, as though the old man had read her thoughts—or else was responding to local gossips, who knew all too well Lady Eleanor's husband, Lord Richard, spent more time in London than he did at Forbes Hall—he added softly, "I do believe the lad's waiting for his father to arrive."

Then we all may be here for a while, Eleanor thought, enjoying the unexpected wave of humor.

The lad's waiting for his father to arrive.

Lad. Son. The next heir to Eden Castle and Eden Point, one continuous line which stretched back to the beginnings of recorded English history.

She gasped with delight and felt strong enough to survive any pain.

"A smile, that's a good sign, my lady," Mrs. Eunice murmured close beside the bed. "I don't have to ask what you were thinking on. I've delivered too many babes not to recognize a mother's love for her own babe."

Eleanor nodded. "I was thinking of him." She smiled. "Thinking of all he could become." Across the bedchamber she saw the doctor conferring with the two strange women.

Suddenly the infant pressed down with such force she couldn't catch her breath. As the pain increased, she leaned back against the pillow and bit down hard, though not on the twisted cloth. Mrs. Eunice had removed it during her moments of ease and she bit down on her own lip instead and tasted blood.

"Flat!" Dr. Brackish called out with a degree of urgency.

She felt Mrs. Eunice remove the large feather pillow at her back and ease her down. For several moments the two worked in silence while the other strange women stood at the foot of the bed and watched.

Why watch? And what right did they have to be here? And where was Richard?

At the height of the pain she thought the saddest thought of all, the fact that, despite everything, she had loved him and no other since that hot September day during the Eden Festivities when John Murrey Eden had invited her parents into the small library at Eden and had emerged four hours later with a marital contract.

"Better?" The gentle inquiry came from Mrs. Eunice.

"Not long now," promised Dr. Brackish. "The lad is growing impatient."

The lad. She liked that.

Geoffrey Richard Forbes Eden, a combination of two houses. And if the thrashing infant were female? Well, she hadn't even considered that possibility.

Then her thoughts of heirs and names were cut short by a series of convulsive pains, like waves breaking on a beach, each wave coming faster than the one before it, perspiration covering her face like sea spray.

"Push, Lady Eleanor. Remember we talked about . . ."

Yes, she remembered, and grabbed fistfuls of bed linens and tried to push against the pain. At the height of agony, she calmly opened her eyes and felt herself bathed in cold sweat, felt hands pulling at something between her legs.

"Now, push, Lady Eleanor!"

At the doctor's urgent command she flattened her head against the bed and bore down as hard as she could on the now squalling, angry infant, who tore at her as though birth was a destiny he'd not quite reckoned with. But it was too late, for suddenly she felt a great rushing and heard the squalling at the same time rise to a shriek. Sweat burned her eyes. She closed them and tried to steady her breathing, waiting less than patiently for the doctor's voice.

"Lady Eleanor, may I present your son, Lord Eden?"

She opened her eyes and saw a red, bloodied, and squiggly piece of infuriated human flesh held suspended in the doctor's hands, while, curiously, the two strange women made notations in small black notebooks.

"Who . . . ?" she began, wishing they would depart and give her her son.

Mrs. Eunice stepped close. "They are official verifiers from Hastings, my lady, hired by Lord Eden to witness and record the birth of his son. You know, quite necessary where lineage is involved."

Eleanor gaped upward, unable for the moment to believe the woman. No, she didn't know. Richard couldn't manage to be here himself, but he'd thought to hire two strange women to witness and testify to the successful delivery of her son.

Her anger crested, as recently the pain had. It was her son, for she had done the work. She opened her eyes to keep careful watch on the two women, who were now examining the small and bloodied hands, recording everything so there could be no question—when Lord Richard did deign to arrive—that this was his son and not an impostor brought in at the last minute.

"Tell them to finish quickly," she ordered. "Then give me my son." The tone of her voice caught the attention of all, even the repulsive ladies, who gazed down on her with surprise.

While she waited out the official inspection, she asked Mrs. Eunice to pass the word of the birth of her son to the servants waiting outside the door, many of whom had been with her family since *her* birth, and who would be happy and relieved to hear of her safe delivery.

"A Christmas babe," Mrs. Eunice beamed. "A good omen."

"I hope so," Eleanor murmured, waiting less than patiently for the two women, who now were in close examination of the infant's genitals, to finish.

Poor thing, Eleanor mourned, regretting his first moments of consciousness would be to submit to such a crude and cold human act.

Talbot House, Dublin January 4, 1875

"That's what the man said, Lord Harrington, the madman, I might add, who only a few moments after that dared to lift his hand in violence against me."

Breathless from her tirade, Rose O'Donnell at last stopped for breath and looked across the expanse of the library. Lord Harrington still wore that empty, vacant glazed look. Holy Mother of Jesus, were all men mad, and had they always been so, or had she just noticed it?

"Lord Harrington?" she ventured. "Did you hear what I just said?" she asked, raising her voice, hoping to penetrate the emptiness.

Still no response, except he seemed to tighten his grip on the bureau where she'd found him working on household bills. She'd only just arrived, still wearing the mud-splattered brown dress of the journey.

A miserable journey it had been, too. She had been plagued every mile of the way by twin torments. One, the fact she'd not taken the time to report the nigger's assault to the police. And, two, that her profitable little game was over before it had ever really gotten started. With Mr. Eden dead, there was, of course, no one interested in any news coming out of Talbot House, and Lord Harrington could rest easy. The boys were his for as long as he—

"Are you . . . certain you understood correctly, Mrs. O'Donnell?"

"I'm certain, Lord Harrington." She nodded vigorously. "What the imposter said was, 'Mr. Eden is dead.' "

"Was . . . there anyone else present?" Lord Harrington asked, still sitting rigidly straight in his chair.

"Just one," said Rose O'Donnell hastily, at last remembering the old crone of a woman who'd just stood placidly by.

"Who?" Lord Harrington demanded.

"A serving woman," she replied. "A hag. I didn't know her name."

"Anyone else? A Mr. Aldwell?"

"No. I know Mr. Aldwell. He wasn't in sight."

"Did Aslam say how John had . . . ?" His voice broke and at the same time he rapidly bowed his head.

For a few moments Rose O'Donnell was prepared to swear the man was deeply moved.

"Was Lord Richard present?" Lord Harrington asked, still probing for additional witnesses.

"I said no, Lord Harrington, and it's no I'll be saying again," Rose snapped, losing what little patience she still had after the tedious, prolonged coach ride.

Now she ached to get out of these filthy clothes, to submerge her weary body in a hip bath of steaming lavender water, and to turn all her energies and attention to forgetting the horrible episode.

"If that's all, Lord Harrington . . ." she murmured, heading back toward the door. She should have inquired after Stephen, but she'd stop off in his chambers on the way up to her own and see for herself. She feared the child had grown worse, for something of sad consequence had occupied Lord Harrington the weeks she'd been gone. She'd never seen a man so morose.

"Wait, Mrs. O'Donnell," he called out, at last rising from his chair. "Please, I must . . ." All at once he sat back down and suddenly pressed his clasped hands against the center of his forehead, making a sound that caused gooseflesh on Rose's arms.

"Sir?" she inquired. "I thought you'd be pleased with news of the villain's death. He's certainly caused you a mountain of grief."

He nodded as though he wasn't going to refute her words. Then, speaking carefully around them, he said, "But in the beginning, I loved him as much as my daughter loved him."

In the beginning, Rose thought wryly. What matter in the beginning? It's what we are and will become that matters.

"Did Aslam say . . . how? When?" Lord Harrington asked, looking up.

"No, he said nothing. Now I've told you everything, and if you'll excuse me, I'm very exhausted and cold and hungry . . ."

"Of course," he murmured.

She sensed an apology in his voice. As she started toward the door, she called back over her shoulder, "I will place an itemized account of my expenses on your bureau come morning." She waited for a response, and when none was forthcoming, she drew open the library door and felt the pronounced chill of the hall.

"I trust Stephen is no worse," she said. "I'll look in on him on my way—"

"No!"

Surprised, she looked back. "I beg your—"

"I said no," he repeated, his voice growing stronger. "He's sleeping."

"Then I'll wait until he awakens."

"No, Mrs. O'Donnell, I don't want . . ."

"What, Lord Harrington?" she asked, her voice hard with a slight edge. She was sick to death of men and their weak purposes and weaker wills. "What precisely is it you want? Tell me."

Under the duress of the direct challenge, the man faltered, as she knew he would. She was about to repeat her intention to stop in at Stephen's chamber when once again the man stopped her.

"I . . . don't want you to see the boy," he said with a directness that alarmed her.

"I said I'll wait until he awakens."

"No. I mean I don't want you to see the boy . . . ever."

Shocked, she thought one word—"ingratitude." "I'm afraid it's my turn to express puzzlement," she pronounced primly.

"I don't want you to see Stephen, or Frederick either. They mustn't know about their father's death. Not yet."

"Then I shan't tell them."

"No, it's more than that. It's . . ."

Again he faltered, and Rose O'Donnell clearly saw the handwriting on the wall. She was being dismissed, although why, she had no idea. And there was that word again in her consciousness—"ingratitude, *male* ingratitude."

"Lord Harrington, please don't confuse the message with the messenger," she said, pleased with herself for coming up with that bit of wisdom.

"I'm not, Mrs. O'Donnell," he said, new kindness in his voice. "And I know what you're thinking. I'm not dismissing you. The truth is that Mr. Parnell has need of your . . . services."

Interested, though distrustful, she held her temper. "Mr. Parnell?" she asked, warning herself not to let her hopes rise too high.

"He has your passage to America. He needs a connecting link that he can trust to run messages to the Skirmishers."

All at once both her heart and her hope vaulted. Dear God, it was her dream come true! But cautious, be cautious. . . .

"He has plenty of loyal men to run his—"

"No. Men are being too closely watched and checked," Lord Harrington said, shaking his head and moving closer. "Mr. Parnell thinks a woman will be able to pass with greater ease."

"Is this . . . true?" she sputtered, still thinking he'd retract part or all of it, that it was merely a lie to serve his own ends.

For the first time since she'd entered his presence, he smiled. "It's true, I swear it," he said. "In fact, as soon as you are rested from your journey, Mr. Parnell will be expecting you in Dublin so that a date for your departure may be set."

Dear Lord, thank You!

She breathed the quick prayer, then turned immediately to the door. "I need no time for rest, Lord Harrington, just a brief interval to restore myself and gather up my belongings. Then, with your permission, I'll be on my way to Dublin."

"Of course with my permission." Lord Harrington nodded, a smile on his face.

For a moment there was something unpleasant that lodged in her consciousness. Why was it he seemed so relieved at the prospect of her depar-

282

ture? Well, no matter. The men of this once grand country were dying, as was the country itself. All the true lifeblood, the men who were still capable of daring, had been sent to America. Now she could shortly follow, there to be reunited with that grandest of all men that God did ever create, Denis Bourke O'Donnell.

"Then I'm off," she said, and started with renewed energy down the cold corridor, and saw ahead not the frayed runner which ran up the creaking staircase, but the shores of America, which she was certain would receive her kindly and make room for the talented, resourceful, and Christian lady she knew she was.

Lord Harrington held his position in the library door until he made certain the distasteful woman had indeed bypassed Stephen's door and was safely ensconced in her own room on the third floor, preparing for her departure from Talbot House, from Dublin, from Ireland, thank God.

He leaned heavily against the door frame, feeling every day of his seventy-six years. Briefly he envied John Murrey Eden for entering the peace of death so prematurely. No, he didn't mean that, and God forgive him. And John's death—my God, it was a waste of one of the most infinitely varied and gifted personalities he'd ever known.

Should the boys be told? Stephen particularly seemed to cling to a very idealized and romantic dream.

"Someday, when Papa is ready, we'll all go back."

To tell the boy now there would be no reunion, no return to Eden, might in a very real way hinder his recovery. No! The news would have to wait until the boy fully regained his strength. Lord Harrington paused outside the closed door in order to adjust to the fact of his cowardice. As he waited, he heard two young piping voices raised in dispute.

"It is so your fault! You ordered the army forward, and they—"

"They would have moved anyway," Stephen protested angrily.

How good it was to hear anger in that small boy's voice that a mere two weeks ago had been too weak to ask for water.

Lord Harrington stood a moment longer, seeing John's face everywhere, in the curious configuration of January sun and shadow through the lace curtains at the far end of the long corridor, in every aspect of his mind and memory. Quickly he pushed open the door.

The two miniature generals were on their knees, the "battlefield" between them. Stephen wore the robe and slippers of his confinement, while Frederick appeared to be lost in a gray hand-me-down sweater from Stephen, which obviously had been handed down several months too soon. The battles—both of them, the one on the board and the one between the two boys—still raged.

"Napoleon would have performed with greater genius had he not been ill," Stephen announced, obviously identifying with the emperor who at Borodino had ordered eighty thousand French, German, Italian, and Polish soldiers to fight to their deaths.

Frederick, one year younger and not naturally as aggressive, was more intelligent and therefore intimately acquainted with all the statistics of that dramatic and fateful battle.

"What difference does a cold make?" Frederick protested, growing every day to resemble his mother, Lila, delicate, fair, light blue eyes, inquisitive, sensitive. "The face of Russia was not transformed at the will of one man. One man can do nothing."

"It wasn't Napoleon's fault," Stephen muttered defensively.

Lord Harrington stood very still, amazed Frederick had briefly taken the upper hand.

"Of course it wasn't," Frederick readily agreed, at last backing off his knees and slumping deep into the chair. "I never said it was. Napoleon did not fire at anyone. All *that* was done by his soldiers. Therefore, it was not he who killed those men."

"That's what I said," Stephen repeated triumphantly, with just a hint of scheming to his voice, as though deep down he knew he hadn't said that at all, but to say it now would make him appear victorious.

Shades of John.

Lord Harrington announced his presence from the door. "May a neutral party join the battle? I promise to keep quiet and not—"

"Grandpapa!" It was Frederick who shrieked the greeting and hurried across the room for a warm embrace.

Lord Harrington was only too happy to receive him, this living part of Lila.

"Stephen is mad at me again," the child mourned, nestling into Lord Harrington's arms. Stephen's approval as older brother meant a great deal to Frederick.

"Why is Stephen mad at you?" he inquired, carrying the boy like an infant back to the large window, where the heavy drapes had been drawn to let in as much January sun as was available.

"For the same old reason," Frederick sighed, imitating adult weariness. "Because I won't shout *'Vive Napoleon!'*"

Lord Harrington smiled and winked at Stephen, who had slouched down in his chair.

"I don't care what he says," Stephen muttered in response to Frederick's accusation. "Napoleon may not have ordained the course of Borodino, but *his* inferior strategies are superior to any similar arrangements conceived by lesser men."

"Agreed," Lord Harrington said quickly, ruffling the boy's hair as he thought again, with ever-increasing pain: *John dead* . . .

How sad, he could never watch these two bright miracles grow. Lord Harrington stood for a moment at the arm of Stephen's chair looking down. The only sounds in the room now were those coming from the crackling fire, the staccato bursts of sleet on the large windowpane and Frederick's soft humming.

"How are you feeling, Stephen?" Lord Harrington asked, still holding Frederick and at the same time caressing Stephen's neck.

In answer, the boy merely shrugged and continued to keep a close vigil on the disagreeable day.

As the silence persisted, Lord Harrington briefly regretted interfering with this second Battle of Borodino. He knew one way to stir life back into this frozen room of failed emperors and failed dreams. Though in the past he'd loathed to do it—because then he hadn't been sure if John Murrey Eden was a threat or not—now he knew corpses couldn't threaten and knew further that nothing pleased the boys as much as tales of their father. So, with the creation of a legend in mind, he urged Stephen to scoot to one side of the massive wing chair and eased down into it, cradling Frederick in one arm and drawing Stephen close with the other.

Briefly he felt Stephen's resistance, like the January wind, but held him tightly despite the resistance, saying quickly, "Let's talk about your papa, shall we?" He launched into the subject that he'd once dreaded and which now caused him to feel mournful.

"Your papa . . ." he mused, pleased at both boys, who were slowly relaxing against him. "Do you know what he was doing the first time I ever saw him?" Not waiting for an answer but sensing their rapt attention, he went right on. "He was sitting flat down in the middle of my garden at Harrington Hall, in the dirt, mind you. A grown man just sitting there like a boy, like both of you, with my daughter—your mother— and both were studying rainbow colors that decorate the backs of earthworms after a May rain."

Calais, France
March 16, 1875

Father John Dudley, age seventy-three, nicknamed "Old Charon" by the French customs officials, stood at the gate leading to the ferry house, as he'd done for the last thirty years, checking not the luggage of boarding passengers for Dover—the French did that thoroughly, if not efficiently— but rather standing there to answer questions. He was capable of answering them in excellent French, better English, flawless German, and magnificent Italian, for in his younger days before he'd become an Anglican priest and long before he'd become Old Charon, he'd studied language and had excelled at it.

On this late winter's evening he drew his monk's robes more closely about him in protection against the damp wind off the water and watched the last passengers hurry by on their way to the ferry house, where, sadly, they thought they would find warmth. The only true warmth on the decaying dock was up there in the French inspector's office, which sat above the loading area, looking down on everything as though from the smug elevation of French bureaucracy.

But at least the passengers were out of the wind in the large crumbling old ferry house until they were permitted to board one of the large packets which plied back and forth across the murky channel waters.

Abruptly he turned toward the end of the long quay leading to the dock house. Something was moving there. Should he go and see? It was such a long distance to make on frozen feet, close to three hundred yards, and he *was* freezing. What if he walked all that distance only to find a bundle of discarded rags caught on the sharp rocks and twisting in the harsh wind like a collapsed old man, for that's what the blowing rags looked like, and undoubtedly what they were.

Suddenly his attention lifted from the small mystery to a large carriage

286

which had just pulled up at the end of the quay and around which appeared to be considerable activity. He squinted harder and saw several footmen arranging steps before the carriage door, saw one unlatch and draw open the door, and saw a child descend. At least from this distance it looked like a child. A few moments later another child emerged, followed by a black-bonneted woman—clearly a nanny—who shepherded them to one side while all waited with what appeared to be nervous anticipation for yet a fourth party to emerge from the carriage.

A lady. Clearly a lady, who stepped hesitantly down the two steps while leaning heavily on the arm of a steward. Her small frame was encased in layers of garments, as though she chilled easily.

Old Charon watched the distant scene, concentrating lovingly on the children until the cold wind caused his eyes to water. He turned away, certain such grandeur did not need him in any way. He stopped his turn briefly to see if the old discarded bundle of rags could still be seen. Gone. Nothing in sight save the large retinue which had just arrived and was now starting down the quay, the children in the lead, each safely tucked away under the protective wings of the black-clad nanny, followed by the woman who continued to lean heavily on two stewards, her head down, her face obscured by the thick black cloak. Though she was walking, her steps were hesitant, the support of her legs questionable, as though if the stewards were to withdraw their support she would surely fall.

Quickly he lowered his head into the coarse fabric of his monk's robes and realized thus far today no one had asked him to identify his ecclesiastical order. He was always secretly pleased when they did, for this gave him an opportunity to respond, "I belong to the Order of Life and worship any god who alleviates pain, compulsion, obsession, and grief."

The two children were still in the lead, though something had distracted them. They had veered close to the edge of the quay, only to be herded back on track by the nursemaid.

Two of them. Two girls? Two daughters—and suddenly an ancient pain like an open wound throbbed at the base of his throat.

Why?

In 1850 old Charon had taken a leave from the flourishing little parish church in Westminster considered by all to be a necessary stepping-stone to the abbey, which in turn was a necessary stepping-stone to Canterbury. He'd also kissed good-bye the three jewels in his personal crown: his wife, Florence, and his two beautiful little daughters, Amy and Trudy.

He had journeyed to Paris, to the Sorbonne to study the great French theologians. The family's plan was that Florence and the two girls would join him the last fortnight for a brief French holiday.

He looked up quickly from the storm of memory to check the slow progress of the entourage which, despite the cold wind, was moving at a snail's pace down the quay. "Hurry!" he breathed to the still-distant group. If only they would hurry, he would be forced to engage them in brief dialogue, thus banishing memory, pushing it back into the past where it belonged.

But memory arrived first, and he saw himself as a young man again who had just alighted from a chaise at the end of this very quay and was now hurrying toward the ferry house and the long pier where people waited to greet incoming passengers.

And there it was. He could see the packet even as he hurried down the quay, his head bursting with plans for the holiday. Then the wind suddenly picked up—where had that wind come from?—and whitecaps danced on black water and . . . What was the matter with the packet? Look! It was rolling first to one side, then the other. And what was that trailing up from the captain's deck, like gray smoke, followed by red, like a red tongue licking out from . . .

Dear God, no!

Old Charon closed his eyes and held on to whatever support he could resurrect from deep within, for in the blowing wind he heard the screams of thirty years ago originating from two sources, from those waiting on the dock to greet friends and families and visitors who were within sight of the land, and those distant cries of terror from those aboard the ferry who, better than anyone else, could see the flames and knew the seriousness of their predicament.

Then had come the explosion, and as it resounded in memory he grasped the sides of his head and covered his ears, foolishly thinking the sound came from without and therefore could be blocked, forgetting momentarily it came from within, from the caves of memory, and therefore could never be blocked, only endured.

He forced himself to watch the burning ferry again, the flaming bodies who jumped too late into the channel, those below deck who never had a chance, and those—like his wife and two daughters—who had simply gone down and whose bodies had never been recovered.

For a moment the wound throbbed, a physical pain sharper than any he'd ever felt. He had tried to return to England, but he had suffered endless nightmares in which he had seen his two young daughters trying to struggle up from the black depths of the channel and they kept calling to him, begging him to save them.

The peace he searched for was not in London or in Paris, and he kept returning *here,* to this place, the French customhouse at the quay. While he'd not found peace—that would never be his, not in this world—he had on occasion found a cessation of pain as he tried to administer to others.

Breathless from the storm of memory, he lifted his head and saw the entourage about one hundred feet away, the woman still leaning heavily on the stewards—ill, was his guess—while in contrast the two young children pranced and skipped down the quay as though to say their youth alone had made them superior.

"Bonjour, monsieur," they called as they came close.

He started to call them back under some false pretense so he could enjoy their new and breathtaking beauty. But the nursemaid was almost upon him, and though old and bowed, she gave him a shy half-smile and a weary look.

He stepped forward, prepared to address her in French, when she bobbed her head and spoke first.

"Monsieur, are we advancing in the proper direction for the evening packet?"

Her English, though not flawless, was understandable, and he nodded quickly. "Yes, madame," he said, raising his voice over the incredible wind. "Straight ahead to the ferry house. The packet leaves at seven."

"Merci." She smiled, clasped her cloak more tightly about her neck, and looked quickly behind, apparently checking on the progress of the lady supported between the two stewards, her heavily veiled head and face obscured not only by the black veils but also by the sharp downward angle of her head. The nursemaid passed him by a step or two, looking first at the children who had run ahead, then behind at the faltering and ill lady.

"May I be of assistance?" Old Charon offered quietly.

The maid looked up gratefully, then shook her head. "Pray for us, if you will," she said. "I fear the countess will be dead before we reach London, and the doctors . . ."

She *was* ill, just as he'd thought.

"Keep a cheerful and hopeful heart, madame," he advised.

"I try, monsieur, I try . . ."

"That's all God requires of us." He stepped closer, selfishly wanting to prolong the brief exchange. "What, may I ask, is the nature of her illness? Your mistress, I mean."

"If we knew that, we could have stayed in Paris," the old woman mourned. "She cannot take food or water or liquid of any sort, and she weeps constantly and claims a pain no French physician can locate or identify."

There was something familiar in the description of the malady, more an ill spirit manifesting itself in the body.

"May I inquire her name," Old Charon asked, "so that I may pray for her?"

"She is the Countess Eugenie Retiffe, only daughter of the Duke Henri Retiffe."

"Who are the children?"

"Her young nephew and niece. Only they, on occasion, can make her smile."

Then the lady was approaching and he could hear her over the wind, the pitiful sound of soft continuous weeping, as though something in the soul or the spirit or both had broken. As she passed by, Old Charon ached to reach out to her, but grief that deep had to be dealt with alone and over a number of years.

"God be with you," he prayed as she passed falteringly by, and hoped she would look up, but she did not. As the stewards led her past, the old nursemaid stepped back to one side, keeping a watchful eye on the lot of them.

"Sir . . ." It was the old nursemaid again, who had taken a few steps after her mistress and now returned to his side. "There's an old man at the head of the quay, dead or dying, we know not which, but he appears to have lost his footing and slipped. Look to him, would you, please?"

Her startling announcement took him by surprise, and he remembered the bundle of blowing rags. When he looked up to thank the old nursemaid for this grim news, she'd already returned to the aid of her mistress.

He forced his stiff joints into action and increased his speed toward the end of the quay. Drawing close, he now observed the bundle of rags had two arms, a scarecrow physique, and a head covered with tangled wet hair where the sea spray battered him. Something was tucked beneath him, elevating his body at an awkward angle, and his feet and legs had slipped into the icy water.

Moving carefully so as not to fall on the rocks, Old Charon started tentatively down, testing each step before he transferred his full weight to it, making certain the rock would hold, all the time looking down on the wretched piece of humanity which now resembled debris the channel might have washed up onto the embankment.

Asking God for strength in excess of his seventy-three years, Old Charon pushed up the long sleeves of his robes, found the man's hand, soiled beyond recognition, and blood-encrusted, as though he'd recently suffered a wound; then quickly he reached down, grabbed him beneath the arms, and pulled. With gratitude he felt the body move. He pulled again, and in the process lifted the torso and shoulders and saw the head fall lifelessly down against the chest. Yes, dead, Old Charon thought sadly, and pulled again, stepping carefully up the shifting rocks, exposing a wicker case.

"Don't worry, my friend," Old Charon soothed. "I'll fetch it for you in a minute."

Breathless from exertion, he dragged the man the rest of the way up, placing him gently face down on the path.

Old Charon bent down, resting his hands on his knees for a closer look. Strange. Not as old a man as he'd thought. Suddenly Charon saw the movement of an eyelid. He stared down for a few additional minutes and was on the verge of turning away to descend the rocky embankment for the wicker case, which clearly had been of great importance to the man, but as he turned, he saw the eyelid move again, as though the man wanted very much to open his eyes.

"Hello!" Old Charon grinned. Gently he turned the man over on his back, newly shocked by how thin he was. His ragged, filthy shirtwaist was open due to lack of buttons, and every rib showed, as did the jutting angles of the collarbone.

It suddenly occurred to Old Charon the only malady which might be plaguing this wretched man was lack of food, insipient starvation.

Hurriedly he tried to draw together as much of the torn fabric as he could in an attempt to protect the man from the biting wind. His coat—while soiled beyond recognition, and torn—was of good quality. Perhaps there was identification in one of those torn pockets. But a cursory examination of the two sashed pockets revealed nothing of interest. Scraps of paper, mostly, two curious yarn circles—one red, one green—a soiled linen handkerchief, and an empty envelope with the name Madame Charvin lettered on it.

"Come on," Old Charon urged, slipping an arm beneath the man's head, elevating it slightly in an attempt to encourage a return to consciousness. "Come on, my friend, you're stuck here for a bit longer. Death doesn't want you, either, for a while." Suddenly the man's eyes opened, and Old Charon found himself staring down into a most remarkable skeletal face, far younger than he had imagined.

"Hello." Old Charon grinned. "I just pulled you out of the channel. I trust that was all right, unless you had plans to swim to Dover."

He waited to see if the man would respond. When he didn't, Old Charon said, "Can you speak, my friend?" He elevated the man's head a bit more. As he did, he saw the dried, split lips try to move. After several moments of tortured effort which produced nothing in the way of recognizable communication, Old Charon lowered him gently back onto the quay.

All at once one bony hand reached for his arm and gripped it with surprising strength, and at last one word emerged through the cracked lips. "C-case . . ." was all he said.

For a moment Old Charon couldn't understand. Then he did. The wicker case which had been abandoned at the edge of the rock embankment. "All right," he agreed, and stood. "I'll fetch your treasure." He saw a look of relief cover the emaciated features.

When Old Charon returned with the case, he saw the man's eyes were open, fixed on the rapidly gathering dusk, squinting as though he had perceived some unfathomable mystery in the heavens.

"Can you walk?" Old Charon asked, placing the wicker case on the man's chest.

But the question went unanswered, for at the feel of the slight weight of the container on his chest, he grasped it to him as one might grasp and hold a beloved woman. At the same time, he tried to raise himself, an impossible task under the best of circumstances. But Old Charon was there to help, and with the man holding on tightly, together they drew him to his feet, where for a moment he wobbled ominously.

"Shall we?" Old Charon bobbed his head toward the end of the quay and the ferry house.

As the man started tentatively forward, another word escaped his lips, a simple one, and easily understood. "Home," was what he whispered.

Old Charon nodded, maintaining his viselike grip. It was his intention to see the man safely settled into the warmth of the ferry house, then fetch a few limited provisions from his own quarters. He still harbored the opinion the man needed food as much as anything, and he would certainly need it for the voyage to Dover, if indeed that was his destination.

Halfway down the quay, pleased he was not carrying a dead man but assisting a live one, Old Charon grew brave. "May I . . . inquire as to your name, sir?" he asked.

They never broke the pace of their limited stride, and the man never lifted his eyes from the footing of the quay. Neither did he respond except to say brokenly, "H-home . . ."

Old Charon nodded affably, as though he'd understood the fragmented message perfectly. "Yes, home. And your name, sir?" As a ploy it failed. For some reason, Old Charon did not suspect the man of withholding his name on purpose. It was simply a matter of his own name being of total unimportance. He was going home, and nothing else mattered.

"Step down," Old Charon directed now as they approached the turnstile which led to the narrow walk, which in turn led to the ferry house. "We will wait in there. It's warmer."

"No."

The objection registered clearly. Surprised, Old Charon looked at the worn face, taut with effort. "Why not?" he asked. "Others will be waiting . . ."

"No."

"Please, sir, you need to get warm. I was going to fetch you—"

"No."

Then they were through the turnstile and heading, not toward the old ferry house, but following the quay farther out into the inky water laced with whitecaps, where the cold wind blew stronger and the stinging spray leaped higher.

"Sir, I beg you," Old Charon shouted above the shrieking wind. But it was no use. Despite his apparent weakness, the man was at last moving under his own power, though he faltered now and then and would have fallen were it not for the unreliable wooden railing which ran the length of the boarding pier.

At some point Old Charon fell back a few steps, baffled and helpless. He watched him make his way to the end and settle stiffly on one of the plain wooden benches. From this distance again he resembled a discarded pile of blowing rags. He bowed his head over the wicker case, his entire frame bent in on itself, a solitary figure of consummate grief.

Suddenly Old Charon shivered, not from cold. In a minute he would go and fetch the man a hard roll and a ticket to Dover. But for a few seconds he wanted to watch the man he had just rescued. For the first time in thirty years Old Charon realized he was in the presence of a man who had suffered a loss even greater than his own.

After a few moments of close and reverent scrutiny, Old Charon bowed his head against the blowing wind and prayed quite simply for a cessation of the pain the man was suffering, and for God's holy power to ease the emptiness caused by some recent and mysterious tragedy.

Forbes Hall,
Kent
March 25, 1875

Richard stood at the casement windows of Eleanor's bedchamber and stared out through the diamond panes at the perverse Kentish spring and heard his three-month-old son suckling at Eleanor's breast. He wondered how long it would be, what penance he would have to serve before God granted him just a semblance of that same contentment, that same peace.

John dead?

"Don't bite," he heard Eleanor whisper softly, lovingly to the perfect infant, who on occasion was inclined to teethe on her full nipple.

Richard started to look back at the always moving tableau, but something prevented him from doing so, a deeper need to deny himself.

Why?

Suddenly he leaned forward and pressed his forehead against the cold window glass.

Aslam.

There was part of the trouble, part of the grief, which had nothing to do with the news of John's death.

John dead?

He still couldn't believe it and had asked Aslam repeatedly for more details, had even dispatched Alex Aldwell back to Paris to see if he could locate Bates, who surely could tell them more. All Aslam had been able to tell him was that he had received a late-night messenger who had not identified himself, in fact who had refused to do so, and had informed him John Murrey Eden's body had been found and disposed of.

Richard stood away from the window, again struck by the bizarre nature of the tale. A late-night messenger? Who?

"He didn't name himself."

293

"And you didn't ask?"

"I asked. He refused to reply."

"Where and how is John dead?"

"He didn't say."

"And you didn't ask?"

"Leave me alone . . ."

Richard closed his eyes against the memory of the angry exchange he'd had with Aslam. It had served no purpose.

Still, if John wasn't dead, then where was he? And where was Bates? Suddenly he turned about in desperate need of new vistas that would be capable of dulling memory.

He found them in the warm ambers, golds, and reds of the roaring fire, in the sweet peace he found on Eleanor's face as she leaned back against the chair while her son pressed a tiny fist into the soft white flesh of her breast and drew on her nipple.

"So you're back with us?" she asked quietly. He thought he saw something slightly cold and defiant in her face, and for a moment didn't know how to deal with either.

"I've always been here," he soothed, at last turning his back on the cold winter. "Why do you say that I've been elsewhere?"

He stopped ten feet from the large overstuffed chair in which she sat and again recorded an expression on her face he couldn't quite interpret. He suspected she had been angry with him since the infant's birth and his own tardy arrival. Why she had been so shocked by the presence of the verifiers, he had no idea. Surely she knew such steps were necessary where direct lineage was concerned.

Knowing, or at least suspecting, he might be detained in London on Christmas, he'd taken steps to see to it a verifier from Hastings would be present, and, to further ensure both the proof and fact of his son's birth, the verifier had brought along a second witness, the wife of the Anglican priest in Hastings. And these two, with nothing and no one to serve save the cause of truth, had attended the birth and had duly recorded all the necessary information to ensure both the child and the family against any and all future disputes concerning his right to the titles, wealth, and land of Eden Point.

Now, thinking on the child, the future lord of Eden Castle, Richard stepped closer and peered inside the soft blue blanket and gazed at his perfectly shaped head, pleasing wide-set blue eyes, and tiny flawless features, like a perfect miniature.

"Would you care to hold your son?" Eleanor asked, observing his close scrutiny.

Richard nodded, grateful to her for not pursuing the unpleasant subject of the past.

"Come, then," she urged. "I believe he's finished dinner and would appreciate a little stroll."

He did love her. He would be willing to swear to anyone he did. . . .

As he bent over her chair, he caught her unique fragrance of hyacinths and allowed his eyes to rest briefly on that one lovely exposed white breast and wondered what it would be like to suckle on that nipple, to taste the warm sweet milk, too.

"Hold him steady, Richard. You're trembling." She laughed as she placed the baby in his outstretched hands.

Then he felt the feather-light weight in his hands, felt it shift and kick, as though it were impatient to move.

"Walk with him," she urged, "he likes that. Mrs. Eunice will be here soon and he won't be ours any longer."

He nodded and lifted his son partially free of the blanket. "He's beautiful," he murmured to no one in particular, unless it was to the babe himself.

John dead.

The thought entered his consciousness like a clever thief, stealing a portion of his sanity with each entrance. *John's sons*. Would they contest Geoffrey for right to the title of Eden Castle? Of course not. Lord Harrington, their grandfather and apparently now permanent guardian, knew better than that. No, there would be no challenge, he was certain of it.

"What are you thinking?" Eleanor asked quietly, apparently seeing the distant look on his face as he studied his son.

He looked back at her where she sat, legs curled to one side, in the large chair, the side of her face resting against the wing, a lovely oval of a face with dark hair, white skin, and violet eyes. They had never really fallen in love. Their marriage had been arranged between her aging and financially destitute parents and John, who knew, first of all, what Richard was and would quite likely always be . . .

"Richard?" Eleanor called again, concerned. "Are you . . . ?"

"I'm fine," he said quickly, coming back to himself and his awareness of the baby, who was beginning to whimper.

"Put him on your shoulder," Eleanor suggested, "and lightly rub his back."

Carefully Richard followed her instructions and observed that his spread palm covered the entirety of the baby's back. "He's so small." He smiled, rubbing the babe and anchoring the wobbling head with his own cheek. He closed his eyes briefly and thought with the strictest of disciplines that he had literally everything, a lovely wife who probably would forgive him one day for missing the birth of their son, a perfect son who would proudly take his place in the long line of Edens, and now—with John's death—Eden Castle as well.

He had all this and more, and yet a deep sense of sorrow was the prevailing emotion as his son grew more restless in his arms. He missed Aslam, had not seen him since the news of John's death had arrived at mid-January.

"Don't crush him, Richard. You're holding him too . . ."

He nodded quickly and paced off the length of the chamber.

"He likes that." Eleanor smiled. "Movement, any movement pleases him. What do you suppose that means?"

Just then a knock sounded at the door and Eleanor took the baby from him. It was Mrs. Eunice.

At some point he shut out the soft babbling music of the woman's voice and allowed his son to be taken from him, and stood, ghostlike, by the far window. It couldn't go on much longer. He needed Aslam, needed his calm, his warmth, his love.

"Richard?" It was Eleanor. He thought she'd left. "You look
. . . ill."

"I'm not."

"What's the matter?"

He shrugged and sorted through his mind for a safe explanation.
"John . . ."

". . . is dead," she completed for him.

"No . . ."

"I don't understand you, Richard. He did terrible things to you, to all of
you. Why should you mourn him and—worse—miss him?"

He heard the harsh indictment and did not try to answer it.

"If ever," Eleanor went on, "you were justified to feel relief at another's
death, this is the time." She stood very close to him now. Where was the
babe? Then he heard the door close and knew Mrs. Eunice had taken him
away and they were alone.

"I can't celebrate the death of any man," he said, trying to move away
from her before she placed demands on him he could not meet.

"Of course not," she readily agreed, "but neither should you subject
yourself and those around you to this senseless mourning."

"I loved him once as a brother."

"Did you love him when you vowed never to return to Eden as long as he
was there?"

"No," he replied, and succeeded in putting a short distance between
them, which she instantly canceled by following after him.

"Richard, what is it? You're trembling."

Suddenly, on hearing the love and kindness and concern in her voice,
knowing he was as entrapped as he'd ever been in his life, and baffled by
his inability to hate the dead man as he had hated the living man, Richard
turned away, enduring a sorrow which extended well beyond the cross-
purposes of this room.

"What is it?" Eleanor asked with undoing consideration, and put her
arms around him, led him to the bed.

"Come," she invited. "I'll ask nothing of you. Just hold me and allow
me to comfort you."

Because she was so beautiful and because in those few words she had
confirmed she knew what he was and still she desired him, and because—
despite the warring factions in his mind and heart—Richard preferred
peace and harmony, and because the longer he focused on that full white
breast the more desperately he wanted it, at last he stretched out beside
her, leaned over her, kissed her nipple and tasted the sweetness of her
milk, and prayed he could satisfy her.

As for himself, he wanted nothing so greedy as satisfaction, just a diminution of the mysterious forces that were on the verge of tearing him
apart.

East London
Salvation Mission,
London
March 25, 1875

Susan felt first hot, then cold, and though she'd been hungry when she'd come down from the second-floor dormitory, now the sight of the farthing breakfast—the sausage lying in a reflecting pool of its own grease and the single yellow eye of the overcooked egg—caused an upheaval in the pit of her stomach which forced her to reach out for the nearest support, which, fortunately, was Cassie Helms's ample arm. Cassie held still and supplied the support but allowed her tongue to move at the speed of an express train.

"You're working too hard. Yes, you are," Cassie scolded. "Even General Booth concedes it can't all be done by one person, and the one who tries is guilty of pride, which works against both God and His will and—"

"I'm . . . fine," Susan murmured.

"Well, you do work too hard, you know," Cassie persisted, guiding Susan to a seat at one of the long tables, where already at six in the morning there were several hundred hungry men and women, all eagerly devouring their breakfast.

Susan tried to shut out the sounds as well as the odor of food. Both were conspiring against her this morning. As dizziness joined the nausea, she clung to the low bench with both hands for fear of falling. She waited out the storm and hoped it would pass soon, for she was desperately needed at the Whitechapel Night Refuge.

Though the job was a hazardous one, exposed all day to various fevers and infections, nonetheless it suited her. Since few of the other workers wanted to go near the sickly outcasts, the refuge was always understaffed, which meant she could serve on consecutive duty shifts. She was certain then to be tired enough to sleep and did not have to pass through that interval of no-man's-land—neither asleep nor awake—when the mind eased slyly backward to Eden, to John.

The name alone was capable of causing new weakness, and she might have toppled from the bench had Cassie not looked up from her own breakfast and seen Susan begin to weaken again.

"Here, now," she said quickly, abandoning her fork with a clatter. She reached out with both hands to steady Susan, who had realized too late she could not stem the encroaching blackness.

"I'm sorry," she whispered, grateful for the firm brace across her back which was Cassie's arm.

"Don't apologize," Cassie comforted. "Anyone can get sick, even you." Then she was standing. "Come on, let's get you back to bed."

"No." The strength in Susan's voice was motivated mostly by fear. She would never survive an idle day in bed with nothing to distract . . .

"N-no," she repeated to the stunned Cassie. "I'm fine. A cup of tea would be—"

"You look terrible," Cassie said bluntly.

"Where I'm going, the men don't seem to mind."

"In my opinion, you shouldn't be going anyplace but—"

"May I join you, sisters?" The male voice, so close and unexpected, came from directly above Susan.

She tried to look up, but there was no need, for Cassie had made the identification, not in so many words but in the hushed tone of voice that all the female workers adopted when the sadly melancholy Lord Simmons came around.

"Oh, of course, sir," Cassie crooned. "I'm afraid Sister Susan is somewhat under the weather. I've been trying to talk her back up the stairs and into bed. Perhaps you can have more luck."

Susan was aware of someone settling on the bench next to her. From her downward vision she saw a single piece of black bread and a mug of tea. Strange fare for a peer of the realm, and once a very rich one, or so she had heard.

Now the deep, quiet male voice that had testified endlessly to the redemptive powers of Jesus Christ asked, "Is this true, Susan? You don't look well."

"I'm . . . fine."

"No, she isn't, sir. She would have just gone all flat twice if I hadn't been there."

"God does not expect us to serve Him beyond our capacity."

"I haven't even approached my capacity yet," Susan said, trying to fill her voice with at least the illusion of strength.

"Oh, I'd say you had," Lord Simmons contradicted. "In fact, you, more than any of us, have probably come the closest to realizing your full—"

"No!" She was the nurse. It was she who must take care of others. And she'd left several old gentlemen—so ill—only the night before. She'd promised them she'd return come morning and help them to bathe . . .

John.

Was he well? Where was he? Would she ever see him again? As the questions exploded in her head, she was capable of answering only one

298

with any degree of certainty, the last one. Would she ever see him again?

Of course not. Get to work. You can't sit here all morning . . .

Following the advice of this wise voice inside her head, she started up from the bench, only to discover she was entrapped by Cassie on one side and by Lord Simmons on the other. It really didn't make any difference, anyway, for the sudden movement to her feet had mysteriously caused all the blood to drain from her head. Suddenly the floor turned to liquid and there was nothing solid on which to stand. As she felt twin fires erupt on her face, as though she had fallen into a fire well, she thought: How strange. She'd never been sick before. Was this sickness? Or was it punishment? God's punishment for her hypocrisy, for surely God knew— even if no one else knew—the motivation behind her great labors was not love for Him, but rather the need to annihilate her pointless love for John Murrey Eden.

Catherine Booth, wife of General William Booth and a woman accustomed to fanaticism in the name of God, stood in her customary place of greeting at the door of the Food and Shelter Mission and saw the policeman point the man toward the mission. She smiled. No public recognition for their works as yet, but at least the police were recognizing them, using them as tools for getting the homeless off the London streets.

She continued to watch as the man started across the street at a halting gait. That he was hungry, there was no doubt. And perhaps ill as well. He appeared to walk with a limp, and what limited strength he did possess seemed to be channeled into grasping that worn wicker case to him, which he held with both arms as though it were a shield against all vicissitudes.

Watching closely as she was, Catherine was the first to see him lose his footing on the uneven cobbles, slip to one knee, a painful descent since he refused to relinquish his hold on the wicker case to break his fall. Alarmed, seeing a large hansom cab bearing down on him from the right, Catherine started forward.

Didn't the driver see him?

Dear God! Looking quickly back into the crowded mission for help, she spied Lord Simmons. He seemed to be carrying a woman, quite an unconscious woman from the limp nature of her hand, the distorted angle of her head.

"Lord Simmons!" she called out, glancing back out into the street, relieved to see the cab had stopped short, but now quite a crowd was gathering around the old man, who had fallen completely, facedown, the wicker case caught beneath him.

Dead? Quite possibly. But he was a child of God and therefore must be loved and tended even in death.

"Lord Simmons!" she called again, finding it difficult to address the man, as he had requested, by simply his given name of Laurence. He looked up, concern on his face for the woman in his arms. He was a good and tireless worker, one of the best, though she doubted if the General fully appreciated him.

Can a leopard change his spots? he'd asked her once regarding Lord

Simmons. A curious question, she'd thought, for a man who preached daily on the faith and power of God.

"Who . . . ?" she asked incompletely, referring to the woman in Lord Simmons' arms. Then she saw for herself.

"She . . . just . . . collapsed," was Cassie's tearful response as Catherine drew near.

Susan. Dear Susan. Catherine felt a deep, genuine affection for the selfless, though driven, little nurse. She felt Susan's forehead with increasing alarm, knew the woman was terribly ill, and called forward two workers who were standing nearby awaiting assignments.

"Will you help Cassie get her to bed?" she asked.

At first she thought Lord Simmons would object. The inclination was there. But the General always preached long and hard on obedience. So he handed Susan over to the receiving arms of others and allowed Catherine to lead him to the door. "Out there." She pointed toward the place where all traffic had come to a halt before the collapsed man.

"Hurry!" she called out to Lord Simmons, who had perceived the crisis and was already on his way across the street.

Catherine watched with held breath. Why these lost souls—old men mostly—moved her so, she couldn't say. But they did. Of course, everyone in need was the responsibility of General Booth's Christian Army, but for Catherine the most poignant of all were the old men, ill, abandoned by their families, to whom they had often dedicated their lives.

"Mrs. Booth, Cassie wants to know if you have summoned the doctor for Susan. She's awful sick."

Catherine looked over her shoulder at the timid voice and saw Flossie, a young girl just in from Cornwall. "Would you fetch him for me, Flossie?" she asked kindly. "He is just around the corner—and please request he see me before he departs. We may have another . . ." Her voice drifted off as she gazed out into the street, where Lord Simmons was bent over the fallen man.

"Mrs. Booth, may I ask what the fascination of the street is this morning?" At the sound of that deep, familiar, and beloved voice, she turned immediately, suffering a moment of guilt for what must appear to be an idle waste of time.

"My dearest," she murmured, touching her husband's arm, impressed anew, as she was every time she saw him after even so short a separation as a few hours, of the magnificence of his face. There were those who thought this man a saint, and others with matching conviction thought him the devil. As far as Catherine was concerned, he was a beloved husband and a true and gifted servant of God.

"It's an old man," she explained. "I saw him start across the street a few minutes ago. He appeared to be heading toward the mission, and halfway across, he collapsed. Lord Simmons went to fetch him—"

"Not 'Lord,' my dear," he corrected. "Laurence. There is but one Lord."

"Of course. I'm sorry," she murmured. "Laurence went to fetch him, and . . ."

But she never had a chance to finish, for suddenly he strode away from her across the sidewalk, heading toward the pavement, an impressive figure in his black coat.

Catherine could see her husband's face clearly as he leaned over the invalid, picked up the man, and carried him out of the street. Lord Simmons followed, carrying the abandoned wicker case.

A peculiar portmanteau, she thought. Then they were upon her, General Booth striding directly past. Why was he taking the old man in here? The infirmary for ill males was around the corner in Whitechapel.

Then, with belated insight, she understood. The sign above the mission was enormous and highly visible. Let the entire traffic of the street see precisely where the fallen man was being carried, as well as who was carrying him. In one highly public act of charity, General Booth was making converts on all sides.

For several moments Catherine stared after her husband, as mesmerized as everyone else on the street. She disliked it, the posturing, and she'd lost count of the number of times General Booth had tried to explain it to her. It made no difference.

Still, there he was, though the door was pushed open and held steady by other staff members. Before passing through, he turned back for yet another tableau, a very moving one, proof this small, struggling mission was following both the letter and the spirit of God's word better and more humanely than all the expensive churches which dotted the city. Last year those churches had allocated two hundred thousand pounds of their income to restore buildings, but had designated nothing toward the nation's poor.

As Lord Simmons approached, she observed he too held back, apparently aware of the significance of the tableau being performed at the door. If the man in General Booth's arms was dead, it made no difference. Let him pose. But if the man in his arms was still alive and in need of medical attention, then the delay in seeking treatment could be more costly than . . .

"Is he alive?" she whispered to Lord Simmons as he drew even with her, in his arms that curious-looking wicker case. She started to inquire as to its nature, but she saw him shake his head.

"I don't know. I could get no response from him. The General will get two staff members to take him out the back and over to Whitechapel."

Of course. Catherine should have known.

When she looked up from her thoughts, she found the doorway to the mission empty. She hurried through the mission door and saw a very worried Cassie Helms standing on the staircase which led up to the second-floor dormitory.

"The doctor, ma'am, has he . . . ?"

"Not yet, Cassie. He'll be here soon."

"She is so ill, so—"

"Shhhh . . . Let's take a look. Maybe there is something the two of us can do to make her more comfortable."

"God wouldn't let her die, would he, ma'am? I . . . don't understand . . ."

At the direct and impossible question, Catherine stopped and looked up. "It is not required of us to understand God's will," she said to Cassie, resuming her climb up the stairs. "All that's asked of us is cheerful obedience, acceptance, and faith. Do you understand?"

The girl nodded and ducked her head.

Catherine sensed tears. With instinctive, warm compassion, she reached out for Cassie's hand and enfolded it between her own. "Don't cry," she comforted. "If you were our Heavenly Father, wouldn't you want to call home a servant as good and true as Susan Mantle?"

"But we need her here, ma'am," the girl wept. She withdrew her hand and ran ahead to the top of the stairs, leaving Catherine with the distinct feeling that, while General Booth's recent theatrical display had succeeded, her quiet words of faith had failed.

Perhaps for some the theatrics of God were necessary. As for whether or not He would spare His servant Susan Mantle, that remained to be seen.

Whitechapel Infirmary
for Men,
London
April 1, 1875

For the first three days he didn't even bother rising to the surface of consciousness. The cool black crystalline depths suited him better, where there were no requirements of thought or feeling.

On the fourth day—although he certainly didn't will it—he opened his eyes and caught a glimpse of the world from which he had been unable to escape. He found himself in a coffinlike bed, and moving his hands slowly in both directions, he could feel the rough, unsanded pine sides. All they had to do was nail the lid on, dig a suitable hole, and the refuse could be discarded.

He considered lifting his head and discounted it as impossible and was forced to content himself with only what he could see on either side. On his left there was nothing, while on his right he saw a bed similar to his own and the sharp bony profile of an old man.

He lay still, closed his eyes and wondered why he was so cold, wondered where he was and why he was too weak to lift his head, wondered . . .

Why was he still alive when Elizabeth was dead?

He realized he had spoken only as the name itself formed on his lips.

"Are you in pain, my friend?"

He at first was uncertain whether the voice belonged to the past or the present.

"Do you feel like taking some nourishment? It might help." The voice didn't go away. In fact, it came closer. "I have something here that belongs to you. I've taken good care of it while you've been ill."

Who the voice belonged to, John had no idea. But as he felt the slight weight of something settle in on his left side, he lowered one hand and saw the wicker case which contained the remnants of Elizabeth's dress.

Elizabeth.

The cry erupted with such force it literally dragged him up to a sitting position. His hollow, feverish eyes closed against the remembered horror he could neither digest nor pass beyond. Thus imprisoned in the coffin bed and in the agony of the past, he flailed upward with both hands, reaching for the wicker case which brought her nearer to him and which had sustained him on his long odyssey.

But as he reached for the wicker case, something intervened, someone on his knees beside the bed, who intercepted his hands, brought them forcibly together, and then moved over him with gentle insistence. Before John could protest, he felt arms move around him, in a crushing embrace. With his hands pinned, it was impossible to reach for the wicker case.

The grief was still increasing, grief to which he'd succumbed countless times in the past few months, but which never seemed to be truly eased. Rather it grew by what it fed on, which were the memories, the lonely, hideous, graphic memories.

He wasn't alone now. The hands that initially had merely intercepted his reach for the wicker case gently pushed him back on the bed. A voice was now flowing over him, a male voice but bearing none of the natural qualities of the species, neither aggressive, nor arrogant, nor challenging.

It was promising him the one state that had persistently eluded him all his life.

Peace.

". . . my friend, it's yours for the taking. Not by might or by power but by God's spirit. There is not enough darkness in the whole world to blot out the shining of one small candle of faith. Do you hear?"

He heard, though the words were not as important to him as the touch of those hands. No one had ever touched him like this before—except Elizabeth when she had rocked him thus once, a long time ago. Yes, Elizabeth . . .

Elizabeth, oh, my dearest . . .

"Easy, friend. God is with you to help you face this hour."

But again something was rising within him, something unendurable, something from which he must find respite soon or . . .

Still whispering, the voice asked, "Father, what has Thou for this Thy servant, and where should he go?"

Father? Papa . . .

"Teach him to walk in a new way, in newness of life."

Papa, Elizabeth is . . . dead.

"Hold on to me, my friend. I'm with you."

The blackness rose about him. The tears came.

"Please, lovest Thou your servant," the quiet voice begged softly, blending with the deep grief. "There is darkness here, but we will find the path that leads to the heart of God."

The encompassing arms, the faint rocking motion, the voice promising peace, all were both unbearable and sustaining. But perhaps with grace and forgiveness and the guidance of this gentle voice promising peace, his long-deafened soul could now hear.

Though she had tragic news to deliver, Catherine waited at the door of the Whitechapel infirmary and saw the moving scene, one which she had

304

witnessed hundreds of times before, General Booth gathering a lost lamb to him with all the love and compassion and sincerity it was possible for one person to feel for another.

At last she saw General Booth stir himself from the stiff position he had held for so long. He rose awkwardly, testing each leg first as though it were necessary to check the circulation before placing full weight upon it. The others went about their various chores. The young woman pushing the breakfast cart turned away and commenced serving the men in the opposite aisle.

Catherine observed a curious look on the faces of all, even the ill old men, who lay back on their beds, a look of shared peace.

She felt it, as well, one more soul brought nearer to God. Perhaps not a true servant yet, but neither would he ever again be the wounded, helpless man he was before.

"Who is he?" she asked softly as General Booth drew near.

"A lost soul," was all he said, touching her arm lightly, affectionately, leading toward the steps which led down to the dormitory below.

A lost soul! She might have guessed that much. Well, there would be time later for identification, perhaps even acquaintances and, best of all, friendships, like Lord Simmons. Many of the men who once had thought themselves dead and who subsequently had known resurrection remained in the Whitechapel mission. According to Lord Simmons, there was no life for him beyond the realm of General Booth and his service to God.

Perhaps that one, lying so still now, one hand resting lightly on that mysterious wicker case, would remain. And serve. And find the peace he had so consistently denied himself.

Catherine jarred herself out of her daydreaming. Sweet Heaven, forgive her. General Booth must be informed of the tragic news. He was needed in the women's infirmary, where Susan Mantle had taken a serious turn for the worse. Dr. Mercer was at a loss to diagnose, beyond the fact she had worked herself in excess of her body's capacity and beyond the fact of the fever itself.

How capricious of God, Catherine thought, as she took a final look at the man sleeping, that He had sent a lost soul to the mission on the same day He took a dedicated, loving servant.

"Please spare her," Catherine prayed quickly, sensing God's presence still lingering in the room. "We need her desperately." Then she hurried down the stairs after General Booth, dreading his initial look of sorrow, responding to tragic news first as a man, then a few minutes later with faith, as a man of God.

"William," she called out, spying him at the bottom of the stairs in conference with Lord Simmons.

She approached quietly and saw a brief look of acknowledgment in Lord Simmons' eyes, but no greeting. Rather, he nodded to General Booth, apparently engrossed in the information being relayed.

"Are you certain?" she heard him inquire, his expression one of surprise.

"No," General Booth said, "I'm not at all certain. But there is a resemblance, and I saw the man a few years ago and—"

"I knew that gentleman as well. It simply couldn't be the same," Lord Simmons said with a degree of authority which crumbled rapidly. "Could

305

it? I mean, he had a large family, to say nothing of his financial empire. His aides would not permit him to descend to the state in which—"

"You did," General Booth said quietly, not meanly, just a matter-of-fact reminder that no man was exempt from falls and descents.

Lord Simmons nodded. "But I was very much on my own. No family certainly no profession, no . . ."

General Booth nodded sharply. "Still, would you check it out for me? Simply a matter of curiosity, that's all. How interesting if indeed we had today rescued one of the richest men in England."

Catherine looked up. Despite her reluctance to eavesdrop, it had been unavoidable. One of the richest men in England? What had he meant by that?

"I shall be happy to, sir. How do I go about it?"

"Call his offices here in London. Say nothing that will give him away. He needs time, obviously. Make a simple inquiry as to his whereabouts. Their answer may tell us what we want to know."

Lord Simmons nodded to everything, and Catherine thought again how unusual these two should get on so well, this blue-blooded peer and the commoner preacher who at thirteen had apprenticed himself to a pawn-broker.

"Then if you'll excuse me," Lord Simmons said quickly with a bit of humor in his eyes, "I'll now go play sleuth."

"No, it's not that," General Booth objected, following after him a few steps. "It always helps us to establish identity if possible. Even in your case . . ."

"I know," Lord Simmons said, a look of remorse on his face now, as though he was sorry for the implication.

Catherine kept her distance by several feet to watch the little drama, feeling curiously disquieted by it.

"General Booth, I must speak with you," she called out, filling her voice with new force as she saw Lord Simmons hurry out the door to fulfill his own mission.

At last he turned to face her, but the vacancy on that normally strong face was alarming. For several moments he looked at her as though she were a stranger.

Alarm increasing, she stepped closer until she was within touching distance of this man who had shared her body and her bed every night since 1855. "William, what is it? Who do you think the man is—besides a lost soul?"

"Ah, Catherine," he murmured at last, covering her hand with his own. "Where have you been?" he inquired, thus confirming her suspicion he was indeed seeing her for the first time.

"Right behind you, William," she said quietly. Near the door she saw two young female staff members, red-eyed and quite upset, who were waiting to escort them back to Susan Mantle's bedside.

The two young aides saw them coming and dabbed quickly at their eyes in an attempt to straighten themselves. She knew it had been their hope she would return with General Booth. Too many of these young country girls ascribed far too much power to William, she knew, and knew further he did nothing to discouraged such adulation.

In that moment he apparently came back to himself and to the fact she

306

was moving him toward a destination. "Catherine, wait. Where are we . . . ? I must return. Upstairs the new man . . ."

As his objections came out in fragments, she continued her firm but gentle pressure and tried to distract him with questions. "Where was Lord Simmons going?"

"On an errand."

"For you?"

"For the mission. . ."

"Will the new man upstairs be all right?"

"I think so. I want Dr. Mercer to . . ."

"Who is he? Do you know?"

Then General Booth stopped, glancing rapidly about as though fearful of listening ears. "I think," he began, smiling in a conspiratorial fashion, "of course, I'm not certain, but I think he may be John Murrey Eden." He stepped back, a look of immense pleasure on his face.

"John Mur . . ." she tried to repeat and couldn't. Surely he was mistaken. The John Murrey firm was the largest construction firm in all of London. One could not walk four blocks in any direction without seeing their large signs proclaiming new structures planned or under way. She bowed her head so he couldn't see the disbelief on her face and decided to change the subject.

"Susan Mantle," she said quietly, feeling new mourning rise within her. "Dr. Mercer said—"

"Dear God, no!" General Booth breathed quickly. "Hurry!" he called to the two aides, who had parted to make way for him. "We must pray as we move toward her." All at once his head fell forward and the two young female aides followed suit.

Only Catherine, bringing up the rear, was relieved in a way the message had been delivered, wishing—in spite of her recent condemnation—General Booth *could* perform a miracle and restore the woman to perfect health. As she followed after the three who were praying aloud, she looked over her shoulder toward the steps that led upward to the men's infirmary.

John Murrey Eden.

Not very likely.

307

Grosvenor Mansion,
London
April 2, 1875

Richard had long since given up asking God to forgive him, though the thought occurred to him every time he shared the large mahogany bed with Aslam. Now, as he stretched pleasurably beneath the coverlet, he felt that lovely tension in every nerve and muscle of his body.

"I do love you, you know," he whispered, drawing Aslam closer, feeling the young man respond, his hand moving slowly down across Richard's chest.

"And I you," came the muffled reply, as Aslam pushed beneath the coverlet. The sensuous exploration conducted by those expert hands continued. The moment wasn't far, and it would be good, and as Richard closed his eyes in an attempt to bring the release to full expression, he heard a loud knocking at the outer door and felt Aslam go rigid.

His hands now grasped Richard's shoulders, the dark eyes which only seconds earlier had been hooded with pleasure now alert, the tension destroyed along with the momentum, both killed by a second loud knocking.

Richard felt Aslam push against him in an attempt to leave the bed. The rapturous expression had disappeared into something terrible. Fear. They both knew all too well the consequences of their actions should they be found out. Sodomites were treated on a par with murderers in English courts. Worse. Murderers were condemned to death, while sodomites were sent to prisons where they were completely at the mercy of other prisoners. Death was usually the result, but it came slowly, mercilessly after weeks of brutality.

"Were . . . you expecting anyone?" Richard whispered as both men pulled frantically at their dressing gowns.

Aslam shook his head—one sharp gesture—and drew the cord about his dressing gown, pulled it tight, and looked quite lost for a moment until the knock came again.

"Be calm," Richard advised. "It's just Maudie, and she . . ."

". . . knows nothing," Aslam whispered, further revealing his depths of fear.

Richard was sorry for the fear and saw himself fifteen years ago. "Go and see what she wants," he directed, touching Aslam lightly on the shoulder. "Go on," he urged the young man, trying to communicate a peace and calm he did not feel.

"You wait here," Aslam said, nodding. "Don't let . . ."

". . . her see me?" Richard concluded, smiling. "She knows I'm here."

"She thinks we're working. It's late, and—"

"No, it's early, not yet nine. We ate early . . ."

For a moment longer they stared at each other across the mussed bed. The knock came again.

Finally Aslam turned toward the door, his expression splintered. When he looked up, all his defenses were in place. Without a word he passed through the door and drew it partially closed behind him, leaving a crack—a thoughtful gesture so Richard might hear and know the nature of the interruption. For Maudie Canfield's sake, Richard hoped it was something of vital importance.

"Well, sir," the woman was saying, "he said it was important—about Mr. Eden, it was—and I knew how worried . . ."

Richard stepped closer to the partially open door, newly alert.

Suddenly into the new silence came a male voice. Someone had managed to talk Maudie Canfield into bringing him right to the very door of Aslam's sanctum. "Let me apologize for myself, sir," Richard heard the voice request. "My name is Lord Simmons . . ."

Following this remarkable announcement, there was a second silence, as though Aslam were awaiting further clues to this bizarre, ill-timed interruption. As for Richard, he thought he detected a familiar ring to both the name and the voice. Lord Simmons? Where had he heard that name before?

"State your business, sir," Aslam demanded with an uncharacteristic lack of grace and diplomacy.

"May I . . . come in?" the man requested gently, a distressing counterpoint to Aslam's rudeness.

Lord Simmons? Where had he heard that name?

"Yes, of course," Aslam responded, his voice utterly lacking in sincerity. "That will be all, Mrs. Canfield," he added.

Richard held his position by the door, head bowed, curious at the mystery yet regretful it had forced itself upon them at this moment.

"Allow me to apologize again."

As the voice broke the silence, Richard was tempted to steal one look through the partially open door.

"No need for apology, Lord Simmons. Just state your business quickly."

"Of course. And it's simple, really."

"Then state it!"

"It concerns Mr. Eden—"

"I'm Mr. Eden."

"No, with all apology. I had reference to Mr. John Murrey Eden."

"Why?"

The bluntness compounded the rudeness, and in the echo of both, the tension grew.

"Why do you inquire about John Murrey Eden?" Aslam demanded.

There was a pause. Richard heard a peculiar break in the man's voice. "Because . . . I know him, you see. Old friends, yes, that's what we are. I've been out of touch for several years, and I . . ." As the voice drifted off into a lack of conclusion, the fact of a lie was confirmed.

Richard debated again the wisdom of stealing one small glance. Perhaps the face that accompanied Lord Simmons would be familiar.

"So you see, if you have any word of him, I'd be most grateful. I came here tonight thinking to find him, and again I can only offer my sincerest apology—"

"He's not here," Aslam interrupted harshly.

Another pause. The man did not retreat so easily.

"I realize that, but could you—?"

"He is dead."

Richard heard clearly the reverberating echo of those dreadful words, unconfirmed but spoken with all the authority of wishful thinking. Aslam wanted him dead, and as no one had been able to find him in the labyrinthian underworld of Paris, Aslam had, some time ago, pronounced him dead.

"I . . ." Lord Simmons tried to speak and couldn't.

Aslam took advantage of the man's disorientation. "Now, if you will excuse me, Lord Simmons, I must . . ."

"Of course. You must forgive me. I'm . . . stunned. May I ask how . . . when?"

"In France. Some months ago. Now, please, I must . . ."

"Of course. Thank you for being so kind."

"No need . . ."

In this muddled exchange, Richard felt a peculiar wave of new mourning, as though he too had heard the tragic news for the first time. Not until he heard the slow measured tread of boots moving toward the outer door did he think to steal a glance. John's unsubstantiated death was not the mystery here. The true mystery was why this man had come at this time with this inquiry.

He grasped the edge of the door, fearful of moving lest the floorboards in the old mansion creak and give him away. Still, he had to take a chance. With the first glance he saw the man full length, as it were, a bewildering portrait, the initial impression that of aristocrat turned commoner, for the apparel was common in cut and fabric, while the angle of the head and body were clearly . . .

Dear God.

Then he remembered. Lord Simmons, of course. Laurence Simmons Family seat in Shropshire. Several months ago all newspapers filled with the scandal—Richard remembered the gossip now—a nobleman who had turned his back on everything to follow Christ, or, more accurately, some zealous evangelist in the East End.

He dared to look more closely, and this time saw his suspicion confirmed. It was Laurence Simmons, once heir to one of the most impressive families and fortunes in the realm.

"Are you certain, Mr. Eden, of John's death?" Lord Simmons inquired a final time. For some reason, he looked genuinely bereft, yet to the best of Richard's knowledge John and Laurence Simmons had never met.

Richard eased back from the door, realizing that in his estrangement from John for the last four years he had no idea who he had seen or known or been associated with.

"Are you asking for substantiation, Lord Simmons?" Aslam demanded.

"No, I merely wanted—"

"Why should I give you substantiation?"

"Of course, you have no—"

"I've extended you the courtesy of an interview at great inconvenience to me."

Oh, for God's sake, Aslam, he's a nobleman. Don't speak to him as if . . .

". . . and I am most grateful, Mr. Eden," Lord Simmons replied, courteous to a fault even under these trying circumstances.

In the silence that followed, Richard peered out again, fascinated by the man who had taken the whimsical teachings of the Bible so seriously.

"Thank you, Mr. Eden," the man said graciously, his manner confident, his face exhibiting a rare peace, as though the serenity were soul-deep.

No response from Aslam. Richard saw Lord Simmons reach for the door, push it open, and leave, closing the door behind him. Even after the echo of boots had long since ceased, no one in the chambers stirred, as though each had fallen into his own trance.

Richard was the first to move. Slowly he drew open the door all the way and reflexively tightened the cord about his dressing gown. He padded with bare feet into the sitting room, all the while keeping his eye on the door, as though the man had been a mirage.

"Laurence Simmons," he repeated softly, still stunned that so radical a man had recently passed in and out of those doors.

"Could you tell me what in the hell that was all about?" Aslam snapped from the shadows.

Without looking at him, still focusing on the door, Richard said quietly, "He wanted to inquire about John."

"I know that."

"And you shouldn't have told him he was dead."

"He is."

"Unsubstantiated."

"Bates says so."

"Bates is bored with Paris and the search and wants to come home."

"Do you . . . think he's dead?"

At last here was the old Aslam, reasonable, polite, ready to listen. At the sound of that tone, Richard turned toward the desk and tried to answer the difficult question with as much integrity as he could muster.

John dead?

"No," he said at last, wishing curiously that Lord Simmons were still here. "No," he repeated, "not until I see a death certificate—or better, the body."

"Then where is he?" Aslam asked.

Richard heard new desperation in the young man's voice, as though there was nothing worse or more threatening than an unaccounted-for John Murrey Eden.

Where was he? Richard had an idea now, but in that instant decided to keep it to himself until he could prove it one way or the other. If John were alive, there was a good chance he was in wretched condition, physical as well as mental and spiritual.

"Richard, what is it?" The voice of concern was Aslam's. Why hadn't he exhibited some of that concern for Lord Simmons, who truly deserved it?

"Nothing," Richard answered. "We'll know sooner or later, won't we? Everything."

"Why did he come here, that man?"

Richard shrugged. "He was a friend of John's . . ."

"John had no friends."

"Maybe he acquired a few in the last four years."

"John was insane during the last four years."

"We don't know that."

"Alex Aldwell said . . ."

Aldwell! Richard hadn't thought on the man. "Is he still in Paris?"

Now Aslam slowly stood and stretched, the bathrobe pulling against his shoulders, then falling open to the waist, revealing the smooth brown chest and tight coils of black hair. "He comes and goes, helping Bates check every lead."

"Is he in London now?"

"I have no idea. I've ceased to need him," Aslam said wearily, and Richard thought it a strange way of phrasing it. "I've found another foreman equally as good, better in some ways."

Richard turned slowly and stared directly down into the dead fire. A queer solution to human need. Simply replace them as one would replace a pair of lost boots with new ones.

"My dearest," Richard said with affectionate simplicity. He extended his hand across the shadows toward the dark face that brooded endlessly. It was several seconds before he felt the comforting pressure of Aslam's hand in his.

"He mustn't be alive, Richard," Aslam whispered, caught in the embrace.

"Why?" Richard asked gently.

"Because he'll try to take the firm away from me, and the fight will be bitter."

Richard noted the strange prophecy. "And who will win?" he asked, now amused by the young man's sense of melodrama.

But there was no response, only a tightening of those arms around him, reminiscent of a child clinging to a father.

"He *is* dead, isn't he, Richard?" came the last plaintive inquiry.

While Richard heard, he refrained from answering because he knew his reply would only cause greater distress. No, he suspected John Murrey

Eden was very much alive—and worse, right here in London. What's more, he had a fair idea where he could be found. How John had managed the difficult journey back from France, Richard had no idea.

Locked inside Aslam's embrace, Richard smiled. Why should such a force of nature as John Murrey Eden be stopped by a mere journey across the waters of the English Channel?

East London
Salvation Mission,
London
April 2, 1875

The first indication she had she might be dying was the thickness of her tongue. The second was her fever. She was on fire, could feel the perspiration streaming down into her matted hair, trickling down her neck, the pillow soaked despite the number of times Cassie had changed the pillow slip.

And, of course, there was that third indication, the fact of General Booth bending over her bed. Who was she to attract the attention and take the time of General Booth—unless, of course, she was dying.

"My dearest," came the deep voice which she'd heard so often from the revival platform.

She tried to acknowledge his presence, but couldn't. It was impossible to form words with that swollen tongue, which seemed to be so enlarged now that surely it was distorting her mouth.

Then Cassie was there again with her plain, good, and now frightened face. Susan wished with all her heart she could reassure the young girl. But she couldn't, and as the cool cloth moved over her forehead, she saw the strong, compassionate face of Catherine Booth.

She closed her eyes, for it hurt to keep them open, and now she felt a hand on her forehead and knew it wasn't Cassie's, yet the touch was cool and encompassing. She shivered in her fever, realizing whose hand it was and recalling there were many workers who considered the touch of that hand to be capable of miracles.

"Susan, can you hear me?"

She nodded, hoping it would suffice.

"Good." General Booth nodded. In the next moment, and to her extreme surprise, he sat on the edge of the cot, his body pressed firmly against her leg—a premeditated intimacy, she suspected, as though he needed to touch her at several points in order to transmit his strength to her.

"Then you must listen to me," he ordered. "You must fight against this poison that is moving through you," he commanded. "You can, you know. You have allowed something to weaken you, to undermine you, even in the act of service. You must fight it, but you won't be alone in the battle. Everyone at this bedside is now praying for the safe deliverance of your body and soul. Tonight at the meeting hundreds will offer similar prayers, and *God . . . will . . . hear!*"

Those three words were delivered like a trumpet call, the soft voice no longer soft in any aspect, but strong and echoing. All the time his hand pressed, palm down, upon her forehead, where his fingers touched she felt a curious tension, as though each fingertip was capable of dispensing its own power.

Thus the weight of his hand on her forehead seemed to be growing lighter. The fingers still touched but were exerting no pressure. She thought she heard someone sniffling close by and knew it was Cassie—poor Cassie, who shed endless tears for the wretched of this earth.

Catherine Booth appeared to be still at prayer. How fond Susan was of this woman who lived eclipsed in the shadow of the remarkable man to whom she was joined for life.

As General Booth continued praying, Susan felt herself beginning to float on the low hard bed. There was no sensation of anything beneath her.

To whom she was joined for life.

Remarkable words, she thought hazily in her delirium. She pressed hard back against the pillow and feared, not death, but the act of dying, prayed it would be brief, and thanked God very privately for allowing her to know this miraculous world and pledged her continuous deep love for the kingdom of God and vowed there were no regrets—save one.

Look after him, wherever he is, she prayed quickly, and wished she might have looked upon him one more time.

"Susan!"

There was that strong voice again, angry-sounding now, and there were others moving closer, something cool pressing upon her forehead, the high collar of her muslin nightgown loosened . . .

"Fetch Dr. Mercer," she heard someone command, and knew there was nothing Dr. Mercer could do, as on so many occasions there had been nothing she could do but sit and watch, helpless, trying to make the patient as comfortable as possible, as slowly all air was blocked from the lungs.

Then there were no more voices, only silence. She thought of the Psalms, one of her favorites: *They that go down into silence . . .*

. . . and knew then what death was and knew as well how near it was at hand, and thought: *Thirty-four years . . .*

. . . and thanked God for the gift of every minute of them.

Whitechapel Infirmary for Men, London April 2, 1875

By reaching with one hand beside his bed, he could feel the edge of the wicker case, and that satisfied him. He realized with a degree of relief that for the first time in countless weeks he was relatively at ease. Of course all aspects of Elizabeth still inhabited his heart, and the memory was still so fresh . . .

But upon awakening yesterday from a deep, prolonged sleep, he'd discovered a new sensation, like a vacuum almost. Not that he had let go of everything that once had been so important to him; it was just that he was unable to recall what those things were. And if he couldn't remember what they were, how could he think on them and strive to attain them again?

And where was he? And how had he come to be here? And was it important that he know the answers to these questions? Or, for now, was it sufficient to concentrate on that single ray of sun over his bed which had slipped in through an unseen window and had now caught, in perfect focus, on the sheer, symmetrical, gossamer beauty of a perfectly formed cobweb hanging suspended from the dark low rafters overhead.

It was a five-sided miracle, as perfectly aligned and designed as though the spider had used a straightedge in its construction—a more skillful intelligence than most of the architects who at one time had been in his employ in the John Murrey firm.

Despite the weakness he felt in all parts of his body, he smiled.

The John Murrey firm! What a colossal bit of arrogance and conceit that had been.

He closed his eyes with confidence and felt deep within a new calm.

"Breakfast, sir? It would do you a world of good."

Slowly he peered up at the plump, pleasant-looking young girl severely dressed in black with a high white collar. She pushed a small cart before her on which sat a large steaming kettle and several teapots covered with brown cozies. The delicious odor reminded John of the kitchen at his father's Ragged School on Oxford Street.

"'Breakfast, sir?' was what I asked," the girl repeated. "You need some nourishment and I got to do these tasks plus me own, plus . . ."

He sensed an overworked staff and nodded to the offer.

"Can you manage, sir, or should I . . . ?"

As the young nurse posed the incomplete question, she placed a steaming bowl of oatmeal and a cup of tea on the upturned crate which served as a table beside the low bed.

"No," he managed, his voice barely a whisper. The awareness of this warm and friendly nurse reminded him of . . .

Susan.

The thought of the name and the accompanying physical image left him strangely weaker.

Susan Mantle.

Something different there, something insistent and nourishing, for indeed she'd dragged him back from the edge, single-handedly.

"I . . . can manage," he whispered, and tried to sit up. His quivering muscles refused to cooperate, everything objecting to movement of any kind.

Apparently she saw the failed effort and grew quite cheery. "Not to worry, sir. Let me pass these out to those 'uns over there, and I'll come right back."

Before he could object or express gratitude, she added, "We're short-handed, don't you see?"

He thought he detected a look of sadness on her face and sensed grief.

"But it's good to see you feeling better, it is." The young girl smiled. "You are, aren't you?"

He nodded and tried again to sit up.

But the young nurse objected. "Oh, no, sir, please stay put—at least till General Booth gets here. You're kind of a special package, you are, and until we find out precisely who you are . . ." Abruptly she broke off. A crimson blush, like a new flame, started along the edges of her jaw and climbed rapidly up her face, leaving her normally rosy cheeks rosier than ever. "I'll be back, sir, I will," she murmured, clearly flustered, having obviously said too much.

John watched, prone again, though amused. Of course they didn't know who he was. He had no papers and, in all honesty, he couldn't account for his actions with any degree of clarity since . . .

Dear God, how it still hurt, that single image, Elizabeth led forward . . .

Again he closed his eyes and knew that while he could never successfully obliterate that image, that sound, he must learn first to accommodate it and then to resist it, though at the moment that possibility seemed so remote. He lacked even the strength to lift his head.

Slowly he slipped one hand out of sight beside the low coffin bed and touched the wicker case in which he carried the fragmented remains of his soul.

317

So! They didn't know who he was. Neither did he. Oh, he knew his name, knew what had happened, did not know how he had journeyed from Paris to London without funds or papers, did not know what direction he would choose now, did not know what he would place into the new vacuum of his personality, did not know . . . anything. Until he did, it occurred to him it might be best to remain silent and anonymous. His name had become like a piece of unnecessary and heavy baggage. Everyone labored mightily under his own preconceptions of who John Murrey Eden was.

Then be someone else for a while—or better, be no one.

Suddenly to his right at the far end of the long aisle of beds he heard voices raised in ugly dispute, one voice in particular—male, belligerent—shouting obscenities at the pleasant young nurse, who appeared to be trying to quiet him with no success.

All the way down the long aisle, John saw his fellow patients, all very old men, glance up apprehensively. As the male voice grew more offensive, threatening the nurse now with physical assault, John saw the old man in the bed directly next to him start to weep very quietly, all the time pleading, "Don't, please!" as though the outline of this argument taking place in the infirmary bore a certain resemblance to one he'd endured in the distant past.

His attention was drawn back to the ruckus at the end of the aisle, which was ugly and growing uglier. The man—possibly just drunk—was out of bed now, threatening the nurse with one powerful hand.

After several minutes when he heard no one approaching, he knew someone had to intervene before it was too late. The young nurse was weeping openly, her strength no match for the man, who at that moment delivered a stunning blow across her face.

Effort must be made, even if he fell flat on his face, which was a distinct possibility. With renewed determination he fought his way up to a sitting position, suddenly grasping the high wooden edges of the coffin bed to hold on while the rest of the large room swirled about him.

A woman's muted moan steadied the room for him, and he swung his legs out and over, aware the young nurse had recovered from that first stunning blow and was now struggling again for her freedom.

Then he was on his feet, moving down the long center aisle, grasping one bed after another for continuous support, at last getting the rhythm of it, as pleased with himself as though he were newly born and taking his first tentative steps.

"No, please!" came the terrified female voice.

John did not approach the man in violence for the simple reason he lacked the energy. With a kind of insistent gentleness he merely reached over a bed and touched the man on his shoulder, more to get his attention than anything else—which he did admirably, for suddenly the man struggled up, arms flailing, the anger which recently had been focused on the terrified nurse now aimed at John.

Though the distance between them was limited, it was momentarily enough. Before the man could move, John extended a hand to the sobbing nurse and helped her up with a one-word instruction. "Go," he said.

Instead, she covered her face with her hands and wept openly, at the same time trying to straighten her long skirt, which had been pushed up by the man's straying hands.

The man was moving like an angry bull around the end of the bed, his face flushed with fury, his hands two ready fists, both inching slowly upward, gathering speed and strength.

"Please, my friend," John said quietly, not necessarily afraid of those fists—he'd dealt with fists all his life—nor did he display any inclination to run. First of all, he had no energy for running, and as long as the young nurse was still in harm's way, he would have to remain.

Suddenly the man stopped just as he rounded the foot of the bed, as though he had collided with an invisible wall. Apparently John's reaction had taken him off guard. For a moment the impasse held, the large man weaving drunkenly on his feet, perspiration running down his face.

Without thinking what he was doing or of the consequences, John again extended a hand, and with wary, distrustful eyes the man watched the hand, his breathing still labored, his mouth open and slack.

"Take it." John smiled, seeing the man wobble anew and reach out for support that did not exist. "Take it," he repeated, his voice a kind command, though he added with a smile, "Take it before we both fall."

For several long moments he heard nothing. Even the young nurse's sobs had grown quiet in the tension of waiting. Like a receding storm, he heard the man's labored breathing, saw the painful confusion on his face confronted suddenly with terms of peace just at the pitch of battle.

"Oh, come on," John repeated, daring to step closer. "We've nothing to gain by this, neither one of us. Years from now you must not wake up, as I did, and remember you have caused pain. Let me spare you that, if I can. Take my hand . . ."

For an instant the look of confusion on the man's face seemed to increase. A middle-aged face, John noted, which bore the scars of several other altercations. Suddenly he shook his head roughly, stepped back, and in his inebriation, misjudged his footing, tottered for a moment on unsteady legs. Reflexively he lifted his face to the ceiling, and his hands shot out searching for support. One, his left, found it in John's offer, their hands grappling for a moment as though the sensation was new to both but intriguing enough not to be abandoned.

When the man regained his balance, the link continued to hold. They gazed at each other with a degree of surprise. Neither spoke, but continued in silence to read the miracle of the other's face until from some source of agony soul-deep, the man commenced to weep. The tears hid in the perspiration until John looked more closely and saw their source and sensed the tears of a lifetime, long repressed, at last set free by one human hand extended in need to need.

"Don't," John murmured. Still using the link of hands, he drew himself close to the sorrow and gently enclosed it.

"Do." He smiled, and felt the man's arms tighten around him in what conceivably was the first human embrace in approximately fifty years of loneliness and living.

By noon that same day, though everyone had lovingly consigned him to , John knew being an invalid no longer suited him. For one thing, it was unnecessary. There was nothing wrong with him that two bowls of Casie's hot oatmeal with burnt-sugar topping hadn't cured.

Then, too, he'd not created one of the largest and most flourishing construction firms in the British Empire without a keen eye for organization. And this organization—whatever its nature and however noble its intentions—was in sad need of overhaul.

Last and most important, he ached to duplicate that rare feeling, combination of peace and warmth mixed with an almost unbearable surge of new life that had visited him as he'd taken the drunken man in his arms and comforted him.

Now wanting to be useful, he sat up with astonishing energy to ask young male worker who was just passing by under a staggering weight of soiled linen, "Do you do those yourself?"

"Indeed I do, sir."

"Do you have another set of those clothes you're wearing?"

Baffled, the young man stepped close and looked down on John as though he hadn't heard correctly. "I . . . beg your pardon?"

"Those clothes," John repeated. "Do you have extras?"

"Wh-why?"

"So you can lend them to me," John exclaimed. He stood up from the low bed to reveal the comic nightshirt that stopped just above his knees. " can't very well help you with the laundry dressed like this."

The slowly dawning look of understanding on the young man's face was gratifying, though in the next moment he was shaking his head as though good sense had intervened. "Oh, I'm not certain General Booth will permit that, sir."

"Why not? I want to help. You need help."

"Still, I think I should check with General Booth."

"Where is General Booth?"

"I'm . . . not certain, sir. I think he's preparing for the afternoon meeting."

"And in the meantime, we're losing valuable time."

"Are you sure you feel . . . ?"

John took a step closer, wanting very much to convince the young man he was capable of helping. "Let me try it," he requested softly. "If the pins go unsteady, I can always return here." He gestured behind him to the low bed.

The young man looked over his shoulder, as though wishing someone with greater authority would appear. But they were alone in the large room except for the dozen or so patients confined to beds.

"Well," he began hesitantly, "General Booth always says a desire to serve is a sure sign of health, mental and physical."

"Good man, your General Booth."

"Oh, he's not mine, sir. He belongs to God, who has lent him to all of us including you."

"Well, then?"

"Oh, all right. I'll be right back." Briefly a very wide, exremely pleasant grin passed between them. There was something about the young man that reminded John of Aslam. They were about the same age, and both were exceedingly sober in the execution of their duties. He watched the young man hurry through the infirmary doors after dropping the enormous bundle of soiled linen at the foot of John's bed.

He stared down at the soiled sheets for several minutes, then looked

320

farther down the aisle, where the drunken man was still sleeping soundly. Curious, the bond he felt for this stranger.

He padded barefoot down the aisle, aware of shifting watery eyes upon him as the old men on both sides charted his passage.

The man was on his stomach, his face turned to the left. John drew up the low three legged stool on which he'd passed most of the early morning, continuouly soothing the man.

"I'm glad to see you're feeling better, John." The voice, so near and so sudden, startled him, causing him to whirl about on the low stool.

For a moment he lost his balance and the room spun about. He half-expected, half-hoped to see the black-bearded visage of General Booth.

"Who . . . ?" he asked, squinting behind into a direct ray of noon sun and finding the face blurred, only the silhouette of a man standing about ten feet from the bed.

In answer to the question came another question. "*Are* you John Murrey Eden?"

Someone knew who he was or had been. "Yes." He nodded. "Who . . . ?"

"My name is Laurence Simmons. I live in London now with General Booth, but my family is from Shropshire."

A tall man, fifties, graying hair and beard, simply dressed like all of General Booth's mission workers. There was an amiable expression of calm and self-possession on his lined face.

"I'm sorry. I don't . . ." John faltered, continuing to struggle for recognition.

"No, please. I didn't expect you to know me, though I was at your beloved Eden some years ago for the Festivities, to see the lovely painting *The Women of Eden*. Alma-Tadema, I believe, wasn't it?"

As the series of names and events from the past bombarded him, John felt momentarily disoriented. Everything was vaguely familiar, yet all seemed dreamlike as well.

"Come, sit," the man invited kindly, taking John's arm to lead him across the aisle to an empty bed.

John looked more closely at the remarkable face of the man who knew so much about him. Still he did not recognize him.

Simmons must have seen the look. "Please, as I said, I didn't expect you to."

"Do you work here?"

"Oh, yes. I've been here for some time."

"Were you . . . ?"

"Dead? Yes, almost. I lived very well on inheritances, but . . ." He looked at the floor through clasped hands. ". . . but there was . . . no . . . core."

"And you found it here?"

The man nodded. "And I continue to find it every day, at the most unexpected moments."

John knew what he was talking about, like this morning.

"I thought it was you, you know," Simmons went on, "when they first brought you in, but you've . . . changed."

"Yes."

"Ill?"

"Once, though not of late."

"No matter," Simmons reassured him, apparently sensing the difficult nature of the conversation. "Well," he exclaimed, and stood to leave, "I wanted to welcome you and to—"

"How long did you say you have been here?"

"Several months."

"And what do you do?"

"Whatever is needed to be done." He stepped away, then turned back smiling. "I'm not certain who I was before I came here. I know I must have responded to a name. Unfortunately, there wasn't even the substance of a man behind it."

Dear God, he'd just described perfectly the vacuum in which John now found himself. "When . . . will it pass, this feeling?"

The man smiled and shook his head. "Can't say. Different for everyone."

John nodded as though he understood, though in truth he understood nothing.

For a moment the silence held. "Would you like for me to help you back to your . . . ?"

"No, no," John said quickly. "I'm waiting for clothes. I . . . feel like moving about."

"Good sign," Simmons exclaimed warmly. For a moment he seemed on the verge of departing. When he was only a few steps down the aisle, he looked back, a curious expression on his face. "You must forgive me . . ." be began.

"For what?"

"For prying."

"I . . . don't understand."

"You had no identification when you were brought in, only a small wicker . . ."

Don't speak on that, not yet.

"I thought I recognized you, but I wasn't certain."

"I've changed."

"Yes, oh, yes. But in order to confirm my suspicions, I called on your house in Grosvenor Square and asked simply for a brief audience with Mr. Eden."

Intrigued, John listened closely. That other life, that other man, kept surfacing.

"And . . . ?" he prompted, seeing a new hesitancy in Simmons' face.

"To my surprise—for I fully expected to be told there was no one there by that name—I was ushered up to the top-floor chamber, where a dark young man greeted me and informed me that you were . . . dead."

For several moments the two men gazed at each other, obviously pondering all the implications of this premature judgment.

"Dead?" John repeated.

"That's what I was told, yes."

Bates. Then John remembered. Bates must have searched for him and, unable to find him, had pronounced him dead. No matter. In a very real

vay he wished that man *could* die. He was partially dead already. If only
he remembering part of him would follow suit.

"What is your wish?" Simmons asked.

Confused, John looked at him. "My . . . wish?" Then he understood.
Did he want to stay dead, or should they announce his resurrection?

"I beg you, do nothing, for now," he requested. "I need time to . . ."
Not certain what he needed time for, he broke off and looked up.

The young man was hurrying down the center aisle carrying a pair of
plain dark trousers and a dark smocklike shirt. As he caught sight of
Simmons, he stopped, a stricken look on his face, as though he'd been
caught in some guilty act.

"It's all right," John called out, urging him forward. "Hand them to
me, then both of you leave. I'll join you in a moment."

Simmons and the young man exchanged a glance. Still doubtful, the
young man asked, "Shouldn't Dr. Mercer see him first?"

But Simmons shook his head no and looked back at John for confirma-
ion.

"Thank you," John said, grateful. He took the clothes, thinking: *He
nformed me that you were dead.*

Perhaps he was.

Then dress and go find out. Dead men did not, as a general rule, do
aundry.

The laundry room was in the subbasement of the Whitechapel Infirma-
y, a low-ceilinged, damp, steamy, satanic place of openfires, billowing
apors, and the burning sting of harsh lye soap. By six o'clock that night
John's hands were chafed and bleeding, his face raw from repeated exposure to the vats of steam, and his eyes aflame from lack of fresh air. But on
he table before him was row after row of clean, neatly folded linen.

"A half-day's supply," Rob commented wearily.

John gaped, unable to believe this inhuman, back-breaking chore would
have to be repeated tomorrow.

"Are you all right, John?" Rob inquired with admirable cheerful-
ness.

John nodded and noticed that only he seemed to be suffering. Rob's
hands were well callused and hardened, surviving the lye soap very well.
And he'd survived very well in all other respects.

"Are you sure you're all right?" Rob asked again thoughtfully. "It's
very hard, I know, if you're not used to it."

"How . . . long does it take to get used to it?"

"Depends." Rob smiled. "My hands bled for about a month before . . ."

John nodded broadly, not wanting to hear more.

"I do thank you," Rob added. "Usually I'm here until much later. With
your help I can now assist General Booth."

"With what?"

"Evening services. You'll come, of course."

John wasn't so certain. He had never cared for preachers, nor had he
fully understood the concept of a beneficent, all-powerful God.

"John, are you—?"

323

"Fine," he cut in, and reached behind to untie the heavy black full-length apron which had done nothing to keep his borrowed garments dry.

"Thank you again," Rob called out, and took the stairs two at a time.

John waited a moment, then followed wearily after, heading toward the narrow stone steps which led up to the kitchen, filled with women cooking large vats of vegetable stew, all of which bore a startling resemblance to the vats of boiling clothes which he had recently presided over in the laundry room.

Slowly he reached out for the banister, felt it creak and give under his weight, and suddenly he saw a world where nothing existed in abundance except want, hunger, illness, and need. Unable at the moment to go on, he sat heavily on the bottom step, briefly resting his head in his hands, and saw one surprising but clear image of the little nurse who had tended him so loyally at Eden, who had cooked, cleaned, and washed for him, alone and unaided.

Susan.

Yes, that was her name.

Then he moved slowly up the narrow staircase again, heading toward the chattering females in the kitchen. Halfway up, he noticed they didn't seem to be chattering as much as they had been at midafternoon when he had gone—on Rob's instructions—to fetch two mugs of tea and plain biscuits.

Now, as he reached the top, he saw no one was minding the steaming kettles, boiling away quite merrily all by themselves. The bulk of the kitchen staff seemed to be huddled around a low chair, from which emanated deep sobs.

He slowed his pace as he approached the women and considered offering whatever help he could. But, not knowing the nature of the problem or the grief, and sensing perhaps the females were better able to handle it, he bowed his head and was in the process of circumventing them on his way back up to the second-floor infirmary, when suddenly a voice called to him.

"Oh, sir, you really shouldn't be up. They said you were, but . . ."

At the sound of the broken voice, he stopped, looked back and, to his surprise, saw plump little Cassie sitting at the center of that knot of hovering women, her eyes red and swollen, tears still seeping out, despite her continuous dabbing at them.

At first he was baffled by the look of such unbearable grief. Then he remembered. Of course. This was a delayed reaction to her terrible ordeal of the morning, when the man had attempted to assault her.

He walked slowly into the congregation of women, to stop a few feet from where Cassie sat. "Are you all right?" He smiled down on her. "I'm very sorry for what happened this morning. I should have been quicker, but . . ."

A slowly gathering look of puzzlement on her face halted his words. "This morning . . ." he prompted, equally puzzled. Then what *was* she crying about?

"Oh . . ." At last an enfeebled light crossed her face. "It wasn't your fault," she said nervously. "Besides, it's over and no harm done."

324

He nodded, still bewildered. Then why was she crying one moment and speaking so clearly the next? "Then you're all right?" he asked, backing away from the staring women.

"No," she murmured. Fresh tears came to take the place of the ones she'd just wiped away.

He looked around at the women with a questioning expression. One, a heavy old auntie with gray hair and a red kerchief tied about her throat, obliged with a brief answer. "It's our friend, don't you know. Dying, that's what she is. God just standing by and lettin' her die." In her crackling voice was a distinct tone of condemnation pointed at God.

"He's the one," Cassie said, over and around fresh sobs. "Remember I told you how he rescued me this morning, how he took that man's hand that had been raised in violence and brought him low with love?"

The explanation was a bit melodramatic, and John sensed the story might grow even more before it blessedly died. Now he felt the combined weight of all their eyes.

Even Cassie stopped weeping and sat sniffling upon her chair. "I thank you, sir." She smiled.

"No need for thanks, Cassie, and I'm sorry your friend is—"

"Would *you* come with me, sir, and see her?" Cassie asked suddenly, a new light of hope on her face.

All about him he heard the females buzzing, discussing the possibilities inherent in such a visitation.

"He may have the touch," one whispered. "I think he does. . . ."

"General Booth says all kind can possess it . . ."

". . . when you least expect it."

He stepped back from the discord of their rising voices. "I . . . possess nothing, I'm afraid," he said quietly, and started back toward the staircase.

"No, please, sir." This voice, so urgent, cut through all the others and summoned his attention. "Just come with me and we'll share a prayer, that's all," Cassie murmured, dabbing at her eyes again. "Dr. Mercer says it's too late for anything else."

"No." His protest was weak and ignored. As he struggled against the voices and what they were saying, he felt himself succumbing to them, some ancient, misplaced hunger for power, to be more than he was and all things to all men, to be beloved, like the ill friend was beloved, to be mourned and missed.

"Will you, sir? It will take only a minute."

Though the wiser voice of reason said no, the child-voice of his heart said: Yes, if you wish. . . . He extended his hand to Cassie. "Come," he said.

"Oh, thank you, sir," she said shyly, and led the way to the stairs, cutting a path through the females, who went along as far as the stairs, then held back, though they continued to look longingly after them, as though they wished they might accompany them.

With mounting dread, John followed after Cassie's ample black skirts, assuming a single-file position as they entered the crowded London street which led from the Whitechapel Infirmary to the main building of the Salvation Mission. Twice he started to call out to her that he'd changed his mind and had best return to the male infirmary but her step seemed to gather momentum and he couldn't quite bring himself to do it. Silently he vowed to see the ill friend, speak a brief prayer—if he could even remember one from his childhood—and hurriedly depart and leave the ill woman to the doctor and to God.

"This way, sir." Cassie smiled back at him, leading the way through the double doors of the Salvation Mission, where hundreds had already gathered for the free evening meal of black bread and vegetable soup.

As they entered the large room filled with long rows of wooden tables, John was struck by the silence. There must have been over three hundred people—men mostly—seated at the wooden benches, and yet the room was silent, except for an occasional cough. Those who had already finished eating continued to sit before their empty bowls, as though, despite the recent nourishment, they were incapable of movement. Either that, or it made no sense to move because they had no place to go.

Observing the vast theater of despair, he allowed Cassie to draw far ahead of him in her own impatience. He looked up to see her waiting less than patiently at the top of the stairs which obviously led up to a second-floor dormitory similar to the one in Whitechapel.

He nodded to say he knew he must hurry, and approached the steps with dread and a growing fatigue, the result of the day's labor. Halfway up, trying to maintain a goodly pace for appearance's sake, he saw Cassie in a close huddle with a short round man with eye spectacles perched on the top of his nose at an angle which defied gravity. Taking advantage of the respite to clear his head and catch his breath, John watched the man speaking, his hands moving constantly for several moments, then abruptly lifting into a shrug and falling to his sides.

Cassie nodded with suspect vigor, as though she wanted to convince the man she understood. Paradoxically, at the same time, she started weeping again.

Too late? He prayed not, but hoped so, for he knew better than anyone he possessed no "touch."

"Oh, please hurry, sir," Cassie sobbed openly, not even making an attempt to disguise her tears. "Dr. Mercer says she's . . ."

John obliged, doubling his speed, not pressing the woman for specifics. He'd find out for himself soon enough.

A few moments later Cassie called out, "In here, sir." She entered a door which led to a large dormitory, the beds of slightly better quality than those in the male infirmary. All were empty—save one. Near the far end of the second aisle he saw a slight figure abed, attended by two women, both garbed in the mission's standard black, both on their knees, one on either side of the bed.

At their approach, one woman looked up, her worn though kind face registering surprise at John's presence. Cassie attempted an incoherent explanation. "It's him, Mrs. Booth, the one what came to me rescue this morning. He has the touch, and I asked if he could . . ." Without a word, the woman rose from her knees with a smile, thus clearing the way for him.

The other, a younger woman whose face remained obscured by her bowed head, held her position, all her concentration focused on the black beads of a rosary which slipped slowly through her fingers. Catholic? He

326

knew nothing of Catholic ritual save that which Lord Harrington had brought with him when he and Lila had moved into Eden Castle.

He shook his head, bewildered why the past wouldn't remain in the past where it belonged, and approached the foot of the bed and slowly looked down upon the small female form, which scarcely made an indentation beneath the cover, her arms pitifully thin atop the blanket, her head pressed back against the pillow, lips dry and cracked, eyes . . .

He blinked. *No!*

Almost in anger he shook his head again, ordering the past to remain in the past, as for one terrifying moment he'd seen the face of the nurse who'd cared for him with such skill. He opened his eyes again and looked into the face again.

No stray fragment from memory this time. The same brow, the same smooth angle of jaw, the same dark brown hair—though instead of being neatly groomed and drawn back, this hair lay spread, mussed upon the pillow—the entire face pale and wasted, save for two fiery fever spots on each cheek.

"Susan . . . ?" he whispered, and heard a gasp coming from behind him, but paid no attention to anything until he could be certain the exact duplication of features was not a cruel trick, an optical illusion, perhaps brought on by the dim evening light which filtered through the high coal-dust-covered windows, or perhaps by his own state of mind and fatigue, the rapid, confusing chain of events which had led him to this place.

"Susan?" he repeated, wanting the woman to either confirm or deny.

Behind him he was aware of soft weeping and Cassie's voice, awed and reverent. "I swear, I never told him her name."

It was she, that miraculous "she" who had lifted the dead Harriet from his arms, who had descended to the unspeakable depths with him, and when she felt they'd gone far enough and it was time to rise, had set a new pace, a new direction, enduring his sullen impatience and arrogance, protecting him against outsiders until he was capable of meeting them on almost equal ground. All this and so much more . . .

Why was she here? What was she doing in this place of illness and disease? He'd left her safely in the West Country off on her circuits. What had drawn her to foul London and this state?

"Susan?" He spoke her name with sad confidence. How the name fit, but the woman who lay before him so still was unaware someone was calling her, that others were already mourning her, that the fever that had ravaged her body would shortly reach her heart and . . .

After the splintered, difficult day, after the hard labor and a despairing glance at how a large percentage of the world passed its hours upon this earth, after all the unwanted yet painfully vivid excursions into the dead past, after the unexpected peace and joy of the morning—after all this, he felt only a benumbing sensation and a strong need to hold her as she had held him on so many occasions.

Without a word, aware of nothing but the searing heat of her hand as he touched it, he reached down with both arms and enclosed her, felt her head wobble bonelessly against his chin, and held her in a cradling embrace, despite the doctor's brief protest.

"He shouldn't. She's contagious. . . ."

327

But no one made a move to stop him. He eased up to the edge of the bed, tightened his grasp on her, and rocked with her gently back and forth, thinking he'd felt her hand lifting.

Of course he hadn't, for it was clear she was dying. Yet he closed his eyes against her fevered brow and vowed to remain with her, to be vigilant, constantly on the lookout for Death. If Death appeared to challenge him, he would make it as clear as possible that Death would have to look elsewhere for his daily quota of the living, that this remarkable woman would be staying on for a while in a world that needed her much more than Death did.

"Remember the headlands at Eden, Susan, how we walked them back and forth and tried to count the seagulls?"

The weeping that surrounded him ceased. He sensed the women on their knees, sensed as well a solid and impenetrable fortress of prayer.

If Death did show up, it would be a memorable battle.

For a lost amount of time she had passed in and out of consciousness like the sun on a May Devon day. There were no real sensations of discomfort, save for the burning heat on her face and in her throat. Other than that, she merely felt as though she were in a fitful sleep, the kind she'd suffered often when she had allowed herself to get overfatigued.

She knew she was dying, and at first that terrified her. But then she remembered she'd worked all her life with the promise of heaven, of unity with God. Now that she was approaching that threshold, why should she be frightened of it?

Clinically speaking—for she was a good professional—the only thing that truly astounded her was that it was taking her so long to die.

Then someone was whispering to her, a deep male voice vaguely reminiscent of . . .

But it couldn't be. What would so grand a man be doing in General Booth's mission? And there was a gentleness, a tone of bereavement in his voice she had never heard in . . .

John? . . .

The thought was so absurd that for one terrifying moment she was afraid her powers of reasoning were slipping as well. Sometimes it happened in a high fever. No, she had no idea who this man was who was speaking her name over and over again, as though he too were struggling for identification.

There it was again, that face and voice that bore a striking resemblance to . . .

Was she dreaming?

If so, this dream was of a different nature than the others. In this one she could see him clearly now, his face, that same strong arrangement of features, yet altered somehow, tempered by something. Suddenly, in addition to being able to see and hear this hallucination, she felt him, felt clearly the press of his arms as they lifted her into his embrace, one broad hand supporting her head, guiding it to a place of safety and comfort beneath his chin.

She closed her eyes and did not attempt to open them again. In this safe fortress, vision was not necessary. Nothing was necessary, no effort of will or discipline on her part. She knew—without knowing how she knew, without caring how she knew—just knew that someone was holding her, that it wasn't a hallucination. This was someone of substance who hurt very much, was not ill in the sense she was but nonetheless bore new and deep wounds.

Three times he spoke her name, and as he continued to hold her, she relaxed and pressed deeper into his arms and thought, with a pleasant mix of seriousness and humor, that perhaps she *was* dead, that perhaps to be held thus by such a man was prelude to heaven.

For three days and two nights Catherine Booth, like all the other workers in General Booth's Salvation Mission, watched the drama taking place in the second-floor infirmary, watched Susan Mantle enter crisis after crisis, the fever raging out of control to the extent blisters formed on her face and body and portions of her hair fell out, her lips cracked and bled.

Early this morning General Booth had visited the sickbed and had suggested softly that God put an end to her suffering and claim her.

A short-lived request that had been, for the man—John, they called him, for he'd said that was his name—rose on unsteady legs from the low chair he had inhabited for three days and two nights and turned on General Booth with such anger that several workers had had to come between the two, placating John while the General made a hasty exit.

Now, as they were approaching the third night, Catherine sensed resolve in the cool April evening, and feared, despite John's obvious devotion and "touch," the laws of nature would be more powerful than the "touch" of a lost soul and Death would claim her. Catherine feared a despondency of spirit within the mission that would have to be dealt with, for the two active participants in this drama had worked their ways into the hearts and souls of everyone.

Convinced it could not go on much longer, and as there were only a few remaining in the common kitchen after the evening meal, she decided to climb the steps to the second-floor infirmary and see for herself what a large portion of the staff was already witnessing. Most had disappeared at discreet intervals throughout the evening. Catherine had known where they were going and had let them go, though it *had* angered General Booth, who had left the mission after dinner without a word.

"Be patient," she had counseled him before he left. "Don't give him more power than he already possesses."

Still angry at this usurpation of his authority, he had stomped out into the night. Where he had gone, she had no idea. But in a way, she was glad he would not be in the building when Death came tonight. She feared that John, weary from the battle, would turn on General Booth, who earlier had worked against him. It was best the two men not meet—at least until John had been able to digest his grief.

Suddenly she heard a rush of footsteps from behind, and looked back in time to see two of the youngest kitchen maids hurrying toward the stairs, their faces flushed with exertion, a patina of sweat on their foreheads which suggested they had recently been bending over caldrons of steaming water.

"Oh, ma'am, I'm sorry. We didn't mean . . ."

They had rushed right past her, not recognizing Catherine standing in her indecision at the bottom of the stairs.

"It's all right." She smiled, following the guidelines she set forth for everyone else. There was no stratification of work or workers here. They all were servants in Christ; therefore, one and all would be treated with the same dignity and respect. "You've finished your chores, of course?" Catherine asked, fascinated by the light of excitement in their eyes, as though they were going to a theatrical or a marionette show.

"Oh, yes, mum," the second replied, and curtsied on the third step. Both continued to inch their way up, as though even a brief delay was intolerable.

Fascinated, Catherine continued to chart their enthusiasm, until at last she was forced to call out, "Wait just a minute, would you, please?" She saw the two exchange a glance of dread, and hastened to reassure them. "No, in a minute you can go up. It's perfectly all right. I just wanted to ask a question of you."

"Of . . . us?" the first girl asked, striking herself lightly on her chest and looking comically incredulous.

Catherine waited for them to give her at least a small portion of their attention, then asked bluntly, directly, "Why are you so eager to watch your friend die?"

All at once a massive look of disbelief passed in unison across both their faces. "Die, mum? Susan ain't gonna die. What makes you say something awful like that?"

Suddenly feeling very much like a faithless heathen, and sorry for having asked the question, Catherine tried to think of a way out, couldn't, and answered as honestly as she knew how. "Because . . . I've seen fever patients before, many times, and when the fever is this bad, without respite, they seldom, if ever—"

"Oh, don't count Susan among what should happen," they protested. The first did most of the talking, though the second contributed her moral support by nodding broadly and continuously. "She ain't like no other, and we all know that, now, don't we? And so when Susan gets sick, Holy God sends someone special to . . ."

Catherine bowed her head, disheartened to hear her fears confirmed. Of course she knew Susan was special, but she also knew she was subjected to the same laws of nature, just like everyone else.

". . . so you see, mum, nothin's going to happen to her, long as him's there, and he don't plan to leave."

"Run along, then," Catherine urged them with a tolerant smile.

"You comin', mum? It will be wonderful to see—General Booth, too, just what he's always preaching to us about, resurrection."

Then they were gone, leaving Catherine stunned at both their claims and her own feeling of doubt. Where had that come from? She was a faithful servant of God, wasn't she? She *did* believe, did practice both the letter and the spirit of God's law.

Susan ain't gonna die. What makes you say something awful like that?

As the conflict grew within her, she felt a kind of paralysis. She continued to grip the banister but seemed incapable of lifting her foot to take the first step, seemed most content in safe inaction, staring unseeing at the worn dark green frayed runners which covered the steps.

When she finally reached the door, she was surprised to find it closed. It never was, in the event one of the patients had to call out to the limited nursing staff.

She listened, thinking to hear something that would give her a clue, heard nothing, and briefly closed her eyes to pray, though now the words seemed hollow. In an attempt to escape from what felt like the husk of herself, she pushed open the door and saw a moving spectacle. Twenty-five, thirty workers on their knees surrounding Susan's bed, all heads bowed save one, the man named John, who sat on the same low chair he'd inhabited for three days and two nights, a basin of water resting on his knees, his hands moving back and forth across her forehead with a cloth he continuously dipped in the basin in an attempt to keep it cool.

She saw the man lean forward, concentrating on Susan's face, whispering something to her—or so Catherine thought, for she heard someone whispering but could not distinguish the words or the source. No one was moving, but the awesome weight of all those eyes focused on one limited arena, that of the low bed and the man who had now, for the first time in three days, abandoned the low stool and was seated on the side of the bed.

The whispering was coming from *him;* Catherine was certain of it now, and occasionally heard a single word before his voice fell into intimacy again. "Eden" and "heather," and once she heard an entire phrase clearly, ". . . the sun on Eden Rising." He spoke on for a few moments in this incredibly soft, private manner. Then, without warning, his voice fell silent as though from exhaustion or despair.

For the rest of them, all that could be said was they gave the impression of being held so fast by a mutual point of interest that no one appeared to be breathing.

The man seated on the edge of the bed whispered something else, cut off this time by a clear and discernible break in his voice. Catherine felt the tension continue to build to an almost unbearable point, saw now, along with everyone else, an incredible movement coming from the man, saw him bend forward over Susan as though he were preparing to . . .

He was.

. . . to lift her, gently at first, as though he were afraid of harming her, then with clear vigor and intent, cradling her as he would a child, his body obscuring everything except one arm, which dangled uselessly at a distorted angle, the white muslin sleeve bearing evidence of the intense fever, the hand beneath the cuff small, pale, and still.

Now Catherine bowed her head along with the others. The brief sense of joy had been annihilated by the clear sight of that one limp hand, which did not speak of life or energy or will, but spoke simply of the draining exhaustion and blessed surrender of death after a painful illness.

God go with her and receive her, for she was a good and faithful servant.

This prayer was Catherine's, very silent, very private, already mourning the gifted little nurse. "Too slight to do any good," had been General

331

Booth's initial judgment, but in a few short months she'd proved herself to be a most valuable, competent, and capable member of General Booth's female staff.

He should be here . . .

Catherine looked up, jarred by the thought that should not have intersected her prayer, and thus was the first to see it, though it was a matter of only seconds before others saw it as well, that one lifeless hand receiving messages from the brain, the fingers flexing once, the hand lifting ever so slowly at first, yet still it came, one arm, one hand lifting, angling around *his* shoulders.

Then the entire hand cupped around the back of that bowed head, the fingers reaching out in an attempt to smooth the mussed hair, coming to rest at last in a gentle cupped and enclosing gesture until it was difficult to tell who was giving succor and support to whom.

To her surprise, Catherine felt her eyes blur. Now throughout the room she heard others weeping, but could not look away from that one delicately cupped white hand which continued to caress the back of his neck in a gesture that signified merely all the love in the world.

East London Salvation Mission, London
April 19, 1875

Never in his life had anything happened so effortlessly, with such a feeling of rightness.

Seated now at her bedside, watching her sleep in a soft glow of late-afternoon April sun, John charted carefully the entire miracle, the way in which the infinitesimally small light brown hairs which fringed her forehead curled into two perfect circles; the manner in which the soft hollows beneath her cheekbones formed two oval pools of purple shadow; the angle at which her head rested upon the pillow, as though someone had just called to her and she was on the verge of responding; that one small but so capable right hand resting atop the cover; the lips, still pale from the fever, slightly parted; the beautiful arch which the shadow of her eyes formed with her eyebrows . . .

He couldn't see enough, for there was so much, every angle and shade, tinge, and tone of her was pure miracle.

He leaned slowly back in his chair. *Please wake up*, he prayed, missing her even in sleep. *Please continue to rest*, he prayed again, knowing it was what she needed, longing for her to become strong and well again.

Briefly he closed his eyes to rest them, and scolded himself for being so . . . adolescent. She'd turned him down once—or rather turned down his gift of the cottage on Eden Rising. She was a talented, practicing professional, dedicated to a life of service. He had no right to expect anything of her, save the kind of loose bond two people have who have been of service to each other.

Still, with new longing, he quickly opened his eyes, missing her even in so brief an interim. He would have to leave soon. Not just her and this bedside, but leave the mission as well. He didn't belong here. He'd hoped

333

once he did, but since the evening of Susan's awakening, when without warning the fever had broken and she had moved of her own volition when all were expecting death, since then too many of the workers had ascribed to him greater powers than he possessed. Several of the young kitchen maids had asked for pieces of his garments to send to ill relatives. Others had asked if he would journey with them to sickbeds of beloved family members, and one, a young scrub girl in scullery who'd recently buried an infant son, had asked him to come with her to visit the grave and see if he could raise the boy.

For a few moments Susan's simple beauty faded as in his mind's eye he saw those plain worn faces, who had no conception of the true nature of their requests or how wasted they were upon John. He'd talked briefly with Laurence Simmons about it, but the man had only counseled patience, truth, and passage of time.

That had been five days ago, and instead of diminishing, the requests were increasing. The only time they left him alone was when he was at Susan's bedside, as though this were the font of the first miracle and therefore sacred.

For several moments longer he stared down on her, his mind and heart torn now between the dilemma of his future, the perfection of the present, this moment, and the awesome weight of his past. If only . . . But he had no right. Gone were the days when he could blindly force his wishes on others. Quickly he bent over, still not fully capable of dealing with memory.

All at once he saw her eyes open, one hand lightly curled beside her head, her eyes still glistening feverishly from the severity of the illness, though Dr. Mercer had reassured him she was well out of danger and needed only rest.

For a moment, under the direct gaze of those eyes, he found he couldn't breathe. While he struggled to form words, she seemed more than content just to watch him, the expression on her face beyond his interpretation.

Suddenly, when he'd least expected it and certainly when he'd least needed it, he felt a tidal wave of heat rush over his face, searing everything in its path, rendering him as inarticulate and mute as a shy schoolboy.

Forever—or so it seemed—they stared at each other. When at last they spoke, they spoke at once, a muddle of voices in which nothing was clear.

"I'm sorry I—"

"I still can't believe—"

As they had started together, they broke off together, and again the room was filled with first a splintered echo, then silence, save for the street sounds outside the window.

She was the first to try again. "I . . . thought of you so often, and worried . . ." She broke off, her lips dry.

He moved back to the bed, still trying to think of something to say in return that did not sound inane or stupid.

"Are you . . . all right?" she asked.

Suddenly he was aware that inquiry should be coming from him to her. He nodded and sat down on the edge of the straight-backed chair. "And you?" He smiled. "You're the one—"

"I . . . must get up," she interrupted, reaching for the cover with one hand to push it back.

"No," he protested, moving quickly to the edge of the bed. "Dr. Mercer says—"

"I couldn't believe it was you."

"And I couldn't believe it was you."

"You've been ill. . . ."

"Just hungry."

"What happened in Paris?"

He bowed his head, expecting the waves of grief to inundate him. "Later," he murmured, pleased that for the first time the waves never developed. "May we speak of it later?"

"Of course. I'm sorry. I shouldn't have . . ."

"No, it's all right. It's just that . . ."

They continued to gaze at each other. Again it was impossible for him to read her expression. It looked amazingly like care and concern, but then, he could be wrong. He knew from experience she cared indiscriminately for the entire human race. Was there anything about her view of him that was different?

She shook her head, briefly closed her eyes, then reopened them.

He realized she was tired and he was intruding. "I'm sorry. I'll . . ."

"John . . ." She'd never addressed him by his Christian name before, and did it now as effortlessly as though she'd addressed him thus always.

He looked down on her, thought he should respond, but again could think of nothing to say, nothing, at least, as eloquent and articulate as the volumes they were both speaking in the silence.

Every time she had awakened during the last few days, she had suffered moments of black dread.

Was he really here? Or had she dreamed it?

So confirmation was always first on the agenda, followed by a desire to speak rationally and coherently to him, as she'd imagined so often she would speak to him if she ever had another chance. But of rationality and coherence in her brain there was little.

Each time upon awakening he was there, right enough, the same face and yet vastly changed; the same frame and torso, yet they too were changed; the same mind and spirit, yet even they were changed. It was as though the old John had escaped his skin, had carelessly left it lying about and someone else was now inhabiting it, someone she did not recognize— therefore the point of confusion.

"John?" she repeated, knowing it was he yet wanting, needing another confirmation.

"I'm here," he obliged, reaching forward to cover her hand with his.

All at once she felt an incredibly strong impulse to smile. For almost a year she'd dreamed of a moment like this, never expecting there was even a remote chance of its coming true. Yet, now that it apparently had, all she could do was gape and repeat his name.

There were so many questions inside her head, she couldn't begin to

335

articulate them. For now, until she regained enough strength to at least make an attempt to solve the mystery, she would have to be content with the dilemma that she had almost died, and in the brief interim while she was gone, this earth had become a paradise.

"Would you . . . care for water?" he asked, apparently as baffled by their prolonged silences as she.

Quickly she shook her head, not wanting to inconvenience him, then abruptly regretted her response. She *was* thirsty, but—more important— if she had allowed him to fetch water, she would have given him something to do, and perhaps have eased both of them.

"Yes," she said, and again apologized. "I'm . . . sorry . . ."

Again a silence grew between them, this one not so good as others, this one speaking of too much uncertainty.

"John, a glass of water would be—"

"I'll get it," he said too eagerly.

She watched him the length of the infirmary as far as she could keep him in view before he disappeared like a sudden deprivation behind the nurses' screen, where a pitcher of fresh water was placed twice daily, generally one of her own chores.

Without a word he extended the glass of water to her and stood back.

"Thank you." She smiled, taking the water, only to discover she was incapable of lifting her head to drink without spilling it.

He saw the dilemma and approached awkwardly, his hands outreaching, wanting to help but not quite certain what they should do.

"Remember how we used to do it?" She smiled, weary of censoring each and every thought, ceaselessly worried that this one was inappropriate, that one too painful. Dear Lord, at this rate they would never converse again. "Back at Eden—you remember—when you were abed. Here, I need a boost, just enough to . . ."

With the help of sign language indicating his arm beneath her neck would make it possible for her to drink, she was delighted to have him respond immediately and felt an absurd schoolgirl flutter beneath her breast as he leaned over her, his left arm gently elevating her head while his right hand held the glass close to her lips. In this intimate position she found it difficult to swallow, and managed only a gulp or two before her throat seemed to constrict, blocking all further passage.

As he continued to tilt the glass toward her lips, she finally was forced to splutter, "Enough . . ."

"I'm sorry . . ."

"It's fine . . ."

"I'm afraid we've spilled . . ."

"I used to do that, too. Remember?"

"Did you get enough?"

"Oh, yes. Thank you."

"I'm afraid I lack your training."

"You do very well."

Silence.

He backed away, taking the half-filled glass of water with him, while she made an attempt to brush the spilled drops from the front of her nightgown.

When she looked up at him again, she found him staring down on her. Suddenly the awkwardness of their encounter seemed so absurd. They knew each other better than certain married couples. Each had witnessed the other in extremity. What was the matter with them now, that neither seemed capable of forming a single sentence?

"John, come . . ." She smiled, exhibiting a calm she did not feel. She assumed she had little to lose at this point. She had tried to eradicate him from her life and thoughts so often in the past. If he left now, what was so different?

At first he didn't seem to hear, continuing to stand a few feet back from the bed, still holding the half-filled glass of water, quite stricken, as though he'd committed an unforgivable crime by spilling a few drops of water. Just when she was about to ask again, he started slowly forward, bringing the glass with him, never once taking his eyes off her face.

Then there was nothing more behind which either could take refuge, no rationalization, no activity, no intrusion from others. In fact, the world seemed to be leaving them painfully alone. For a moment she studied his face and weakened, as though his presence were sapping her strength. "Thank you for your . . . attention," she began simply.

"No need," he said with mock brusqueness.

She waited a moment, giving him a chance to speak further if he wished to speak. Obviously he didn't. "May I ask a question?" she went on with new hesitation. She didn't want to pry, but somehow she wanted very much to start filling in some of the empty places of the last few months.

He nodded.

"How did . . . you come to be here? In London. At General Booth's."

He shook his head, smiling, as though what she was asking for was far too much. "It would take forever . . ."

"I'm not going anyplace."

The expression with which he viewed her changed, grew more sober. The smile faded. "I'm not certain I can . . ."

She understood both the tone and the hesitancy and moved them quickly past both. "You've changed," she began, thinking it a safe comment, only to realize she had thrust him right back into the spotlight.

Abruptly he strode to the beds on the opposite side, in several determined steps. "I don't understand what goes on here," he said from this distant point. "Sometimes I find it all very moving, then at other times it seems small and bitter, feuding and unnatural. . . ." As his voice drifted off, he gave a helpless shrug.

The silence held. From her bed Susan found herself continuously moved by all aspects of him. "I'm not certain," she began quietly, "that we do ourselves a service when we try rationally to understand the workings of the heart. Everyone here," she went on, "is here because they want to be. No one has been pressed or forced into service. As you've observed, there are workers from all walks of life. The only common bond between them is a . . . need to serve."

"A need?"

"Yes, a need."

"Doesn't that imply that the act of service is more *self*-serving?"

337

She smiled at the ancient dilemma. It had bothered her in the past, the selfish nature of selflessness. "I don't know," she confessed, "why the act of easing pain should bring pleasure, but it does, doesn't it?"

Still maintaining the distance between them, he said a peculiar thing. "You were so kind to me last year at Eden."

"You were very ill," she said, masking her surprise. Conversing with him was like chasing a ball of mercury.

"And very difficult."

"Yes, sometimes."

"Susan, I have committed crimes . . ."

"We all have."

"Mine are worse."

"Perhaps." She listened carefully, feeling her pulse quicken. She found herself incapable of taking her eyes off him, as though he were the last man on earth and she had to record everything, every feature, commit it to memory against the day when he would be gone from her.

"Elizabeth is dead."

The simple words simply delivered moved across the room and struck her with painful accuracy.

Could she withstand it? She had to.

For never again would she ever back off from this awesome man.

He was moving slowly toward her now.

God, give me strength, she prayed quickly.

"How? Please tell me about it."

And John did, until the room was completely dark, save for the mysterious light source that is always visible in early darkness, and until she felt bruised upon the pillow.

Incredibly, once he started speaking, he never moved, never even once changed positions from the slumped one he'd initially assumed in the chair. His voice throughout most of the tale was a monotone, as though a dead man were speaking, his head never lifting, the only visible manifestation of the ordeal in his hands, which seemed to contain and exhibit energy for the whole body, clasping and unclasping, clenching, unclenching, restless as birds in flight.

So real had been his words that she felt as though she recently had been a lodger at Monsieur DuCamp's, felt outrage that men like General Montaud were permitted to draw breath upon this earth, felt she would have liked Madame Charvin very much and was grateful to her, as was John, for providing him with that final hope. A chance had been taken and the gamble had failed. At stake had been Elizabeth's life. . . .

She looked up at him where he sat in the chair as though the prolonged detailed account had left him drained. What could she say? What could she possibly say? It was a miracle he hadn't taken safe refuge in madness or death. As far as his family was concerned, apparently they did indeed think him dead, a judgment which seemed to suit John for a while. And why not?

Old Bates had undoubtedly launched a search. Briefly she saw an image of the grasshopperlike old man who last year had begrudgingly been kind to her. And Charley Spade. What had become of the hulking young man who'd been selected to assist Mr. Eden?

She looked at him through the lengthening shadows and saw, not "Mr. Eden," saw instead a frightened, lonely, and confused man. Elizabeth would have known and recognized that expression on his face. It was a lost-child look and must have visited him repeatedly as a child.

She tried again to conceive of adequate words, again failed, and settled for the most eloquent of all, extending her hand to his, where it rested upon his knee.

The trembling was over, the fingers still and cold. It might have been the hand of a dead man, except as she touched him, covered the coldness with her own hand, she felt it stir, felt the fingers flex and intertwine with hers until the link was complete.

With no words spoken, the past had been defeated, the present accepted, the future plotted.

East London
Salvation Mission,
London
May 1, 1875

"I won't have it!" General Booth thundered, slamming down his Bible
upon his bureau with such force Catherine heard the spine crack and saw
several pages break loose from their bindings and slide across the surface
of his desk.

Quickly she placed her mending on the floor and went to the door and
closed it, not wanting General Booth's irrational voice to carry beyond the
four walls of their private flat near the rear of the mission on Whitechapel. She leaned against the closed door for a moment, wishing the laws of
matrimony did not require she shut herself in with her husband's rage.
She'd much rather be downstairs where the "offense" was going on, where
two people—when they least expected it and most needed it—were falling
hopelessly, shamelessly in love.

"How long have you known about it?" General Booth demanded, turning on her in his fury—again a husband's right and prerogative.

"Since the beginning," she admitted calmly.

"They told you?"

"They told me nothing, my dearest." She smiled and went back to her
mending, hoping, praying he not interfere in any way. The man John
Murrey Eden had gained a considerable foothold in the past month in the
affections of the workers, as well as the men who frequented the mission.
"It's been there all along for anyone with eyes to see," she said, settling
again in her armless rocker and retrieving the basket of mending. With
the first stitch she instantly regretted her previous claim.

"I have eyes," he bellowed, really quite out of sorts, annoyed such a
miracle had taken place within his mission that he'd had nothing to do
with, had indeed expressly forbidden to happen.

"Of course you do." She nodded quickly, still fearful his voice was carrying despite the closed door.

"Then why didn't *I* see?"

"Because, my darling, as you have eloquently pointed out so often in the past, we tend to hear only what we want to hear and see only what we want to see."

He seemed to think on this for a moment, his bruised ego temporarily assuaged with her diplomatic use of the word "eloquently."

She watched, needle poised, fearful of another outburst. There had been several observations he'd failed to make in the last few weeks, not only the growing, irresistible affection that was blossoming between John Murrey Eden and Susan Mantle, but also the developing—and more dangerous—loss of staff loyalty. Almost imperceptibly—and certainly without seeking it—John Murrey Eden was garnering that to himself, along with Susan Mantle's affection.

"Well, I won't have it," General Booth repeated, gathering up the scattered pages of his Bible and looking at them for a moment with a bewildered expression as though he wasn't quite certain how it had happened.

"Please, my dear," she entreated softly, "let them alone. It's for the best. I've heard kitchen gossip. I don't think they plan to remain—"

"I won't let Susan go."

"I don't think you have much choice."

"It is *my* mission," he shouted angrily at her. "Have you forgotten that as well?"

A curious "as well," she thought, bowing her head over her mending, a mild refuge from the storm of his anger. Obviously he too had witnessed the shifting of loyalty. Even Lord Simmons, who used to come to this very flat daily for afternoon tea, had preferred of late to sit communally at the long board table with John Murrey Eden and Susan Mantle and the several hundreds of others who wandered in off the street for a mug of tea and a plain biscuit.

"I have forgotten nothing, dearest," Catherine soothed, resuming her mending, thinking a demeanor of calm would help with the difficult moment. "It's just that—"

But she was never given a chance to finish, as fresh outrage erupted from the man crouched before his bureau, still clutching the loose pages from his Bible as though he didn't quite know what to do with them.

"No!" he exclaimed, filling the single word with Old Testament fury. "Obedience to me is essential," he pronounced, leaving his bureau to pace rapidly back and forth in the limited area of their sitting room.

She looked up, astonished. Surely he didn't know what he was saying—and if he did know, did he mean it?

"William," she cautioned, glancing toward the door, wishing there was another one she might close, at least until he regained his senses. "William, I must argue—"

"Don't . . . argue, Catherine," he exploded, turning on her and pointing his finger directly at her. "Argument never opened the eyes of the blind. Do not argue, but pray."

With a suddenness that startled her, he dropped to his knees as if he'd been felled, lifted his face to the ceiling, shut his eyes, and commenced to pray, not speaking clearly enough for her to hear—which was just as well, for she had no desire to hear, had only one clear desire, and that was to leave the room and take refuge elsewhere—at least until he'd regained his senses. But of course she couldn't do that. Sometimes it seemed to her that her only function as a wife and a woman was to bear captive witness to the mercurial moods of this irrational and brilliant man.

She placed her mending to one side, knelt by her chair, and joined him in prayer, though she was wise enough to know their divine entreaties were probably very different in nature. General Booth prayed those who had strayed be returned to *his* fold and *his* good sense, while she was praying that for the sake of future peace within General Booth's Salvation Mission, it would be best if two of his most effective and dedicated workers moved on, found a haven somewhere else, for she could not stand idly by and watch William Booth be destroyed by any man, not even so effective a convert as John Murrey Eden.

She closed her eyes and tried to dismiss the persistent and pleasing image of the two who now moved through the mission like two warming rays of light. To the best of her knowledge, it had been three days since anyone had sought out General Booth for counsel or prayer.

And this was the cause of his fury, though he would not admit it, not to her and—more importantly—never to himself.

London
May 5, 1875

Several weeks ago Lord Richard had made the suggestion and had asked Alex not to say anything about it to Aslam, but simply to put on an appropriate disguise and visit the mission on Whitechapel Street to see if . . .

But there had been no time until now for such a massive waste of time, and reviewing the absurd command in his mind as he made his way through the crowded East End, Alex tried not to breathe the obnoxious fumes of his "costume" and wondered if he himself hadn't gone a little balmy to be engaged in such a dubious activity.

John alive? Living in a mission in the East End?

He shook his head and instantly regretted it, as the sudden gesture seemed only to release fresh fumes from the disreputable trousers and coat he had purchased from a ragman for a king's ransom. He cut a tentative path through the jostling street traffic and tried not to think on the rationality of what he was doing, for of rationality there was none. Still, Lord Richard had requested it—several times—and Alex did owe the Eden family a great deal. . . .

John alive?

The astonishing suggestion continued to cartwheel through his mind. Where had Lord Richard acquired even the seed for such an unfounded suspicion?

Bates's last communication from France had claimed the decomposed remains of a man had been pulled from the Seine last month. Though identification had been impossible, the height had matched and the police had raised next to the body a partially decayed wicker basket. For some reason, Bates felt certain that was the identifying factor.

343

Puzzling, all of it. Why would John be carrying about a wicker basket?

Hurry! Check on Lord Richard's madness and then . . .

And why was it all so secretive? And why didn't he want Aslam to know?

As mystery compounded mystery, Alex hurried down the pavement, still not certain what he hoped to find in the Whitechapel mission. At that moment he glanced up to find himself approaching the mission, a large three-story building painted in horizontal stripes of blue and white, a large sign proclaiming "Salvation Mission—Food and Shelter."

He paused—not through choice, but because, as well as he could determine, a long queue was beginning to form, unruly here at the outer edges, all men, or at least as far as he could tell, but up close to the mission door perfectly formed and well organized.

Well, then, if what he needed to find out resided behind that large blue-and-white-painted door, then he'd best fall in line with the other lost souls and bring this absurd excursion to its conclusion.

Two hours later Alex was seated at the far end of one of the low long tables, the bowl of thin vegetable soup still before him. It wasn't bad, for he'd tasted it and he had consumed almost all the large chunk of freshly baked dark bread, constantly searching every face for one that bore even a slight resemblance to the man he once had known and loved.

Suddenly intercepting his thoughts as well as his line of vision was a vaguely familiar face—not male, but female.

All at once one of the women on the serving line spied her as well and hurried to her side in a solicitous manner, appearing to be insisting upon something which the woman resisted with equal determination, until the two females joined the entreaties of the second woman. At last the three determined wenches guided her to a stool against the far wall, insisting she sit; and finally—with a surrendering laugh—she sat, still mopping at her brow with the hem of her apron.

Where had he seen her?

Frustrated, Alex tore off another piece of brown bread and munched. If he could just clear his head, he could place the woman in memory, or at least . . .

What now?

All at once there seemed to be a similar gathering coming down the stairs at the far end of the large hall, a moving knot of people—mostly men this time—laughing and talking with some irresistible force at the center. From this distance Alex couldn't see it all and decided it didn't matter. He'd seen enough. This clearly was a preaching place, and preaching never had appealed to him, had appealed less to John, who had reserved certain choice epithets for—

My God!

Halfway up from the low table he remembered where he'd seen the woman. Of course, he could be mistaken—probably was—but if he wasn't, it was the nurse, the same one who had cared for John after Harriet's death. But was it? And how could it be? That woman had been a circuit nurse in the West Country, a dedicated and stubborn soul, as he remembered.

There was nothing more to stay for or to hope for. Lord Richard's

344

whimsical suspicion had proven groundless. Now perhaps he'd tell Alex precisely what had given him such an absurd notion in the first place.

These thoughts took him to within a few feet of the front door, where two young female workers hurried past, chattering, their tongues moving as fast as their feet, fragments of their gentle debate floating back as they hurried past:

"Well, how do you know?"

"I just know, that's all. He doesn't like that sort of thing."

"Then I'll ask Susan to ask him. She's the only one who can get him to do anything."

Susan!

That was her name, the nurse's name. Susan Something-or-other. Baffled that the puzzle pieces seemed to be falling into place without his efforts, Alex stopped to watch the two young nurses as they hurried toward the kitchen. Still watching the distant drama, Alex decided there probably were thousands of Susans in London and again started toward the door and the rapidly falling dusk.

He stopped for one last backward look and saw the ever-growing crowd at the end of the hall. Then he heard one clear female voice rise, lifting above the confusion of voices.

"Susan, he's here." With that the group appeared to move toward the stairs, leaving the young woman sitting alone.

Frustrated by the distance, Alex moved closer until only fifty feet and the barrier of two tables separated him from the kitchen. There he sat slowly down, drew low the flat worn shapeless hat, thinking at that moment he did not choose to be recognized. Then he saw clearly it *was* her, though she had changed. She looked thin and pale, as though she'd recently been ill.

All at once the chattering fell silent. Something at the center had commanded their attention and willingly they had given it. Even the young nurse looked up.

Alex shifted his attention back to the steps and at last caught a partial glimpse of the core, a tall gaunt man with scattered gray in his fair hair and beard. Suddenly this man turned his back on the crowd and in a curious movement started to back his way through his supplicants, once, twice shaking his head, as though he were rejecting their adoration as gently as possible.

Without warning the man increased his speed and drew completely away from the group and turned, facing Alex directly for only a moment, then looked into the kitchen, where he saw the woman. With one brief gesture the man motioned her forward and she obeyed instantly. Their hands joined out of sight in the fold of her skirts and the man looked back toward the still-clamoring crowd, touching his hand to his forehead in a kind of salute.

In that moment, in that gesture, Alex knew.

It *was* John, resurrected from the dead or never dead at all, mysteriously transported from Paris to London, aged, thin—but all these alterations superficial compared to a larger one which Alex could not readily identify but which had made recognition so difficult.

Still, it was John, and Alex continued to gape forward, needing almost constant substantiation, watching closely as he exchanged a few words

345

with the nurse, who nodded only once and quickly removed her apron, dropping it over a near chair, then rejoining him at the door, where he was still fending off the large group who seemed only to want to be near him.

For the width of the room the crowd followed after them until at last they disappeared around the partition. The crowd came to a halt and shuffled aimlessly for a few moments, as though they'd lost their compasses.

As for Alex, he wasn't faring so well himself. The identification had been positive. It was John. But how changed he was. Anyone else might not have even recognized him.

Leave now! Stay! Tell Lord Richard! Tell no one!

As the conflicting voices swirled through his head, he felt paralyzed by an inability to act. As the men started to drift past him, still searching for something to fill the vacuum of their lives, Alex bowed his head to ensure his own safety and heard whispered voices:

"He touched my arm. Did you see?"

"He said he would speak to us later."

Alex closed his eyes. What was this new John Murrey Eden up to? Should he stay and find out? Did he want to know?

As new questions arose to take the place of all the previous, unanswered ones, Alex at last found the strength to push up from the low table, and still keeping his head down, stumble toward the door, playing no role now, feeling genuinely undone by what he had seen.

He could say in all honesty he was certain of absolutely nothing except one fact, that John Murrey Eden *was* alive. He and the world would have to deal with that unalterable fact as they had always dealt with it, slowly, cautiously, and with the greatest of care.

Though sadly lacking in physical beauty, it had become their favorite spot, this high, creaking exterior wooden staircase that overlooked the dark alley behind the mission, a place where cats prowled for rats, and dogs for cats, where the rays of the sun seldom penetrated the dank darkness of surrounding structures. It was to this questionable place they now retreated, seeking it out only because it assured them of a moment's privacy.

John led the way without speaking, and she followed, maintaining the same silence, understanding it but saving her words until they were seated on the top steps, which led through a window and into a long corridor, which in turn led back into the infirmary, where recently he had presided over her . . . resurrection.

Quickly she corrected her thought. *That* was the trouble, the reason for his despondency. "It will pass, John," she soothed, sitting on the top step and tucking her skirts beneath her, regretful the words sounded so empty and inadequate.

He sat slowly beside her, resting his head in his hands. Behind this barrier he shook his head. "It's getting worse, and I haven't the vaguest idea how to deal with it or put a stop to it. They are attributing me with powers I do not possess, have never possessed, will never possess. I . . ." He broke off in a new despair and shook his head again.

"Please be patient with them, John, and with yourself," she counseled quietly, hearing the street sounds coming from the front of the mission, as though from a distance, like the rumor of a world.

"I can't allow it to go on," he protested.

"There's nothing you can do to alter what you are."

"I am not what they think."

"How do you know what they think?"

"I see how they look at me."

"With love and respect and—"

"I am not a god, Susan. I can't work miracles."

"In their eyes you can."

"Then their vision is faulty and I refuse to be responsible."

"What do you think they see in you?"

For the first time the rapid exchange faltered. Suddenly he stood, as though to move away from the question. He walked down several steps and peered over the railing into the garbage-strewn passage below.

She waited, giving him all the time he needed. After several moments when there still was no response, she drew a deep breath and offered an answer.

"They see in you a man who has endured and survived many crucibles, more than they, perhaps." She paused to see if he would comment in any way. He seemed more content to lean heavily against the railing, his arms braced, head down, eyes fixed on the darkness below.

"They also see," she went on, "a man who, in spite of everything that has happened, still believes in himself."

At this he looked sharply at her, as though she'd lost her mind.

Oh, you do, John, and you know you do. Your strength at the core is the most incredible I've ever known . . . in anyone, save one." She paused. "You knew her as well. Miss Nightingale. She, like you, possessed an unshakable faith in her own unique vision and individuality. Oh, setbacks would discourage her temporarily, but never for long, and certainly never permanently. She would always—"

"Miss Nightingale has reason to believe in herself. Her life has been exemplary from start to finish. Mine has not." The voice that spoke was a monotone. His attention was still largely fixed on the shadows below.

"All the more reason for them to see in you—"

"—something that does not exist!" Anger surfaced from someplace. As he spoke, he pushed away from the railing, looking restlessly about the limited area. "I don't want to go backward, Susan," he said. As quickly as the anger had surfaced, it passed and left him slumped against the side of the building, hands shoved into his pockets, the late-evening sun caught in his long fair hair and beard.

"Once I thought I could do everything, create everything, control everything." He seemed to collapse against the wall, head bowed, face obscured. "In the process of this . . . madness," he concluded, his voice low, "I came very close to destroying everyone I'd ever loved." He sat heavily on the step, resting his arms on his knees and covering his face with his hands.

She watched for several moments, her heart aching for him, and understood more clearly now why the adoration of the workers and staff disturbed him. He had accurately assessed his weakness, which paradoxically was his strength, his great ability to reach and control people. If he

347

could deny his own power, then he would never again be guilty of misusing it.

Studying him, she tried to conceive of the turmoil within, perhaps worse now than ever before, the world cruelly presenting him with the greatest temptation that could befall him, people willing and eager to be controlled and manipulated.

Still, he mustn't run from it. That was no solution.

Slowly she moved down until she was seated beside him. "John," she began, longing to touch him but deciding against it, "the past is over. Whatever you did or didn't do is of value to you now only as a lesson. The regret you have expressed today indicates a new awareness . . ."

He appeared to be listening. She hoped she was making sense.

"Something led you here, wouldn't you say, where your strength could be put to the greatest use among those less fortunate than yourself." She *was* preaching. She loathed the sound of it and broke off abruptly, moving back up to the top of the landing, vowing privately not to say another word. How presumptuous of her to tell him what he should do with his life. She hadn't done such a tremendous job of directing her own.

For several minutes only the distant street sounds filled the silence. Suddenly she heard movement and looked up to see him standing as though on the brink of a new idea, certainly new energy.

"Then you suggest I stay here and deal with it?" he asked, not looking back at her but posing the question straight ahead to the rapidly falling dusk.

Under the duress of the question she faltered. "Why . . . I . . . but I'm in no position to . . ."

"Will you stay with me?" he asked, still not looking at her.

She blinked at him, longing to see his face. Perhaps there was a clue there. "I . . . don't understand."

He shrugged and at last looked back at her over his shoulder. "What I said. We seem to fall apart with predictable regularity, you and I, and we both do a pretty fair job of putting the other back together again. I just thought it would save time and be wise to stay conveniently . . . close."

"I'm . . . not sure I . . . under—"

"You're not going to turn me down again, are you?" he asked, and sat on the step directly below her, the dying rays of the sun highlighting the rugged beauty of his face, that face so close now, staring at her with such intensity she found breathing difficult.

"Eden Rising," he said by way of explanation. "I gave you that decrepit cottage once, remember, and you turned it down."

Of course she remembered. But what was he asking now? She must understand before she replied.

"Well?" He smiled up at her, obviously not at all aware of her confusion.

"I'm . . . not certain that I . . . what do you mean, will I . . . stay with you?"

"Here. At the mission. Help me. Be with me. Talk with me, like we're doing now."

She nodded. "Of course I'll do all those—"

"Marry me."

348

"—things." Neatly she completed the sentence, then quietly disinte-
rated. "M-marry," she tried to repeat.

"Me."

She met his intense gaze directly and felt a searing heat scorch her face,
elt her mouth go dry. No matter how hard she tried, she couldn't get her
ongue to form words, which was just as well, for there wasn't one coher-
nt thought in her head.

He reached up, lightly took her hand, and, incredibly, apologized.
'Look, I don't think either one of us planned on it . . ."

"No."

"It just seems to be the most sensible solution."

"You don't even know who I am."

"Who are you?"

"The daughter of an Exeter farmer."

He grinned, a *Eureka!* expression covering his face. "Perfect! All my
fe I've been looking for the daughter of an Exeter farmer. Perfect. And
ou don't know who I am."

She felt her heart racing beneath the plain black dress and hoped it
vasn't visible. "Who . . . are you?" she asked, playing the foolish game,
eeling herself drowning in his smile and the sensation of his hand on
ers.

His grin broadened. "A bastard. Not even a legitimate Eden." He
ooked up expectantly at her.

She realized he was waiting for her to repeat his claim. And she did
Perfect. All my life I've been looking for a bastard."

His grin exploded into a laugh, and she joined him, finding it difficult to
elieve this same man had been hopelessly caught in his own despair less
han ten minutes ago.

The laugh died and left them staring at each other. The astonishment
he felt was mirrored in his face. Doubt surfaced. It was either a magical
vening or an insane one.

"John, I . . ."

"I can offer you nothing—"

"I require nothing."

"—except my love and devotion."

"They will suffice."

"I . . . am difficult sometimes."

"I know."

He seemed surprised by her ready agreement, then pleased by it. "Then
vill you?" he concluded on a deep breath. "Marry me."

It was inconceivable what was happening. "Yes."

For a moment she saw the slight relief of a smile on his face.

"When?" he asked, moving to the heart of the matter.

"We must ask General Booth first," she cautioned. "There are a few
narried couples here, and he doesn't always object, but he does like to
e—"

"Fine. We'll go all the way to Canterbury if that is required."

"No, that won't be necessary." She smiled. She no longer fought her
esire to touch him, and slowly raised one shy hand to that brow she'd
reamed of so often. With the tip of her finger she traced the length of one
ncient scar that ran across his forehead and wondered how it had hap-

pened and vowed with moving simplicity that never again would she allow him to endure any kind of pain alone.

As her hand moved down the side of his face, she saw a peculiar tightening about his eyes. In a sudden gesture of pure need he pressed her hand against his lips and she saw tears in the corners of his closed eyes.

Without quite knowing how it happened, she found herself in his arms, her face pressed against his shoulder, a fortress from which she could withstand anything the world had to offer.

He'd had no plan of this, no thought in his mind of marriage. In fact, his only desire as they'd left the common room had been a permanent escape from all those people who attributed to him more power than it was good for one man to possess.

When had the concept of marriage entered his mind?

As he held her and enjoyed her closeness, he tried to move backward through this brief encounter to discover at precisely what point his mind had effortlessly suggested marriage. The fact she was a farmer's daughter from Exeter was unimportant. The fact she had "preached" was unimportant. The fact she had attempted to counsel him was unimportant.

Then when? At what point had the mind said marriage?

Then he remembered. It hadn't been his mind at all that had made the suggestion. It had been his heart and it had spoken to him at the exact moment she'd moved away from him, back up to the top of the staircase at the exact moment she had withdrawn, clearly fearful she'd said too much. At the precise moment she had "left him alone," as it were, then he'd found her withdrawal a deprivation of such enormous proportions he'd followed her back to the top of the stairs and had suggested . . . marriage.

She sat beside him now, his arm about her shoulder, their hands interlaced.

He considered speaking. Perhaps she needed reassurance. Perhaps he shouldn't have mentioned marriage. He'd so failed his first wife. "Susan . . ."

By way of response she tightened her grip on his hand.

"I will try to be a good husband," he whispered.

"And I a good wife."

"Are you afraid?"

"Terrified."

"So am I."

On this bizarre declaration of love, they continued to sit, huddled together, foreheads touching like two children exhausted at the end of a long and difficult day.

Catherine knew the purpose of the meeting and thought once she should warn General Booth. But how could he not know? Everyone in the mission knew, and he would have to be blind not to see the new light in their eyes, the way their fingers touched at the slightest provocation, and—most important—the new peace they took with them everywhere and so generously shared with others.

She paced outside his study on the second floor of the mission. He's late, she thought, so perhaps he *does* know. Her brooch watch said half-past one. The meeting had been scheduled for two, prearranged only yesterday by Mr. Eden and Susan. She thought she'd seen General Booth mark it down on his ledger, but she wasn't certain, as she had been so captivated by the two, so newly impressed with the miracle of love.

Behind her she heard a step on the stair and looked quickly over her shoulder, hoping it was the General. Instead it was the two who somehow had transformed this grim mission into a magical enchantment.

"We had an appointment with General Booth." Susan smiled. "I guess we are early . . ."

"No, General Booth is late," Catherine replied, bobbing her head in greeting to Mr. Eden, who was maintaining a distance behind.

Susan glanced back at John. A question seemed to pass between them. Then, as though she were the appointed spokesman, she said simply, "We can wait for a few minutes."

Suddenly Catherine found herself hoping General Booth did not arrive. He'd been so churlish and short-tempered of late.

"You're looking well, Susan." Catherine smiled, leaning lightly against the wall outside the General's study.

"Thank you. I'm feeling well."

Beyond Susan, Catherine saw Mr. Eden pacing at the top of the steps. The man looked none too strong himself, gaunt and lost in the borrowed oversized clothes of Lord Simmons.

"And you, Mr. Eden?" she asked, wishing to engage him in just a brief conversation before General Booth arrived.

"I'm well, thank you," he said rather stiffly, as though he felt uncomfortable.

Catherine sensed their presence here was largely Susan's idea, and Mr. Eden, at best, was humoring her. Mr. Eden was not a man who easily asked another man for permission to do anything, which accounted for the pinched look on his face.

"I can't imagine where General Booth could be," Catherine said weakly, finding the ever-increasing silence awkward.

"We are a bit early," Susan murmured, though they weren't at all, as Catherine's watch now said two, straight up.

Catherine laughed. "General Booth is always assailing me for my lack of promptness . . ."

"Susan, we can come back later." This stern voice came from the man pacing at the top of the stairs.

She saw the small objection on Susan's face. "Let's wait a few more minutes, John, please."

The request was so softly spoken, no one could have resisted it. And no one did, though he abandoned his pacing and took up a vigil at the window at the far end of the corridor, which looked down on the street.

Susan smiled at Catherine, glanced toward the closed study door, then looked away. It really was becoming too awkward. Perhaps it would be easier if she departed, thus leaving them alone to talk freely. With this in mind, Catherine pushed away from the wall. "If you will excuse me, I'll go and see if I can locate . . ."

At that moment she heard something behind her, the sound of a key turning in a lock coming from the study, as though someone were . . .

She was aware of Susan's close attention now—as well as Mr. Eden's, who heard the lock turning from the end of the corridor and drew nearer in fascination with the sound and the realization someone had been in the study all the time.

Catherine started to speak, then changed her mind. She'd never known the study door to be locked before. General Booth always believed in openness and preached openness. Was it General Booth, she wondered and approached the door cautiously.

Long before she saw the black coat sleeve and the familiar hand, she *knew* and closed her eyes to the significance of the locked door and her husband's tightly drawn face.

At last he emerged full portrait into the afternoon shadows of the second-floor corridor, his Bible clutched at its customary position in the crook of his arm, pushing the door all the way open with his leg, then standing framed in the open doorway, as though to give them all the benefit of his appearance.

For the moment all three seemed too stunned to speak. Catherine rallied first. "General Booth, I had no idea. I . . . was waiting—"

"Why?" he interrupted, not looking directly at her but seeming to concentrate on Mr. Eden, who continued to stand near the staircase at the farthest removed distance. "Why are all of you standing about? Surely there is enough work to occupy one and all. If not, there are endless tasks at the new colony off the Strand. Come with me and I shall see to it that—"

"General, please," Catherine begged, fearing that tone, that look, that inability to hear or see anything save what he wanted to hear and see.

At her interruption he halted his progress through the door and looked sharply at her. For a moment she saw not one softening angle of husbandly love, saw only suspicion and distrust, as though she'd joined the enemy' camp.

"I'm late now as it is, Mrs. Booth. While others may have time to stand about, I assure you God's work keeps me quite busy."

"These two," she said in a tone of apology, "they made an appointment to see you just yesterday, do you remember? It was to have been at two o'clock."

As she gestured toward Susan and Mr. Eden, she saw him follow her direction, saw a neutral expression on his face, as though two strangers were standing in the corridor. Under the force of such a glare, Susan looked away. Mr. Eden held his position.

"I remember no such appointment," General Booth said briskly.

In that moment Catherine knew he did indeed know of the impending request to marry. Not only knew but had already made his decision.

"General Booth, please see them," Catherine entreated quietly, wishing she might have a moment alone with him to help him see what a disastrous mistake he was making.

But: "I have no time, Mrs. Booth. I am late as it is, and now, if you will . . ."

This time his steps took him as far as the staircase, into direct confrontation with Mr. Eden, who stood for a moment as though blocking his passage down. At the last minute he stepped aside and apparently captured General Booth's attention with his quiet calm.

"We did make an appointment, sir, yesterday. It was at about this same hour."

At this General Booth stopped, looked back, and on his face Catherine saw anger—and something else. Not fear, surely. . . .

"Are you disputing my word, sir?"

Catherine thought she saw a slight smile on Mr. Eden's face.

"No, not disputing it . . ."

"Then let me pass."

"I'm not blocking your passage, though all we require of you is a simple word. . . ."

Resigned and fearful, Catherine held her position close to the study door. She knew her husband well enough to know nothing could infuriate him more than that one subtle smile, unless it was Mr. Eden's calm demeanor.

Faring less well, Susan Mantle had withdrawn to a position close to the wall and now stood, head down, her back braced against the surface, palms flattened. She appeared to be concentrating on aligning the points of her black shoes, but Catherine knew better than that, could feel too clearly the woman's pain of embarrassment.

Why was all this necessary?

In a surge of anger, she pushed out of her own embarrassed lethargy. "General Booth," she called out, her voice forceful, a sound of fake bravado, "none of this is necessary. Their request is simple. They wish to marry. Give them your blessing and everyone can—"

Although no word was spoken, it was the look in his eye as he glared at her—part shock she would speak to him like that and the rest fury—that cut her off. She'd never seen such a look and thought quite lucidly for just a moment: *He is . . . insane.*

In the awesome silence, she was aware of the other two and the growing feeling of alarm that was spreading throughout the quiet corridor.

Beyond General Booth's shoulder she saw Mr. Eden bow his head, though at the same time he spoke quietly. "As I understand it, it is your policy to approve or disapprove of all marriages. Is that correct?"

General Booth turned on Mr. Eden's voice, as though it alone were capable of doing him damage. "It is," he thundered, and the hand that held the Bible shook.

"Then give us permission"—Mr. Eden smiled courteously—"and I assure you we shan't detain you a moment."

"Never!"

The single word came like a volley fired from a cannon and seemed to echo endlessly throughout the long, shadowy corridor. Surely the word had been heard all over Whitechapel as well, for it had been clearly heard here. Though no one could have possibly mistaken either the word or its meaning, all three stared at General Booth as though somehow they hadn't heard correctly or needed clarification.

Mr. Eden smiled, a quick nervous smile, and spoke for all three. "I'm afraid I . . . don't understand."

"How much clearer need I make it?" General Booth went on, moving at last, finding energy in the confusion of the others. "To your request to marry Susan Mantle I said, 'No.' In fact I absolutely forbid it." At the

353

conclusion of this madness, he started down the steps as though confident there would be neither rebuttal nor argument.

Of course he was wrong on both counts. While Susan seemed too stunned to speak, Mr. Eden did not. As General Booth marched down to the first landing five steps below, Mr. Eden followed after, more than followed, pursued, for the smile was gone and in its place Catherine saw a painful mix of regret and relief, as though he'd held himself in check for too long and now looked forward to and dreaded the release.

"No explanation, sir?" he asked, only a step or two before he caught up with General Booth and reached out for his shoulder, as though physically to restrain him from proceeding on down the steps.

Catherine held her position, fearful for both of them, regretful this was happening, yet at the moment powerless to stop it. She saw Susan push away from her safe harbor near the wall and walk unsteadily to the top of the stairs.

"It isn't necessary, John," she said softly.

"No, forgive me, Susan, but you're wrong. It is necessary and important," Mr. Eden protested with grim but unfailing politeness. "I have never fully understood this . . . abridgment of personal liberty, why two people must seek permission from a third for something that concerns and involves only—"

"Your inability to understand is neither shocking nor surprisng," General Booth interrupted.

"Then enlighten me, please," Mr. Eden requested, still wielding the upper hand merely because of his calm demeanor, while General Booth appeared to be on the verge of a seizure.

"Gladly"—General Booth nodded with suspect eagerness—"though I think it would be best if Miss Mantle—"

"—remained where she is," Mr. Eden cut in. "Since your decision affects her future as well as mine, I think she has a right to hear."

"Suit yourselves," General Booth said. He shifted the Bible from one hand to the other, in the process placing his hand meticulously atop the newel post while everyone else in the corridor waited with checked tempers.

A performance, Catherine thought, and wondered what was the point and tried to see a need for meddling in people's lives in this fashion, could find none, and prayed briefly God would show General Booth the error of his ways before it was too late and the grand works of a lifetime were destroyed in one moment of egomaniacal weakness.

"Then speak, sir," Mr. Eden invited. "We all are curious about the reason for your denial."

"Simple," General Booth said with suspect ease that belied his trembling hands. "When we took you into the refuge, we knew nothing about you, could find no papers, nothing. I asked you repeatedly to speak that first day, to inform us as to—"

"I have no memory of that day," Mr. Eden said quickly in the manner of an apology.

"Of course not," Catherine agreed, drawing nearer to the top of the stairs and the confrontation. "I was there. I saw he had fallen senseless onto the pavement—"

General Booth said nothing but raised a restraining hand in her direc-

354

tion and with that one gesture made it clear she was to hold her tongue.

In the ensuing silence she saw Mr. Eden and Susan exchange a glance. Its precise nature she couldn't determine, still smarting from her own reprimand.

"Please go on," Mr. Eden urged.

"Gladly," General Booth said.

The weight of authority seemed to be shifting. It was Mr. Eden now who looked weak and defeated.

"Our doors are open to one and all," General Booth said magnanimously with a matching gesture, arms outstretched. Everyone is welcome to sit at table, to rest in peace, comfort, and quiet. Everyone, that is, except a . . . criminal, a fugitive from the law." These last words were delivered coldly, with a bluntness that shocked.

Again Mr. Eden gave him a look of pure bewilderment. "Criminals? I . . . don't understand."

"That day we found you in front of the mission, Mr. Eden, you had one possession which you were clutching to your person, a wicker case which unfortunately contained evidence of criminal activity."

From where Catherine stood, she saw the slow draining of color from Mr. Eden's face. "You . . . had no right," she heard him say on diminished breath.

Apparently General Booth heard nothing and went right on, gesturing with the Bible now, as he frequently did during revivals. "Out of human compassion I have refrained from notifying the proper authorities until you had the strength and the opportunity to explain what precisely . . ."

Something in Mr. Eden's face caused him momentarily to halt. At the same time, Catherine was aware of Susan moving closer, passing her by, and starting directly down the stairs.

"We are very fond of Susan here at the mission," General Booth went on. "Naturally I can't stand idly by and see her become involved with a man of questionable activity who—"

At last Susan spoke, though her voice was scarcely recognizable. "General Booth, you . . . don't understand. Please—"

"No. I understand perfectly," he said with conviction. To Mr. Eden he added imperiously, "I offer you two alternatives. Either meet with the authorities and tell them precisely how you came to possess that blood-stained gown, or else leave the mission immediately." At the end of the pronouncement he tucked the Bible under his arm and started to walk away as though he wasn't even concerned with the man's answer.

As for Mr. Eden, he stood absolutely motionless, head bowed. Then he lifted one hand to Susan, who stared down at it for a moment. His face was a mask of grief. Finally Susan came down the three short steps and took the hand offered to her.

With no words spoken, the two started down the stairs, keeping close to the wall on the left in an effort to avoid contact with General Booth, who continued to watch them as though hoping Mr. Eden would give him an excuse to respond.

But clearly Mr. Eden was finished speaking for the day. Catherine saw and envied the strength with which he gripped Susan's hand, the purpose with which he led her past General Booth, who, despite the fact he'd had the last word, looked defeated.

"Mr. Eden!"

The two continued down the steps. But General Booth would not leave them alone. "Sir! I demand a response!"

Fearful the ugly scene would shortly be played out for the benefit of all the staff and the men in the crowded common room below, Catherine gathered her courage and her wits about her and started after them, determined, if nothing else, to avoid a public spectacle that would do dangerous damage to the mission and irreparable damage to General Booth.

"Wait, please," she called out.

Only then did Mr. Eden halt his steps and look back.

"My intention, sir, is to leave here at your request. I will always be grateful to you and to this mission for taking me in, for giving me back my strength and my judgment. I had hoped to serve with you for a while, like Lord Simmons, but clearly that was not meant to be." For the first time he paused.

In this silence Catherine saw Susan's head bowed.

"I will find another place to serve, though," Mr. Eden went on. "I want you to know that—"

Without looking at either of them, General Booth said in a voice remarkable for its tonelessness, "I forbid you to go with him, Miss Mantle. Did you hear? I absolutely forbid it."

If either Susan or Mr. Eden heard, they gave no indication of it.

"Did you hear me?" General Booth ranted. "I forbid it. Do not proceed another step in his company or you, too, will find yourself out on the street."

Then Catherine could stand it no longer, the shouting, the senseless infliction of pain on people who had borne quite enough. "General Booth, I beg you to consider—"

Apparently he was in no mood to consider anything, and now followed after the two going downstairs, using the Bible as an object with which to gesture angrily. "I demand a response," he cried. "Don't turn your backs on me. I am God here, and as such I demand the same reverence and respect you so lavishly give to Him. Miss Mantle, do you hear me? Do not proceed another step, do not associate yourself with such a man, do not . . ."

Let them go, Catherine thought, and sat wearily on the steps to cover her face with her hands, hearing General Booth's echoing madness, hearing as well the sudden shocked silence coming from the large room below.

Dear God, he is good. He can affect men's lives . . .

Why was it God couldn't keep a thing pure for more than a generation?

No answer. Just an echoing silence and the awesome sense of something powerful in nature gone awry, that and the equally moving suspicion that Mr. Eden was on the verge of going home to peace.

How she feared the one and how she envied the other.

* * *

356

Susan had no idea where he was leading her, didn't really care, just so long as it was away from that judgmental voice which had followed them down the stairs, through the dining hall in tidal waves of embarrassed silence, and even out onto the crowded pavement of Whitechapel.

Now, for the first time, she was blessedly aware of only street sounds, no penetrating voice topping the rattle of wheels and cries of vendors.

She was newly aware of John's hand clasping hers, literally dragging her through the crowds on the pavement. She followed because she had no choice in any sense of the word, though she wondered if *he* knew where he was leading her.

Abruptly he turned to the left, taking her with him, and started off at a rapid pace down Regiment Street, where he didn't once look back but proceeded straight on. Now she suspected he did have a destination in mind and felt him lead her toward the small low wooden gate which led into the cloisters of Saint Stephen's.

Of course. She should have thought of it herself, a quiet green haven, at the center of Whitechapel Street, a place where abandoned and lost men used to sleep before General Booth opened his mission.

He did perform sacred work. . . .

Not until they were inside the gate did John release her hand, and only then to check the latch, as though he wanted to lock them in or lock the world out.

She withdrew quietly to the center of the cloister, to a spot near a wooden bench where over the years initials had been carved by the bored, hungry, and lonely. As she sat she saw a crudely carved heart encircling two sets of initials and lovingly ran her finger over the memento of past love.

She looked up, thinking to call it to his attention, feeling it might be best to break the tension of the moment with a change of subject. To her surprise, she saw him still standing by the gate, his back to her, his position obscuring his face.

Then slowly he turned, a shy, sad smile altering his features. Without a word he drew near to the bench, never taking his eyes off her. She could not even begin to estimate the joy it would be to live with that face every day for the rest of her life.

Still without words, he sat close beside her and reached for her hand, which was open and available to him, and enclosed it between his own. She found the gesture so gentle and loving she went down on her knees before him, a position of intimacy, yet it seemed the most natural thing in the world.

"John, look at me," she pleaded softly. "Are you all right?" she asked, despite the fact she had not as yet elicited any response.

At last a faint smile broke through the fatigue. Slowly he looked down on her and made brief eye contact. "I'm fine . . . though I don't . . ." He broke off and shook his head, lifting his eyes to the limited spires of little Saint Stephen's, a local Anglican church which over the years had fallen on hard times. No parishioners.

"I don't understand," John said, "any of it. There was a time when I could have told you the direction of my entire life, the master plan, as it were, all my accomplishments to thirty years of age, to forty, to fif-

357

ty . . ." He broke off and shook his head again, looking down. "Now?" he said. "I can't tell you with any degree of conviction what I will be doing for the next . . . fifteen minutes."

She smiled. "I suspect," she began, "that you have just described the condition of a large part of the human race."

He appeared to be listening to what she was saying. "I feel lost," he confessed. "I was so certain the mission was where we—"

"I'm afraid we were wrong," she said. "Like you, I had hoped. But God clearly—"

"Do you believe that?" he interrupted. "That God's hand was behind that . . . maniac's words?"

"Of course I believe it," she said, settling comfortably on her heels, "and so do you," she added, "more or less."

Either he heard the amusement in her voice or placed it there because he needed it. "Did you know that I was tempted to hit him, to do him physical harm?"

"But you didn't," she said.

"No, but only because I walked away instead, and even as I did, somewhere inside me was a voice which called out, 'Coward!' "

"Did you feel like a coward?"

He looked down on her, an expression of bewilderment on his face. "No," he said with quiet amazement. "In fact, it was one of the hardest things I've ever done in my life."

She nodded. "Good." She started to say more, but he went on.

"He *is* insane, you know."

She hesitated a moment before confirming or denying. She'd known for a long time about General Booth's proclivity—not just to follow God and His teachings, but occasionally to become God. She also knew, for she'd borne witness for months longer than John, that General Booth possessed a power not of this earth to affect and change men's lives. If he was mad and malicious, he was also quite sane and saintly.

"I don't know," she confessed, looking directly up at him, surprised to see him return her gaze with matching directness. "I thought once . . ." She broke off under his gaze.

His right hand lifted to cup gently about her face, his thumb caressing her cheek. "I'm . . . sorry about you," he murmured.

"I don't understand . . ."

"You were dismissed as well."

Relieved, she clasped his hand, which still was exploring the side of her face. "I wouldn't have stayed on, anyway. Not without you."

The quiet confession caused a look of incredulity to appear on his face. "Then we're both on the streets." He smiled.

"It appears that way."

"What do you suggest?"

"What do *you* suggest?"

"I don't want to go back to being who and what I was," he whispered, so close she could feel his breath upon her skin. For several moments he seemed as content as she, without any further questions or answers. "Then what do you suggest?" he asked finally, not relaxing his hold on her.

"Let's go home," she said, touching the back of his neck.

"Home?" he repeated. "I thought you hated that . . . tomb. Wasn't that what you called it once?"

Had she? Probably.

"Not the castle," She smiled. "The cottage on Eden Rising. You gave it to me once, remember? For services rendered. I accept it now, on one condition."

"What?" She sensed clearly his relief—and something else, excitement—at the suggestion.

"That I can convert one room into a small clinic and that North Devon people will always have access to it"—she hesitated, wondering if her heart was beating thunderously loud because of her daring or her happiness—"because I don't think it would be . . . feasible for me to travel the circuit anymore."

"No."

"And this way I can still see my patients and watch over the children at the same time."

"What . . . children?"

"Ours."

"Children?"

"We do plan to have them, I hope. All my life I've wanted—"

She was interrupted in a most pleasurable way, by renewed strength in his arms, by one hand lifting her face and by the force of his lips upon hers, canceling all words, though that was no great loss, for inside the warm moisture of his mouth she found all her answers.

Yes, they would go home to Eden Rising. Yes, she could convert a room into a small clinic. Yes, the circuit was out of the question, and, yes, most definitely, there would be children.

Grosvenor Square,
London
May 6, 1875

Shocked and disbelieving, Bates looked at Aldwell. "Are you . . . certain?" he gasped.

"Certain." Aldwell smiled.

Bates continued to stare at him in the high heat of the May day. In a
way, he wished Alex Aldwell hadn't confided in him. True, it eased his
guilt and his grief. But it seemed as though all his life either rumors of
John Murrey Eden or the man himself had stepped in and altered Bates's
destiny.

Weary from his ghastly trip across the channel, Bates had wanted only
to make his report to Lord Richard and Master Aslam, then to leave
immediately for his cottage in Mortemouth, where he planned to spend
what was left of his days doing nothing more strenuous than watching the
tide go out and come in.

Now, as he stood on the pavement in front of the Grosvenor Square
mansion, he blinked at Aldwell and felt a curious and wholly unexpected
surge of joy at the news.

"Are you absolutely certain, sir?" he asked, aware of Charley Spade
and Jason lounging atop the high seat of the carriage, which Lord Richard said they might take back to Eden Point with them.

Even Jason had elected to go with them back to North Devon, as an
unholy alliance had developed between him and Charley Spade, leaving
Bates feeling like the harried father of two unruly childen. Well, he'd
managed to keep them under control for four months in Paris. He could
manage for another week or two, then, as far as he was concerned, it
would be too soon if he ever saw them again in his life.

"You are . . . certain?" he asked Aldwell again, and wondered why they were discussing such momentous news on the pavement outside the mansion beyond the hearing of Lord Richard and Master Aslam.

Again Aldwell nodded, looking extremely pleased with himself. "I wasn't at first, but I stayed long enough to find out. I saw him, and I saw her as well—"

"Her?"

"The nurse that old Reverend Christopher sent up when John was—"

Bates nodded. Susan was her name. He hadn't cared for her at first. But she'd worked like four men nursing Mr. Eden back to health, and in Bates's book anyone who did not shirk his duties warranted at least a degree of respect. "Were they together?" Bates asked.

Aldwell nodded. "It didn't appear that way at first." He shook his head and looked down at the sun-drenched pavement at his feet. "I . . . couldn't believe my eyes," he said quietly. "He's very changed."

Bates kept quiet as his mind instantly conjured up a vision of John Murrey Eden, an image that had tortured him every day since that tragic morning of Elizabeth Eden's execution. "I . . . can't believe it," Bates murmured apologetically, lifting one hand to his forehead, hoping to ease the sense of confusion from which he was suffering, and to ease, as well, Aldwell's own sense of incredulity.

"Was he . . . I mean, did he appear to be . . . ?"

"Thin. Terribly thin."

Bates nodded and wondered why his hand was trembling. He hid it quickly in his pocket, but Aldwell saw and asked, "Are you all right, Bates? I know it's a shock. It was a shock to me, seeing him standing there when I'd been told he was in a French grave."

"The detective was an idiot," Bates snapped. "I never quite believed him, but I never dreamed Mr. Eden could have successfully made it back to England."

"Of course, I didn't speak with him," said Aldwell. "But somehow I had the feeling he . . ."

"What?"

Adlwell shrugged. "I don't know. If he'd wanted us to know of his whereabouts, he would have come here, wouldn't he? It was almost as if he were in hiding."

"And that's why you haven't told . . . the others?" Bates nodded toward the mansion, at last understanding at least one aspect of the mystery.

Aldwell nodded. "Precisely. I assure you John didn't seem addled. He knew where he was, and if he'd wanted Lord Richard to know he had returned, then it would have been a simple matter to—"

Bates interrupted. "But how is he living? How did he manage to cross the channel without papers or funds? How did he find . . . ? What did you call it?"

"A charity mission. The man running it is alternately viewed as a saint and the devil."

"Do you know him?"

"Oh, my, no. Only by reputation. Booth is his name, and he prefers to be called General Booth, though he had nothing to do with the military He is waging a war for God—or so he claims in newsprint. . . ."

The more Bates heard, the more the mystery was compounded. John Murrey Eden had never endured such nonsense. "How did Mr Eden . . . ?" Bates began, and never finished, aware of the repetition of his questions.

Sympathetically Aldwell nodded. "I know," he commiserated. "I've mulled it over a thousand times since I saw him. All I can say is that he appeared the same, and yet very changed." Abruptly he looked at Bates "I have told no one but you."

"I'm grateful."

"I sensed you felt responsible for his . . . death."

"I do. . . . I did. . . .'"

"No need now."

"No."

The rapid exchange came to an equally rapid halt as self-consciously both men looked across the pavement to where Charley Spade and Jason were lounging, legs propped up against the wind guard, both apparently impervious to the incredible news.

"Should I tell them?" Bates asked, without looking at Aldwell, continuing to feel as uncertain of this new information as he'd ever felt in his life.

Alive! John Murrey Eden alive! Why was he so shocked?

Again Aldwell shrugged. "I'll leave that decision up to you. I still think that when he's ready, John will come forward."

Bates nodded in agreement. But *did* he agree? What had happened to Mr. Eden in Paris could not be easily absorbed by any man, a nightmare which even Bates relived every night with awesome regularity.

For several moments they stood on the pavement, each locked in his own thoughts. Bates watched Aldwell pace two or three steps away from him, then retrace his steps to come back with a fresh apology.

"I'm sorry if I—"

"No, I'm truly grateful."

"What will you do now?"

An unanswerable question. "Go home, I suppose."

"Without . . . ?"

"As you said, when Mr. Eden is ready . . ."

"Yes."

"Where . . . did you say this . . . mission was located?"

Aldwell followed the rapid flight of a flock of birds across the high May sky. "In Whitechapel, not far from Regiment Street."

Bates nodded quickly.

"Then you do plan to . . . ?"

"No, I . . . don't think so. As long as he's well . . ."

Aldwell smiled. "I know now why I told only you. Despite everything that he is and has done and might do, you love him as much as I."

Bates blinked up at the curious declaration, started to refute it and couldn't, and yet didn't quite know what to make of those times in his life when he gladly would have killed John Murrey Eden.

"Time's passing," he said vaguely. "I'd best get those two back to North Devon before they wreak further havoc on the world."

"Safe journey, then." Aldwell smiled, extending his hand. "I'm sure we will meet again."

Bates took his hand. "I'm sure we will."

"Then, again, safe journey."

"Thank you, sir, for . . . everything." At that, Bates stepped off onto the pavement, heading toward the carriage, where Charley Spade and Jason spied him. Both sat quickly upright, clearly eager to be on the road.

Bates had wages in his pocket for both men, for their dubious assistance in Paris. In truth, they had spent most of their time at a little sidewalk café across from Notre Dame, drinking endless absinthes and watching the passing parade of French beauties. Wisely Bates decided to withhold their wages until they arrived safely in Mortemouth. If they wished, they could drink themselves senseless at the Green Man.

At his approach, Charley Spade called down, "The guv didn't go too hard on you, did he, sir?"

"No, Charley, not at all."

"It ain't our fault, is it? I mean, losing Mr. Eden like that . . ."

Bates bowed his head and thought how painful those words would have been a scant ten minutes ago. Now?

"No, of course it isn't our fault. They understood . . ."

"Good. Then shall we head toward God's country and the West?"

Bates nodded quickly, as eager as they to shake the dust of filthy London from his boots. But seconds before he ducked his head to enter the carriage, an instinct as strong as he'd ever suffered in his life sliced down upon him.

What harm would it do? Just a glimpse to confirm the rumor. And a chance to see for himself that the man was *well*.

"Sir?" It was Charley Spade again, awaiting directions so he might pass them on to Jason, who held the reins wrapped tightly about his hands. "The western route, shall it be? If we hurry, we can make Salisbury by—"

"No," Bates said quietly. "Whitechapel, if you please, near Regiment Street."

"Whitecha . . ."

Bates ducked quickly into the carriage and didn't linger to deal with the confusion on Charley's face. How could he deal with another man's confusion when he couldn't even deal with his own?

For all those years, he had thought he'd hated John Murrey Eden.

Whitechapel Street,
London
May 6, 1875

Aware they were no longer welcome at the mission, yet not having a thought in his head how they could get to Eden, John sat on the side stoop of an abandoned building fifty yards from the mission door, the wicker case—his only possession—tucked beneath his legs, waiting for Susan, who had more friends to say good-bye to than he did. He wondered why, with all the problems facing him, he felt such peace and unity with himself, with his father, who now seemed literally to inhabit him. He saw that strong paternal face in every shadow, every high white cloud, every reflection.

Slowly he leaned back, lifting his face to the mild May breeze. Despite his closed eyes, he saw simultaneously an image of his two sons, followed quickly by an image of his father. Curious juxtaposition. Edward Eden hadn't lived long enough to know young Frederick or Stephen. He would have loved them both. He'd loved all children. John recalled how frequently in the Ragged School he would scoop up as many as his arms would hold. . .

As for John, he'd hated the children then.

But you're my papa!

I am indeed.

Then love only me!

A stray particle of dust, a fleck of lint, a bit of the past, something stung his eyes.

Why should that youthful need stir him so? Before the excursion into memory became too painful, he sat up straight, his elbows propped on his knees, and stared intently at the pavement between his legs.

Susan had told him not to worry, that she had small savings which would purchase them outside passage on a coach to Exeter. And once in

364

Exeter they could always fetch her landau and old Betts, both of which he'd left in the care of a cousin.

Susan . . .

Thinking on her and feeling her absence, he looked toward the front of the mission a short distance away. The men were beginning to queue up for the evening meal. Orderly, bowed, gaunt, they always reminded John of his father. And thoughts of his father always reminded him of Elizabeth.

Abruptly he stood, as though a change of position would help him move away from the tyranny of memory. But it didn't. The image simply moved with him, a recall so complete he could smell the damp courtyard at La Rochelle, could hear the curiously subdued voices all around, could feel the terror mounting.

Slowly he sat down again, undone by memory. He pressed both hands to his face and felt the wicker case against the backs of his legs. In need, he glanced toward the door of the mission and saw a small delegation just emerging—a half-dozen, perhaps more—all clustered about a very familiar center.

Susan.

She was beloved here, he knew that. Perhaps it was wrong of him to take her away. But it had been her decision. He vowed now to see to it that it remained that way. No more interference in any life, save his own.

From this distance she looked so small. The recent fever had left her weak. The North Devon air would be good for her, good for both of them.

He recognized Catherine Booth standing close beside her. And plump Cassie was there, and all of the kitchen staff. The tall gentleman would be Lord Simmons.

At last he saw her glance in his direction. He saw her accept a final embrace from poor Cassie, who apparently was weeping torrents of tears.

In her hand Susan carried a bulky portmanteau. Ah, at last there was a legitimate excuse to go to her.

He reached down to retrieve his own wicker case, and just as he looked up, he saw a carriage—most out of place in Whitechapel Street—draw up slowly before the pavement of the mission. From where he stood, it seemed to possess a kind of faded elegance, as though it had been highly fashionable about five years ago.

Susan, who had just pulled free of Cassie's last embrace, looked closely at the two men who sat atop the high seat of the carriage.

What in the . . . ?

Everyone on the pavement now seemed to be focused on the confrontation. At that moment the carriage door pushed open. A black-coated arm evolved first, then a shoulder, then a matchstick-thin torso, and at last the whole man.

John felt Susan's surprise, saw her rush forward with characteristic warmth to clasp the man's hand, then turn abruptly to point directly at him.

"Bates!" John whispered, incredulous, and at that moment identified as well the two mismatched bookends atop the high carriage seat, Jason and Charley Spade. Bates had stood beside him on that bleak morning. Bates had endured all with him, the only man in the world who knew precisely the nature and cast of that most intolerable nightmare.

"Bates?" John grinned, wanting confirmation. As he saw the old man quicken his step, he saw a breaking emotion as pronounced as his own.

"S-sir?" Bates managed. "Are you . . . well?"

John replied as honestly as possible. "I think so, Bates. I used to count on you to tell me that."

A quick smile creased Bates's thin lips and was canceled as he ducked his head. "We're all here, sir," he said on a fresh breath, and at the same time gestured over his shoulder toward the two men who continued to sit frozen atop the carriage seat.

At the gesture, John saw Charley Spade stand as if answering a roll call. Jason waved, his hand lingering in midair for a few seconds, as though he wanted to wave again.

"I . . . recognized the young lady," Bates said, still awkward.

"Susan?" John inquired, and wished he knew a way to put the man at ease. "We are going to be married," he announced simply.

"I say." Bates brightened. John saw the continuing pleasure on his face and was pleased by it. "Here in London?" Bates asked, daring to step closer, as though not wanting to miss the reply.

"No. At Eden, or—more accurately—Mortemouth. Susan suggested Reverend Christopher."

"Of course. Ideal." Bates ducked his head and apparently caught sight of the wicker case. For a moment the color left the man's face. "We . . . were so worried, sir," he muttered.

John nodded and thought what a considerate way to deal with a truant. "I'm sorry, Bates, to have bolted like that."

"It's nothing."

"But I felt I had—"

"I know. I know."

"Who told you I was here?"

It seemed time to change the subject. Perhaps one day they could discuss what had happened in Paris, but not now.

Since the initial greeting they had moved closer together. Now it was Bates who bridged the distance first with a single step. "Aldwell," he said. "Alex Aldwell. A decent man . . ."

"He is." John nodded in full agreement. "But how did Aldwell . . . ?"

As one answer simply provoked more questions, John looked toward the mission, surprised to see everyone still waiting and watching, including Susan, who had ventured several yards away from her friends, yet still a distance from where he stood talking to Bates. The sight of her standing alone—in a no-man's-land, as it were—moved him.

"Excuse me, Bates, just a moment, if you will." He ignored Bates' puzzled expression and started slowly toward her, trying to read her expression and, in lieu of that, trying to memorize every angle and slant of her features. Then he was before her, unmindful of everything save her desirable presence.

"Shall we go home?" he inquired softly.

"I'd like that."

"Bates?" he called out, extending a hand to the old man, who still seemed too stunned to move, "when are you taking that . . . curiosity back to Eden?" He gestured broadly toward the old road-weary carriage.

Bates gaped a moment, as though not understanding the question. "Now, sir. We were on our way out of London when we stopped here to see . . ."

Now?

He looked down on Susan, who held her portmanteau in one hand, her valise in the other. "Why not?" She smiled. "If it's all right with Charley and . . ."

John nodded and walked back to Bates. "Would it be all right if we . . . ?"

At once Bates beamed. "Nothing would give us greater pleasure, sir. Nothing in this world, I assure you."

Then John was aware of Susan coming up behind him, saw Bates bob his head and blush crimson. "Ma'am," he murmured, "it's very good to see you again."

"And you, Mr. Bates." She smiled. "You're looking well."

Abruptly John walked back to the carriage and extended a hand up to both men. "Charley . . ."

Charley Spade was in a state of awe. He shook his head. "Gawd, I never thought I'd lay me eyes on you again, Mr. Eden. You ain't a ghost, are you?"

John laughed. "Sometimes I feel like one."

"We looked, sir," Spade went on. "Didn't we, Jason?"

Jason nodded. "Good to see you again, sir," he said in that clipped East Indian speech.

Charley Spade bent down. "What is it you're doing in a place like this, sir?" he whispered, as though he didn't want to offend anyone.

John smiled. "Leaving it, primarily. We're going back to Eden," he added, extending his hand to Susan, who came up alongside him.

A broad grin spread across Charley's face. "That's where we're headed, it is, Jason and me and old Bates. We've had enough of cities for a while, ain't we?"

Jason nodded broadly.

"Here, now," Charley went on, "why don't you come with us? We got this big carriage and . . ." Abruptly he stopped talking and hopped down from the high seat to take Susan's luggage and toss both pieces into the backseat of the carriage. "There. It's settled," he said, still grinning. "It is all right, ain't it, sir? I mean, I was hired to escort Mr. Eden to Paris and back again. Well, the 'back again' part is just coming a little later."

Bates nodded. "My thoughts exactly, Charley." To Susan and John he instructed, "You two sit back here, and I'll ride up here to keep an eye on these two."

So it was settled, though John felt such a draining emotion that for a moment he closed his eyes.

"Are you all right?" Susan whispered, taking his arm.

He nodded, and he was. It was just that sometimes he felt so foreign inside his own skin. This world was so simple, so comprehensible. That other world had had to be dealt with and subdued every day, every hour, constant assessments of the status of enemies, the aggression of competi-

367

tion, constant vigilance against new assaults. Then the mind had never rested, had schemed long into the nights, and had awakened early in the morning.

"Sir, a word, if I might . . ." The request came from Bates, who held the carriage door while Susan settled in by the far window.

"Of course." John smiled.

"Sir, my request is simple. If you are returning to Eden, obviously you will be reopening the castle and will be in need of a . . ." The man broke off. "What I'm trying to say, sir, is that we would consider it an honor if we could serve you again in any capacity. . . ."

John looked toward the carriage and saw Susan listening.

"No," he said, and saw the surprised, shocked expressions on all three faces, and said it again. "No. Never again will anyone 'serve' me or do work I could not do for myself." He felt Susan's hand tighten around his. "And we do not intend to reopen Eden Castle, Bates," he went on. "I'll leave that to someone else."

"I . . . don't understand."

"Our destination is Eden Rising and the cottage there. We intend to repair and inhabit it, enclosing the west portico for a small clinic so Susan can . . . continue to serve."

"I see, sir," Bates murmured, the disappointment showing despite his claim of understanding.

"Now," John continued, drawing a deep breath, "there will be much work involved in such an undertaking, and while I refuse your offer to serve me, I'd be most grateful if you and Charley and Jason would work alongside me. But I swear to God I'll set a fast pace."

At first nothing moved on anyone's face. All three expressions were identically blank.

"Well?" John urged.

At last Bates stirred, though his first words were little more than splut-terings. "I say, sir. I mean, yes, of course. I think I speak for all of . . . I say, yes, we will join you, won't we?"

"Then let's go." John smiled, walking away from the carriage back to where he'd left the wicker case. As he stopped to retrieve it, he was aware of everyone watching and was sorry for this sad note coming at such a happy time. When they arrived at Eden he would bury the wicker case containing Elizabeth's gown in the Eden graveyard next to his father, then try to put the past behind him.

When he returned to the carriage he saw Bates standing beside the open door. "Mr. Eden, I—"

"My name is John." John extended his hand to the man as though they were meeting for the first time.

Bates nodded, though something seemed to be pinching—the past, his training . . .

Then John had an idea. "What's your given name, Bates? Your Chris-tian name. What did your mother call you?"

All at once the old man blushed crimson. "Bates is my name, sir. It will do."

"No. If we're to work side by side, you call me John and I'll call you . . ." He extended his hand as though waiting for Bates to fill in the missing word.

368

With growing reluctance, Bates maintained an embarrassed silence. Finally, with head bowed, he muttered something John couldn't hear.

"I beg your pardon?"

"Percival," Bates repeated, a dark cloud of embarrassment gathering on his brow, which remained until John, fighting against a smile, lost the battle and gave in, until he was laughing openly and Bates with him and Susan and even the two atop the carriage, laughing like fools, like people who had called the world's bluff and who—at least for the time being— appeared to be winning.

Mortemouth,
North Devon
May 11, 1875

Standing before an ancient pier glass, courtesy of Meg Winchombe, surrounded by half a dozen women from Mortemouth who made continuous adjustments to her lovely white silk wedding dress—a miracle of a dress, really, which had been put together in the last three days by Sarah and Martha Turner, artisan seamstresses of Mortemouth—Susan turned slowly on cue while all checked the length of the hem.

As she turned, she suffered an almost overwhelming sense of miracle and remembered this was where it all started, with Reverend Christopher's urgent midnight call.

"Hold still, Susan," Martha Turner scolded.

Susan obeyed and studied once again that strange woman who stared back at her from the pier glass.

Mrs. John Murrey Eden . . .

Soon—in less than twenty minutes—it would be a reality, so she'd better adjust to it. On that gentle self-scolding, she drew her attention back to the ladies.

Meg Winchombe saw something in Susan's face. "Now, don't go scared on us, Susan. You're a lovely bride and deserve the best." The others looked up from their adjustments and nodded in agreement, were still nodding when Meg added ominously, "Of course, only time will tell if you got the best."

"I believe I did, Meg," she said quietly, feeling no real need to defend John. She knew what difficulty they were having accepting him as he was now. Most still distrusted him, recalling the imperious monster of Eden, who bore absolutely no resemblance to this thin, slightly bowed, unfailingly courteous man she was marrying within the hour.

370

Meg nodded, her prim blue hat with the single peacock feather bobbing up and down. "Well, you'll have to forgive us if we content ourselves with waiting and seeing."

Susan nodded and realized it would take time and hoped John would be as patient with them as he had been with the staff at the mission. As the endless fussing continued, she asked of anyone who cared to answer, "What time is it? We mustn't be late."

"Three-forty-five," said Meg Winchombe. "Fifteen whole minutes. Can't you wait?" There was a touch of innuendo in both her smile and voice. "And don't be too disappointed. Mr. Eden just simply don't look like the man he used to be, if you get me point."

Susan got it. How could she miss it? But the indomitable Meg leaned closer, persistent if not tactful. "Do you have any notion of what will happen tonight? In this very room?" With excited eyes Meg gestured about the small room which Reverend Christopher had said she and John might share after the wedding until the cottage was completed.

"Of course I do, Meg." Susan smiled, wishing the woman would change the subject.

"Have you ever received a man?"

"No," Susan murmured, blushing.

A knowing grin passed among the ladies of Mortemouth. "Well, what you lack in experience, Mr. Eden can more than make up for." Meg grinned.

Susan felt her embarrassment vault and was grateful to Martha Turner, the eldest at seventy, who scolded, "Leave it be, Meg. What Susan and her husband do tonight is between them, and that's as it should be."

The reprimand was harsh, though lovingly delivered, and a repentant Meg busied herself with something behind Susan and apologized lightly. "Sorry, love. Didn't mean to cause no harm."

"You didn't," Susan smiled.

They all worked in silence for several moments, a few still making adjustments to the hem, Meg concentrating on the sheer veil which had been lent to Susan by Meg's aunt. In fact, almost everything had been lent or donated. John's good black suit was courtesy of Bates, who, thrilled over being asked to serve as best man, had thrown himself wholeheartedly into the ceremony. The plain gold ring which John would place on her finger shortly was the gracious gift of Reverend Christopher, who had been positively ecstatic when he'd heard the news, insisting Mr. Eden allow him to offer his dear mother's wedding ring which was serving no purpose locked in the small trunk at the foot of his bed.

In this and in countless other ways their generosity had been moving. Of course Susan knew they were pleased she and John were settling in their community and so close, merely at the top of the cliff walk, behind the old castle in the small cottage on Eden Rising.

At the thought of the cottage she closed her eyes and saw it—not as it was at present—as it could be, restored and shining, the side portico enclosed to form her own clinic.

"There!" a female voice pronounced close by.

She opened her eyes to the pier glass, to the reflection of a woman she failed to recognize at first. Was happiness capable of doing all that?

"And don't forget these." Martha Turner smiled, presenting her with a stunning bouquet of white roses mixed with heather.

With a smile of thanks, Susan accepted the flowers, and again realized how much had been given to her by these people. At that moment she heard a knock at the door.

"Susan? Are you ready? Time . . ."

Reverend Christopher.

"Is John—?" she called out through the door, and was not given a chance to finish.

"Nervous as a cat," Reverend Christopher called back. "Mr. Bates and the others are doing their best to calm him."

Poor John, she thought, wanting all at once to get it over with. She took a final look in the mirror and wished her parents were still alive.

"You look beautiful," Meg murmured.

To her surprise, she discovered she *was* beautiful. The simple white silk dress—a marvel of tailoring—followed perfectly the contours of her waist and breasts, the tapered sleeves ending in delicate points over her wrists, the tiny buttons of the bodice stopping short at her breasts, leaving a smooth white oval of neck and shoulders, the entire effect enhanced by the lovely lace veil.

Martha Turner smiled. "Don't look like no Susan Mantle I ever knew."

"It's the same, I assure you."

The knock came again. "It is time, Susan. Church is filled and Mrs. Hawkins is priming the organ."

Meg Winchombe drew open the door. On the other side stood Reverend Christopher, dressed in his fancy black clerical robes, his large Bible cradled in his arm. On his face Susan saw a most rewarding expression, a joyous look accompanied by whispered words.

"It's Mrs. John Murrey Eden, I believe."

With all fears and apprehensions banished, Susan took his arm and went forward to make the statement a reality.

It was approaching nine o'clock when the last well-wisher took his leave from the small garden which fronted the church which had served as the site of one of the most joyous wedding celebrations Mortemouth had ever witnessed.

Exhilarated as she'd never been before in her life, Susan hugged old Martha Turner and thanked her again for the very special wedding gift of the gown. And there were so many others to thank as well. As out of thin air, all evening special treats had appeared on the long table which ran the length of the garden, a lovely table covered with a white linen cloth—courtesy of Sarah Hensley—fresh bouquets of colorful garden flowers and culinary treats of every description. There were plump roasted chickens, rounds of cheddar cheese, every kind of freshly baked rolls and scones, bowls of ripe fruit and small round barrels of churned butter and clotted cream, pickled herring and sweets in the form of tarts, puddings and small brown cakes, and one beautiful wedding cake with surprises of candied fruit baked throughout.

Now, as Susan waved a final time to Martha Turner, she stood up straight and drew a deep breath, looking around, a little surprised to find the garden emptied except for a familiar circle of men seated at various angles of repose on the steps of the church.

In the gathering dusk, confident they weren't aware of her watching them, she turned to drink in the peace of the evening, luxuriating in the happiness of her heart, and to study from a distance the most remarkable man God had ever created.

Still in his borrowed dress blacks, though the tie had been loosened, John Eden sat at the center of the group, knees raised, listening to something Mr. Bates was saying. Charley Spade was there, as well as Jason, Reverend Christopher, Tom Babcock, and two or three others she didn't recognize in the falling dusk.

She knew they were discussing the renovation of the cottage on Eden Rising. As the whole village had joined forces to make this day memorable, so now they seemed equally willing to lend a shoulder, tools, and time to the reconstruction of the cottage. She knew that all were vastly pleased "the nurse" was settling in their village—accidents and illnesses could now be dealt with immediately. No more waiting for "their turn" on the circuit. Then, too, she suspected there was considerable curiosity about John Murrey Eden, and even more fascination that the clinic would be located on Eden ground, that once-forbidding stronghold of wealth and power at the top of the cliff walk.

Tom Babcock was speaking as though reinforcing an argument. "I just don't think they'll use it. Some won't, I know. They're afraid, some of them, because that's been forbidden to them all their lives, don't you see?"

Mystified both by his intensity and by what he said, Susan looked up and tried to discern the nature of the debate.

Nothing. All heads were now bowed in what seemed to be deep gloom. She focused directly on John, relishing every angle and aspect of that bowed head, wishing, whatever the nature of the problem, they could solve it quickly and John could bid them good night.

Reverend Christopher eased back on the top step. "Well," he began with a light, palms-up gesture, "it doesn't have to be solved now, does it? We all have time—"

Without looking, Mr. Bates replied, "The restoration will go quickly, but I see no need for so drastic an action, none at—"

Suddenly John stood, stretching his hands over his head. "No, I think Tom's right. I think we must do it, and I, for one, will look forward to it. To prove it, I will strike the first blow."

Mr. Bates protested. "Oh, sir, you can't."

"I don't know why not."

"Still, I don't think it would be . . . suitable."

"You heard the men, Mr. Bates. As far as I can see, there's no other way."

"It will weaken the fortress."

Bates looked both saddened and worried, a curious counterpoint to John, who looked almost deliriously happy, the confidence of a right solution on his face. Though she hadn't the foggiest notion what they were talking about, she reveled in his face. He must have worn that expression as a small boy.

Now he looked at Reverend Christopher. "What do you think?" he inquired.

The old priest shrugged, his most characteristic gesture, wanting peace at all costs. "I suppose it would be the most reasonable—"

"Of course it would," John cut in. "Then it's settled." To Charley Spade and Jason he said, "Bring your heaviest tools and all the help you can dredge up." He stopped and laughed. "Tell them what it's for, and I predict the entire village will be on hand." For the first time he looked up, saw Susan, and discernibly faltered.

Susan saw on his face the love with which he had received her at the altar of the church. She treasured the expression and knew the time had come to withdraw from people, however kind and well-wishing. Under the intensity of his gaze she felt her knees go weak and abandoned the linen tea towel with which she had been covering a platter of cherry tarts and drew near the steps and the lounging men, who all stood at once.

Suddenly nervous under their collective stares, she ducked her head and confessed, "I haven't an idea what you're talking about. But it sounds serious."

Tom Babcock scooped off his low-brimmed hat before he answered. "Access to your clinic, Miss Mantle . . . or rather . . ." Too late he remembered her new name and, embarrassed, didn't try for a correction.

She smiled in an attempt to put him at ease. "I . . . don't understand."

"Tom, here," said John, "claims that entrance through the gatehouse and across the open courtyard of the great hall will intimidate and frighten many people. They simply won't make the trip."

"What was . . . the other suggestion?" she asked.

"Simple." He grinned. "Knock a sizable hole in the south wall near the cottage. We would have a magnificent view of all of Eden Rising, and your patients could avoid that great pile of stone altogether."

Her initial reaction resembled Bates's, shocked, conservative. She looked more closely at John and announced quietly, "I think it's a splendid idea." Extending her hand to him, she waited as he made his way down the steps and through the men.

Then he was before her, all the dark emotion in those eyes focused directly down on her. She did well to speak. "It's . . . late . . ."

He nodded.

"Shall we?"

He looked back at the men, who suddenly—and to her extreme embarrassment—were grinning. "Will you excuse us?" he asked.

She walked ahead of him, leading the way down the narrow walk which led to the back of the church. Just before she reached the door, he caught up with her and took her hand. "Come, not here. Let's . . . walk."

"Wait a minute." She smiled, removed her veil, placing it carefully on the stoop, and loosened her hair.

He removed the black coat and draped it across the stoop with her veil. Thus unencumbered, they started off around the rear of the church.

The cliff walk loomed ahead of them like a narrow, twisting artery.

She led the way, running part of the time, though stopping halfway up to look back and see him right behind her, maintaining a good brisk walk and covering the same ground. "Not fair," she called out. "You have a longer stride."

At the top of the walk they both stopped for breath, each turned in a different direction. She was facing out over the channel, enjoying the cooling breeze, while he gazed in the opposite direction, toward Eden Castle.

He reached back for her hand, and she tried to still her fears. As they approached the gatehouse, a bleak thought occurred to her. "You're not . . . going in, are you?"

"No," he reassured her, though he stood for a moment longer and peered through at the empty courtyard, the darkened and deserted castle beyond. Then he was leading her again around to the south wall, that immense long and unbroken stone barrier that had made the castle a fortress. "Does this place alarm you?" he asked softly, apparently seeing something on her face.

She nodded, honest at least.

As they slipped through the low door that led into the vast courtyard of the great hall, he again reached for her hand. He was standing very near now, so near she could hear his breathing. With no words spoken, he took her in his arms, drew her close, and she felt his lips, at first gentle and testing, felt them grow more insistent.

She responded with the needs of a lifetime, and at the end of the kiss when he whispered, "Let's go home," she was prepared to make her way back down the cliff walk to Mortemouth.

Instead, with his arm securely about her waist, he started off in the opposite direction, toward the little-used path which led past the outbuildings and barns, directly into the rich farmlands of Eden Rising and the cottage.

"Do you know where we're going?" he asked, his breath forming a light caress on her cheek.

"I think so."

"Do you mind?"

She looked at him, surprised. "I think it's perfect."

A few minutes later she saw the open meadow which signaled the beginning of Eden Rising, and saw, just on the other side, the cottage that would be their home. They both increased their pace, following the narrow track across the high, blowing meadow grasses, until at last she tore loose from his grasp, and without looking to see if he was following, broke into a run.

The wind caught in her hair, loosened it, and she lifted her face to the sky and saw a solid canopy of stars. About fifty feet from the cottage he caught up with her. Breathing heavily, he drew her into his arms and gasped, "I love you. I swear to God, I love you." There was an intensity in his voice that matched her own. At the end of the kiss he stepped back and she saw the need on his face.

As though by mutual consent, her fingers struggled nervously down the small buttons that Meg Winchombe a few hours earlier had struggled to button.

Their eyes never shifted from the other's face as he too began to pull off the white shirtwaist, the obstruction of garments pressed into new service as they fell onto the soft grasses, spread out by each in turn until they formed a second softness. At last they stood before each other and she was in his arms again, every nerve alive to new sensations, a pleasurable pain erupting at the pit of her stomach and moving out in circles.

He guided her down onto the carpet formed by discarded garments, still down, until she relaxed onto the unorthodox bed and closed her eyes to yet a new sensation, his lips on her breast. As she clasped him to her, she felt a sudden shooting sensation moving back and forth between her breasts and the pit of her stomach, something reacting to the sensation of his body, his weight upon her, the manner in which he gently pushed between her legs.

She received him, in one clean penetration that caused her to gasp, feeling him push more deeply inside her, still deeper, the emptiness filled, though far from satisfied, something beginning to ache within her as his hands explored all aspects of her body, new sensations which caused the growing tension to increase.

He was whispering close by her ear, but she couldn't hear, occupied by the seismic explosions which were tearing through her, each accompanied by a strange paralysis, until she thought she could not bear it if the sensations subsided. At that moment a paroxysm whose size and nature she had never felt before seized her—and seized him as well. They had no choice but to cling to each other until breath and reason returned and the pleasurable pain subsided.

She felt more alive than she'd ever felt in her life, pressed him to her and lifted her legs over his as though to lock him into her for all time. After a moment the tension started to build again, the warm core deep in her stomach began to move and push deeper. Before she closed her eyes, the better to savor the new explosion, she looked straight up into the heavens and knew that thanks were due.

After all, the designs were God's, as were the instincts. Give God the credit . . .

Eden Rising, North Devon May 18, 1875

Standing on a grassy knoll fifty yards from the cottage, John shook his head, amazed and moved by the willingness of strangers to help them. For the first few days he'd recognized all the faces. Bates, of course, who had assumed the role of official overseer, and the indomitable Charley Spade, whose irrepressible whistling could be heard the length of the headlands, and Jason, as lighthearted as John had ever seen him, freed from the limitations London had placed on him.

But yesterday more had come, men John had never seen before. They came with their tools and materials, their wives with covered picnic baskets. At times John looked up, fearful if he didn't keep the miraculous scene in sight it would disappear. But it was still there, accompanied now by a new sound, the pickaxes and sledgehammers attacking the south wall, providing a new, ready access from the moors directly to the cottage, thus eliminating the need for the villagers to use the gatehouse.

John heard the noise clearly over the whistling wind. A true breach in the wall, the first since it had been erected in the tenth century. He smiled as he thought of all his Eden ancestors turning in their graves. One would be pleased, though. His father. John had never before felt his presence so strongly.

Papa . . .

Before the good memory overtook him, dragging along with it the bad ones, he started back toward the cottage and caught sight of the one person largely responsible for such peace.

Susan had just emerged from the front door of the cottage, a child in tow. The clinic was open now, though the portico yet required a sturdy roof. But, as she'd said that morning, as long as there were children, there

377

would be scrapes, cuts, and splinters. She stopped on the top step, speaking to the child.

John saw it was a boy about nine, a conspicuous white bandage on his hand, which he lovingly protected like a wound of honor. The little boy nodded solemnly to everything she was saying. Suddenly she bent over and kissed the top of his head and sent him running down the steps.

The mere sight of her moved him. She stood for a moment, stretching, one hand smoothing the band of her apron, the other tucking up a strand of hair the wind had worried loose. He saw her lift her head to the sky, as though for a deep breath before moving on to the next task.

As she turned back into the cottage, she caught sight of him standing a distance away. Slowly she started down the steps, never lifting her eyes from his. He saw the soft smile on her face, the way the wind was blowing her long skirt, outlining her legs, reminding him of their intimacy every night, splendid love, perfect love, mutually satisfying.

"I missed you," she called out, bringing her beauty and goodness nearer.

When she was close enough, he simply opened his arms, and without a word, she walked into them. He buried his face in her hair and felt her cling to him.

Still caught in the embrace, he heard her whisper, "Are you all right?"

"No."

She drew back, alarm on her face. "What's the matter? Are you ill?"

"Yes."

She pressed a professional hand to his forehead, checking for fever, and he smiled and confessed, "Ill . . . with love."

He took her face in his hands, looked down, and felt such overwhelming desire for her. "Where can we go?" he whispered.

She laughed softly. "I'm afraid the cottage is overrun. Tonight, though . . ."

He nodded. "Tonight." The pickaxes grew louder, the shattering of stone more pronounced. "Come on"—he grinned, grabbing her hand—"I want you to see this."

Hand in hand, they walked back toward the cottage, where eight women were setting up a long table on the side of the cottage protected from the wind, getting ready to serve the noon meal.

"Who was the little boy?" John asked after Susan had greeted all the women.

"Sam Oden's," she replied. "Tim is his name. Why do you ask?"

"He reminded me of Stephen, my son, and Frederick," he answered without hesitation.

His sons.

He had had sons, and had lost them . . .

As they approached the south wall, where the battering was going on, he saw Mr. Bates standing to one side in shirt sleeves, a look of consummate horror on his face at what was taking place. At least a dozen men were putting their backs, shoulders, and souls and hearts into the destruction of the obstructing wall.

"Come on, Mr. Bates," John called out in high spirits, "grab a sledgehammer. I'm sure one of these men . . ." At their approach, he saw that instantaneous reaction from the men, a reaction he loathed, but one, according to Susan, it would take time to obliterate, a look which spoke of master and servants.

To his left he saw Charley Spade, bent over, gasping for breath, exhausted from trying to break through the wall.

"Here, Charley, let me spell you," John offered.

Without argument the large man yielded his sledgehammer as the others moved back as though to clear a space for John.

"No, stay as you are," he called out. "Come on, all together now." As he waved them forward, they came, grins beginning to replace the soberness on their faces.

John stepped directly up to the wall, part of which already lay in shattered fragments over the ground but not yet wholly penetrated. He grasped the sledgehammer firmly, swung it up over his shoulder, and brought it down with one teeth-rattling blow, felt the remaining stones give, and saw for the first time daylight coming from the other side, a jagged glimpse of the moors which had not been seen from this angle since the tenth century.

All at once a great cry went up from the men watching. A few more well-placed blows from the others shattered the wall even more, until at last a breach ten feet wide opened Eden to the world, and the world to Eden.

Eden Rising,
North Devon
July 28, 1875

For Bates every day dawned like a new miracle, and frequently his eagerness to arrive at the cottage on Eden Rising would drag him out of bed before dawn, when, with the aid of a single candle, he'd fix his first cup of morning tea, then dress quickly and scramble up the cliff walk.

This morning was like all the others, though marred by a new sadness. The job was done. Today was to be more a celebration than a workday. But what a job they had accomplished. Despite his years and aching joints, he hurried up the cliff walk, wanting to see it all as the sun first struck it, that modest temple which he suspected contained two of the happiest people in the world.

Sometimes, watching Susan and John, Bates would think with regret on the loneliness of his own existence. But no woman would have had him, then or now, and so he'd adjusted to his small cottage down in Mortemouth very well. And besides, what loneliness? Both Susan and John had told him repeatedly there would always be countless jobs, daily jobs, that would need doing, and as long as he wanted to be with them, he had a place, a family.

Breathless from the effects of that miraculous word and all that it implied, he stopped at the top of the cliff walk and glanced toward the eastern horizon, over the rim of the world—or so it seemed—and saw the first rose-colored streaks in the night sky.

For several moments Bates suffered a sharp nostalgia. As there was no need to rush, he walked slowly to the still-barred gatehouse and the ruins of the castle beyond. Why must the world of Eden Castle die? When it had worked, it had worked beautifully, all people by nature secure, knowing their places, servants well treated, happy to serve those they respected, masters compassionate and wise, guiding and leading more than ordering

If this new John Murrey Eden ever chose to be master of Eden Castle again . . .

But no. Bates knew better than that. Nothing, he suspected, could ever pry John away from the cottage on Eden Rising. If anyone resurrected Eden Castle, it would have to be Lord Richard, John's half-brother—and how much Bates would love to reunite those two men. For a moment the idea nagged at him—a dream really, the family all returned under happier circumstances.

"No," he scoffed aloud, pushed away from the bars of the gatehouse, and looked back, mourning the death of that world.

By the time he walked the length of the south wall to the place where the new gate had been created, the sun had risen and was shedding rays of pink, gold, and purple over everything—most specifically the cottage that rested peacefully on Eden Rising, glistening under its new coat of whitewash, the contrasting brown window and door trim, the fenced-in barn area boasting chickens, goats, and one good milk cow, all bartered for Susan's services. Now Bates heard the rooster proclaim the morning from the same yard.

And a fine morning it would be, all of Mortemouth invited to the official opening of the clinic, that spotless little room, which once had been an open portico, now filled with Susan's equipment, a magic room where pain might be eased and hope renewed. He saw the first wisp of smoke coming from the large fieldstone chimney. Someone up, preparing breakfast.

Bates stood a few minutes, safely concealed behind the wall at the very edge of the gate. Unless he missed his guess, Susan would come through that back door in a moment on her way to feed the chickens. He always enjoyed watching her, the confident way she moved, still as stubborn as on that first bleak night so long ago when she had insisted he direct her to the top of Eden Castle, where John was mindless with grief.

Startled by the sudden clear image of the beginning, Bates shook his head to dispel all negative feelings on this day and heard the latch on the back door of the cottage slide open.

A moment later, there she was, a pail of feed in one hand, a broad white apron tied over what appeared to be a special dress for this special day. She paused for a moment in the first warming rays of the morning sun to lift her face heavenward.

There was the source of John's new peace and serenity.

He swallowed hard and heard her voice, "Good morning, Mr. Bates. You're up early. Best come in for a cup of tea and some fresh scones."

How had she known he was here, in hiding behind the wall?

"Mr. Bates?"

"Coming."

Sheepishly he emerged into full view, smoothing back his thinning hair, baffled—as he had been every morning for the past month—at her ability to detect him in his place of concealment behind the wall.

It was seven o'clock in the evening, and for the first time since seven o'clock that morning Susan sat, exhausted, in one of the chairs John and Mr. Bates had arranged on the grassy knoll fronting the cottage, to enjoy the peace of the evening, the warmth of good friends who had come this day, and—the richest sight of all—John, like an overgrown child himself, seated on the clinic steps surrounded by an adoring group of children, captivating them with melodramatic and slightly exaggerated tales of his adventures in India.

Close to Susan sat Mr. Bates, puffing on a pipe like a ready-made grandfather. Now, as John's voice drifted into her range of hearing, she asked Bates softly, "Did all that really happen?"

Mr. Bates smiled and let a thin trail of smoke escape from the corner of his mouth. "If John says it did, it did."

She nodded, enjoying the old man's company, finding it hard to believe this was the same pompous man who had reluctantly led her into Eden Castle a year ago. Transformations all about—and within as well, for she too had changed.

At the sound of John's laughter, she looked up suddenly to see him enclosing a small boy in his embrace.

"He misses his sons," she said quietly.

Bates nodded immediately, as though he'd made the same observation. "They are all he talks about during the workday. I've even considered writing to Alex Aldwell," he went on, quite hesitant, "and . . ."

Susan leaned forward. "And what?" she prompted. Once, not too long ago, the same idea had occurred to her. "And what, Mr. Bates?" she urged, keeping her voice down, not wanting it to travel as far as the cottage steps.

Abruptly the old man fell maddeningly silent. He appeared to stare with a fixed gaze at the group on the steps.

"Mr. Bates, please. Do you think Mr. Aldwell might . . . ?"

Even as she spoke, he shook his head. "Oh, Aldwell will do whatever we ask, I'm certain." He paused and looked at her with a directness that startled. "The problem is, what do we want to ask?"

For a moment they stared at each other. She realized it was John's radical transformation that was causing the problem. If it were merely reported, it would not be believed. Even seeing it as she was now, still on occasion she shared the startled bewilderment of the villagers.

"Well?" Mr. Bates asked. "I'll write a letter, if you'll phrase it."

Was that a challenge or an offer? She looked sharply at him. "I want him reunited with his family, most specifically his sons."

"My desires precisely." The old man nodded. "But they may not be shared by the family. Unhappily, that man succeeded admirably in driving them all away." He bobbed his head toward John.

She rushed to correct him. "No, Mr. Bates, that's just the point. It wasn't that man. That man is gone forever." They both looked in the direction of the storyteller.

"So do I do it?" Mr. Bates asked with a degree of apprehension in his voice.

She looked back at him. "What's the worst that can happen?"

"That they'll all ignore us."

"They've done that for years."

"Precisely."

"You think Mr. Aldwell is the one?"

"Oh, yes. He's the connecting link between all members of the family."

382

"And what will be your message?" she asked, suddenly aware Mr. Bates had obviously given this a great deal of thought.

He shook his head. "A request, simple and direct, for the family to return to Eden for the purpose of meeting Mr. and Mrs. John Murrey Eden, now in residence in the cottage on Eden Rising."

"And whom will you ask that he send it to?" she asked.

"Lord Harrington is in residence in Dublin, I believe. He has custody of John's sons."

John's sons . . .

"And, of course," Bates went on, "Lord Richard and Lady Eleanor in Kent. I understand there is a new child, a son." The old man beamed. "Continuity, you know."

She smiled and nodded. *Please, God, a child* . . .

"And Lady Mary and her American husband," Bates continued, "though of course the distance from America undoubtedly would be too great for them. Does that meet with your approval?" Mr. Bates asked.

"Yes, it does," she murmured.

"Then I'll do it tonight and post it tomorrow."

"Good."

"And then will come the hardest part."

"What?"

"Waiting."

At last she looked at him, hearing a new seriousness in his voice.

"And I would suggest," he went on, "that you say nothing to John . . ."

"No, of course not."

"If they refuse to come, we can shoulder the disappointment for him."

"Yes."

They were whispering furtively back and forth and apparently John saw them and suffered an attack of curiosity. He concluded his story in the next few minutes and stood up among the children, keeping his eyes on Susan and Mr. Bates.

"Enough! He sees us," Mr. Bates ordered. "Do you want to read the messages before—?"

"No. You'll handle it well, I know."

"No more. He's coming."

She looked up and saw he was dragging a trail of children behind him, carrying one in his arms, a little girl who was running her small hand through his hair. Still several yards away, he called out, "You two look very secretive over here."

Susan could not reply, but Mr. Bates did. "We were discussing the possibility of a second garden. Susan wants to try one, anyway. I offered to help turn the plot."

Hesitantly she nodded. Not a bad idea.

Then he was upon them, the children scrambling everyplace, surrounding him, a few grasping for his hands, others his arms, the young ones content with clinging to his legs.

"Susan, I'm taking these monkeys home. Do you want to . . . ?"

"No need." Bates smiled, rising stiffly from his comfortable chair. "I must go as well, and I'm going in that very direction. I'll deliver each to the proper doorstep."

John seemed hesitant. "Are you sure?"

"Of course I'm sure. Otherwise I wouldn't have offered." Bates looked about at the laughing, chattering children who were now darting off in several directions. He viewed the chaos a moment, then stood erect. "But we shall do it my way." Suddenly he clapped his hands exactly twice in two ear-shattering explosions which instantly summoned every child's attention.

"All right, line up," he commanded. "Now!" It was the "now!" that set most of them into motion. With startling obedience they fell into line behind him.

Susan smiled, thinking he'd probably organized the enormous staff of Eden Castle with the same air of authority.

John moved behind her and put his arms about her waist, drawing her back against him, and confirmed her suspicion. "Give Bates something to organize and he's never happier."

Finally all was ready, and on Mr. Bates's command the parade started, with the tall, lean man in the lead, like a grasshopper Pied Piper, his young and uneven "tail" elongating behind him, marching toward the new gate in the south wall. Susan and John watched until the last one had passed through the gate.

John, with his arms still about her, tightened them and drew her closer still.

"They adore you," she murmured, leaning back against him, certain sensations beginning to grow under the influence of his closeness.

"It's reciprocal," he said, and tightened his arms about her even more.

She felt his breath near her left ear and knew that all remaining chores would have to wait. As his lips commenced a teasing path down the side of her cheek, on down her neck, and across her shoulder, one of her last coherent thoughts was for Bates and the message which would be posted tomorrow.

Dear God, let them come . . .

At that moment she felt his hands turning her about, felt his lips on her forehead, moving directly down until they found their proper home on hers.

Though close, they were not close enough, and without a word he scooped her up, cradling her in his arms. She clung to him, knew their destination, and approved of it—more than approved, wondered if she could survive until they reached it.

Grosvenor Square, London
August 4, 1875

Lord Richard was aware of Alex Aldwell and Aslam staring at him as he read the remarkable message from Bates. Although he'd read it twice, he read it again because he needed time to form a response.

"I don't trust him," came the flat, clipped condemnatory voice from behind the desk. Aslam. The young man seemed unduly agitated.

"Well, I do," countered Aldwell, "but then, you didn't see him down at that mission like I did." He shook his head. "I tell you it wasn't the same man who—"

"But what does he truly want?" Aslam went on, implying the letter was a scheme.

"I don't think he wants anything," Aldwell replied.

"Surely you don't believe that?"

"Yes, I do."

Richard heard the pause in the arguing voices, then heard a question which involved him.

"Richard, what do you think?" Aslam asked quietly.

He looked up from the prim penmanship, not quite ready to get involved in open debate. "I . . . don't know," he faltered. "In a way, I've always expected such a letter would come. I didn't know from whom, and generally I envisaged it on the occasion of John's . . . death."

"He's far from dead." Aldwell smiled. "According to the letter, he has initiated half a dozen projects, including the clinic."

Interested, Richard glanced down at the part of the letter which described the free clinic, the shared farmlands, the pooling of equipment to produce larger crops so the community would no longer be totally dependent upon the whims of the herring. Also the letter mentioned a "wife."

"Who is the woman?" he asked, remembering Lila and fearing for any woman unfortunate enough to fall in love with John.

"Oh, that one." Alex grinned. "I've had dealings with her." Abruptly he stood and moved to the sideboard, where with careful deliberation he poured a small snifter of brandy. "Her name is Susan. She's a nurse, and one does not encounter her lightly."

He lifted the snifter as though in toast to the absent Susan, took a brief swallow, made a wry face at it, then returned to the settee, where Richard was still studying Bates's letter.

"You know her, then?" Richard asked.

"Of course I know her," Aldwell boasted. "In fact, I could have predicted last year when John was so ill and she was caring for him that he might at last have met his match."

For a moment the large room was quiet, save for the street sounds floating up from four floors below. It had been mercilessly hot of late, and the casements were pushed open all the way to receive the maximum breeze. Richard felt the heat, felt a single drop of perspiration course down the small of his back, and recalled Eden, the place of his birth, the scene of his childhood, the longings and fears he'd suffered in that drafty old castle.

He looked back up in an attempt to gauge Aslam's reaction. That he was upset, there was no doubt. John had always intimidated him, a kind of spiritual bullying. Now, of course, he felt threatened anew. The man himself had apparently come roaring up out of a premature grave, wanting . . . What?

As the unanswered question echoed bleakly through Richard's mind, he saw the continued alarm on Aslam's face and wished he could alleviate it. But he couldn't, for two reasons. One, there had never been any successful way to predict what John Murrey Eden would do under any given circumstances, and, two, for all Richard knew, Aslam's fears were perfectly justified. He really couldn't believe a man like John would be content forever to preside over a rural free clinic and a row of cabbages.

At the preposterous thought Richard smiled. On the other side of the room Aldwell and Aslam were still at it, one terribly threatened, the other terribly pleased, while Richard sat at the far end of the settee puzzled, lost in indecision.

What if Bates had lied or exaggerated? What if Aslam's fears *were* well-grounded? Did he really want to take his wife and son into close proximity with a monster who was well known for his unique ability to destroy people?

"Gentlemen," he said, suddenly rising, weary of hearing the bickering voices, weary of the debate raging in his own heart, "Mr. Bates set September 6 as the date of reunion. There's time to make a prudent decision, and I think for all concerned it must be the most prudent decision we are capable of making."

As he spoke, he saw approval on Aslam's face, disappointment on Aldwell's. He was sorry for that, but between now and the date specified in Bates's letter he had much thinking to do. What if Bates's words were true? He disliked hating anyone or anything. If only John had not given him such just cause. . . . Still, hate must ultimately be transformed into forgiveness if life was to flow again.

Now, without warning, as though his soul were testing him, he thought of the man he had first loved, Bertie Nichols—driven to suicide by John Murrey Eden. The memory took a deadly toll. The world had been denied that rare man and his gifted presence by John's arrogant self-righteousness. Despite the hot breeze which fluttered the casement curtains, Richard for a moment felt only the chill of recall, that winter night in Cambridge when he'd gone to Bertie's flat and found him hanging, his face already swollen and distorted.

Dear God, he'd not expected it to still be so painful. For a moment he couldn't breathe. In a sorrowing instant of perception he realized he'd spent all the intervening years since Bertie's death trying to find another Bertie. He never had and he never would.

Slowly he sat back down on the settee, saw Bates's letter in his hand and stared at it as though curious how it came to be there. Suddenly—though he once thought he'd expended all his hate for John Murrey Eden—he crushed the letter and hurled it across the room, watched it fall under a low footstool, and made no attempt to retrieve it.

As he bowed his head in an attempt to deal with the ancient grief, he was aware of the others watching.

"Richard, are you all right?"

He nodded to Aslam. It was all he could manage.

The next question came tentatively from the sideboard. "Will you be returning to Eden with me in September?" Aldwell asked. "It would mean a lot to John."

At that he looked up. Did he really give a damn what meant a lot to John?

When he didn't answer, Alex prodded again. "Will you? Be going back to Eden, I mean."

He gaped up at the direct question. Would he be going to Eden? He thought on it for a moment, then answered truthfully.

"I . . . don't know. . . ."

Talbot House,
Dublin, Ireland
August 19,1875

Who was it said that all discord was harmony not understood?

Lord Harrington couldn't recall, and decided whoever said it was a fool anyway, as he sat behind his writing bureau, dreading the weekly post of bills overdue, and decided further he was more than ready for a particle of understanding, for the discord in his household was beginning to take a dreadful toll, of himself, of his limited staff and—most important of all—of his two grandsons.

He looked up through the mullioned windows, which gave a perfect view of the meadowlands, which generally were the boys' favorite haunt. At first he couldn't see them and started up out of his chair.

Then he spied them where he least wanted them to be, near the big oak with the half-dozen men Charles Parnell had transferred out to Talbot House several days ago—along with four large sealed crates which the men had hidden in the barn under bales of scattered hay.

Arms. Of that Lord Harrington was certain, both from the size and weight of the crates and from the care with which the men had handled them. As he had tried to quiz Parnell about both the men and the guns, he had been dismissed as though he were nothing more than a curious child.

The men need a safe refuge for a few days; then they and their cargo will be gone.

Gazing with fixed vision out of the window, Lord Harrington recalled the words as well as the voice and face of the man who had spoken them. His good friend Charles Parnell was changing, had changed. His dislike of the British had escalated into full-fledged hatred. Now he couldn't abide anything British and was advocating, both publicly and privately, a full-scale attack on British imperialism.

Lord Harrington suspected that his tools were the motley crew just beyond the big oak, who were lounging in various positions of relaxation, his grandsons in slavish attendance, apparently clinging to every word that was said, though from what Lord Harrington had heard earlier, they were scarcely capable of speaking the King's English. Rabble, all of them, ex-convicts he was certain, hired to perform unsavory services and ask no questions.

For a moment longer Lord Harrington stared at the bizarre scene, the meadow idyllic and green in summer ripeness, marred by that one ugly knot of humanity. Even the innocence of his grandsons seemed to be in the very process of becoming corrupt.

Yet what could he do? He was indebted to Charles Parnell, who had lent him funds when he'd left England so hurriedly, taking his grandsons away from the influence of their father. Parnell had even located and acquired this secluded estate for him outside Dublin. In the past, anything Lord Harrington or his grandsons had ever needed had been instantly supplied by Parnell himself. Now perhaps it was time for Lord Harrington to return some of the kindness and accommodation.

He shook his head and broke the line of vision that was causing him such trouble, closed his eyes a moment to rest them, and in that instant saw a perfect and clear image of Eden Castle.

John . . . dead.

Could the woman Rose O'Donnell be believed? If so, then would it be safe to return the boys to their family seat? And who was in residence now at Eden, and would they welcome the sons of John Murrey Eden, or would they . . . ?

As always, there were no answers to his questions. With a sigh he returned to his bureau and began to sort through the various envelopes. One from his estate agent in Wiltshire, who was having trouble liquidating his English property because of taxes; and of course there were the endless bills, more each month; and an announcement for an auction over in Trilby; and . . .

Hello, what was this? He placed the bills to one side and a small, thin envelope slipped from the larger ones. He saw instantly its difference, an English stamp, a worn, well-traveled look to the envelope, and—most important—an unfamiliar hand. He lifted it free of the others, pushed back in his chair, and angled the penmanship toward the bright August sun. Not until he turned it over and saw the familiar crest of the Grosvenor Square mansion in London did his excitement mount, along with a curious sense of dread.

Who? News of John? Aslam? What and why?

Even as his mind presented these frantic questions, his hand was splitting the seal, drawing back the flap, and pulling free several pages of correspondence, pages which did not seem to be of a piece.

He unfolded the first, a rather lengthy two pages which appeared to have been extremely well read and which were addressed to Lord Richard Eden.

Lord Richard?

Even before he commenced reading, he turned to the second page and saw at the bottom a neat, proper signature of one Percival Bates.

Percival Bates?

He looked up, confident he had never heard that name in his life Bates. . . . John's old butler years ago was a Bates, if he remembered correctly. One and the same?

Then he began to read. He read straight through the remarkable document, then read it again, then a third time, and was just commencing the fourth when suddenly he placed the pages heavily on his bureau, aware for the first time he was in need of a deep breath of air.

It *was* from the old butler Bates, though a very different Bates, who spoke of hideous matters. John's terrible illness, his long recuperation and ultimate excursion to Paris in search of Elizabeth, his ordeal—and this Lord Harrington could not bear to read again, could not even think on it.

Elizabeth . . . executed?

It was the words in combination that did the damage. Needing help to perceive them, he bowed his head into his hands, made the sign of the cross upon his forehead, and prayed for the salvation of Elizabeth's soul.

Minutes later, far from being restored, but curious about the second note, he opened this second letter and found the gold-embossed Eden seal at the top of the page and Lord Richard's elegant penmanship informing him of Bates's request to reunion at Eden Castle the sixth of September 1875.

No! Never!

He looked up from reading, still mystified. John alive? Perhaps. John changed? Never! John's soul reformed? Not possible. Living in the cottage on Eden Rising? There was no cottage on Eden Rising, only a shack in the process of falling down, beaten to earth by years of weather and neglect. And living with his . . . wife?

Wife! That angered him most of all. How many wives was a man entitled to destroy? The monster had already destroyed one, his beloved Lila.

Reformation, redemption, forgiveness—these were the themes of old Bates's letter. Exaggerated, all exaggerated, no doubt.

Suddenly from outside the window he heard a cry, followed by the sound of men laughing, and looked up to see Stephen suspended, one man holding his ankles, another his wrists, swinging him through the air, his protestations clear but no one one paying the least attention to them, little Frederick standing to one side, frightened, while the pleas of both boys were ignored by the laughing, jeering, bored men.

Enough!

In mounting anger, Lord Harrington pushed away from the bureau with such force his chair tilted and clattered backward. He didn't stop to right it. He stopped for nothing except to retrieve the curious letters which had arrived from London.

"Stop it!" he shouted, running across the green. "Stop it, I say, this moment!" he shouted again and thought: Why not take the boys back to Eden? Then thought, no, he mustn't, for John Murrey Eden had killed their mother. Thought: Yes, go and see if the monster *has* changed. Thought: No. And took his confusion and the debate with him as he increased his speed in an attempt to arrive before Stephen was hurt, all the time shouting, "Stop it! You must stop it. He's not been well. . . ."

Eden Rising,
North Devon
September 6, 1875

Concealment had been the most difficult problem of the day. Unfortu-
ately, Susan had never been very good at concealing anything from any-
ne. Yet since early morning until now—late afternoon—she'd had to
onceal everything: the large amounts of foodstuffs she'd prepared if and
hen they came; her own physical disposition, of which she knew the
ause but John as yet did not. Most difficult of all, she'd been forced to
onceal her own nervous state, as well as that of Mr. Bates, who had come
ery close to driving her crazy as every hour he had gone to check the road
ading off the moors, prompting John to comment, perplexed, "What's
he matter with him?"

Compounding all this had been the constant stream of patients who had
assed through the clinic on this day, one of the busiest since they'd
pened. As luck would have it, all the children in Mortemouth had chosen
his day to cut their fingers on whittling knives, fall and scrape both knees,
at too many green apples.

Now, at five o'clock, Susan looked up to see the small whitewashed
linic empty, not an ailing child or adult in sight. At first she couldn't
elieve it; then a sudden draining fatigue washed over her. She reached
ut for a chair and sat slowly, trying not to hear the silence coming from
e porch outside or the world beyond.

If they were coming, they should have been here by now.

She rose slowly and gathered up a bouquet of wildflowers one of the
hildren had brought her, pushed open the door and felt that pleasurable
arly-autumn freshness in the late-afternoon air. The sun was still high
nd warm and very golden, but somewhere close behind the warmth and
e gold was the ominous gray sense of winter.

She stood on the top step of the porch and consciously breathed deeply,
oked to her left . . . and saw him.

John.

He was in the garden seventy-five yards away, turning the soil in preparation for it to lie fallow during the winter months. It had been a marvelous garden and he'd produced enough squash, tomatoes, onions, lettuce, and cabbage to feed themselves and anyone else who came to the door. She continued to watch, very grateful now neither she nor Mr. Bates had given him a hint as to their hopes for this day. Once they had considered telling him, but both had decided against it in the event . . .

Quickly she looked toward the new gate in the south wall, thinking she'd seen movement. She'd seen movement, all right. Mr. Bates, his hoe still in hand from where he'd been working with John in the garden, making what was easily his hundredth trip to check the road.

As Bates turned about, he apparently caught sight of her, and glancing first toward the garden to see if John was watching, he hurried to her "The bastards!" he cursed under his breath as he stopped short of the steps.

"There's time yet," she soothed, unconvincingly. "Maybe they were . . . delayed."

"Maybe no one's coming," the old man snapped, as though it were her fault.

"Well, we knew we were taking a gamble from the beginning."

"I should have delivered the letter to Aldwell in person. Or, better still insisted upon a reply of some sort."

He looked so disappointed she moved down the steps to offer comfort "Don't blame yourself, Mr. Bates."

"But they should have given him a chance."

"Perhaps they will, in time. The wounds were deep—you said so your self."

"Bastards!" Bates grumbled again, and glanced back toward the garden and the man working. "He is so . . . changed," he marveled quietly, depth of emotion in his voice that moved her. Before she could reply, he went on. "You didn't know him in those days, Susan. He was . . ." Unable to say precisely what he had been, the old man faltered and broke off. "Now . . . I've never known a man so kind, so . . ." He shrugged embarrassed. "I just think they should . . . give him a chance, that' all."

Suddenly she felt such a depth of gratitude to this man who had started out as an enemy and had now become the best friend they had. Realizing she'd never expressed this gratitude, she started to speak, when suddenly he warned, "He sees us. I'd better get back."

She looked down toward the garden to see John staring up at them.

"Back to work," Bates muttered, and started off, dragging his hoe behind him like a dejected schoolboy.

Susan was left to watch the two men meet and exchange a few words then resume their labors, carefully turning the rich soil that would supply them with another garden next spring.

The cycles of life and death.

You didn't know him then, Susan . . .

No, she didn't, but she knew him now, frequently watched him with patients in the clinic, saw his gentleness, his almost desperate need to touch, as though only now had he discovered the vast love that was stored unused, within him.

Dear God, please let someone come, she prayed quickly, then went to prepare tea for the two men working in the garden.

At seven o'clock that evening she was in the clinic rolling bandages for the next day, aware of John waiting for her on the steps outside to join him for their evening walk along the headlands, an end-of-the-day ritual that had become important to both of them.

Where Mr. Bates had gone to after tea, she had no idea. Probably back down into Mortemouth or to the Green Man to dull his massive disappointment in several glasses of stout. Her own disappointment was massive as well, though she'd tried to work it off, to keep her mind away from it, and to concentrate on the man himself.

Hurry! Complete the bandages! She wanted to walk with him, to feel his hand around hers, to stop as they frequently did at the farthest point for a kiss. Sometimes they talked quite volubly of everything under the sun, and at other times they were silent the length of the headlands and back again. Sometimes she'd watch him as he studied the massive facade of Eden Castle, a look of bemusement on his face, as though he knew something now he'd never known before.

Hurry! She wanted to be with him.

"Susan?"

At the sound of his voice coming through the open door, she looked up. "What is it, John? I'm almost finished."

"Bad news, I'm afraid. I think you have another patient. There's someone coming." From where she stood she could see his line of vision, eyes focused on the gate, squinting at someone who had just appeared.

Fatigued and disappointed, she closed her eyes and wondered who it could be and hoped the ailment could be treated rapidly and simply.

She smoothed down her apron and tried to digest her disappointment at this delay and joined him on the porch, gazing with him toward the gate. At that moment she saw a solitary man silhouetted against the fiery evening sun. Quite large, he was, and he paused now and seemed to return their stare. From this distance she couldn't recognize him.

"Who is . . . ?"

"I can't tell."

Suddenly the man waved and started directly toward them. Because of the blinding setting sun and the angle of shadows, identification still was impossible. But he didn't walk as though there was anything wrong. In fact, he appeared to increase his speed, waving again, and at last—in what appeared to be great exuberance—he scooped off his hat and did a peculiar thing. He tossed it up into the air. Just gave it one gigantic upward spiral and . . .

All at once her attention was no longer focused on the rapidly approaching man but rather on John, who squinted into the sun, his face taut with inner tension as though he'd already made an identification but needed one clear confirmation.

From a distance she heard the man shout, "John, is that you?"

Then she saw John start slowly forward, a faint hint of a smile beginning to alter the confusion on his face. She heard him whisper a name. Though it was only a whisper and only a single name, she heard such an incredible weight of love and pleasure behind it.

"Aldwell" was what he'd said. Daring to hope, she looked for herself, and saw that it was.

As the mountainous man drew closer, his ruddy face was a map of delight. He shouted again, "John, don't you know me?"

At that the tentative grin on John's face splintered and he was on his feet, down the stairs, and moving toward his old friend with the same degree of delight that Aldwell was moving toward him.

Susan saw beyond the imminent reunion to the gate, where Mr. Bates stood, Though his features were obscured by distance, she could sense his extreme pleasure.

She looked back at the two men approaching each other, more slowly now, and saw to her amazement that in the last instant they had stopped short of each other. Brief words were exchanged—she couldn't hear what, but it didn't matter, for in the next moment John opened his arms, as did Alex, and they embraced each other. Susan found herself grinning at nothing at all and felt a tickling in her nose. She rubbed it away just as the two started back toward her, their arms still about each other.

As she went down the steps to greet Mr. Aldwell, she recalled their first awkward meeting, when John had been ill. There had been tense moments between them then. She hoped he'd forgotten or forgiven by now.

"Mr. Aldwell . . ." She smiled in greeting, wondering if he had news of the others, who obviously were not coming. She extended her hand in greeting and found it totally ignored as he enclosed her in a massive bear hug as earlier he had embraced John.

"Well, you've gone and done it now." He smiled down on her at the end of the embrace.

Blushing, she looked up. "I don't . . ."

"You should have been content just to be his nursemaid. Now you've gone and become his wife. Heaven help you."

She laughed and reached back for John's hand. "Heaven has already helped me, Mr. Aldwell."

She heard John, just marveling, "I can't believe it," clearly delighted to see his old friend. "What are you doing wandering so far afield of London?"

"Come to see you, I have, " Aldwell blustered abruptly, then stopped, and she suspected both men were assessing each other with new intensity. Aldwell leaned back against the banister that led up to the clinic. To John he said, "If you feel half as good as you look, I'd say you were restored."

She felt John's arm about her waist and heard his voice. "I feel whole, Alex," he said quietly, simply. "For the first time in my life. I consider myself the most blessed man in the universe."

His words hung like a benediction on the still evening air. Susan bowed her head and saw Aldwell do the same. No one spoke for several minutes.

Then, as though he knew he had to restore the small gathering to high good spirits, John stepped to Aldwell's side, a new lightness in his voice and manner. "Well, come on, man, where's your luggage? Of course you're staying with us. But be warned, I'll work you during the day like a common laborer, and it will do you good, I . . ."

Though Aldwell was smiling and nodding, his attention seemed to be focused on the gate.

She looked in that direction and saw Mr. Bates standing back, as though there was someone concealed behind the wall. Apparently John had yet to notice the splintered focus, continuing to talk volubly of projected plans.

Suddenly Alex interrupted. "John, there is someone waiting who wants very much to see you."

John fell silent and looked quizzical at the curious announcement, then followed Aldwell's gaze back to the gate, where . . .

Susan blinked in an attempt to clear her vision and knew someone else had come and felt the beginning warmth of forgiveness.

She saw John focus once again on the gate, at the spot where she saw a man—this one slight of build, hesitant. Once through the gate, he paused as though he'd collided with an invisible barrier. Following behind him she saw a woman, stylishly dressed, and following behind her a short, squat figure in black carrying what appeared to be a baby in her arms.

"Do you know who it is, John?" Aldwell asked quietly.

Still squinting, John shook his head, though something suggested to Susan he knew very well who it was and was frightened.

The small entourage had resumed speed, was now walking rapidly toward them. The lady lifted high her skirts over the grassy terrain and turned back twice to check on the progress of the nursemaid and the babe.

Whereas before John had gone forward to meet Alex, now he held his position, watching the approaching party with a splintered expression of pleasure, disbelief, and apprehension.

Susan saw Alex step back as though to remove himself from the impending encounter, and she did the same, easing subtly back to the bottom step. She could see the approaching group clearly now. The man in the lead had fixed his eyes on John and had never lifted them, his expression stern, though his face seemed pale, drained of color. Still they came, walking now with determination, drawing nearer, until at last the man stopped less than four feet from where John stood.

She could see John's face and failed to see the joy with which he'd greeted Alex Aldwell. Now, unfortunately, she saw a degree of pain and remorse.

Would they never speak?

Someone would have to move soon. Some silences were good. This one was not.

Just when she felt certain no one could endure like this a moment longer, the gentleman ducked his head and stepped still closer. "Do . . . you play marbles?" he asked John quite seriously, though his voice was hushed.

At once the tension on John's face broke, and along with it broke his composure. "On . . . occasion."

The gentleman grinned and boasted, "I have four blue cat's-eyes. Do you want to . . . ?"

But he couldn't finish, for suddenly John reached out for him with surprising strength and both men concealed their faces in the embrace itself.

Susan saw Alex turn away and concentrate with undue effort on the gravel path at his feet. Nor was she faring too well, nor was the lady, nor was anyone who watched the two in close embrace. Susan gave herself a few moments. She knew who they were: Lord Richard and his wife, Lady

Eleanor, and their infant son. She assumed the reference to the game of marbles had something to do with a memory from their boyhood.

The reunion was sweet, as both men seemed more than content to stand forever in the embracing forgiveness. "Welcome home, Richard," she heard John murmur at last in a voice that was scarcely recognizable.

Lord Richard did well to nod, and only then drew Eleanor forward, presenting her to John and the company, then went himself and took the baby, a plump cherub, from the nursemaid's arms and introduced both. "My wife, Eleanor, and our son, Geoffrey."

At that Susan stepped forward and greeted the pretty woman. "Welcome to Eden Rising." She smiled. "How glad we are to see you. . . ."

Eleanor looked pleased and took the baby from Lord Richard to cradle him close. "We meant to arrive earlier. But it's difficult traveling with a child. More stops . . ."

Susan nodded, understanding, and thought of the extra foodstuffs she'd prepared for the past two weeks tucked safely away in the kitchen. Tarts and meat pies. What a lovely picnic they would have on the grassy meadow of Eden Rising.

To Eleanor she invited, "Come inside. You must be exhausted."

Though the woman nodded, she held up a restraining hand and looked back toward the place where Lord Richard and John were still standing, Richard talking softly, his hands shoved easily into his pockets. "Look," Eleanor whispered, close at her side.

Susan followed the direction of her gaze back to the gate. Standing there, with Bates close at hand, she saw a dignified old gentleman, his gleaming white hair visible despite the distance. But of greater importance to her were the two young boys he clasped by the hands, all three gaping at the activity about the cottage.

It was Eleanor who directed John's attention toward these newcomers. "John, I believe . . ."

That's all she said, for he looked up from his quiet conversation with Richard, peered into the distance at the three standing at the gate, and whatever it was he was saying to Richard was promptly forgotten. He started forward, a look on his face Susan had never seen before. Then he was running to be reunited with himself, with his sons, who broke loose from their grandfather and were now racing pell-mell toward John, the tallest crying out, "Papa! Papa!" over and over again.

The collision was magnificent, the two boys threatening to topple John. But he regained his balance at the last minute and scooped them both up in his arms, a struggling, laughing, weeping reunion which concluded in a curious, almost ritualistic silence. John dropped heavily to his knees, releasing both boys, then inviting them back into his embrace one at a time, the youngest, Frederick, first, who appeared to approach the kneeling man with a degree of hesitancy but then was in his arms, his small face buried in John's shoulder. Then Stephen, who needed no second invitation and now clung to his father as though to a lifeline.

Susan was aware of the embarrassment of indisposition that issued from all and tried to ease it. "Mr. Aldwell, there are pitchers of ale and lemonade in the ice house. Would you . . . ?"

The big man looked so grateful. She saw Eleanor stripping off her lovely ink feather bonnet and pushing up her sleeves to ask almost plaintively, Please, let me do something."

Susan nodded, understanding, and motioned the nursemaid carrying he babe to come inside. As the women passed before her into the large oomy kitchen, she looked back in time to see John standing again, clutchng his sons by the hand, all going forward to greet the distinguished-ooking gentleman, who must be Lord Harrington.

By eight-thirty everyone was groaning pleasurably, satiated with good ood and drink, stretched out in varying positions of relaxation on the reen-velvet lawn.

There had been only one minor flaw in the perfect reunion. According o Alex, repeated messages had been sent to Mary, John's cousin in Amer-a. And there had been no response. To this sad news John nodded quick-, as though to say he understood.

And Alex said further, rather hurriedly, as though to get it over with, And Aslam could not get away. You know the pressing demands of the rm . . ."

Again John nodded and gazed out at the evening too long and ultimate- bowed his head, only to be drawn back into the life of the moment by tephen and Frederick, who challenged him to a race on the headlands. ohn laughed and drew them close, seeming literally to gain strength from heir closeness. "All right, you're on."

Before the race was launched it was decided Eleanor and the children ould spend the night in the cottage, while the men would find adequate ouches in the castle. Besides, Lord Richard was anxious to chart the pecifics of restoration ahead of him, for, to John's great pleasure, he nnounced he was indeed coming home to stay.

Now, as the others wandered off toward the castle, torches in hand, ohn, Susan, and the two boys cut a straight path through to the head- nds, the boys racing ahead, though stopping to examine everything, very leaf, every curiously shaped stump, every stone, endlessly curious.

She grasped John's hand and felt it tighten about hers in a loving accu- tion. "I suppose you were in on this plot."

She nodded. "Yes, I hope you're not angry."

He drew her close and kissed her forehead. "Why should I be angry ith you for giving me the most perfect day of my life?"

Quickly she returned the kiss and saw Stephen and Frederick twenty rds ahead turn back, as though fascinated by the intimacy.

"What do you think of them?" John asked.

"I think they are perfect," she said. "Stephen is a mirror-image reflec- on."

He nodded, pleased. "And bright, They are so —"

"Papa, come! Let's race!"

As the boys drifted back, Susan and John stepped out onto the vast xpanse of the headlands, the view uncluttered in all directions, a pano- ma of breathtaking beauty.

"Papa, come!" the boys shouted impatiently.

"Go on," Susan urged. "Go show them how to run. A boy's first race ould always be with his father."

397

He looked down on her, and she thought in that one look was enough love to warm her for the rest of her life.

"John?" she called out just as he started away. She waited until he looked back. "A favor?" she asked.

"Anything."

"Hold in reserve a portion of your love for your third child. . . ."

For a moment she wasn't certain he'd understood. Then he started slowly back toward her, his hands reaching out. "Oh, my dearest!" he whispered, and drew her to him.

Beyond his shoulder she saw his two young sons approaching shyly, again drawn to the sight of two adults embracing.

"Come," she invited, stood back, and urged them forward. "There's room."

They hesitated and looked at each other as though to confirm the wisdom of becoming a part of such closeness. Stephen rallied first, though Frederick was right behind him, and as the boys pushed eagerly against them, she drew them close.

In that protective cocoon she vowed silently to fill the small cottage on Eden Rising with as much love, understanding, and compassion as the four walls would hold.

Then she felt John tighten his grasp on all of them, and felt, as well, the channel breeze enfold them like a caring hand.